About the Author

Tana French grew up in Ireland, Italy, the US and Malawi, and has lived in Dublin since 1990. She trained as an actress at Trinity College, Dublin, and has worked in theatre, film and voiceover. *In the Woods* is her first novel.

Praise for IN THE WOODS:

'A real show-stopper of a thriller . . . French tightens the tension slowly until squealing point; Ryan's increasingly taut relationship with Maddox is woven cunningly around the crime plot. A splendid, page-turning debut.'

She

'The most breathtakingly brilliant and close-to-perfect thriller I've read for a long time. I stayed up until three in the morning two nights running unable to put it down.'

Sophie Hannah

'A taut debut from Tana French, IN THE WOODS is crime fiction at its best.'

Instyle UK Magazine

'Tana French's IN THE WOODS is a terrific debut . . . French's psychological insights into the damaged policeman's torment combine grippingly with the clammy atmosphere that surrounds the lethal woods. As an example of a novel in which the past returns to haunt the present, this scores very high marks.'

Marcel Berlins, *The Times*

IN THE WOODS

TANA FRENCH

HODDER

First published in Great Britain in 2007 by Hodder & Stoughton
A division of Hodder Headline

This paperback edition published in 2007

A Hodder paperback

24

A CIP catalogue record for this title
is available from the British Library

ISBN 978 0 340 92476 1

Typeset in Plantin by Hewer Text UK Ltd, Edinburgh
Printed and bound by Clays Ltd, St Ives plc

Hodder Headline's policy is to use papers that are natural, renewable
and recyclable products and made from wood grown in sustainable
forests. The logging and manufacturing processes are expected to
conform to the environmental regulations of the country of origin.

Hodder & Stoughton Ltd
A division of Hodder Headline
338 Euston Road
London NW1 3BH

For my father, David French,
and my mother, Elena Hvostoff-Lombardi

'Probably just somebody's nasty black poodle. But I've always wondered . . . What if it really was Him, and He decided I wasn't worth it?'

Tony Kushner, *A Bright Room Called Day*

Grateful acknowledgement is made for permission to reprint from the following copyrighted work:

Extract from 'At the British War Cemetery, Bayeux', from *Collected Poems 1951–2000* by Charles Causley, published by Macmillan. Copyright © Estate of Charles Causley 2000, reprinted by permission of David Higham Associates, 5–8 Lower John Street, Golden Square, London W1F 9HA.

PROLOGUE

Picture a summer stolen whole from some coming-of-age film set in small-town 1950s. This is none of Ireland's subtle seasons mixed for a connoisseur's palate, water-colour nuances within a pinch-sized range of cloud and soft rain; this is summer full-throated and extravagant in a hot pure silkscreen blue. This summer explodes on your tongue tasting of chewed blades of long grass, your own clean sweat, Marie biscuits with butter squirting through the holes and shaken bottles of red lemonade picnicked in tree houses. It tingles on your skin with BMX wind in your face, ladybug feet up your arm; it packs every breath full of mown grass and billowing washing-lines; it chimes and fountains with bird calls, bees, leaves and football-bounces and skipping-chants, *One! two! three!* This summer will never end. It starts every day with a shower of Mr Whippy notes and your best friend's knock at the door, finishes it with long slow twilight and mothers silhouetted in door-ways calling you to come in, through the bats shrilling among the black-lace trees. This is Everysummer decked in all its best glory.

Picture an orderly little maze of houses on a hill, only a few miles from Dublin. Someday, the government de-clared, this will be a buzzing marvel of suburban vitality, a plan-perfect solution to overcrowding and poverty and every urban ill; for now it is a few handfuls of cloned semi-d's, still new enough to look startled and gauche on their hillside. While the government rhapsodised about McDonald's and multi-screens, a few young families – escaping from the tenements and outdoor toilets that went unmentioned in 1970s Ireland, or dreaming big back gardens and hopscotch roads for their children, or just buying as close to home as a teacher's or bus driver's salary would let them – packed bin liners and bumped along a two-track path, grass and daisies growing down the middle, to their mint-new start.

That was ten years ago, and the vague strobe-light dazzle of chain stores and community centres conjured up under 'infrastructure' has so far failed to materialise (minor politicians occasionally bellow in the Dáil, unreported, about shady land deals). Farmers still pasture cows across the road, and night flicks on only a sparse constellation of lights on the neighbouring hillsides; behind the estate, where the someday plans show the shopping centre and the neat little park, spreads a square mile and who knows how many centuries of wood.

Move closer, follow the three children scrambling over the thin membrane of brick and mortar that holds the wood back from the semi-d's. Their bodies have the perfect economy of latency; they are streamlined and unselfconscious, pared to light flying machines. White tattoos – lightning-bolt, star, A – flash where they cut plasters into shapes and let the sun brown around them. A flag of white-blond hair flies out: toehold, knee on the wall, up and over and gone.

The wood is all flicker and murmur and illusion. Its silence is a pointillist conspiracy of a million tiny noises – rustles, flurries, nameless truncated shrieks; its emptiness teems with secret life, scurrying just beyond the corner of your eye. Careful: bees zip in and out of cracks in the leaning oak; stop to turn any stone and strange larvae will wriggle irritably, while an earnest thread of ants twines up your ankle. In the ruined tower, someone's abandoned stronghold, nettles thick as your wrist seize between the stones, and at dawn rabbits bring their kittens out from the foundations to play on ancient graves.

These three children own the summer. They know the wood as surely as they know the micro-landscapes of their own grazed knees; put them down blindfolded in any dell or clearing and they could find their way out without putting a foot wrong. This is their territory, and they rule it wild and lordly as young animals; they scramble through its trees and hide-and-seek in its hollows all the endless day long, and all night in their dreams.

They are running into legend, into sleepover stories and nightmares parents never hear. Down the faint lost paths you would never find alone, skidding round the tumbled stone walls, they stream calls and shoelaces behind them like comet-trails. And who is it waiting on the riverbank with his hands in the willow branches, whose laughter tumbles swaying from a branch high above, whose is the face in the undergrowth in the corner of your eye, built of light and leaf-shadow, there and gone in a blink?

These children will not be coming of age, this or any other summer. This August will not ask them to find hidden reserves of strength and courage as they confront the complexity of the adult world and come away sadder and wiser and bonded for life. This summer has other requirements for them.

I

What I warn you to remember is that I am a detective. Our relationship with truth is fundamental but cracked, refracting confusingly like fragmented glass. It is the core of our careers, the endgame of every move we make, and we pursue it with strategies painstakingly constructed of lies and concealment and every variation on deception. The truth is the most desirable woman in the world and we are the most jealous lovers, reflexively denying anyone else the slightest glimpse of her. We betray her routinely, spending hours and days stupor-deep in lies, and then turn back to her holding out the lover's ultimate Möbius strip: *But I only did it because I love you so much.*

I have a pretty knack for imagery, especially the cheap, facile kind. Don't let me fool you into seeing us as a bunch of *parfit gentil* knights galloping off in doublets after Lady Truth on her white palfrey. What we do is crude, crass and nasty. A girl gives her boyfriend an alibi for the evening when we suspect him of robbing a northside Centra and stabbing the clerk. I flirt with her at first, telling her I can see why he would want to stay home when he's got her; she is peroxided and greasy, with the flat, stunted features of generations of malnutrition, and privately I am thinking that if I were her boyfriend I would be relieved to trade her even for a hairy cellmate named Razor. Then I tell her we've found marked bills from the till in his classy white tracksuit bottoms, and he's claiming that she went out that evening and gave them to him when she got back.

I do it so convincingly, with such delicate cross-hatching of discomfort and compassion at her man's betrayal, that finally her faith in four shared years disintegrates like a sandcastle and through tears and snot, while her man sits with my partner in the next interview room saying nothing except 'Fuck off, I was home with Jackie,' she tells me everything from the time he left the house to the details of his sexual shortcomings. Then I pat her gently on the shoulder and give her a tissue and a cup of tea, and a statement sheet.

This is my job, and you don't go into it – or, if you do, you don't last – without some natural affinity for its priorities and demands. What I am telling you, before you begin my story, is this – two things: I crave truth. And I lie.

This is what I read in the file, the day after I made detective. I will come back to this story again and again, in any number of different ways. A poor thing, possibly, but mine own: this is the only story in the world that nobody but me will ever be able to tell.

On the afternoon of Tuesday 14 August 1984, three children – Germaine (Jamie) Elinor Rowan, Adam Robert Ryan and Peter Joseph Savage, all aged twelve – were playing in the road where their houses stood, in the small County Dublin town of Knocknaree. As it was a hot, clear day, many residents were in their gardens, and numerous witnesses saw the children at various times during the afternoon, balancing along the wall at the end of the road, riding their bicycles and swinging on a tyre-swing.

Knocknaree was at that time very sparsely developed, and a sizeable wood adjoined the estate, separated from it by a five-foot wall. Around 3.00 p.m. the three children left their bicycles in the Savages' front garden, telling Mrs Angela Savage – who was in the garden hanging washing on the line – that they were going to play in the wood. They did this often and knew that part of the wood well, so Mrs Savage was not worried that they would become lost. Peter had a wristwatch, and she told him to be home by 6.30 for his tea. This conversation was confirmed by her next-door neighbour, Mrs Mary Therese Corry, and several witnesses saw the children climbing over the wall at the end of the road and going into the wood.

When Peter Savage had not returned by 6.45 his mother called around to the mothers of the other two children, assuming he had gone to one of their houses. None of the children had returned. Peter Savage was normally reliable, but the parents did not at that point become worried; they assumed that the children had become absorbed in a game and forgotten to check the time. At approximately five minutes to seven Mrs Savage went around to the wood by the road, walked a little way in and called the children. She heard no answer and neither saw nor heard anything to indicate any person was present in the wood.

She returned home to serve tea to her husband, Mr Joseph Savage, and their four younger children. After tea Mr Savage and Mr John Ryan, Adam Ryan's father, went a little further into the wood, called the children and again received no response. At 8.25, when it was beginning to grow dark, the parents became seriously worried that the children might have become lost, and Miss Alicia Rowan (Germaine's mother, a single parent), who had a telephone, rang the police.

A search of the wood began. There was at this point some fear that the children might have run away. Miss

Rowan had decided that Germaine was to go to boarding-school in Dublin, remaining there during the week and returning to Knocknaree at weekends; she had been scheduled to leave two weeks later, and all three children had been very upset at the thought of being separated. However, a preliminary search of the children's rooms revealed that no clothing, money or personal items appeared to be missing. Germaine's piggy bank, in the form of a Russian doll, contained £5.85 and was intact.

At 10.20 p.m., a policeman with a torch found Adam Ryan in a densely wooded area near the centre of the wood, standing with his back and palms pressed against a large oak tree. His fingernails were digging into the trunk so deeply that they had broken off in the bark. He appeared to have been there for some time but had not responded to the searchers' calling. He was taken to hospital. The Dog Unit was called in and tracked the two missing children to a point not far from where Adam Ryan had been found; there the dogs became confused and lost the scent.

When I was found I was wearing blue denim shorts, a white cotton T-shirt, white cotton socks and white lace-up running shoes. The shoes were heavily bloodstained, the socks less heavily. Later analysis of the staining patterns showed that the blood had soaked through the shoes from the inside outwards; it had soaked through the socks, in lesser concentrations, from the outside in. The implication was that the shoes had been removed and blood had spilled into them; some time later, when it had begun to coagulate, the shoes had been replaced on my feet, thus transferring blood to the socks. The T-shirt showed four parallel tears, between three and five inches in length, running diagonally across the back from the mid-left shoulder-blade to the right back ribs.

I was uninjured except for some minor scratches on my calves, splinters (later found to be consistent with the wood of the oak tree) under my fingernails, and a deep abrasion on each kneecap, both beginning to form scabs. There was some uncertainty as to whether the grazes had been made in the wood or not, as a younger child (Aideen Watkins, aged five) who had been playing in the road stated that she had seen me fall from a wall earlier that day, landing on my knees. However, her statement varied with retelling and was not considered reliable. I was also near-catatonic: I made no voluntary movement for almost thirty-six hours and did not speak for a further two weeks. When I did, I had no memory of anything between leaving home that afternoon and being examined in the hospital.

The blood on my shoes and socks was tested for ABO type – DNA analysis was not a possibility in Ireland in 1984 – and found to be type A positive. My blood was also found to be type A positive; however, it was judged to be unlikely that the abrasions on my knees, although deep, could have drawn enough blood to cause the heavy soaking in the running shoes. Germaine Rowan's blood had been tested prior to an appendectomy two years earlier, and her records showed that she was also A positive. Peter Savage, though no blood type was on record for him, was eliminated as the source of the stains: both his parents were found to be type O, making it impossible that he could be anything else. In the absence of conclusive identification, investigators could not eliminate the possibility that the blood had come from a fourth individual, nor the possibility that it originated from multiple sources.

The search continued throughout the night of 14 August and for weeks thereafter – teams of volunteers combed the nearby fields and hills, every known bog-hole and bog drain in the area was explored, divers searched the river that ran through the wood – with no result. Fourteen months later, Mr Andrew Raftery, a local resident walking his dog in the wood, spotted a wristwatch in the undergrowth about two hundred feet from the tree where I had been found. The watch was distinctive – the face showed a cartoon of a footballer in action, and the second hand was tipped with a football – and Mr and Mrs Savage identified it as having belonged to their son Peter. Mrs Savage confirmed that he had been wearing it on the afternoon of his disappearance. The watch's plastic strap appeared to have been torn from the metal face with some force, possibly by catching on a low branch when Peter was running. The Technical Bureau identified a number of partial fingerprints on the strap and face; all were consistent with prints found on Peter Savage's belongings.

Despite numerous police appeals and a high-profile media campaign, no other trace of Peter Savage and Germaine Rowan was ever found.

I became a policeman because I wanted to be a murder detective. My time in training and in uniform – Templemore College, endless complicated physical exercises, wandering around small towns in a cartoonish Day-glo jacket, investigating which of the three unintelligible local delinquents had broken Mrs McSweeney's garden-shed window – all felt like an embarrassing daze scripted by Ionesco, a trial by tedium I had to endure, for some dislocated bureaucratic reason, in order to earn my actual job. I never think about those years and cannot remember them with any clarity. I made no friends; to me my detachment from the whole process felt involuntary and inevitable, like the side effect of a sedative drug, but the other cops read it as deliberate superciliousness, a studied sneer at their solid rural backgrounds and solid rural ambitions. Possibly it was. I recently found a diary entry from college in which I described my classmates as 'a herd of mouth-breathing culchie fucktards who wade around in a miasma of cliché so thick you can practically smell the bacon and cabbage and cow shite and altar candles'. Even assuming I was having a bad day, I think this shows a certain lack of respect for cultural differences.

When I made the Murder squad, I had already had my new work clothes – beautifully cut suits in materials so fine they felt alive to your fingers, shirts with the subtlest of blue or green pinstripes, rabbit-soft cashmere scarves – hanging in my wardrobe for almost a year. I love the unspoken dress code. It was one of the things that first fascinated me about the job – that and the private, functional, elliptical shorthand: latents, trace, Forensics. One of the Stephen King small towns where I was posted after Templemore had a murder: a routine domestic-violence incident that had escalated beyond even the perpetrator's expectations, but, because the man's previous girlfriend had died in suspicious circumstances, the Murder squad sent down a pair of detectives. All the week they were there, I had one eye on the coffee machine whenever I was at my desk, so I could get my coffee when the detectives got theirs, take my time adding milk and eavesdrop on the streamlined, brutal rhythms of their conversation: when the Bureau comes back on the tox, once the lab IDs the serrations. I started smoking again so I could follow them out to the car park and smoke a few feet from them, staring blindly at the sky and listening. They would give me brief unfocused smiles, sometimes a flick of a tarnished Zippo, before dismissing me with the slightest angle of a shoulder and going back to their subtle, multidimensional strategies. Pull in the ma first, then give him an hour or two to sit at home worrying about what she's saying, then get him back in. Set up a scene room but just walk him through it, don't give him time for a good look.

Contrary to what you might assume, I did not become a detective on some quixotic quest to solve my childhood mystery. I read the file once, that first day, late on my own in the squad room with my desk lamp the only pool of light (forgotten names setting echoes flicking like bats around my head as they testified in faded Biro that Jamie had kicked her mother because she didn't want to go to boarding-school, that 'dangerous-looking' teenage boys spent evenings hanging around at the edge of the wood, that Peter's mother once had a bruise on her cheekbone), and then never looked at it again. It was these arcana I craved, these near-invisible textures like a Braille legible only to the initiated. They were like thoroughbreds, those two Murder detectives passing through Ballygobackwards; like trapeze artists honed to a sizzling shine. They played for the highest stakes, and they were experts at their game.

I knew that what they did was cruel. Humans are feral and ruthless; this, this watching through cool intent eyes and delicately adjusting one factor or another till a man's fundamental instinct for self-preservation cracks, is savagery in its most pure, most polished and most highly evolved form.

We heard about Cassie days before she joined the squad, probably before she even got the offer. Our grapevine is ridiculously, old-ladyishly efficient. Murder is a high-pressure squad and a small one, only twenty permanent members, and under any added strain (anyone leaving, anyone new, too much work, too little work) it tends to develop a tinge of cabin-fevery hysteria, full of complicated alliances and frantic rumours. I am usually well out of the loop, but the Cassie Maddox buzz was loud enough that even I picked up on it.

For one thing she was a woman, which caused a certain amount of poorly sublimated outrage. We are all well trained to be horrified by the evils of prejudice, but there are deep stubborn veins of nostalgia for the 1950s (even among people my age; in much of Ireland the 50s didn't end until 1995, when we skipped straight to Thatcher's 80s), when you could scare a suspect into confession by threatening to tell his mammy and the only foreigners in the country were med students and work was the one place where you were safe from nagging females. Cassie was only the fourth woman Murder had taken on, and at least one of the others had been a huge mistake (a deliberate one, according to some people) who had entered squad lore when she nearly got herself and her partner killed by freaking out and throwing her gun at a cornered suspect's head.

Also, Cassie was only twenty-eight and only a few years out of Templemore. Murder is one of the élite squads, and nobody under thirty gets taken on unless his father is a politician. Generally you have to spend a couple of years as a floater, helping out wherever someone is needed for legwork, and then work your way up through at least one or two other squads. Cassie had less than a year in Drugs under her belt. The grapevine claimed, inevitably, that she was sleeping with someone important, or alternatively that she was someone's illegitimate daughter, or – with a touch more originality – that she had caught someone important buying drugs and this job was a payoff for keeping her mouth shut.

I had no problem with the idea of Cassie Maddox. I had only been in Murder a few months, but I disliked the New Neanderthal locker-room overtones, competing cars and competing aftershaves and subtly bigoted jokes justified as 'ironic', which always made me want to go into a long pedantic lecture on the definition of irony. On the whole I prefer women to men. I also had complicated private insecurities to do with my own place on the squad. I was almost thirty-one and had two years as a floater and two in Domestic Violence, so my appointment was less sketchy than Cassie's, but I sometimes thought the brass assumed I was a good detective in the mindless pre-programmed way that some men will assume a tall, slim, blonde woman is beautiful even if she has a face like a hyperthyroid turkey: because I have all the accessories. I have a perfect BBC accent, picked up at boarding-school as protective camouflage, and all that colonisation takes a while to wear off: even though the Irish will cheer for absolutely any team playing against England, and I know a number of pubs where I couldn't order a drink without risking a glass to the back of the head, they still assume that anyone with a stiff upper lip is more intelligent, better educated and generally more likely to be right. On top of this I am tall, with a bony, rangy build that can look lean and elegant if my suit is cut just right, and fairly good-looking in an offbeat way. Central Casting would definitely think I was a good detective, probably the brilliant maverick loner who risks his neck fearlessly and always gets his man.

I have practically nothing in common with that guy, but I wasn't sure anyone else had noticed. Sometimes, after too much solitary vodka, I came up with vivid paranoid scenarios in which the superintendent found out I was actually a civil servant's son from Knocknaree and I got transferred to Intellectual Property Rights. With Cassie Maddox around, I figured, people were much less likely to spend time having suspicions about me.

When she finally arrived, she was actually sort of an anticlimax. The lavishness of the rumours had left me with a mental picture of someone on the same TV-drama scale, with legs up to here and shampoo-ad hair and possibly a catsuit. Our superintendent, O'Kelly, introduced her at Monday-morning parade, and she stood up and said something standard about being delighted to join the squad and hoping she'd live up to its high standards; she was barely medium height, with a cap of dark curls and a boyish, slim, square-shouldered build. She wasn't my type – I have always liked girlie girls, sweet tiny bird-boned girls I can pick up and whirl around in a one-armed hug – but there was something about her: maybe the way she stood, weight on one hip, straight and easy as a gymnast; maybe just the mystery.

'I heard her family are Masons and they threatened to have the squad dissolved if we didn't take her on,' said Sam O'Neill, behind me. Sam is a stocky, cheerful, unflappable guy from Galway. I hadn't had him down as one of the people who would get swept up in the rumour tsunami.

'Oh for God's sake,' I said, falling for it. Sam grinned and shook his head at me, and slid past me to a seat. I went back to looking at Cassie, who had sat down and propped one foot against the chair in front of her, leaning her notebook on her thigh.

She wasn't dressed like a murder detective. You learn by osmosis, as soon as you set your sights on the job, that you are expected to look professional, educated, discreetly expensive with just a soupçon of originality. We give the taxpayers their money's worth of comforting cliché. We mostly shop at Brown Thomas, during the sales, and occasionally come into work wearing embarrassingly identical soupçons. Up until then, the wackiest our squad had got was this cretin called Quigley, who sounded like Daffy Duck with a Donegal accent and wore slogan T-shirts (MAD BASTARD) under his suits because he thought he was being daring. When he eventually realised that none of us were shocked, or even remotely interested, he got his mammy to come up for the day and take him shopping at BT.

That first day I put Cassie in the same category. She was wearing combats and a wine-coloured woollen jumper with sleeves that came down past her wrists, and clunky trainers, and I put this down as affectation: *Look, I'm too cool for your conventions*. The spark of animosity this ignited increased my attraction to her. There is a side of me that is most intensely attracted to women who annoy me.

I didn't register her very much over the next couple of weeks, except in the general way that you do register any decent-looking woman when you're surrounded by men. She was being shown the ropes by Tom Costello, our resident grizzled veteran, and I was working on a homeless man found battered to death in an alleyway. Some of the depressing, inexorable flavour of his life had leaked over into his death, and it was one of those cases that are hopeless from the start – no leads, nobody saw anything, nobody heard anything, whoever killed him was probably so drunk or high he didn't even remember doing it – so my gung-ho newbie sparkle was starting to look a little patchy. I was also partnered with Quigley, which wasn't working out; his idea of humour was to re-enact large segments of *Wallace and Gromit* and then do a Woody Woodpecker laugh to show you they were funny, and it was dawning on me that I'd been teamed up with him not because he would be friendly to the new boy but because nobody else wanted him. I didn't have the time or the energy to get to know Cassie. Sometimes I wonder how long we might have gone on like that. Even in a small squad, there are always people with whom you never get beyond nods and smiles in corridors, simply because your paths never happen to cross anywhere else.

We became friends because of her moped, a cream 1981 Vespa that somehow, in spite of its classic status, reminds me of a happy mutt with some border collie in its pedigree. I call it the Golf Cart to annoy Cassie; she calls my battered white Land Rover the Compensation Wagon, with the odd compassionate remark about my girlfriends, or the Eco-mobile when she is feeling bolshie. The Golf Cart chose a viciously wet, windy day in September to break down outside work. I was on my way out of the car park and saw this little dripping girl in a red rain jacket, looking like Kenny out of *South Park*, standing beside this little dripping bike and yelling after a bus that had just drenched her. I pulled over and called out the window, 'Could you use a hand?'

She looked at me and shouted back, 'What makes you think that?' and then, taking me completely by surprise, started to laugh.

For about five minutes, as I tried to get the Vespa to start, I fell in love with her. The oversized raincoat made her look about eight, as though she should have had matching wellies with ladybugs on them, and inside the red hood were huge brown eyes and rain-spiked lashes and a face like a kitten's. I wanted to dry her gently with a big fluffy towel, in front of a roaring fire. But then she said,

'Here, let me – you have to know how to twist the thingy,' and I raised an eyebrow and said, 'The *thingy*? Honestly, *girls*.'

I immediately regretted it – I have never been talented at banter, and you never know, she could have been some earnest droning feminist extremist who would lecture me in the rain about Amelia Earhart. But Cassie gave me a deliberate, sideways look, and then clasped her hands with a wet spat and said in a breathy Marilyn voice, 'Ohhh, I've always *dreamed* of a knight in shining armour coming along and rescuing little me! Only in my dreams he was good-looking.'

What I saw transformed with a click like a shaken kaleidoscope. I stopped falling in love with her and started to like her immensely. I looked at her hoodie jacket and said, 'Oh my God, they're about to kill Kenny.' Then I loaded the Golf Cart into the back of my Land Rover and drove her home.

She had a studio flat, which is what landlords call a bedsit where there is room to have a friend over, on the top floor of a semi-dilapidated Georgian house in Sandymount. The road was quiet; the wide sash window looked out, over rooftops, to Sandymount beach. There were wooden bookshelves crammed with old paperbacks, a low Victorian sofa upholstered in a virulent shade of turquoise, a big futon with a patchwork duvet, no ornaments or posters, a handful of shells and rocks and chestnuts on the window-sill.

I don't remember very many specifics about that evening, and according to Cassie neither does she. I can remember some of the things we talked about, a few piercingly clear images, but I could give you almost none of the actual words. This strikes me as odd and, in certain moods, as very magical, linking the evening to those fugue states that over the centuries have been blamed on fairies or witches or aliens, and from which no one returns unchanged. But those lost, liminal pockets of time are usually solitary; there is something about the idea of a shared one that makes me think of twins, reaching out slow blind hands in a gravity-free and wordless space.

I know I stayed for dinner – a studenty dinner, fresh pasta and sauce from a jar, hot whiskey in china mugs. I remember Cassie opening a huge wardrobe that took up most of one wall, to pull out a towel for me to dry my hair. Someone, presumably her, had slotted bookshelves inside the wardrobe. The shelves were set at odd, off-kilter heights and packed with a wild variety of objects: I didn't get a proper look, but there were chipped enamel saucepans, marbled notebooks, soft jewel-coloured jumpers, tumbles of scribbled paper. It was like something in the background of one of those old illustrations of fairy-tale cottages.

I do remember finally asking, 'So how did you end up in the squad?' We had been talking about how she was settling in, and I thought I had dropped it in pretty casually, but she gave me a tiny, mischievous smile, as though we were playing draughts and she had caught me trying to distract her from a clumsy move.

'Being a girl, you mean?'

'Actually, I meant being so young,' I said, although of course I had been thinking of both.

'Costello called me "son" yesterday,' Cassie said. ' "Fair play to you, son." Then he got all flustered and stammery. I think he was afraid I'd sue.'

'It was probably a compliment, in its own way,' I said.

'That's how I took it. He's quite sweet, really.' She tucked a cigarette in her mouth and held out her hand; I threw her my lighter.

'Someone told me you were undercover as a hooker and ran into one of the brass,' I said, but Cassie just tossed the lighter back to me and grinned.

'Quigley, right? He told me you were an MI6 mole.'

'What?' I said, outraged and falling straight into my own trap. 'Quigley is a cretin.'

'Gee, you think?' she said, and started to laugh. After a moment I joined in. The mole thing bothered me – if anyone actually believed it, they would never tell me anything again – and being taken for English infuriates me to an irrational degree, but I sort of enjoyed the absurd idea of me as James Bond.

'I'm from *Dublin*,' I said. 'I got the accent at boarding-school in England. And that lobotomised bogger knows it.' Which he did; in my first weeks on the squad he had pestered me so monotonously about what an English guy was doing in the Irish police force, like a child poking you in the arm and droning 'Why? Why? Why?', that I had finally broken my need-to-know rule and explained the accent. Apparently I should have used smaller words.

'What are you doing working with him?' Cassie asked.

'Quietly losing my mind,' I said.

Something, I'm still not sure what, had made up Cassie's mind. She leaned sideways, switching her mug to the other hand (she swears we were drinking coffee by that stage and claims that I only think it was hot whiskey because we drank it so often that winter, but I know, I remember the sharp prongs of a clove on my tongue, the heady steam), and pulled up her top to just under her breast. I was so startled that it took me a moment to realise what she was showing me: a long scar, still red and raised and spidered with stitch-marks, curving along the line of a rib. 'I got stabbed,' she said.

It was so obvious that I was embarrassed nobody had thought of it. A detective wounded on duty gets his or her choice of assignment. I suppose we had overlooked this possibility because normally a stabbing would have practically shorted out the grapevine; we had heard nothing about this.

'Jesus,' I said. 'What happened?'

'I was undercover in UCD,' Cassie said. This explained both the clothes and the information gap – undercover are serious about secrecy. 'That's how I made detective so fast. There was a ring dealing on campus, and Drugs wanted to find out who was behind it, so they needed people who could pass for students. I went in as a psychology postgrad. I did a few years of psychology at Trinity before Templemore, so I could talk the talk, and I look young.'

She did. There was a specific clarity about her face that I've never seen in anyone else; her skin was poreless as a child's, and her features – wide mouth, high round cheekbones, tilted nose, long curves of eyebrow – made other people's look smudged and blurry. As far as I could tell she never wore make-up, except for a red-tinted lip balm that smelled of cinnamon and made her seem even younger. Few people would have considered her beautiful, but my tastes have always leaned towards bespoke rather than brand-name, and I took far more pleasure in looking at her than at any of the busty blonde clones whom magazines, insultingly, tell me I should desire.

'And your cover got blown?'

'*No*,' she said, indignant. 'I found out who the main dealer was – this brain-dead rich boy from Blackrock, studying business, of course – and I spent months making friends with him, laughing at his crap jokes, proof-reading his essays. Then I suggested maybe I could deal to the girls, they'd be less nervous about buying drugs from another woman, right? He liked the idea, everything was going great, I was dropping hints that maybe it would be simpler if I met the supplier myself instead of getting the stuff through him. Only then Dealer Boy started snorting a little too much of his own speed – this was in May, he had exams coming up. He got paranoid, decided I was trying to take over his business and stabbed me.' She took a sip of her drink. 'Don't tell Quigley, though. The operation's still going on, so I'm not supposed to talk about it. Let the poor little fucker enjoy his illusions.'

I was secretly terribly impressed, not only by the stabbing (after all, I told myself, it wasn't as though she had done something outstandingly brave or intelligent; she had just failed to dodge fast enough) but by the dark, adrenalin-paced thought of undercover work and by the utter casualness with which she told the story. Having worked hard to perfect an air of easy indifference, I recognise the real thing when I see it.

'Jesus,' I said again. 'I bet he got a good going-over when they brought him in.' I've never hit a suspect – I find there's no need to, as long as you make them think you might – but there are guys who do, and anyone who stabs a cop is likely to pick up a few bruises en route to the station.

She cocked an eyebrow at me, amused. 'They didn't. That would've wrecked the whole operation. They need him to get to the supplier; they just started over with a new undercover.'

'But don't you want him taken down?' I said, frustrated

by her calm and by my own creeping sense of naïveté. 'He *stabbed* you.'

Cassie shrugged. 'After all, if you think about it, he had a point: I *was* only pretending to be his friend to screw him over. And he was a strung-out drug dealer. That's what strung-out drug dealers do.'

After that my memory grows hazy again. I know that, determined to impress her in my turn, and never having been stabbed or involved in a shoot-out or anything, I told her a long and rambling and mostly true story about talking down a guy who was threatening to jump off the roof of a block of flats with his baby, back when I was in Domestic Violence (really, I think I must have been a little drunk: another reason I'm so sure we had hot whiskey). I remember a passionate conversation about Dylan Thomas, I think, Cassie kneeling up on the sofa and gesturing, her cigarette burning away forgotten in the ashtray. Bantering, smart but tentative as shy circling children, both of us checking covertly after each riposte to make sure we hadn't crossed any line or hurt any feelings. Firelight and the Cowboy Junkies, Cassie singing along in a sweet rough undertone.

'The drugs you got from Dealer Boy,' I said, later. 'Did you actually sell them to students?'

Cassie got up to put on the kettle. 'Occasionally,' she said.

'Didn't that bother you?'

'Everything about undercover bothered me,' Cassie said. 'Everything.'

When we went into work the next morning we were friends. It really was as simple as that: we planted seeds without thinking, and woke up to our own private beanstalk. At break-time I caught Cassie's eye and mimed a cigarette and we went outside to sit cross-legged at either end of a bench, like bookends. At the end of the shift she waited for me, bitching to the air about how long I took to get my things together ('It's like hanging out with Sarah Jessica Parker. Don't forget your lip-liner, sweetie, we don't want the chauffeur to have to go back for it again'), and said 'Pint?' on the way down the stairs. I can't explain the alchemy that transmuted one evening into the equivalent of years held lightly in common. The only way I can put it is that we recognised, too surely even for surprise, that we shared the same currency.

As soon as she finished learning the ropes with Costello, we partnered up. O'Kelly put up a bit of a fight – he didn't like the idea of two shiny new rookies working together, and it meant he would have to find something else to do with Quigley – but I had, by sheer luck rather than shrewd detection, found someone who had heard someone bragging about killing the homeless guy, so I was in O'Kelly's good books, and I took full advantage of it. He warned us that he would give us only the simplest cases and the no-hopers, 'nothing that needs real detective work', and we nodded meekly and thanked him again, aware that murderers aren't considerate enough to ensure that the complex cases come up in strict rotation. Cassie moved her stuff to the desk beside mine, and Costello got stuck with Quigley and gave us sad reproachful looks for weeks, like a martyred Labrador.

Over the next couple of years we developed, I think, a good reputation within the squad. We pulled in the suspect from the alley beating and interrogated him for six hours – although, if you deleted every recurrence of 'Ah, fuck, man' from the tape, I doubt it would run over forty minutes – until he confessed. He was a junkie called Wayne ('*Wayne*,' I said to Cassie, while we were getting him a Sprite and watching him pick his spots in the one-way glass. 'Why didn't his parents just tattoo "Nobody in my family has ever finished secondary school" on his forehead at birth?') and he had beaten up the homeless guy, who was known as Beardy Eddie, for stealing his blanket. After he signed his statement, Wayne wanted to know if he could have his blanket back. We handed him over to the uniforms and told him they would look into it, and then we went back to Cassie's with a bottle of champagne and stayed up talking till six in the morning, and came into work late and sheepish and still a little giggly.

We went through the predictable process where Quigley and a few of the others spent a while asking me whether I was shagging her and whether, if so, she was a goer; once it dawned on them that I genuinely wasn't, they moved on to her probable dykehood (I have always considered Cassie to be very clearly feminine, but I could see how, to a certain kind of mind, the haircut and the lack of make-up and the boys'-department corduroys would add up to Sapphic tendencies). Cassie eventually got bored of this and tidied things up by appearing at the Christmas party with a strapless black velvet cocktail dress and a bullishly handsome rugby player named Gerry. He was actually her second cousin and happily married, but he was heartily protective of Cassie and had no objection to gazing adoringly at her for an evening if it would smooth her career path.

After that, the rumours faded and people more or less left us to our own devices, which suited us both. Contrary to appearances, Cassie is not a particularly social person, any more than I am; she is vivacious and quick with banter and can talk to anyone, but given the choice she preferred my company to that of a big group. I slept on her sofa a lot. Our solve rate was good and rising; O'Kelly stopped threatening to split us up every time we were late turning in paperwork. We were in the courtroom to see Wayne found guilty of manslaughter ('Ah, *fuck*, man'). Sam O'Neill drew a deft little caricature of the two of us as Mulder and Scully (I still have it, somewhere) and Cassie stuck it to the side of her computer, next to a bumper sticker that said 'Bad cop! No doughnut!'

In retrospect, I think Cassie came along at just the right time for me. My dazzling, irresistible outsider's vision of the Murder squad had not included things like Quigley, or gossip, or interminable circular interrogations of junkies with six-word vocabularies and dentist's-drill accents. I had pictured a tensile, heightened mode of existence, everything small and petty bush-fired away by a readiness so charged it snapped sparks, and the reality had left me bewildered and let down, like a child opening a glittering Christmas present and finding woolly socks inside. If it hadn't been for Cassie, I think I might have ended up turning into that detective on *Law and Order*, the one who has ulcers and thinks everything is a government conspiracy.

2

We caught the Devlin case on a Wednesday morning in August. It was, according to my notes, 11.48, so everyone else was out getting coffee. Cassie and I were playing Worms on my computer.

'Ha,' said Cassie, sending one of her worms bopping over to mine with a baseball bat and thwacking him off a cliff. My worm, Groundsweeper Willy, yelled 'Och, ye big mammy's boy!' at me on his way down towards the ocean.

'I let you do that,' I told her.

'Course you did,' said Cassie. 'No real man could actually be beaten by a little girl. Even the worm knows it: only a raisin-balled, testosterone-free creampuff could—'

'Fortunately I'm secure enough in my masculinity that I don't feel remotely threatened by—'

'Shh,' said Cassie, turning my face back towards the monitor. 'Nice boy. Shush, look pretty and play with your worm. God knows nobody else is going to.'

'I think I'll transfer somewhere nice and peaceful, like ERU,' I said.

'ERU needs fast response times, sweetie,' Cassie said. 'If it takes you half an hour to decide what to do with an imaginary worm, they're not gonna want you in charge of hostages.'

At that point O'Kelly banged into the squad room and demanded, 'Where is everyone?' Cassie hit Alt-Tab fast;

one of her worms was named O'Smelly and she had been purposefully sending him into hopeless situations, to watch him get blown up by exploding sheep.

'Break,' I said.

'Bunch of archaeologists found a body. Who's up?'

'We'll have it,' said Cassie, shoving her foot off my chair so that hers shot back to her own desk.

'Why us?' I said. 'Can't the pathologist deal with it?'

Archaeologists are required by law to call the police if they find human remains at a depth of less than nine feet below ground level. This is in case some genius gets the idea of concealing a murder by burying the corpse in a fourteenth-century graveyard and hoping it gets marked down as medieval. I suppose they figure that anyone who has the enterprise to dig down more than nine feet without getting spotted deserves a little leeway for sheer dedication. Uniforms and pathologists get called out fairly regularly, when subsidence and erosion have brought a skeleton close to the surface, but usually this is only a formality; it's relatively simple to distinguish between modern and ancient remains. Detectives are called only in exceptional circumstances, usually when a peat bog has preserved flesh and bone so perfectly that the body has all the clamouring immediacy of a fresh corpse.

'Not this time,' said O'Kelly. 'It's modern. Young female, looks like murder. Uniforms asked for us. They're only in Knocknaree, so you won't need to stay out there.'

Something strange happened to my breath. Cassie stopped shoving things into her satchel and I felt her eyes flick to me for a split second. 'Sir, I'm sorry, we really can't take on another full murder investigation right now. We're bang in the middle of the McLoughlin case and—'

'That didn't bother you when you thought this was just an afternoon off, Maddox,' said O'Kelly. He dislikes Cassie for a series of mind-numbingly predictable reasons – her sex, her clothes, her age, her semi-heroic record – and the predictability bothers her far more than the dislike. 'If you had time for a day out down the country, you have time for a serious murder investigation. The Tech Bureau are already on their way.' And he left.

'Oh, shit,' said Cassie. 'Oh, shit, the little wanker. Ryan, I'm so sorry. I just didn't think—'

'It's fine, Cass,' I said. One of the best things about Cassie is that she knows when to shut up and leave you alone. It was her turn to drive, but she picked out my favourite unmarked – a '98 Saab that handles like a dream – and threw me the keys. In the car, she dug her CD-holder out of her satchel and passed it to me; driver chooses the music, but I tend to forget to bring any. I picked the first thing that looked as if it had a hard pounding bass, and turned it up loud.

I hadn't been to Knocknaree since that summer. I went to boarding-school a few weeks after Jamie should have gone – not the same school; one in Wiltshire, as far away as my parents could afford – and when I came back at Christmas we lived in Leixlip, out on the other side of Dublin. Once we hit the dual carriageway, Cassie had to dig out the map and find the exit, then navigate us down potholed side roads with grass verges, hedges grown wild and scraping at the windows.

Obviously, I have always wished I could remember what happened in that wood. The very few people who know about the whole Knocknaree thing invariably suggest, sooner or later, that I should try hypnotic regression, but for some reason I find the idea distasteful. I'm deeply suspicious of anything with a whiff of the New-Age about it – not because of the practices themselves, which as far as I can tell from a safe distance may well have a lot to them, but because of the people who get involved, who always seem to be the kind who corner you at parties to explain how they discovered that they are survivors and deserve to be happy. I worry that I might come out of hypnosis with that sugar-high glaze of self-satisfied enlightenment, like a seventeen-year-old who's just discovered Kerouac, and start proselytising strangers in pubs.

The Knocknaree site was a huge field set on a shallow slope, down the side of a hill. It was stripped to bare earth, churned up by indecipherable archaeological scribblings – trenches, giant anthills of soil, Portakabins, scattered fragments of rough stone wall like outlines for some lunatic maze – that made it surreal, post-nuclear. It was bordered on one side by a thick stand of trees, on another by a wall, tidy gables peeking over it, that ran from the trees to the road. Towards the top of the slope, near the wall, techs were clustered around something cordoned off by blue-and-white crime-scene tape. I probably knew every one of them, but the context translated them – white boiler suits, busy gloved hands, nameless delicate instruments – into something alien and sinister and possibly CIA-related. The one or two identifiable objects looked picture-book solid and comforting: a low whitewashed cottage just off the road, with a black-and-white sheepdog stretched in front of it, paws twitching; a stone tower covered in ivy that rippled like water in the breeze. Light fluttered off the dark slice of a river cutting across one corner of the field.

trainer heels dug into the earth of the bank, leaf-shadows

dappling a red T-shirt, fishing-rods of branches and string,
slapping at midges: Shut up! You'll scare the fish! –

This field was where the wood had been, twenty years
ago. The strip of trees was what was left of it. I had lived in
one of the houses beyond the wall.

I had not expected this. I don't watch Irish news; it
always morphs into a migraine blur of identical sociopath-
eyed politicians mouthing meaningless white noise, like
the gibber you get when you play a 33-rpm record at
45. I stick to foreign news, where distance gives enough
simplification for the comforting illusion that there is
some difference between the various players. I had
known, by vague osmosis, that there was an archaeological site somewhere around Knocknaree and that there
was some controversy about it, but I hadn't picked up
the details, or the exact location. I had not been expecting
this.

I parked in a lay-by across the road from the Portakabin
cluster, between the Bureau van and a big black Merc –
Cooper, the State pathologist. We got out of the car and I
stopped to check my gun: clean, loaded, safety on. I wear a
shoulder holster; anywhere more obvious feels gauche, a
legal equivalent of flashing. Cassie says fuck gauche, when
you are five foot five and young and female a little blatant
authority isn't a bad thing, and wears a belt. Often the
discrepancy works for us: people don't know who to worry
about, the little girl with the gun or the big guy apparently
without, and the distraction of deciding keeps them off
balance.

Cassie leaned against the car and dug her smokes out of
her satchel. 'Want one?'

'No, thanks,' I said. I went over my harness, tightened
the straps, made sure none of them were twisted. My

fingers seemed thick and clumsy, detached from my body. I did not want Cassie to point out that, whoever this girl was and whenever she had been killed, it was unlikely that the murderer was skulking behind a Portakabin needing to be taken at gunpoint. She tipped her head back and blew smoke up into the branches overhead. It was your basic Irish summer day, irritatingly coy, all sun and skidding clouds and jack-knifing breeze, ready at any second to make an effortless leap into bucketing rain or blazing sun or both.

'Come on,' I said. 'Let's get into character.' Cassie put out her smoke on the sole of her shoe and tucked the butt back into the packet, and we headed across the road.

A middle-aged guy in an unravelling jumper was hovering between the Portakabins, looking lost. He perked up when he saw us.

'Detectives,' he said. 'You must be the detectives, yes? Dr Hunt . . . I mean, Ian Hunt. Site director. Where would you like to – well, the office or the body or . . .? I'm not sure, you know. Protocol and things like that.' He was one of those people whom your mind instantly starts turning into a cartoon: scribbled wings and beak and ta-da, Professor Yaffle.

'Detective Maddox, and this is Detective Ryan,' Cassie said. 'If it's all right, Dr Hunt, maybe one of your colleagues could give Detective Ryan an overview of the whole site, while you show me the remains?'

Little bitch, I thought. I felt jittery and dazed at the same time, as if I had a massive stone-over and had tried to clear it with way too much caffeine; the light jinking off fragments of mica in the rutted ground looked too bright, tricky and fevered. I was in no mood to be protected. But one of Cassie's and my unspoken rules is that, in public at least, we do not contradict each other. Sometimes one of us takes advantage of it.

'Um . . . yes,' said Hunt, blinking at us through his glasses. He somehow gave the impression of constantly dropping things – lined yellow pages, chewed-looking tissues, half-wrapped throat lozenges – even though he wasn't holding anything. 'Yes, of course. They're all . . . Well, Mark and Damien usually do the tours, but you see Damien's . . . Mark!' He aimed it in the general direction of the open door of a Portakabin, and I had a fleeting glimpse of a bunch of people crowded around a bare table: army jackets, sandwiches and steaming mugs, clods of earth on the floor. One of the guys tossed down a hand of cards and started disentangling himself from the plastic chairs.

'I told them all, stay in there,' said Hunt. 'I wasn't sure . . . Evidence. Footprints and . . . fibres.'

'That's perfect, Dr Hunt,' Cassie said. 'We'll try to clear the scene and let you get back to work as soon as possible.'

'We've only got a few weeks left,' said the guy at the Portakabin door. He was short and wiry, with a build that would have looked almost childishly slight under a heavy jumper; he was wearing a T-shirt, though, with muddy combats and Doc boots, and below the sleeves his muscles were complex and corded as a featherweight's.

'Then you'd better get a move on and show my colleague around,' Cassie told him.

'Mark,' said Hunt. 'Mark, this detective needs a tour. The usual, you know, around the site.'

Mark eyed Cassie for another moment, then gave her a nod; she had apparently passed some private test. He moved on to me. He was somewhere in his mid-twenties, with a long fair ponytail and a narrow, foxy face with very green, very intense eyes. Men like him – men who are obviously interested purely in what they think of other people, not in what other people think of them – have always made me violently insecure. They have a kind of gyroscopic certainty that makes me feel bumbling, affected, spineless, in the wrong place in the wrong clothes.

'You'll want wellies,' he told me, giving my shoes a sardonic look: QED. His accent had a hard border-country edge. 'Spares in the tools shed.'

'I'll be fine as I am,' I said. I had an idea that archaeological digs involved trenches several feet deep in mud, but I was damned if I was going to spend the morning clumping around after this guy with my suit trailing off ludicrously into someone's discarded wellies. I wanted something – a cup of tea, a smoke, anything that would give me an excuse to sit still for five minutes and figure out how to do this.

Mark raised one eyebrow. 'Fair enough. Over this way.'

He headed off between the Portakabins without checking whether I was behind him. Cassie, unexpectedly, grinned at me as I followed him – a mischievous *Gotcha!* grin, which made me feel a little better. I scratched my cheek at her, with my middle finger.

Mark took me across the site, along a narrow path between mysterious earthworks and clumps of stones. He walked like a martial artist or a poacher, a long, easy, balanced lope. 'Medieval drainage ditch,' he said, pointing. A couple of crows shot up from an abandoned wheelbarrow full of dirt, decided we were harmless and went back to picking through the earth. 'And that's a Neolithic settlement. This site's been inhabited more or less nonstop since the Stone Age. Still is. See the cottage, that's eighteenth-century. It was one of the places where they planned the 1798 Rebellion.' He glanced over his shoulder at me, and I had an absurd impulse to explain my accent and inform him that I was not only Irish but from just around the corner, so there. 'The guy who lives there now is descended from the guy who built it.'

We had reached the stone tower in the middle of the site. Arrow-slits showed through gaps in the ivy, and a section of broken wall sloped down from one side. It looked vaguely, frustratingly familiar, but I couldn't tell whether this was because I actually remembered it or because I knew I should.

Mark pulled a packet of tobacco out of his combats and started rolling a cigarette. There was masking tape wrapped around both his hands, at the base of the fingers. 'The Walsh clan built this keep in the fourteenth century, added a castle over the next couple of hundred years,' he said. 'This was all their territory, from those hills over there' – he jerked his head at the horizon, high overlapping hills furred with dark trees – 'to a bend in the river down beyond that grey farmhouse. They were rebels, raiders. In the seventeenth century they used to ride into Dublin, all the way to the British barracks in Rathmines, grab a few guns, whack the heads off any soldiers they saw, and then leg it. By the time the British got organised to go after them, they'd be halfway back here.'

He was the right person to tell the story. I thought of rearing hooves, torchlight and dangerous laughter, the rising pulse of war drums. Over his shoulder I could see Cassie, up by the crime-scene tape, talking to Cooper and taking notes.

'I hate to interrupt you,' I said, 'but I'm afraid I won't have time for the full tour. I just need a very basic overview of the site.'

Mark licked the Rizla, sealed his rollie and found a lighter. 'Fair enough,' he said, and started pointing. 'Neolithic settlement, Bronze Age ceremonial stone, Iron Age round-house, Viking dwellings, fourteenth-century keep, sixteenth-century castle, eighteenth-century cottage.' 'Bronze Age ceremonial stone' was where Cassie and the techs were.

'Is the site guarded at night?' I asked.

He laughed. 'Nah. We lock the finds shed, obviously, and the office, but anything really valuable goes back to head office right away. And we started locking the tools shed a month or two ago – some of our tools went missing, and we found out the farmers had been using our hoses to water their fields in dry weather. That's it. What's the point of guarding it? In a month it'll all be gone anyway, except for this.' He slapped the wall of the tower; something scuttled in the ivy above our heads.

'Why's that?' I asked.

He stared at me, giving it an impressive level of incredulous disgust. 'In a month's time,' he said, enunciating clearly for me, 'the fucking government is going to bulldoze this whole site and build a fucking motorway over it. They graciously agreed to leave a fucking traffic island for the keep, so they can wank off about how much they've done to preserve our heritage.'

I remembered the motorway now, from some news report: a bland politician being shocked at the archaeologists who wanted the taxpayer to pay millions to redesign the plans. I had probably changed the channel at that point. 'We'll try not to delay you for too long,' I said. 'The dog at the cottage: does he bark when people come to the site?'

Mark shrugged and went back to his cigarette. 'Not at us, but he knows us. We feed him scraps and all. He might if someone went too near the cottage, specially at night, but probably not for someone up by the wall. Off his territory.'

'What about cars – does he bark at them?'

'Did he bark at yours? He's a sheepdog, not a guard dog.' He sent out a narrow ribbon of smoke between his teeth.

So the killer could have come to the site from any direction: by road, from the estate, even along the river if he liked making things difficult. 'That's all I need for now,' I said. 'Thanks for your time. If you'll wait with the others, we'll come and update you in just a few minutes.'

'Don't walk on anything that looks like archaeology,' Mark said, and loped off back to the Portakabins. I headed up the slope towards the body.

The Bronze Age ceremonial stone was a flat, massive block, maybe seven feet long by three wide by three high, chipped from a single boulder. The field around it had been crudely bulldozed away – not too long ago, judging by the way the ground gave under my shoes – but a cushion around the stone had been left untouched, so that it rode high like an island amid the churned earth. On top of it, something flashed blue and white between the nettles and long grass.

It wasn't Jamie. I had more or less known this already – if there had been a chance it might be, Cassie would have come to tell me – but it still blew my mind empty. This girl had long dark hair, one plait thrown across her face. That was all I noticed, at first, the dark hair. It didn't even occur to me that Jamie's body wouldn't have been in this condition.

I had missed Cooper: he was picking his way back towards the road, shaking his foot like a cat on every step. A tech was taking photos, another was dusting the table for prints; a handful of local uniforms were fidgeting and chatting with the morgue guys, over by their stretcher. The grass was scattered with triangular numbered markers. Cassie and Sophie Miller were crouching beside the stone table, looking at something on the edge. I knew it was Sophie right away; that backboard-straight posture cuts through the anonymous coveralls. Sophie is my favourite crime-scene tech. She is slim and dark and demure, and on her the white shower cap looks like she should be bending over wounded soldiers' beds with cannon-fire in the background, murmuring something soothing and giving out sips of water from a canteen. In actual fact, she is quick and impatient and can put anyone from superintendents to prosecutors in their place with a few crisp words. I like incongruity.

'Which way?' I called, at the tape. You don't walk on a crime scene until the Bureau guys say you can.

'Hi, Rob,' Sophie shouted, straightening up and pulling down her mask. 'Hang on.'

Cassie reached me first. 'Only been dead a day or so,' she said quietly, before Sophie caught up. She looked a little pale around the mouth; kids do that to most of us.

'Thanks, Cass,' I said. 'Hi, Sophie.'

'Hey, Rob. You two still owe me a drink.' We had promised to buy her cocktails if she got the lab to fast-track some blood analysis for us, a couple of months before. Since then we'd all been saying 'We have to meet up for that drink' on a regular basis, and never getting around to it.

'Come through for us on this one and we'll buy you dinner as well,' I said. 'What've we got?'

'White female, ten to thirteen,' Cassie said. 'No ID. There's a key in her pocket, looks like a house key, but that's it. Her head's smashed in, but Cooper found pete-chial haemorrhaging and some possible ligature marks on her neck, too, so we'll have to wait for the post for cause of death. She's fully dressed, but it looks like she was probably raped. This one's weird all round, Rob. Cooper says she's been dead somewhere around thirty-six hours, but there's been practically no insect activity, and I don't see how the archaeologists could have missed her if she'd been there all yesterday.'

'This isn't the primary scene?'

'No way,' Sophie said. 'There's no spatter on the rock, not even any blood from the head wound. She was killed somewhere else, probably kept for a day or so and then dumped.'

'Find anything?'

'Plenty,' she said. 'Too much. It looks like the local kids hang out here. Cigarette butts, beer cans, a couple of Coke cans, gum, the ends of three joints. Two used condoms. Once you find a suspect, the lab can try matching him to all this stuff – which will be a nightmare – but to be honest I think it's just your basic teenage debris. Footprints all over the place. A hair-clip. I don't think it was hers – it was shoved right down into the dirt at the base of the stone, and it looks like it's been there a good while – but you might want to check. It doesn't look like it belonged to some teenager; it's the all-plastic kind, with a plastic strawberry on the end, and you'd usually see them on younger kids.'

blonde wing lifting

I felt as though I had tilted sharply backwards; I had to stop myself jerking for balance. I heard Cassie say quickly, somewhere on the other side of Sophie, 'Probably not hers. Everything she's wearing is blue and white, right down to the hair elastics. This kid coordinated. We'll check it out, though.'

'Are you OK?' Sophie asked me.

'I'm fine,' I said. 'I just need coffee.' The joy of the new, hip, happening, double-espresso Dublin is that you can blame any strange mood on coffee deprivation. This never worked in the era of tea, at least not at the same level of street cred.

'I'm going to get him an IV caffeine drip for his birthday,' said Cassie. She likes Sophie too. 'He's even more useless without his fix. Tell him about the rock.'

'Yeah, we found two interesting things,' said Sophie. 'There's a rock about this size' – she cupped her hands: about eight inches wide – 'that I'm pretty sure is one of the weapons. It was in the grass by the wall. Hair and blood and bone fragments all over one end of it.'

'Any prints?' I asked.

'No. A couple of smudges, but they look like they came from gloves. The interesting parts are where it was – up by the wall; could mean he came over it, from the estate, although that could be what we're meant to think – and the fact that he bothered dumping it. You'd think he'd just rinse it and stick it in his garden, rather than carrying it as well as a body.'

'Couldn't it have been in the grass already?' I asked. 'He might have dropped the body on it, maybe getting her over the wall.'

'I don't think so,' said Sophie. She was shifting her feet delicately, trying to nudge me towards the stone table; she wanted to get back to work. I looked away. I am not squeamish about bodies, and I was pretty sure I had seen even worse than this one – a toddler, the year before, whose father kicked him until he basically broke in half – but I still felt weird, light-headed, as though my eyes weren't focusing clearly enough to take in the image. *Maybe I really do need coffee*, I thought. 'It was blood-side down. And the grass underneath it is fresh, still alive; the rock hadn't been there long.'

'Plus, she wasn't bleeding any more by the time she was brought here,' Cassie said.

'Oh, yeah – the other interesting thing,' Sophie said. 'Come look at this.'

I bowed to the inevitable and ducked under the tape. The other techs glanced up and moved back from the stone to give us room. They were both very young, barely more than trainees, and suddenly I thought of how we must look to them: how much older, how aloof, how much more confident in the little arts and negotiations of adulthood. It steadied me somehow, the image of two Murder detectives with their practised faces giving away nothing, walking shoulder to shoulder and in step towards this dead child.

She was lying curled on her left side, as though she had fallen asleep on the sofa under the peaceful murmurs of adult conversation. Her left arm was flung out over the edge of the rock; her right fell across her chest, the hand bent under at an awkward angle. She was wearing smoke-blue combats, the kind with tags and zippers in peculiar places, and a white T-shirt with a line of stylised cornflowers printed on the front, and white trainers. Cassie was right, she had taken trouble: the thick plait trailing across her cheek was secured with a blue silk cornflower. She was small and very slight, but her calf showed taut and muscular where one leg of the combats was rucked up. Ten to thirteen sounded about right: her breasts were just beginning, barely denting the folds of the T-shirt. Blood was caked on her nose and mouth and the tips of her front teeth. The breeze whirled the soft, curling fronds at her hairline.

Her hands were covered in clear plastic bags, tied at the wrists. 'Looks like she fought,' Sophie said. 'A couple of nails were broken off. I wouldn't bet on finding DNA under the others – they look pretty clean – but we should get fibres and trace off her clothes.'

For a moment I was dizzied by the impulse to leave her there: shove the techs' hands away, shout at the hovering morgue men to get the hell out. We had taken enough toll on her. All she had left was her death and I wanted to leave her that, that at least. I wanted to wrap her up in soft blankets, stroke back her clotted hair, pull up a duvet of falling leaves and little animals' rustles. Leave her to sleep, sliding away forever down her secret underground river, while breathing seasons spun dandelion seeds and moon-phases and snowflakes above her head. She had tried so hard to live.

'I have that same T-shirt,' Cassie said quietly, at my shoulder. 'Penney's kids' department.' I had seen it on her before, but I knew she wouldn't wear it again. Violated, that innocence was too vast and final to allow any tongue-in-cheek claim of kinship.

'Here's what I wanted to show you,' said Sophie briskly. She doesn't approve of either sentimentality or graveyard humour at crime scenes. She says they waste time that should be spent working on the damn case, but the implication is that coping strategies are for wimps. She pointed to the edge of the stone. 'Want gloves?'

'I won't touch anything,' I said, and crouched in the grass. From this angle I could see that one of the girl's eyes was a slit open, as if she was only pretending to be asleep, waiting for her moment to jump up and yell, *Boo! Fooled you!* A shiny black beetle ticked a methodical path over her forearm.

A groove about a finger wide had been carved around the top of the stone, an inch or two from the edge. Time and weather had worn it smooth, almost glossy, but in one place the maker's handmade chisel had slipped, gouging a chunk out of the side of the groove and leaving a tiny, jagged overhang. A smear of something dark, almost black, clung to the underside.

'Helen here spotted it,' Sophie said. The girl tech glanced up and gave me a shy proud smile. 'We've swabbed, and it's blood – I'll let you know if it's human. I doubt it has anything to do with our body; her blood had dried by the time she was brought here, and anyway I'd bet this is years old. It could be animal, or it could be from some teenage scrap or whatever, but still, it's interesting.'

I thought of the delicate hollow by Jamie's wrist-bone, the brown back of Peter's neck bordered by white after a haircut. I could feel Cassie not looking at me. 'I don't see how it could be connected,' I said. I stood up – it was getting hard to balance on my heels without touching the table – and felt a quick head-rush.

Before we left the site I stood on the little ridge above the girl's body and turned full circle, imprinting an overview of the scene on my mind: trenches, houses, fields, access and angles and alignments. Along the estate wall, a thin rim of trees had been left untouched, presumably to shield the residents' aesthetic sensibilities from the uncompromisingly archaeological view. One had a broken piece of blue plastic rope heavily knotted around a high branch, a couple of feet dangling. It was frayed and mildewed and implied

sinister Gothic history – lynch mobs, midnight suicides –
but I knew what it was. It was the remnant of a tyre-swing.

Though I had come to think of Knocknaree as though it
had happened to another and unknown person, some part
of me had been here all along. While I doodled in Templemore or sprawled on Cassie's futon, that relentless child
had never stopped spinning in crazy circles on a tyre-
swing, scrambling over a wall after Peter's bright head,
vanishing into the wood in a flash of brown legs and
laughter.

There was a time when I believed, with the police and the
media and my stunned parents, that I was the redeemed
one, the boy borne safely home on the ebb of whatever
freak tide carried Peter and Jamie away. Not any more. In
ways too dark and crucial to be called metaphorical, I never
left that wood.

3

I don't tell people about the Knocknaree thing. I don't see why I should; it would only lead to endless salacious questioning about my nonexistent memories or to sympathetic and inaccurate speculation about the state of my psyche, and I have no desire to deal with either. My parents know, obviously, and Cassie, and a boarding-school friend of mine called Charlie – he's a merchant banker in London now; we still keep in touch, occasionally – and this girl Gemma whom I went out with for a while when I was about nineteen (we spent a lot of our time together getting much too drunk, plus she was the intense angsty type and I thought it would make me sound interesting); nobody else.

When I went to boarding-school I dropped the Adam and started using my middle name. I'm not sure whether this was my parents' idea or mine, but I think it was a good one. There are five pages of Ryans in the Dublin phone book alone, but Adam is not a particularly common name and the publicity was overwhelming (even in England: I used to scan furtively through the newspapers I was supposed to be using to light prefects' fires, rip out anything relevant, memorise it later in a toilet cubicle before flushing it away). Sooner or later, someone would have made the connection. As it is, nobody is likely to link up Detective Rob and his English accent with little Adam Ryan from Knocknaree.

I knew, of course, that I should tell O'Kelly, now that I was working on a case that looked like it might be connected to that one, but to be frank I never for a second considered doing it. It would have got me booted off the case – you are very definitely not allowed to work on anything where you might be emotionally involved – and probably questioned all over again about that day in the wood, and I failed to see how this would benefit either the case or the community in general. I still have vivid, disturbing memories of being questioned the first time round: male voices with a rough undertow of frustration yammering faintly at the edges of my hearing, while in my mind white clouds drifted endlessly across a vast blue sky and wind sighed through some huge expanse of grass. That was all I could see or hear, the first couple of weeks afterwards. I don't remember feeling anything about this at the time, but in retrospect the thought was a horrible one – my mind wiped clean, replaced by a test pattern – and every time the detectives came back and tried again it resurfaced, by some process of association, seeping in at the back of my head and frightening me into sullen, uncooperative edginess. And they did try – at first every few months, in the school holidays, then every year or so – but I never had anything to tell them, and around the time I left school they finally stopped coming. I felt that this had been an excellent decision, and I could not for the life of me see how reversing it at this stage would serve any useful purpose.

And I suppose, if I'm being honest, it appealed both to my ego and to my sense of the picturesque, the idea of carrying this strange, charged secret through the case unsuspected. I suppose it felt, at the time, like the kind of thing that enigmatic Central Casting maverick would have done.

I rang Missing Persons, and they came up with a possible ID almost immediately. Katharine Devlin, age twelve, four foot nine, slim build, long dark hair, hazel eyes, reported missing from 29 Knocknaree Grove (I remembered that, suddenly: all the streets in the estate called Knocknaree Grove and Close and Place and Lane, everyone's post constantly going astray) at 10.15 the previous morning, when her mother went to wake her and found her gone. Twelve and up is considered old enough to be a runaway, and she had apparently left the house of her own accord, so Missing Persons had been giving her a day to come home before sending in the troops. They already had the press release typed up, ready to send to the media in time for the evening news.

I was disproportionately relieved to have an ID, even a tentative one. Obviously I had known that a little girl – especially a healthy well-groomed little girl, in a place as small as Ireland – can't turn up dead without someone coming forward to claim her; but a number of things about this case were giving me the willies, and I think a superstitious part of me had believed that this child would remain as nameless as if she had dropped from thin air and that her DNA would turn out to match the blood from my shoes and a variety of other *X-Files*-type stuff. We got an ID shot from Sophie – a Polaroid, taken from the least disturbing angle, to show to the family – and headed back to the Portakabins.

Hunt popped out of one of them as we approached, like the little man in old Swiss clocks. 'Did you . . . I mean, it is definitely murder, is it? The poor child. Awful.'

'We're treating it as suspicious,' I said. 'What we'll need to do now is have a quick word with your team. Then we'd like to speak to the person who found the body. The others can go back to work, as long as they stay outside the boundaries of the crime scene. We'll speak with them later.'

'How will . . . Is there something to show where it – where they shouldn't be? Tape, and all that.'

'There's crime-scene tape in place,' I said. 'If they stay outside it, they'll be fine.'

'We'll need to ask you for the lend of somewhere we can use as an on-site office,' Cassie said, 'for the rest of the day and possibly a bit longer. Where would be best?'

'Better use the finds shed,' said Mark, materialising from wherever. 'We'll need the office, and everywhere else is soupy.' I hadn't heard the term before, but the view through the Portakabin doors – layers of mud crazed with boot-prints, low sagging benches, teetering heaps of farming implements and bicycles and luminous yellow vests that reminded me uncomfortably of my time in uniform – provided a fair explanation.

'As long as it has a table and a few chairs, that'll be fine,' I said.

'Finds shed,' said Mark, and jerked his head towards a Portakabin.

'What's up with Damien?' Cassie asked Hunt.

He blinked helplessly, mouth open in a caricature of surprise. 'What . . . Damien who?'

'Damien on your team. Earlier you said that Mark and Damien usually do the tours, but Damien wouldn't be able to show Detective Ryan around. Why's that?'

'Damien's one of the ones who found the body,' said Mark, while Hunt was catching up. 'Gave them a shock.'

'Damien what?' said Cassie, writing.

'Donnelly,' Hunt said happily, on sure ground at last. 'Damien Donnelly.'

'And he was with someone when he found the body?'

'Mel Jackson,' Mark said. 'Melanie.'

'Let's go talk to them,' I said.

The archaeologists were still sitting around the table in their makeshift canteen. There were fifteen or twenty of them; their faces turned towards the door, intent and synchronised as baby birds', when we came in. They were all young, early twenties, and they were made younger by their grungy-student clothes and by a windblown, outdoorsy innocence that, although I was pretty sure it was illusory, made me think of kibbutzniks and Waltons. The girls wore no make-up and their hair was in plaits or ponytails, tightened to be practical rather than cutesy; the guys had stubble and peeling sunburns. One of them, with a guileless teacher's-nightmare face and a woolly cap, had got bored and started melting stuff onto a broken CD with a lighter flame. The result (bent teaspoon, coins, smoke-packet cellophane, a couple of crisps) was surprisingly pleasing, like one of the less humourless manifestations of modern urban art. There was a food-stained microwave in one corner, and a small inappropriate part of me wanted to suggest that he put the CD in it, to see what would happen.

Cassie and I started to speak at the same time, but I kept going. Officially she was the primary detective, because she was the one who'd said 'We'll have it'; but we have never worked that way, and the rest of the squad had grown used to seeing 'M & R' scribbled under 'Primary' on the case board, and I had a sudden, stubborn urge to make it clear that I was just as capable of leading this investigation as she was.

'Good morning,' I said. Most of them muttered something. Sculptor Boy said loudly and cheerfully, 'Good afternoon!' – which, technically, it was – and I wondered which of the girls he was trying to impress. 'I'm Detective Ryan, and this is Detective Maddox. As you know, the body of a young girl was found on this site earlier today.'

One of the guys let his breath out in a little burst and caught it again. He was in a corner, sandwiched protectively between two of the girls, clutching a big steaming mug in both hands; he had short brown curls and a sweet, frank, freckled boy-band face. I was pretty sure this was Damien Donnelly. The others seemed subdued (except Sculptor Boy) but not traumatised, but he was white under the freckles and holding the mug way too hard.

'We'll need to talk to each of you,' I said. 'Please don't leave the site until we have. We may not have a chance to get to all of you for a while, so please bear with us if we need you to stay a bit late.'

'Are we, like, suspects?' said Sculptor Boy.

'No,' I said, 'but we need to find out if you have any relevant information.'

'Ahhh,' he said, disappointed, and slumped back in his chair. He started to melt a square of chocolate onto the CD, caught Cassie's eye and put the lighter away. I envied him: I have often wanted to be one of those people who can take anything, the more horrific the better, as a deeply cool adventure.

'One other thing,' I said. 'Reporters will probably start arriving at any minute. Do not talk to them. Seriously. Telling them anything, even something that seems insignificant, could damage our whole case. We'll leave you our cards, in case at any point you think of anything we should know. Any questions?'

'What if they offer us, like, millions?' Sculptor Boy wanted to know.

The finds shed was less impressive than I'd expected. In spite of what Mark had said about taking away the valuable stuff, I think my mental image had included gold cups and skeletons and pieces of eight. Instead there were two chairs, a wide desk spread with sheets of drawing paper, and an incredible quantity of what appeared to be broken pottery, stuffed into plastic bags and crammed onto those perforated DIY metal shelves.

'Finds,' said Hunt, flapping a hand at the shelves. 'I suppose . . . Well, no, maybe some other time. Some very nice jettons and clothing hooks.'

'We'd love to see them another day, Dr Hunt,' I said. 'Could you give us about ten minutes and then send Damien Donnelly in to us?'

'Damien,' said Hunt, and wandered off. Cassie shut the door behind him. I said, 'How on earth does he run a whole excavation?' and started clearing away the drawings: fine, delicately shaded pencil sketches of an old coin, from various angles. The coin itself, sharply bent on one side and patchy with encrustations of earth, sat in the middle of the desk in a Ziploc bag. I found space for them on top of a filing cabinet.

'By hiring people like that Mark guy,' Cassie said. 'I bet he's plenty organised. What was with the hair-clip?'

I squared off the edges of the drawings. 'I think Jamie Rowan was wearing one that matched that description.'

'Ah,' she said. 'I wondered. Is that in the file, do you know, or do you just remember it?'

'What difference does that make?' It came out sounding snottier than I'd intended.

'Well, if there's a link, we can't exactly keep it to ourselves,' Cassie said reasonably. 'Just for example, we're going to have to get Sophie to check that blood against the '84 samples, and we're going to have to tell her why. It would make things a whole lot simpler to explain if the link was right there in the file.'

'I'm pretty sure it is,' I said. The desk rocked; Cassie found a blank sheet of paper and folded it to wedge under the leg. 'I'll double-check tonight. Hold off on talking to Sophie till then, OK?'

'Sure,' said Cassie. 'If it's not there, we'll find a way round it.' She tested the desk again: better. 'Rob, are you OK with this case?'

I didn't answer. Through the window I could see the morgue guys wrapping the body in plastic, Sophie pointing and gesturing. They barely had to brace themselves to lift the stretcher; it looked almost weightless as they carried it away towards the waiting van. The wind rattled the glass sharply in my face and I spun round. I wanted, suddenly and fiercely, to shout 'Shut the hell up,' or 'Fuck this case, I quit,' or something, something reckless and unreasonable and dramatic. But Cassie was just leaning against the desk and waiting, looking at me with steady brown eyes, and I have always had an excellent brake system, a gift for choosing the anticlimactic over the irrevocable every time.

'I'm fine with it,' I said. 'Just kick me if I get too moody.'

'With pleasure,' Cassie said, and grinned at me. 'God, though, look at all this stuff . . . I hope we do get a chance to have a proper look. I wanted to be an archaeologist when I was little, did I ever tell you?'

'Only about a million times,' I said.

'Lucky you've got a goldfish memory, then, isn't it? I

used to dig up the back garden, but all I ever found was a little china duck with the beak broken off.'

'It looks like I should have been the one digging out the back,' I said. Normally I would have made some remark about law enforcement's loss being archaeology's gain, but I was still feeling too nervy and dislocated for any decent level of back-and-forth; it would only have come out wrong. 'I could have had the world's biggest private collection of pottery bits.'

'Now there's a chat-up line,' said Cassie, and dug out her notebook.

Damien came in awkwardly, with a plastic chair bumping along from one hand and his mug of tea still clutched in the other. 'I brought this . . .' he said, using the mug to gesture uncertainly at his chair and the two we were sitting on. 'Dr Hunt said you wanted to see me?'

'Yep,' said Cassie. 'I would say, "Have a seat," but you already do.'

It took him a moment; then he laughed a little, checking our faces to see if that was OK. He sat down, started to put his mug on the table, changed his mind and kept it in his lap, looked up at us with big obedient blue eyes. This was definitely Cassie's baby. He looked like the type who was accustomed to being taken care of by women; he was shaky already, and being interrogated by a guy would probably send him into a state where we would never get anything useful out of him. I got out a pen, unobtrusively.

'Listen,' Cassie said soothingly, 'I know you've had a bad shock. Just take your time and walk us through it, OK? Start with what you were doing this morning, before you went up to the stone.'

Damien took a deep breath, licked his lips. 'We were, um, we were working on the medieval drainage ditch.

Mark wanted to see if we could follow the line a little further down the site. See, we're, we're sort of cleaning up loose ends now, 'cause it's coming up to the end of the dig—'

'How long's the dig been going on?' Cassie asked.

'Like two years, but I've only been on it since June. I'm in college.'

'I used to want to be an archaeologist,' Cassie told him. I nudged her foot, under the table; she stood on mine. 'How's the dig going?'

Damien's face lit up; he looked almost dazzled with delight, unless dazzled was just his normal expression. 'It's been amazing. I'm so glad I did it.'

'I'm so jealous,' Cassie said. 'Do they let people volunteer for just, like, a week?'

'Maddox,' I said stuffily, 'can you discuss your career change later?'

'Sor-*ry*,' said Cassie, rolling her eyes and grinning at Damien. He grinned back, bonding away. I was taking a vague, unjustifiable dislike to Damien. I could see exactly why Hunt had assigned him to give the site tours – he was a PR dream, all blue eyes and diffidence – but I have never liked adorable, helpless men. I suppose it's the same reaction Cassie has to those baby-voiced, easily impressed girls whom men always want to protect: a mixture of distaste, cynicism and envy. 'OK,' she said, 'so then you went up to the stone . . .?'

'We needed to take back all the grass and soil around it,' Damien said. 'The rest of that bit got bulldozed last week, but they left a patch round the stone, because we didn't want to risk the bulldozer hitting it. So after the tea break Mark told me and Mel to go up there and mattock it back while the others did the drainage ditch.'

'What time was that?'

'Tea break ends at quarter past eleven.'

'And then . . .?'

He swallowed, took a sip from his mug. Cassie leaned forward encouragingly and waited.

'We, um . . . There was something on the stone. I thought it was a jacket or something, like somebody had forgotten their jacket there? I said, um, I said, "What's that?" so we went closer and . . .' He looked down into his mug. His hands were shaking again. 'It was a person. I thought she might be, you know, unconscious or something, so I shook her, her arm, and um . . . she felt weird. Cold and, and stiff. And I put my head down to see if she was breathing, but she wasn't. There was blood on her, I saw blood. On her face. So I knew she was dead.' He swallowed again.

'You're doing great,' Cassie said gently. 'What did you do then?'

'Mel said, "Oh my God," or something, and we ran back and told Dr Hunt. He told us all to go into the canteen.'

'OK, Damien, I need you to think carefully,' Cassie said. 'Did you see anything that seemed weird today, or over the last few days? Anyone unusual hanging around, anything out of place?'

He gazed into space, lips slightly parted; took another sip of his tea. 'This probably isn't the kind of thing you mean . . .'

'Anything could help us,' Cassie told him. 'Even the tiniest thing.'

'OK.' Damien nodded earnestly. 'OK, on Monday I was waiting for the bus home, out by the gate? And I saw this guy come down the road and go into the estate. I don't know why I even noticed him, I just . . . He sort of looked around before he went into the estate, like he was checking if anyone was watching him or something.'

'What time was this?' Cassie asked.

'We finish at half-five, so maybe twenty to six? That was the other weird thing. I mean, there's nothing round here that you can get to without a car, except the shop and the pub, and the shop closes at five. So I wondered where he was coming from.'

'What did he look like?'

'Sort of tall, like six foot. In his thirties, I guess? Heavy. I think he was bald. He had on a dark-blue tracksuit.'

'Would you be able to work with a sketch artist to come up with a drawing of him?'

Damien blinked fast, looking alarmed. 'Um . . . I didn't see him all that well. I mean, he was coming from up the road, on the other side of the estate entrance. I wasn't really looking – I don't think I'd remember . . .'

'That's all right,' Cassie said. 'Don't worry about it, Damien. If you feel like you might be able to give us some more details, let me know, OK? Meanwhile, just take care of yourself.'

We got Damien's address and phone number, gave him a card (I wanted to give him a lollipop too, for being such a brave boy, but they're not standard department issue) and shooed him back to the others, with orders to send in Melanie Jackson.

'Sweet kid,' I said non-committally, testing.

'Yeah,' said Cassie drily. 'If I ever want a pet, I'll keep him in mind.'

Mel was a lot more useful than Damien. She was tall and skinny and Scottish, with muscled brown arms and sandy hair in a messy ponytail, and she sat like a boy, feet planted firmly apart.

'Maybe you know this already, but she's from the estate,' she said straight away. 'Or from somewhere round here, anyway.'

'How do you know?' I asked.

'The local kids come around the site sometimes. There's not much else for them to do during the summer. They mostly want to know if we've found buried treasure, or skeletons. I've seen her a few times.'

'When was the last time?'

'Maybe two, three weeks ago.'

'Was she with anyone?'

Mel shrugged. 'Nobody that I remember. Just a bunch of other kids, I think.'

I liked Mel. She was shaken but refusing to show it; she was fidgeting with an elastic band, cat's-cradling it into shapes between her callused fingers. She told basically the same story as Damien, but with a lot less coaxing and petting.

'At the end of the tea break, Mark told me to go mattock back around the ceremonial stone so we could see the base. Damien said he'd go too – we don't usually work on our own, it's boring. Partway up the slope we saw something blue and white on the stone. Damien said, "What's that?" and I said, "Somebody's jacket, maybe." When we got a bit closer I realised it was a kid. Damien shook her arm and checked whether she was breathing, but you could tell she was dead. I never saw a dead body before, but—' She bit the inside of her cheek, shook her head. 'It's bullshit, isn't it, when they say, "Oh, he looked like he was just sleeping"? You could tell.'

We think about mortality so little, these days, except to

flail hysterically at it with trendy forms of exercise and high-fibre cereals and nicotine patches. I thought of the stern Victorian determination to keep death in mind, the uncompromising tombstones: *Remember, pilgrim, as you pass by, As you are now so once was I; As I am now so will you be* . . . Now death is uncool, old-fashioned. To my mind the defining characteristic of our era is spin, everything tailored to vanishing point by market research, brands and bands manufactured to precise specifications; we are so used to things transmuting into whatever we would like them to be that it comes as a profound outrage to encounter death, stubbornly unspinnable, only and immutably itself. The body had shocked Mel Jackson far more deeply than it would have the most sheltered Victorian virgin.

'Could you have missed the body if it had been on the stone yesterday?' I asked.

Mel glanced up, wide-eyed. 'Ah, shit – you mean it was there all the time we were . . .?' Then she shook her head. 'No. Mark and Dr Hunt went round the whole site yesterday afternoon, to make a list of what needs doing. They'd have seen it – her. We only missed it this morning because we were all down the bottom of the site, at the end of the drainage ditch. The way the hill slopes, we couldn't see the top of the stone.'

She hadn't seen anyone or anything unusual, including Damien's weirdo: 'But I wouldn't have anyway. I don't take the bus. Most of us who aren't from Dublin live in this house they rented for us, a couple of miles down the road. Mark and Dr Hunt have cars, so they drive us back. We don't go past the estate.'

The 'anyway' interested me: it suggested that Mel, like me, had her doubts about the sinister tracksuit. Damien struck me as the type who would say just about anything if he thought it would make you happy. I wished I had thought of asking him whether the guy had been wearing stilettos.

Sophie and her baby techs had finished up with the ceremonial stone and were working their way outwards in a circle. I told her that Damien Donnelly had touched the body and leaned over it; we'd need his prints and hair, for elimination. 'What an idiot,' Sophie said. 'I suppose we should be thankful he didn't decide to cover her up with his coat.' She was sweating in her boiler suit. The boy tech covertly ripped a page out of his sketchbook, behind her back, and started over.

We left the car at the site and walked round to the estate by the road (I still remembered, somewhere in my muscles, going over the wall: where the foothold was, the scrape of the concrete on my kneecap, the jar of landing). Cassie demanded to go to the shop on the way; it was well past two o'clock and we might not have another chance at lunch for a while. Cassie eats like a teenage boy and hates missing meals, which normally I enjoy – women who live on weighed portions of salad annoy me – but I wanted to get today over with as quickly as possible.

I waited outside the shop, smoking, but Cassie came out with two sandwiches in plastic cartons and handed one to me. 'Here.'

'I'm not hungry.'

'Eat the damn sandwich, Ryan. I'm not carrying you home if you faint.' I have in fact never fainted in my life, but I do tend to forget to eat until I start getting irritable or spacy.

'I said I'm not *hungry*,' I said, hearing the whine in my

voice, but I opened the sandwich anyway: Cassie had a point, it was likely to be a very long day. We sat on the kerb and she pulled a bottle of lemon Coke out of her satchel. The sandwich was officially chicken and stuffing, but it tasted mainly of plastic wrapper, and the Coke was warm and too sweet. I felt slightly sick.

I don't want to give the impression that my life was blighted by what happened at Knocknaree, that I drifted through twenty years as some kind of tragic figure with a haunted past, smiling sadly at the world from behind a bittersweet veil of cigarette smoke and memories. Knocknaree didn't leave me with night terrors or impotence or a pathological fear of trees or any of the other good stuff that, in a made-for-TV movie, would have led me to a therapist and redemption and a more communicative relationship with my supportive but frustrated wife. To be honest, I could go for months on end without ever thinking about it. Occasionally some newspaper or other would run a feature on missing people and there they would be, Peter and Jamie, smiling from the cover of a Sunday supplement in grainy photographs made premonitory by hindsight and overuse, between vanished tourists and runaway housewives and all the mythic, murmuring ranks of Ireland's lost. I'd see the article and notice, detachedly, that my hands were shaking and it was hard to breathe, but this was purely a physical reflex and only lasted a few minutes anyway.

I suppose the whole thing must have had its effects on me, but it would be impossible – and, to my mind, pointless – to figure out exactly what they were. I was twelve, after all, an age at which kids are bewildered and amorphous, transforming overnight, no matter how stable their lives are; and a few weeks later I went to boarding-school, which shaped and scarred me in far more dramatic, obvious ways. It would feel naïve and basically cheesy to un-weave my personality, hold up a strand and squeal: *Golly, look, this one's from Knocknaree!* But here it was again, all of a sudden, resurfacing smugly and immovably in the middle of my life, and I had absolutely no idea what to do with it.

'That poor kid,' Cassie said suddenly, out of nowhere. 'That poor, poor little *kid.*'

The Devlins' house was a flat-fronted semi with a patch of grass in front, exactly like all the others on the estate. All of the neighbours had made frantic little declarations of individuality via ferociously trimmed shrubs or geraniums or something, but the Devlins just mowed their lawn and left it at that, which in itself argued a certain level of originality. They lived halfway up the estate, five or six streets from the site; far enough that they had missed the uniforms, the techs, the morgue van, all the terrible, efficient bustle that in one glance would have told them everything they needed to know.

When Cassie rang the bell, a man about forty answered. He was a few inches shorter than me, starting to thicken around the middle, with neatly clipped dark hair and big bags under his eyes. He was wearing a cardigan and khaki trousers and holding a bowl of cornflakes, and I wanted to tell him that this was all right, because I already knew what he would learn over the next few months: this is the kind of thing people remember in agony all their lives, that they were eating cornflakes when the police came to tell them their daughter was dead. I once saw a woman break down on the witness stand, sobbing so hard they had to call a recess and give her a sedative shot, because when her boyfriend was stabbed she was at a yoga class.

'Mr Devlin?' Cassie said. 'I'm Detective Maddox, and this is Detective Ryan.'

His eyes widened. 'From Missing Persons?' There was mud on his shoes, and the hems of his trousers were wet. He must have been out looking for his daughter, somewhere in the wrong fields, come in to get something to eat before he tried again and again.

'Not exactly,' Cassie said gently. I mostly leave these conversations to her, not just out of cowardice but because we both know she is much better at it. 'May we come in?'

He stared at the bowl, put it down clumsily on the hall table. A little milk slopped onto sets of keys and a child's pink cap. 'What do you mean?' he demanded; fear put an aggressive edge on his voice. 'Have you found Katy?'

I heard a tiny sound and looked over his shoulder. A girl was standing at the foot of the stairs, holding onto the banister with both hands. The interior of the house was dim even in the sunny afternoon, but I saw her face, and it transfixed me with a bright shard of something like terror. For an unimaginable, swirling moment I knew I was seeing a ghost. It was our victim: it was the dead little girl on the stone table. I heard a roaring noise in my ears.

A split second later, of course, the world righted itself, the roaring subsided and I realised what I was seeing. We wouldn't be needing the ID shot. Cassie had seen her as well. 'We're not sure yet,' she said. 'Mr Devlin, is this Katy's sister?'

'Jessica,' he said hoarsely. The little girl edged forward; without taking his eyes from Cassie's face, Devlin reached back, caught her shoulder and pulled her into the doorway. 'They're twins,' he said. 'Identical. Is this— Have you— Did you find a girl who looks like this?' Jessica stared somewhere between me and Cassie. Her arms hung limply by her sides, hands invisible under an oversized grey jumper.

'Please, Mr Devlin,' Cassie said. 'We need to come in and speak with you and your wife in private.' She flicked a glance at Jessica. Devlin looked down, saw his hand on her shoulder and moved it away, startled. It stayed frozen in mid-air, as if he had forgotten what to do with it.

He knew, by that point; of course he knew. If she had been found alive, we would have said so. But he moved back from the door automatically and made a vague gesture to one side, and we went into the sitting-room. I heard Devlin say, 'Go back upstairs to your Auntie Vera.' Then he followed us in and closed the door.

The terrible thing about the sitting-room was how normal it was, how straight out of some satire on suburbia. Lace curtains, a flowery four-piece suite with those little covers on the arms and headrests, a collection of ornate teapots on top of a dresser, everything polished and dusted to an immaculate shine: it seemed – victims' homes and even crime scenes almost always do – far too banal for this level of tragedy. The woman sitting in an armchair matched the room: heavy in a solid shapeless way, with a helmet of permed hair and big, drooping blue eyes. There were deep lines from her nose to her mouth.

'Margaret,' Devlin said. 'They're detectives.' His voice was taut as a guitar string, but he didn't go to her; he stayed by the sofa, fists clenched in the pockets of his cardigan. 'What is it?' he demanded.

'Mr and Mrs Devlin,' Cassie said, 'there's no easy way to say this. The body of a little girl has been found on the archaeological site beside this estate. I'm afraid we think she's your daughter Katharine. I'm so sorry.'

Margaret Devlin let out her breath as if she'd been hit in

the stomach. Tears began to fall down her cheeks, but she didn't seem to notice.

'Are you sure?' Devlin snapped. His eyes were huge. 'How can you be sure?'

'Mr Devlin,' Cassie said gently, 'I've seen the little girl. She looks exactly like your daughter Jessica. We'll be asking you to come see the body tomorrow, to confirm her identity, but there's no doubt in my mind. I'm sorry.'

Devlin swung towards the window, away again, pressed a wrist against his mouth, lost and wild-eyed. 'Oh God,' said Margaret. 'Oh God, Jonathan—'

'What happened to her?' Devlin cut in harshly. 'How did she – how—'

'I'm afraid it looks as if she was murdered,' Cassie said.

Margaret was heaving herself up out of the chair, in slow, underwater movements. 'Where is she?' The tears were still pouring down her face, but her voice was eerily calm, almost brisk.

'She's with our doctors,' Cassie said gently. If Katy had died differently, we might have taken them to her. But as it was, her skull smashed open, her face covered in blood . . . At the post-mortem, the morgue guys would wash off at least that gratuitous layer of horror.

Margaret looked around, dazed, patting mechanically at the pockets of her skirt. 'Jonathan. I can't find my keys.'

'Mrs Devlin,' Cassie said, putting a hand on her arm. 'I'm afraid we can't take you to Katy yet. The doctors need to examine her. We'll let you know as soon as you can see her.'

Margaret twitched away from her and moved in slow motion towards the door, dragging a clumsy hand across her face to smear the tears away. 'Katy. Where is she?' Cassie shot a glance of appeal over her shoulder at

Jonathan, but he was leaning both palms against the window-pane and staring out, unseeing, breathing too fast and too hard.

'Please, Mrs Devlin,' I said urgently, trying to unobtrusively get between her and the door. 'I promise we'll take you to Katy as soon as we can, but at the moment you can't see her. It's simply not possible.'

She stared at me, red-eyed, her mouth hanging open. '*My baby*,' she gasped. Then her shoulders slumped and she started to weep, in deep, hoarse, unrestrained sobs. Her head fell back and she let Cassie take her gently by the shoulders and ease her back into her chair.

'How did she die?' Jonathan demanded, still staring fixedly out the window. The words were blurred, as if his lips were numb. 'What way?'

'We won't know that until the doctors have finished examining her,' I said. 'We'll keep you informed of every development.'

I heard light footsteps running down the stairs; the door flew open, and a girl stood in the doorway. Behind her Jessica was still in the hall, sucking a lock of hair and staring in at us.

'What is it?' said the girl breathlessly. 'Oh, God – is it Katy?'

Nobody answered. Margaret pressed a fist to her mouth, turning her sobs into terrible choking sounds. The girl looked from face to face, her lips parted. She was tall and slim, with chestnut curls tumbling down her back, and it was hard to tell how old she was – eighteen or twenty, maybe, but she was made up far more expertly than any teenager I'd ever known, and she was wearing tailored black trousers and high-heeled shoes and a white shirt that looked expensive, with a purple silk scarf flung round her neck. She had a kind of vital, electric presence that filled the room. In that house, she was utterly, startlingly incongruous.

'Please,' she said, appealing to me. Her voice was high and clear and carrying, with a newsreader accent that didn't match Jonathan and Margaret's soft, small-town working-class. 'What's happened?'

'Rosalind,' Jonathan said. His voice came out rough, and he cleared his throat. 'They found Katy. She's dead. Someone killed her.'

Jessica made a small, wordless noise. Rosalind stared at him for a moment; then her eyelids fluttered and she swayed, one hand going out to the door frame. Cassie got an arm around her waist and supported her to the sofa.

Rosalind leaned her head back against the cushions and gave Cassie a weak, grateful smile; Cassie smiled back. 'Could I have some water?' she whispered.

'I'll get it,' I said. In the kitchen – scrubbed linoleum, varnished faux-rustic table and chairs – I turned on the tap and had a quick look around. Nothing noteworthy, except that one high cupboard held an array of vitamin tubs and, at the back, an industrial-sized bottle of Valium with a label made out to Margaret Devlin.

Rosalind sipped the water and took deep breaths, one slim hand to her breastbone. 'Take Jess and go upstairs,' Devlin told her.

'Please, let me stay,' Rosalind said, lifting her chin. 'Katy was my sister – whatever happened to her, I can . . . I can listen to it. I'm all right now. I'm sorry for being so . . . I'll be fine, really.'

'We'd like Rosalind and Jessica to stay, Mr Devlin,' I said. 'It's possible they might know something that could help us.'

'Katy and I were very close,' Rosalind said, looking up at me. Her eyes were her mother's, big and blue, with that touch of a droop at the outer corners. They shifted, over my shoulder: 'Oh, Jessica,' she said, holding out her arms. 'Jessica, darling, come here.' Jessica edged past me, with a flash of bright eyes like a wild animal's, and pressed up against Rosalind on the sofa.

'I'm very sorry to intrude at a time like this,' I said, 'but there are some questions we need to ask you as soon as possible, to help us find whoever did this. Do you feel able to talk now, or shall we come back in a few hours?'

Jonathan Devlin pulled over a chair from the dining-table, slammed it down and sat, swallowing hard. 'Do it now,' he said. 'Ask away.'

Slowly we took them through it. They had last seen Katy on Monday evening. She had had a ballet class in Stillorgan, a few miles in towards the centre of Dublin, from five o'clock till seven. Rosalind had met her at the bus stop at about 7.45 p.m. and walked her home. ('She said she'd had a lovely time,' Rosalind said, her head bent over her clasped hands; a curtain of hair fell across her face. 'She was such a wonderful dancer . . . She had a place in the Royal Ballet School, you know. She would have been leaving in just a few weeks . . .' Margaret sobbed, and Jonathan's hands gripped the arms of his chair convulsively.) Rosalind and Jessica had then gone to their Aunt Vera's house, across the estate, to spend the night with their cousins.

Katy had had her tea – baked beans on toast and orange juice – and then walked a neighbour's dog: her summer job, to earn money towards ballet school. She had got back at approximately ten to nine, taken a bath and then watched television with her parents. She had gone to bed at ten o'clock, as usual during the summer, and read for a few minutes before Margaret told her to turn out the light. Jonathan and Margaret watched more television and went to bed a little before midnight. On his way to bed Jonathan, as a matter of routine, checked that the house was secure: doors locked, windows locked, chain on the front door.

At 7.30 the next morning, he got up and left for work – he was a senior teller in a bank – without seeing Katy. He noticed that the chain was off the front door, but he assumed that Katy, who was an early riser, had gone to her aunt's house to have breakfast with her sisters and cousins. ('She does that sometimes,' Rosalind said. 'She likes fry-ups, and Mum . . . well, in the mornings Mum's too tired to cook.' A terrible, rending sound from Margaret.) All the girls had keys to the front door, Jonathan said, just in case. At 9.20, when Margaret got up and went to wake Katy, she was gone. Margaret waited for a while, assuming, like Jonathan, that Katy had woken early and gone to her aunt's; then she rang Vera, just to be sure; then she rang all Katy's friends, and finally she rang the police.

Cassie and I perched awkwardly on the edges of arm-chairs. Margaret cried, quietly but continuously; after a while Jonathan went out of the room and came back with a box of tissues. A birdlike, pop-eyed little woman – Auntie Vera, I assumed – tiptoed down the stairs and hovered uncertainly in the hallway for a few minutes, wringing her hands, then slowly retreated to the kitchen. Rosalind rubbed Jessica's limp fingers.

Katy, they said, had been a good child, bright but not outstanding in school, passionate about ballet. She had a temper, they said, but she hadn't had any arguments with family or friends recently; they gave us the names of her best friends, so we could check. She had never run away from home, nothing like that. She had been happy lately, excited about going away to ballet school. She wasn't into boys yet, Jonathan said, she was only twelve, for God's sake; but I saw Rosalind dart a sudden glance at him and then at me, and I made a mental note to talk to her without her parents.

'Mr Devlin,' I said, 'what was your relationship with Katy like?'

Jonathan stared. 'What the fuck are you accusing me of?' he said heavily. Jessica let out a high, hysterical yelp of laughter, and I jumped. Rosalind pursed her lips and shook her head at her, frowning, then gave her a pat and a tiny reassuring smile. Jessica bowed her head and put her hair back in her mouth.

'Nobody's accusing you of anything,' Cassie said firmly, 'but we have to be able to say we've explored and eliminated every possibility. If we leave anything out, then when we catch this person – and we will – the defence can make that into reasonable doubt. I know answering these questions will be painful, but I promise you, Mr Devlin, it would be even more painful to see this person acquitted because we didn't ask them.'

Jonathan took a breath through his nose, relaxed a fraction. 'My *relationship* with Katy was great,' he said. 'She talked to me. We were close. I . . . maybe I made a pet of her.' A twitch from Jessica, a swift up-glance from Rosalind. 'We argued, the way any father and daughter do, but she was a wonderful daughter and a wonderful girl, and I loved her.' For the first time his voice cracked; he jerked his head up angrily.

'And you, Mrs Devlin?' Cassie said.

Margaret was shredding a tissue in her lap; she looked

up, obedient as a child. 'Sure, they're all great,' she said. Her voice was thick and wobbly. 'Katy was . . . a dote. She was always an easy child. I don't know what we'll do without her.' Her mouth convulsed.

Neither of us asked Rosalind or Jessica. Kids are unlikely to be frank about their siblings when their parents are around, and once a kid lies, especially a kid as young and as confused as Jessica, the lie becomes fixed in its mind and the truth recedes into the background. Later, we would try to get the Devlins' permission to speak to Jessica – and, if she was under eighteen, Rosalind – on her own. I didn't get the sense this would be easy.

'Can any of you think of anyone who might want to harm Katy for any reason?' I asked.

For a moment nobody said anything. Then Jonathan shoved his chair back and stood up. 'Jesus,' he said. His head swung back and forth, like a baited bull's. 'Those phone calls.'

'Phone calls?' I said.

'Christ. I'll kill him. You said she was found on the dig?'

'Mr Devlin!' Cassie said. 'You need to sit down and tell us about the phone calls.'

Slowly he focused on her. He sat down, but I could still see an abstracted quality in his eyes, and I would have been willing to bet he was privately considering the best way to hunt down whoever had made these calls. 'You know about the motorway going over the archaeological site, right?' he said. 'Most people around here are against it. A few are more interested in how much the value of their houses would go up, with it going right past the estate, but most of us . . . That should be a heritage site. It's unique and it's ours, the government has no right to destroy it without even asking us. There's a campaign here in

Knocknaree, Move the Motorway. I'm the chairman; I set it up. We picket government buildings, write letters to politicians – for all the good it does.'

'Not much response?' I said. Talking about his cause was steadying him. And it intrigued me: he had seemed at first like a downtrodden little man, not the type to lead a crusade, but there was clearly more to him than met the eye.

'I thought it was just bureaucracy, they never want to make changes. But the phone calls made me wonder . . . The first one was late at night; the guy said something like, "You thick bastard, you have no idea what you're messing with." I thought he had a wrong number, I hung up on him and went back to bed. It was only after the second one that I remembered and connected it up.'

'When was this first call?' I said. Cassie was writing.

Jonathan looked at Margaret; she shook her head, dabbing her eyes. 'Sometime in April – late April, maybe. The second one was on the third of June, around half-one in the morning – I wrote it down. Katy – there's no phone in our bedroom, it's in the hall, and she's a light sleeper – she got there first. She says when she answered he said, "Are you Devlin's daughter?" and she said, "I'm Katy," and he said, "Katy, tell your father to back off the bloody motorway, because I know where you live." Then I took the phone off her, and he said something like, "Nice little girl you've got there, Devlin." I told him never to ring my house again, and hung up.'

'Can you remember anything about his voice?' I asked. 'Accent, age, anything? Did it sound familiar at all?'

Jonathan swallowed. He was concentrating ferociously, clinging to the subject like a lifeline. 'It didn't ring any bells. Not young. On the high side. A country accent, but not one I could pin down – not Cork or the North, nothing distinctive like that. He sounded . . . I thought maybe he was drunk.'

'Were there any other calls?'

'One more, a few weeks ago. The thirteenth of July, two in the morning. I took it. The same guy said, "Don't you—"' He glanced at Jessica. Rosalind had an arm round her, rocking her soothingly and murmuring in her ear. ' "Don't you effing well listen, Devlin? I warned you to leave the effing motorway alone. You'll regret this. I know where your family lives." '

'Did you report this to the police?' I asked.

'No,' he said brusquely. I waited for a reason, but he didn't offer one.

'You weren't worried?'

'To be honest,' he said, glancing up with a terrible mixture of misery and defiance, 'I was delighted. I thought it meant we were getting somewhere. Whoever he was, he wouldn't have bothered ringing me if the campaign hadn't been a real threat. But now . . .' Suddenly he hunched towards me, staring me in the eye, fists pressed together. I had to fight not to lean back. 'If you find out who made those calls, tell me. You tell me. I want your word.'

'Mr Devlin,' I said, 'I promise you we'll do everything in our power to find out who it was and whether he had anything to do with Katy's death, but I can't—'

'He scared Katy,' Jessica said, in a small hoarse voice. I think we all jumped. I was as startled as if one of the armchairs had contributed to the conversation; I had been beginning to wonder if she was autistic or handicapped or something.

'Did he?' Cassie said quietly. 'What did she say?'

Jessica gazed at her as if the question was incomprehensible. Her eyes started to slide away again; she was retreating back into her private daze.

Cassie leaned forward. 'Jessica,' she said, very gently, 'is there anyone else Katy was scared of?'

Jessica's head swayed a little, and her mouth moved. A thin hand reached out and caught a pinch of Cassie's sleeve.

'Is this real?' she whispered.

'Yes, Jessica,' Rosalind said softly. She detached Jessica's hand and gathered the child close against her, stroking her hair. 'Yes, Jessica, it's real.' Jessica stared out under her arm, her eyes wide and unfocused.

They had no internet access, which eliminated the deeply depressing possibility of some chat-room wacko from halfway around the world. They also had no alarm system, but I doubted that would turn out to be relevant: Katy hadn't been snatched from her bed by some intruder. We had found her fully and carefully dressed – yes, she always coordinated, Margaret said; she'd picked that up from her ballet teacher, whom she worshipped – in outdoor clothes. She had switched off her light and waited till her parents were asleep, and then, sometime in the night or the early morning, she had got up and got dressed and gone somewhere. Her house key had been in her pocket: she had been expecting to come back.

We searched her room anyway, partly for any clues to where she might have gone, and partly because of the brutal, obvious possibility that Jonathan or Margaret had killed her and then staged it to look as if she had left the house alive. She had shared a room with Jessica. The window was too small and the light bulb too dim, which added to the creepy feeling the house was giving me. The wall on Jessica's side, a little eerily, was covered in sun-shiny, idyllic art prints: Impressionist picnics, Rackham fairies, landscapes from the cheerier parts of Tolkien ('I gave her all those,' said Rosalind, from the doorway. 'Didn't I, pet?' Jessica nodded, at her shoes). Katy's wall, less surprisingly, had a strict ballet theme: photos of Baryshnikov and Margot Fonteyn that looked like they'd been cut from TV guides, a newsprint picture of Pavlova, her acceptance letter from the Royal Ballet School; a pretty nice pencil drawing of a young dancer, with 'To Katy, 21/03/03. Happy Birthday! Love, Daddy' scribbled on the corner of the pasteboard mount.

The white pyjamas Katy had worn on Monday night were tangled on her bed. We bagged them just in case, along with the sheets and her mobile phone, which was in her bedside locker, switched off. She hadn't kept a diary – 'She started one a while ago, but after a couple of months she got bored and "lost" it,' Rosalind said, putting the word in quotation marks and giving me a small, sad, knowing smile, 'and she never bothered to start another' – but we took school copybooks, an old homework diary, anything whose scribbles might give us some hint. Each of the girls had a tiny wood-effect desk, and on Katy's there was a little round tin holding a jumble of hair elastics; I recognised, with a small sudden pang, two silk cornflowers.

'Phew,' said Cassie, when we got out of the estate onto the road. She rubbed her hands through her hair, messing up her curls.

'I've seen that name somewhere, not too long ago,' I said. 'Jonathan Devlin. As soon as we get back, let's run him through the computer and see if he's got a record.'

'God, I almost hope it turns out to be that simple,' Cassie

said. 'There is something deeply, deeply fucked up in that house.'

I was glad – relieved, actually – that she had said it. I'd found a number of things about the Devlins disturbing – Jonathan and Margaret hadn't touched once, had barely looked at each other; where you would expect a bustle of curious, comforting neighbours, there had been nobody but shadowy Auntie Vera; each member of the household appeared to come from a completely different planet – but I was so edgy that I wasn't sure I could trust my own judgment, so it was good to know Cassie had felt something off-kilter too. It wasn't that I was having a breakdown or losing my mind or anything, I knew I would be fine once I got a chance to go home and sit down by myself and take all this in; but that first glimpse of Jessica had practically given me a heart attack, and the realisation that she was Katy's twin hadn't been as reassuring as you might think. This case was too full of skewed, slippery parallels, and I couldn't shake the uneasy sense that they were somehow deliberate. Every coincidence felt like a sea-worn bottle slammed down on the sand at my feet, with my name engraved neatly on the glass and inside a message in some mockingly indecipherable code.

When I first went to boarding-school I told my dorm-mates I had a twin brother. My father was a good amateur photographer, and one Saturday that summer when he'd seen us trying out a new stunt on Peter's bike – speeding along their knee-high garden wall and sailing off the end – he made us do it again and again, half the afternoon while he crouched on the grass changing lenses, until he'd used up a whole roll of black-and-white film and got the shot he wanted. We're in mid-air; I am driving and Peter is on the handlebars with his arms spread wide, and both of us have our eyes screwed tight shut and out mouths open (high, rough-edged boy-yells) and our hair is streaming out in fiery haloes, and I'm pretty sure that just after the photo was taken we went tumbling and skidding across the lawn and my mother gave out to my father for encouraging us. He angled the shot so that the ground is out of the picture and we look like we're flying, gravity-free against the sky.

I glued the photo to a piece of cardboard and propped it on my bedside locker, where we were allowed two family pictures, and told the other boys detailed stories – some true, some imagined and I'm sure utterly implausible – about the adventures my twin and I had during the holidays. He was at a different school, I said, one in Ireland; our parents had read that it was healthier for twins to be separated. He was learning to ride horses.

By the time I came back for second year I had realised that it was only a matter of time before the twin story got me into excruciatingly embarrassing trouble (some classmate meeting my parents on Sports Day, asking chirpily why Peter hadn't come too), so I left the photo at home – tucked into a slit in my mattress, like some dirty secret – and stopped mentioning my brother, in the hope that everyone would forget I had had one. When this kid called Hull – he was the type to pull the limbs off small furry animals in his spare time – sensed my discomfort and latched on to the subject, I finally told him my twin had been thrown off a horse over the summer and died of concussion. I spent much of that year in terror that the rumour about Ryan's dead brother would reach the teachers and, through them, my parents. In hindsight, of course, I'm fairly sure that it did, and that the teachers, already briefed on the Knocknaree saga, decided to be sensitive and understanding – I still cringe when I think about it – and let the rumour die out in its own time. I think I had a narrow escape: a couple of years further into the 80s and I would probably have been sent to kiddie counselling and forced to share my feelings with hand puppets.

Still, I regretted having to get rid of my twin. I'd found it comforting, the knowledge that Peter was alive and riding horseback, somewhere in a couple of dozen minds. If Jamie had been in the photo, I would probably have made us triplets and had a much harder time working my way out of that one.

By the time we got back to the site, the reporters had arrived. I gave them the standard preliminary spiel (I do this part, on the basis that I look more like a responsible adult than Cassie does): body of a young girl, name not being released till all the relatives are informed, treating it as a suspicious death, anyone who may have any information please contact us, no comment no comment no comment.

'Was this the work of a satanic cult?' asked a large woman in unflattering ski pants, whom we'd met before. She was from one of those tabloids with a penchant for punny headlines using alternative spellings.

'There's absolutely no evidence to indicate that,' I said snottily. There never is. Homicidal satanic cults are the detective's version of yetis: no one has ever seen one and there is no proof that they exist, but one big blurry footprint and the media turn into a gibbering, foaming pack, so we have to act as though we take the idea at least semi-seriously.

'But she was found on an altar that the Druids used for human sacrifice, wasn't she?' the woman demanded.

'No comment,' I said automatically. I had just realised

what the stone table reminded me of, that deep groove round the edge: the autopsy tables in the morgue, grooved to drain away blood. I had been so busy wondering whether I recognised it from 1984, it hadn't even occurred to me that I recognised it from a few months ago. Jesus.

Eventually the reporters gave up and started drifting off. Cassie had been sitting on the steps of the finds shed, blending into the scenery and keeping an eye on things. When she saw the large journalist homing in on Mark, who had come out of the canteen heading for the Portaloo, she got up and wandered towards them, making sure Mark could see her. I saw him catch her eye, over the reporter's shoulder; after a minute Cassie shook her head, amused, and left them to it.

'What was that all about?' I asked, fishing out the key to the finds shed.

'He's giving her a lecture about the site,' said Cassie, dusting off the seat of her jeans and grinning. 'Every time she tries to ask anything about the body, he says, "Hang on," and goes into a rant about how the government is about to destroy the most important discovery since Stonehenge, or starts explaining Viking settlements. I'd love to stay and watch; I think she may finally have met her match.'

The rest of the archaeologists had very little to add, except that Sculptor Boy, whose name was Sean, felt we should consider the possibility of vampire involvement. He sobered up a lot when we showed him the ID shot, but although he, like the others, had seen Katy or possibly Jessica around the site a few times – sometimes with other kids her age, sometimes with an older girl matching Rosalind's description – none of them had seen anyone odd watching her or anything like that. None of them had seen anything sinister at all, in fact, although Mark added, 'Except for the politicians who show up to have their photos taken in front of their heritage before they pimp it out. Do you want descriptions?' Nobody remembered the Tracksuit Shadow, either, which reinforced my suspicion that he had been either some perfectly normal guy from the estate out for a walk, or else Damien's imaginary friend. You get people like this in every investigation, people who end up wasting huge amounts of your time with their compulsion to say whatever they think you want to hear.

The archaeologists from Dublin – Damien, Sean and a handful of others – had all been at home on Monday and Tuesday nights; the rest had been in their rented house, a couple of miles from the dig. Hunt, who of course turned out to be pretty lucid on anything archaeological, had been home in Lucan with his wife. He confirmed the large reporter's theory that the stone where Katy had been dumped was a Bronze Age sacrificial altar. 'We can't be sure whether the sacrifices were human or animal, naturally, although the . . . um . . . the *shape* certainly suggests they may have been human. The right dimensions, you know. Very rare artefact. It implies that this hill was a site of immense religious importance in the Bronze Age, yes? Such a terrible shame . . . this road.'

'Have you found anything else to suggest this?' I asked. If he had, it would be months before we could disentangle our case from the media-versus-New-Age frenzy.

Hunt gave me a wounded look. 'Absence of evidence is not evidence of absence,' he told me reproachfully.

He was the last interview. As we were putting our stuff away, the boy tech knocked on the door of the Portakabin and stuck his head in. 'Um,' he said. 'Hi. Sophie says to tell you we're finishing up for today and there's one more thing you might want to see.'

They'd packed up the markers and left the altar stone alone in its field again, and at first the whole site looked deserted; the reporters had long since moved on, and all the archaeologists had gone home except Hunt, who was clambering into a muddy red Ford Fiesta. Then we came out from among the Portakabins, and I saw a flash of white between the trees.

The familiar, uneventful routine of the interviews had settled my mood considerably (Cassie calls these preliminary background interviews the nuthin' stage of a case: nobody saw nuthin', nobody heard nuthin', nobody did nuthin'), but still I felt something zip down my spine as we stepped into the wood. Not fear: more like the sudden shot of alertness when someone wakes you by calling your name, or when a bat shrills past just too high to be heard. The undergrowth was thick and soft, years of fallen leaves sinking under my feet, and the trees grew heavily enough to filter the light into a restless green glow.

Sophie and Helen were waiting for us in a tiny clearing, maybe a hundred yards in. 'I left it for you to take a look at,' Sophie said, 'but I want to bag all this shit before the light starts going. I'm not setting up the lighting rig.'

Someone had been using the place as a campsite. A sleeping-bag-sized patch had been cleared of sharp branches, and the layers of leaves were pressed flat; a few yards away were the remains of a campfire, in a wide circle of bare earth. Cassie whistled.

'Is this our kill site?' I asked, without much hope: for that, Sophie would have interrupted the interviews.

'Not a chance,' she said. 'We've done a fingertip search:

no signs of a struggle and not a drop of blood – there's a big spill of something near the fire, but it tests negative, and from the smell I'm pretty sure it's red wine.'

'That's one upmarket camper,' I said, raising my eyebrows. I had been picturing some bucolic homeless guy, but market forces mean that 'wino', in Ireland, is a metaphorical term: your average down-and-out alcoholic goes for hard cider or cheap vodka. I wondered briefly about a couple, with an adventurous streak or nowhere else to go, but the flattened patch was barely wide enough for one person. 'Find anything else?'

'We'll go through the ash in case someone was burning bloody clothes or something, but it looks like straight wood. We've got bootprints, five cigarette butts and this.' Sophie handed me a Ziploc bag labelled in felt-tip. I held it up to the shifting light, and Cassie tiptoed to look over my shoulder: a single long, fair, wavy hair. 'Found it near the fire,' Sophie said, and jerked her thumb at a plastic evidence marker.

'Any idea how recently this place was used?' Cassie asked.

'The ash hasn't been rained on. I'll check rainfall for this area, but I know where I live it rained early Monday morning, and I'm only about two miles away. It looks like someone stayed here either last night or the night before.'

'Can I see those cigarette butts?' I asked.

'Be my guest,' said Sophie. I found a mask and tweezers in my case and squatted by one of the markers near the fire. The butt was from a rollie, made thin and smoked down low; someone was being careful with tobacco.

'Mark Hanly smokes rollies,' I said, straightening up. 'And has long fair hair.'

Cassie and I looked at each other. It was past six o'clock,

O'Kelly would be on the phone demanding a briefing any minute, and the conversation we needed to have with Mark was likely to take a while, even assuming we could disentangle the side roads and find the archaeologists' house.

'Forget it, let's talk to him tomorrow,' Cassie said. 'I want to go see the ballet teacher on the way in. And I'm starving.'

'It's like having a puppy,' I told Sophie. Helen looked shocked.

'Yes, but a pedigree one,' Cassie said cheerfully.

As we headed back across the site towards the car (my shoes were a mess, just like Mark had said they would be – there was red-brown muck grained into every seam – and they had been fairly nice shoes; I comforted myself with the thought that the killer's footwear would be in the same unmistakeable condition), I looked back at the wood and saw that flutter of white again: Sophie and Helen and the boy tech, moving back and forth among the trees as silently and intently as ghosts.

4

The Cameron Dance Academy was above a video shop in Stillorgan. On the street outside, three kids in baggy trousers were flipping skateboards on and off a low wall and yelling. The assistant teacher – an extremely pretty young woman called Louise, in a black leotard and black pointe shoes and a full, calf-length black skirt; Cassie gave me an amused look as we followed her up the stairs – let us in and told us Simone Cameron was just finishing up a class, so we waited on the landing.

Cassie drifted over to a cork noticeboard on the wall, and I looked around. There were two dance studios, with little round windows in the doors: in one, Louise was showing a bunch of toddlers how to be butterflies or birds or something; in the other, a dozen little girls in white leotards and pink tights were crossing the floor in pairs, in a series of jumps and twirls, to the 'Valse des Fleurs' on an old scratchy record player. As far as I could tell there was, to put it mildly, a wide range of ability. The woman teaching them had white hair pulled back in a tight bun, but her body was as spare and straight as a young athlete's; she was wearing the same black outfit as Louise and holding a pointer, tapping at the girls' ankles and shoulders and calling instructions.

'Look at this,' Cassie said quietly.

The poster showed Katy Devlin, though it took me a

second to recognise her. She was wearing a gauzy white smock and had one leg raised behind her in an effortless, impossible arc. Below her it said, in a large font, 'Send Katy to the Royal Ballet School! Help Her Make Us Proud!' and gave the details of the fundraiser: St Alban's Parish Hall, 20 June, 7.00 p.m., An Evening of Dance with the Pupils of the Cameron Dance Academy. Tickets €10/€7. All Proceeds will go to Pay Katy's Fees. I wondered what would happen to the money now.

Under the poster was a newspaper clipping, with an arty soft-focus shot of Katy at the barre; her eyes, in the mirror, gazed out at the photographer with an ageless, intent gravity. 'Dublin's Tiny Dancer Takes Wing', *The Irish Times*, 23 June: ' "I guess I'll miss my family, but I still can't wait," Katy says. "I've wanted to be a dancer ever since I was six. I can't believe I'm really going. Sometimes when I wake up I think maybe I dreamed it." ' No doubt the article had brought in donations towards Katy's fees – another thing we'd have to check up on – but it had done us no favours at all: paedophiles read morning papers too, and it was an eye-catching photo, and the field of potential suspects had just widened to include most of the country. I glanced at the other notices: tutu for sale, size 7–8; would anyone living in the Blackrock area be interested in setting up a carpool to and from the Intermediate class?

The studio door opened and a flood of matching little girls streamed past us, all chattering and shoving and shrieking at once. 'Can I help you?' Simone Cameron asked, in the doorway.

She had a beautiful voice, deep as a man's without being in the least mannish, and she was older than I had thought: her face was bony and deeply, intricately lined. I realised that she probably took us for parents coming to ask about dance classes for our daughter, and for a moment I had a wild impulse to play along with it, ask about fees and schedules and go away, leave her her illusion and her star pupil a little longer.

'Ms Cameron?'

'Simone, please,' she said. She had extraordinary eyes, almost golden, huge and heavy-lidded.

'I'm Detective Ryan, and this is Detective Maddox,' I said for the thousandth time that day. 'Could we speak to you for a few minutes?'

She brought us into the studio and set out three chairs in a corner. A mirror took up the whole of one long wall, three barres running along it at different heights, and I kept catching my own movements out of the corner of my eye. I angled my chair so I couldn't see it.

I told Simone about Katy – it was definitely my turn to do this part. I had expected her to cry, I think, but she didn't: her head went back a little and the lines in her face seemed to get even deeper, but that was all.

'You saw Katy in class on Monday evening, didn't you?' I said. 'How did she seem?'

Very few people can hold a silence, but Simone Cameron was unusual: she waited, not moving, one arm thrown over the back of her chair, until she was ready to speak. After a long time she said, 'Very much as usual. Slightly overexcited – it was a few minutes before she could settle and concentrate – but this was natural: she was to leave for the Royal Ballet School in a few weeks. She'd been growing more and more excited about it all summer.' She turned her head away, very slightly. 'She missed her class yesterday evening, but I simply assumed she was ill again. If I had rung her parents—'

'By yesterday evening she was dead,' Cassie said gently. 'There was nothing you could have done.'

'Ill again?' I asked. 'Had she been ill recently?'

Simone shook her head. 'Not recently, no. But she isn't a strong child.' Her eyelids dropped for a moment, hooding her eyes: 'Wasn't.' Then she looked up at me again. 'I've taught Katy for six years now. For several of those years, beginning when she was perhaps nine, she was ill very often. So was her sister Jessica, but her illnesses were colds, coughs – she, I think, is simply delicate. Katy suffered from periods of vomiting, diarrhoea. Sometimes it was serious enough to need hospitalisation. The doctors thought it was some form of chronic gastritis. She should have gone to the Royal Ballet School last year, you know, but she had an acute attack at the end of the summer, and they operated on her to find out more; by the time she recovered, it was too far into the term for her to catch up. She had to re-audition this spring.'

'But recently these attacks had disappeared?' I asked. We would need Katy's medical records, fast.

Simone smiled, remembering; it was a small, wrenching thing, and her eyes flicked away from us. 'I was worried about whether she would be healthy enough for the training – dancers can't afford to miss many classes through illness. When Katy was accepted again this year, I kept her after class one day and warned her that she would have to keep seeing a doctor, to find out what was wrong. Katy listened, and then she shook her head and said – very solemnly, like a vow – "I'm not going to get sick any more." I tried to impress upon her that this wasn't something she could ignore, that her career might depend on this, but that was all she would say. And, in fact, she hasn't been ill since. I thought perhaps she had simply outgrown whatever it was; but the will can be a powerful thing, and Katy is – was – strong-willed.'

The other class was letting out; I heard parents' voices on the landing, another rush of small feet and chatter. 'You taught Jessica as well?' Cassie said. 'Did she audition for the Royal Ballet School?'

In the early stages of an investigation, unless you have an obvious suspect, all you can do is find out as much about the victim's life as possible and hope something sets off alarm bells; and I was pretty sure Cassie was right, we needed to know more about the Devlin family. And Simone Cameron wanted to talk. We see this a lot, people desperate to keep talking because when they stop we will leave and they will be left alone with what has happened. We listen and nod and sympathise, and file away everything they say.

'I taught all three of the sisters, at one time or another,' Simone said. 'Jessica seemed quite competent when she was younger, and she worked hard, but as she grew she became cripplingly self-conscious, to the point where any individual exercises seemed to be a painful ordeal for her. I told her parents I thought it would be better if she didn't have to go through this any more.'

'And Rosalind?' Cassie asked.

'Rosalind had some talent, but she lacked application and wanted instant results. After a few months she switched to, I believe, violin lessons. She said it was by her parents' choice, but I thought it was because she was bored. We see this quite often with young children: when they aren't immediately proficient, and when they realise how much hard work is involved, they become frustrated and leave. Frankly, neither of them would ever have been Royal Ballet School material in any case.'

'But Katy . . .' Cassie said, leaning forward.

Simone looked at her for a long time. 'Katy was . . . *sérieuse*.'

That was what gave her voice some of its distinctive quality: somewhere, far back, there was a touch of French shaping the intonations. 'Serious,' I said.

'More than that,' said Cassie. Her mother was half French, and as a child she spent summers with her grand-parents in Provence; she says she's forgotten most of her spoken French at this point, but she still understands it. 'A professional.'

Simone inclined her head. 'Yes. She loved even the hard work – not only for the results it brought, but for its own sake. A real talent for dance is not common; the tempera-ment to make a career of it is much rarer. To find both at once . . .' She looked away again. 'Sometimes, on evenings when only one studio was being used, she would ask if she could come in and practise in the other.'

Outside, the light was beginning to dim towards evening; the skateboard kids' calls floated up, faint and crystalline through the glass. I thought of Katy Devlin alone in the studio, watching the mirror with detached absorption as she moved in slow spins and dips; the lift of a pointed foot; street lamps throwing saffron rectangles across the floor, Satie's *Gnossiennes* on the crackly record player. Simone seemed pretty *sérieuse* herself, and I wondered how on earth she had ended up here: above a shop in Stillorgan with the smell of grease wafting up from the chipper next door, teaching ballet to little girls whose mothers thought it would give them good posture or wanted framed pictures of them in tutus. I realised, suddenly, what Katy Devlin must have meant to her.

'How did Mr and Mrs Devlin feel about Katy going to ballet school?' Cassie asked.

'They were very supportive,' Simone said, without hesitation. 'I was relieved, and also surprised; not every parent is willing to send a child that age away to school, and most, with good reason, are opposed to their children becoming professional dancers. Mr Devlin, in particular, was very much in favour of Katy going. He was close to her, I think. I admired this, that he wanted what was best for her even if it meant letting her go away.'

'And her mother?' Cassie said. 'Was she close to her?'

Simone gave a little one-shouldered shrug. 'Less, I think. Mrs Devlin is . . . rather vague. She always seemed bewildered by all of her daughters. I think perhaps she isn't very intelligent.'

'Have you noticed anyone strange hanging around in the past few months?' I asked. 'Anyone who worried you?' Ballet schools and swimming clubs and scout troops are paedophile magnets. If someone had been looking for a victim, this was the obvious place where he might have spotted Katy.

'I understand what you mean, but no. We look for this. About ten years ago a man used to sit on a wall up the hill and look into the studio through binoculars. We complained to the police, but they did nothing until he tried to convince one little girl to get into his car. Since then we're very watchful.'

'Did anyone take an interest in Katy to a level that you felt was unusual?'

She thought, shook her head. 'No one. Everyone admired her dancing, many people supported the fundraiser we held to help with her fees, but no one person more than others.'

'Was there any jealousy of her talent?'

Simone laughed, a quick hard breath through her nose.

'These are not stage parents we have here. They want their daughters to learn a little ballet, enough to be pretty; they don't want them to make a career of it. I'm sure a few of the other little girls were envious, yes. But enough to kill her? No.'

She looked, suddenly, exhausted; her elegant pose hadn't changed, but her eyes were glazed with fatigue. 'Thank you for your time,' I said. 'We'll contact you if we need to ask you any more questions.'

'Did she suffer?' Simone asked abruptly. She wasn't looking at us.

She was the first person to ask. I started to give the standard non-answer involving the post-mortem results, but Cassie said, 'There's no evidence of that. We can't be sure of anything yet, but it seems to have been quick.'

Simone turned her head with an effort and met Cassie's eyes. 'Thank you,' she said.

She didn't get up to see us out, and I realised it was because she wasn't sure she could do it. As I closed the door I caught a last glimpse of her through the round window, still sitting straight-backed and motionless with her hands folded in her lap: a queen in a fairy tale, left alone in her tower to mourn her lost, witch-stolen princess.

' "I'm not going to get sick any more," ' Cassie said, in the car. 'And she stopped getting sick.'

'Will-power, like Simone said?'

'Maybe.' She didn't sound convinced.

'Or she could have been making herself sick,' I said. 'Vomiting and diarrhoea are both pretty easy to induce. Maybe she was looking for attention, and once she got into ballet school she didn't need to any more. She was getting plenty of attention without being sick – newspaper articles, fundraisers, the lot . . . I need a cigarette.'

'Junior Munchausen's syndrome?' Cassie reached into the back, dug around in my jacket pockets and found my smokes. I smoke Marlboro Reds; Cassie has no particular brand loyalty but generally buys Lucky Strike Lights, which I consider to be girl cigarettes. She lit two and passed one to me. 'Can we pull medical records on the two sisters as well?'

'Dodgy,' I said. 'They're alive, so there's confidentiality. If we got the parents' consent . . .' She shook her head. 'Why, what are you thinking?'

She opened her window a few inches, and the wind blew her fringe sideways. 'I don't know . . . The twin, Jessica – the bunny-in-headlights thing could just be stress from Katy being missing, but she's way too thin. Even through that big huge jumper you could tell she's half the size of Katy, and Katy was no heifer. And then the other sister . . . There's something off about her, too.'

'Rosalind?' I said.

There must have been something funny in my tone. Cassie shot me an oblique glance. 'You liked her.'

'Yes, I suppose I did,' I said, defensive and not sure why. 'She seemed like a nice girl. She's very protective of Jessica. What, you didn't?'

'What's that got to do with it?' Cassie said coolly and, I felt, a little unfairly. 'Regardless of who likes her, she dresses funny, she wears too much make-up—'

'She's well groomed, so there's something wrong with her?'

'Please, Ryan, do us both a favour and grow up; you know exactly what I mean. She smiles at inappropriate times, and, as you spotted, she wasn't wearing a bra.' I had noticed that, but I hadn't realised that Cassie had as well, and the dig irritated me. 'She may well be a very *nice girl*, but there's something off there.'

I didn't say anything. Cassie threw the rest of her cigarette out the window and dug her hands into her pockets, slumped in her seat like a sulky teenager. I turned on dipped headlights and sped up. I was annoyed with her and I knew she was annoyed with me too, and I wasn't sure quite how this had happened.

Cassie's mobile rang. 'Oh for God's sake,' she said, looking at the screen. 'Hello, sir . . . Hello? . . . Sir? . . . Bloody phones.' She hung up.

'Reception?' I said coldly.

'The fucking reception is fine,' she said. 'He just wanted to know when we'd be back and what was taking us so long, and I didn't feel like talking to him.'

I can usually hold a sulk for much longer than Cassie, but I couldn't help it, I laughed. After a moment Cassie did too.

'Listen,' she said, 'I wasn't being bitchy about Rosalind. More like worried.'

'Are you thinking sexual abuse?' I realised that, somewhere in the back of my mind, I had been wondering about the same thing, but I disliked the thought so much that I had been avoiding it. One sister over-sexual, one badly underweight, and one, after various unexplained illnesses, murdered. I thought of Rosalind's head bent over Jessica's and felt a sudden, unaccustomed surge of protectiveness. 'The father's abusing them. Katy's coping strategy is making herself sick, either out of self-hatred or to lessen the chances of abuse. When she gets into ballet school, she decides she needs to be healthy and the cycle has to stop; maybe she confronts the father, threatens to tell. So he kills her.'

'It plays,' said Cassie. She was watching the trees flash past on the verge; I could only see the back of her head. 'But so does, for example, the mother – if it turns out Cooper was wrong about the rape, obviously. Munchausen's by proxy. She seemed way at home in the victim role, did you notice?'

I had. In some ways grief anonymises as powerfully as a Greek tragedy mask, but in others it pares people to the essentials (and this is, of course, the real and icy reason why we try to tell families about their losses ourselves, rather than leaving it to the uniforms: not to show how much we care, but to see how they react), and we had borne bad news often enough to know the usual variations. Most people are shocked senseless, struggling for their footing, with no idea how to do this; tragedy is new territory that comes with no guide, and they have to work out, step by dazed step, how to negotiate it. Margaret Devlin had been unsurprised, almost resigned, as though grief was her familiar default state.

'So basically the same pattern,' I said. 'She's making one or all of the girls sick, when Katy gets into ballet school she tries to put her foot down, and the mother kills her.'

'It could explain why Rosalind dresses like a forty-year-old, too,' Cassie said. 'Trying to be a grown-up to get away from her mother.'

My mobile rang. 'Ah, *fuck*, man,' we both said, in unison.

I did the bad-reception routine, and we spent the rest of the drive making a list of possible lines of inquiry. O'Kelly likes lists; a good one might distract him from the fact that we hadn't rung him back.

We work out of the grounds of Dublin Castle, and in

spite of all the colonial connotations this is one of my favourite perks of the job. Inside, the rooms have been lovingly refurbished to be exactly like every corporate office in the country – cubicles, fluorescent lighting, staticky carpet and institution-coloured walls – but the outsides of the buildings are listed and still intact: old, ornate red brick and marble, with battlements and turrets and worn carvings of saints in unexpected places. In winter, on foggy evenings, crossing the cobblestones is like walking through Dickens – hazy gold street lamps throwing odd-angled shadows, bells pealing in the cathedrals nearby, every footstep ricocheting into darkness; Cassie says you can pretend you're Inspector Abberline working on the Ripper murders. Once, on a ringingly clear full-moon night in December, she turned cartwheels straight across the main courtyard.

There was a light in O'Kelly's window, but the rest of the building was dark: it was past seven, everyone else had gone home. We sneaked in as quietly as we could. Cassie tiptoed up to the squad room to run Mark and the Devlins through the computer, and I went down to the basement, where we keep the old case files. It used to be a wine cellar, and the crack Corporate Design Squad hasn't got around to it yet, so it's still all flagstones and columns and low-arched bays. Cassie and I have a pact to take a couple of candles down there someday, in spite of the electric lighting and in defiance of safety regulations, and spend an evening looking for secret passageways.

The cardboard box (Rowan G., Savage P., 33791/84) was exactly as I had left it more than two years before; I doubt anyone had touched it since. I pulled out the file and flipped to the statement Missing Persons had taken from Jamie's mother and, thank God, there it was: blond hair, hazel eyes, red T-shirt, cut-off denim shorts, white trainers, red hair-clips decorated with strawberries.

I shoved the file under my jacket, in case I ran into O'Kelly (there was no reason why I shouldn't have it, especially now that the link to the Devlin case was definite, but for some reason I felt guilty, furtive, as if I were absconding with some taboo artefact), and went back up to the squad room. Cassie was at her computer; she had left the lights off so O'Kelly wouldn't spot them.

'Mark's clean,' she said. 'So's Margaret Devlin. Jonathan has one conviction, just this February.'

'Kiddie porn?'

'Jesus, Ryan. You have a melodramatic mind. No, disturbing the peace: he was protesting about the motorway and crossed a police line. Judge gave him a hundred-quid fine and twenty hours of community service, then upped it to forty when Devlin said that as far as he was concerned he had just been arrested for performing a community service.'

That wasn't where I'd seen Devlin's name, then: as I've said, I had had only the vaguest idea that the motorway controversy even existed. But it did explain why he hadn't reported the threatening phone calls. We would not have seemed like allies to him, especially not on anything related to the motorway. 'The hair-clip's in the file,' I said.

'Nice one,' said Cassie, with a shade of a question in her voice. She was shutting down the computer and turned to look at me. 'Are you pleased?'

'I'm not sure,' I said. It was, obviously, nice to know that I wasn't losing my mind and imagining things; but now I was wondering whether I had actually remembered it at all or only seen it in the file, and which of those possibilities I

liked less, and wishing I had just kept my mouth shut about
the damn thing.

Cassie waited; in the evening light through the window her
eyes looked huge, opaque and watchful. I knew she was
giving me a chance to say, *Fuck the hair-clip, let's forget we ever
found it.* Even now the temptation, tired and profitless though
it may be, is to wonder what would have happened if I had.

But it was late, I had had a long day, I wanted to go
home, and being handled with kid gloves – even by Cassie
– has always made me itch; cutting short this whole line of
inquiry seemed like so much more effort than simply
leaving it to run its course. 'Will you ring Sophie about
the blood?' I asked. In that dim room, it seemed all right to
admit this much weakness at least.

'Sure,' said Cassie. 'Later, though, OK? Let's go talk to
O'Kelly before he has an aneurysm. He texted me while
you were in the basement; I didn't think he even knew how
to do that, did you?'

I rang O'Kelly's extension and told him we were back, to
which he said, 'About fucking time. What did you do, stop
for a quickie?' and then told us to get into his office pronto.

The office has only one chair apart from O'Kelly's own,
one of those faux-leather ergonomic things. The implication is that you shouldn't take up too much of his space or
time. I sat in the chair, and Cassie perched on a table
behind me. O'Kelly gave her an irritated look.

'Make it fast,' he said. 'I've to be somewhere at eight.'
His wife had left him the year before; since then the
grapevine had picked up a series of awkward attempts
at relationships, including one spectacularly unsuccessful
blind date where the woman turned out to be an ex-hooker
he had arrested regularly in his Vice days.

'Katharine Devlin, age twelve,' I said.

'The ID's definite, so?'

'Ninety-nine per cent,' I said. 'We'll have one of the parents view the body when the morgue's patched her up, but Katy Devlin was an identical twin, and the surviving twin looks exactly like our victim.'

'Leads, suspects?' he snapped. He had a sort of nice tie on, ready for his date, and he was wearing too much cologne; I couldn't place it, but it smelled expensive. 'I'm going to have to give a fucking press conference tomorrow. Tell me you've got something.'

'She was hit over the head and asphyxiated, probably raped,' Cassie said. The fluorescent lighting smudged grey under her eyes. She looked too tired and too young to be saying the words so calmly. 'We won't know anything definite till the post-mortem tomorrow morning.'

'Fucking *tomorrow*?' O'Kelly said, outraged. 'Tell that shite Cooper to give this priority.'

'Already did, sir,' said Cassie. 'He had to be in court this afternoon. He said first thing tomorrow is the best he can do.' (Cooper and O'Kelly hate each other; what Cooper had actually said was, 'Kindly explain to Mr O'Kelly that his cases aren't the only ones in the world.') 'We've identified four primary lines of inquiry, and—'

'Good, that's good,' said O'Kelly, grabbing drawers open and rummaging for a pen.

'First, there's the family,' said Cassie. 'You know the stats, sir: most murdered kids are killed by their parents.'

'And there's something odd about that family, sir,' I said. This was my line; we had to get the point across, in case we ever needed a little leeway in investigating the Devlins, but if Cassie had said it O'Kelly would have gone off into a long snide boring routine about women's intuition. We were good at O'Kelly by this time. Our counterpoint has been polished to the seamlessness of a Beach Boys harmony – we can sense exactly when to swap the roles of front man and back-up, good cop and bad cop, when my cool detachment needs to strike a balancing note of gravitas against Cassie's bright ease – and it is for use even against our own. 'I can't put my finger on it, but there's something up in that house.'

'Never ignore a hunch,' said O'Kelly. 'Dangerous.' Cassie's foot, swinging casually, nudged my back.

'Second,' she said, 'we're going to have to at least check out the possibility of some kind of cult.'

'Oh, God, Maddox. What, did *Cosmo* run an article on Satanism this month?' O'Kelly's disregard for cliché is so sweeping that it almost has its own panache. I find this entertaining or irritating or mildly comforting, depending on my mood, but at least it makes it very easy to prepare your script in advance.

'I think it's a load of rubbish too, sir,' I said, 'but we've got a murdered little girl on a sacrificial altar. The reporters were asking about it already. We'll have to eliminate it.' It is, obviously, difficult to prove that something does not exist, and saying it without solid proof just brings out the conspiracy theorists, so we take a different tack. We would spend several hours finding ways in which Katy Devlin's death didn't match the putative MO of a hypothetical group (no bloodletting, no sacrificial garment, no occult symbols, yada yada yada), and then O'Kelly, who luckily has absolutely no sense of the absurd, would explain all this to the cameras.

'Waste of time,' O'Kelly said. 'But yeah, yeah, do it. Talk to Sex Crime, talk to the parish priest, whoever, just get it out of the way. What's third?'

'Third,' Cassie said, 'is a straight-up sex crime – a paedophile who killed her either to stop her talking or because killing is part of his thing. And if things point that way, we're going to have to look at the two kids who disappeared at Knocknaree in 1984. Same age, same location, and right beside our victim's body we found a drop of old blood – lab's working on matching it to the '84 samples – and a hair-clip that fits the description of one the missing girl was wearing. We can't rule out a connection.' This was definitely Cassie's line. I am, as I've said, a pretty good liar, but just hearing her say it made my heart rate go up annoyingly, and in many ways O'Kelly is more perceptive than he pretends to be.

'What, a serial sex killer? After twenty years? And how do you know about this hair-clip anyway?'

'You told us to familiarise ourselves with cold cases, sir,' said Cassie virtuously. It was true, he had – I think he heard it in a seminar, or maybe on *CSI* – but he told us a lot of things, and anyway none of us ever had time. 'And the guy could have been out of the country, or in prison, or he only kills when he's under a lot of stress—'

'We're *all* under a lot of stress,' said O'Kelly. 'Serial killer. That's all we need. What's next?'

'Fourth is the one that could get dodgy, sir,' said Cassie. 'Jonathan Devlin, the father, runs the Move the Motorway campaign in Knocknaree. Apparently that's pissed off a few people. He says he's had three anonymous phone calls in the last couple of months, threatening his family if he doesn't back off. We're going to have to find out who has a serious stake in that motorway going through Knocknaree.'

'Which means fucking about with property developers and County Councils,' said O'Kelly. 'Jesus.'

'We'll need as many floaters as we can get, sir,' I said, 'and I think we'll need someone else from Murder.'

'Too bloody right, you will. Take Costello. Leave him a note; he's always in early.'

'Actually, sir,' I said, 'I'd like to have O'Neill.' I have nothing against Costello, but I definitely did not want him on this one. Apart from the fact that he was basically dreary and this case was depressing enough without him, he was the dogged type who would go through the old case file with a fine-tooth comb and start trying to trace Adam Ryan.

'I'm not putting three rookies on a high-profile case. You two are only on this because you spend your breaks surfing for porn, or whatever you were doing, instead of getting some fresh air like everyone else.'

'O'Neill's hardly a rookie, sir. He's been in Murder for seven years.'

'And we all know why,' said O'Kelly, nastily. Sam made the squad at twenty-seven; his uncle is a mid-level politician, Redmond O'Neill, who is usually junior Minister for Justice or the Environment or something. Sam deals with it well: whether by nature or by strategy, he is placid, reliable, everyone's favourite back-up, and this deflects most of the potential for snide commentary. He still gets the odd bitchy remark, but these are usually reflexive, like O'Kelly's had been, rather than actively malicious.

'That's exactly why we need him, sir,' I said. 'If we're going to poke our noses into County Council business and all the rest of it without making too many waves, we need someone who's got contacts in that circle.'

O'Kelly glanced at the clock, moved to smooth his comb-over and then thought better of it. It was twenty to eight. Cassie recrossed her legs, settled more comfortably on the table. 'I guess there could be pros and cons,' she said. 'Maybe we should discuss—'

'Ah, whatever, have O'Neill,' said O'Kelly irritably. 'Just get the job done and don't let him piss anyone off. I want reports on my desk every morning.' He stood up and started patting papers into rough piles: we were dismissed.

Out of absolutely nowhere I felt a sudden sweet shot of joy, piercing and distilled as the jolt I imagine heroin users get when the fix hits the vein. It was my partner bracing herself on her hands as she slid fluidly off the desk, it was the neat practised movement of flipping my notebook shut one-handed, it was my superintendent wriggling into his suit jacket and covertly checking his shoulders for dandruff, it was the garishly lit office with a stack of marker-labelled case files sagging in the corner and evening rubbing up against the window. It was the realisation, all over again, that this was real and it was my life. Maybe Katy Devlin, if she had made it that far, would have felt this way about the blisters on her toes, the pungent smell of sweat and floor-wax in the dance studios, the early-morning breakfast bells raced down echoing corridors. Maybe she, like me, would have loved the tiny details and the inconveniences even more dearly than the wonders, because they are the things that prove you belong.

I remember that moment because, if I am honest, I have them so seldom. I am not good at noticing when I'm happy, except in retrospect. My gift, or fatal flaw, is for nostalgia. I have sometimes been accused of demanding perfection, of rejecting heart's desires as soon as I get close enough that the mysterious impressionistic gloss disperses into plain solid dots, but the truth is less simplistic than that. I know very well that perfection is made up of frayed, off-struck mundanities. I suppose you could say my real weakness is a kind of longsightedness: usually it is only at a distance, and much too late, that I can see the pattern.

5

Neither of us felt like a pint. Cassie rang Sophie's mobile and gave her the story about recognising the hair-clip from her encyclopaedic knowledge of cold cases – I got the sense Sophie didn't really buy it, but didn't much care either way. Then she went home to type up a report for O'Kelly, and I went home with the old file.

I share a purpose-built apartment in Monkstown with an unspeakable woman named Heather, a civil servant with a little-girl voice that always sounds as though she is about to burst into tears. At first I found it appealing; now it just makes me nervous. I moved in because I liked the idea of living near the sea, the rent was affordable, and I fancied her (five foot nothing, tiny build, big blue eyes, hair down to her arse) and harboured Hollywood-style fantasies of a beautiful relationship blossoming to our mutual amazement. I stay because of inertia and because by the time I discovered her array of neuroses I had started saving for an apartment of my own, and her flat was – even after we both worked out that Harry and Sally were never going to materialise, and she raised my rent – the only one in the greater Dublin area that would allow me to do that.

I unlocked the door, shouted 'Hi' and made a dive for my room. Heather beat me to it: she appeared in the kitchen doorway with incredible speed and quavered, 'Hi, Rob, how was your day?' Sometimes I have this mental picture of her sitting in the kitchen hour after hour, folding the hem of the tablecloth into perfect little pleats, poised to leap out of her chair and fasten on to me as soon as she hears my key in the lock.

'Fine,' I said, keeping my body language pointed towards my room and unlocking my door (I installed the lock a few months after I moved in, ostensibly to prevent hypothetical burglars from making off with confidential police files). 'How are you?'

'Oh, I'm all right,' Heather said, pulling her pink fleece dressing-gown more closely around herself. The martyred tone meant I had two options: I could say 'Great' and go into my room and close the door, in which case she would sulk and bang pans for days to register her displeasure at my lack of consideration, or I could say 'Are you OK?' in which case I would have to spend the next hour listening to a blow-by-blow account of the outrages perpetrated by her boss or her sinuses or whatever it was that was currently making her feel hard done by.

Fortunately I have an Option C, though it has to be saved for emergencies. 'Are you sure?' I said. 'There's this awful flu going round at work, and I think I'm coming down with it. I hope you don't get it too.'

'Oh my God,' said Heather, her voice going up another octave and her eyes getting even bigger. 'Rob, pet, I so don't mean to be rude, but I'd probably better stay away from you. You know I just get colds so easily.'

'I understand,' I said reassuringly, and Heather disappeared back into the kitchen, presumably to add horse-sized capsules of vitamin C and echinacea to her frenetically balanced diet. I went into my room and closed the door.

I poured myself a drink – I keep a bottle of vodka and one of tonic behind my books, to avoid cosy convivial 'drinkies' with Heather – and spread out the old case file on my desk. My room is not conducive to concentration. The whole building has the cheap, mean-spirited feel of so many new Dublin developments – ceilings a foot too low, frontage flat and mud-coloured and hideous in an utterly unoriginal way, bedrooms insultingly narrow as if designed to rub in the fact that you can't afford to be picky – and the developer saw no need to waste insulation on us, so every footstep from above or musical selection from below echoes through our entire flat, and I know far more than I need to about the sexual tastes of the couple next door. Over four years I've more or less got used to it, but I still find all the basic premises of the place offensive.

The ink of the statement sheets was faded and spotty, almost illegible in places, and I tasted fine dust settling on my lips. The two detectives who had headed the case were both retired by this time, but I made a note of their names – Kiernan and McCabe – in case we, or rather Cassie, needed to talk to them at some stage.

One of the most startling things about the case, to modern eyes, is how slow our families were to become worried. Nowadays parents are on the phone to the police as soon as a child's mobile goes unanswered; Missing Persons have become jaded from taking too many reports on children kept after school or lingering over video games. It seems ingenuous to say that the 1980s were a more innocent time, given all that we now know about industrial schools and revered priests and fathers in rocky, lonely corners of the country. But then these were only unthinkable rumours happening somewhere else, people held on to their innocence with a simple and passionate tenacity, and it was perhaps no less real for being chosen and for carrying its own culpability; and Peter's mother called us from the edge of the wood, wiping her hands on her apron, and then left us to our absorbing game and went home to make the tea.

I found Jonathan Devlin in the margins of a minor witness statement, halfway through the pile. Mrs Pamela Fitzgerald of 27 Knocknaree Drive – oldish, by the cramped, curlicued handwriting – had told the detectives that a group of rough-looking teenagers hung around the edge of the wood, drinking and smoking and courting and sometimes hurling terrible abuse at passers-by, and that you weren't safe walking your own road these times, and that what they needed was a good clatter round the ear. Kiernan or McCabe had scribbled names down the side of the page: Cathal Mills, Shane Waters, Jonathan Devlin.

I flipped through the sheets to see if any of them had been interviewed. Outside my door I could hear the rhythmic, invariable sounds of Heather going through her nightly routine: determinedly cleansing and toning and moisturising, brushing her teeth for the dentist-prescribed three minutes, genteelly blowing her nose an inexplicable number of times. Bang on schedule at five to eleven, she tapped on my door and cooed, 'Night-night, Rob,' in a coy stage-whisper. 'Night,' I called back, adding a cough at the end.

The three statements were brief and almost identical, except for margin notes that described Waters as 'v. nervous' and Mills as 'uncooperative' [*sic*]. Devlin hadn't warranted any comment. On the afternoon of 14 August they had drawn their dole and then gone by bus to the pictures in Stillorgan. They had got back to Knocknaree around seven – when we were already late for tea – and gone knacker-drinking in a field near the wood till around midnight. Yes, they had seen the searchers, but they had simply moved behind a hedge to be out of sight. No, they hadn't seen anything else unusual. No, they hadn't seen anyone who could confirm their whereabouts that day, but Mills had offered (presumably in a spirit of sarcasm, but they took him up on it) to lead the detectives to the field and show them the empty cider cans, which did indeed prove to be located in the spot he identified. The young man who had been working the box office at the Stillorgan cinema appeared to be under the influence of controlled substances and wasn't sure whether he remembered the three guys or not, even when the detectives searched his pockets and gave him a stern lecture about the evils of drugs.

I didn't get the impression that the 'youths' – I hate that word – had been serious suspects. They weren't exactly hardened criminals (the local uniforms cautioned them for public intoxication on a semi-regular basis, and Shane Waters had been given six months' probation for shoplifting when he was fourteen, but that was it), and why would they want to make a couple of twelve-year-olds disappear? They had simply been there, and vaguely unsavoury, so Kiernan and McCabe had checked them out.

The bikers, we had called them, although I'm unsure whether any of them actually had motorbikes; probably they just dressed as though they did. Black leather jackets, unzipped at the wrists and trimmed with metal studs; stubble and long hair, and one of them had the inevitable mullet. High Doc boots. T-shirts with logos on the fronts – Metallica, Anthrax. I thought those were their names, till Peter told me they were bands.

I had no idea which one had become Jonathan Devlin; I couldn't connect the sad-eyed man with the little paunch and the desk slump to any of the lean, sun-blurred, looming teenagers in my memory. I had forgotten all about them. I don't think the bikers had entered my mind once in twenty years, and I intensely disliked the thought that they had been there all along in spite of this, just waiting for their cue to pop up neatly as jacks-in-the-box, bobbing and grinning, and make me jump.

One of them wore shades all year round, even in the rain. Sometimes he offered us Juicy Fruit gum, which we took, at arm's length, even though we knew they had stolen it from Lowry's shop. 'Don't go near them,' my mother said, 'don't answer if they talk to you,' and wouldn't tell me why. Peter asked Metallica if we could have a drag of his cigarette, and he showed us how to hold it and laughed when we coughed. We stood in the sun, just out of reach, stretching to see the insides of their magazines; Jamie said one of them had a girl all nude. Metallica and Shades flicked plastic lighters, had competitions to see who could hold his finger over the flame longest. When they left, in the evening, we went over and smelled the squashed cans left behind in the dusty grass: sour, stale, grown-up.

I woke up because someone was screaming below my window. I sat up hard, my heart banging against my ribs. I had been dreaming, something tangled and feverish where Cassie and I were in a crowded bar and a guy in a tweed cap was yelling at her, and for a moment I thought it was her voice I had heard. I was disorientated, it was dark, heavy late-night silence; and someone, a girl or a child, was screaming again and again outside.

I went to the window and cautiously hooked the curtain open an inch. The complex where I live is made up of four identical apartment buildings around a little square of grass with a couple of iron benches, the kind of thing estate agents call a 'communal recreation area', although nobody ever uses it (the couple in the ground-floor flat had lazy evening cocktails *al fresco* a couple of times, but people complained about the noise, and the management company put up a narky sign in the foyer). The white security lights gave the garden an eerie night-scope glow. It was empty; the slants of shadow in the corners were too low to hide anyone. The scream came again, high and chilling and very close, and an atavistic prickle went up my spine.

I waited, shivering a little in the cold air striking off the glass. After a few minutes something moved in the shadows, blacker against the black, then detached itself and stepped out onto the grass: it was a big dog-fox, alert and scrawny in his sparse summer coat. He raised his head and screamed again, and for a moment I imagined I caught his wild, alien scent. Then he trotted across the grass and disappeared through the front gate, pouring between the bars as sinuously as a cat. I heard his shrieks moving away into the darkness.

I was dazed and half-asleep and keyed up with leftover adrenalin, and my mouth tasted foul; I needed something cold and sweet. I went out to the kitchen to look for juice. Heather, like me, sometimes has trouble sleeping, and I found myself almost hoping she would be awake and still wanting to complain about whatever it was, but there was no light under her door. I poured myself a glass of her orange juice and stood in front of the open fridge for a long time, holding the glass to my temple and swaying slightly in the flickering neon light.

In the morning it was pouring rain. I texted Cassie to say I'd pick her up – the Golf Cart tends to go catatonic in wet weather. When I beeped my horn outside her flat, she ran down wearing a Paddington Bear duffel coat and carrying a thermos of coffee.

'Thank God it didn't do this yesterday,' she said. 'Bye-bye evidence.'

'Look at this,' I said, giving her the Jonathan Devlin stuff.

She sat cross-legged in the passenger seat and read, occasionally passing me the thermos. 'Do you remember these guys?' she said, when she'd finished.

'Vaguely. Not well, but it was a small neighbourhood and they were hard to miss. They were the nearest thing we had to juvenile delinquents.'

'Did they strike you as dangerous?'

I thought about this for a while, as we crawled down Northumberland Road. 'Depends what you mean,' I said. 'We were wary of them, but I think that was mainly because of their image, not because they ever did anything to us. I remember them being fairly tolerant of us, actually. I can't see them having made Peter and Jamie disappear.'

'Who were the girls? Were they interviewed?'

'What girls?'

Cassie flicked back to Mrs Fitzgerald's statement. 'She said "courting". I'd say it's a safe bet that involved girls.'

She was right, of course. I wasn't too clear on the exact definition of 'courting', but I was pretty sure it would have excited a fair amount of comment if Jonathan Devlin and his mates had been doing it with each other. 'They're not in the file,' I said.

'What about you, do you remember them?'

We were still on Northumberland Road. The rain was sheeting down the windows so heavily it looked like we were underwater. Dublin was built for pedestrians and carriages, not for cars; it's full of tiny winding medieval streets, rush hour lasts from seven in the morning till eight at night, and at the first hint of bad weather the whole city goes into prompt, thorough gridlock. I wished we had left a note for Sam.

'I think so,' I said eventually. It was nearer to a sensation than to a memory: powdery lemon bonbons, dimples, flowery perfume. *Metallica and Sandra, sitting in a tree* . . . 'One of them might have been called Sandra.' Something inside me flinched at the name – acrid taste like fear or shame at the back of my tongue – but I couldn't find why.

Sandra: round-faced and buxom, giggles and pencil skirts that rode up when she perched on the wall. She seemed very grown-up and sophisticated to us; she must have been all of seventeen or eighteen. She gave us sweets out of a paper bag. Sometimes there was another girl there, tall, with big teeth and lots of earrings – Claire, maybe? Ciara? Sandra showed Jamie how to put on mascara, in a little heart-shaped mirror. Afterwards Jamie kept blinking, as though her eyes felt strange, heavy. 'You look pretty,' Peter said. Later Jamie decided she hated it. She washed it off in the river, scrubbing away the panda-rings with the hem of her T-shirt.

'Green light,' Cassie said quietly. I inched forward another few feet.

We stopped at a newsagent's and Cassie ran in and got the papers, so we could see what we were dealing with. Katy Devlin was front-page news in every one of them, and they all seemed to be focusing on the motorway link – 'Knocknaree Protest Leader's Daughter Murdered', that kind of thing. The large tabloid reporter (whose story was headlined DIG BIGWIG'S DAUGHTER SLAUGHTER, a hyphen away from libel) had thrown in a few coy references to Druidic ceremonies but stayed clear of full-scale Satanism hysteria; she was obviously waiting to see which way the wind blew. I hoped O'Kelly would do his stuff well. Nobody, thank Christ, had mentioned Peter and Jamie, but I knew it was only a matter of time.

We palmed off the McLoughlin case (the one we had been working till we got this call: two God-awful little rich boys who had kicked another to death when he jumped the queue for a late-night taxi) on Quigley and his brand-new partner McCann, and went to find ourselves an incident room. The incident rooms are too small and always in demand, but we had no trouble getting one: children take priority. By that time Sam had got in – he had been held up in traffic as well; he has a house somewhere in Westmeath, a couple of hours out of town, which is as near as our generation can afford to buy – so we grabbed him and briefed him, with full harmonies and the official hair-clip story, while we set up the incident room.

'Ah, Jesus,' he said, when we finished. 'Tell me it wasn't the parents.'

Every detective has a certain kind of case that he or she finds almost unbearable, against which the usual shield of practised professional detachment turns brittle and un-trustworthy. Cassie, though nobody else knows this, has nightmares when she works rape-murders; I, displaying a singular lack of originality, have serious trouble with mur-dered children; and, apparently, family killings gave Sam the heebie-jeebies. This case could turn out to be perfect for all three of us.

'We haven't a clue,' Cassie said, through a mouthful of marker cap; she was scribbling a timeline of Katy's last day across the whiteboard. 'We might have a better idea once

Cooper comes back with the results from the post, but right now it's wide open.'

'We don't need you to look into the parents, though,' I said. I was Blu-tacking crime-scene photos to the other side of the board. 'We want you to take the motorway angle – trace the phone calls to Devlin, find out who owns the land around the site, who has a serious stake in the motorway staying put.'

'Is this because of my uncle?' Sam asked. He has a tendency to directness that I've always found slightly startling, in a detective.

Cassie spat out the marker cap and turned to face him. 'Yeah,' she said. 'Is that going to be a problem?'

We all knew what she was asking. Irish politics are tribal, incestuous, tangled and furtive, incomprehensible even to many of the people involved. To an outside eye there is basically no difference between the two main parties, which occupy identical self-satisfied positions on the far right of the spectrum, but many people are still passionate about one or the other because of which side their great-grandfathers fought on during the Civil War, or because Daddy does business with the local candidate and says he's a lovely fella. Corruption is taken for granted, even grudgingly admired: the guerrilla cunning of the colonised is still ingrained into us, and tax evasion and shady deals are seen as forms of the same spirit of rebellion that hid horses and seed potatoes from the British.

And a huge amount of the corruption centres on that primal, clichéd Irish passion, land. Property developers and politicians are traditionally bosom buddies, and just about every major land deal involves brown envelopes and inexplicable re-zoning and complicated transactions through offshore accounts. It would be a minor miracle if there weren't at least a few favours to friends woven into the Knocknaree motorway, somewhere. If there were, it was unlikely that Redmond O'Neill didn't know about them, and equally unlikely that he would want them to come out.

'No,' Sam said, promptly and firmly. 'No problem.' Cassie and I must have looked dubious, because he glanced back and forth between us and laughed. 'Listen, lads, I've known him all my life. I *lived* with them for a couple of years when I first came up to Dublin. I'd know if he was into anything dodgy. He's straight as a die, my uncle. He'll help us out any way he can.'

'Perfect,' Cassie said, and went back to the timeline. 'We're having dinner at my place. Come over around eight and we'll swap updates.' She found a clean corner of whiteboard and drew Sam a little map of how to get there.

By the time we had the incident room organised, the floaters were starting to arrive. O'Kelly had got us about three dozen of them, and they were the cream of the crop: up-and-comers, alert and smooth-shaven and dressed for success, tipped to make good squads as soon as the openings arose. They pulled out chairs and notebooks, slapped backs and resurrected old in-jokes and chose their seats like kids on the first day of school. Cassie and Sam and I smiled and shook hands and thanked them for joining us. I recognised a couple of them – an uncommunicative dark guy from Mayo called Sweeney, and a well-fed Corkman with no neck, O'Connor or O'Gorman or something, who compensated for having to take orders from two non-Corkonians by making some incomprehensible but clearly triumphalistic comment about Gaelic football. A lot of the others looked familiar, but the names went straight out of my head the moment their hands slid away from mine, and the faces merged into one big, eager, intimidating blur.

I've always loved this moment in an investigation, the moment before the first briefing begins. It reminds me of the focused, private buzz before a curtain goes up: orchestra tuning, dancers backstage doing last-minute stretches, ears pricked for the signal to throw off their wraps and leg-warmers and explode into action. I had never been in charge of an investigation anything like this size before, though, and this time the sense of anticipation just made me edgy. The incident room felt too full, all that primed and cocked energy, all those curious eyes on us. I remembered the way I used to look at Murder detectives, back when I was a floater praying to be borrowed for cases like this one: the awe, the bursting, almost unbearable aspiration. These guys – a lot of them were older than I was – seemed to me to have a different air about them, a cool, unconcealed assessment. I've never liked being the centre of attention.

O'Kelly slammed the door behind him, slicing off the noise instantaneously. 'Right, lads,' he said, into the silence. 'Welcome to Operation Vestal. What's a vestal when it's at home?'

Headquarters picks the names for operations. They range from the obvious through the cryptic to the down-right weird. Apparently the image of the little dead girl on the ancient altar had piqued someone's cultural tendencies. 'A sacrificial virgin,' I said.

'A votary,' said Cassie.

'Jesus fuck,' said O'Kelly. 'Are they *trying* to make everyone think this was some cult thing? What the fuck are they reading up there?'

★   ★   ★

Cassie gave them a run-down on the case, skipping lightly over the 1984 connection – just an off-chance, something she could check out in her spare time – and we handed out jobs: go door-to-door through the estate, set up a tip line and a roster for manning it, get a list of all the sex offenders living near Knocknaree, check with the British cops and with the ports and airports to see if anyone dodgy had come over to Ireland in the last few days, pull Katy's medical records, her school records, run full background checks on the Devlins. The floaters snapped smartly into action, and Sam and Cassie and I left them to it and went to see how Cooper was getting on.

We don't normally watch the autopsies. Someone who was at the crime scene has to go, to confirm that this is in fact the same body (it's happened, toe-tags getting mixed up, the pathologist ringing a startled detective to report his finding of death from liver cancer), but mostly we palm this off on uniforms or techs and just go through the notes and photos with Cooper afterwards. By squad tradition you attend the post-mortem in your first murder case, and although supposedly the purpose is to impress you with the full solemnity of your new job, nobody is fooled: this is an initiation rite, as harshly judged as any primitive tribe's. I know an excellent detective who, after fifteen years on the squad, is still known as Arkle because of the speed with which he left the morgue when the pathologist removed the victim's brain.

I made it through mine (a teenage prostitute, thin arms layered with bruises and track-marks) without flinching, but I was left with no desire to repeat the experience. I go only in those few cases – ironically, the most harrowing ones – that seem to demand this small, sacrificial act of devotion. I don't think anyone ever quite gets over that first time, really, the mind's violent revolt when the pathologist slices the scalp and the victim's face folds away from the skull, malleable and meaningless as a Halloween mask.

Our timing was a little off: Cooper was just coming out of the autopsy room in his green scrubs, a waterproof gown held away from him between finger and thumb. 'Detectives,' he said, raising his eyebrows. 'What a surprise. If only you'd let me know you were planning to come, I would of course have waited until you managed to fit us in.'

He was being snotty because we were too late for the post-mortem. It was, in all fairness, not even eleven o'clock, but Cooper gets into work between six and seven, leaves by three or four, and likes you to remember it. His morgue assistants all hate him for this, which doesn't bother him because he mostly hates them too. Cooper prides himself on instant, unpredictable dislikes; as far as we've been able to figure out so far, he dislikes blonde women, short men, anyone with more than two earrings and people who say 'you know' too much, as well as various random people who don't fit into any of these categories. Fortunately he had decided to like me and Cassie, or he would have made us go back to work and wait until he sent over the post-mortem results (handwritten – Cooper writes all his reports in spidery fountain pen, an idea I sort of like but don't have the courage to try out in the squad room). There are days when I worry, secretly, that in a decade or two I might wake up and discover I've turned into Cooper.

'Wow,' Sam said, trying. 'Finished already?' Cooper gave him a chilly glance.

'Dr Cooper, I'm so sorry to burst in on you at this hour,' Cassie said. 'Superintendent O'Kelly wanted to go over a few things, so we had a hard time getting away.' I nodded wearily and raised my eyes to the ceiling.

'Ah. Well, yes,' Cooper said. His tone implied that he found it slightly tasteless of us to mention O'Kelly at all.

'If by any chance you have a few moments,' I said, 'would you mind talking us through the results?'

'But of course,' Cooper said, with an infinitesimal, long-suffering sigh. Actually, like any master craftsman, he loves showing off his work. He held the autopsy-room door open for us and the smell hit me, that unique combination of death and cold and rubbing alcohol that sends an instinctive animal recoil through you every time.

Bodies in Dublin go to the city morgue, but Knocknaree is outside the city limits; rural victims are simply brought to the nearest hospital, and the post-mortem is done there. Conditions vary. This room was windowless and grubby, layers of grime on the green floor-tiles and nameless stains in the old porcelain sinks. The two autopsy tables were the only things in the room that looked post-1950s; they were bright stainless steel, light flaring off those grooved edges.

Katy Devlin was naked under the merciless fluorescent lights and too small for the table, and she looked somehow much deader than she had the previous day; I thought of the old superstition that the soul lingers near the body for a few days, bewildered and unsure. She was grey-white, like something out of Roswell, with dark blotches of lividity down her left side. Cooper's assistant had already sewn her scalp back together, thank God, and was working on the Y incision across her torso, big sloppy stitches with a needle the size of a sailmaker's. I felt a momentary, crazy pang of guilt at being late, at leaving her all on her own – she was so small – through this final violation: we should have been there, she should have had someone to hold her hand while

Cooper's detached, gloved fingers prodded and sliced. Sam, to my surprise, crossed himself unobtrusively.

'Pubescent white female,' Cooper said, brushing past us to the table and motioning the assistant away, 'aged twelve, so I'm told. Height and weight both on the low side, but within normal limits. Scars indicating abdominal surgery, possibly an exploratory laparotomy, some time ago. No obvious pathology; as far as I can tell, she died healthy, if you'll pardon the oxymoron.'

We clustered around the table like obedient students; our footsteps threw small flat echoes off the tiled walls. The assistant leaned against one of the sinks and folded his arms, chewing stolidly on a piece of gum. One arm of the Y incision still gaped open, dark and unthinkable, the needle stuck casually through a flap of skin for safekeeping.

'Any chance of DNA?' I asked.

'One step at a time, *if* you please,' Cooper said fussily. 'Now. There were two blows to the head, both ante-mortem – before death,' he added sweetly to Sam, who nodded solemnly. 'Both were struck with a hard, rough object with protrusions but no distinct edges, consistent with the rock Ms Miller presented to me for inspection. One was a light blow to the back of the head, near the crown. It caused a small area of abrasion and some bleeding, but no cracks to the skull.' He turned Katy's head to one side, to show us the little bump. They had cleaned the blood off her face, to check for any injuries underneath, but there were still faint swipes of it across her cheek.

'So maybe she dodged, or she was running away from him while he was swinging,' Cassie said.

We don't have profilers. When we really need one we bring one over from England, but most of the time a lot of the Murder guys just use Cassie, on the dubious basis that she studied psychology at Trinity for three and a half years. We don't tell O'Kelly this – he considers profilers to be one step up from psychics, and only grudgingly lets us listen even to the English guys – but I think she's probably fairly good at it, although presumably this is for reasons unrelated to her years of Freud and lab rats. She always comes up with a couple of useful new angles, and usually turns out to be quite close to the mark.

Cooper took his time thinking about it, to punish her for interrupting. Finally he shook his head judiciously. 'I consider that unlikely. Had she been moving when this blow was struck, one would expect peripheral grazing, but there was none. The other blow, in contrast . . .' He tilted Katy's head to the other side and hooked back her hair with one finger. On her left temple a patch of skin had been shaved to expose a wide, jagged laceration, splinters of bone poking out. Someone, Sam or Cassie, swallowed.

'As you see,' Cooper said, 'the other blow was far more forceful. It landed just behind and above the left ear, causing a depressed skull fracture and a sizeable subdural haematoma. Here and here' – he flicked his finger – 'you'll observe the peripheral grazing to which I referred, at the proximal edge of the primary impact point: as the blow was struck, she appears to have turned her head away, so the weapon skidded along her skull briefly before achieving its full impact. Do I make myself clear?'

We all nodded. I glanced covertly across at Sam and was heartened by the fact that he looked like he was having a hard time, too.

'This blow would have been sufficient to cause death within hours. However, the haematoma had progressed very little, so we can safely say that she died of other causes within a short time of receiving this injury.'

'Can you tell whether she was facing towards him or away from him?' Cassie asked.

'The indications are that she may have been prone when the harder blow was struck: there was considerable bleeding, and the flow was directed inwards across the left side of the face, with some pooling apparent around the central line of the nose and mouth.' This was good news, if I can use the term at all in this context: there would be blood at the scene, if we ever found it. Also, it meant we were probably looking for someone left-handed, and, while this wasn't Agatha Christie and real cases seldom hinge on that kind of thing, at this point any tiny lead was an improvement.

'There was a struggle – prior to this blow, I may add: it would have rendered her unconscious immediately. There are defensive wounds to the hands and forearms – bruising, abrasions, three broken fingernails on the right hand – probably inflicted by the same weapon as she warded off blows.' He lifted one of her wrists between finger and thumb, turned over her arm to show us the scrapes. Her fingernails had been clipped off short and taken away for analysis; on the back of her hand was a stylised flower with a smiley face in the middle, drawn in faded marker. 'I also found bruising around the mouth and toothmarks on the insides of the lips, consistent with the perpetrator pressing a hand over her mouth.'

Outside, down the corridor, a woman's high voice was giving out about something; a door slammed. The air in the autopsy room felt thick and too still, hard to breathe. Cooper glanced around at us, but nobody said anything. He knew this wasn't what we wanted to hear. In a case like this, the one thing you can hope for is that the victim never knew what was happening.

'When she was unconscious,' Cooper said coolly, 'some material, probably plastic, was placed around her throat and twisted at the top of the spine.' He tilted her chin back: there was a faint, broad mark around her neck, striated where the plastic had buckled into folds. 'As you see, the ligature mark is well defined, hence my conclusion that it was put in place only when she had been immobilised. She shows no signs of strangulation, and I consider it unlikely that the ligature was tight enough to cut off the airway; however, petechial haemorrhaging in the eyes and on the surface of the lungs indicates that she did in fact die of anoxia. I would hypothesise that something along the lines of a plastic bag was placed over her head, twisted at the back of the neck and held in place for several minutes. She died of suffocation, complicated by blunt-force trauma to the head.'

'Hang on,' Cassie said suddenly. 'So she wasn't raped after all?'

'Ah,' Cooper said. 'Patience, Detective Maddox; we're coming to that. The rape was post-mortem, and was performed using an implement of some kind.' He paused, discreetly enjoying the effect.

'Post-*mortem*?' I said. 'You're sure?' This was a relief in the obvious way, eliminating some of the most excruciating mental images; but, at the same time, it did imply a special level of wacko. Sam's face was pulled into an unconscious grimace.

'There are fresh abrasions to the exterior of the vagina and to the first three inches of the interior, and a fresh tear in the hymen, but there was no bleeding and no inflammation. Post-mortem, beyond a doubt.' I felt the collective, panicky flinch – none of us wanted to see this, the thought was obscene – but Cooper gave us a tiny amused glance and stayed where he was, at the head of the table.

'What kind of implement,' Cassie said. She was staring at the mark on Katy's throat, intent and expressionless.

'Inside the vagina we found particles of earth and two minute splinters of wood, one severely charred, the other overlaid with what appears to be thin, clear varnish. I would postulate something at least four inches in length and approximately one to two inches in diameter, made of lightly varnished wood, with considerable wear, a burn mark of some kind and no sharp edges – a broom handle, something along those lines. The abrasions were discrete and well defined, implying a single insertion. I found nothing to suggest that there was also penile penetration. The rectum and mouth showed no signs of any sexual assault.'

'So no body fluids,' I said grimly.

'And there appeared to be no blood or skin beneath her fingernails,' said Cooper, with faint, pessimistic satisfaction. 'The tests are incomplete, of course, but I feel I should warn you not to place too much hope in the possibility of DNA samples.'

'You checked the rest of the body for semen, too, right?' Cassie said.

Cooper gave her an austere look and didn't bother answering. 'After death,' he said, 'she was placed in much the same position in which we found her, lying on her left side. There was no secondary lividity, indicating that she remained in this pose for at least twelve hours. The relative lack of insect activity leads me to believe that she was in an enclosed space, or possibly wrapped tightly in some material, for a considerable proportion of the time before discovery of the body. All this will be included in my notes, of course, but for now . . . Do you have any questions?'

The dismissal was delicate but clear. 'Anything new on time of death?' I asked.

'The gastrointestinal contents allow me to be a little more precise than I was at the scene – if, that is, you can determine the time of her last meal. She had eaten a chocolate biscuit only a few minutes before her death, and a full meal – the digestive process was fairly advanced, but beans appear to have been a component – approximately four to six hours earlier.'

Baked beans on toast, at around eight. She had died somewhere between midnight and two o'clock, give or take. The biscuit must have come either from the Devlins' kitchen, sneaked on her way out of the house, or from her killer.

'My team should have her cleaned up within a few minutes,' Cooper said. He straightened Katy's head with a precise, satisfied flourish. 'If you'd like to notify the family.'

We stood outside the hospital and looked at each other. 'Haven't been to one of those in a while,' Sam said softly.

'And now you remember why,' I said.

'Post-*mortem*,' Cassie said, frowning absently back at the building. 'What the hell was this guy *doing*?'

Sam went off to find out more about the motorway, and I phoned the incident room and told two of the floaters to take the Devlins to the hospital. Cassie and I had already seen their first, crucial reaction to the news, we neither needed nor wanted to see it again; and we did need, urgently, to talk to Mark Hanly.

'Want to bring him in?' I said, in the car. There was no

reason why we couldn't interrogate Mark in the finds shed, but I wanted him off his territory and on ours, partly as a form of unreasonable revenge for my ruined shoes.

'Oh yeah,' said Cassie. 'He said they only have a few weeks left, didn't he? If I've got Mark right, the fastest way to get him talking is to waste his work day.'

We used the drive to make O'Kelly a nice long list of reasons why we did not feel that Knocknaree For Satan had been responsible for Katy Devlin's death. 'Don't forget "no ritual positioning",' I said. I was driving again; I was still edgy enough that, without something to do, I would have chain-smoked all the way to Knocknaree.

'And no . . . slaughtered . . . livestock,' Cassie said, writing.

'He is not going to say that at the press conference. "We didn't find a dead chicken"?'

'Bet you a fiver he does. He won't even miss a beat.'

The day had changed while we were in with Cooper: the rain had spent itself and a hot, benevolent sun was already drying the roads. The trees in the lay-by were glittering with leftover raindrops, and when we got out of the car the air smelled new, washed clean, vital with wet earth and leaves. Cassie pulled off her jumper and tied it around her waist.

The archaeologists were spread out across the bottom half of the site, doing energetic things with mattocks and shovels and wheelbarrows. Their jackets were thrown over rocks and some of the guys had stripped off their T-shirts, and – presumably in reaction to yesterday's shock and hush – they were all in a giddy mood. A ghetto-blaster was pumping out the Scissor Sisters at full volume, and they were singing along, in between mattock-blows; one girl was using her shovel as a microphone. Three of them were having a water fight, shrieking and dodging with bottles and a hose.

Mel heaved a full wheelbarrow up the side of a huge heap of earth, caught it expertly on her thigh while she changed her grip to empty it out. On her way back down, she got a hoseful of water in the face. 'You bastards!' she screamed, dropping the wheelbarrow and chasing after the little red-headed girl holding the hose. The redhead shrieked and ran, but she caught a foot in the coils; Mel grabbed her in a headlock and they wrestled for the hose, laughing and spluttering, wide arcs of water flying everywhere.

'Ah, deadly,' one of the guys called. 'Lesbo action.'

'Where's the camera?'

'Here, is that a hickey on your neck?' the redhead shouted. 'Lads, Mel's got a hickey!' A burst of congratulatory whoops and laughter.

'Fuck off,' Mel yelled, bright red and grinning.

Mark called something sharp at them all and they shouted back, cheekily – 'Ooo, touchy!' – and drifted back to work, shaking sparkling fans of water out of their hair. I felt a sudden, unexpected surge of envy, for the unselfconscious freedom of their shouting and tussling, the satisfying arc and thud of the mattocks, their muddy clothes left to dry in the sun as they worked; for the loose-limbed, efficient assurance of it all. 'Not a bad way to make a living,' Cassie said, tipping her head back and smiling a private little smile up at the sky.

The archaeologists had spotted us; one by one they lowered their tools and looked up, shielding their eyes against the sun with bare forearms. We picked our way across to Mark under their collective, startled gaze. Mel stood up out of a trench, puzzled, swiping hair off her face and leaving a muddy streak; Damien, kneeling among his protective phalanx of girls, still looked woebegone and faintly bedraggled, but Sean the sculptor perked up when he saw us, and waved his shovel. Mark leaned on his mattock like some taciturn old mountainy man, squinting at us inscrutably.

'Yeah?'

'We'd like a word with you,' I said.

'We're working. Can it not wait till lunch?'

'No. Bring your things; we're going back to headquarters.'

His jaw tightened and for a moment I thought he was going to argue, but then he tossed down the mattock, wiped his face with his T-shirt and headed off up the hill. 'Bye,' I said to the archaeologists, as we followed him. Not even Sean answered.

In the car Mark pulled out his tobacco packet. 'No smoking,' I said.

'What the fuck?' he demanded. 'You both smoke. I saw you yesterday.'

'Department cars count as workplaces. It's illegal to smoke in them.' I wasn't even making this up; it takes a committee to come up with something that ludicrous.

'Ah, what the hell, Ryan, let him have a cigarette,' Cassie said. She added in a nicely judged undertone, 'It'll save us having to take him out for a smoke break for a few hours.' I caught Mark's startled glance in the rear-view mirror. 'Can I have a rollie?' she asked him, twisting round to lean between the seats.

'How long is this going to take?' he said.

'That depends,' I told him.

'On *what*? I don't even know what this is *about*.'

'We'll get to that. Settle down and have your smoke before I change my mind.'

'How's the dig going?' Cassie asked sociably.

One corner of Mark's mouth twisted sourly. 'How do you think? We've got four weeks to do a year's work. We've been using *bull*dozers.'

'And that's not a good thing?' I said.

He glared at me. 'Do we look like the fucking Time Team?'

I wasn't sure how to answer that, given that as far as I was concerned he and his buddies did in fact look exactly like the fucking Time Team. Cassie turned on the radio; Mark lit up and blew a noisy, disgusted stream of smoke out of the window. It was obviously going to be a long day.

I didn't say much on the drive back. I knew it was very possible that Katy Devlin's killer was sulking in the back seat of the car, and I wasn't sure how I felt about this. In a lot of ways, of course, I would have loved him to be our guy: he had been getting right up my nose, and if it was him then we could get rid of this eerie, dicey case almost before it began. It could be over that afternoon; I could put the old file back in the basement – Mark, who in 1984 had been about five and living somewhere very far from Dublin, was not a viable suspect – collect my pat on the back from O'Kelly, take back the taxi-rank wankers from Quigley and forget all about Knocknaree.

And yet, somehow, that felt all wrong. Partly it was the crashing, embarrassing anticlimax of the idea – I had spent much of the past twenty-four hours trying to prepare myself for wherever this case might take me, and I had expected something a lot more dramatic than one inter-rogation and an arrest. It was more than that, though. I am not superstitious, but if the call had come in a few minutes earlier or later, after all, or if Cassie and I hadn't just discovered Worms, or if we had wanted a smoke, this case would have gone to Costello or someone, never to us, and it seemed impossible that so powerful and heady a thing could be coincidence. I had a sense of things stirring, rearranging themselves in some imperceptible but crucial way, tiny unseen cogs beginning to shift. Deep down, I think – ironic as it may seem – a part of me couldn't wait to see what would happen next.

6

By the time we got back to work, Cassie had managed to extract the information that bulldozers were used only in emergencies because they destroy valuable archaeological evidence and that the Time Team were a bunch of unprofessional hacks, as well as the end of a rollie Mark had made her, which meant that if necessary we could match his DNA to the butts from the clearing without getting a warrant. It was pretty clear who was going to be the good cop today. I frisked Mark (clench-jawed, shaking his head) and put him in an interview room, while Cassie left our Satan-Free Knocknaree list on O'Kelly's desk.

We let Mark simmer for a few minutes – he slouched in his chair and drummed an increasingly irritable riff on the table with his index fingers – before we went in. 'Hi again,' said Cassie cheerfully. 'Do you want tea or coffee?'

'No. I *want* to get back to my *job*.'

'Detectives Maddox and Ryan, interviewing Mark Conor Hanly,' Cassie told the video camera, high up in a corner. Mark whipped round, startled; then he grimaced at the camera and eased back into his slump.

I pulled up a chair, threw a sheaf of crime-scene shots on the table and ignored them. 'You are not obliged to say anything unless you wish to do so, but anything you do say will be taken down in writing and may be used in evidence. Got it?'

'What the fuck— Am I under *arrest*?'

'No. Do you drink red wine?'

He shot me a brief, sarcastic glance. 'Are you offering?'

'Why don't you want to answer the question?'

'That is my answer. I drink whatever's going. Why?' I nodded thoughtfully and wrote this down.

'What's with the tape?' Cassie asked curiously, leaning across the table to point at the masking tape wrapped around his hands.

'For blisters. Plasters don't stay on, when you're using a mattock in the rain.'

'Couldn't you just wear gloves?'

'Some people do,' Mark said. His tone implied that these people lacked testosterone, in one way or another.

'Would you have any objection to letting us see what's underneath?' I said.

He gave me a fishy look, but he unwound the tape, taking his time, and dropped it on the table. He held up his hands with a sardonic flourish. 'See anything you like?'

Cassie leaned further forward on her arms, took a good look, gestured to him to turn his hands over. I couldn't see any scrapes or fingernail marks, only the remains of large blisters, half-healed, at the base of each finger. 'Ow,' Cassie said. 'How'd you get those?'

Mark shrugged dismissively. 'Usually I have calluses, but I was out for a few weeks there, hurt my back – had to stick to cataloguing finds. My hands went soft. When I went back to work, this is what I got.'

'Must have driven you mental, not being able to work,' Cassie said.

'Aye, it did all right,' Mark said briefly. 'Shite timing.'

I picked up the masking tape between finger and thumb

and dropped it in the bin. 'Where were you Monday night?' I asked, leaning against the wall behind Mark.

'In the team house. Like I told you yesterday.'

'Are you a member of Move the Motorway?' Cassie asked.

'Yeah, I am. Most of us are. Your man Devlin came round a while back, asking us if we wanted to join up. It's not illegal yet, as far as I know.'

'So you know Jonathan Devlin?' I asked.

'That's what I just said. We're not bosom buddies, but yeah, I know the man.'

I leaned over his shoulder and flicked through the crime-scene photos, giving him glimpses but not leaving him time for a proper look. I found one of the more disturbing shots and flipped it across to him. 'But you told us you didn't know her.'

Mark held the photo between the tips of his fingers and gave it a long, impassive look. 'I told you I'd seen her around the dig but I didn't know her name, and I don't. Should I?'

'I think you should, yes,' I said. 'She's Devlin's daughter.'

He spun to stare at me for a second, brows knitting; then he looked back at the photo. After a moment he shook his head. 'Nah. I met a daughter of Devlin's at a protest, back in spring, but she was older. Rosemary, Rosaleen, something.'

'What did you think of her?' Cassie asked.

Mark shrugged. 'Good-looking girl. Talked a lot. She was working the membership table, signing people up, but I don't think she was really into the campaign; more into flirting with the fellas. She never bothered showing up again.'

'You found her attractive,' I said, wandering over to the one-way glass and checking my shave in the reflection.

'Pretty enough. Not my type.'

'But you noticed that she wasn't at any subsequent protests. Why were you looking for her?'

I could see him, in the glass, staring suspiciously at the back of my head. Finally he shoved the photo away and settled back in his chair, chin jutting. 'I wasn't.'

'Did you make any attempt to get in contact with her again?'

'No.'

'How did you know she was Devlin's daughter?'

'I don't remember.'

I was starting to get a bad feeling about this. Mark was impatient and pissed off, and the shower of disconnected questions was making him wary, but he didn't seem remotely nervous or scared or anything like that; his main feeling about the whole thing appeared to be irritation. Basically, he wasn't acting like a guilty man.

'Listen,' Cassie said, tucking one foot up under her, 'what's the real story on the dig and the motorway?'

Mark laughed, a mirthless little snort. 'It's a lovely bedtime story. The government announced the plans in 2000. Everyone knew there was plenty of archaeology around Knocknaree, so they brought in a team to do a survey. The team came back, said the site was way more important than anyone had thought and only an idiot would build on it, the motorway would have to be moved. The government said that was very interesting, thanks very much, and they weren't moving it an inch. It took massive rows before they'd even allow an *excavation*. Finally they were gracious enough to say OK, we could do a two-year dig – it'd take at *least* five years to do that site justice. Since then there's been thousands of people fighting this every way we can – petitions, demonstrations, lawsuits. The government doesn't give a fuck.'

'But why?' Cassie asked. 'Why don't they just move the thing?'

He shrugged, his mouth twisting savagely. 'Don't ask me. We'll find out all about it in some tribunal, when it's ten or fifteen years too late.'

'What about Tuesday night?' I said. 'Where were you?'

'*The team house.* Can I go now?'

'In a while,' I told him. 'When was the last time you spent the night on the site?'

His shoulders stiffened, almost imperceptibly. 'I've never spent the night on the site,' he said, after a moment.

'Don't split hairs. The wood beside the site.'

'Who said I've ever slept there?'

'Look, Mark,' Cassie told him, suddenly and bluntly, 'you were in the wood either Monday night or Tuesday night. We can prove it with forensic evidence if we have to, but that's going to waste a lot of our time, and believe me, we'll make sure it wastes plenty of yours. I don't think you killed that girl, but we need to know when you were in the wood, what you were doing there and whether you saw or heard anything useful. So we can spend the rest of the day trying to drag it out of you, or you can just get it over with and go back to work. Your call.'

'What forensic evidence?' Mark demanded sceptically.

Cassie gave him a little mischievous smile and pulled the rollie, neatly encased in a Ziploc bag, out of her pocket. She waved it at him. 'DNA. You left your butts at your campsite.'

'Jesus,' Mark said, staring at it. He looked like he was deciding whether or not to be furious.

'Just doing my job,' she said cheerfully, pocketing the bag.

'Jesus,' he said again. He bit his lip, but he couldn't hide the grudging smile tugging at one corner of his mouth. 'And I walked straight into it. You're some woman, all the same.'

'So they tell me. About sleeping in the wood . . .'

Silence. Finally Mark stirred, glanced up at the clock on the wall, sighed. 'Yeah. I've spent the odd night there.'

I moved back around the table, sat down and opened my notebook. 'Monday or Tuesday? Or both?'

'Monday, only.'

'What time did you get there?'

'About half-ten. I lit a fire and went to sleep when it burned down, around two o'clock.'

'Do you do that on every site?' Cassie asked. 'Or just Knocknaree?'

'Just Knocknaree.'

'Why?'

Mark watched his fingers, drumming slowly on the table again. Cassie and I waited.

'You know what it means, Knocknaree?' he said eventually. 'Hill of the king. We're not sure when the name originated, but we're pretty sure it's a pre-Christian religious reference, not a political one. There's no evidence of any royal burials or dwelling-places on the site, but we found Bronze Age religious artefacts all over the place – the altar stone, votive figurines, a gold offering-cup, remains of animal sacrifices and some possible human ones. That used to be a major religious site, that hill.'

'Who were they worshipping?'

He shrugged, drumming harder. I wanted to slam a hand down over his fingers.

'So you were keeping vigil,' Cassie said quietly. She was leaning back casually in her chair, but every line of her face was alert and intent, focused on him.

Mark moved his head uncomfortably. 'Something like that.'

'The wine you spilled,' Cassie said. He glanced up sharply, then cut his eyes away again. 'A libation?'

'I suppose.'

'Let me see if I have this right,' I said. 'You decide to sleep a few yards from where a little girl gets murdered, and you feel we should believe you were there for religious reasons.'

Suddenly he caught fire, throwing himself forward and jabbing a finger at me, fast and feral. I flinched before I could stop myself. 'Come here, Detective, you listen to me. I don't believe in the Church, do you get me? Any Church. Religion exists to keep people in their place and paying into the collection plate. I had my name taken off the Church register the day I turned eighteen. And I don't believe in any government. They're the same as the Church, every one of them. Different words, same goal: keep the poor under your thumb and supporting the rich. The only things I believe in are out on that there dig.' His eyes were narrow, incandescent, eyes for behind a rifle atop a doomed barricade. 'There's more to worship on that site than in any fucking church in the world. It's *sacrilege* that they're about to run a motorway over it. If they were about to tear down Westminster Abbey to build a car park, would you blame people for keeping vigil there? Then *don't fucking patronise me* for doing the same thing.' He stared me out of it until I blinked, then flung himself back in the chair and folded his arms.

'I take it that was a denial that you had anything to do

with the murder,' I said coolly, when I was sure my voice was under control. For some reason, that little rant had got to me more than I liked to admit. Mark raised his eyes to the ceiling.

'Mark,' Cassie said. 'I know exactly what you mean. I feel the same way about what I do.' He gave her a long, hard green stare, without moving, but finally he nodded. 'But you've got to see Detective Ryan's point: a lot of people won't have a clue what you're on about. To them, it's going to look suspicious as hell. We need to eliminate you from the investigation.'

'You want me to take a lie-detector test, I will. But I wasn't even *there* on Tuesday night. I was there on *Monday*. What does that have to do with anything?' I got that sinking feeling again. Unless he was a lot better at this than I thought, he was taking it for granted that Katy had died on Tuesday night, the night before her body had appeared on the site.

'OK,' Cassie said. 'Fair enough. Can you prove where you were from the time you left work on Tuesday till you went back in on Wednesday morning?'

Mark sucked his teeth and picked at a blister, and I suddenly realised he looked embarrassed; it made him seem much younger. 'Yeah, actually, I can. I went back to the house, took a shower, had dinner with the rest of the lads, we played cards and had a few cans in the garden. You can ask them.'

'And then?' I said. 'What time did you go to bed?'

'Most people went in around one.'

'And can anyone vouch for your whereabouts after that? Do you share a room?'

'Nah. I've a room to myself, because of being assistant site director. I stayed up a while longer, in the garden. I was talking with Mel. I was with her till breakfast.' He was doing his best to sound blasé, but all that arrogant self-possession had vanished; he looked prickly and self-conscious and about fifteen. I was dying to laugh. I didn't dare look at Cassie.

'All night?' I said, maliciously.

'Yeah.'

'In the garden? Wasn't that a little chilly?'

'We went inside at maybe three o'clock. After that we were in my room, till eight. That's when we get up.'

'Well, well, well,' I said sweetly. 'Most alibis aren't nearly that enjoyable.' He shot me a poisonous look.

'Let's go back to Monday night,' Cassie said. 'While you were in the wood, did you see or hear anything unusual?'

'No. But it's dark out there – country-dark, not your city-dark. No street lights or nothing. I wouldn't have seen someone ten feet away. And I mightn't have heard them, either; there are plenty of noises anyway.' Dark, and wood-noises: that trill went down my spine again.

'Not necessarily in the wood,' Cassie said. 'On the dig, or on the road, maybe? Was anyone out there after, say, half-eleven?'

'Hang on, now,' Mark said suddenly, almost reluctantly. 'Out on the site. There was someone.'

Neither Cassie nor I moved, but I felt the electric spark of alertness shoot between us. We had been about ready to give up on Mark, check his alibi and put him on a question-mark list and send him back to his mattock, at least for now – in the urgent first days of an investigation, you have no time to waste on any but the most crucial things – but he had our full attention again.

'Could you give us a description?' I asked.

He glanced at me with dislike. 'Yeah. They looked a lot like a torch. It was *dark*.'

'Mark,' said Cassie. 'From the beginning?'

'Someone carrying a torch cut across the site, from the estate towards the road. That's it. All I saw was the torch-beam.'

'What time?'

'I wasn't looking at my watch. One, maybe? A little before?'

'Think back. Could you tell anything about them at all – maybe their height, from the angle of the torch?'

He thought, eyes narrowing. 'Nah. It looked fairly low to the ground, but the dark fucks up your sense of perspective, yeah? They were moving slow enough, but anyone would; you've seen the site, it's all ditches and bits of wall.'

'Big torch or small?'

'Small beam, not that strong. It wasn't one of those big heavy yokes with the handle. Just a little torch.'

'When you first saw it,' Cassie said, 'it was up by the estate wall – where, at the end farthest from the road?'

'Somewhere around there, yeah. I figured they'd come out of the back gate, or maybe over the wall.' The back gate of the estate was at the end of the Devlins' street, only three houses away. He could have seen Jonathan or Margaret, slowed down by a body and looking for a place to leave it; or Katy, slipping through the dark to meet someone, armed with nothing but a torch-beam and a house key that would never be able to take her home.

'And they went out to the road.'

Mark shrugged. 'They cut down that way, diagonal across the site, but I didn't see where they ended up. The trees got in the way.'

'Do you think whoever it was saw your fire?'

'How would I know?'

'OK, Mark,' Cassie said, 'this is important. Did you see a car go past around that time? Or maybe a car stopped on the road?'

Mark took his time. 'Nah,' he said, finally and definitely. 'A couple went past when I first got there, but nothing after about eleven. They go to bed early around there; all the lights on the estate are out by midnight.'

If he was telling the truth, then he had just done us a huge favour. Both the kill site and the secondary scene – wherever Katy's body had been hidden through Tuesday – were almost definitely within walking distance of the estate, quite probably on it, and our field of suspects no longer included most of the population of Ireland. 'Are you sure you would have noticed if a car had gone past?' I asked.

'I noticed the torch, didn't I?'

'Which you've only just remembered,' I said.

His lip curled. 'My memory's grand, thanks. I didn't think it was important. This was *Monday* night, yeah? I didn't even pay much attention. I thought it was someone heading home from a mate's house, maybe, or one of the local kids going to meet someone – they hang out on the site at night, sometimes. Not my problem, either way. They weren't giving me any hassle.'

At this point Bernadette, the squad administrator, tapped on the interview-room door; when I opened it, she said disapprovingly, 'Detective Ryan, there's a telephone call for you. I told the person you couldn't be disturbed, but she said it was important.' Bernadette has been with Murder for something like twenty-four years, her entire working life. She has a petulant marsupial face, five work outfits (one for each day of the week, which is helpful if you're too tired to remember what day it is) and, we all think, a Smithers-style hopeless passion for O'Kelly. There's a squad sweepstake on when they'll finally get together.

'Go ahead,' said Cassie. 'I can finish up here – Mark, we just need to take your statement. Then we can give you a lift back to work.'

'I'll take the bus.'

'No you won't,' I said. 'We need to verify your alibi with Mel, and it's not exactly verification if you have a chance to talk to her first.'

'For fuck's *sake*,' Mark snapped, thudding back in his chair. 'I'm not making it *up*. Ask anyone. It was all round the team before we even got up.'

'Don't worry, we will,' I said cheerfully, and left him and Cassie to it.

I went back to the incident room and waited for Bernadette to put the call through, which she did in her own time, to show me it wasn't her job to come looking for me. 'Ryan,' I said.

'Detective Ryan?' She sounded breathless and bashful, but I knew the voice instantly. 'It's Rosalind. Rosalind Devlin.'

'Rosalind,' I said, flipping my notebook open and hunting for a pen. 'How are you?'

'Oh, I'm fine.' A small, brittle laugh. 'Well, actually, no, I'm not. I'm devastated. But I think we're all still in shock, really. It hasn't sunk in yet. You never imagine something like this happening, do you?'

'No,' I said gently. 'I know how you must be feeling. Can I do anything to help?'

'I was wondering . . . do you think I could come in and talk to you sometime? Only if it's no trouble. There's

something I need to ask you.' A car went by in the background; she was outside somewhere, on a mobile or a pay
phone.

'Of course. This afternoon?'

'No,' she said hastily. 'No – not today. You see, they'll be
back any minute, they've only gone to . . . to view the . . .'
Her voice trailed off. 'Could I come tomorrow? Sometime
in the afternoon?'

'Whenever you like,' I said. 'Let me give you my mobile
number, OK? Then you can reach me any time you need
to. Just give me a ring tomorrow, and we'll meet up.'

She took it down, murmuring the numbers under her
breath. 'I have to go,' she said hurriedly. 'Thank you,
Detective Ryan. Thank you so much,' and, before I could
say goodbye, she was gone.

I checked the interview room: Mark was writing, and
Cassie had managed to make him laugh. I flipped my
fingernails against the glass. Mark's head snapped up, and
Cassie threw me a tiny smile and a fractional shake of her
head: apparently they were managing to get by without me.
This, as you might expect, was fine with me. Sophie would
be waiting for the blood sample we'd promised her; I left
Cassie a 'Back in 5' Post-it on the door of the interview
room, and went down to the basement.

Evidence-storage procedures in the early 80s, especially
for cold cases, were not sophisticated. Peter and Jamie's
box was on a high shelf and I had never taken it down
before, but I knew, from the lumpy shifting when I had
pulled out the main file from the top, that there were other
things in there, and those had to be whatever evidence
Kiernan and McCabe and their team had collected. The
case had four other boxes, but they were labelled, in neat

black lettering as careful as a child's: 2) Questionaires, 3) Questionaires, 4) Statements, 5) Leads. Either Kiernan or McCabe couldn't spell. I tugged the main box off the shelf, dust-motes fountaining through the bare light bulb's glare, and dumped it on the floor.

It was half-full of plastic evidence bags, furred with thick layers of dust that gave the objects inside a shadowy, sepia-toned look, like mysterious artefacts found by chance in a centuries-sealed chamber. I pulled them out gently, one by one, blew on them and laid them in a row on the flagstones.

There was very little, for a major case. A child's watch, a glass tumbler, a dull-orange Donkey Kong game, all coated in what looked like fingerprint powder. Various scraps of trace evidence, mainly dried leaves and chips of bark. A pair of white gym socks stippled with dark brown, with neat square holes where swatches had been razored out for testing. A grubby white T-shirt; faded denim shorts, the hems starting to fray. Last of all the trainers, with their childish scuff-marks and their stiff, black, buckled lining. They were the padded kind, but the blood had soaked almost all the way through: the outsides had tiny dark stains spreading from the stitching-holes, splashes around the top, faint brownish patches where it lay just beneath the surface.

I had been bracing myself quite hard for this, actually. I think I'd had some vague idea that seeing the evidence would trigger a dramatic flash flood of memories; I hadn't exactly expected to end up in a foetal position on the basement floor, but there was a reason I'd picked a moment when no one was likely to come looking for me. In the event, though, I realised with a definite sense of anticlimax that none of this stuff looked even remotely familiar – except, of all things, Peter's Donkey Kong game, which was presumably only there for fingerprint comparison and which ignited a brief and fairly useless flare of memory (me and Peter sitting on sunlit carpet working a button each, concentrated and elbowing, Jamie leaning over our shoulders and yelping excited instructions) so intense I could practically hear the game's brisk, bossy chirrups and beeps. The clothes, though I knew they were mine, rang no bells whatsoever. It seemed inconceivable that I had actually got up one morning and put them on. All I could see was the pathos of them – how small the T-shirt was, the Biro Mickey Mouse on the toe of one trainer. Twelve had seemed terrifyingly grown-up, at the time.

I picked up the T-shirt bag between finger and thumb and turned it over. I had read about the rips across the back, but I had never seen them before, and somehow I found them more shocking even than those terrible shoes. There was something unnatural about them – the perfect parallels, the neat shallow arcs; a stark, implacable impossibility. *Branches?* I thought, staring blankly down at them. Had I jumped out of a tree, or ducked through bushes, and somehow caught my shirt on four sharp twigs at once? My back itched, between the shoulder-blades.

Suddenly and compulsively, I wanted to be somewhere else. The low ceiling pressed down claustrophobically and the dusty air was hard to breathe; it was oppressively quiet, only the odd ominous vibration in the walls when a bus went past outside. I practically threw all the stuff back into the box, heaved it onto its shelf and snatched up the shoes, which I had left on the floor, ready to send to Sophie.

It was only then that it hit me, there in the chilly basement with half-forgotten cases all around and tiny sharp crackles coming from the box as the plastic bags settled: the immensity of what I had set in motion. Somehow, what with everything that was on my mind, I had failed to think this through. The old case seemed such a private thing that I had forgotten it could have implications in the outside world, too. But I (what the hell, I wondered, had I been thinking?) was about to take these shoes up to the buzzing incident room and put them in a padded envelope and tell one of the floaters to take them to Sophie.

It would have happened anyway, sooner or later – missing-child cases are never closed, it was only a matter of time before someone thought of running the old evidence through new technology. But if the lab managed to get DNA off the trainers, and especially if they somehow matched it to the blood from the altar stone, this would no longer be just a minor lead in the Devlin case, a long shot between us and Sophie: the old case would explode back into active status. Everyone from O'Kelly up would want to make a huge deal of this shiny new high-tech evidence: the Gardaí never give up, no unsolved case is ever closed, the public can rest assured that behind the scenes we are moving in our own mysterious ways. The media would leap on the possibility of a serial child-killer in our midst. And we would have to follow through; we would need DNA samples from Peter's parents and Jamie's mother and – oh, God – from Adam Ryan. I looked down at the shoes and had a sudden mental image of a car, brakes come loose, drifting down a hill: slowly at first, harmless, almost comic, then gathering momentum and transforming into a merciless wrecking ball.

7

We took Mark back to the site and left him to brood darkly in the back of the car while I talked to Mel and Cassie had a quick word with their housemates. When I asked her how she'd spent Tuesday night, Mel went sunburn-red and couldn't look at me, but she said she and Mark had talked in the garden till late, ended up kissing and spent the rest of the night in his room. He had only left her once, for no more than two minutes, to go to the bathroom. 'We've always got on great – the others used to take the piss out of us about it. I guess it was on the cards.' She also confirmed that Mark occasionally spent the night away from the house, and that he'd told her he slept in Knocknaree wood: 'I don't know if any of the others would know that, though. He's kind of private about it.'

'You don't find it a little odd?'

She shrugged clumsily, rubbing at the back of her neck. 'He's an intense guy. That's one of the things I like about him.' God, she was young; I had a sudden urge to pat her shoulder and remind her to use protection.

The rest of the housemates told Cassie that Mark and Mel had been the last ones left in the garden Tuesday night, that they had come out of his room together the next morning and that everyone had spent the first few hours of the day, until Katy's body turned up, mercilessly giving them grief about it. They also said Mark sometimes stayed out, but they didn't know where he went. Their versions of 'an intense guy' ranged from 'a little weird' through 'a total slave-driver'.

We got more plasticky sandwiches from Lowry's shop and had lunch sitting on the estate wall. Mark was organising the archaeologists into some new activity, gesturing in big militant jerks like a traffic cop. I could hear Sean complaining vociferously about something, and everyone else yelling at him to shut up and stop skiving and get a grip.

'I swear to God, Macker, if I find it on you I'm going to shove it so far up your hole—'

'Ooh, Sean's PMSing.'

'Have you checked up *your* hole?'

'Maybe the cops took it away with them, Sean, better lie low for a while.'

'Get to work, Sean,' Mark shouted across.

'I can't *work* without my fucking *trowel!*'

'Borrow one.'

'Spare over here,' someone yelled. A trowel flew spinning from hand to hand, light spiking off the blade, and Sean caught it and settled down to work, still grumbling.

'If you were twelve,' Cassie said, 'what would get you out here in the middle of the night?'

I thought of the faint gold circle of light, bobbing like a will-o'-the-wisp among the severed tree-roots and the shards of ancient walls; the silent watcher in the wood. 'We did it a couple of times,' I said. 'Spent the night in our tree house. This was all woods, back then, right up to the road.' Sleeping-bags on rough boards, torch-beams close against comic books. A rustle, and the beams skidding up to cross on a pair of golden eyes, rocking wild and luminous only a few trees away; all of us yelling, and

Jamie leaping up to fire a spare satsuma as the thing bounded away with a crash of leaves—

Cassie glanced at me over her juice carton. 'Yeah, but you were with your mates. What would get you out here on your own?'

'Meeting someone. A dare. Possibly getting something important that I'd forgotten here. We'll talk to her friends, see if she said anything to them.'

'This wasn't a random thing,' Cassie said. The archaeologists had put the Scissor Sisters back on and one of her feet swung, absently, in time with the beat. 'Even if it wasn't the parents. This guy didn't go out and pick up the first vulnerable kid he saw. He put a lot of planning into this. He wasn't just looking to kill a kid; he was after Katy.'

'And he knew the place pretty well,' I said, 'if he could find the altar stone in the dark, carrying a body. It's looking more and more like a local boy.' The wood was gay and sparkly in the sunlight, all birdsong and flirting leaves; I could feel the rows upon rows of identical, trim, innocuous houses ranged behind me. *This fucking place*, I almost said, but I didn't.

After the sandwiches we went looking for Auntie Vera and the cousins. It was a hot, still afternoon, but the estate had an eerie *Marie Celeste* emptiness, all the windows tightly closed and not a single kid playing; they were all inside, confused and antsy and safe under their parents' eyes, trying to eavesdrop on the adult whispers and find out what was going on.

The Foleys were an unprepossessing bunch. The fifteen-year-old settled into an armchair and folded her arms, hitching up her bust like someone's mammy, and gave us a pale, bored, supercilious stare; the ten-year-old looked like a cartoon pig and chewed gum with her mouth open, wriggling her rump on the sofa and occasionally flicking the gum out on her tongue and then back into her mouth again. Even the youngest was one of those deeply unnerving toddlers who look like bonsai adults; it had a prim, pudgy face with a beaky nose, and it stared at me from Vera's lap, its lips pursing, and then retracted its chin disapprovingly into the folds of its neck. I had a nasty conviction that, if it said anything, its voice would be a deep, forty-a-day rasp. The house smelled of cabbage. I could not fathom why on earth Rosalind and Jessica would choose to spend any time there, and the fact that they had bothered me.

With the exception of the toddler, though, they all told the same story. Rosalind and Jessica, and sometimes Katy, spent the night there every few weeks or so ('I'd love to have them more often, of course I would,' said Vera, pinching tensely at a corner of a slipcover, 'but I simply can't, not with my nerves, you know'); less often, Valerie and Sharon stayed with the Devlins. Nobody was sure whose idea this particular sleepover had been, although Vera thought vaguely that it might have been Margaret who suggested it. On Monday night Rosalind and Jessica had come over somewhere around half-eight, watched television and played with the baby (I couldn't imagine how; the kid had barely moved all the time we were there, it must have been like playing with a large potato), and gone to bed around eleven, sharing a camp bed in Valerie and Sharon's room.

This, apparently, was where the trouble had started: unsurprisingly, they had all four been up talking and giggling most of the night. 'Now they're lovely girls, Officers, I'm not saying that, but sometimes the young people don't realise how much of a *strain* they can put on us old folks, isn't that right?' Vera tittered frantically and nudged the middle kid, who squirmed further away on the sofa. 'I had to go in to them half a dozen times to tell them to be quiet – I can't bear noise, you know. It must have been *half-two* in the morning, can you imagine, before they finally went off to sleep. And by that time, of course, my nerves were in such a state that I couldn't settle at all, I had to get up and make myself a cup of tea. I didn't get a wink of sleep. I was shattered the next morning. And then when Margaret rang, sure, we were all going frantic, weren't we, girls? But I never imagined . . . sure, I thought she was only . . .' She pressed a thin, twitching hand over her mouth.

'Let's go back to the night before,' Cassie said to the oldest kid. 'What did you and your cousins talk about?'

The kid – Valerie, I think – rolled her eyes and pulled up her lip to show what a stupid question this was. 'Stuff.'

'Did you talk about Katy at all?'

'I don't *know*. Yeah, I guess. Rosalind was saying how brilliant it was that she was going to ballet school. I don't see what's so great about it.'

'What about your aunt and uncle? Did you mention them?'

'Yeah. Rosalind was saying they're horrible to her. They never let her do anything.'

Vera gave a breathless little hoot. 'Oh, now, Valerie, don't be saying that! Sure, Officers, Margaret and Jonathan would do anything for those girls, they've themselves worn out—'

'Oh, yeah, *sure*. I guess that's why Rosalind ran away, because they were too *nice* to her.'

Cassie and I both started to jump on this at once, but Vera got there first. 'Valerie! What did I tell you? We don't talk about that. It was all a misunderstanding, only. Rosalind was a very bold girl to be worrying her poor parents like that, but it's all forgiven and forgotten . . .'

We waited for her to run down. 'Why did Rosalind run away?' I asked Valerie.

She twitched one shoulder. 'She was sick of her dad bossing her around. I think maybe he hit her or something.'

'*Valerie!* Now, Officers, I don't know where she's getting this. Jonathan would never lay a finger on those children, so he wouldn't. Rosalind's a sensitive girl; she had an argument with her daddy, and he didn't realise how upset she was . . .'

Valerie sat back and stared at me, a smug smile creeping through the professional boredom. The middle kid wiped her nose on her sleeve and examined the result with interest.

'When was this?' Cassie asked.

'Ah, I wouldn't remember. A long time ago – last year, I think it was—'

'May,' said Valerie. '*This* May.'

'How long was she gone?'

'Like three days. The police came and everything.'

'And where had she been, do you know?'

'She went off somewhere with a fella,' Valerie said, smirking.

'She did *not*,' Vera snapped shrilly. 'She was only saying that to put the heart across her poor mother, God forgive her. She was staying with that friend of hers from school, what's her name, Karen. She came home after the weekend and no harm done.'

'What*ever*,' Valerie said, doing the one-shouldered shrug again.

'Want my tea,' the toddler stated firmly. I had been right: it had a voice like a bassoon.

This, in all probability, explained something I had been meaning to check out: why Missing Persons had been so quick to assume that Katy was a runaway. Twelve is borderline, and normally they would have given her the benefit of the doubt, started the search and the media fireworks immediately rather than waiting the twenty-four hours. But running away tends to spread through families, the younger children getting the idea from the older. When Missing Persons ran the Devlins' address through their system, they would have come up with Rosalind's escapade and assumed that Katy had done the same thing, had a spat with her parents and stormed off to a friend's house; that she, like Rosalind, would be back as soon as she calmed down, and no harm done.

I was, callously, very glad that Vera had been up all Monday night. Though it was almost too horrible to admit, I had had moments of worry about both Jessica and Rosalind. Jessica didn't look very strong, but she definitely did look unbalanced, and the cliché about insanity lending strength has some basis in fact, and she could hardly have failed to be jealous of all the adulation Katy was getting. Rosalind was highly strung and fiercely protective of Jessica, and if Katy's success had been sending Jessica further and further into her daze . . . I knew Cassie had been thinking the same things, but she hadn't mentioned them either, and for some reason this had been getting on my nerves.

'I want to know why Rosalind ran away from home,' I said, as we headed back down the Foleys' drive. The middle kid had her nose squashed up against the living-room window and was making faces at us.

'And where she went,' said Cassie. 'Can you talk to her? I think you'll get more out of her than I would.'

'Actually,' I said, a little awkwardly, 'that was her on the phone, earlier. She's coming in to see me tomorrow afternoon. She says there's something she wants to talk about.'

Cassie turned from stuffing her notebook into her satchel and gave me a long look I couldn't read. For a moment I wondered if she was miffed that Rosalind had asked for me instead of her. We were both used to Cassie being the families' favourite, and I felt a juvenile, shameful spark of triumph: *Someone likes me best, so there.* My relationship with Cassie has a brother-and-sister tinge that works well for us, but occasionally it does lead to sibling rivalry. But then she said, 'Perfect. You can bring up the running-away thing without it seeming like a big deal.'

She swung her satchel onto her back and we headed off down the road. She was looking out over the fields with her hands in her pockets, and I couldn't tell whether she was annoyed with me for not telling her about Rosalind Devlin's phone call earlier – which, in all fairness, I should have done. I gave her a little nudge with my elbow, testing. A few steps later she flipped up a foot behind her and kicked me in the arse.

We spent the rest of the afternoon going door-to-door through the estate. Door-to-door is boring, thankless work and the floaters already had it covered, but we wanted to get a feel for what the neighbours thought of the Devlins. The general consensus was that they were a decent family but kept themselves firmly to themselves, which hadn't gone down very well: in a place the size and social class of Knocknaree, any kind of reserve is considered a general insult, half a step from the unforgivable sin of snobbery.

But Katy herself was different: the Royal Ballet School place had made her Knocknaree's pride, their own personal cause. Even the obviously poor households had sent someone to the fundraiser, everyone needed to describe her dancing to us; a few people cried. A lot of people were part of Jonathan's Move the Motorway campaign and gave us edgy, resentful looks when we asked about him. A few went into outraged speeches about how he was trying to stop progress and undermine the economy, and got special little stars beside their names in my notebook. Most people were of the opinion that Jessica wasn't the full shilling.

When we asked if they had seen anything suspicious, they offered us the usual set of local weirdos – an old guy who yelled at bins, two fourteen-year-olds with a reputation for drowning cats in the river – and irrelevant ongoing feuds and non-specific things that went bump in the night. A number of people, none of them with any useful information, mentioned the old case; until the dig and the motorway and Katy came along, it had been Knocknaree's one claim to fame. I thought I half-recognised a few names, a couple of faces. I gave them my best professional blank look.

After an hour or so of this we got to 27 Knocknaree Drive and found Mrs Pamela Fitzgerald – still, incredibly, very much alive and kicking. Mrs Fitzgerald was great. She was eighty-eight, skinny and half-blind and bent almost double; she offered us tea, ignored our refusals and shouted to us from the kitchen while she prepared a loaded, trembling tray, and then demanded to know whether we had found her purse that some young one had robbed off her in town three months ago, and why not. It was a bizarre sensation, after reading her faded handwriting in the old file, to watch her complain about her swollen ankles ('I'm a martyr to them, so I am') and indignantly refuse to let me take the tray. It was as if Tutankhamun or Miss Havisham had wandered into the pub one night and started bitching about the head on the pints.

She was from Dublin, she told us – 'a Liberties girl, born and bred and buttered' – but she had moved to Knocknaree twenty-seven years ago, when her husband ('God rest him') retired from his job as a train driver. The estate had been her microcosm ever since, and I was pretty sure she could recite every coming and going and scandal in its history. She knew the Devlins, of course, and approved of them: 'Ah, they're a lovely family altogether. She was always a great girl, Margaret Kelly, never a bit of worry to her mammy, only for' – she leaned sideways to Cassie and lowered her voice conspiratorially – 'only for coming up pregnant that time. And do you know, love, the government and the Church do always be going on about what a shocking thing this teenage pregnancy is, but what I say is, every now and then it's no harm. That Devlin lad used to be a bit of a bowsie, so he did, but the moment he got that young one in the family way – sure, he wasn't the same fella at all. He got a job for himself, and a house, and they'd a lovely wedding. It was the making of him. It's only terrible what's after happening that poor child, may she rest in peace.'

She crossed herself and patted my arm. 'And you're after coming all the way from England to find out who done it? Aren't you great? God bless you, young fella.'

'The old heretic,' I said, when we got outside. Mrs Fitzgerald had cheered up my day immensely. 'I hope I have that much zip when I'm eighty-eight.'

We knocked off just before six and went to the local pub – Mooney's, next to the shop – to watch the news. We had only covered a small part of the estate, but we had a handle on the general atmosphere, and it had been a long day; the meeting with Cooper seemed to have happened at least forty-eight hours before. I had a dizzy urge to keep going until we got to my old road – see if Jamie's mother answered their door, what Peter's brothers and sisters looked like now, who was living in my old room – but I knew this would not be a good idea.

We had timed it well: as I carried our coffee over to the table, the barman turned up the volume on the TV and the news came on with a sweep of synthetic music. Katy was the lead story; the studio presenters looked suitably grave, their voices vibrating at the end of each sentence to indicate tragedy. The arty *Irish Times* shot flashed up in a corner of the screen.

'The young girl found dead yesterday on the controversial archaeological site at Knocknaree has been identified as Katharine Devlin, aged twelve,' intoned the male presenter. Either the colour on the TV set was off or he had used too much fake tan; his face was orange, the whites of his eyes spookily bright. The old guys at the bar stirred, tilting their faces slowly up to the screen, their glasses clicking down. 'Katharine had been missing from her nearby home since early Tuesday morning. Gardaí have confirmed that the death is suspicious, and have appealed to anyone with information to come forward.' The tip-line number came up across the bottom of the screen, white lettering on a blue banner. 'Orla Manahan is live at the scene.'

Cut to a blonde with frozen hair and an overhanging nose, standing in front of the altar stone, which didn't appear to be doing anything that demanded live coverage. People had already started leaving tributes propped against it: flowers wrapped in coloured cellophane, a pink teddy bear. In the background a stray piece of crime-scene tape, overlooked by Sophie's team, fluttered forlornly from a tree.

'This is the place where, just yesterday morning, little Katy Devlin's body was found. In spite of her youth, Katy was a well-known figure in the small, close-knit community of Knocknaree. She had just been awarded a place at the prestigious Royal Ballet School, where she was due to begin her studies in only a few weeks. Today, local residents were devastated at the tragic death of the little girl who was *all* of their pride and joy.'

A shaky hand-held camera on an old woman with a flowery headscarf, outside Lowry's shop. 'Ah, it's awful.' A long pause while she looked down and shook her head, her mouth working; a guy on a bike went past behind her, gawking at the camera. 'It's only terrible. We're all saying prayers for the family. How could anyone want to harm that gorgeous wee girl?' There was a low, angry murmur from the old men at the bar.

Back to the blonde. 'But this may not be the first violent death Knocknaree has seen. Thousands of years ago, this stone' – she swept her arm out, like an estate agent displaying a fitted kitchen – 'was a ceremonial altar where archaeologists say the Druids may have practised human sacrifice. This afternoon, however, Gardaí said there was no evidence that Katy's death was the work of a religious cult.'

Cut to O'Kelly, in front of an imposing piece of pasteboard with a Garda seal stamped on it. He was wearing a vile checked jacket that, on camera, seemed to ripple and heave of its own accord. He cleared his throat and went through our list, non-existent dead livestock and all. Cassie held out a hand, not taking her eyes off the screen, and I found a fiver.

The orange presenter again. 'And Knocknaree holds yet *another* mystery. In 1984, two local children . . .' The screen filled up with those overused school pictures: Peter grinning wickedly from under his fringe, Jamie – she hated photos – giving the photographer a dubious, humouring-the-adults half-smile.

'Here we go,' I said, trying to make it sound light and wry.

Cassie took a sip of her coffee. 'Are you going to tell O'Kelly?' she asked.

I had been waiting for this, and I knew all the reasons why she had to ask, but still it hit me with a jolt. I glanced at the guys at the bar; they were intent on the screen. 'No,' I said. 'No. I'd be off the case. I want to work this one, Cass.'

She nodded, slowly. 'I know. If he finds out, though.'

If he found out, there was a pretty good chance that both of us would be reverted back to uniform, or at the very least thrown off the squad. I had been trying not to think about this. 'He won't,' I said. 'How could he? And if he does, we'll both say you had no idea.'

'He wouldn't believe that for a second. And anyway that's not the point.'

Fuzzy old footage of a cop with a hyperactive German shepherd, plunging into the wood. A diver pulling himself out of the river, shaking his head. 'Cassie,' I said. 'I know what I'm asking. But please; I need to do this. I won't fuck it up.'

I saw her lashes flicker and realised that my tone had come out more desperate than I intended. 'We don't even know for sure that there's a link,' I said, more quietly. 'And if there is, I could end up remembering something that's useful to the investigation. Please, Cass. Back me up on this one.'

She was silent for a moment, drinking her coffee and gazing thoughtfully at the TV. 'Is there any chance that a really determined reporter could . . .?'

'No,' I said briskly. I had, as you would expect, thought about this a lot. Even the file didn't mention my new name or my new school, and when we moved my father gave the police my grandmother's address; she died when I was about twenty, and the family sold her house. 'My parents are unlisted, and my number's listed under Heather Quinn—'

'And these days your name's Rob. We should be fine.'

The 'we', and the practical, considering tone – as if this were just another routine complication, in the same category as a reluctant witness or a suspect gone on the run – warmed me. 'If it all goes horribly wrong, I'll let you fend off the paparazzi,' I said.

'Cool. I'll learn karate.'

On the screen the old footage was over, and the blonde was working up to a big finish. '. . . But, for now, all the people of Knocknaree can do is wait . . . and hope.' They panned to the altar stone for a long moment, poignantly, and then cut back to the studio, and the orange presenter started giving the latest update on some endless depressing tribunal.

We dumped our stuff at Cassie's and went for a walk on the beach. I love Sandymount strand. It's pretty enough on the rare summery afternoons, brochure-blue sky and all the girls in camisoles and red shoulders, but for some reason I love it most of all on your bog-standard Irish days, when wind blows rain-spatter in your face and everything blurs into elusive, Puritan half-tones: grey-white clouds, grey-green sea off on the horizon, great sweep of bleached-fawn sand edged with a scatter of broken shells, wide abstract curves of dull silver where the tide is coming in unevenly. Cassie was wearing sage-green cords and her big russet duffel coat, and the wind was turning her nose red. A large earnest girl in shorts and a baseball cap – probably an American student – was jogging on the sand in front of us; up on the promenade, an underage mother in a track-suit heaved along a twin pushchair.

'So what are you thinking?' I asked.

I meant about the case, obviously, but Cassie was in a giddy mood – she generates more energy than most people, and she'd been sitting indoors most of the day. 'Will you listen to him? A woman asking a guy what he's thinking is the ultimate crime, she's clingy and needy and he runs a mile, but when it's the other—'

'Behave yourself,' I said, pulling her hood over her face.

'Help! I'm being oppressed!' she yelled through it. 'Call the Equality Commission.' The pushchair girl gave us a sour look.

'You're overexcited,' I told Cassie. 'Calm down or I'll take you home with no ice cream.'

She shook back the hood and took off down the strand in a long chain of cartwheels and flips, her coat tumbling around her shoulders. My initial impression of Cassie was satisfyingly spot-on: she did gymnastics for eight years as a kid and was apparently quite good. She quit because competitions and routines bored her; it was the moves themselves she loved, their taut, sprung, risky geometry, and fifteen years later her body still remembers almost all of them. When I caught up with her she was breathless and dusting sand off her hands.

'Better?' I asked.

'Much. You were saying?'

'The case. Work. Dead person.'

'Ah. That,' she said, instantly serious. She pulled her coat straight and we wandered on down the strand, scuffing at half-buried shells.

'I was wondering,' Cassie said, 'what Peter Savage and Jamie Rowan were like.'

She was watching a ferry, small and neat as a toy, chug determinedly across the horizon line; her face, tipped up to the soft rain, was unreadable. 'Why?' I said.

'I'm not sure. Just wondering.'

I thought about the question for a long time. My memories of them had rubbed thin with overuse, worn to frail colour transparencies flickering on the walls of my mind: Jamie scrambling intent and surefooted up to a high branch, Peter's laugh arcing out of the *trompe-l'oeil* dazzle of green ahead. Through some slow sea-change they had become children out of a haunting storybook, bright myths from a lost civilisation; it was hard to believe they had once been real and my friends.

'In what sense?' I said eventually and inanely. 'Personality, or looks, or what?'

Cassie shrugged. 'Whichever.'

'They were both about the same height as me,' I said. 'Average height, I suppose, whatever that is. They both had a slim build. Jamie had white-blond hair, cut in a bob, and a snub nose. Peter had light-brown hair, that floppy cut that little boys have when their mothers cut it for them, and green eyes. I think he would probably have been very handsome.'

'And their personalities?' Cassie glanced up at me; the wind flattened her hair sleek as a seal's against her head.

Occasionally when we go for walks she links a hand through my arm, but I knew she wouldn't do it now.

In my first year of boarding-school I thought about them all the time. I was wildly, devastatingly homesick; I know every child is, in that situation, but I think my wretchedness went well beyond the norm. It was a constant agony, consuming and debilitating as a toothache. At the start of every term I had to be extracted howling and struggling from the car and dragged inside while my parents drove away. You'd think this kind of thing would have made me a perfect target for bullies, but actually they left me severely alone, recognising, I suppose, that nothing they could do would make me feel any worse. It wasn't that the school was hell on earth or anything, in fact I think it was probably pretty OK as these places go – a smallish school in the countryside, with an elaborate fag system and an obsession with house points and various other clichés – but I wanted, more than I have ever wanted anything in my life, to go home.

I coped, in the grand tradition of children everywhere, by retreating into my imagination. I sat on wobbly chairs through droning assemblies and pictured Jamie fidgeting beside me, conjured up every detail of her, the shape of her kneecaps, the tilt of her head. At night I lay awake for hours, boys snoring and muttering all around me, and concentrated with every cell in my body until I knew, beyond any doubt, that when I opened my eyes Peter would be in the next bed. I used to float messages in cream-soda bottles down the stream that ran through the school grounds: 'To Peter and Jamie. Please come back please. Love Adam.' I knew, you see, that I had been sent away because they had disappeared; and I knew that if they were to run back out of the wood some evening, grubby and nettle-stung and demanding their tea, I would be allowed to come home.

'Jamie was a tomboy,' I said. 'Very shy of strangers, especially adults, but physically absolutely fearless. You two would have liked each other.'

Cassie gave me a sideways half-grin. 'In 1984 I was only ten, remember? You guys wouldn't have talked to me.'

I had come to think of 1984 as a separate, private world; it came as something of a shock to realise that Cassie had been there too, only a few miles away. At the moment when Peter and Jamie disappeared she had been playing with her own friends or riding a bike or eating her tea, oblivious to what was happening and to the long, complicated paths that would lead her to me and to Knocknaree. 'Of course we would have,' I said. 'We would have said, "Give us your lunch money, you little twit."'

'You do that anyway. Go on about Jamie.'

'Her mother was sort of a hippie – long floaty skirts and long hair, and she used to give Jamie yoghurt with wheat-germ in it for her break at school.'

'Ewww,' Cassie said. 'I didn't even know you could *get* wheatgerm in the eighties. Supposing you wanted to.'

'I think she may have been illegitimate – Jamie, not her mother. Her father wasn't in the picture. A few kids used to pick on her about it, till she beat one of them up. I asked my mother where Jamie's dad was, after that, and she told me not to be nosy.' I had asked Jamie, too. She had shrugged and said, 'Who cares?'

'And Peter?'

'Peter was the leader,' I said. 'Always, even when we were tiny kids. He could talk to anyone, he was always talking us out of trouble – not that he was a smart-arse, I don't think he was, but he was confident and he liked people. And he was kind.'

There was a kid on our road, Willy Little. The name would have caused him enough trouble all by itself – I wonder what on earth his parents were thinking – but on top of that he had Coke-bottle glasses, and he had to wear thick hand-knitted jumpers with bunnies across the front all year round because there was something wrong with his chest, and he started most of his sentences with 'My mother says . . .' We had cheerfully tortured him all our lives – drawing the obvious pictures on his school copy-books, spitting on his head out of trees, saving up droppings from Peter's rabbit and telling him they were chocolate raisins, that kind of thing – but the summer we were twelve Peter made us stop. 'It's not fair,' he said. 'He can't help it.'

Jamie and I sort of saw his point, although we did argue that Willy could perfectly well have called himself Bill and quit telling people what his mother thought about things. I felt guilty enough to offer him half a Mars bar the next time I saw him, but understandably he gave me a suspicious look and scuttled away. I wondered, absently, what Willy was doing these days. In the movies he would have been a Nobel-prize-winning genius with a supermodel wife; this being real life, he was probably making a living as a medical-research guinea pig and still wearing bunny jumpers.

'That's rare,' Cassie said. 'Most kids that age are vicious. I'm sure I was.'

'I think Peter was an unusual kid,' I said.

She stopped to pick up a bright-orange cockleshell and examine it. 'There's still a chance they could be alive, isn't there?' She dusted sand off the shell against her sleeve, blew on it. 'Somewhere.'

'I suppose there is,' I said. Peter and Jamie, out there somewhere, specks of faces blurring into some vast moving throng. When I was twelve this was in some ways the worst possibility of all: that they had simply kept running that day, left me behind and never once looked back. I still have a reflexive habit of scanning for them in crowds – airports, gigs, train stations; it's faded a lot now, but when I was younger it would build to something like panic and I would end up whipping my head back and forth like a cartoon character, terrified that the one face I missed might be one of them. 'I doubt it, though. There was a lot of blood.'

Cassie was putting the shell in her pocket; she glanced up at me for a second. 'I don't know the details.'

'I'll leave you the file,' I said. Annoyingly, it took an effort to say it, as if I were handing over my diary or something. 'See what you think.'

The tide was starting to come in. Sandymount beach slopes so gradually that at low tide the sea is almost invisible, a tiny grey edge far off on the horizon; it swoops in dizzyingly fast, from all directions at once, and sometimes people get stranded. In a few minutes it would be up to our feet. 'We'd better head back,' Cassie said. 'Sam's coming over for dinner, remember?'

'Oh, that's right,' I said, without much enthusiasm. I do like Sam – everyone likes Sam, except Cooper – but I wasn't sure I was in the mood for other people. 'Why did you invite him?'

'The case?' she said sweetly. 'Work? Dead person?' I made a face at her; she grinned back.

The two sticky toddlers in the pushchair were whacking at each other with luridly coloured toys. 'Britney! Justin!' the mother screamed over their yells. 'Shurrup or I'll kill the fucking pair of yous!' I got an arm around Cassie's neck and managed to pull her a safe distance away before we both burst out laughing.

I did eventually settle into boarding-school, by the way. When my parents dropped me off for the beginning of second year (me weeping, begging, clutching the car door handle as the disgusted housemaster plucked me up by the waist and prised my fingers away one by one) I recognised that, no matter what I did or how I pleaded, they were never going to let me come home. After that I stopped being homesick.

I had very little choice. My unrelenting misery in first year had worn me almost to breaking point (I had grown used to flashes of dizziness every time I stood up, moments when I couldn't remember a classmate's name or the way to the dining hall) and even thirteen-year-old resilience has its limits; a few more months of that and I would probably have ended up having some kind of embarrassing nervous breakdown. But when it comes to the crunch I have, as I say, excellent survival instincts. That first night of second year I sobbed myself to sleep, and then I woke up the next morning and decided that I would never be homesick again.

After that I found it, to my slight surprise, quite easy to settle in. Without really paying attention, I had picked up much of the bizarre, inbred school slang ('scrots' for juniors, 'mackos' for teachers), and my accent went from County Dublin to Home Counties within a week. I made friends with Charlie, who sat next to me in Geography and had a round solemn face and an irresistible chuckle; when we got old enough, we shared a study and experimental joints that his brother at Cambridge gave him and long, confused, yearning conversations about girls. My academic work was mediocre at best – I had bent myself so fiercely to the idea of school as an eternal, inescapable fate that I had trouble imagining anything beyond it, so it was hard to remember why I was supposed to be studying – but I turned out to be a pretty good swimmer, good enough for the school team, which got me a lot more respect from both masters and boys than good exam results would have. In fifth year they even made me a prefect; I tend to attribute this, like my Murder appointment, to the fact that I looked the part.

I spent a lot of the holidays at Charlie's home in Herefordshire, learning to drive on his dad's old Mercedes (jolting country roads, the windows wide open, Bon Jovi blaring on the car stereo and both of us singing along out of tune at the top of our lungs) and falling in love with his sisters. I found I no longer particularly wanted to go home. The house in Leixlip was flimsy and dark and smelled of damp, and my mother had arranged my stuff all wrong in my new bedroom; it felt awkward and temporary, like hurriedly assembled refugee accommodation, not like a home. All the other kids on the street had dangerous-looking haircuts and made unintelligible fun of my accent.

My parents had noticed the change in me, but rather than being pleased that I had settled in at school, as you'd expect, they seemed taken aback, nervous of the unfamiliar, self-contained person I was becoming. My mother tiptoed around the house and asked me timidly what I would like for my tea; my father tried to start man-to-man chats that always ran aground, after much throat-clearing and newspaper-rattling, on my vacant, passive silence. I understood, rationally, that they had sent me to boarding-school to protect me from the unrelenting waves of journalists and futile police interviews and curious classmates, and I was aware that this had probably been an excellent decision; but some part of me believed, unassailably and wordlessly and perhaps with a fleck of justice, that they had sent me away because they were afraid of me. Like some monstrously deformed child who should never have lived beyond infancy, or a conjoined twin whose other half died under the knife, I had – simply by surviving – become a freak of nature.

8

Sam arrived bang on time, looking like a kid on a first date – he had even slicked down his fair hair, ineffectually, with a cowlick at the back – and carrying a bottle of wine. 'There you go,' he said, presenting it to Cassie. 'I didn't know what you were cooking, but the guy in the offie said this will go with just about anything.'

'That's perfect,' Cassie told him, turning down the music (Ricky Martin, in Spanish; she has this boppy mix that she turns up loud when she's cooking or doing housework) and heading for the wardrobe to find wineglass equivalents. 'I'm only making pasta anyway. Corkscrew's in that drawer. Rob, sweetie, you have to actually *stir* the sauce, not just hold the spoon in the pan.'

'Listen, Martha Stewart, am I doing this or are you?'

'Neither, apparently. Sam, are you having wine or are you driving?'

'Maddox, it's tinned tomatoes and basil, it's hardly *haute cuisine*—'

'Did they surgically remove your palate at birth, or did you have to cultivate such an utter lack of refinement? Sam, wine?'

Sam looked a little bemused. Sometimes Cassie and I forget that we can have that effect on people, especially when we're off duty and in a good mood, which we were. I know this sounds odd, given what we had been doing all day, but in the squads with a high horror quota – Murder, Sex Crime, Domestic Violence – either you learn to switch off, or you transfer to Art and Antiques. If you let yourself think too much about the victims (what went through their minds in their last seconds, all the things they'll never do, their devastated families), you end up with an unsolved case and a nervous breakdown. I was, obviously, having a harder time than usual switching off; but it was doing me good, the comforting routine of making dinner and annoying Cassie.

'Um, yes, please,' Sam said. He looked around awkwardly for somewhere to put his coat; Cassie took it and tossed it on the futon. 'My uncle has a house in Ballsbridge – yeah, yeah, I know,' he said, as we both gave him mock-impressed looks, 'and I still have a key. I sometimes stay the night if I'm after having a few pints.' He looked from one to the other of us, waiting for us to comment.

'Good,' said Cassie, diving into the wardrobe again and coming up with a glass tumbler that said 'Nutella' on the side. 'I hate when some people are drinking and some aren't. It makes the conversation go all lopsided. What the hell did you do to Cooper, by the way?'

Sam laughed, relaxed and rummaged for the corkscrew. 'I swear, that wasn't my fault. My first three cases all came in at five in the evening; I rang him just when he was getting home.'

'Uh-oh,' Cassie said. '*Bad* Sam.'

'You're lucky he'll talk to you,' I said.

'Barely,' said Sam. 'He still pretends he can't remember my name. He calls me Detective Neary or Detective O'Nolan – even on the *stand*. Once he called me a different name every time he mentioned me, and the judge got so confused he almost declared a mistrial. Thank God he likes the pair of ye.'

'It's Ryan's cleavage that does it,' said Cassie, nudging me out of the way with her hip and throwing a handful of salt into the pan of water.

'I'll buy a Wonderbra, so,' Sam said. He uncorked the bottle deftly, poured the wine and put glasses into our free hands. 'Cheers, lads. Thanks for inviting me over. Here's to a quick solve and no nasty surprises.'

After dinner we got down to business. I made coffee; Sam insisted on washing up. Cassie had the post-mortem notes and photos spread out on her coffee table, an old wooden chest beeswaxed to a shine, and she was sitting on the floor flipping back and forth, eating cherries from the fruit bowl with her other hand. I love watching Cassie when she's concentrating. Utterly focused, she is as absent and un-selfconscious as a child – twisting a finger in a curl at the back of her head, pulling her legs into effortlessly odd angles, flipping a pen around her mouth and abruptly pulling it out to murmur something to herself.

'While we're waiting for the Amazing Psychic Woman over there,' I said to Sam – Cassie gave me the finger without looking up – 'how was your day?'

Sam was rinsing plates with neat, bachelor efficiency. 'Long. Hold music, and all these civil servants telling me I needed to speak to someone else and then putting me through to voicemail. It's not going to be as easy as it sounds, finding out who owns that land. I did talk to my uncle, asked him if this Move the Motorway was actually having any effect.'

'And?' I said, trying not to sound cynical. I had nothing against Redmond O'Neill in particular – I had a vague image of a big, ruddy man with a shock of silver hair, but that was all – but I do have a firm general mistrust of politicians.

'He said no. Basically, he says, they're just a nuisance—' Cassie glanced up, raised an eyebrow. 'I'm only quoting. They've been to court a few times, trying to stop the motorway; I've still to check the exact dates, but Red says the hearings were at the end of April, the beginning of June and the middle of July. That matches the phone calls to Jonathan Devlin.'

'Apparently someone thought they were more than just a nuisance,' I said.

'This last time, a few weeks ago, Move the Motorway got an injunction, but Red says it'll be thrown out on appeal. He's not worried.'

'Well, that's nice to know,' Cassie said sweetly.

'That motorway will do a lot of good, Cassie,' Sam said gently. 'There'll be new houses, new jobs—'

'I'm sure it will. I just don't see why it couldn't do all that good a few hundred yards to one side.'

Sam shook his head. 'I wouldn't know, sure. I don't understand all that stuff. But Red does, and he says it's badly needed.'

Cassie was opening her mouth to say something else, but I caught the glint in her eye. 'Stop being a brat and profile,' I told her.

'OK,' she said, as we brought over the coffee, 'the main interesting thing is that it looks to me like this guy's heart wasn't in it.'

'What?' I said. 'Maddox, he smacked her twice over the head and then suffocated her. She was very, very dead. If he hadn't been serious about it—'

'No, hang on,' Sam said. 'I want to hear this.' My job in

the amateur profiling sessions is to play devil's advocate, and Cassie is well able to shut me up if I get over-enthusiastic, but Sam has an ingrained, old-fashioned chivalry that I find admirable as well as slightly annoying. Cassie shot me a wicked sideways look and smiled at him.

'Thanks, Sam. *As* I was saying. Look at the first blow: it was only a tap, barely enough to knock her over, never mind knock her out. She had her back to him, she wasn't moving, he could have smashed her head in; but he didn't.'

'He didn't know how much force it would take,' Sam said. 'He hadn't done this before.' He sounded unhappy. This may seem callous, but we often prefer the signs to point to a serial offender. That way there might be other cases to cross-check with, more evidence to collate. If our guy was a first-timer, we had nothing to go on but this.

'Cass?' I said. 'You think he's a virgin?' I realised, as I said it, that I had no idea what I wanted the answer to be.

She reached for the cherries absently, her eyes still on the notes, but I saw her eyelashes flicker: she knew what I was asking. 'I'm not sure. He hasn't done this often, or recently, or he wouldn't have been this tentative about it. But he could have done it once or twice before, a while ago. We can't rule out a link to the old case.'

'It's unusual for a serial killer to take twenty years off,' I said.

'Well,' Cassie said, 'he wasn't too crazy about doing it this time. She fights, he gets a hand over her mouth, he hits her again – maybe as she's trying to crawl away, something like that – and this one knocks her out. But, instead of keeping on hitting her with the rock – even though they've been struggling and his adrenalin must be through the roof at this stage – he drops it and suffocates her. He doesn't even strangle her, which would be a whole lot simpler: he uses a plastic bag, and from behind so he won't have to see her face. He's trying to distance himself from the crime, make it seem less violent. Gentler.' Sam grimaced.

'Or he doesn't want to make a mess,' I said.

'OK, but then why hit her at all? Why not just jump her and stick the bag over her head? I think he wanted her out cold because he didn't want to see her suffer.'

'Maybe he wasn't confident that he'd be able to subdue her unless he knocked her out right away,' I said. 'Maybe he's not very strong – or, again, he's a first-timer and he doesn't know what it'll take.'

'Fair enough. Maybe a little of all three. I agree that we're looking for someone with no known history of violence – someone who never even got into fights in the schoolyard, wouldn't be considered physically aggressive at all – and probably no history of sexual assault, either. I don't think the rape was really a sex crime.'

'What, because he used an object?' I said. 'You know some of them can't get it up.' Sam blinked, startled, took a sip of coffee to cover it.

'Sure, but then he would've been more . . . thorough.' We all winced. 'From what Cooper said, it was a token gesture: one thrust, no sadism, no frenzy, only a couple of inches' worth of abrasion, barely tore the hymen. And it was post-mortem.'

'That could be by choice. Necrophilia.'

'Jesus,' Sam said, putting the coffee down.

Cassie looked for her cigarettes, changed her mind and took one of my strong ones. Her face, momentarily off guard as she tilted it to the lighter flame, looked tired and quenched; I wondered if that night she would dream about Katy Devlin, pinned down and trying to scream. 'He'd have kept her for longer. And, again, there'd be signs of more comprehensive sexual assault. No: he didn't want to do it. He did it because he had to.'

'Staging a sex crime to put us on the wrong track?'

Cassie shook her head. 'I don't know . . . If that was it, you'd expect him to make a point of it: strip her, pose her with her legs spread. Instead, he pulls her combats up again, *zips* them . . . No, I was thinking maybe something more along the lines of schizophrenia. They're almost never violent, but if you get one off his meds and in a full-on paranoid phase, you never know. He could have believed, for some reason of his own, that she had to be killed and raped, even though he hated doing it. That would explain why he tried not to hurt her, why he used an object, why it didn't look more like a sex crime – he didn't want her exposed, and he didn't want anyone thinking of him as a rapist – even why he left her on the altar.'

'How's that?' I took the cigarette packet back and tilted it at Sam, who looked like he could do with one, but he shook his head.

'I mean, he could've dumped her in the woods or somewhere, where she might not have been found for ages, or even just on the ground. Instead, he went out of his way to put her on that altar. It could be a display thing, but I don't think so: he didn't pose her, except to leave her lying on her left side, so the head injury was hidden – again, trying to minimise the crime. I think he was trying to treat her with care, respect – keep her away from animals, make sure she was found soon.' She reached for the ashtray. 'The good thing is, if it's a schizophrenic falling apart, he should be fairly easy to spot.'

'What about a hired killer?' I asked. 'That would explain the reluctance, too. Someone – maybe the mystery phone caller – hired him to do it, but he didn't have to like the job.'

'Actually,' Cassie said, 'a hired killer – not a professional; an amateur who needed the money badly – might fit even better. Katy Devlin sounded like a fairly copped-on kid, wouldn't you say, Rob?'

'She sounds like the most well-adjusted person in that whole family.'

'Yeah, to me too. Smart, focused, strong-willed—'

'Not the type to go off at night with a stranger.'

'Exactly. Especially not a stranger who's clearly not all there. A schizophrenic going to pieces probably wouldn't be able to act normal enough to get her to go anywhere with him. More likely this person is presentable, pleasant, good with kids – someone she'd known for a while. Someone she felt comfortable with. He didn't seem like a threat.'

'Or she,' I said. 'How much did Katy weigh?'

Cassie flipped through the notes. 'Seventy-eight pounds. Depending on how far she was carried, yeah, a woman could have done it, but it would have to be a pretty strong woman. Sophie didn't find any drag marks at the dump site. Just statistically speaking, I'd bet on a guy.'

'But we're eliminating the parents?' Sam said hopefully.

She made a face. 'No. Say one of them was abusing her and she was threatening to tell: either the abuser or the other parent could have felt she had to die, in order to protect the whole family. Maybe they tried to stage a sex crime but didn't have the heart to do it thoroughly . . . Basically, the only thing I'm more or less sure of is that we're not looking for a psychopath or a sadist – our guy couldn't dehumanise her and didn't enjoy seeing her suffer. We're looking for someone who didn't want to do it, someone who felt he was doing it out of necessity. I don't think he'll insert himself into the investigation – he won't be getting off on all the attention, nothing like that –

and I don't think he'll do it again any time soon, not unless he feels threatened somehow. And he's almost definitely local. A real profiler could probably be a lot more specific, but . . .'

'You got your degree at Trinity, right?' Sam said.

Cassie gave a quick shake of her head, reached for more cherries. 'I dropped out in fourth year.'

'Why'd you do that?'

She spat a cherry stone into her palm and gave Sam a smile I knew, an exceptionally sweet smile that scrunched up her face till you couldn't see her eyes. 'Because what would you people do without me?'

I could have told him she wouldn't answer. I had asked her that question several times, over the years, and got answers ranging from 'There was nobody of your calibre to annoy,' through 'The food in the Buttery sucked.' There has always been something enigmatic about Cassie. This is one of the things I like in her, and I like it all the more for being, paradoxically, a quality that isn't readily apparent, elusiveness brought to so high a level it becomes almost invisible. She gives the impression of being startlingly, almost childishly open – which is true, as far as it goes: what you see is in fact what you get. But what you don't get, what you barely glimpse: this is the side of Cassie that fascinated me always. Even after all this time I knew there were rooms inside her that she had never let me guess at, let alone enter. There were questions she wouldn't answer, topics she would discuss only in the abstract; try to pin her down and she would skim away laughing, as nimbly as a figure skater.

'You're good,' Sam said. 'Degree or no degree.'

Cassie raised one eyebrow. 'Wait and see if I'm right before you say that.'

'Why did he keep her for a day?' I asked. This had been bothering me all along – because of the obvious hideous possibilities, and because of the nagging suspicion that, if he hadn't needed to get rid of her for some reason, he might have kept her for longer, kept her forever; she might have vanished as silently and finally as Peter and Jamie had.

'If I'm right about all the other stuff, the distancing himself from the crime, then it wasn't because he wanted to. He would've wanted to get rid of her as soon as possible. He kept her because he didn't have a choice.'

'He lives with someone and had to wait till they were out of the way?'

'Yeah, could be. But I was wondering if maybe the dig wasn't a random choice. Maybe he *had* to dump her there – either because it's part of whatever grand plan he's following, or because he doesn't have a car and the dig was the only place handy. That would fit in with what Mark said about not seeing a car go past – and it would mean the kill site's somewhere very nearby, probably in one of the houses at that end of the estate. Maybe he tried to dump her on Monday night, but Mark was there in the woods, with his fire. The killer could have seen him and been scared off; he had to hide Katy and try again the next night.'

'Or the killer could have *been* him,' I said.

'Alibi for Tuesday night.'

'From a girl who's mad about him.'

'Mel's not the ditzy stand-by-your-man type. She's got a mind of her own, and she's plenty smart enough to realise how important this is. If Mark had jumped out of bed halfway through the action to take a nice long walk, she'd have told us.'

'He could have an accomplice. Either Mel or someone else.'

'And what, they hid the body on the grassy knoll?'

'What's your boy's motive?' Sam enquired. He had been eating cherries and watching us with interest.

'His motive is he's several hundred yards out of his tree,' I told him. 'You didn't hear him. He's perfectly normal on most things – normal enough to reassure a kid, Cass – but get him talking about the site and he starts going on about sacrilege and worship . . . The site's under threat from this motorway: maybe he thought a nice human sacrifice to the gods, just like old times, would get them to step in and save it. When it comes to this site, he's *batty*.'

'If this turns out to be a pagan sacrifice,' Sam said, 'dibs I not be the one to tell O'Kelly.'

'I vote we get him to tell O'Kelly himself. And we sell tickets.'

'Mark is not batty,' Cassie said firmly.

'Oh, he is too.'

'He is *not*. His work is the centre of his life. That's not batty.'

'You should have seen them,' I told Sam. 'Honestly, it was more like a date than an interrogation. Maddox nodding away, fluttering her eyelashes, telling him she knew *exactly* how he feels—'

'Which I do, actually,' Cassie said. She abandoned Cooper's notes and pulled herself backwards onto the futon. 'And I did not either flutter my eyelashes. When I do, you won't miss it.'

'You know how he feels? What, you pray to the Heritage God?'

'*No*, you big eejit. Shut up and listen. I have a theory about Mark.' She kicked off her shoes, tucked her feet up under her.

'Oh God,' I said. 'Sam, I hope you're not in a hurry.'

'I always have time for a good theory,' Sam said. 'Can I have a drink to go with it, if we've finished working?'

'Wise move,' I told him.

Cassie shoved me with her foot. 'Find whiskey or something.' I slapped her foot away and got up. 'OK,' she said, 'we all need to believe in something, right?'

'Why?' I demanded. I found this both intriguing and mildly disconcerting; I am not religious, and as far as I knew Cassie wasn't either.

'Oh, because we *do*. Every single society in the world, ever, has had some form of belief system. But now . . . How many people do you know who're Christian – not just going to church, but actually Christian, like trying to do things the way Jesus would've? And it's not like people can have faith in political ideologies. Our government doesn't even *have* an ideology, as far as anyone can tell—'

' "Brown Envelopes for the Boys," ' I said, over my shoulder. 'That's an ideology, of sorts.'

'Hey,' said Sam mildly.

'Sorry,' I said. 'I didn't mean anyone specific.' He nodded.

'Neither did I, Sam,' said Cassie. 'I just meant there isn't one overall philosophy. So people have to make their own faith.'

I had found whiskey, Coke, ice and three glasses; I juggled them all back to the coffee table in one go. 'What, you mean Religion Lite? All those New-Age yuppies having tantric sex and feng shui-ing their SUVs?'

'Them too, but I was thinking of the people who make a religion out of something completely different. Like money – actually, that's the nearest thing the government has to an ideology, and I'm not talking about brown envelopes, Sam. Nowadays it's not just unfortunate if you have a low-paid job, have you noticed? It's actually *irresponsible*: you're not a good member of society, you're being very very naughty not to have a big house and a fancy car.'

'But if anyone asks for a raise,' I said, whapping the ice tray, 'they're being very very naughty to threaten their employer's profit margin, after everything he's done for the economy.'

'Exactly. If you're not rich, you're a lesser being who shouldn't have the gall to expect a living wage from the decent people who are.'

'Ah, now,' Sam said. 'I don't think things are that bad.'

There was a small, polite silence. I collected stray ice cubes from the coffee table. Sam by nature has a Pollyanna streak, but he also has the kind of family that owns houses in Ballsbridge. His views on socioeconomic matters, though sweet, could hardly be considered objective.

'The other big religion these days,' Cassie said, 'is bodies. All those patronising ads and news reports about smoking and drinking and fitness—'

I was pouring, looking at Sam for a signal to stop; he lifted a hand, smiled at me as I passed him the glass. 'Those always make me want to see how many cigarettes I can fit in my mouth at once,' I said. Cassie had stretched her legs across the futon; I moved them out of the way so I could sit down, put them back across my lap and started making her drink, lots of ice and lots of Coke.

'Me too. But those reports and stuff aren't just saying things are unhealthy – they're saying they're morally *wrong*. Like you're somehow a better person, spiritually, if you have the right body-fat percentage and exercise for an hour a day – and there's that awful condescending set of ads where smoking isn't just a stupid thing to do, it's literally the *devil*. People need a moral code, to help them make decisions. All this bio-yoghurt virtue and financial self-righteousness are just filling the gap in the market. But the problem is that it's all *backwards*. It's not that you do the right thing and hope it pays off; the morally right thing is by definition the thing that gives the biggest pay-off.'

'Drink your drink,' I said. She was lit up and gesturing, leaning forward, her glass forgotten in her hand. 'What does this have to do with batty Mark again?'

Cassie made a face at me and took a sip of her drink. 'Look: Mark believes in archaeology – in his heritage. That's his faith. It's not some abstract set of principles, and it's not about his body or his bank account; it's a concrete part of his whole life, every day, whether it pays off or not. He *lives* in it. That's not batty, that's *healthy*, and there's something seriously wrong with a society where people think it's weird.'

'The guy poured a fucking *libation* to some *Bronze Age god*,' I said. 'I don't think there's anything particularly wrong with me for considering that a little odd. Back me up here, Sam.'

'Me?' Sam had settled back into the sofa, listening to the conversation and reaching out to finger the tumble of shells and rocks on the windowsill. 'Ah, I'd say he's just young. He should get himself a wife and a few kids. That'd settle him.'

Cassie and I looked at each other and started to laugh. 'What?' Sam demanded.

'Nothing,' I said, 'honestly.'

'I'd love to get you and Mark together over a couple of pints,' Cassie said.

'I'd soon sort him out,' Sam said serenely, sending Cassie and me into a fresh fit of giggles. I leaned back into the futon and took a sip of my drink. I was enjoying this conversation. It was a good evening, a happy evening; soft rain was pittering at the windows and Billie Holiday was playing in the background and I was glad, after all, that Cassie had invited Sam. I was starting to like him a lot more actively. Everyone, I decided, should have a Sam around.

'Do you seriously think we can eliminate Mark?' I asked Cassie.

She sipped her drink, balanced the glass on her stomach. 'Actually, I honestly do,' she said. 'Regardless of the battiness question. Like I said, I get this very strong sense that whoever did this was in two minds about it. I can't imagine Mark being in two minds about anything – at least, not anything important.'

'Lucky Mark,' Sam said, smiling at her across the coffee table.

'So,' Sam asked, later, 'how did you and Cassie meet?' He leaned back on the sofa and reached for his glass.

'What?' I said. It was sort of a weird question, out of the blue like that, and to be honest I had half-forgotten he was there. Cassie buys good booze, silky Connemara whiskey that tastes like turf-smoke, and we were all a little tipsy. The conversation was starting, comfortably, to ebb. Sam had been stretching to read the titles of the battered paperbacks on the bookshelf; I had been lying back on the futon, thinking about nothing more taxing than the music. Cassie was in the bathroom. 'Oh. When she joined the squad. Her bike broke down one evening and I gave her a lift.'

'Ah. Right,' Sam said. He looked slightly flustered, which wasn't like him. 'That's what I thought at first, sure: that you hadn't met before. But then it seemed like you'd known each other for ages, so I just wondered were you old friends or . . . you know.'

'We get that a lot,' I said. People tended to assume we were cousins or had grown up next door to each other or something along those lines, and it always filled me with a private, unreasonable happiness. 'We just hit it off well, I suppose.'

Sam nodded. 'You and Cassie,' he said, and cleared his throat.

'What'd I do?' Cassie demanded suspiciously, shoving my feet out of the way and sliding back into her seat.

'God only knows,' I said.

'I was only asking Rob whether the two of ye knew each other before you joined Murder,' Sam explained. 'From college or something.'

'I didn't go to college,' I said. I had a feeling that I knew what he had been going to ask me. Most people do ask, sooner or later, but I hadn't had Sam down as the inquisitive type, and I wondered why, exactly, he wanted to know.

'Seriously?' Sam said, startled and trying not to show it. This is what I mean about the accent. 'I thought Trinity, maybe, and you had classes together, or . . .'

'Didn't know him from Adam,' Cassie said blandly, which after a frozen instant sent her and me into helpless, snorting, juvenile giggles. Sam shook his head, smiling.

'One as mad as the other,' he said, and got up to empty the ashtray.

I had told Sam the truth: I never went to college. I came out of my A levels, miraculously, with a B and two Ds – enough to have got me into some course somewhere, probably, except that I hadn't even filled in an application form. I told people I was taking a gap year, but the truth was that I wanted to do nothing, absolutely nothing, for as long as possible, maybe for the rest of my life.

Charlie was going up to London to study economics, so I went with him: there was nowhere else I particularly needed or wanted to be. His father was paying his share of the rent on a sparkly apartment with hardwood floors and a doorman, and there was no way I could afford my half, so I got a dingy little bedsit in a semi-dangerous area and Charlie got a flatmate, a Dutch exchange student who would be going home at Christmas. The plan was that by then I would have a job and be able to join him, but long before Christmas it became clear that I wouldn't be moving anywhere – not just because of money, but because I had, unexpectedly, fallen in love with my bedsit and my private, free-floating, wayward life.

After boarding-school, the solitude was intoxicating. On my first night there I lay on my back on the sticky carpet for hours, in the murky orange pool of city glow coming through the window, smelling heady curry-spices spiralling across the corridor and listening to two guys outside yelling at each other in Russian and someone practising stormy flamboyant violin somewhere, and slowly realising that there was not a single person in the world who could see me or ask me what I was doing or tell me to do anything else, and I felt as if at any moment the bedsit might detach itself from the building like a luminous soap-bubble and drift off into the night, bobbing gently above the rooftops and the river and the stars.

I lived there for almost two years. Most of the time I was on the dole; occasionally, when they started hassling me or when I wanted money to impress a girl, I spent a few weeks working in furniture removals or construction. Charlie and I had, inevitably, drifted apart – starting, I think, with his look of polite, horrified fascination when he first saw the bedsit. We met for pints every couple of weeks, and sometimes I went to parties with him and his new friends (this is where I met most of the girls, including angsty Gemma with the drink problem). They were nice guys, his friends from uni, but they spoke a language I neither knew nor regretted, full of inside jokes and abbreviations and backslapping, and I found it hard to make myself pay attention.

I'm not sure what exactly I did for those two years. A lot of the time, I think, nothing. I know this is one of the unthinkable taboos of our society, but I had discovered in myself a talent for a wonderful, unrepentant laziness, the kind most people never know after childhood. I had a prism from an old chandelier hanging in my window, and I could spend entire afternoons lying on my bed and watching it flick tiny chips of rainbow around the room.

I read a lot. I always have, but in those two years I gorged myself on books with a voluptuous, almost erotic gluttony. I would go to the local library and take out as many as I could, and then lock myself in the bedsit and read solidly for a week. I went for old books, the older the better – Tolstoy, Poe, Jacobean tragedies, a dusty translation of Laclos – so that when I finally resurfaced, blinking and dazzled, it took me days to stop thinking in their cool, polished, crystalline rhythms.

I watched a lot of TV, too. In my second year there I became fascinated with late-night true-crime documentaries, mostly on the Discovery Channel: not with the crimes themselves, but with the intricate structures of their unravelling. I loved the taut, steady absorption with which these men – sharp FBI Bostonians, potbellied Texas sheriffs – carefully disentangled threads and joined jigsaw pieces, until at last everything fell into place and the answer rose at their command to hang in the air before them, shining and unassailable. They were like magicians, throwing a handful of scraps into a top hat and tapping it and whipping out – flourish of trumpets – a perfect, silken banner; only this was a thousand times better, because the answers were real and vital and there were (I thought) no illusions.

I knew it wasn't like that in real life, at least not all the time, but it struck me as a breathtaking thing to have a job where even that possibility existed. When, all in the same month, Charlie got engaged and the dole informed me they were cracking down on people like me and this guy with a thing for bad rap music moved in downstairs, it seemed like the obvious response to go back to Ireland, apply to Templemore Training College and start becoming a detective. I didn't miss the bedsit – I think I had been starting to get bored anyway – but I still remember those marvellous, self-indulgent two years among the happiest times of my life.

Sam left around 11.30; Ballsbridge is only a few minutes' walk from Sandymount. He gave me a quick, questioning look as he pulled on his coat. 'Which way are you walking?'

'You've probably missed the last DART,' Cassie told me easily. 'You can kip on my sofa if you want.'

I could have said I planned to take a taxi home, but I decided she had probably called it right: Sam wasn't Quigley, we wouldn't come in the next day to a gleeful little flurry of smirks and single entendres. 'I think I have, actually,' I said, checking my watch. 'Would that be all right?'

If Sam was startled, he covered it well. 'See ye in the morning, so,' he said cheerfully. 'Sleep tight.'

'He fancies you,' I told Cassie, when he had left.

'God, you're predictable,' she said, digging in the wardrobe for the spare duvet and the T-shirt I keep there.

'"Oh, I want to hear what *Cassie* has to say, oh Cassie you're sooo good at this—"'

'Ryan, if God had wanted me to have a horrible pubescent brother, he would have given me one. Also your Galway accent sucks.'

'Do you fancy him, too?'

'If I did, I would have done my famous trademark trick where I tie a cherry stem in a knot with my tongue.'

'You do not either. Show me.'

'I was *joking*. Go to bed.'

We pulled out the futon; Cassie turned on the bedside lamp and I switched off the overhead light, leaving the bedsit small and warm and shadowy. She found the knee-length T-shirt she sleeps in and took it into the bathroom to change. I tucked my socks into my shoes and pushed them out of the way under the sofa, stripped to my boxers, pulled on my T-shirt and settled myself under the spare duvet. We had the routine down pat by this time. I could hear her splashing water on her face and singing to herself, something folk-songy I didn't recognise, in a minor key. 'To the Queen of Hearts is the Ace of Sorrow, he's here today, he's gone tomorrow . . .' She had pitched it too low; the bottom note disappeared into a hum.

'Do you really feel that way about our job?' I asked, when she came out of the bathroom (small bare feet, smooth calves muscled like a boy's). 'The way Mark feels about archaeology?'

I had been saving the question till Sam left. Cassie gave me a quizzical little sideways grin. 'I have never poured booze on the squad-room carpet. Cross my heart.'

I waited. She slid into bed and leaned up on one elbow, her cheek on her fist; the glow of the bedside lamp edged her with light, so that she looked translucent, a girl in a stained-glass window. I wasn't sure she was going to answer, even without Sam there, but after a moment she said, 'We're dealing with truth, finding truth. That's serious business.'

I thought about this. 'Is that why you don't like lying?' This is one of Cassie's quirks, especially odd in a detective. She omits things, eludes questions with open mischief or so subtly you hardly notice her doing it, spins misleading phrases with a conjurer's expertise; but I had never known her to lie outright, not even to a suspect.

She shrugged, one-shouldered. 'I'm not very good with paradox.'

'I think I am, actually,' I said thoughtfully.

Cassie rolled over onto her back and laughed. 'You should put that in a personal ad. Male, six foot, good with paradox—'

'Abnormally studly—'

'Seeks his very own Britney for—'

'Ew!'

She cocked an eyebrow at me, innocently. 'No?'

'Give me some credit. Britney is exclusively for those with cheap tastes. It would have to be Scarlett Johansson at *least.*'

We laughed, subsided. I sighed comfortably and arranged myself around the sofa's familiar quirks; Cassie reached out one arm to turn off the lamp. 'Night. Sleep tight.'

'Sweet dreams.'

Cassie sleeps as lightly and easily as a kitten; after a few seconds I heard her breathing slow and deepen, the tiny catch at the top of each breath that told me she had drifted off. I am the opposite: once I'm asleep it takes an extra-loud alarm clock or a kick in the shins to wake me, but it can be hours of tossing and fidgeting before I get there. But somehow I always found it easier to sleep at Cassie's, in spite of the lumpy, too-short sofa and the grouchy creaks and ticks of an old house settling for the night. Even now, when I'm having trouble falling asleep, I try to imagine myself back on that sofa: the soft, worn flannel of the duvet cover against my cheek, a spicy tang of hot whiskey still warming the air, the tiny rustles of Cassie dreaming across the room.

A couple of people clattered into the house, shushing each other and giggling, and went into the flat downstairs; peaks of conversation and laughter filtered up, faint and muffled, through the floor. I matched the rhythm of my breathing to Cassie's and felt my mind sliding pleasurably down into dreamy, nonsensical tangents – Sam was explaining how to build a boat, and Cassie was sitting on a window ledge between two stone gargoyles and laughing. The sea is several streets away and there was no way I could have heard it, but I imagined I did all the same.

9

In my memory, we spent a million nights in Cassie's flat, the three of us. The investigation only lasted a month or so, and I'm sure there must have been days when one or another of us was off doing something else; but over time those evenings have coloured the whole season for me, like a brilliant dye flowering slowly through water. The weather dipped in and out of an early, bitter autumn; wind whined through the roof-space, and raindrops seeped in the warped sash windows and trickled down the panes. Cassie would light a fire and we would all spread out our notes on the floor and bat theories back and forth, then take turns getting dinner – mainly pasta variations from Cassie, steak sandwiches from me, surprisingly exotic experiments from Sam: lavish tacos, some Thai thing with spicy peanut sauce. We would have wine with dinner, move on to whiskey in various forms afterwards; when we started to get tipsy, we would pack the case file away and kick off our shoes and put on music and talk.

Cassie, like me, is an only child, and we were both enthralled by Sam's stories about his childhood – four brothers and three sisters piled into an old white farmhouse in Galway, playing mile-wide games of Cowboys and Indians and sneaking out at night to explore the haunted mill, with a big quiet father and a mother dealing out oven-warm bread and raps with a wooden spoon and counting heads at mealtimes to make sure nobody had fallen into the stream. Cassie's parents died in a car crash when she was five, and she was brought up by a gentle, older aunt and uncle, in a ramshackle house in Wicklow, miles from anything. She talks about reading unsuitable books from their library – *The Golden Bough*, Ovid's *Metamorphoses*; *Madame Bovary*, which she hated but finished anyway – curled up in a window seat on the landing, eating apples from the garden, with soft rain going past the panes. Once, she says, she wriggled under an ancient and hideous wardrobe and found a china saucer, a George VI penny and two letters from a World War I soldier whose name nobody recognised, with bits blacked out by censors. I don't remember much from before I was twelve, and after that my memories are mainly arranged in rows – rows of grey-white dormitory beds, rows of echoing, bleach-smelling cold showers, rows of boys in archaic uniforms droning Protestant hymns about duty and constancy. To both of us, Sam's childhood was something out of a storybook; we pictured it in pencil drawings, apple-cheeked children with a laughing sheepdog jumping around them. 'Tell us about when you were little,' Cassie would say, snuggling into the futon and pulling her jumper sleeves down over her hands to hold her hot whiskey.

In many ways, though, Sam was the odd man out in these conversations, and a part of me was pleased at this. Cassie and I had spent two years building our routine, our rhythm, our subtle private codes and indicators; Sam was, after all, there by our favour, and it seemed only fair that he should play a supporting role, present but not too present. It never seemed to bother him. He would stretch out on the sofa, tilting his whiskey glass to make the firelight throw spots of amber on his jumper, and watch and smile as

Cassie and I argued over the nature of Time, or T.S. Eliot, or scientific explanations for ghosts. Adolescent conversations, no doubt, and made more so by the fact that Cassie and I brought out the brat in each other ('Bite me, Ryan,' she would say, narrowing her eyes at me across the futon, and I would grab her arm and bite her wrist till she yelled for mercy), but I had never had them in my adolescence and I loved them, I loved every moment.

I am, of course, romanticising; a chronic tendency of mine. Don't let me deceive you: the evenings may have been roast chestnuts around a cosy turf fire, but the days were a grim, tense, frustrating slog. Officially we were on the nine-to-five shift, but we were in before eight every morning, seldom left before eight at night, took work home with us – questionnaires to correlate, statements to read, reports to write. Those dinners started at nine o'clock, ten; it was midnight before we stopped talking shop, two in the morning by the time we had unwound enough to go to bed. We developed an intense, unhealthy relationship with caffeine and forgot what it was like not to be exhausted. On the first Friday evening, a very new floater called Corry said, 'See you Monday, lads,' and got a round of sardonic laughter and slaps on the back, as well as a humourless 'No, Whatsyourname, I'll see you at eight tomorrow morning and don't be late,' from O'Kelly.

Rosalind Devlin hadn't come in to see me that first Friday, after all. Around five o'clock, edgy from waiting and unaccountably worried that something might have happened to her, I rang her mobile. She didn't answer. She was with her family, I told myself, she was helping with the funeral arrangements or looking after Jessica or crying in her room; but that unease stayed with me, tiny and sharp as a pebble in my shoe.

On the Sunday we went to Katy's funeral, Cassie and Sam and I. The thing about murderers being irresistibly drawn to the graveside is mostly legend, but still, the off-chance was worth it, and anyway O'Kelly had told us to go on the grounds that it was good PR. The church had been built in the 1970s, when concrete was an artistic statement and when Knocknaree was supposed to become a major metropolis any day now; it was huge and chill and ugly, gauche semi-abstract Stations of the Cross, echoes creeping dismally up to the angled concrete ceiling. We stood at the back, in our best unobtrusive dark clothes, and watched as the church filled up: farmers holding flat caps, old women in headscarves, trendy teenagers trying to look blasé. The little white coffin, gold-trimmed and terrible, in front of the altar. Rosalind stumbling up the aisle, shoulders heaving, supported by Margaret on one side and Auntie Vera on the other; behind them Jonathan, glassy-eyed, guided Jessica towards the front pew.

Candles guttered in an unceasing draught; the air smelled of damp and incense and dying flowers. I was light-headed – I had forgotten to eat breakfast – and the whole scene had the glass-covered quality of memory. It took me a while to realise that this was, in fact, for good reason: I had attended Mass here every Sunday for twelve years, had quite possibly sat through a memorial service for Peter and Jamie in one of the cheap wooden pews. Cassie blew into her hands, surreptitiously, to warm them.

The priest was very young and solemn, trying painfully hard to rise to the occasion with his frail seminary arsenal of clichés. A choir of pale little girls in school uniforms – Katy's schoolmates; I recognised some of the faces –

huddled shoulder to shoulder, sharing hymn sheets. The hymns had been chosen to offer comfort, but their voices were thin and uncertain and a few of them kept breaking down. 'Be not afraid, I go before you always; come, follow me . . .'

Simone Cameron caught my eye on her way back from Communion and gave me a tiny stiff nod; her golden eyes were bloodshot, monstrous. The family filed out of their pew one by one and laid mementoes on the coffin: a book from Margaret, a stuffed toy shaped like a ginger cat from Jessica, from Jonathan the pencil drawing that had hung above Katy's bed. Last of all Rosalind knelt down and placed a pair of small pink ballet shoes, bound together by their ribbons, on the lid. She stroked the shoes gently and then bent her head onto the coffin and sobbed, her warm brown ringlets tumbling over the white and gold. A faint, inhuman wail rose from somewhere in the front pew.

Outside, the sky was grey-white and wind was whipping leaves off the trees in the churchyard. Reporters were leaning over the railings, cameras firing in swift bursts. We found a discreet corner and scanned the area and the crowd, but unsurprisingly no one rang any alarm bells. 'Some turnout,' Sam said quietly. He was the only one of us who had gone up for Communion. 'Let's get film off some of these lads tomorrow, check if anyone's here who shouldn't be.'

'He's not here,' Cassie said. She dug her hands into her jacket pockets. 'Not unless he has to be. This guy won't even be reading the newspapers. He'll change the subject if anyone starts talking about the case.'

Rosalind, moving slowly down the church steps with a handkerchief pressed to her mouth, raised her head and saw us. She shook off the supporting arms and ran across the grass, long black dress fluttering in the wind. 'Detective Ryan . . .' She caught my hand in both of hers and raised a tear-stained face to me. 'I can't bear it. You have to catch the man who did this to my sister.'

'Rosalind!' Jonathan called hoarsely, somewhere, but she didn't look away. Her hands were long-fingered and soft and very cold. 'We'll do everything we can,' I said. 'Will you come in and talk to me tomorrow?'

'I'll try. I'm sorry about Friday, but I couldn't . . .' She glanced quickly over her shoulder. 'I couldn't get away. Please find him, Detective Ryan – please . . .'

I felt, more than heard, the spatter of the cameras. One of the photos – Rosalind's anguished, upturned profile, an unflattering shot of me with my mouth open – made it onto the front page of a tabloid the next morning, with 'Please Give My Sister Justice' below it in letters an inch high, and Quigley gave me grief about it all week.

In the first two weeks of Operation Vestal we did everything you can think of, everything. Between us and the floaters and the local uniforms, we talked to everyone who lived within a four-mile radius of Knocknaree and anyone who had ever known Katy. There was one diagnosed schizophrenic on the estate, but he had never hurt anyone in his life, even when he was off his meds, which he hadn't been in three years. We checked out every Mass card the Devlins got and tracked down every person who'd contributed towards Katy's fees, and set up surveillance to see who brought flowers to lay on the altar stone.

We interviewed Katy's best friends – Christina Murphy, Elisabeth McGinnis, Marianne Casey: red-eyed, shaky, brave little girls, with no useful information to offer, but I found them disconcerting nevertheless. I have no time for people who sigh about how quickly children grow up nowadays (my grandparents, after all, were working full-time by sixteen, which I think trumps any number of body-piercings in the adulthood stakes), but all the same: Katy's friends had a poised, savvy awareness of the outside world that jarred with the happy animal oblivion I remembered enjoying at that age. 'We wondered if Jessica had a learning disability, maybe,' Christina said, sounding about thirty, 'but we didn't want to ask. Did . . . I mean, was it a paedophile that killed Katy?'

The answer to this appeared to be no. In spite of Cassie's feeling that this hadn't really been a sex crime, we checked out every convicted sex offender in south Dublin, as well as plenty whom we've never been able to convict, and we spent hours with the guys who have the thankless job of tracking and trapping paedophiles online. The guy we mostly talked to was called Carl. He was young and skinny, with a lined white face, and he told us that after eight months on this job he was already thinking of quitting: he had two kids under seven, he said, and he couldn't look at them the same way any more, he felt too dirty to hug them good night after a day of doing what he did.

The network, as Carl called it, was buzzing with speculation and titillation about Katy Devlin – I'll spare you the details – and we read through hundreds of pages of chat transcripts, dispatches from a dark and alien world, but we came up empty. One guy seemed to empathise a little too strongly with Katy's killer ('I think he just LOVED HER TO MUCH she didn't understand so he got UPSET') but when she died he had been online, discussing the relative physical merits of East Asian versus European little girls. Cassie and I both got very drunk that night.

Sophie's gang went over the Devlins' house with a fine-tooth comb – ostensibly collecting fibres and so on, for elimination purposes, but they reported back that they had found no bloodstains and nothing matching Cooper's description of the rape weapon. I pulled financial records: the Devlins lived modestly (one family holiday, to Crete, four years earlier on a credit-union loan; Katy's ballet lessons and Rosalind's violin; a '99 Toyota) and had almost no savings, but they weren't in any debt, their mortgage was almost paid off, they had never even fallen into arrears on their phone bill. There was no dodgy activity on their bank account and no insurance policy on Katy's life; there was nothing.

The tip line got a record number of calls, an incredible percentage of which were utterly useless: the people whose neighbours looked funny and refused to join the Residents' Association, the people who had seen sinister men hanging around halfway across the country, the usual assorted wackjobs who had had visions of the murder, the other set of wackjobs explaining at length how this was God's judgement on our sinful society. Cassie and I spent a full morning on one guy who rang up to tell us that God had punished Katy for her immodesty in exhibiting herself, dressed only in a leotard, to thousands of *Irish Times* readers. We had high hopes of him, actually – he refused to talk to Cassie, on the grounds that women shouldn't be working and that her jeans were also immodest (the objective standard for female modesty, he informed me vehemently, was Our Lady of Fatima). But his alibi was impeccable: he had spent the Monday night in the minuscule red-light district off Baggot Street, drunk as a skunk, shrieking fire and brimstone at the hookers and writing down their clients' plate numbers and getting forcibly removed by the pimps and starting all over again, until the cops had finally thrown him in a cell to sleep it off at around four in the morning. Apparently this happened every few weeks or so; everyone concerned knew the drill and was happy to confirm it, with the odd pungent remark about the guy's probable sexual proclivities.

Those were strange weeks, strange disjointed weeks. Even after all this time, I find it difficult to describe them to you. They were so full of little things, things that at the time seemed insignificant and disconnected as the jumble of objects in some bizarre parlour game: faces and phrases and sitting-rooms and phone calls, all running together into a single strobe-light blur. It was only much later, in the stale cold light of hindsight, that the little things rose up and rearranged themselves and clicked neatly into place to form the patterns we should have seen all along.

And then, too, it was so excruciating, that first phase of Operation Vestal. The case was, though we refused to admit this even to ourselves, going nowhere. Every lead I found ran me into a dead end; O'Kelly kept giving us rousing, arm-waving speeches about how we couldn't afford to drop the ball on this one and when the going gets tough the tough get going; the papers were screaming for justice and printing photo enhancements of what Peter and Jamie would look like today if they had unfortunate haircuts. I was as tense as I have ever been in my life. But perhaps the real reason I find it so difficult to talk about those weeks is that – in spite of all that, and of the fact that I know this to be a self-indulgence I cannot afford – I miss them still.

Little things. We pulled Katy's medical records, of course, straight away. She and Jessica had been a couple of weeks premature, but Katy, at least, had rallied well, and until she was eight and a half she had had nothing but the normal childhood stuff. Then, out of nowhere, she had started getting sick. Stomach cramping, projectile vomiting, diarrhoea for days on end; once she had ended up in the emergency room three times in one month. A year ago, after a particularly bad attack, the doctors had done an exploratory laparotomy – the surgery Cooper had spotted, the one that had kept her out of ballet school. They had diagnosed 'idiopathic pseudo-obstructive bowel disease with atypical lack of distension'. Reading between the lines, I got the sense that this meant they had ruled out everything else and had absolutely no idea what was wrong with this kid.

'Munchausen's by proxy?' I asked Cassie, who was reading over my shoulder, arms folded on the back of my chair. She and I and Sam had staked out a corner of the incident room, as far as possible from the tip line, where we could have a modicum of privacy as long as we kept our voices down.

She shrugged, made a face. 'It could be. But there's stuff that doesn't fit. Most Munchausen's mothers have a background around the edges of medicine – nurse's aide, something like that.' Margaret, according to the background check, had left school at fifteen and worked in Jacobs' biscuit factory until she got married. 'And check out the admission records. Half the time Margaret's not even the one bringing Katy into the hospital: it's Jonathan, Rosalind, Vera, once it's a *teacher* . . . For Munchausen's-by-proxy mothers, the whole *point* is the attention and sympathy they get from doctors and nurses. She wouldn't let someone else be at the centre of all that.'

'So we rule out Margaret?'

Cassie sighed. 'She doesn't match the profile, but that's

not definitive; she could be the exception. I just wish we could have a look at the other girls' records. These mothers don't usually target one kid and leave the others alone. They skip from kid to kid, to avoid suspicion, or else they start with the oldest and then move on to the next when the first one gets old enough to kick up a fuss. If it's Margaret, there'll be something weird in the other two's files – like maybe this spring, when Katy stopped getting sick, something went wrong with Jessica . . . Let's ask the parents if we can look at them.'

'No,' I said. All the floaters seemed to be talking at once and the noise was like a heavy fog coating my brain; I couldn't focus. 'So far, the Devlins don't know they're suspects. I'd rather keep it that way, at least until we have something solid. If we go asking them for Rosalind and Jessica's medical records, it's bound to tip them off.'

'Something solid,' Cassie said. She looked down at the pages spread out on the table, the jumble of computerised headings and scribbled handwriting and photocopy-smudges; at the whiteboard, which had already blossomed into a multicoloured tangle of names, phone numbers, arrows and question-marks and underlining.

'Yeah,' I said. 'I know.'

The Devlin girls' school records had that same ambiguous, mocking quality. Katy was bright but not outstanding, solid Bs with the occasional C in Irish or A in PE; no behavioural problems bigger than a tendency to talk in class, no red flags except the stark patches of absence. Rosalind was more intelligent, but also more erratic: streams of straight As, broken up by clumps of Cs and Ds and frustrated teachers' comments about lacking effort and skipping class. Jessica's file, unsurprisingly, was the thickest. She had been in the happy class since she and Katy were nine, but Jonathan had apparently hassled the health board and the school into running a battery of tests on her: her IQ was somewhere between 90 and 105, and there were no neurological problems. 'Non-specific learning disability with autistic features,' the file claimed.

'What do you think?' I asked Cassie.

'I think this family just keeps getting weirder. Going by this, you'd swear that, if one of them's being abused, it's Jessica. Perfectly normal kid up until she's around seven; then all of a sudden, bam, her schoolwork and her social skills start going downhill. That's way too late for the onset of autism, but it's a textbook reaction to some kind of ongoing abuse. And Rosalind – all that upsy-downsy stuff could just be normal teenage mood swings, but it could also be a response to something weird going on at home. The only one who looks just fine – well, fine psychologically – is Katy.'

Something dark loomed up in the corner of my vision and I whipped around, sending my pen skittering across the floor. 'Whoa,' Sam said, startled. 'It's only me.'

'Jesus,' I said. My heart was racing. Cassie's eyes, across the table, gave away nothing. I retrieved my pen. 'I didn't realise you were there. What've you got?'

'The Devlins' phone records,' Sam said, waving a sheaf of paper in each hand. 'Out and in.' He put the two bundles on the table and squared off the edges carefully. He had colour-coded the numbers; the pages were striped with neat lines of highlighter pen.

'For how long?' Cassie asked. She leaned across the table, looking at the pages upside down.

'Since March.'

'That's it? For six months?'

That was the first thing I had noticed, too: how thin the piles were. A family of five, three adolescent girls; surely the line should have been busy non-stop, someone constantly yelling for someone else to get off the phone. I thought of the underwater hush in the house the day Katy was found, Auntie Vera hovering in the hall. 'Yeah, I know,' Sam said. 'Maybe they use mobiles.'

'Maybe,' Cassie said. She didn't sound convinced. I wasn't either: almost without exception, when a family cuts itself off from the rest of the world it's because something is badly wrong. 'But that's expensive. And there's two phones in that house, one in the downstairs coat closet and one on the upstairs landing, with a cord long enough that you could take it into any of the bedrooms. You wouldn't need to use a mobile for privacy.'

We had gone through Katy's mobile records already. She had had an allowance, ten euros of credit every second Sunday. She had mostly used it on text messages to her friends, and we had reconstructed long, cryptically abbreviated conversations about homework, classroom gossip, *American Idol*; not one unidentified number, not one red flag.

'What's the highlighter?' I asked.

'I cross-referenced against the known associates, tried to split up the calls by family member. Looks like Katy's the one used the phone most: all those numbers in yellow are her mates.' I flipped pages. The yellow highlighter took up at least half of each one. 'The blue is Margaret's sisters – one in Kilkenny, Vera across the estate. The green's Jonathan's sister in Athlone, the nursing home where their mammy's living, and committee members of Move the Motorway. The purple's Rosalind's friend Karen Daly, the one she stayed with when she ran away. The calls between them start to dry up after that. I'd say Karen wasn't too pleased about being put in the middle of family hassle, except that she kept ringing Rosalind for a few weeks after; Rosalind just wasn't ringing her back.'

'Maybe she wasn't allowed to,' I said. It might have been just the start Sam had given me, but my heart was still going too fast and there was a sharp, animal taste of danger in my mouth.

Sam nodded. 'The parents might've seen Karen as a bad influence. Anyway, that's all the calls accounted for, except a bunch from a phone company trying to get them to switch provider – and these three.' He spread out the pages of incoming calls: three stripes of pink highlighter. 'The dates, times and lengths match what Devlin gave us. They're all from payphones.'

'Dammit,' Cassie said.

'Where?' I asked.

'City centre. The first one's on the quays, down near the IFSC; second one's on O'Connell Street. Third one's halfway between, also on the quays.'

'In other words,' I said, 'our caller's not one of the local boys who have their knickers in a twist over the value of their houses.'

'I wouldn't say so. Going by the times, he's ringing on his way home from the pub. I suppose a Knocknaree fella could drink in town, but it doesn't sound likely, not as a regular thing. I'll have the lads check, to make sure, but for now I'm guessing this is someone whose interest in the motorway is business, not personal. And if I was a betting man, I'd put money on him living somewhere along the quays.'

'Our killer's almost definitely local,' Cassie said.

Sam nodded. 'My boy could've hired a local to do the

job, though. That's what I'd have done.' Cassie caught my
eye: the thought of Sam earnestly toddling off in search of a
hit man was irresistible. 'When I find out who owns that
land, I'll see if any of them have been talking to anyone
from Knocknaree.'

'How are you getting on with that?' I asked.

'Ah, sure,' Sam said cheerfully and vaguely. 'I'm working on it.'

'Hang on,' Cassie said suddenly. 'Who does Jessica
phone?'

'No one,' Sam said, 'as far as I can tell,' and he patted the
papers gently into a stack and took them away.

All that was on the Monday, almost a week after Katy had
died. In that week, neither Jonathan nor Margaret Devlin
had phoned us to ask how the investigation was going. I
wasn't complaining, exactly – some families ring four or
five times a day, desperate for answers, and there are few
things more excruciating than telling them we have none –
but all the same: it was another small unsettling thing, in a
case that was already much too full of them.

Rosalind finally came in on Tuesday, at lunchtime. No
phone call, no arrangement, just Bernadette informing me
with faint disapproval that there was a young woman to see
me; but I knew it was her, and the fact that she had shown
up out of the blue like that smacked of desperation somehow, of some clandestine urgency. I dropped what I was
doing and went downstairs, ignoring the enquiring raised
eyebrows from Cassie and Sam.

Rosalind was waiting in Reception. She had an emerald
shawl wrapped tightly around her; her face, turned to look
out the window, was wistful and faraway. She was too
young to know it, but she made a lovely picture: the fall of

chestnut curls and the splash of green, poised against the sunlit brick and stone of the courtyard. Block out the defiantly utilitarian lobby, and the scene could have come straight off a Pre-Raphaelite greeting card.

'Rosalind,' I said.

She spun from the window, a hand going to her chest. 'Oh, Detective Ryan! You startled me . . . Thank you so much for seeing me.'

'Any time,' I said. 'Come upstairs and we'll talk.'

'Are you sure? I don't want to be any trouble. If you're too busy, just tell me and I'll go.'

'You're no trouble at all. Can I get you a cup of tea? Coffee?'

'Coffee would be lovely. But do we have to go in there? It's such a lovely day, and I'm a little claustrophobic – I don't like to tell people, but . . . Couldn't we go outside?'

It wasn't standard procedure; but then, I reasoned, she wasn't a suspect, or even necessarily a witness. 'Sure,' I said, 'just give me a second,' and ran upstairs for the coffee. I'd forgotten to ask her how she took it, so I added a little milk and put two sachets of sugar in my pocket, in case.

'Here you go,' I said to Rosalind, downstairs. 'Shall we find somewhere in the garden?'

She took a sip of coffee and tried to hide a quick little moue of distaste. 'I know, it's foul,' I said.

'No, no, that's fine – it's just that . . . well, I don't take milk, usually, but—'

'Oops,' I said. 'Sorry about that. Want me to get you another one?'

'Oh, no! It's all right, Detective Ryan, honestly – I didn't really need coffee. You have this one. I don't want to put you to any trouble; it's wonderful of you to see me, you mustn't go out of your way . . .' She was talking too fast, too high and chatty, hands flying, and she held my eyes for too long without blinking, as if she had been hypnotised. She was badly nervous, and trying hard to cover up.

'It's no problem at all,' I said gently. 'I'll tell you what: let's find somewhere nice to sit, and then I'll get you another cup of coffee. It'll still be foul, but at least it'll be black. How does that sound?' Rosalind smiled up at me gratefully, and for a moment I had a startled sense that this small act of consideration had moved her almost to tears.

We found a bench in the gardens, in the sun; birds were twittering and rustling in the hedges, darting out to wrestle with discarded sandwich crusts. I left Rosalind there and went back up for the coffee. I took my time, to give her a chance to settle down, but when I got back she was still sitting on the edge of the bench, biting her lip and picking the petals off a daisy.

'Thank you,' she said, taking the coffee and trying to smile. I sat down beside her. 'Detective Ryan, have you . . . have you found out who killed my sister?'

'Not yet,' I said. 'But it's early days. I promise you, we're doing absolutely everything we can.'

'I know you'll catch him, Detective Ryan. I knew the minute I saw you. I can tell an awful lot about people from first impressions – sometimes it actually scares me, how often I'm right – and I knew right away that you were the person we needed.'

She was looking up at me with pure, unblemished faith in her eyes. I was flattered, of course I was, but at the same time, this level of trust made me very uncomfortable. She was so sure, and so desperately vulnerable; and, although you try not to think this way, I knew there was a chance this case would never be solved, and I knew exactly what that would do to her.

'I had a dream about you,' Rosalind said, then glanced down, embarrassed. 'The night after Katy's funeral. I hadn't slept more than an hour a night since she vanished, you know. I was – oh, I was frantic. But seeing you that day . . . it reminded me not to give up. That night I dreamed you knocked on our door and told me you'd caught the man who did this. You had him in the police car behind you, and you said he'd never hurt anyone again.'

'Rosalind,' I said. I couldn't take this. 'We're doing our best, and we won't give up. But you have to prepare yourself for the possibility that it might take a very long time.'

She shook her head. 'You'll find him,' she said simply.

I let it go. 'You said there was something you wanted to ask me?'

'Yes.' She took a deep breath. 'What happened to my sister, Detective Ryan? Exactly?'

Her eyes were wide and intent, and I wasn't sure how to handle this: if I told her, would she break down, collapse, scream? The gardens were full of chattery office workers on their lunch break. 'I should really let your parents tell you about it,' I said.

'I'm eighteen, you know. You don't need their permission to talk to me.'

'Still.'

Rosalind bit her bottom lip. 'I asked them. He . . . they . . . they told me to shut up.'

Something zipped through me – anger, alarm bells, compassion, I'm not sure. 'Rosalind,' I said, very gently, 'is everything all right at home?'

Her head flew up, mouth open in a little O. 'Yes,' she said, in a small, uncertain voice. 'Of course.'

'Are you sure?'

'You're very kind,' she said shakily. 'You're so good to me. It's . . . everything's fine.'

'Would you be more comfortable talking to my partner?'

'No,' she said sharply, with what sounded like disapproval in her voice. 'I wanted to talk to you because . . .' She turned the cup in circles in her lap. 'I felt like you cared, Detective Ryan. About Katy. Your partner didn't really seem to care, but you – you're different.'

'Of course we both care,' I said. I wanted to put a reassuring arm around her, or a hand on hers, or something, but I've never been good at that stuff.

'Oh, I know, I know. But your partner . . .' She gave me a self-deprecating little smile. 'I guess I'm a bit scared of her. She's so aggressive.'

'My *partner*?' I said, startled. 'Detective *Maddox*?' Cassie has always been the one with a reputation for being good with the families. I get stiff and tongue-tied, but she always seems to know the right thing to say and the gentlest way to say it. Some families still send her sad, valiant, grateful little cards at Christmas.

Rosalind's hands fluttered helplessly. 'Oh, Detective Ryan, I don't mean it in a bad way. Being aggressive is a good thing, isn't it – especially in your job? And I'm probably much too sensitive. It was just how she went on at my parents – I know she had to ask all those questions, but it was the *way* she asked them, so coldly . . . Jessica was really upset. And she was smiling at me like it was all . . . Katy's death wasn't a *joke*, Detective Ryan.'

'Very far from it,' I said. I was mentally skimming through that awful session in the Devlins' sitting-room, trying to work out what the hell Cassie had done to get this kid so upset. The only thing I could think of was that she had given Rosalind an encouraging smile, when she sat her down on the sofa. In retrospect, I supposed that could have been a little inappropriate, although hardly enough to warrant this kind of reaction. Shock and grief often do make people overreact in skewed, illogical ways; but still, this level of jumpiness strengthened my feeling that there was something up in that house. 'I'm sorry if we gave the impression—'·

'No, oh no, not you – you were wonderful. And I know Detective Maddox can't have meant to seem so – so harsh. Really, I do. Most aggressive people are just trying to be strong, aren't they? They just don't want to be insecure, or needy, or anything like that. They're not actually *cruel*, underneath.'

'No,' I said, 'probably not.' I had a hard time thinking of Cassie as needy; but then, I had never thought of her as aggressive, either. I realised, with a sudden small shot of unease, that I had no way of knowing how Cassie came across to other people. It was like trying to tell whether your sister is pretty, or something: I could no more be objective about her than about myself.

'Have I offended you?' Rosalind looked up at me nervously, pulling at a ringlet. 'I have. I'm sorry, I'm sorry – I'm always putting my foot in it. I open my silly mouth and everything just comes out, I never learn—'

'No,' I said, 'it's fine. I'm not offended at all.'

'You are. I can tell.' She threw her shawl more closely around her shoulders and flipped her hair out from under it, her face tight and withdrawn.

I knew if I lost her now I might never have another chance. 'Honestly,' I said, 'I'm not. I was just thinking about what you said. It's very insightful.'

She played with the fringe of the shawl, not meeting my eyes. 'But isn't she your girlfriend?'

'Detective Maddox? No no no,' I said. 'Nothing like that.'

'But I thought from the way she—' She clapped a hand over her mouth. 'Oh, there I go again! *Stop*, Rosalind!'

I laughed; I couldn't help it, we were both trying so hard. 'Come on,' I said. 'Take a deep breath and we'll start over.'

Slowly she relaxed back onto the bench. 'Thank you, Detective Ryan. But, please . . . what exactly happened to Katy? I keep imagining, you see . . . I can't bear not knowing.'

And so (because what could I say to that?) I told her. She didn't faint or go into hysterics, or even burst into tears. She listened in silence, with her eyes – blue eyes, the colour of faded denim – fixed on mine. When I had finished she put her fingers to her lips and stared out into the sunshine, at the neat patterns of hedges, the office workers with their plastic containers and gossip. I patted her shoulder awkwardly. The shawl was cheap stuff, once you touched it, prickly and synthetic, and the childish, pathetic gallantry of it went to my heart. I wanted to say something to her, something wise and profound about how few deaths can match the refined agony of being the one left behind, something that she could remember when she was alone and sleepless and uncomprehending in her room; but I couldn't find the words.

'I'm so sorry,' I said.

'So she wasn't raped?'

There was a flat, hollow note in her voice. 'Drink your coffee,' I said, with some obscure notion about hot drinks being good for shock.

'No, no . . .' She waved her hand distractedly. 'Tell me. She wasn't raped?'

'Not exactly, no. And she was already dead, you know. She didn't feel a thing.'

'She didn't suffer much?'

'Hardly at all. She was knocked out almost immediately.'

Suddenly Rosalind bent her head over the coffee cup, and I saw her lips quivering. 'I feel awful about it, Detective Ryan. I feel as if I should have protected her better.'

'You didn't know.'

'But I should have known. I should have been there, not having fun with my cousins. I'm a terrible sister, aren't I?'

'You are not responsible for Katy's death,' I said firmly. 'It sounds to me as though you were a wonderful sister to her. There's nothing you could have done.'

'But—' She stopped, shook her head.

'But what?'

'Oh . . . I should have known. That's all. Never mind.' She smiled tentatively up at me, through her hair. 'Thank you for telling me.'

'My turn,' I said. 'Can I ask you a couple of things?'

She looked apprehensive, but she took a deep breath and nodded.

'Your father said Katy wasn't into boys yet,' I said. 'Is that true?'

Her mouth opened, then closed again. 'I don't know,' she said, in a small voice.

'Rosalind, I know this isn't easy for you. But if she was, we need to know.'

'Katy was my *sister*, Detective Ryan. I don't want to – to say things about her.'

'I know,' I said gently. 'But the best thing you can do for her now is to tell me anything that might help me find her killer.'

Finally she sighed, a tremulous little breath. 'Yes,' she

said. 'She liked boys. I don't know who, exactly, but I heard her and her friends teasing each other – about boyfriends, you know, and who they'd kissed . . .'

The thought of twelve-year-olds kissing startled me, but I remembered Katy's friends, those knowing, disconcerting little girls. Maybe Peter and Jamie and I had just been backward. 'Are you positive? Your father seemed pretty sure.'

'My father . . .' There was a tiny frown-line between Rosalind's eyebrows. 'My father worshipped Katy. And she – sometimes she took advantage of that. She didn't always tell him the truth. That made me very sad.'

'OK,' I said. 'OK. I understand. You've done the right thing by telling me.' She nodded, just a slight inclination of the head. 'I need to ask you one more thing. You ran away from home in May, right?'

The frown deepened. 'I didn't exactly *run away*, Detective Ryan. I'm not a child. I spent a weekend with a friend.'

'Who was that?'

'Karen Daly. You can ask her, if you'd like. I'll give you her number.'

'There's no need,' I said, ambiguously. We had already talked to Karen – a timid, pasty-faced girl, not at all what I would have expected a friend of Rosalind's to be – and she had confirmed that Rosalind had been with her all weekend; but I have a fairly good nose for deception, and I was pretty sure there was something Karen wasn't telling me. 'Your cousin thought you might have spent the weekend with a boyfriend.'

Rosalind's mouth tightened into a displeased little line. 'Valerie has a dirty mind. I know a lot of other girls do things like that, but I'm not other girls.'

'No,' I said. 'You're not. But your parents didn't know where you were?'

'No. They didn't.'

'Why was that?'

'Because I didn't feel like telling them,' she said sharply. Then she glanced up at me and sighed, and her face softened. 'Oh, Detective, don't you ever feel that – that you just need to get away? From everything? That it's all just too much?'

'I do,' I said, 'yes. So the weekend away wasn't because anything bad had happened at home? We've been told you had a fight with your father . . .'

Rosalind's face clouded over, and she looked away. I waited. After a moment, she shook her head. 'No. I . . . nothing like that.'

My alarm bells were going off again, but her voice had tightened and I didn't want to push her, not yet. I wonder now, of course, whether I should have; but I can't see that, in the long run, it would have made any difference to anything at all.

'I know you're having a very hard time right now,' I said, 'but don't run away again, OK? If things are getting on top of you, or if you just want to talk, give Victim Support a ring, or call me – you have my mobile number, right? I'll do whatever I can to help.'

Rosalind nodded. 'Thank you, Detective Ryan. I'll remember that.' But her face was withdrawn, subdued, and I had the sense that, in some obscure but critical way, I had let her down.

Cassie was in the squad room, photocopying statements. 'Who was that?'

'Rosalind Devlin.'

'Huh,' Cassie said. 'What did she say?'

For some reason, I didn't feel like telling her the details. 'Nothing much. Just that, no matter what Jonathan thought, Katy was into boys. Rosalind didn't know any names; we'll need to talk to Katy's mates again and see if they can give us more. She also said Katy told lies, but then, most kids do.'

'Anything else?'

'Not really.'

Cassie turned from the photocopier, a page in her hand, and gave me a long look I couldn't read. Then she said, 'At least she's talking to you. You should stay in touch with her; she might open up more as you go.'

'I did ask her whether there was anything wrong at home,' I said, a little guiltily. 'She said no, but I didn't believe her.'

'Hmm,' Cassie said, and went back to photocopying.

But when we talked to Christina and Marianne and Beth again, the next day, they were all adamant: Katy had had no boyfriends and no particular crushes. 'We used to tease her about guys sometimes,' Beth said, 'but not really, you know? Just messing.' She was a red-headed, cheerful-looking kid, already sprouting boisterous curves, and when her eyes filled with tears she seemed bewildered by them, as if crying was still an unfamiliar thing. She fished in the sleeve of her jumper and pulled out a tattered tissue.

'She might not have told us, though,' said Marianne. She was the quietest of the bunch, a pale fairy of a girl vanishing into her funky teenage clothes. 'Katy's – Katy was very *private* about stuff. Like the first time she auditioned for ballet school, we didn't even know about it till she got accepted, remember?'

'Um, hel-*lo*, not the same thing,' Christina said, but she had been crying too and the stuffed nose took most of the authority off her voice. 'We couldn't exactly have missed a *boyfriend*.'

The floaters would re-interview every boy on the estate and in Katy's class, of course, just in case; but I realised that, at some level, this was exactly what I had been expecting. This case was like an endless, infuriating street-corner shell game: I knew the prize was in there somewhere, right under my eye, but the game was rigged and the dealer much too fast for me, and every sure-thing shell I turned over came up empty.

Sophie rang me as we were leaving Knocknaree, to say that the lab results were back. She was walking somewhere; I could hear the mobile jolting and the fast, decisive taps of her shoes.

'I've got your results on the Devlin kid,' she said. 'The lab's got a six-week backlog and you know what they're like, but I got them to jump this one up the queue. I practically had to sleep with the head geek before he'd do it.'

My heart rate picked up. 'Bless you, Sophie,' I said. 'We owe you another one.' Cassie, driving, glanced across at me; I mouthed, 'Results.'

'Tox screen was negative: she wasn't drugged, drunk or on any medication. She was covered in trace, mostly outdoor stuff – dirt, pollen, the usual. It's all consistent with the soil composition around Knocknaree, even – this is the good part – even the stuff that was inside her clothes and stuck to the blood. So stuff she didn't just pick up at the dump site. Lab says there's some super-rare plant in that wood that doesn't grow anywhere else nearby – it got the plant geek very turned on, apparently – and the pollen wouldn't blow more than a mile or so. The odds are she was in Knocknaree the whole time.'

'That fits with what we have,' I said. 'Get to the good stuff.'

Sophie snorted. 'That *was* the good stuff. The footprints are a dead end: half of them match the archaeologists, and the ones that don't are too blurry to be any use. Practically all the fibres are consistent with stuff we pulled from the home; a handful of unidentified ones, but nothing distinctive. One hair on the T-shirt matching the idiot who found her, two that match the mother – one on the combats, one on a sock, and she probably does the washing, so no big deal there.'

'Any DNA? Or fingerprints or anything?'

'Ha,' Sophie said. She was eating something crunchy, probably crisps – Sophie lives mainly on junk food. 'A few bloody partials, but they came off a rubber glove – surprise, surprise. So no epithelials, either. And no semen and no saliva, and no blood that doesn't match the kid.'

'Great,' I said, my heart slowly sinking. I had fallen for the con all over again, I had got my hopes up, and I felt suckered and stupid.

'Except for that old spot Helen found. They got a blood type off it: it's A positive. Your victim's O neg.'

She paused for another mouthful of crisps, while my stomach did something complicated. 'What?' she demanded, when I said nothing. 'That's what you wanted to hear, isn't it? Same as the blood from the old case. OK, so it's tentative, but at least it's a link.'

'Yeah,' I said. I could feel Cassie listening; I turned my shoulder to her. 'That's great. Thanks, Sophie.'

'We've sent the swabs and those shoes off for DNA

testing,' Sophie said, 'but I wouldn't hold your breath if I were you. I bet it's all degraded to fuck. Who stores blood evidence in a *basement*?'

Cassie, by unspoken agreement, was following up on the old case while I concentrated on the Devlins. McCabe had died several years before, a heart attack, but she went to see Kiernan. He was retired and living in Laytown, a little commuter village up along the coast. He was well into his seventies, with a ruddy, good-humoured face and the comfortably sloppy build of a rugby player gone to seed, but he brought Cassie for a long walk on the wide empty beach, seagulls and curlews screaming, while he told her what he remembered about the Knocknaree case. He seemed happy, Cassie said that evening, as she lit the fire and I spread mustard on ciabatta rolls and Sam poured the wine. He had taken up woodworking, there was sawdust on his soft worn trousers; his wife had wrapped a scarf around his neck and kissed his cheek as he went out.

He remembered the case, though, every detail. In all Ireland's brief disorganised history as a nation, fewer than half a dozen children have gone missing and stayed that way, and Kiernan had never been able to forget that two of these had been given into his hands and he had failed them. The search, he told Cassie (a little defensively, she said, as though this was a conversation he had had many times in his mind), had been massive: dogs, helicopters, divers; policemen and volunteers had combed miles of wood and hill and field in every direction, starting at dawn every morning for weeks and going on into the late summer twilights; they had followed leads to Belfast and Kerry and even Birmingham; and all the time a nagging whisper had insisted, in Kiernan's ear, that they were looking in the wrong directions, that the answer was right in front of them all along.

'What's his theory?' Sam asked.

I flipped the last steak onto its roll and handed round the plates. 'Later,' Cassie said, to Sam. 'Enjoy your sandwich first. How often does Ryan do something that's worth appreciating?'

'You are speaking to two talented men here,' I told her. 'We can eat *and* listen, at the same time.' It would have been nice to hear this story in private first, obviously, but by the time Cassie had got back from Laytown it had been too late for that. The thought had already killed my appetite; the thing itself wasn't going to make much difference. Besides, we always talked about the case over dinner, and today was not going to be any different if I could help it. Sam appears blithely unaware of subtext and emotional cross-currents, but I sometimes wonder if anyone can be quite as oblivious as all that.

'I'm impressed,' Cassie said. 'OK' – her eyes went to me for a second; I looked away – 'Kiernan's theory was that they never left Knocknaree. I don't know if you guys remember this, but there was a third kid . . .' She leaned sideways to check her notebook, open on the arm of the sofa. 'Adam Ryan. He was with the other two that afternoon, and they found him in the wood, a couple of hours into the search. No injuries, but there was blood in his shoes and he was pretty shaken up; he couldn't remember anything. So Kiernan figured that, whatever happened, it must have been either in the wood or very nearby, otherwise how had Adam got back there? He thought someone – someone local – had been watching them for a while. The guy approached them in the wood, maybe lured them back to his house, and attacked them. Probably he hadn't planned to kill them; maybe he tried to molest them and something went wrong. At some point during the attack, Adam escaped and ran back into the wood – which probably means they were either in the wood itself, in one of the estate houses that back onto it, or in one of the farmhouses nearby; otherwise he'd have gone home, right? Kiernan thinks the guy panicked and killed the other two children, possibly stashed the bodies in his house until he saw his chance and then either dumped them in the river or buried them, in his garden or, more likely – there were no reports of unexplained digging in the area over the next few weeks – in the wood.'

I took a bite of my sandwich. The taste, pungent and bloody, almost made me retch. I forced it down, unchewed, with a swallow of wine.

'Where's young Adam these days?' Sam enquired.

Cassie shrugged. 'I doubt he'd be able to tell us anything. Kiernan and McCabe kept going back to him for years, but he never remembered any more. In the end they gave up, figured the memory was gone for good. The family moved out of the area; Knocknaree gossip says they emigrated to Canada.' All of which was true, as far as it went. This was both more difficult and more ridiculous than I had expected. We were like spies, communicating over Sam's head in careful, stilted code.

'They must have been going mental,' Sam said. 'An eyewitness right there . . .' He shook his head and took a big bite of sandwich.

'Yeah, Kiernan said it was frustrating, all right,' Cassie said, 'but the kid was doing his best. He even participated in a reconstruction, with two local kids. They were hoping it would help him remember what he and his mates had done that afternoon, but he froze up as soon as he got into the wood.' My stomach flipped. I had no memory of this at all. I put down my sandwich; suddenly and intensely, I wanted a cigarette.

'Poor little bastard,' Sam said peacefully.

'Was this what McCabe thought, too?' I asked.

'No.' Cassie licked mustard off her thumb. 'McCabe thought it was a tourist killer – some guy who was only here for a few days, probably over from England, maybe for work. See, they couldn't find a single good suspect. They did almost a thousand questionnaires, hundreds of interviews, ruled out all the known perverts and weirdos in south Dublin, accounted for every local man's movements down to the minute . . . You know what it's like: you almost always come up with a suspect, even if you don't have enough to charge him. They had *nobody*. Every time they got a lead, they ran bang into a dead end.'

'That sounds familiar,' I said grimly.

'Kiernan thinks it was because someone gave the guy a fake alibi so he never really made it onto their radar, but McCabe figured it was because he wasn't there to find. His theory was that the kids were playing by the river and followed it to where it comes out on the other side of the wood – it's a long walk, but they'd done it before. There's a little back road that goes right past that stretch of the river. McCabe thought someone was driving by, saw the kids and tried to drag them or lure them into his car. Adam fought, got away and ran back into the wood, and the guy drove off with the other two. McCabe talked to Interpol and the British police, but they didn't come up with anything useful.'

'Kiernan and McCabe,' I said, 'both thought the children were murdered, then.'

'McCabe wasn't sure, apparently. He thought there was

a chance someone had abducted them – maybe someone mentally ill and desperate to have kids, or maybe . . . Well. At first they thought they might have just run away, but two twelve-year-olds with no money? They'd have been found within days.'

'Well, Katy was no random tourist killing,' Sam said. 'He had to set up the meeting, keep her somewhere for the day . . .'

'Actually,' I said, impressed by the pleasant, everyday tone of my voice, 'I can't really see the old case as a car snatch, either. As far as I remember, the shoes were only put back on the kid after the blood in them had started to congeal. In other words, the abductor spent some time with all three of them, in the area, before one got away. To me, that says local.'

'Knocknaree's a small place,' Sam said. 'What are the odds of two different child-murderers living there?'

Cassie balanced her plate on her crossed legs, linked her hands behind her neck and arched stiffness out of it. There were dark shadows under her eyes; I realised suddenly that her afternoon with Kiernan had hit her hard, and that her reluctance to tell the story might not have been just for my sake. There is a specific tiny compression to the corners of her mouth when she is holding something back, and I wondered what Kiernan had told her that she wasn't saying.

'They even searched the trees, you know that?' she said. 'After a few weeks, some smart floater remembered an old case where a kid climbed a hollow tree and fell into a hole in the trunk; he wasn't found till forty years later. Kiernan and McCabe had people checking every tree, shining torches into hollows . . .'

Her voice drifted off and we fell silent. Sam munched his

sandwich with even, unhurried appreciation, put down the plate and sighed contentedly. Finally Cassie stirred, held out a hand; I put her smoke packet into it. 'Kiernan still dreams about it, you know,' she said quietly, fishing out a cigarette. 'Not as much as he used to, he said; only every few months, since he retired. He dreams that he's searching for the two kids in the wood at night, calling them, and someone leaps out of the bushes and rushes at him. He knows it's the person who took them, he can see his face – "clear as I see you," he said – but when he wakes up, he can't remember it.'

The fire cracked and spat sharply. I caught it out of the corner of my eye and whipped round; I was sure I had seen something shoot out of the fireplace into the room, some small, black, clawed thing – baby bird, maybe, fallen down the chimney? – but there was nothing there. When I turned back Sam's eyes were on me, grey and calm and somehow sympathetic, but he only smiled and leaned across the table to refill my glass.

I was having trouble sleeping, even when I got the opportunity. I often do, as I've said, but this was different: in those weeks I kept finding myself trapped in some twilight zone between sleep and waking, unable to force my way into either. 'Look out!' voices said suddenly and loudly in my ear; or, 'I can't hear you. What? What?' I half-dreamed dark intruders moving stealthily around the room, riffling through my work notes and fingering the shirts in my wardrobe; I knew they couldn't be real, but it took me a panicky eternity to drag myself awake to either confront or dispel them. Once I woke to find myself slumped against the wall by my bedroom door, pawing crazily at the light switch, my legs barely able to hold me up. My head was swimming and there was a muffled moaning sound coming from somewhere, and it was a long time before I realised that it was my voice. I turned on the light, and my desk lamp, and crawled back into bed, where I lay, too shaken to go back to sleep, until my alarm went off.

In this limbo I kept hearing children's voices, too. Not Peter's and Jamie's, or anything: this was a group of children a long way off, chanting playground rhymes that I didn't remember ever having known. Their voices were gay and uncaring and too pure to be human, and underneath them were the brisk expert rhythms of complicated hand-clapping. *Say say my playmate, come out and play with me, climb up my apple tree . . . Two, two, the lily-white boys, clothed all in green-o, one is one and all alone and evermore shall be so . . .* Sometimes their faint chorus stayed in my head all day, a high inescapable underscore to whatever I was doing. I lived in mortal dread that O'Kelly would catch me humming one of the rhymes.

Rosalind phoned my mobile that Saturday. I was in the incident room; Cassie had gone off to talk to Missing Persons; behind me, O'Gorman was bellowing about some guy who had failed to give him proper respect during the door-to-door. I had to press the phone to my ear to hear her. 'Detective Ryan, it's Rosalind . . . I'm so sorry to bother you, but do you think you might have the time to come talk to Jessica?'

City noises in the background: cars, loud conversation, the frenetic beeping of a pedestrian signal. 'Of course,' I said. 'Where are you?'

'We're in town. Could we meet you in the Central Hotel bar in, say, ten minutes? Jessica has something to tell you.'

I dug out the main file and started flipping through it for

Rosalind's date of birth: if I was going to talk to Jessica, I needed an 'appropriate adult' present. 'Are your parents with you?'

'No, I . . . no. I think Jessica might be more comfortable talking without them, if that's all right.'

My antennae prickled. I had found the page of family stats: Rosalind was eighteen, and appropriate as far as I was concerned. 'No problem,' I said. 'I'll see you there.'

'Thank you, Detective Ryan, I knew I could come to you – I'm sorry to rush you, but we really should get home before—' A beep, and she was gone: either her battery or her credit had run out. I wrote Cassie a 'Back soon' note and left.

Rosalind had good taste. The Central bar has a stubbornly old-fashioned feel – ceiling mouldings, huge comfortable armchairs taking up inefficient quantities of space, shelves of weird old books in elegant bindings – that contrasts satisfyingly with the manic overdrive of the streets below. Sometimes I used to go there on Saturdays, have a glass of brandy and a cigar – this was before the smoking ban – and spend the afternoon reading the 1938 *Farmer's Almanac* or third-rate Victorian poems.

Rosalind and Jessica were at a table by the window. Rosalind's curls were caught up loosely and she was wearing a white outfit, long skirt and gauzy ruffled blouse, that blended perfectly with the surroundings; she looked as if she had just stepped in from some Edwardian garden party. She was leaning over to whisper in Jessica's ear, one hand stroking her hair in a slow, soothing rhythm.

Jessica was in an armchair, her legs curled under her, and the sight of her hit me all over again, almost as hard as it had that first time. The sun streaming through the high window held her in a column of light that transformed her into a radiant vision of someone else, someone vivid and eager and lost. The fine crooked Vs of her eyebrows, the tilt of her nose, the full, childish curve of her lip: the last time I had looked into that face, it had been empty and blood-smeared on Cooper's steel table. She was like a reprieve; like Eurydice, gifted back to Orpheus from the darkness for a brief miraculous moment. I wanted, so intensely it took my breath away, to reach out and lay a hand on her soft dark head, to pull her tightly against me and feel her slight and warm and breathing, as if by protecting her hard enough I could somehow undo time and protect Katy too.

'Rosalind,' I said. 'Jessica.'

Jessica flinched, eyes widening sharply, and the illusion was gone. She was holding something, a sachet of sugar from the bowl in the middle of the table; she shoved the corner into her mouth and started to suck on it.

Rosalind's face lit up at the sight of me. 'Detective Ryan! It's so good to see you. I know it was short notice, but – oh, sit down, sit down . . .' I pulled up another armchair. 'Jessica saw something I think you should know about. Didn't you, pet?'

Jessica shrugged, an awkward wriggle.

'Hi, Jessica,' I said, softly and as calmly as I could. My mind was shooting in a dozen directions at once: if this had anything to do with the parents then I would have to find somewhere for the girls to go, and Jessica was going to be terrible on the stand . . . 'I'm glad you decided to tell me. What did you see?'

Her lips parted; she swayed, a little, in her chair. Then she shook her head.

'Oh, dear . . . I thought this might happen.' Rosalind sighed. 'Well. She told me that she saw Katy—'

'Thanks, Rosalind,' I said, 'but I really need to hear this from Jessica. Otherwise it's hearsay, and that's not admissible in court.'

Rosalind stared blankly, taken aback. Finally she nodded. 'Well,' she said, 'of course, if that's what you need, then . . . I just hope . . .' She bent over Jessica and tried to catch her eye, smiling; hooked her hair back behind her ear. 'Jessica? Darling? You really need to tell Detective Ryan what we talked about, sweetheart. It's important.'

Jessica ducked her head away. 'Don't remember,' she whispered.

Rosalind's smile tightened. 'Come on, Jessica. You remembered just fine earlier on, before we came *all the way out here* and dragged Detective Ryan away from *work*. Didn't you?'

Jessica shook her head again and bit down on the sugar packet. Her lip was trembling.

'It's all right,' I said. I wanted to shake her. 'She's just a little nervous. She's been having a hard time. Right, Jessica?'

'We've *both* been having a hard time,' Rosalind said sharply, 'but *one* of us has to act like an adult instead of like a stupid little girl.' Jessica shrank deeper into her oversized jumper.

'I know,' I said, in what I hoped was a soothing tone, 'I know. I understand how hard this is—'

'No, actually, Detective Ryan, you don't.' Rosalind's crossed knee was jiggling angrily. 'Nobody can possibly understand what this is like. I don't know why we came in. Jessica can't be bothered to tell you what she saw, and you obviously don't think that matters. We might as well go.'

I couldn't lose them. 'Rosalind,' I said urgently, leaning forward across the table, 'I'm taking this very seriously. And I do understand. Honestly, I do.'

Rosalind laughed bitterly, fumbling under the table for her purse. 'Oh, I'm sure. Put that thing down, Jessica. We're going home.'

'Rosalind, I *do*. When I was about Jessica's age, two of my best friends disappeared. I know what you're going through.'

Her head came up and she stared at me.

'I know it's not the same as losing a sister—'

'It isn't.'

'But I do know how hard it is to be the one left behind. I'm going to do whatever it takes to make sure you get some answers. OK?'

Rosalind kept staring for another long moment. Then she dropped her purse and laughed, a breathless burst of relief. 'Oh – oh, Detective Ryan!' Before she thought, she had reached across the table and caught my hand. 'I *knew* there was a reason why you're the perfect person for this case!'

I hadn't looked at it this way before, and the thought was warming. 'I hope you're right,' I said.

I gave her hand a squeeze; it was intended to be reassuring, but she suddenly realised what she had done and pulled away, in an embarrassed flutter. 'Oh, I didn't mean to—'

'Tell you what,' I said, 'you and I can talk for a while, until Jessica feels ready to explain what she saw. How's that?'

'Jessica? Pet?' Rosalind touched Jessica's arm; she jumped, eyes wide. 'Do you want to stay here for a bit?'

Jessica thought about this, gazing up into Rosalind's face. Rosalind smiled down at her. Finally she nodded.

I bought coffee for Rosalind and me and a 7-Up for Jessica. Jessica held her glass in both hands and stared, as if hypnotised, at the bubbles floating upwards, while Rosalind and I talked.

Frankly, I hadn't expected to take much pleasure in a teenager's conversation, but Rosalind was an unusual kid. The initial shock of Katy's death had worn off and for the first time I got a chance to see what she was really like: outgoing, bubbly, all sparkle and dash, ridiculously bright and articulate. I wondered where the girls like this had been when I was eighteen. She was naïve, but she knew it; she told jokes on herself with such zest and mischief that – in spite of the context, and my creeping worry that this level of innocence would get her into trouble one day, and Jessica sitting there watching invisible booglies like a cat – my laughter was real.

'What are you going to do when you leave school?' I asked. I was genuinely curious. I couldn't picture this girl in some nine-to-five office.

Rosalind smiled, but a sad little shadow passed across her face. 'I'd love to study music. I've been playing the violin since I was nine, and I do a little bit of composing; my teacher says I'm . . . well, he says I shouldn't have any trouble getting into a good course. But . . .' She sighed. 'It's expensive, and my – my parents don't really approve. They want me to do a secretarial course.'

But they had been behind Katy's Royal Ballet School ambitions, all the way. In Domestic Violence I had seen cases like this, where parents choose a favourite or a scapegoat (*I made a bit of a pet of her*, Jonathan had said, that first day) and siblings grow up in utterly different families. Few of them end well.

'You'll find a way,' I said. The idea of her as a secretary was ludicrous; what the hell was Devlin thinking? 'A scholarship or something. It sounds like you're good.'

She ducked her head modestly. 'Well. Last year the National Youth Orchestra performed a sonata I wrote.'

I didn't believe her, of course. The lie was transparent – something that size, someone would have mentioned it during the door-to-door – and it went straight to my heart as no sonata ever could have; because I recognised it. *That's my twin brother, his name's Peter, he's seven minutes older than me* . . . Children – and Rosalind was little more – don't tell pointless lies unless the reality is too much to bear.

For a moment I almost said as much. *Rosalind, I know something's wrong at home; tell me, let me help* . . . But it was too soon; she would just have thrown all her defences up again, it would have undone everything I had managed to do. 'Well done,' I said. 'That's pretty impressive.'

She laughed a little, embarrassed; glanced up at me under her lashes.

'Your friends,' she said timidly. 'The ones who disappeared. What happened?'

'It's a long story,' I said. I had painted myself into this one, and I had no idea how to get out of it. Rosalind's eyes were starting to turn suspicious, and, while there was not a chance in hell that I was going to go into the whole Knocknaree thing, the last thing I wanted was to lose her trust after all this.

Jessica, of all people, saved me: she shifted a little in the armchair, stretched out a finger to Rosalind's arm.

Rosalind didn't seem to notice. 'Jessica?' I said.

'Oh – what is it, sweetheart?' Rosalind bent towards her. 'Are you ready to tell Detective Ryan about the man?'

Jessica nodded stiffly. 'I saw a man,' she said, her eyes not on me but on Rosalind. 'He talked to Katy.'

My heart rate started to pick up. If I had been religious, I would have been lighting candles to every saint in the calendar for this: just one solid lead. 'That's great, Jessica. Where was this?'

'On the road. When we were coming back from the shop.'

'Just you and Katy?'

'Yes. We're allowed.'

'I'm sure you are. What did he say?'

'He said' – Jessica took a deep breath – 'he said, "You're a very good dancer," and Katy said, "Thank you." She likes when people say she's a good dancer.'

She looked anxiously up at Rosalind. 'You're doing wonderfully, pet,' Rosalind said, stroking her hair. 'Keep going.'

Jessica nodded. Rosalind touched her glass, and Jessica took an obedient sip of her 7-Up. 'Then,' she said, 'then he said, "And you're a very pretty girl," and Katy said, "Thank you." She likes that, too. And then he said . . . he said . . . "My little girl likes dancing too, but she broke her leg. Do you want to come see her? It would make her very happy." And Katy said, "Not now. We have to go home." So then we went home.'

You're a pretty girl . . . These days, there are very few men who would say something like that to a twelve-year-old. 'Do you know who the man was?' I asked. 'Had you ever seen him before?'

She shook her head.

'What did he look like?'

Silence; a breath. 'Big.'

'Big like me? Tall?'

'Yeah . . . um . . . yeah. But big like this, too.' She stretched out her arms; the glass wobbled precariously.

'A fat man?'

Jessica giggled, a sharp, nervous sound. 'Yeah.'

'What was he wearing?'

'A, a tracksuit. A dark-blue one.' She glanced at Rosalind, who nodded encouragingly.

Shit, I thought. My heart was speeding. 'What was his hair like?'

'No. He didn't have hair.'

I made a quick, fervent mental apology to Damien: apparently he hadn't, after all, just been telling us what we wanted to hear. 'Was he old? Young?'

'Like you.'

'When did this happen?'

Jessica's lips parted, moved soundlessly. 'Huh?'

'When did you and Katy meet the man? Was it just a few days before Katy went away? Or a few weeks? Or a long time ago?'

I was trying to be sensitive, but she flinched. 'Katy didn't go away,' she said. 'Katy got killed.' Her eyes were starting to lose focus. Rosalind shot me a reproachful look.

'Yes,' I said, as gently as I could, 'she did. So it's very important for you to try and remember when you saw this man, so we can find out if he's the one who killed her. Can you do that?'

Jessica's mouth fell a little open. Her eyes were unreachable, gone.

'She told me,' Rosalind said softly, over her head, 'that this happened a week or two before . . .' She swallowed. 'She's not sure of the exact date.'

I nodded. 'Thank you so much, Jessica,' I said. 'You've been very brave. Do you think you would know this man if you saw him again?'

Nothing; not a flicker. The sugar packet hung loosely in

her curled fingers. 'I think we should go,' Rosalind said, looking worriedly from Jessica to her watch.

I watched from the window as they walked away down the street: Rosalind's decisive little steps and the delicate sway of her hips, Jessica dragging along behind her by the hand. I looked at the back of Jessica's silky bent head and thought of those old stories where one twin is hurt and the other, miles away, feels the pain. I wondered if there had been a moment, during that giggly girls' night at Auntie Vera's, when she had made some small, unnoticed sound; if all the answers we wanted were locked away behind the strange dark gateways of her mind.

You're the perfect person for this case, Rosalind had said to me, and the words were still ringing in my head as I watched her go. Even now, I wonder whether subsequent events proved her completely right or utterly and horribly wrong, and what criteria one could possibly use to tell the difference.

10

Over the next few days, I spent practically every waking moment searching for the mystery tracksuit. Seven guys around Knocknaree matched the description, such as it was – tall, heavily built, thirties, bald or skinheaded. One of them had a minor record, left over from his wild youth: possession of hash, indecent exposure – my heart skipped a beat when I saw that, but all he had done was have a slash down a laneway just as an earnest young cop was passing. Two said they might have been going into the estate on their way home from work at about the time Damien had given us, but they weren't sure.

None of them would admit to having talked to Katy; all of them had alibis, more or less, for the night of her death; none of them had a dancing daughter with a broken leg, or anything like a motive, as far as I could discover. I got photos and did line-ups for Damien and Jessica, but they both gave the array of photographs the same dazed, hunted look. Damien finally said he didn't think any of them was the man he had seen, while Jessica pointed tentatively to a different picture every time she was asked and finally turned catatonic on me again. I had a couple of floaters go door-to-door, asking everyone in the estate whether they had had a visitor matching the description: nothing.

A couple of the alibis were uncorroborated. One guy claimed he had been online till almost three in the morning, on a bikers' forum, discussing the maintenance of classic Kawasakis. Another said he had been on a date in town, missed the half-twelve Nitelink and waited for the two o'clock one in Supermac's. I stuck their photos up on the whiteboard and set about trying to break the alibis, but every time I looked at them I got the same feeling, a specific and unsettling feeling that I was starting to associate with this whole case: the sensation of another will meeting mine at every turn, something sly and obstinate, with reasons of its own.

Sam was the only one getting anywhere. He was out of the office a lot, interviewing people – County Council members, he said, surveyors, farmers, members of Move the Motorway. At our dinners he was vague about where all this was taking him: 'I'll show you in a few days,' he said, 'when it starts to make sense.' I sneaked a glance at his notes once, when he went to the bathroom and left them on his desk: diagrams and shorthand and little sketches in the margins, meticulous and indecipherable.

Then on Tuesday – a muggy, petulant, drizzly morning, Cassie and I grimly going through the floaters' door-to-door reports again in case we had missed something – he came in with a big roll of paper, the heavy kind that children use to make Valentines and Christmas decorations in school. 'Right,' he said, pulling Sellotape out of his pocket and starting to stick the paper to the wall in our corner of the incident room. 'Here's what I've been doing all this time.'

It was a huge map of Knocknaree, beautifully detailed: houses, hills, the river, the wood, the keep, all sketched in fine pen and ink with the delicate, flowing precision of a children's-book illustrator. It must have taken him hours. Cassie whistled.

'Thank you, thankyouverymuch,' Sam said in a deep Elvis voice, grinning. We both abandoned our stacks of reports and went over for a closer look. Much of the map had been divided into irregular blocks, shaded in coloured pencil – green, blue, red, a few in yellow. Each block held a tiny, mysterious jumble of abbreviations: *Sd J. Downey-GII 11/97; rz ag-ind 8/98*. I cocked an interrogative eyebrow at Sam.

'I'll explain it now.' He bit off another piece of tape and secured the last corner. Cassie and I sat on the edge of the table, where we were close enough to see the details.

'OK. See this?' Sam pointed to two parallel dashed lines curving across the map, cutting through the wood and the dig. 'That's where the motorway's going to be. The government announced the plans in March of 2000 and bought the land off local farmers over the next year, under a compulsory purchase order. Nothing dodgy there.'

'Well,' Cassie said. 'Depending on your point of view.'

'Shh,' I told her. 'Just look at the pretty picture.'

'Ah, you know what I mean,' Sam said. 'Nothing you wouldn't expect. Where it gets interesting is the land around the motorway. That was all agricultural land too, up until late 1995. Then, bit by bit, over the next four years, it started getting bought up and rezoned, from agricultural to industrial and residential.'

'By clairvoyants who knew where the motorway was going to be, five years before it was announced,' I said.

'That's not actually that dodgy either,' Sam said. 'There was talk about a motorway coming into Dublin from the south-west – I've found newspaper articles – starting in about 1994, when the Celtic Tiger kicked in. I talked to a couple of surveyors, and they said this was the most obvious route for a motorway, because of topography and settlement patterns and a load of other things. I didn't understand the whole of it, but that's what they said. There's no reason why property developers couldn't have done the same thing – got wind of the motorway and hired surveyors to tell them where it was likely to go.'

Neither of us said anything. Sam glanced from me to Cassie and flushed slightly. 'I'm not being naïve. Yeah, they might have been tipped off by someone in government – but, then again, they might not. Either way, it's not something we can prove, and I don't think it means anything to our case.' I tried not to smile. Sam is one of the most efficient detectives on the squad, but it was very sweet, somehow, how earnest he was about it all.

'Who bought the land?' Cassie asked, relenting.

Sam looked relieved. 'A bunch of different companies. Most of them don't exist, not really; they're just holding companies, owned by other companies that are owned by other companies. That's what's been taking all my time – trying to find out who actually owns the bloody land. So far I've traced each buy back to one of three companies: Global Irish Industries, Futura Property Consultants and Dynamo Development. The blue bits here are Global, see; the green ones are Futura, and the red are Dynamo. I'm having a hell of a time finding out who's behind them, though. Two of them are registered in the Czech Republic, and Futura's in Hungary.'

'Now that does sound dodgy,' Cassie said. 'By any definition.'

'Sure,' Sam said, 'but it's most likely tax evasion. We can pass all this on to the Revenue, but I don't see how it can have anything to do with our case.'

'Unless Devlin had found out about it and was using it to put pressure on someone,' I said.

Cassie looked sceptical. 'Found out how? And he would've told us.'

'You never know. He's weird.'

'You think everyone's weird. First Mark—'

'I'm only getting to the interesting bit,' said Sam. I made a face at Cassie and turned towards the map before she could make one back. 'So by March of 2000, when the motorway is announced, these three companies own almost all the land around this section of it. But four farmers had held out – those are the yellow bits. I tracked them down; they're in Louth now. They'd seen what way things were going, and they knew these buyers were offering pretty good prices, above the going rate for agricultural land; that was why everyone else had taken the money. They talked it over – they're all mates, these four – and decided to hold onto their land and see if they could work out what was going on. When the motorway plans were announced, obviously, they copped why these fellas wanted their land so badly: for industrial estates and residential developments, now that the motorway was going to make Knocknaree accessible. So these lads figured they'd get the land rezoned themselves, double or triple its value overnight. They applied to the County Council for rezoning – one of them applied *four times* – and got refused, every time.'

He tapped one of the yellow blocks, half-full of tiny calligraphic notes. Cassie and I leaned forward to read them: *M. Cleary, app rz ag-ind: 5/2000 ref, 11/2000 ref, 6/ 2001 ref, 1/2002 ref; sd M. Cleary-FPC 8/2002; rz ag-ind 10/2002.*

Cassie took it in with a brief nod and leaned back on her hands, her eyes still on the map. 'So they sold up,' she said quietly.

'Yeah. For around the same price as the others got – good for agricultural land, but a long way under the going rate for industrial or residential. Maurice Cleary wanted to stay put, out of sheer bloody-mindedness as much as anything else – said he wasn't going to be forced off his land by any eejit in a suit – but he got a visit from some fella from one of the holding companies, who explained to him that they'd be building a pharmaceutical plant backing onto his farm and they couldn't guarantee that chemical waste wouldn't seep into the water and poison his cattle. He took it as a threat – I don't know whether he was right or not, but he sold up anyway. As soon as the Big Three bought the land – under various other names, but it all traces back to them – they applied for rezoning, and got it.'

Cassie laughed, a small angry breath.

'Your Big Three had the County Council in their pockets all the way,' I said.

'Looks like.'

'You've talked to the County Councillors?'

'Ah, yeah. For all the good it did me. They were very polite and all, but they talked in circles. They could keep going for hours without giving me a single straight answer.' I slid my eyes sideways and caught Cassie's covert, amused glance: Sam, living with a politician, should have been used to this by now. 'They said the rezoning decisions were – hang on . . .' He flipped pages in his notebook. ' "Our decisions were on all occasions intended to further the best interests of the community as a whole, as determined based upon the information made available to us at the relevant points in time, and were not impacted by any form of favouritism." This wasn't part of a letter or anything; your man actually *said* that to me. In conversation, like.' Cassie mimed sticking a finger down her throat.

'How much does it take to buy a County Council?' I asked.

Sam shrugged. 'For that many decisions, over that amount of time, it must have added up to a decent old figure. The Big Three had a lot of money sunk in that land, one way or another. They wouldn't have been best pleased at the idea of the motorway moving.'

'How much damage would it actually do them?'

He pointed to two dotted lines, just cutting across the north-west corner of the map. 'According to my surveyors, that's the nearest logical alternative route. That's the one Move the Motorway wants. It's a good two miles away, four or five in some places. The land to the north of the original route would still be accessible enough, but these lads all have plenty on the south side as well, and its value would go right down. I talked to a couple of estate agents, pretended I was interested in buying; they all said industrial land right on the motorway was worth up to twice as much as industrial land three miles off it. I haven't done the exact maths, but it could add up to millions in the difference.'

'That'd be worth a few threatening phone calls,' Cassie said softly.

'There are people,' I said, 'to whom that would be worth a few extra grand for a hit man.'

Nobody said anything for a few moments. Outside, the drizzle was starting to clear; a watery shaft of sun fell across the map like a helicopter's searchlight, picked out a stretch of the river, rippling with delicate pen-strokes and shaded over with a dull red haze. Across the room, the floater manning the tip line was trying to get rid of someone too voluble to let him finish his sentences. Finally Cassie said, 'But why Katy? Why not go after Jonathan?'

'Too obvious, maybe,' I said. 'If Jonathan had been murdered, we'd have gone straight after any enemies he might have made through the campaign. With Katy, it can be set up to look like a sex crime, so our attention is diverted away from the motorway angle, but Jonathan still gets the message.'

'Unless I can find out who's behind these three companies, though,' Sam said, 'I've hit a dead end. The farmers don't know any names, the County Council claim they don't either. I've seen a couple of deeds of sale and applications and that, but they were signed by lawyers – and the lawyers say they can't release their clients' names to me without permission from the clients.'

'Jesus.'

'What about journalists?' Cassie said suddenly.

Sam shook his head. 'What about them?'

'You said there were articles about the motorway as far back as 1994. There must be journalists who followed the story, and they'd have a pretty good idea who bought up the land, even if they're not allowed to print it. This is *Ireland*; there's no such thing as a secret.'

'Cassie,' Sam said, his face lighting up, 'you're a gem. I'm buying you a pint for that.'

'Want to read my door-to-door reports for me instead? O'Gorman structures sentences like George Bush; most of the time I haven't a clue what he's on about.'

'Listen, Sam,' I said, 'if this pans out, we'll both be buying you pints for a very long time.' Sam bounded over to his end of the table, giving Cassie a clumsy, happy pat on the shoulder on his way, and started rooting through a file of newspaper clippings like a dog with a brand-new scent, and Cassie and I went back to our reports.

We left the map taped to the wall, where it got on my

nerves for reasons I couldn't quite define. It was the perfection of it, I think, the fragile, enchanting detail: tiny leaves curling in the wood, knobbly little stones in the wall of the keep. I suppose I had some kind of subconscious idea that one day I'd happen to glance up at it and catch two minute, laughing faces ducking out of sight among the pen-and-ink trees. Cassie drew a property developer, with a suit and horns and little dripping fangs, in one of the yellow patches; she draws like an eight-year-old, but I still jumped about a foot every time I caught the bloody thing leering at me in the corner of my eye.

I had started trying – for the first time, really – to remember what had happened in that wood. I prodded tentatively around the edges of it, barely acknowledging even to myself what I was doing, like a kid picking at a scab but afraid to look. I went for long walks – mostly in the early hours of the morning, on nights when I wasn't staying at Cassie's and couldn't sleep – wandering through the city for hours in something like a trance, listening for delicate little noises in the corners of my mind. I would come to, dazed and blinking, to find myself staring up at the tacky neon sign of an unfamiliar shopping centre, or the elegant gables of some Georgian home in the swankier part of Dun Laoghaire, with no idea how I had got there.

To some extent, at least, it worked. Unleashed, my mind threw out great streams of images like a slide show running on fast-forward, and gradually I learned the knack of reaching out to catch one as they flew past, holding it lightly and watching as it unfurled in my hands. Our parents bringing us into town to shop for First Communion clothes; Peter and I, natty in our dark suits, doubled over howling with unfeeling laughter when Jamie – after a long, whispered battle with her mother – came out of the girls' dressing-room wearing a meringue and a look of horrified loathing. Mad Mick, the local nutter, who wore overcoats and fingerless gloves all year round and whispered to himself in an endless stream of small, bitter curses – Peter said Mick was crazy because when he was young he had done rude things with a girl and she was going to have a baby, so she hanged herself in the wood and her face went black. One day Mick started screaming, outside Lowry's shop. The cops took him away in a police car, and we never saw him again. My desk in school, old deep-grained wood with an obsolete hole in the top for an inkwell, worn shiny and inlaid with years of doodles: a hurley stick, a heart with the initials inside scribbled over, 'Des Pearse was here 12/10/67'. Nothing special, I know, nothing that helped with the case; barely worth mentioning. But remember, I was used to taking it for granted that the first twelve years of my life were more or less gone for good. To me every salvaged scrap seemed tremendously potent and magical, a fragment of Rosetta Stone carved with just one tantalising character.

And on occasion I did manage to remember something that, if not useful, could at least be called relevant. *Metallica and Sandra, sitting in a tree* . . . We, I realised gradually and with an odd sense of insult, had not been the only people who claimed the wood as our territory and brought our private business there. There was a clearing deep in the wood, not far from the old castle – first bluebells in spring, swordfights with whippy branches that left long red weals on your arms, a tangled clump of bushes that by the end of summer was heavy with blackberries – and sometimes, when we had nothing more interesting to do, we used to spy on the bikers there. I remembered only one specific incident, but it had the taste of habit: we had done this before.

A hot summer day, sun on the back of my neck and the taste of Fanta in my mouth. The girl called Sandra was lying on her back in the clearing in a patch of flattened grass, with Metallica half on top of her. Her shirt was coming off her shoulder so her bra strap showed black and lacy. Her hands were in Metallica's hair and they were kissing with their mouths wide open. 'Ewww, you could catch germs that way,' Jamie whispered, by my ear.

I pressed myself closer against the ground, feeling grass print criss-cross patterns on my stomach where my T-shirt had twisted up. We breathed through our mouths, to be quieter.

Peter made a long kissing noise, just soft enough that they couldn't hear him, and we clamped our hands over our mouths, shaking with giggles, elbowing to make each other be quiet. Shades and the tall girl with five earrings were on the other side of the clearing. Anthrax mostly stayed at the edge of the wood, kicking the wall and smoking and throwing stones at beer cans. Peter held up a pebble, grinning; he flicked it, and it rattled into the grass only inches from Sandra's shoulder. Metallica, breathing hard, didn't even look up, and we had to duck our faces down into the long grass till we could stop laughing.

Then Sandra turned her head and she was looking at me; straight at me, through the long grass stalks and the chicory. Metallica was kissing her neck and she didn't move. Somewhere near my hand a grasshopper was ticking. I looked back at her and felt my heart banging slowly against the ground.

'Come on,' Peter whispered urgently, 'Adam, come *on*,'

and their hands pulled my ankles. I wriggled backwards, scratching my legs on brambles, back into the deep shadow of the trees. Sandra was still looking at me.

There were other memories, ones I still find it difficult to think about. I remembered, for example, going down the stairs of our house without touching them. I can recall this in perfect detail: the ribbed texture of the wallpaper with its fading bouquets of roses, the way a shaft of light came through the bathroom door and down the stairwell, catching on dust-motes, to glow a deep auburn in the polish of the banister; the deft, accustomed flick of my hand with which I pushed off the rail to float serenely downstairs, my feet swimming slowly three or four inches above the carpet.

I remembered, too, the three of us finding a secret garden, somewhere in the heart of the wood. Behind some hidden wall or doorway, it had been. Fruit trees run wild, apple, cherry, pear; broken marble fountains, trickles of water still bubbling along tracks green with moss and worn deep into the stone; great ivy-draped statues in every corner, feet wild with weeds, arms and heads cracked away and scattered among long grass and Queen Anne's lace. Grey dawn light, the swish of our feet and dew on our bare legs. Jamie's hand small and rosy on the stone folds of a robe, her face upturned to look into blind eyes. The infinite silence. I was very well aware that if this garden had existed it would have been found when the archaeologists did their initial survey, and the statues would have been in the National Museum by now, and Mark would have done his level best to describe them to us in detail, but this was the problem: I remembered it, all the same.

★   ★   ★

The guys from Computer Crime rang me early Wednesday morning: they had finished trawling through our last Tracksuit Shadow suspect's computer, and they confirmed that he had, in fact, been online when Katy died. With a certain amount of professional satisfaction, they added that, although the poor bastard shared the house and the computer with both his parents and his wife, e-mails and discussion-board posts showed that each of the occupants made characteristic spelling and punctuation errors. The posts made while Katy was dying matched our suspect's pattern to a T.

'Buggery,' I said, hanging up and putting my face in my hands. We already had security footage of the Nitelink guy in Supermac's, dipping chips into barbecue sauce with the glacial concentration of the very drunk. Deep down, a part of me had been expecting this, but I was feeling pretty ropey – no sleep, not enough coffee, nagging headache – and it was way too early in the morning to find out that my one good lead had gone south.

'What?' Cassie asked, looking up from whatever she was doing.

'The Kawasaki Kid's alibi checked out. If this guy Jessica saw is our man, he's not from Knocknaree, and I don't have the first clue where to look for him. I'm back to bloody square one.'

Cassie tossed down a handful of paper and rubbed her eyes. 'Rob, our guy's local. Everything's pointing that way.'

'Then who the fuck is Tracksuit Boy? If he's got an alibi for the murder and he just happened to talk to Katy one day, why hasn't he said so?'

'Assuming,' Cassie said, glancing at me sideways, 'he actually exists.'

A flare of disproportionate, almost uncontrollable fury shot through me. 'Sorry, Maddox, but what the hell are you talking about? Are you suggesting that Jessica made the whole thing up, just for laughs? You've barely seen those girls. Do you have any idea quite how devastated they are?'

'I'm saying,' Cassie said coolly, her eyebrows lifting, 'that I can think of circumstances in which they might feel they had a very good reason to make up a story like that.'

In the fraction of a second before I lost my temper altogether, the penny dropped. '*Shit*,' I said. 'The parents.'

'Hallelujah. Signs of intelligent life.'

'Sorry,' I said. 'Sorry for biting your head off, Cass. The parents . . . Shit. If Jessica thinks one of their parents did it, and she made up this whole thing—'

'Jessica? You think she could come up with something like this? She can hardly *talk*.'

'OK, then Rosalind. She comes up with Tracksuit Boy to take our attention off her parents, coaches Jessica – the whole Damien thing is just a coincidence. But if she bothered to do that, Cass . . . if she went to this much hassle, she must know something pretty bloody definitive. Either she or Jessica must have seen something, heard something.'

'On the Tuesday . . .' Cassie said, and checked herself; but the thought passed between us all the same, too horrible to be voiced. On that Tuesday, Katy's body must have been somewhere.

'I need to talk to Rosalind,' I said, going for the phone.

'Rob, don't chase her. She'll only back off. Let her come to you.'

She was right. Kids can be beaten, raped, abused in any number of unthinkable ways, and still find it all but impossible to betray their parents by asking for help. If Rosalind was shielding Jonathan or Margaret or both, then her whole world would crumble when she told the truth, and she needed to come to that in her own time. If I tried to push her, I would lose her. I put the phone down.

But Rosalind didn't ring me. After a day or two my self-restraint ran out and I called her mobile – for a variety of reasons, some more inchoate and troubling than others, I didn't want to phone the land line. There was no answer. I left messages, but she never rang me back.

Cassie and I went down to Knocknaree on a grey, mean afternoon, to see if the Savages or Alicia Rowan had anything new to tell us. We were both pretty badly hung over – this was the day after Carl and his internet freak show – and we talked very little in the car. Cassie drove; I stared out the window at leaves whipping in a fast, un-trustworthy wind, spurts of drizzle spattering the glass. Neither of us was at all sure I should be there.

At the last minute, when we had turned onto my old road and Cassie was parking the car, I wimped out of going to Peter's house. This was not because the road had overwhelmed me with a sudden flood of memories, or anything like that – quite the contrary: it reminded me strongly of every other road in the estate, but that was about it, and this left me feeling off-balance and at a strong disadvantage, as if Knocknaree had got one up on me yet again. I had spent an awful lot of time at Peter's house, and in some obscure way I felt his family was more likely to recognise me if I was unable to recognise them first.

I watched from the car as Cassie went up to Peter's door and rang the bell, and as a shadowy figure ushered her inside. Then I got out of the car and walked down the road to my old home. The address – 11 Knocknaree Way, Knocknaree, County Dublin – came back to me in the automatic rattle of something learned by rote.

It was smaller than I remembered; narrower; the lawn was a cramped little square, rather than the vast, cool expanse of green I had been picturing. The paintwork had been redone not too long ago, gay butter-yellow with a white trim. Tall red and white rosebushes were dropping their last petals by the wall, and I wondered if my father had planted them. I looked up at my bedroom window and in that instant it clicked home: I had lived here. I had run out that door with my book-bag on school mornings, leaned out of that window to yell down to Peter and Jamie, learned to walk in that garden. I had been riding my bike up and down this very road, until the moment when the three of us had climbed the wall at the end and run into the wood.

There was a neat little silver Polo in the driveway, and a blond kid, maybe three or four, was pedalling a plastic fire truck around it and making siren noises. When I reached the gate he stopped and gave me a long, solemn look.

'Hello,' I said.

'Go away,' he told me, eventually and firmly.

I wasn't sure how to respond to this, but as it turned out I didn't have to: the front door opened and the kid's mother – thirties, also blonde, pretty in a standardised kind of way – hurried down the drive and put a protective hand on his head. 'Can I help you?' she asked.

'Detective Robert Ryan,' I said, finding my ID. 'We're investigating the death of Katharine Devlin.'

She took the ID and scrutinised it carefully. 'I'm not sure how I can help,' she said, handing it back to me. 'We already talked to the other detectives. We didn't see anything; we barely know the Devlins.'

Her eyes were still wary. The kid was starting to get bored, making vrooming noises under his breath and wiggling his steering-wheel, but she held him in place with a hand on his shoulder. Faint, sparkling music – Vivaldi, I think – was drifting through the open front door, and for a moment I came dizzyingly close to asking her: *There are just a few things I'd like to confirm with you; would it be all right if I came in for a moment?* I told myself Cassie would worry if she came out of the Savages' house and found me gone. 'We're just double-checking everything,' I said. 'Thank you for your time.'

The mother watched me leave. As I got back into the car, I saw her scooping up the fire truck under one arm and the kid under the other and taking them both inside.

I sat in the car for a long time, looking out at the road and feeling that I would be able to deal with this a lot better if only my hangover would go away. At last Peter's door opened, and I heard voices: someone was walking Cassie down the drive. I whipped my head around and pretended to be staring in the opposite direction, deep in thought, until I heard the door close.

'Nothing new,' Cassie said, leaning in at the car window. 'Peter didn't mention being scared of anyone, or getting hassle from anyone. Smart kid, knew better than to go anywhere with a stranger; a little overconfident, though, which could have got him into trouble. They don't have any suspicions of anybody, except they wondered if it could be the same person who killed Katy. They were sort of upset about that.'

'Aren't we all,' I said.

'They seem like they're doing OK.' I hadn't been able to bring myself to ask this, but I did want, rather badly, to know. 'The father wasn't happy about having to go over it all again, but the mother was lovely. Peter's sister Tara still lives at home; she was asking after you.'

'Me?' I said, feeling an irrational little skip of panic in my stomach.

'She wanted to know if I had any idea how you were doing. I told her the cops had lost track of you, but as far as we knew you were fine.' Cassie gave me a sly grin. 'I think she might have sort of fancied you, back then.'

Tara: a year or two younger than us, sharp elbows and sharp eyes, the kind of kid who was always ferreting out something to tell her mother. Thank God I hadn't gone in there. 'Maybe I should go talk to her after all,' I said. 'Is she good-looking?'

'Just your type: a fine strapping girl with good child-bearing hips. She's a traffic warden.'

'Of course she is,' I said. I was starting to feel better. 'I'll get her to wear her uniform on our first date.'

'Way too much information. OK: Alicia Rowan.' Cassie straightened up and checked her notebook for the house number. 'Want to come?'

It took me a moment to be sure. But we hadn't spent much time at Jamie's house, as far as I remembered. When we were indoors, it was mostly at Peter's – his home was cheerfully noisy, full of brothers and sisters and pets, and his mother baked ginger biscuits, and his parents had bought a TV on hire-purchase and we were allowed to watch cartoons. 'Sure,' I said. 'Why not?'

Alicia Rowan answered the door. She was still beautiful, in a faded, nostalgic way – delicate bones, hollow cheeks, straggling blonde hair and huge, haunted blue eyes – like some forgotten film star whose looks have only gained pathos over time. I saw the small, worn spark of hope and fear light in her eyes when Cassie introduced us, then fade at Katy Devlin's name.

'Yes,' she said, 'yes, of course, that poor little girl . . . Do they – do you think it had something to do . . .? Please, come in.'

As soon as we got inside the house I knew this had been a bad idea. It was the smell of it – a wistful blend of sandalwood and camomile that went straight for my subconscious, setting memories flickering like fish in murky water. Weird bread with bits in it, for tea; a painting of a naked woman, on the landing, that made us elbow and snicker. Hiding in a wardrobe, arms round my knees and flimsy cotton skirts drifting like smoke against my face, 'Forty-nine, fifty!' somewhere in the hall.

She brought us into the sitting-room (hand-woven throws over the sofa, a smiling Buddha in smoky jade on the coffee table: I wondered what 1980s Knocknaree had made of Alicia Rowan) and Cassie did the preliminary spiel. There was – of course; I don't know how I had failed to expect this – a whacking great framed photo of Jamie on the mantelpiece, Jamie sitting on the estate wall squinting into sunlight and laughing, the wood rising all black and green behind her. On either side of it were little framed snapshots and one of them had three figures, elbows hooked around one another's necks, heads tilted together in paper crowns, some Christmas or birthday . . . *I should have grown a beard or something*, I thought wildly, looking away, *Cassie should have given me time to*—

'In our file,' Cassie said, 'the initial report says you called the police saying that your daughter and her friends had run away. Is there any particular reason why you assumed they'd run away, rather than, say, getting lost or having an accident?'

'Well, yes. You see . . . Oh, God.' Alicia Rowan ran her hands through her hair – long, boneless-looking hands. 'I was going to send Jamie to boarding-school, and she didn't want to go. It makes me sound so horribly selfish . . . I suppose I was. But I truly did have my reasons.'

'Ms Rowan,' Cassie said gently, 'we're not here to judge you.'

'Oh, no, I know, I know you're not. But one judges oneself, doesn't one? And you'd really . . . oh, you'd have to know the whole story to understand.'

'We'd be glad to hear the whole story. Anything you can tell us might help.'

Alicia nodded, without much hope; she must have heard those words so many times, over the years. 'Yes. Yes, I see that.'

She drew a deep breath and let it out slowly, eyes closed, over a count of ten. 'Well . . .' she said. 'I was only seventeen when I had Jamie, you see. Her father was a friend of my parents, and very much married, but I was desperately in love with him. And it all felt very sophisticated and daring, having an affair – hotel rooms, you know, and cover stories – and I didn't believe in marriage anyway. I thought it was an outdated form of oppression.'

Her father. He was in the file – George O'Donovan, a Dublin solicitor – but thirty-odd years later she was still shielding him. 'But then you discovered you were pregnant,' Cassie said.

'Yes. He was horrified, and my parents found out the whole story and *they* were horrified. They all said I must give the baby up for adoption, but I wouldn't. I put my foot down. I said I would keep the baby and raise her all by myself. I thought of it as a bit of a blow for women's rights, I think: a rebellion against the patriarchy. I was very young.'

She had been lucky. In Ireland in 1972, women were given life sentences in asylums or Magdalen laundries for far less. 'That was a brave thing to do,' Cassie said.

'Oh, thank you, Detective. Do you know, I think I was quite a brave person, back then. But I wonder if it was the right decision. I used to think – if I had given Jamie up for adoption, you see . . .' Her voice trailed off.

'Did they come round in the end?' Cassie asked. 'Your family and Jamie's father?'

Alicia sighed. 'Well, no. Not really. In the end they said I could keep the baby, as long as we both stayed well out of all their lives. I had disgraced the family, you see; and, of course, Jamie's father didn't want his wife to find out.' There was no anger in her voice, nothing but a simple, sad puzzlement. 'My parents bought me this house – nice and far away; I'm from Dublin originally, from Howth – and gave me a bit of money now and then. I sent Jamie's father letters to tell him how she was getting on, and photographs. I was positive that sooner or later he would come round and want to start seeing her. Maybe he would have. I don't know.'

'And when did you decide she should go to boarding-school?'

Alicia wrapped her fingers in her hair. 'I . . . oh, dear. I don't like thinking about this.'

We waited.

'I had just turned thirty, you see,' she said eventually. 'And I realised I didn't like what I had become. I was waiting tables in a café in town while Jamie was at school, but it really wasn't worth it, with the bus fares, and I had no education so I couldn't get any other job . . . I realised I didn't want to spend the rest of my life like that. I wanted something better, for me and for Jamie. I . . . oh, in many ways I was still a child myself. I'd never had a chance to grow up. And I *wanted* to.'

'And for that,' Cassie said, 'you needed a little time to yourself?'

'Yes. Oh, exactly. You understand.' She squeezed Cassie's arm gratefully. 'I wanted a proper career, so I wouldn't have to rely on my parents, but I didn't know *what* career. I needed a chance to figure it out. And once I did, I knew I would probably have to do some kind of course, and I couldn't simply leave Jamie on her own all the time . . . It would have been different if I'd had a husband, or family. I had a few friends, but I couldn't expect them to—'

She was twisting her hair tighter and tighter around her fingers. 'Makes sense,' Cassie said, matter-of-factly. 'So you had just told Jamie your decision . . .'

'Well, I told her first in May, when I decided. But she took it very badly. I tried to explain, and I brought her up to Dublin to show her around the school, but that only made things worse. She hated it. She said the girls there were all stupid and didn't talk about anything except boys and clothes. Jamie was a bit of a tomboy, you see, she loved being outdoors in the wood all the time; she hated the thought of being cooped up in a city school and having to do exactly what everyone else did. And she didn't want to leave her best friends. She was very close to Adam and Peter – the little boy who vanished with her, you know.' I fought down the impulse to hide my face behind my notebook.

'So you argued.'

'Heavens, yes. Well, really it was more like a *siege* than a battle. Jamie and Peter and Adam absolutely *mutinied*. They sent the entire adult world to Coventry for weeks – wouldn't speak to us parents, wouldn't even look at us, wouldn't speak in class – every bit of homework Jamie did had "Don't send me away" written across the top . . .'

She was right: it had been a mutiny. LET JAMIE STAY, red block letters across squared paper. My mother trying helplessly to reason with me while I sat cross-legged and unresponsive on the sofa, picking at the skin around my fingernails, my stomach squirming with excitement and terror at my own daring. *But we won*, I thought in confusion, *surely we won*: whoops and high-fives on the castle wall, Coke cans raised high in a triumphant toast— 'But you stuck by your decision,' Cassie said.

'Well, not exactly. They did wear me down. It was terribly difficult, you know – all the estate talking about it, and Jamie making it sound as though she were being sent off to the orphanage from *Annie* or somewhere – and I didn't know what to do . . . In the end I said, "Well, I'll think about it." I told them not to worry, we would sort something out, and they called off their protest. I truly did think about waiting another year, but my parents had offered to pay Jamie's school fees, and I couldn't be sure they'd still feel the same way in a year's time. I know this makes me sound like a terrible mother, but I really did think—'

'Not at all,' Cassie said. I shook my head automatically. 'So, when you told Jamie she would be going after all . . .'

'Oh, dear, she just . . .' Alicia twisted her hands together. 'She was devastated. She said I had lied to her. Which I hadn't, you know, really I hadn't . . . And then she stormed out to find the others, and I thought, "Oh, Lord, now they'll stop speaking again, but at least it's only for a week or two" – I had waited until the last minute to tell her, you see, so she could enjoy her summer. And then, when she didn't come home, I assumed . . .'

'You assumed she'd run away,' Cassie said gently. Alicia nodded. 'Do you still feel that's a possibility?'

'No. I don't know. Oh, Detective, one day I think one thing, and the next . . . But there was her piggy bank, you see – she would have taken that, wouldn't she? And Adam was still in the wood. And if they'd run away, surely by now she would have . . . would have . . .'

She turned away sharply, a hand going up to shield her face. 'When it occurred to you that she might not have run away,' Cassie said, 'what was your first thought?'

Alicia did the cleansing-breath thing again, folded her hands tightly in her lap. 'I thought her father might just possibly have . . . I *hoped* he had taken her. He and his wife couldn't have children, you know, so I thought maybe . . . But the detectives looked into it, and they said no.'

'In other words,' Cassie said, 'there was nothing that made you think anyone might have harmed her. She hadn't been scared of anyone, or upset about anything, in the previous weeks.'

'Not really, no. There had been one day – oh, a couple of weeks earlier – when she ran in from playing early, looking a bit shaken up, and she was awfully quiet all evening. I asked her if anything had happened, if anyone had been bothering her, but she said no.'

Something dark leaped in my mind – home early, *No, Mammy, nothing's wrong* – but it was far too deep to catch. 'I did tell the detectives,' Alicia said, 'but that didn't give them very much to go on, did it? And it might have been nothing, after all. She might just have had a little spat with the boys. Perhaps I should have been able to tell whether it was something serious or not . . . But Jamie was quite a reserved child, quite private. It was hard to tell, with her.'

Cassie nodded. 'Twelve's a complicated age.'

'Yes, it is; it really is, isn't it? That was the thing, you see: I don't think I'd realised that she was old enough to – well, to feel so *strongly* about things. But she and Peter and Adam . . . they'd done everything together since they were babies. I don't think they could imagine life without one another.'

The wave of pure outrage blindsided me. *I shouldn't be here*, I thought. *This is utterly fucked up*. I should have been sitting in a garden down the road, barefoot with a drink in my hand, swapping the day's work stories with Peter and Jamie. I had never thought about this before, and it almost knocked me over: all the things we should have had. We should have stayed up all night together studying and stressing out before our Leaving Cert, Peter and I should have argued over who got to bring Jamie to our debs and slagged her about how she looked in her dress. We should have come weaving home together, singing and laughing and inconsiderate, after drunken college nights. We could have shared a flat, taken off Interrailing around Europe, gone arm-in-arm through dodgy fashion phases and low-rent gigs and high-drama love affairs. Two of us might have been married by now, given the other one a godchild. I had been robbed blind. I bent my head over my notebook so that Alicia Rowan and Cassie wouldn't see my face.

'I still keep her bedroom the way she left it,' Alicia said. 'In case – I know it's silly, of course I do, but if she did come home, I wouldn't want her to think . . . Would you like to see it? There might be – the other detectives might have missed something . . .'

A flash of the bedroom slapped me straight across the face – white walls with posters of horses, yellow curtains blowing, a dream-catcher hanging above the bed – and I knew I had had enough. 'I'll wait in the car,' I said. Cassie gave me a quick glance. 'Thank you for your time, Ms Rowan.'

I made it out to the car and put my head down on the steering-wheel until the haze cleared from my eyes. When I looked up I saw a flutter of yellow, and adrenalin spiked through me as a white-blond head moved between the curtains; but it was only Alicia Rowan, turning the little vase of flowers on the windowsill to catch the last of the grey afternoon light.

'The bedroom's eerie,' Cassie said, when we were out of the estate and negotiating the twisting little back roads. 'Pyjamas on the bed and an old paperback open on the floor. Nothing that gave me any ideas, though. Was that you, in the photo on the mantelpiece?'

'Presumably,' I said. I was still feeling like hell; the last thing I wanted to do was analyse Alicia Rowan's decor.

'What she said about Jamie coming in upset one day. Do you remember what that was about?'

'Cassie,' I said, 'we've been through this. Once more, with feeling: I remember sweet shining fuck-all. As far as I'm concerned, my life began when I was twelve and a half and on a ferry to England. OK?'

'Jesus, Ryan. I was just asking.'

'And now you know the answer,' I said, putting the car up a gear. Cassie threw up her hands, switched the radio on to something loud and left me to it.

A couple of miles later I took a hand off the wheel and rumpled Cassie's hair.

'Fuck off, dickface,' she said, without rancour.

I grinned, relieved, and pulled one of her curls. She smacked my hand away. 'Listen, Cass,' I said, 'I need to ask you something.'

She gave me a suspicious look.

'Do you think the two cases are linked, or not? If you had to make a guess.'

Cassie thought about this for a long time, looking out the window at the hedges and the grey sky, clouds chasing fast. 'I don't know, Rob,' she said at last. 'There are things that don't match up. Katy was left where she'd be found right away, while . . . That's a big difference, psychologically. But maybe the guy was haunted by the first time, figured he might feel less guilty if he made sure the family got the body back this time round. And Sam's right: what are the odds of two different child-killers in the same place? If I had to put money on it . . . I honestly don't know.'

I hit the brakes, hard. I think both Cassie and I yelled. Something had darted across the road in front of the car – something dark and low to the ground, with the sinuous gait of a weasel or a stoat, but much too big for either – and disappeared into the overgrown hedge on the other side.

We slammed forward in our seats – I had been going much too fast for a one-lane back road – but Cassie is fanatical about seat-belts, which might have saved her parents' lives, and we were both wearing ours. The car came to a stop skewed at a wild angle across the road, one wheel inches from the ditch. Cassie and I sat still, stunned. On the radio some girl band ululated with insane cheer, on and on.

'Rob?' Cassie said breathlessly, after a minute. 'Are you OK?'

I couldn't make my hands release their grip on the steering-wheel. 'What the hell was that?'

'What?' Her eyes were wide and frightened.

'The animal,' I said. 'What was it?'

Cassie was looking at me with something new in her eyes, something that scared me almost as badly as the creature had. 'I didn't see an animal.'

'It went straight across the road. You must have missed it. You were looking out the side.'

'Yeah,' she said, after what felt like a very long time. 'Yeah, I guess I was. A fox, maybe?'

Sam had found his journalist within a few hours: Michael Kiely, sixty-two and semi-retired after a moderately successful career – he had sort of peaked in the late 80s, when he discovered that a government minister had nine family members on his payroll as 'consultants', and had never quite recaptured those dizzy heights. In 2000, when the plans for the motorway were announced, Kiely had written a snide article suggesting that it had already achieved its primary goal: there were a lot of happy property developers in Ireland that morning. Apart from an oratorical two-column letter from the Minister for the Environment, explaining that this motorway would essentially make everything perfect forever, there had been no follow-up.

It had taken Sam a few days to persuade Kiely to meet him, though – the first time he mentioned Knocknaree, Kiely shouted, 'Do you take me for a fool, boy?' and hung up – and even then, Kiely refused to be seen with him anywhere in town. He made him trek out to a spectacularly downmarket pub somewhere on the far side of Phoenix Park: 'Safer, my boy, so much safer.'

He had a swooping nose and an artfully windswept

mane of white hair – 'sort of poetic-looking,' Sam said, dubiously, over dinner that evening. Sam had bought him a Bailey's and brandy ('Good God,' I said – I had been having a hard time eating anyway; 'Oo,' said Cassie, eyeing her booze shelf speculatively) and tried to bring up the motorway, but Kiely flinched and held up a hand, eyelids fluttering in exquisite pain: 'Your voice, my boy, lower your voice . . . Oh, there's something there, no doubt about it. But someone – no names, no pack drill – someone had me ordered off the story almost before it began. Legal reasons, they said, no proof of anything . . . Absurd. Rubbish. It was purely, poisonously personal. This town, my boy: this dirty old town has a long memory.'

By the second round, though, he had loosened up a little and was in a reflective mood. 'Some might say,' he told Sam, leaning forward in his chair and gesturing expansively, 'some might say *that place* was bad news from the first. So much initial rhetoric, you know, about how it was going to be a new urban hub, and then – after all the houses in that lone estate had been sold – it simply fell through. They said the budget wouldn't allow for any further development. Some might say, my boy, that the only purpose of the rhetoric was to ensure that the houses sold for much more than one might expect of an estate in the middle of nowhere. Not I, of course. I've no *proof*.'

He finished his drink and eyed the empty glass wistfully. 'All I'll say is that there's been something just a *little* off-kilter about that place all along. Do you know, the rate of injuries and fatalities during construction was almost three times the national average? Do you believe, my boy, that a place can have a will of its own – that it can rebel, so to speak, against human mismanagement?'

'Whatever one may say about Knocknaree,' I said, 'it did

not put a fucking plastic bag over Katy Devlin's head.' I was glad Kiely was Sam's problem and not mine. Normally I find this kind of absurdity entertaining, but the way I was feeling that week, I would probably have kicked the guy in the shin.

'What did you say?' Cassie asked Sam.

'I said yes, of course,' he said serenely, trying to wind fettuccine onto his fork. 'I'd've said yes if he'd asked me did I believe little green men were running the country.'

Kiely had drunk his third round – Sam was going to have fun trying to get this one through expenses – in silence, chin sunk on his chest. Finally he had put on his coat, shaken Sam's hand in a long, fervent grasp, murmured, 'Don't look at it until you're in a safe place,' and swept out of the pub, leaving a twist of paper in Sam's palm.

'The poor bastard,' Sam said, rummaging in his wallet. 'I think he was grateful to have someone listen to him for once. The way he is, he could shout a story from the rooftops and no one would believe a word of it.' He extracted something tiny and silver, holding it carefully between finger and thumb, and passed it to Cassie. I put down my fork and leaned in over her shoulder.

It was a piece of silver paper, the kind you pull out of a fresh cigarette packet, rolled into a tight, precise scroll. Cassie opened it out. On the back was written, in crabbed, smudged black felt-tip: 'Dynamo – Kenneth McClintock. Futura – Terence Andrews. Global – Jeffrey Barnes & Conor Roche.'

'Are you sure he's reliable?' I asked.

'Mad as a brush,' Sam said, 'but he's a good reporter, or he used be. I'd say he wouldn't have given me these unless he was sure of them.'

Cassie ran her fingertip over the scrap of paper. 'If these

check out,' she said, 'this is the best lead we've got so far. Fair play, Sam.'

'He got into a car, you know,' Sam said, sounding faintly worried. 'I didn't know whether to let him drive, after all that drink, but . . . I might need to talk to him again, sure; I need to keep him on side. I wonder should I ring and see did he get home OK?'

The next day was Friday, two and a half weeks into the investigation, and early that evening O'Kelly called us into his office. Outside the day was crisp and biting, but sun was streaming through the big windows and the incident room was warm, so that from inside you could almost believe it was still summer. Sam was in his corner, scribbling between hushed phone calls; Cassie was running someone through the computer; I and a couple of floaters had just done a coffee run and were passing out mugs. The room had the intent, busy murmur of a classroom. O'Kelly put his head around the door, stuck a finger-and-thumb circle into his mouth and whistled shrilly; when the murmur died away, he said, 'Ryan, Maddox, O'Neill,' jerked his thumb over his shoulder and slammed the door behind him.

Out of the corner of my eye I could see the floaters exchanging covert eyebrow-raises. We had been expecting this for a couple of days now, or at least I had. I had been rehearsing the scene in my head on the drives to work and in the shower and even in my sleep, waking myself up arguing. 'Tie,' I said to Sam, motioning; his knot always edged its way towards one ear when he was concentrating.

Cassie took a quick swig of her coffee and blew out a breath. 'OK,' she said. 'Let's go.' The floaters went back to whatever they had been doing, but I could feel their eyes following us, all the way out of the room and down the corridor.

'So,' O'Kelly said, as soon as we got into his office. He was already sitting behind his desk, fiddling with some awful chrome executive toy left over from the 80s. 'How's Operation What-d'you-call-it going?'

None of us sat down. We gave him an elaborate exegesis of what we had done to find Katy Devlin's killer, and why it hadn't worked. We were talking too fast and too long, repeating ourselves, going into details he already knew: we could all feel what was coming, and none of us wanted to hear it.

'Sounds like you've all the bases covered, all right,' O'Kelly said, when we finally ran down. He was still playing with his horrible little toy, click click click . . . 'Got a prime suspect?'

'We're leaning towards the parents,' I said. 'One or the other of them.'

'Which means you've nothing solid on either one.'

'We're still investigating, sir,' Cassie said.

'And I've four main men for the threatening phone calls,' Sam said.

O'Kelly glanced up. 'I've read your reports. Watch where you step.'

'Yes, sir.'

'Grand,' O'Kelly said. He put down the chrome thing. 'Keep at it. You don't need thirty-five floaters for that.'

Even though I had been expecting it, it still hit me with a thud. The floaters had never really stopped making me edgy, but all the same: giving them up felt so horribly significant, such an irrevocable first step of retreat. Another few weeks, this meant, and O'Kelly would be putting us back into the rota, giving us new cases, Operation Vestal would become something we worked in scraps of free time; a few months more and Katy would be relegated to the basement and the dust and the cardboard boxes, dragged out every year or two if we got a good new lead. RTÉ would do a cheesy documentary on her, with a breathy voiceover and creepy credit music to make it clear that the case remained unsolved. I wondered whether Kiernan and McCabe had listened to these same words in this room, probably from someone playing with the same pointless toy.

O'Kelly felt the mutiny in our silence. 'What,' he said.

We gave it our best shot, our most earnest, most eloquent prepared speeches, but even as I was speaking I knew it was no good. I prefer not to remember most of what I said; I'm sure by the end I was babbling. 'Sir, we always knew this wasn't going to be a slam-dunk case,' I finished. 'But we're getting there, bit by bit. I really think it would be a mistake to drop it now.'

'Drop it?' O'Kelly demanded, outraged. 'When did you hear me say anything about dropping it? We're dropping nothing. We're scaling back, is all.'

Nobody answered. He leaned forward and steepled his fingers on the desk. 'Lads,' he said, more softly, 'this is simple cost-benefit analysis. You've got the good out of the floaters. How many people have ye left to interview?'

Silence.

'And how many calls did the tip line get today?'

'Five,' Cassie said, after a moment. 'So far.'

'Any of them any good?'

'Probably not.'

'There you go.' O'Kelly spread his hands. 'Ryan, you said yourself this isn't a slam-dunk case. That's just what I'm telling you: there are quick cases and slow cases, and this one'll take time. Meanwhile, though, we've had three new murders since, there's some class of a drug war going on up the north side, and I've people ringing me left and right wanting to know what I'm doing with every floater in Dublin town. Do you see what I'm saying?'

I did, all too well. Whatever else I may say about O'Kelly, I have to give him this: an awful lot of supers would have taken this one away from Cassie and me, right at the beginning. Ireland is still, basically, a small town; usually we have a fair idea whodunit almost from the start, and most of the time and effort goes not into identifying him but into building a case that will stick. Over the first few days, as it became clear that Operation Vestal was going to be an exception and a high-profile one at that, O'Kelly must have been tempted to send us back to our taxi-rank brats and hand it over to Costello or one of the other thirty-year guys. I don't generally think of myself as naïve, but when he hadn't, I had put it down to some stubborn, grudging loyalty – not to us personally, but to us as members of his squad. I had liked the thought. Now I wondered if there might have been more to it than that: if some battle-scarred sixth sense of his had known, all along, that this one was doomed.

'Keep one or two of them,' O'Kelly said, magnanimously. 'For the tip line and legwork and that. Who do you want?'

'Sweeney and O'Gorman,' I said. I had a fairly good handle on the names, by this time, but at that moment those were the only two I could remember.

'Go home,' O'Kelly said. 'Take the weekend off. Go for a few pints, get some sleep – Ryan, your eyes are like piss-holes in the snow. Spend some time with your girlfriends or whatever you've got. Come back on Monday and start fresh.'

Out in the corridor, we didn't look at one another. Nobody made any move to go back to the incident room. Cassie leaned against the wall and scuffed up the carpet pile with the toe of her shoe.

'He's right, in a way,' Sam said finally. 'We'll be grand on our own, so we will.'

'Don't, Sam,' I said. 'Just don't.'

'What?' Sam asked, puzzled. 'Don't what?' I looked away.

'It's the idea of it,' Cassie said. 'We shouldn't be snookered on this case. We've the body, the weapon, the . . . We should *have* someone by now.'

'Well,' I said, 'I know what I'm going to do. I am going to find the nearest non-horrible pub and get absolutely legless. Anyone joining me?'

We went to Doyle's, in the end: overamplified 80s music and too few tables, suits and students shouldering at the bar. None of us had any desire to go to a police pub where, inevitably, everyone we met would want to know how Operation Vestal was going. On about the third round, as I was coming back from the jacks, I bumped elbows with a girl and her drink splashed over, splattering us both. It was her fault – she had reared back laughing at something one of her friends had said, and knocked straight into me – but she was extremely pretty, the tiny ethereal type I always go for, and she gave me a soft appreciative look while we were both apologising and comparing damage, so I bought her another drink and struck up a conversation.

Her name was Anna and she was doing a Master's in art history; she had a cascade of fair hair that made me think of warm beaches, and one of those floaty white cotton skirts, and a waist I could have got my hands around. I told her I was a professor of literature, over from a university in England to do research on Bram Stoker. She sucked on the rim of her glass and laughed at my jokes, showing little white teeth with an engaging overbite.

Behind her, Sam grinned and raised an eyebrow and Cassie did a panting, puppy-eyed impression of me, but I didn't care. It had been a ridiculously long time since I had slept with anyone and I badly wanted to go home with this girl, sneak giggling into some student flat with art posters on the walls, wind that extravagant hair round my fingers and let my mind shimmer into blankness, lie in her sweet safe bed all night and most of tomorrow and not once think about either of these fucking cases. I put a hand on Anna's shoulder to guide her out of the way of a guy precariously manoeuvring four pints, and gave Cassie and Sam the finger behind her back.

The tide of people threw us closer and closer. We had got off the subject of our respective studies – I wished I knew more about Bram Stoker – and were onto the Aran Islands (Anna and a bunch of friends, the previous summer; the beauties of nature; the joy of escaping urban life in all its superficiality), and she had started touching my wrist to emphasise her points, when one of her friends detached himself from the howling group and came over to stand behind her.

'You all right, Anna?' he demanded ominously, putting an arm around her waist and giving me a bullocky stare.

Out of his line of vision, Anna rolled her eyes at me, with a conspiratorial little smile. 'Everything's *fine*, Cillian,' she said. I didn't think he was her boyfriend – she hadn't been acting taken, at any rate – but if he wasn't then he clearly wanted to be. He was a big guy, handsome in a heavy-set way; he had obviously been drinking for some time and was itching for an excuse to invite me to take it outside.

For a moment I actually considered it. *You heard the lady, pal, go back to your little buddies . . .* I glanced over at Sam and Cassie: they had given up on me and were deep in an intent conversation, heads bent close to hear through the noise, Sam illustrating something with a finger on the table. I was suddenly, viciously sick of myself and my professorial alter ego, and, by association, of Anna and whatever game she was playing with me and this Cillian guy. 'I should get back to my girlfriend,' I said, 'sorry again for spilling your drink,' and turned away from the startled pink O of her mouth and the confused, reflexive flare of belligerence in Cillian's eyes.

I slipped my arm around Cassie's shoulders for a moment as I sat down, and she gave me a suspicious look. 'Get shot down?' Sam asked.

'Nah,' said Cassie. 'I'm betting he changed his mind and told her he had a girlfriend. Hence the touchy-feely stuff. Next time you pull that one, Ryan, I'm gonna snog the face off Sam and let your lady friend's mates beat you up for messing with her head.'

'Deadly,' Sam said happily. 'I like this game.'

At closing time, Cassie and I went back to her flat. Sam had gone home, it was a Friday and we didn't have to get up the next morning; there seemed no reason to do anything but lie on the sofa, drinking and occasionally changing the music and letting the fire burn down to a whispering glow.

'You know,' said Cassie idly, fishing a piece of ice out of

her glass to chew on, 'what we've been forgetting is that kids think differently.'

'What are you on about?' We had been talking about Shakespeare, something to do with the fairies in *A Midsummer Night's Dream*, and my mind was still there. I half-thought she was going to come up with some late-night analogy between the way children think and the way people thought in the sixteenth century, and I was already preparing a rebuttal.

'We've been wondering how he got her to the kill site – no, knock it off and listen.' I was shoving at her leg with my foot and whining, 'Shut up, I'm off duty, I can't hear you, la la la . . .' I was hazy with vodka and lateness and I had decided I was sick of this frustrating, tangled, intractable case. I wanted to talk about Shakespeare some more, or maybe play cards. 'When I was eleven a guy tried to molest me,' Cassie said.

I stopped kicking and lifted my head to look at her. 'What?' I said, a little too carefully. This, I thought, this, finally, was Cassie's secret locked room, and I was at last going to be invited in.

She glanced over at me, amused. 'No, he didn't actually do anything to me. It was no big deal.'

'Oh,' I said, feeling silly and, obscurely, a little miffed. 'What happened, then?'

'Our school was going through this craze for marbles – everyone played marbles all the time, all through lunch, after school. You carried them around in a plastic bag and it was a big thing, how many you had. So this one day I'd been kept after school—'

'You? I'm astounded,' I said. I rolled over and found my glass. I wasn't sure where this story was going.

'Fuck off; just because you were Prefect Perfect. Anyway I was leaving, and one of the staff – not a teacher; a groundskeeper or a cleaning guy or something – came out of this little shed and said, "Do you want marbles? Come on in here and I'll give you marbles." He was an old guy, maybe sixty, with white hair and a big moustache. So I sort of edged around the door of the shed for a while, and then I went in.'

'God, Cass. You silly, silly thing,' I said. I took another sip, put down my glass and pulled her feet into my lap to rub them.

'No, I told you, nothing happened. He went behind me and put his hands through under my arms, like he was going to lift me up, only then he started messing with the buttons on my shirt. I said, "What are you doing?" and he said, "I keep my marbles up on that shelf. I'm going to pick you up so you can get them." I knew something was very badly wrong, even though I had no idea what, so I twisted away and said, "I don't want any marbles," and legged it home.'

'You were lucky,' I said. She had slim, high-arched feet; even through the soft thick socks she wore at home, I could feel the tendons, the small bones moving under my thumbs. I pictured her at eleven, all knees and bitten nails and solemn brown eyes.

'Yeah, I was. God knows what could've happened.'

'Did you tell anyone?' I still wanted more from the story; I wanted to extract some rending revelation, some terrible, shameful secret.

'No. I felt too icky about the whole thing, and anyway I didn't even know what to tell. That's the point: it never occurred to me that it had anything to do with sex. I *knew* about sex, my friends and I talked about it all the *time*, I knew something was wrong, I knew he was trying to undo my shirt, but I never put it together. Years later, when I was like eighteen, something reminded me of it – I saw some kids playing marbles, or something – and it suddenly hit me: Oh my God, that guy was trying to *molest* me!'

'And this has what to do with Katy Devlin?' I asked.

'Kids don't connect things in the same ways grown-ups do,' said Cassie. 'Give me your feet and I'll do them.'

'I wouldn't. Can't you see the smell-waves off my socks?'

'God, you're disgusting. Don't you ever change them?'

'When they stick to the wall. In accordance with bachelor tradition.'

'That's not tradition. That's reverse evolution.'

'Go on, then,' I said, unfolding my feet and shoving them at her.

'No. Get a girlfriend.'

'What are you wittering about now?'

'Girlfriends aren't allowed to care if you have Stilton socks. Friends are.' All the same, she gave her hands a quick, professional shake and took hold of my foot. 'Plus, you might be less of a pain in the arse if you got more action.'

'Look who's talking,' I said, realising as I spoke that I had no idea how much action Cassie got. There had been a semi-serious boyfriend before I knew her, a barrister called Aidan, but he had somehow faded from the scene around the time she joined Drugs; relationships seldom survive undercover work. Obviously I would have known if she'd had a boyfriend since, and I like to think I would have known if she'd even been dating someone, whatever that means, but beyond that I had no idea. I had always assumed that was because there was nothing to know, but suddenly I wasn't sure. I glanced encouragingly at

Cassie, but she was kneading my heel and giving me her best enigmatic smile.

'The other thing,' she said, 'is why I went in there in the first place.' Cassie has a mind like a cloverleaf flyover: it can spin off in wildly divergent directions and then, by some Escherian defiance of dimension, swoop dizzily back to the crux. 'It wasn't just for the marbles. He had this very thick country accent, Midlands I think, and it sounded like he might have said, "Do you want marvels?" I mean, I knew he *hadn't*, I knew he'd said "marbles", but a part of me thought just maybe he was one of those mysterious old men out of stories, and inside the shed would be shelves and shelves of scrying-glasses and potions and ancient parchments and tiny dragons in cages. I *knew* it was only a shed and he was only a groundskeeper, but at the same time I thought this might just be my chance to be one of the children who go through the wardrobe into the other world, and I couldn't stand the thought of spending the rest of my life knowing I'd missed it.'

How can I ever make you understand Cassie and me? I would have to take you there, walk you down every path of our secret shared geography. The truism says it's against all the odds for a straight man and woman to be real friends, platonic friends; we rolled thirteen, threw down five aces and ran away giggling. She was the summertime cousin out of storybooks, the one you taught to swim at some midge-humming lake and pestered with tadpoles down her swimsuit, with whom you practised first kisses on a heather hillside and laughed about it years later over a clandestine joint in your granny's cluttered attic. She painted my fingernails gold and dared me to leave them that way for work. I told Quigley that she thought Croke

Park stadium should be turned into a shopping centre, and watched her try to decipher his outraged splutter. She cut up the packaging of her new mouse mat and stuck the part that said TOUCH ME – FEEL THE DIFFERENCE to the back of my shirt, and I wore it half the day before I noticed. We climbed out her window and down the fire escape and lay on the roof of the extension below, drinking improvised cocktails and singing Tom Waits and watching the stars spin dizzily around us.

No. These are stories I like to think about, small bright currency and not without value; but above all that and underlying everything we did, she was my partner. I don't know how to tell you what that word, even now, does to me; what it means. I could tell you about going room by room, guns two-handed at arm's length, through silent houses where a suspect could be armed and waiting behind any door; or about long nights on surveillance, sitting in a dark car drinking black coffee from a thermos and trying to play gin rummy by the light of a street lamp. Once we chased two hit-and-run joyriders through their own territory – graffiti and rubbish-dump wastelands whipping past the windows, sixty miles per hour, seventy, I floored it and stopped looking at the speedometer – until they spun into a wall, and then we held the sobbing fifteen-year-old driver between us, promising him that his mother and the ambulance would be there soon, while he died in our arms. In a notorious tower block that would redraw the outlines of your image of humanity, a junkie pulled a syringe on me – we weren't even interested in him, it was his brother we were after, and the conversation had seemed to be proceeding along normal lines until his hand moved too fast and suddenly there was a needle against my throat. While I stood frozen and sweating and wildly praying that neither of us would sneeze, Cassie sat down cross-legged on the reeking carpet, offered the guy a cigarette and talked to him for an hour and twenty minutes (in the course of which he demanded, variously, our wallets, a car, a fix, a Sprite and to be left alone); talked to him so matter-of-factly and with such frank interest that finally he dropped the syringe and slid down the wall to sit across from her, and he was starting to tell her his life story when I got my hands under control enough to slap the cuffs on him.

The girls I dream of are the gentle ones, wistful by high windows or singing sweet old songs at a piano, long hair drifting, tender as apple blossom. But a girl who goes into battle beside you and keeps your back is a different thing, a thing to make you shiver. Think of the first time you slept with someone, or the first time you fell in love: that blinding explosion that left you crackling to the fingertips with electricity, initiated and transformed. I tell you that was nothing, nothing at all, beside the power of putting your lives, simply and daily, into each other's hands.

11

That weekend I went over to my parents' house for Sunday dinner. I do this every few weeks, although I'm not really sure why. We're not close; the best we can do is a mutual state of amicable and faintly puzzled politeness, like people who met on a package holiday and can't figure out how to end the connection. Sometimes I bring Cassie with me. My parents love her – she teases my father about his gardening, and sometimes when she helps my mother in the kitchen I hear my mother laugh, full-throated and happy as a girl – and drop hopeful little hints about how close we are, which we cheerfully ignore.

'Where's Cassie today?' my mother asked after dinner. She had made macaroni and cheese – she has some idea that this is my favourite dish (which it may well have been, at some point in my life) and she cooks it, as a small timid expression of sympathy, whenever something in the papers indicates that a case of mine isn't going well. Even the smell of it makes me claustrophobic and itchy. She and I were in the kitchen; I was washing up and she was drying. My father was in the sitting-room, watching a Columbo movie on TV. The kitchen was dim and we had the light on, though it was only mid-afternoon.

'I think she went to her aunt and uncle's,' I said. Actually, Cassie was probably curled up on her · sofa, reading and eating ice-cream out of the carton – we hadn't had much time to ourselves, the last couple of weeks, and Cassie, like me, needs a certain amount of solitude – but I knew it would upset my mother, the thought of her spending a Sunday alone.

'That'll be nice for her: a bit of minding. The pair of you must be shattered.'

'We're pretty tired,' I said.

'All that back and forth to Knocknaree.'

My parents and I don't talk about my work, except in the most general terms, and we never mention Knocknaree. I looked up sharply, but my mother was tilting a plate to the light to look for wet streaks.

'It's a long drive, all right,' I said.

'I read in the paper,' my mother said carefully, 'that the police were talking to Peter and Jamie's families again. Was that yourself and Cassie?'

'Not the Savages. I talked to Ms Rowan, though, yes. Does this look clean to you?'

'It's grand,' my mother said, taking the baking dish out of my hand. 'How's Alicia now?'

There was something in her voice that made me look up again, startled. She caught my gaze and flushed, wiping hair away from her cheek with the back of her wrist. 'Ah, we used be great friends. Alicia was . . . well, I suppose she was almost like a little sister to me. We got out of touch, after. I was just wondering how she was, is all.'

I had a fast, queasy flash of retrospective panic: if I had known that Alicia Rowan and my mother had been close, I would never have gone near that house. 'I think she's all right,' I said. 'As much as one could expect. She still has Jamie's room the way it was.'

My mother clicked her tongue unhappily. We washed up in silence for some time: clink of cutlery, Peter Falk cunningly interrogating someone in the next room. Outside the window, a pair of magpies landed on the grass and started picking over the tiny garden, discussing it raucously as they went.

'Two for joy,' my mother said automatically, and sighed. 'I suppose I've never forgiven myself for losing touch with Alicia. She'd no one else. She was such a sweet girl, a real innocent – she was still hoping Jamie's father would leave his wife, after all that time, and they'd be a family . . . Did she ever marry?'

'No. But she doesn't seem unhappy, really. She teaches yoga.' The suds in the basin had turned lukewarm and clammy; I reached for the kettle and added more hot water.

'That's one reason we moved away, you know,' my mother said. She had her back to me, sorting cutlery into a drawer. 'I couldn't face them – Alicia and Angela and Joseph. I had my son back safe and sound, and they were going through hell . . . I could hardly go out of the house, in case I'd meet them. I know it sounds mad, but I felt guilty. I thought they must hate me for having you safe. I don't see how they could help it.'

This took me aback. I suppose all children are self-centred; it had never occurred to me, at any rate, that the move might have been for anyone's benefit but my own. 'I never really thought about that,' I said. 'Selfish brat that I was.'

'You were a little dote,' my mother said, unexpectedly. 'The most affectionate child that ever lived. When you came in from school or playing, you'd always give me a massive hug and a kiss – even when you were almost as big as me – and say, "Did you miss me, Mammy?" Half the time you'd have something for me, a pretty stone or a flower. I still have most of them kept.'

'Me?' I was glad I hadn't brought Cassie. I could practically see the wicked glint in her eye if she'd heard this.

'Yes, you. That's why I was so worried when we couldn't find you that day.' She gave my arm a sudden, almost violent little squeeze; even after all these years, I heard the strain in her voice. 'I was panicking, you know. Everyone was saying, "Sure, they've only run away from home, children do that, we'll have them found in no time . . ." But I said, "No. Not Adam." You were a sweet boy; kind. I knew you wouldn't do that to us.'

Hearing the name cast in her voice sent something through me, something fast and primeval and dangerous. 'I don't remember myself as a particularly angelic child,' I said.

My mother smiled, out the kitchen window; the abstracted look on her face, remembering things I didn't, made me edgy. 'Ah, not angelic. But thoughtful. You were growing up fast, that year. You made Peter and Jamie stop tormenting that poor wee boy, what was his name? The one with the glasses and the awful mammy who did the flowers for the church?'

'Willy Little?' I said. 'That wasn't me, that was Peter. I would have been perfectly happy to go on tormenting him till the cows came home.'

'No, that was you,' my mother said firmly. 'The three of you did something or other that made him cry, and it upset you so badly, you decided you'd have to leave the poor boy alone. You were worried that Peter and Jamie wouldn't understand. Do you not remember?'

'Not really,' I said. Actually, this bothered me more than anything in this whole uncomfortable conversation. You'd think I'd have preferred her version of the story to my own, but I didn't. It was entirely possible, of course, that she had unconsciously recast me as the hero, or that I had done it myself, lied to her at the time; but over the past few weeks I had come to think of my memories as solid, shining little things, to be hunted out and treasured, and it was deeply unsettling to think that they might be fool's gold, tricky and fog-shaped and not at all what they seemed. 'If there aren't any more dishes, I should probably go in and talk to Dad for a while.'

'He'll like that. Off you go – I can finish up here. Bring a couple of cans of Guinness with you; they're in the fridge.'

'Thanks for the dinner,' I said. 'It was delicious.'

'Adam,' my mother said suddenly, as I turned to leave; and that swift treacherous thing hit me under the breast-bone again, and oh God how I wanted to be that sweet child for one more moment, how I wanted to spin round and bury my face in her warm toast-smelling shoulder and tell her through great tearing sobs what these last weeks had been. I thought of what her face would look like if I actually did it, and bit my cheek hard to keep back an insane crack of laughter.

'I just wanted you to know,' she said timidly, twisting the dishcloth in her hands. 'We did our best for you, after. Sometimes I worry that we did it all wrong . . . But we were afraid that whoever had – you know – that whoever it was would come back and . . . We were just trying to do what would be best for you.'

'I know, Mum,' I said. 'It's fine,' and, with the sensation of some huge and narrow escape, I went out to the sitting-room to watch Columbo with my father.

'How's work treating you?' my father said, during an ad break. He rummaged down the side of a cushion for the remote control and lowered the sound on the TV.

'Fine,' I said. On the screen, a small child sitting on a toilet was conversing vehemently with a green, fanged cartoon creature surrounded by vapour trails.

'You're a good lad,' my father said, staring at the TV as if mesmerised by this. He took a swig from his can of Guinness. 'You've always been a good lad.'

'Thanks,' I said. Clearly he and my mother had had some kind of conversation about me, in preparation for this afternoon, although for the life of me I couldn't figure out what it might have entailed.

'And work's all right for you.'

'Yes. Fine.'

'That's grand, so,' my father said, and turned the volume up again.

I got back to the apartment around eight. I went into the kitchen and started making myself a sandwich, ham and Heather's low-fat cheese – I'd forgotten to go shopping. The Guinness had left me bloated and uncomfortable – I'm not a beer drinker, but my father gets worried if I ask for anything else; he considers men drinking spirits to be a sign of either incipient alcoholism or incipient homosexuality – and I had some hazy paradoxical idea that eating something would soak up the beer and make me feel better. Heather was in the sitting-room. Her Sunday evenings are devoted to something she calls 'Me Time', a process involving *Sex and the City* DVDs, a wide variety of mystifying implements and a lot of bustling between the bathroom and the sitting-room with a look of grim, righteous determination.

My phone beeped. Cassie: *Give me a lift 2 court 2moro? Grown-up clothes + golf cart + weather = very bad look.*

'Oh, *shit*,' I said aloud. The Kavanagh case, an old

woman beaten to death in Limerick during a break-in, sometime the year before: Cassie and I were giving evidence first thing in the morning. The prosecutor had been in to prep us, and we'd reminded each other on Friday and everything, but I'd promptly managed to forget all about it.

'What's wrong?' Heather piped eagerly, hurrying out of the sitting-room at the prospect of an opening for conversation. I threw the cheese back into the fridge and slammed the door on it, not that that would do much good: Heather knows to a millimetre how much of everything she has left, and once sulked till I bought her a new bar of fancy organic soap because I'd come in drunk and washed my hands with hers. 'Are you all right?' She was in her dressing-gown, with what looked like cling-film wrapped around her head, and she smelled of a headache-inducing array of flowery, chemical things.

'Yeah, fine,' I said. I hit Reply and started texting Cassie back: *As opposed to what? See you at 8.30ish.* 'I just forgot I'm in court tomorrow.'

'Uh-oh,' said Heather, widening her eyes. Her nails were a tasteful pale pink; she waved them around to dry them. 'I could help you get ready. Go over your notes with you, or something.'

'No, thanks.' Actually, I didn't even have my notes. They were somewhere at work. I wondered whether I should drive in and get them, but I told myself I was probably still over the limit.

'Oh . . . OK. That's all right.' Heather blew on her nails and peered at my sandwich. 'Oh, did you go shopping? It's actually your turn to buy toilet bleach, you know.'

'I'm going tomorrow,' I said, gathering up my phone and my sandwich and heading for my room.

'Oh. Well, I suppose it can wait till then. Is that my cheese?'

I extricated myself from Heather – not without difficulty – and ate my sandwich, which unsurprisingly didn't undo the effects of the Guinness. Then I poured myself a vodka and tonic, following the same general logic, and lay on my back on the bed to run through the Kavanagh case in my mind.

I couldn't focus. All the peripheral details bounced into my head promptly, vividly and uselessly – the flickering red light of the Sacred Heart statue in the victim's dark sitting-room, the two teenage killers' stringy little fringes, the awful clotted hole in the victim's head, the damp-stained flowery wallpaper in the B&B where Cassie and I had stayed – but I couldn't remember a single important fact: how we had tracked down the suspects or whether they had confessed or what they had stolen, or even their names. I got up and walked around my room, stuck my head out of the window for some cold air, but the harder I tried to concentrate, the less I remembered. After a while I couldn't even be positive whether the victim's name was Philomena or Fionnuala, although a couple of hours earlier I had known it without having to think (Philomena Mary Bridget).

I was stunned. Nothing like this had ever happened to me before. I think I can say, without flattering myself, that I've always had an ironically good memory, the parroty kind that can absorb and regurgitate large amounts of information without much effort or understanding. This is how I managed to pass my A levels, and also why I hadn't freaked out too badly at the realisation that I didn't have my notes – I'd forgotten to go over them before, once or twice, and never been caught out.

And it wasn't as if I were trying to do anything particularly out of the ordinary, after all. In Murder you get used to juggling three or four investigations at once. If you pull a child murder or a dead cop or something high-priority like that, you can hand off your open cases, the way we'd handed off the taxi-rank thing to Quigley and McCann, but you still have to deal with all the aftermath of the closed ones: paperwork, meetings with prosecutors, court dates. You develop a knack for filing away all the salient facts at the back of your mind, ready to whip out at any moment if you should need them. The basics of the Kavanagh case should have been there, and the fact that they weren't sent me into a silent, animal panic.

About two o'clock I became convinced that, if I could just get a good night's sleep, everything would fall into place in the morning. I had another shot of vodka and turned off the light, but every time I closed my eyes the images zipped around my head in a frenetic, unstoppable procession – Sacred Heart, greasy perpetrators, head wound, creepy B&B . . . Around four, I suddenly realised what a cretin I had been not to go pick up my notes. I switched on the light and fumbled blindly for my clothes, but as I was tying my shoes I noticed my hands wobbling and remembered the vodka – I was definitely not in the right form for smooth-talking my way out of a breathalyser – and then slowly became aware that I was way too fuzzy to make any sense of my notes even if I had them.

I went back to bed and stared at the ceiling some more. Heather and the guy in the next flat snored in syncopation; every now and then a car went past the gates of the complex, sending grey-white searchlights arcing across my walls. After a while I remembered my migraine tablets and took two of them, on the grounds that they always knock me out – I tried not to consider the possibility that this might be a side effect of the migraines themselves. I finally fell asleep around seven, just in time for my alarm.

When I beeped my horn outside Cassie's, she ran down wearing her one respectable outfit – a chic little Chanel trouser suit, black with rose-pink lining, and her grandmother's pearl earrings – and bounced into the car with what I considered an unnecessary amount of energy, although she was probably just in a hurry to get out of the drizzle. 'Hi, you,' she said. She was wearing make-up; it made her look older and sophisticated, unfamiliar. 'No sleep?'

'Not much. Do you have your notes?'

'Yeah. You can have a look at them while I'm in – who's up first, actually, me or you?'

'I can't remember. Will you drive? I need to go over this.'

'I'm not insured on this thing,' she said, eyeing the Land Rover with disdain.

'So don't hit anyone.' I clambered woozily out of the car and went round to the other side, rain splattering off my head, while Cassie shrugged and slid into the driver's seat. She has nice handwriting – faintly foreign-looking, somehow, but firm and clear – and I am very used to it, but I was so tired and hung over that her notes didn't even look like words. All I could see was random, indecipherable squiggles arranging and rearranging themselves on the page as I watched, like some kind of bizarre Rorschach test. In the end I fell asleep, my head juddering gently off the cool window-pane.

I was, of course, first on the stand. I really don't have the heart to go into the dozen ways in which I made a fool of myself: stammering, mixing up names, screwing up timelines and having to go back and painstakingly correct myself from the beginning. The prosecutor, MacSharry, looked confused at first (we'd known each other a while, and normally I am pretty good on the stand), then alarmed and finally furious, under the urbane veneer. He had this huge blown-up photo of Philomena Kavanagh's body – it's a standard trick, try to horrify the jury into needing to punish someone, and I was vaguely surprised that the judge had allowed it in – and I was supposed to point out each injury and match it to what the suspects had said in their confessions (apparently they had, in fact, confessed). But for some reason it was the final straw. It vaporised what little composure I had left: every time I looked up I saw her, heavy and battered, skirt rucked up around her waist, mouth open in a powerless howl of reproach at me for letting her down.

The courtroom was like a sauna, steam from drying coats fogging the windows; my scalp prickled with heat and I could feel droplets of sweat sliding down my ribs. By the time the defence attorney finished cross-examining me he had a look of incredulous, almost indecent glee, like a teenager who's managed to get into a girl's knickers when the most he hoped for was a kiss. Even the jury – shifting, shooting one another covert sideways looks – seemed embarrassed for me.

I came off the stand shaking all over. My legs felt like jelly; for a second I thought I was going to have to grab at a railing to stay upright. You're allowed to watch the trial after you've finished giving evidence, and Cassie would be surprised not to see me there, but I couldn't do it. She didn't need moral support: she would do just fine, and childish as it sounds this made me feel even worse. I knew the Devlin case was bothering her, and Sam too, but both of them were managing to keep on top of things without even seeming to put much effort into it. I was the only one who was twitching and gibbering and spooking at shadows like a bit part in *One Flew Over the Cuckoo's Nest*. I didn't think I could bear to sit in the courtroom and watch Cassie matter-of-factly, unconsciously, clean up the mess I had made of several months' work.

It was still raining. I found an uncompromisingly dingy little pub down a side-street – three guys at a corner table pegged me as a cop with one glance and shifted seamlessly to a new topic of conversation – ordered a hot whiskey and sat down. The barman thumped my drink in front of me and went back to the racing pages without volunteering my change. I took a long swallow, burning the roof of my mouth, leaned my head back and closed my eyes.

The dodgy guys in the corner had moved on to someone's ex-girlfriend. 'So I says to her, there's nothing in the support order about dressing him like P fucking Diddy, if you want him to wear Nikes you can bleeding buy them yourself. . . .' They were eating toasted sandwiches; the salty, chemical smell made me feel sick. Outside the window the rain bucketed down a gutter.

Strange though it may seem, I had only just realised, up there on the stand with the flare of panic in MacSharry's eyes, that I was falling apart. I had been aware that I was sleeping less than usual and drinking more, that I was snappy and distracted and possibly sort of seeing things, but no specific incident had seemed particularly ominous or alarming in itself. It was only now that the whole pattern rose up and swooped at me, violently, garishly clear, and it scared me to death.

All my instincts were shrieking at me to get off this horrible, treacherous case, get as far away from it as possible. I was owed quite a lot of holiday time, I could use some of my savings to rent a little apartment in Paris or Florence for a few weeks, walk on cobblestones and spend all day listening peacefully to a language I didn't understand and not come back until the whole thing was over. But I knew, with dreary certainty, that this was impossible. It was too late to pull out of the investigation; I could hardly tell O'Kelly that it had suddenly dawned on me, weeks into the case, that I was actually Adam Ryan, and any other excuse would imply that I'd lost my nerve and would basically end my career. I knew I needed to do something, before people started noticing that I was going to pieces and the little men in white coats rolled up to take me away, but I could not for the life of me think of one single thing that would do the slightest bit of good.

I finished my hot whiskey and ordered another. The barman turned on snooker on the TV; the commentator's low, genteel murmur blended soothingly with the rain. The three guys left, slamming the door behind them, and I heard a burst of raucous laughter from outside. Eventually the barman cleared away my glass sort of pointedly, and I realised that he wanted me to leave.

I went to the bathroom and splashed water on my face. In the greenish, dirt-flecked mirror I looked like something out of a zombie film – mouth open, huge dark bags under my eyes, hair standing up in spiky tufts. *This is ridiculous*, I thought, with a horrible rush of dizzy, detached amazement. *How did this happen? How the hell did I end up here?*

I went back to the courthouse parking lot and sat in the car, eating Polo mints and watching people hurry by with their heads down and their coats pulled tight. It was dark as evening, rain slanting through dipped headlights, street lamps already on. Finally my phone beeped. Cassie: *Whatsastory? Where are you?* I texted back, *In car*, and reached over to flip on the tail lights so she could find me. When she saw me in the passenger seat, she did a little double take and ran round to the other side.

'Sheesh,' she said, wriggling behind the wheel and shaking rain out of her hair. A drop had got caught in her eyelashes and a black mascara tear trickled to her cheekbone, making her look like a modish little Pierrette. 'I'd forgotten what a pair of wankstains they are. They started snickering when I talked about them pissing on her bed; their lawyer was making faces at them to try and shut them up. What happened to you? Why am I driving?'

'I have a migraine,' I said. Cassie was flipping down the sun-visor to check her make-up, but her hand stopped short and her eyes, round and apprehensive, met mine in the mirror. 'I think I fucked up, Cass.'

She would have heard anyway. MacSharry would be on the phone to O'Kelly as soon as he got a chance, and by the end of the day it would be all round the squad. I was so tired I was almost dreaming; for a moment I allowed myself to wonder, wistfully, whether this might actually be some vodka-induced nightmare from which I would wake to my alarm and my appointment in court.

'How bad is it?' she asked.

'I'm pretty sure I made an utter balls of it. I couldn't even see straight, never mind think straight.' This was, after all, true.

She slowly angled the mirror into place, licked her finger and rubbed away the Pierrette teardrop. 'I meant the migraine. Do you need to go home?'

I thought longingly of my bed, hours of undisturbed sleep before Heather came home and wanted to know where her toilet bleach was, but the thought soured quickly: I would only end up lying there rigidly, hands clenched on the sheets, going over and over the courtroom in my head. 'No. I took my tablets once I got out. It's not one of the bad ones.'

'Should I find a pharmacy or have you got enough to last you?'

'I have plenty, but it's better already. Let's go.' I was tempted to go into more detail about the horrors of my imaginary migraine, but the whole art of lying is knowing when to stop, and I've always had sort of a flair for this. I had no idea, and still don't, whether Cassie believed me. She reversed out of the parking space in a swift, dramatic curve, rain skidding off the windshield wipers, and nudged her way into the traffic.

'How did you get on?' I asked suddenly, as we inched down the quays.

'OK. I get the feeling their lawyer's trying to claim the confessions were coerced, but the jury'll never buy it.'

'Good,' I said. 'That's good.'

My phone leapt into hysterical life almost the instant we reached the incident room. O'Kelly, telling me to get into his office; MacSharry hadn't wasted much time. I gave him the migraine story. The one joy of migraines is that they make a perfect excuse: they're disabling, they're not your fault, they can last as long as you need them to and nobody can prove you don't have one. At least I really did look sick. O'Kelly made a few derisive comments about headaches being 'womany shite', but I regained a little of his respect by bravely insisting on staying in work.

I went back to the incident room. Sam was just getting in from somewhere, soaked through, his tweed overcoat smelling faintly of wet dog. 'How'd it go?' he asked. His tone was casual, but his eyes slid to me, over Cassie's shoulder, and then quickly away again: the grapevine had already been doing its thing.

'Fine. Migraine,' Cassie said, tilting her head at me. By this stage I was starting to feel as if I really did have a migraine. I blinked, trying to focus.

'The old migraine's a terrible man,' Sam said. 'My mammy gets them. Sometimes she has to lie in a dark room for days, with ice on her head. Are you all right to be working?'

'I'm fine,' I said. 'What have you been up to?'

Sam glanced at Cassie. 'He's OK,' she said. 'That trial would give anyone a headache. Where've you been?'

He peeled off his dripping coat, gave it a doubtful look and discarded it on a chair. 'I went and had little chats with the Big Four.'

'O'Kelly's going to love that,' I said. I sat down and pressed my temples between finger and thumb. 'I should warn you, he's not in the best of moods as it is.'

'No, it's grand. I told them the protesters had been giving a few of the motorway brigade some hassle – I didn't get specific, but I've a feeling they may think I meant vandalism – and I was just checking that they were all right.' Sam grinned, and I realised he was bursting with excitement about his day and was keeping it contained only because he knew about mine. 'They all got fierce jumpy about how I knew they were involved with Knocknaree, but I acted like it was no big deal – had a little chat, made sure none of them had been targeted by the protesters, told them to mind themselves and left. Not one of them even thanked me, do you believe that? Right bunch of charmers, this lot.'

'So?' I enquired. 'I think we all assumed that much.' I didn't mean to be snotty, not really, but every time I closed my eyes I saw Philomena Kavanagh's body, and every time I opened them I saw the crime-scene shots of Katy all over the whiteboard behind Sam's head, and I really wasn't in the mood for him and his results and his tact.

'So,' Sam said, unfazed, 'Ken McClintock – the boy behind Dynamo – was in Singapore all through April; that's where all the cool property developers are hanging out this year, don't you know. That's one down: he wasn't making any anonymous calls from Dublin phones. And remember what Devlin said about your man's voice?'

'Nothing particularly useful, as I recall,' I said.

'Not very deep,' said Cassie, 'country accent, but nothing distinctive. Probably middle-aged.' She was reared back in her chair, knees crossed, arms folded negligently behind her; in her elegant court get-up she looked almost deliberately incongruous in the incident room, like something out of some clever avant-garde fashion shoot.

'Spot on. Now Conor Roche from Global, he's a Corkman, accent you could cut with a knife – Devlin would have spotted it straight off. And his partner, Jeff Barnes, he's English, and he's got a voice like a bear besides. That leaves us with' – Sam circled the name on the whiteboard, with a deft, happy flourish – 'Terence Andrews of Futura, fifty-three, from Westmeath, squeaky little tenor voice on him. And guess where he lives?'

'Town,' Cassie said, starting to smile.

'Penthouse apartment on the quays. He drinks in the Gresham – I told him to mind himself walking back, you never know with these left-wing types – and all three payphones are directly on his route home. I've got my boy, lads.'

*　　＊　　＊*

I don't remember what I did for the rest of the day; sat at my desk and played with paper, I suppose. Sam headed out on another of his mysterious errands and Cassie went off to follow up some unpromising lead, taking O'Gorman with her and leaving silent Sweeney to man the tip line, for which I was devoutly grateful. After the bustle of the previous few weeks, the near-empty incident room had an eerie, derelict feel to it, the vanished floaters' desks still strewn with leftover paperwork and coffee mugs they had forgotten to take back to the canteen.

I sent Cassie a text saying I wasn't feeling well enough for dinner at her place; I couldn't bear the thought of all that solicitous tact. I left work just in time to get home before Heather – she 'does her Pilates' on Monday evenings – wrote her a note saying I had a migraine and locked myself in my room. Heather tends her health with the kind of tenacious, minute dedication some women devote to flowerbeds or china collections, but the upside of this is that she accords other people's ailments the same awed respect as her own: she would leave me alone for the evening and keep the sound on the television down.

On top of everything else, I couldn't shake the feeling that had blown away my last chance in the courtroom: the steadily growing feeling that MacSharry's photo of Philomena Kavanagh reminded me of something, though I had no idea what. This sounds like a minor problem, especially in light of the kind of day I had had, and no doubt for someone else it would have been. Most people have no reason to know how memory can turn rogue and feral, becoming a force of its own and one to be reckoned with.

Losing a chunk of your memory is a tricky thing, a deep-sea quake triggering shifts and upheavals too far distant from the epicentre to be easily predictable. From that day on, any nagging little half-remembered thing shimmers with a bright aura of hypnotic, terrifying potential: this could be trivia, or it could be The Big One that blows your life and your mind wide open. Over the years, like someone living on a fault line, I had come to trust the equilibrium of the status quo, to believe that if The Big One hadn't come by now then it wasn't coming; but since we caught the Katy Devlin case little rumbles and tremors had been building ominously, and I was no longer anything like sure. The photo of Philomena Kavanagh spread-eagled and wide-mouthed could have been reminding me of some scene from a TV show or of something terrible enough to wipe my mind blank for twenty years, and I had no way of knowing which it was.

In the event, it turned out to be neither. It hit me somewhere in the middle of the night, as I was drifting in and out of a fitful, twitchy doze; hit me so hard that it knocked me awake and upright, heart pounding. I grabbed for the switch on my bedside lamp, stared at the wall while little transparent squiggles swirled in front of my eyes.

Even before we were near the clearing we could tell something was different, something was wrong. The noises were tangled and jagged, too many layers of them, grunts and gasps and squeaks stifled to small, wild bursts more menacing than a roar. 'Get down,' Peter hissed, and we flattened ourselves closer against the ground. Roots and fallen twigs scrabbled at our clothes and my feet were boiling in my trainers. A hot day, hot and still, the sky blazing blue in and out of the branches. We slid through the undergrowth in slow motion: dust in my mouth, slashes of sun, a fly's horrible persistent dance loud as a chainsaw against my ear. Bees at the wild blackberries a few yards away, and a trickle of sweat running down my back. Peter's elbow in the corner of my vision, angling forward as carefully as a cat's; Jamie's quick eye-blink, close behind a grain-topped stalk of grass.

There were too many people in the clearing. Metallica was holding Sandra's arms down against the ground and Shades was holding her legs, and Anthrax was on top of her. Her skirt was twisted up around her waist and there were huge ladders all down her tights. Her mouth past Anthrax's moving shoulder was frozen wide and black, criss-crossed with slices of red-gold hair. She was making weird noises, like she was trying to scream and choking instead. Metallica hit her once, neatly, and she stopped.

We ran, not caring that they could see us, not hearing the yells – 'Jesus Christ!', 'Get the fuck out!' – until afterwards. Jamie and I saw Sandra the next day, down at the shop. She was wearing a big jumper and had dark smudges under her eyes. We knew she had seen us, but none of us looked at each other.

It was some ungodly hour of the night, but I rang Cassie's mobile anyway.

'Are you all right?' she said, sounding tousled and sleepy.

'I'm fine. I've got something, Cass.'

She yawned. 'Jesus. This better be good, git-face. What time is it?'

'I don't know. Listen. Sometime that summer, Peter and Jamie and I saw Jonathan Devlin and his friends raping a girl.'

There was a pause. Then Cassie said, sounding a lot more awake, 'Are you sure? You could have misinterpreted—'

'No. I'm positive. She tried to scream and one of them hit her. They were holding her down.'

'Did they see you guys?'

'Yes. Yes. We ran, and they yelled after us.'

'Fucking hell,' she said. I could feel her slowly realising: a raped little girl, a rapist in the family, two witnesses vanished. We were only a few steps away from an arrest warrant. 'Fucking hell . . . Well done, Ryan. Do you know the girl's name?'

'Sandra something.'

'The one you mentioned before? We'll start tracking her down tomorrow.'

'Cassie,' I said, 'if this pans out, how the hell do we explain how we knew?'

'Listen, Rob, don't worry about that yet, OK? If we find Sandra, she'll be all the witness we need. Otherwise we go at Devlin hard, hit him with all the details, freak him out till he confesses . . . We'll find a way.'

It almost undid me, her unquestioning assumption that the details would be correct. I had to swallow hard to keep my voice from cracking. 'What's the statute of limitations on rape? Can we get him for that even if we don't have enough evidence on the other stuff?'

'Can't remember. We'll figure all that out in the morning. Are you going to be able to sleep, or are you too hyper?'

'Too hyper,' I said. I was almost hysterically jittery; I felt as though someone had injected sherbet into my bloodstream. 'Talk for a while?'

'Sure,' Cassie said. I heard her curl up more comfortably in bed, sheets rustling; I found my vodka bottle and tucked the phone under my ear while I poured a shot.

She told me about a time when she was nine and

convinced all the other local kids that a magic wolf lived in the hills near the village. 'I said I'd found a letter under my floorboards telling me that he'd been there for four hundred years, and there was a map tied around his neck that would show us where to find treasure. I organised all the kids into a posse – God, I was a bossy little bitch – and every weekend we all went off up into the hills looking for this wolf. We were running away screaming every time we saw a sheepdog and falling into streams and having a brilliant time . . .'

I stretched out in bed and sipped my drink. The adrenalin was draining away and the low rhythms of Cassie's voice were soothing; I felt warm and comfortably exhausted, like a kid after a long day. 'And it wasn't a German shepherd or anything, either,' I'm sure I heard her say, 'it was way too big and it looked completely different, wild,' but I was already asleep.

12

In the morning we started trying to trace a Sandra or Alexandra Something who had lived in or near Knocknaree in 1984. It was one of the more frustrating mornings of my life. I rang the census bureau and got a nasal, uninterested woman who said she couldn't release any information to me without a court order. When I started getting passionate about the fact that a murdered child was involved, and she realised I wasn't going to go away, she told me I needed to speak to someone else, put me on hold (*Eine Kleine Nachtmusik*, apparently played with one finger on a vintage Casio) and finally transferred me to an identical uninterested woman who went through the identical process.

Opposite me, Cassie was trying to get hold of the Dublin South-West electoral register for 1988 – by which time I was pretty sure Sandra would have been old enough to vote, but probably not old enough to have moved away from home – with much the same results; I could hear a saccharine quacking sound telling her, at intervals, that her call was important to them and would be answered in rotation. She was bored and restless, changing position every thirty seconds: sitting cross-legged, perching on the table, swivelling her chair around and around until she got tangled up in the phone cord. I was blurry-eyed from lack of sleep, and sticky with sweat – the central heating was up to full, although it wasn't even a cold day – and just about ready to scream.

'Well, *fuck* this,' I said finally, slamming down the phone. I knew *Eine Kleine Nachtmusik* would be playing in my head for weeks. 'This is bloody pointless.'

'Your irritation is important to us,' Cassie droned, looking at me upside down with her head tipped backwards over her headrest, 'and *will* be exacerbated *in* rotation. *Thank* you for holding.'

'Even if these morons ever give us anything, it won't be on disk or in a *data*base. It'll be five million shoeboxes full of paper and we'll have to go through every single fucking name. It'll take weeks.'

'And she's probably moved and got married and emigrated and died anyway, but have you got a better idea?'

Suddenly I had a brainwave. 'Actually, I do,' I said, grabbing my coat. 'Come on.'

'Hello? Where are we going?'

I spun Cassie's chair around to face the door as I went past. 'We are going to talk to Mrs Pamela Fitzgerald. Who's your favourite genius?'

'Leonard Bernstein, actually,' Cassie said, happily banging down her phone and bouncing out of her chair, 'but you'll do for today.'

We stopped at Lowry's and bought Mrs Fitzgerald a tin of shortbread, to make up for the fact that we still hadn't found her purse. Big mistake: that generation is compulsively competitive about generosity, and the biscuits meant she had to get a bag of scones out of the freezer and defrost them in the microwave and butter them and decant jam into a battered little dish, while I sat on the edge of her slippery sofa manically jiggling one knee until Cassie gave me a hairy look and I forced myself to stop. I knew I had to eat the damn things, too, or the 'Ah, go on' phase could last for hours.

Mrs Fitzgerald watched sharply, screwing up her eyes to peer at us, until we had each swallowed a sip of tea – it was so strong I could feel my mouth shrivelling – and a bite of scone. Then she sighed with satisfaction and settled back into her armchair. 'I love a nice white scone,' she said. 'Them fruit ones get stuck in my falsies.'

'Mrs Fitzgerald,' Cassie said, 'do you remember the two children who disappeared in the wood, about twenty years ago?' I resented, suddenly and fiercely, the fact that I needed her to say this, but I didn't have the nerve to do it myself. I was superstitiously certain that some shake in my voice would give me away, make Mrs Fitzgerald suspicious enough to look harder at me and remember that third child. Then we really would have been there all day.

'I do, of course,' she said indignantly. 'Terrible, that was. They never found hide nor hair of them. No proper funeral nor nothing.'

'What do you think happened to them?' Cassie asked suddenly.

I wanted to kick her for wasting time, but I did, grudgingly, understand why she had asked. Mrs Fitzgerald was like a sly old woman from a fairy tale, peering out of some dilapidated cottage in the woods, mischievous and watchful; you couldn't help half-believing she would give you the answer to your riddle, even though it might be in a form too cryptic to unravel.

She inspected her scone thoughtfully, took a bite and dabbed at her lips with a paper napkin. She was making us wait, enjoying the suspense. 'Some mentaller threw them in the river,' she said at last. 'God rest them. Some unfortunate fella who should never have been let out.'

I noticed that my body was having the old, infuriating automatic reaction to this conversation: shaking hands, racing pulse. I put down my cup. 'You believe they were murdered, then,' I said, deepening my voice to make sure it stayed under control.

'Sure, what else, young fella? My mammy, may she rest in peace – she was still alive then; she died three year after, of the influenza – she always said it was the pooka took them. But she was fierce old-fashioned, God love her.' This one took me by surprise. The pooka is an ancient child-scarer out of legend, a wild mischief-making descendant of Pan and ancestor of Puck. He had not been on Kiernan and McCabe's list of persons of interest. 'No, they went into the river, or otherwise your lot would've found the bodies. There's people say they still haunt the wood, poor wee things. Theresa King from the Lane saw them only last year, when she was bringing in her washing.'

I hadn't been expecting this one, either, though I probably should have been. Two children vanished forever in the local wood; how could they have failed to become part of Knocknaree folklore? I don't believe in ghosts, but the thought – small flitting shapes at dusk, wordless calls – still sent a bright icy chill through me, along with a strange twinge of outrage: how dared some woman from the Lane see them, instead of me?

'At the time,' I said, aiming the conversation back on track, 'you told the police that three rough young men used to hang around the edge of the wood.'

'Little gurriers,' Mrs Fitzgerald said with relish. 'Spitting on the ground and all. My father always said that was a sure sign of bad rearing, spitting. Ah, but two of them turned out all right in the end, so they did. Concepta Mills's young fella does the computers now. He's after moving into town – Blackrock, *if* you don't mind. Knocknaree wasn't good enough for him. The Devlin lad, sure, we were talking about him already. He's the father of that poor wee girl Katy, God rest her soul. A lovely man.'

'What about the third boy?' I asked. 'Shane Waters?'

She pursed her lips and took a prim sip of tea. 'I wouldn't know about the likes of him.'

'Ah . . . turned out badly, did he?' Cassie said confidentially. 'Could I take another scone, Mrs Fitzgerald? These are the nicest ones I've had in ages.' They were the only ones she'd had in ages. She dislikes scones on the grounds that they 'don't taste like food'.

'Go on, love; sure, you could do with a bit of meat on you. There's plenty more where those came from. Now that my daughter's after buying me the microwave, I do make six dozen at once and put them away in the freezer till I need them.'

Cassie made a flatteringly big deal of choosing her scone, took a huge bite and said, 'Mmm.' If she ate enough of them that Mrs Fitzgerald felt the need to go heat up more, I was going to brain her. She swallowed her mouthful and said, 'Does Shane Waters still live in Knocknaree?'

'Mountjoy Gaol,' said Mrs Fitzgerald, giving the words their full sinister weight. 'That's where he's living. Himself and another fella robbed a petrol station with a knife; terrified the life out of the poor young fella working there. His mammy always said he wasn't a bad lad, just easily led, but there's no call for that kind of carry-on.' I wished, fleetingly, that we could introduce her to Sam. They would have liked each other.

'You told the police there were girls who used to hang around with them,' I said, getting my notebook ready.

She sucked disapprovingly on her dentures. 'Brazen hussies, the pair of them. I didn't mind showing a bit of leg myself, in my day – no better way to make the boys look, amn't I right?' She winked at me and laughed, a rusty cackle, but it lit up her face and you could see, still, that she had been pretty; a sweet, cheeky, bright-eyed girl. 'But the get-up on them young ones, sure, it was a waste of money altogether. They might as well have been in the nip, for all the difference them clothes made. Nowadays all the young ones are at it, with their belly tops and their hot shorts and what-have-you, but back then there was still a bit of decency.'

'Would you remember their names?'

'Wait now till I think. One of them was Marie Gallagher's oldest. She's in London these fifteen year, comes back now and again to show off her fancy clothes and her fancy job, but Marie says at the end of the day she's only some class of a secretary. She always did have notions of herself.' My heart sank – *London* – but Mrs Fitzgerald took a hearty slurp of her tea and raised a finger. 'Claire, that's it. Claire Gallagher, still; she never married. She was going out with a divorced fella for a few years, put the heart across Marie, but it didn't last.'

'And the other girl?' I said.

'Ah, her; she's still here. Lives with her mammy in the Close, up the top of the estate – the rough end, if you know what I mean. Two childer and no husband. Sure, what else would you expect? If you go looking for trouble, you'll never have far to look. One of the Scullys, she is. Jackie's the one married that Wicklow lad, Tracy's the one works in the betting shop – Sandra; that's herself. Sandra Scully.

Finish that scone,' she ordered Cassie, who had surreptitiously put it down and was trying to look as if she'd forgotten it was there.

'Thank you very much, Mrs Fitzgerald. You've been a great help,' I said. Cassie took the opportunity to jam the rest of her scone in her mouth and wash it down with tea. I put my notebook away and stood up.

'Wait a moment, now,' said Mrs Fitzgerald, flapping a hand at me. She stumped into the kitchen and came back with a plastic bag of frozen scones, which she pressed into Cassie's hand. 'There, now. That's for you. No, no, no' – over Cassie's protests; personal tastes in food aside, we're not supposed to take gifts from witnesses – 'they'll do you good. You're a lovely girl. Share them with your fella there if he behaves himself.'

The rough end of the estate (I had never been there before, as far as I remembered; all our mothers had warned us to stay away) wasn't actually that different from the good end. The houses were a little dingier, there were weeds and daisies growing in some of the gardens. The wall at the end of Knocknaree Close was sprinkled with graffiti, but it was pretty mild stuff – LIVERPOOL RULES, MARTINA + CONOR 4EVER, JONESY IS GAY, mostly done in what looked like coloured marker; almost quaint, really, compared to what you get in your true hard-core areas. If for some reason I had had to leave my car there overnight, I wouldn't have panicked.

Sandra answered the door. For a moment I wasn't sure; she didn't look the way I remembered her. She had been one of those girls who bloom early and fade, bewildered, into blowsiness within a few years. In my hazy mental image she was firm and voluptuous as a ripe peach, haloed in glossy, red-gold 80s curls, but the woman at the door was overblown and sagging, with a weary, suspicious look and hair dyed to dull brassiness. A swift, tiny pang of loss went through me. I almost hoped it wasn't her.

Then she said, 'Can I help you?' Her voice was deeper and rough around the edges, but I knew the sweet, breathy tone. ('Here, which of them's your fella?' A sparkly fingernail moving from me to Peter, while Jamie shook her head and said, 'Ewww!' Sandra had laughed, feet kicking up from against the wall: 'You'll change your mind soon enough!')

'Ms Sandra Scully?' I said. She nodded warily. I saw her peg us as cops, well before our IDs were out, and get ready to go on the defensive. Somewhere in the house a toddler was yelling and banging on something metallic. 'I'm Detective Ryan, and this is Detective Maddox. She'd like to speak with you for a few minutes.'

I felt Cassie shift almost imperceptibly beside me, clocking the signal. If I hadn't been sure, I would have said 'we', and we would both have gone through the routine Katy Devlin questions with her until I made up my mind one way or the other. But I was sure, and Sandra was likely to be more comfortable talking about this without a guy in the room.

Sandra's jaw hardened. 'Is this about Declan? Because you can tell that old bitch I took the stereo off him after the last time, so if she's hearing anything it's the voices in her head.'

'No, no, no,' Cassie said easily. 'Nothing like that. We're just working on an old case, and we thought you might remember some bits and pieces that could help us out. Can I come in?'

She stared Cassie out of it for a moment, then gave a

defeated little shrug. 'Do I have a choice?' She stepped back, opening the door a fraction wider; I smelled something frying.

'Thanks,' Cassie said. 'I'll try not to take too much of your time.' As she went into the house she glanced over her shoulder and gave me a tiny, reassuring wink. Then the door slammed behind her.

She was gone a long time. I sat in the car and chain-smoked until I ran out of cigarettes; then I bit my cuticles and drummed *Eine Kleine Nachtmusik* on the steering-wheel and picked dirt out of the dashboard with my car key. I wished crazily that I had thought of putting a wire on Cassie, or something, just in case there was a moment when it might help if I went in there. It wasn't that I didn't trust her; but she hadn't been there that day, and I had, and Sandra appeared to have turned into a pretty tough cookie somewhere along the way, and I couldn't be positive that Cassie would know the right questions to ask. I had the windows rolled down and I could still hear the toddler yelling and banging; then Sandra's voice, raised sharply, and a smack, and the toddler howling, more in outrage than in pain. I remembered her neat little white teeth when she laughed, the mysterious shadowy valley in the V of her top.

After what felt like hours I heard the door close, and Cassie came down the drive with a snap in her step. She got into the car and blew out her breath. 'Well. You were bang on. It took her a while to start talking, but once she did . . .'

My heart was pounding, whether with triumph or panic I couldn't tell. 'What'd she say?'

Cassie already had her cigarettes out and was rummaging for a lighter. 'Drive around the corner or something.

She didn't like the car sitting outside; she says it looks like a cop car and the neighbours'll talk.'

I got us out of the estate, parked in the lay-by opposite the dig, bummed one of Cassie's girl smokes and found a light. 'So?'

'Do you know what she said?' Cassie rolled down the window violently and blew smoke out of it, and I suddenly realised she was furious, furious and shaken. 'She said, "It wasn't rape or anything, they just made me do it." She said it like *three times*. Thank God the kids are too young to be anything to do with—'

'Cass,' I said, as calmly as I could. 'From the beginning?'

'The beginning is she started going out with Cathal Mills when she was sixteen and he was nineteen. He was, God knows why, considered extremely cool, and Sandra was mad about him. Jonathan Devlin and Shane Waters were his best mates. Neither of them had a girlfriend, Jonathan was into Sandra, Sandra liked him, and one fine day about six months into the *relationship* Cathal tells her that Jonathan wants to, and I quote, "do her" and that he thinks this would be a lovely idea. Like he's giving his mate a sip of his beer or something. Jesus, this was the eighties, they didn't even have *condoms*—'

'Cass—'

She threw the lighter out of the window at a tree. Cassie has a pretty good arm; it cracked off the trunk and flew into the undergrowth. I had seen her in a temper before – I tell her it's her French grandfather's fault, Mediterranean lack of self-control – and I knew she'd settle down now she'd taken it out on the tree. I made myself wait. She thumped back against her seat, drew on her cigarette and, after a moment, gave me a sheepish sideways grin.

'You owe me a lighter, prima donna,' I told her. 'Now what's the story?'

'And you still owe me last year's Christmas present. Anyway. Sandra actually didn't have much of a problem with the idea of shagging Jonathan. It happened once or twice, everyone was a little embarrassed afterwards, they got over it, everything was fine—'

'When was this?'

'The beginning of that summer: June of 'eighty-four. Apparently Jonathan went out with some girl for a while soon after – must be Claire Gallagher – and Sandra thinks he returned the favour. She had a big row with Cathal about that, but the whole thing had her so confused that eventually she just decided to forget it.'

'Jesus,' I said. 'Apparently I was living in the middle of *The Jerry Springer Show*. "Teenage Wife-Swappers Speak Out."' Only a few yards and a few years away, Jamie and Peter and I had been giving each other dead arms and aiming lawn darts at the Carmichaels' horrible yappy Jack Russell. All these private, parallel dimensions, underlying such an innocuous little estate; all these self-contained worlds layered onto the same space. I thought of the dark strata of archaeology underfoot; of the fox outside my window, calling out to a city that barely overlapped with mine.

'Then, though,' Cassie said, 'Shane found out and wanted to play too. Cathal was of course fine with this, but Sandra wasn't. She didn't like Shane – "that spotty little wanker", she called him. I get the feeling he was a bit of a reject, but the other two hung around with him out of habit, because they'd all been mates since they were tiny kids. Cathal kept trying to convince her – I can't wait to find out what Cathal's internet history looks like, can you?

– she kept saying she'd think about it, and finally they jumped her in the woods, Cathal and our boy Jonathan held her down and Shane raped her. She's not sure of the exact date, but she knows she had bruises on her wrists and she was worried about whether they'd be gone by the time school started back, so it has to have been sometime in August.'

'Did she see us?' I asked, keeping my voice level. The fact that this story was starting to dovetail with my own was disorientating but also, horribly, tremendously exciting.

Cassie looked at me; her face gave away nothing, but I knew she was checking whether I was OK with all this. I tried to look casual. 'Not properly. She was . . . well, you know the state she was in. But she remembers hearing someone in the undergrowth, and then the guys yelling. Jonathan ran after you, and when he came back he said something like, "Bloody kids."'

She tapped ash out of the window. I could tell by the set of her shoulders that she hadn't finished. Across the road on the dig, Mark and Mel and a couple of the others were doing something with rods and yellow measuring tapes, yelling back and forth. Mel laughed, hearty and clear, and called, 'You wish!'

'And?' I said, when I couldn't stand it any longer. I was trembling like a gun dog holding a point. As I say, I don't hit suspects, but my mind was racing with melodramatic images of slamming Devlin up against a wall, screaming into his face, punching answers out of him.

'You know something?' Cassie said. 'She didn't even break up with Cathal Mills. She went out with him for another few months, till *he* dumped *her*.'

I almost said, *Is that all?* 'I think the statute of limitations is different if she was a minor,' I said instead. My mind was going a hundred miles an hour, flying through interrogation strategies. 'We might still have time. He sounds like the kind of guy I'd love to arrest in the middle of a board meeting.'

Cassie shook her head. 'There's not a chance she'll press charges. She thinks it was basically all her own fault for sleeping with him in the first place.'

'Let's go talk to Devlin,' I said, starting the car.

'Just a sec,' Cassie said. 'There's something else. It might be nothing, but . . . After they finished, Cathal – honestly, I think we should investigate him anyway, we're bound to find something we can charge him with – Cathal said, "That's my girl," and gave her a kiss. She was sitting there shaking and trying to pull her clothes straight and get her head together. And they heard something in the trees, just a few yards away. Sandra says she's never heard anything like it. Like an enormous bird flapping its wings, she said, only she's positive it was a *voiced* sound, a call. They all jumped and yelled, and then Cathal shouted something like, "Those fucking kids messing about again," and threw a stone into the trees, but it kept going. It was in the shadows, they couldn't see anything. They were paralysed, totally freaked out, they all just sat there screaming. Finally it stopped and they heard it moving away into the woods – it sounded big, she said, at least the size of a person. They legged it home. And there was a smell, Sandra says, a strong animal smell – like goats or something, or what you get at the zoo.'

'What the *hell*?' I said. I was utterly taken aback.

'It wasn't you guys messing, then.'

'Not that I recall,' I said. I remembered running hard, my own breathing rasping in my ears, unsure what was happening but knowing that something was horribly wrong; remembered the three of us staring at each other, panting, at the edge of the wood. I seriously doubted that we would have decided to go back to the clearing and make weird flapping noises and a smell of goat. 'She probably imagined it.'

Cassie shrugged. 'Sure, she might have. But I sort of wondered if there could've actually been some kind of wild animal in the wood.'

Ireland's most ferocious form of wildlife is probably badgers, but there are regular flurries of atavistic rumour, usually somewhere in the Midlands: dead sheep found with their throats torn out, late-night travellers crossing paths with huge slouching shadows or glowing eyes. Mostly these turn out to be rogue sheepdogs or pet kitties seen in tricky lighting, but some go unexplained. I thought, unwillingly, of the rips across the back of my T-shirt. Cassie, without exactly believing in the mysterious wild animal, has always been fascinated by it – because its lineage goes back to the Black Dog that stalked medieval wayfarers, and because she loves the idea that not every inch of the country is mapped and regulated and monitored by CCTV, that there are still secret corners of Ireland where some untamed thing the size of a puma might be going about its hidden business.

I like the thought too, normally, but I had no time for it just then. All through this case, since the moment the car crested the hill and we saw Knocknaree spread out in front of us, the opaque membrane between me and that day in the wood had been slowly, relentlessly thinning; it had grown so fine that I could hear the small furtive movements on the other side, beating wings and tiny scrabbling feet like a moth battering against your cupped hands. I had no room for left-field theories about escaped exotic pets or leftover elk or the Loch Ness Monster or whatever the hell Cassie had in mind.

'No,' I said. 'No, Cass. We practically lived in that wood; if there was anything bigger than a fox in there, we would have known. And the searchers would have found some sign of it. Either some voyeur with bad BO was watching them, or she imagined the whole thing.'

'Fair enough,' Cassie said, neutrally. I started the car again. 'Hang on; how are we going to do this?'

'I am not fucking sitting in the car for this one,' I told her, hearing my voice rise dangerously.

She raised her eyebrows a fraction. 'I was thinking *I* should, actually – well, not sit in the car, but drop you off and go talk to the cousins some more or something, and you can text me when you want me to pick you up. You and Devlin can have a guy chat. He's not going to talk about a rape if I'm there.'

'Oh,' I said, a little awkwardly. 'OK. Thanks, Cass. That sounds good.'

She got out of the car and I started sliding over to the passenger side, thinking she wanted to drive; but she went over to the trees and kicked around in the undergrowth until she spotted my lighter. 'Here,' she said, getting back into the car and giving me a little one-sided smile. 'Now I want my Christmas present.'

13

As I pulled up in front of the Devlins' house, Cassie said, 'Rob, maybe you've already thought of it, but this could point in a whole other direction.'

'How so?' I said absently.

'You know what I was saying about the token feel to Katy's rape – how it didn't seem like a sexual thing? You've given us someone who has a non-sexual motive for wanting Devlin's daughter to be raped, and who'd *have* to use an implement.'

'Sandra? Suddenly, after twenty years?'

'All the publicity about Katy – the newspaper article, the fundraiser . . . That could've set her off.'

'Cassie,' I said, taking a deep breath, 'I'm just a simple small-town boy. I prefer to concentrate on the obvious. The obvious, right now, is Jonathan Devlin.'

'I'm only saying. It might come in useful.' She reached over and ruffled my hair, quickly and clumsily. 'Go for it, small-town boy. Break a leg.'

Jonathan was home, alone. Margaret had taken the girls to her sister's, he said, and I wondered how long ago and why. He looked awful. He had lost so much weight that his clothes and his face sagged loosely, and his hair was cut even shorter, tight to his head; it gave him a lonely, desperate look, somehow, and I thought of ancient civilisations where the bereaved offered their hair on loved ones' funeral pyres. He motioned me to the sofa and took an armchair opposite me, leaning forward with his elbows on his knees, his hands clasped in front of him. The house felt deserted; there was no smell of cooking food, no TV or washing machine in the background, no books left open on chair-arms, nothing to imply that when I arrived he had been doing anything at all.

He didn't offer me tea. I asked how they were getting on ('How do you think?'), explained that we were following up various leads, fended off his terse questions about specifics, asked if he had thought of anything else that might be relevant. The wild urgency I'd felt in the car had vanished as soon as he opened the door; I felt calmer and more lucid than I had in weeks. Margaret and Rosalind and Jessica could have come back at any moment, but somehow I was sure they wouldn't. The windows were grimy, and the late-afternoon sun filtering through them slid confusingly off glass-fronted cabinets and the polished wood of the dining table, giving the room a streaky, underwater luminescence. I could hear a clock ticking in the kitchen, heavy and achingly slow, but apart from that there wasn't a sound, even outside the house; all of Knocknaree might have gathered itself up and vanished into thin air, except me and Jonathan Devlin. It was just the two of us, facing each other across the little ringed coffee table, and the answers were so close I could hear them scuffling and twittering in the corners of the room; there was no need to hurry.

'Who's the Shakespeare fan?' I asked eventually, putting my notebook away. It wasn't relevant, obviously, but I thought it might lower his guard a little, and it had been intriguing me.

Jonathan frowned, irritated. 'What?'

'Your daughters' names,' I said. 'Rosalind, Jessica, Katharine with an A; they're all out of Shakespeare comedies. I assumed it was deliberate.'

He blinked, looking at me for the first time with something like warmth, and half-smiled. It was a rather engaging smile, pleased but shy, like a boy who's been waiting for someone to notice his new Scout badge. 'Do you know, you're the first person ever to pick up on that? Yeah, that was me.' I raised an encouraging eyebrow. 'I went through a kind of self-improvement patch, I suppose you'd call it, after we got married – trying to work my way through all the things you're supposed to read: you know, Shakespeare, Milton, George Orwell . . . I wasn't mad about Milton, but Shakespeare – he was hard going, but I read my way through the lot, in the end. I used tease Margaret that if the twins were a boy and a girl we'd have to call them Viola and Sebastian, but she said they'd be laughed out of it at school . . .'

His smile faded and he looked away. I knew this was my chance, now while he liked me. 'They're beautiful names,' I said. He nodded absently. 'One more thing: are you familiar with the names Cathal Mills and Shane Waters?'

'Why?' Jonathan asked. I thought I caught a flicker of wariness in his eyes, but his back was to the window and it was hard to tell.

'They've been mentioned in the course of our investigation.'

His eyebrows went down sharply and I saw his shoulders stiffen like a fighting dog's. 'Are they suspects?'

'No,' I said firmly. Even if they had been, I wouldn't have told him – not just because of procedure, but because he was way too volatile. That furious, spring-loaded tension: if he was innocent, of Katy's death at least, then one hint of uncertainty in my voice and he would probably have shown up on their doorsteps with an Uzi. 'We're just following up every lead. Tell me about them.'

He stared at me for another second; then he slumped, leaning back in the chair. 'We were friends when we were kids. We've been out of touch for years now.'

'When did you become friends?'

'When our families moved out here. Nineteen seventy-two, it would have been. We were the first three families on the estate, up at the top end – the rest was still being built. We had the whole place to ourselves. We used play on the building sites, after the builders had gone home – it was like a huge maze. We would have been six, seven.'

There was something in his voice, some deep, accustomed undercurrent of nostalgia, that made me realise what a lonely man he was; not just now, not just since Katy's death. 'And how long did you remain friends?' I asked.

'Hard to say, exactly. We started going our separate ways when we were nineteen, about, but we kept in touch for a while longer. Why? What does this have to do with anything?'

'We have two separate witnesses,' I said, keeping my voice expressionless, 'who say that, in the summer of 1984, you, Cathal Mills and Shane Waters participated in the rape of a local girl.'

He whipped upright, his hands jerking into fists. 'What – what the *fuck* does that have to do with Katy? Are you accusing – what the *fuck*!'

I gazed blandly back and let him finish. 'I can't help noticing that you haven't denied the allegation,' I said.

'And I haven't admitted to a bloody thing, either. Do I need a lawyer for this?'

No lawyer in the world would let him say another word. 'Look,' I said, leaning forward and switching to an easy, confidential tone, 'I'm from the Murder squad, not Sex Crime. I'm only interested in a twenty-year-old rape if—'

'Alleged rape.'

'Fair enough, alleged rape. I don't care either way unless it has some bearing on a murder. That's all I'm here to find out.'

Jonathan caught his breath to say something; for a second I thought he was going to order me to leave. 'We need to get one thing straight if you're going to spend another second in my house,' he said. 'I never laid a finger on any of my girls. Never.'

'Nobody's accused you of—'

'You've been dancing around it since the first day you came here, and I don't like insinuations. I love my daughters. I hug them good night. That's it. I've never once touched any of them in any way that anyone could call wrong. Is that clear?'

'Crystal,' I said, trying not to let it sound sarcastic.

'Good.' He nodded, one sharp, controlled jerk. 'Now, about this other thing: I'm not stupid, Detective Ryan. Just assuming that I did something that might land me in gaol, why the hell would I tell you about it?'

'Listen,' I said earnestly, 'we're considering the possibility' – *Bless you, Cassie* – 'that the victim might have had something to do with Katy's death, as revenge for this rape.' His eyes widened. 'It's only an outside chance and we have absolutely no solid evidence, so I don't want you to put too much weight on this. In particular, I don't want you to contact her in any way. If we do turn out to have a case, that could ruin the whole thing.'

'I wouldn't contact her. Like I said, I'm not stupid.'

'Good. I'm glad that's understood. But I do need to hear your version of what happened.'

'And then what? You charge me with it?'

'I can't guarantee you anything,' I said. 'I'm certainly not going to arrest you. It's not up to me to decide whether to file charges – that's down to the DPP and the victim – but I doubt she'll be willing to come forward. And I haven't cautioned you, so anything you say wouldn't be admissible in court anyway. I just need to know how it happened. It's up to you, Mr Devlin. How badly do you want me to find Katy's killer?'

Jonathan took his time. He stayed where he was, leaning forward, hands clasped, and gave me a long, suspicious glare. I tried to look trustworthy and not blink.

'If I could make you understand,' he said finally, almost to himself. He pulled himself restlessly up from the chair and went to the window, leaned back against the glass; every time I blinked his silhouette rose up in front of my eyelids, bright-edged and looming against the barred panes. 'Have you any friends you've known since you were a little young fella?'

'Not really, no.'

'Nobody knows you like people you grew up with. I could run into Cathal or Shane tomorrow, after all this time, and they'd still know more about me than Margaret does. We were closer than most brothers. None of us had what you'd call a happy family: Shane never knew his da, Cathal's was a waster who never did a decent day's work in his life, my parents were both drunks. I'm not saying any of this as an excuse, mind you; I'm only trying to tell you what we were like. When we were ten we did the blood-brothers thing – did you ever do that? Cut your wrists, press them together?'

'I don't think so,' I said. I wondered, fleetingly, whether we had. It felt like the kind of thing we would have done.

'Shane was scared to cut himself, but Cathal talked him into it. He could sell holy water to the Pope, Cathal.' He was smiling, a little; I could hear it in his voice. 'When we saw *The Three Musketeers* on the telly, Cathal decided that would be our motto: All for one and one for all. We had to have each other's back, he said, there was nobody else on our side. He was right, too.' His head turned towards me, a brief, measuring look. 'What are you – thirty, thirty-five?'

I nodded.

'You missed the worst of it. When we left school, it was the early eighties. This country was on its knees. There were no jobs, none. If you couldn't go into Daddy's business, you emigrated or went on the dole. Even if you had the money and the points for college – and we didn't – that just put it off for a few years. We'd nothing to do only hang around, nothing to look forward to, nothing to aim for; nothing at all, except each other. I don't know if you understand what a powerful thing that is. Dangerous.'

I wasn't sure what I thought of the direction in which this appeared to be going, but I felt a sudden, unwelcome dart of something like envy. In school I had dreamed of friendships like this: the steel-tempered closeness of soldiers in battle or prisoners of war, the mystery attained only by men *in extremis*.

Jonathan took a breath. 'Anyway. Then Cathal started going out with this girl – Sandra. It felt strange, at first: we'd all been out with girls here and there, but none of us had ever had a serious girlfriend before. But she was lovely, Sandra was; lovely. Always laughing, and this innocence about her – I think probably she was my first love, as well

. . . When Cathal said she fancied me too, wanted to be with me, I couldn't believe my luck.'

'This didn't strike you as – well, slightly odd, to say the least?'

'Not as odd as you'd think. It sounds mad now, yeah; but we'd always shared everything. It was a rule with us. This just felt like more of the same. I was going out with a girl for a while around the same time, sure, and she went with Cathal, not a bother on her – I think she only went out with me in the first place because he was taken. He was a lot better-looking than I was.'

'Shane,' I said, 'appears to have fallen out of the loop.'

'Yeah. That was where it all went wrong. Shane found out, and he went mental. He was always mad about Sandra too, I think; but more than that, he felt like we'd betrayed him. He was devastated. We had huge rows about it practically every day, for weeks and weeks. Half the time he wouldn't even talk to us. I was miserable, felt like everything was falling apart – you know how it is when you're that age, any little thing is the end of the world . . .'

He stopped. 'What happened then?' I said.

'Then Cathal got it into his head that, since it was Sandra had come between us, it would have to be Sandra brought us together again. He was obsessed, wouldn't stop talking about it. If we were all with the same girl, he said, it'd be the final seal on our friendship – like the blood-brothers thing, only stronger. I don't know, any more, if he really believed that, or if he just . . . I don't know. He had an odd streak in him, Cathal, especially when it came to things like . . . Well. I had my doubts, but he kept on and on about it, and of course Shane was behind him all the way . . .'

'It didn't occur to any of you to ask Sandra's opinion about this?'

Jonathan let his head fall back against the glass, with a soft bump. 'We should have,' he said quietly, after a moment. 'God knows we should have. But we lived in a world of our own, the three of us. Nobody else seemed real – I was wild about Sandra, but it was the same way I was wild about Princess Leia or whoever else we fancied that week, not the way you love a real woman. Not an excuse – there's no excuse for what we did, none. But a reason.'

'What happened?'

He rubbed a hand over his face. 'We were in the wood,' he said. 'The four of us; I wasn't with Claire any more. In this clearing where we used to go sometimes. I don't know would you remember, but we had a beauty of a summer that year – hot as Greece or somewhere, never a cloud in the sky, bright till half-ten at night. We spent every day outside, in the wood or hanging around at the edge of it. We were all burned black, I looked like an Italian student only for these mad white patches round my eyes from my sunglasses . . .

'It was late one afternoon. We'd all been in the clearing all day, drinking and having a few joints. I think we were pretty much off our faces; not just the cider and the gear, but the sun, and the giddy way you get when you're that age . . . I'd been arm-wrestling with Shane – he was in a half-decent mood for once – and I'd let him win, and we were messing, pushing each other and fighting on the grass, you know the way young fellas do. Cathal and Sandra were yelling, cheering us on, and then Cathal started tickling Sandra – she was laughing and screaming. They rolled under our feet, then; we went over in a heap on top of them. And all of a sudden Cathal yelled, "*Now!*" . . .'

I waited for a long time. 'Did all three of you rape her?' I asked quietly, in the end.

'Shane, only. Not that that makes it any better. I helped hold her . . .' He took a fast breath between his teeth. 'I've never known anything like it. I think maybe we went a little out of our minds. It didn't feel real, you know? It was like a nightmare, or a bad trip. It went on forever. It was blazing hot, I was sweating like a pig, light-headed. I looked round at the trees and they were closing in on us, shooting out brand-new branches, I thought they were about to wrap round us and swallow us up; and all the colours looked wrong, off, like in one of those colourised old films. The sky had gone almost white and there were things shooting across it, little black things. I looked back – I felt like I should warn the others that something was happening, something was wrong – and I was holding . . . holding her, but I couldn't feel my hands, they didn't look like mine. I couldn't work out whose hands those were. I was terrified. Cathal was there across from me and his breathing sounded like the loudest thing in the world, but I didn't recognise him, I couldn't remember who the hell he was or what we were doing. Sandra was fighting and there were these noises and – Jesus. For a second I swear I thought we were hunters and this was a, an animal we'd brought down, and Shane was killing it . . .'

I was starting to dislike the tone of this. 'If I understand you correctly,' I said coldly, 'you were under the influence both of alcohol and of illegal drugs at the time, you may quite possibly have been suffering from heatstroke, and you were presumably in a state of considerable excitement. Don't you think these factors might have had something to do with this experience?'

Jonathan's eyes went to me for a moment; then he shrugged, a defeated little twitch. 'Yeah, sure,' he said quietly. 'Probably. Again, I'm not saying any of this is an excuse. I'm only telling you. You asked.'

It was an absurd story, of course, melodramatic and self-serving and utterly predictable: every criminal I have ever interrogated had a long convoluted story proving conclusively that it wasn't actually his fault or at least that it wasn't as bad as it looked, and most of them were a whole lot better than this one. What bothered me was that some tiny part of me believed it. I wasn't at all convinced about Cathal's idealistic motives, but Jonathan: he had been lost somewhere in the wild borderlands of nineteen, half in love with his friends with a love passing the love of women, desperate for some mystical rite that would reverse time and put their disintegrating private world back together. It would not have been difficult for him to see this as an act of love, however dark and twisted and untranslatable to the harsh outside world. Not that this made any difference: I wondered what else he would have done for his cause.

'And you're no longer in any contact with Cathal Mills and Shane Waters?' I asked; a little cruelly, I know.

'No,' he said quietly. He looked away, out the window, and laughed, a mirthless little breath. 'After all that, eh? Cathal and I send Christmas cards; the wife signs his name to theirs. I haven't heard from Shane in years. I wrote him the odd letter, but he never wrote back. I stopped trying.'

'You started drifting apart not long after the rape.'

'It was a slow thing, took years. But yeah, when you come down to it, I suppose it started with that day in the woods. It was awkward, after – Cathal wanted to talk about it over and over, it made Shane nervous as a cat on hot bricks; I felt guilty as hell, didn't even want to think about it . . . Ironic, isn't it? Here we thought it was going to be the thing that brought us together forever.' He shook his head quickly, like a horse twitching off a fly. 'But I'd say we might have gone our separate ways anyway, sure. It happens. Cathal moved away, I got married . . .'

'And Shane?'

'I'm betting you know Shane's in gaol,' he said drily. 'Shane . . . Listen, if that poor thick bastard had been born ten years later, he'd have been grand. I'm not saying he'd be some great success story, but he'd have a decent job and maybe a family. He was a casualty of the eighties. There's a whole generation out there that fell through the cracks. By the time the Celtic Tiger came along it was too late for most of us, we were too old to start over. Cathal and I were just lucky. I was shite at everything else but good at maths, A in my Leaving Cert, so I finally managed to get a job in the bank. And Cathal went out with some rich young one who had a computer and taught him how to use it, for the laugh; a few years later, when everyone was crying out for people who knew computers, he was one of the few in the country who could do more than turn the bloody things on. He always did land on his feet, Cathal. But Shane . . . he'd no job, no education, no prospects, no family. What did he have to lose by robbing?'

I was finding it hard to feel any particular sympathy towards Shane Waters. 'In the minutes immediately after the rape,' I said, almost against my will, 'did you hear anything out of the ordinary – possibly a sound like a large bird flapping its wings?' I left out the part about it being a voiced sound. Even at moments like this, there is a limit to how weird I am prepared to appear.

Jonathan gave me a funny look. 'The wood was full of birds, foxes, what have you. I wouldn't have noticed one more or less – especially not just then. I don't know if I've given you any idea of the state we were all in. It wasn't just me, you know. It was like we were coming down off acid. I was shaking all over, couldn't see straight, everything kept sliding sideways. Sandra was – Sandra was gasping, like she couldn't breathe. Shane was lying on the grass just staring up at the trees and twitching. Cathal started laughing, he was staggering around the clearing howling, I told him I'd punch the face off him if he didn't—' He stopped.

'What is it?' I asked, after a moment.

'I'd forgotten,' he said slowly. 'I don't – sure, I don't like to think about the thing anyway. I'd forgotten . . . If it was anything, mind you. The way our heads were, it could easily have been just imagination.'

I waited. Finally he sighed, made an uneasy movement like a shrug. 'Well. The way I remember it, I grabbed Cathal and told him to shut up or I'd hit him, and he stopped laughing and caught me by my T-shirt – he looked half crazy, for a second there I thought it was going to turn into a fight. But there was still someone laughing – not one of us; away in the trees. Sandra and Shane both started screaming – maybe I did too, I don't know – but it just got louder and louder, this huge voice laughing . . . Cathal let go of me and shouted something about those kids, but it didn't sound—'

'Kids?' I said coolly. I was fighting a violent impulse to get the hell out of there. There was no reason why Jonathan should recognise me – I had just been some little kid hanging around, my hair had been a lot fairer then, I had a different accent and a different name – but I felt suddenly horribly naked and exposed.

'Ah, there were these kids from the estate – little kids, ten, twelve – who used to play in the wood. Sometimes they'd spy on us; throw things and then run, you know the way. But it didn't sound like any kid to me. It sounded like a man – a young fella, maybe, around our age. Not a child.'

For a split second I almost took the opening he had offered. The flash of wariness had dissolved and the quick little whispers in the corners had risen to a silent shout, so close, close as breath. It was on the tip of my tongue: *Those kids, weren't they spying on you that day? Weren't you worried they would tell? What did you do to stop them?* But the detective in me held me back. I knew I would only get one chance, and I needed to come to it on my own territory and with all the ammunition I could bring.

'Did any of you go to see what it was?' I asked, instead.

Jonathan thought for a moment, his eyes hooded and intent. 'No. Like I said, we were all in some kind of shock anyway, and this was more than we could handle. I was frozen, couldn't have moved if I'd wanted to. It kept getting louder, till I thought the whole estate would be out to see what was going on, and we were still yelling . . . Finally it stopped – moved off into the woods, maybe, I don't know. Shane kept screaming, till Cathal smacked him across the back of the head and told him to shut up. We got out of there as fast as we could. I went home, nicked some of my da's booze and got drunk as a lord. I don't know what the others did.'

So much for Cassie's mysterious wild animal, then. But there had quite possibly been someone in the woods that day, someone who, if he had seen the rape, had in all probability seen us too; someone who might have been there again, a week or two later. 'Do you have any suspicion as to who the person laughing might have been?' I asked.

'No. I think Cathal asked us about that, later. He said we needed to know who it was, how much they had seen. I've no idea.'

I stood up. 'Thanks for your time, Mr Devlin,' I said. 'I may need to ask you a few more questions about this at some stage, but that's all for now.'

'Wait,' he said suddenly. 'Do you think Sandra killed Katy?'

He looked very short and pathetic, standing there at the window with his hands balled in his cardigan pockets, but he still had a kind of forlorn dignity about him. 'No,' I said. 'I don't. But we have to investigate every possibility thoroughly.'

Jonathan nodded. 'I suppose that means you've no real suspect,' he said. 'No, I know, I know, you can't tell me . . . If you're talking to Sandra, tell her I'm sorry. We did a terrible thing. I know it's a bit late to be saying that, I should've thought of it twenty years ago, but . . . tell her, all the same.'

That evening I went out to Mountjoy to see Shane Waters. I'm sure Cassie would have come with me if I'd told her I was going, but I wanted to do this, as much as possible, on my own. Shane was rat-faced and nervy, with a repulsive little moustache, and he still had spots. He reminded me of Wayne the junkie. I tried every tactic I knew and promised him everything I could think of – immunity, early release on the armed robbery – banking on the fact that he wasn't smart enough to know what I could and couldn't deliver, but (always one of my blind spots) I'd underestimated the power of stupidity: with the infuriating mulishness of someone who has long ago given up trying to analyse possibilities and ramifications, Shane stuck to the one option he understood. 'I don't know nothing,' he told me, over and over, with a kind of anaemic self-satisfaction that made me want to scream. 'And you can't prove I do.'

Sandra, the rape, Peter and Jamie, even Jonathan Devlin: 'Don't know what you're talking about, man.' I finally gave up when I realised I was in serious danger of throwing something.

On my way home I swallowed my pride and phoned Cassie, who didn't even try to pretend she hadn't guessed where I'd gone. She had spent her evening eliminating Sandra Scully from the inquiry. On the night in question, Sandra had been working in a call centre in town. Her supervisor and everyone else on the shift confirmed that she had been there until just before two in the morning, when she had clocked out and caught a Nitelink home. This was good news – it tidied things up, and I hadn't liked thinking of Sandra as a possible murderess – but it gave me a complicated little pang, the thought of her in an airless fluorescent cubicle, surrounded by part-timing students and actors waiting for the next gig.

I won't go into details, but we put a considerable amount of effort and ingenuity, most of it more or less legal, into identifying the worst possible time to go talk to Cathal Mills. He had some high position with a gibberish title, in a company that provided something called 'corporate e-learning software localisation solutions' (I was impressed: I hadn't thought it was possible for me to dislike him any more than I already did), so we walked in on him halfway through a crucial meeting with a big potential client. Even the building was creepy: long windowless corridors and flights of stairs that stripped your sense of direction to nothing, tepid canned air with too little oxygen, a low witless hum of computers and suppressed voices, huge tracts of cubicles like a mad scientist's rat-mazes. Cassie shot me a wide-eyed, horrified look as we followed some droid through the fifth set of swipe-card swing doors.

Cathal was in the boardroom, and he was easy to identify: he was the one with the PowerPoint presentation. He was still a handsome guy – tall and broad-shouldered, with bright blue eyes and hard, dangerous bones – but fat was starting to blur his waist and hang under his jaw; in a few more years he would have coarsened into piggishness. The new client was four identical, humourless Americans in inscrutable dark suits.

'Sorry, fellas,' Cathal said, giving us an easy, warning smile, 'the boardroom's being used.'

'It is indeed,' Cassie told him. She had dressed for the occasion, in ripped jeans and an old turquoise camisole that said 'Yuppies Taste Like Chicken' in red across the front. 'I'm Detective Maddox—'

'And I'm Detective Ryan,' I said, flipping out my ID. 'We'd like to ask you a few questions.'

The smile didn't budge, but a savage flash shot across his eyes. 'This isn't a good time.'

'No?' Cassie enquired sociably, lounging against the table so that the PowerPoint image vanished into a blob on her camisole.

'*No.*' He cut his eyes sideways at the new client, who stared disapprovingly into space and shuffled papers.

'This looks like a good place to talk,' she said, surveying the boardroom appreciatively, 'but we could go back to headquarters if you'd prefer.'

'What's this about?' Cathal demanded. It was a mistake, and he knew it as soon as the words were out. If we had said anything off our own bat, in front of the clones, it would have been an invitation to a harassment claim, and he looked like the type who would sue; but hey, he had asked.

'We're investigating a child-murder,' Cassie said sweetly. 'There's a possibility it's linked to the alleged rape of a young girl, and we have reason to believe you might be able to help us with our enquiries.'

It only took him a fraction of a second to recover. 'I can't imagine how,' he said, gravely. 'But if it's a question of a murdered child, then of course, anything I can do . . . Fellas' – this to the client – 'I apologise for this interruption, but I'm afraid duty calls. Let me get Fiona to show you around the building. We'll pick up here in just a few minutes.'

'Optimism,' Cassie said approvingly. 'I like that.'

Cathal shot her a filthy look and hit a button on an object that turned out to be an intercom. 'Fiona, could you come down to the boardroom and give these gentlemen a tour of the building?'

I held the door open for the clones, who filed out with prim poker-faces unchanged. 'It's been a pleasure,' I told them.

'Were they *CIA*?' Cassie whispered, not quite quietly enough.

Cathal already had his mobile out. He phoned his lawyer – kind of ostentatiously; I think we were supposed to be intimidated – and then flipped his phone shut and tilted his chair back, legs spread wide, checking Cassie out with slow, deliberate enjoyment. For a giddy second I was tempted to say something to him – *You gave me my first cigarette, do you remember?* – just to see his brows draw sharply downwards, the greasy smirk fall away from his face. Cassie batted her lashes and gave him a mock-flirtatious smile, which pissed him off: he banged down the chair and shot his wrist out of his sleeve to check his Rolex.

'In a hurry?' Cassie enquired.

'My lawyer should be here within twenty minutes,'

Cathal said. 'Let me save us all some time and hassle, though: I'll have nothing to say to you then either.'

'Awww,' Cassie said, perching on the desk with her backside on a pile of paperwork; Cathal eyeballed her, but decided not to rise to the bait. 'We're wasting a whole twenty minutes of Cathal's valuable time, and all he ever did was gang-rape a teenage girl. Life is so unfair.'

'Maddox,' I said.

'I've never raped a girl in my life,' Cathal said, with a nasty little smile. 'Never needed to.'

'See, that's what's interesting, Cathal,' Cassie said confidentially. 'You look to me like you used to be a pretty good-looking guy. So I can't help wondering – do you have some problems with your sexuality? A lot of rapists do, you know. That's why you need to rape women: you're desperately trying to prove to yourselves that you're actually real men, in spite of the little problem.'

'Maddox—'

'If you know what's good for you,' Cathal said, 'you'll shut your mouth right now.'

'What is it, Cathal? Can't get it up? In the closet? Under-endowed?'

'Show me your ID,' Cathal snapped. 'I'm going to file a complaint about this. You'll be out on your arse before you know what hit you.'

'*Maddox*,' I said sharply, doing O'Kelly. 'A word with you. *Now*.'

'You know, Cathal,' Cassie told him sympathetically, on her way out, 'medical science can help with most of that stuff, these days.' I grabbed her arm and shoved her through the door.

In the corridor I chewed her out, keeping my voice low but carrying: stupid bitch, have some respect, he's not even a suspect, yada yada yada. (The 'not a suspect' part was actually true: along the way we had learned, to our disappointment, that Cathal had spent the first three weeks of August drumming up business in the US and had some fairly impressive credit-card bills to prove it.) Cassie gave me a grin and an A-OK sign.

'I'm really sorry about that, Mr Mills,' I said, going back into the boardroom.

'I don't envy you your job, mate,' Cathal said. He was furious, red spots high on his cheekbones, and I wondered if Cassie had actually hit the mark, somewhere in there; if Sandra had told her some little detail she hadn't shared.

'Tell me about it,' I said, sitting down opposite him and running a weary hand over my face. 'She's a token, obviously. I wouldn't even bother filing a complaint; the brass are scared to reprimand her in case she runs to the Equality Commission. The lads and I will sort her out, though, believe me. Just give us time.'

'You know what that bitch needs, don't you?' Cathal said.

'Hey, we all know what she needs,' I said, 'but would you want to get close enough to give it to her?'

We shared a manly little snigger. 'Listen,' I said, 'I should tell you there's not a chance of us arresting anyone for this alleged rape. Even if the story's true, the statute of limitations ran out years ago. I'm working a murder case; I don't give a fuck about this other thing.'

Cathal pulled a packet of tooth-whitening gum out of his pocket, tossed a piece into his mouth and jerked the pack at me. I hate gum, but I took a piece anyway. He was calming down, the high colour fading. 'You looking into what happened to the Devlin kid?'

'Yeah,' I said. 'You know her father, right? Did you ever meet Katy?'

'Nah. I knew Jonathan when we were kids, but we don't stay in touch. His wife's a nightmare. It's like trying to make conversation with wallpaper.'

'I've met her,' I said, with a wry grin.

'So what's all this about a rape?' Cathal asked. He was cracking easily at his gum, but his eyes were wary, animal.

'Basically,' I said, 'we're checking out anything in the Devlins' lives that smells funny. And we hear you and Jonathan Devlin and Shane Waters did something dodgy to a girl in the summer of '84. What's the real story?' I would have liked to spend a few more minutes on the male bonding, but we didn't have time. Once his lawyer got there, my chance would be over.

'Shane Waters,' Cathal said. 'Now there's a name I haven't heard in a while.'

'You don't have to say anything till your lawyer gets here,' I said, 'but you're not a suspect in this murder. I know you weren't in the country that week. I just want all the information I can get about the Devlins.'

'You think Jonathan knocked off his own kid?' Cathal looked amused.

'You tell me,' I said. 'You know him better than I do.'

Cathal leaned his head back and laughed. It eased his shoulders and took twenty years off him, and for the first time he looked familiar to me: the cruel, handsome cut of his lips, the tricky glitter in his eyes. 'Listen, mate,' he said, 'let me tell you something about Devlin. The man's a fucking pussy. He probably still acts the hard man, but don't let that fool you: he's never taken a risk in his life without me there to give him a shove. That's why he's where he is today, and I'm' – he tilted his chin at the boardroom – 'I'm here.'

'So this rape wasn't his idea.'

He shook his head and wagged a finger at me, grinning: *Nice try.* 'Who told you there was a rape?'

'Come on, man,' I said, grinning back, 'you know I can't tell you that. Witnesses.'

Cathal cracked his gum slowly and stared at me. 'OK,' he said finally. The traces of the smile were still hanging at the corners of his mouth. 'Let's put it this way. There was no rape, but if – let's just say – there had been, Jonner would never in a million years have had the balls to think of it. And, *if* it had ever happened, he would've spent the next few weeks so scared he was practically shitting his pants, convinced that someone had seen it and was going to go to the cops, babbling on about how we were all going to gaol, wanting to turn himself in . . . The guy doesn't have the nerve to kill a kitten, never mind a kid.'

'And you?' I said. 'You wouldn't have been worried that these witnesses would rat you out?'

'Me?' The grin broadened again. 'Not a chance, mate. If, hypothetically, any of this had ever happened, I would've been fucking delighted with myself, because I would have known I was going to get away with it.'

'I vote we arrest him,' I said, that evening at Cassie's. Sam was in Ballsbridge, at a champagne-reception-cum-dance for his cousin's twenty-first, so it was just the two of us, sitting on the sofa drinking wine and deciding how to go after Jonathan Devlin.

'For what?' Cassie demanded, reasonably. 'We can't get him on the rape. We might just possibly maybe have enough to pull him in for questioning on Peter and Jamie, except we don't have a witness who can put them at the rape scene, so we can't show a motive. Sandra didn't see you guys, and if you come forward, it'll compromise your involvement in this whole case, besides which O'Kelly will cut off your bollocks and use them for Christmas decorations. And we don't have a single thing linking Jonathan to Katy's death – just some stomach trouble that might or might not have been abuse and might or might not have been him. All we can do is ask him to come in and talk to us.'

'I'd just like to get him out of that house,' I said slowly. 'I'm worried about Rosalind.' It was the first time I had put this unease into words. It had been building in me, gradually and only half-acknowledged, ever since that first hurried phone call she had made, but over the past two days it had risen to a pitch I couldn't ignore.

'Rosalind? Why?'

'You said our guy won't kill unless he feels threatened. That fits with everything we've heard. According to Cathal, Jonathan was petrified that we'd tell someone about the rape; so he goes after us. Katy decided to stop getting sick, maybe threatened to tell, so he kills her. If he finds out Rosalind's been talking to me . . .'

'I don't think you need to be too worried about her,' Cassie said. She finished her wine. 'We could be completely wrong about Katy; it's all guesswork. And I wouldn't put too much weight on anything Cathal Mills says. He strikes me as a psychopath, and they lie easier than they tell the truth.'

I raised my eyebrows. 'You only met him for about five minutes. What, you're diagnosing the guy? He just struck me as a prick.'

She shrugged. 'I'm not saying I'm sure about Cathal. But they're surprisingly easy to spot, if you know how.'

'Is this what they taught you at Trinity?'

Cassie held out her hand for my glass, got up to refill

them. 'Not exactly,' she said, at the fridge. 'I knew a psychopath once.'

Her back was to me, and if there was an odd undertone in her voice I didn't catch it. 'I did see this thing on the Discovery Channel where they said up to five per cent of the population are psychopaths,' I said, 'but most of them don't break the law so they never get diagnosed. How much would you bet that half the government—'

'Rob,' Cassie said. 'Shut up. Please. I'm trying to tell you something here.'

This time I did hear the strain. She came over and gave me my glass, took hers to the window and leaned back on the sill. 'You wanted to know why I dropped out of college,' she said, very evenly. 'In second year I made friends with this guy in my class. He was popular, quite good-looking and very charming and intelligent and interesting – I didn't fancy him or anything like that, but I guess I was flattered that he was paying all this attention to me. We used to skip all our classes and spend hours over coffee. He brought me presents – cheap ones, and some of them looked used, but we were broke students, and hey, it's the thought that counts, right? Everyone thought it was sweet, how close we were.'

She took a sip of her drink, swallowed hard. 'I worked out pretty fast that he told a lot of lies, mostly for no real reason, but I knew – well, he'd told me – that he'd had a terrible childhood and that he'd been bullied in school, so I figured he'd got into the habit of lying to protect himself. I thought – Jesus Christ – I thought I could help: if he knew he had a friend who'd stick by him no matter what, he'd get more secure and wouldn't need to lie any more. I was only eighteen, nineteen.'

I was afraid to move, even to put down my glass; I was

terrified that any tiny movement would be the one that would send her pushing herself up off the windowsill and spinning the subject away with some flippant comment. There was an odd, taut set to her mouth that made her look much older, and I knew she had never told this story to anyone, ever before.

'I didn't even notice I was drifting away from all the other friends I'd made, because he went into this cold sulk if I spent time with them. He went into the cold sulk a lot, actually, for any reason or none, and I would have to spend ages trying to figure out what I'd done and apologising and making up for it. When I went to meet him I never knew whether he'd be all hugs and compliments or all cold shoulder and disapproving looks; there was no logic to it. Sometimes the things he pulled – just little things: borrowing my lecture notes just before exams, then forgetting to bring them back in for days, then claiming he'd lost them, then getting outraged when I saw them sticking out of his bag; that kind of thing . . . it made me so furious I wanted to kill him with my bare hands, but he was lovely just often enough that I didn't want to stop hanging around with him.' A tiny, crooked twist of a smile. 'I didn't want to hurt him.'

It took her three tries to light a cigarette; Cassie, who had told me about getting stabbed without so much as tensing up. 'Anyway,' she said, 'this went on for almost two years. In January of fourth year he made a pass at me, in my flat. I turned him down – I have no idea why, by that time I was so confused I barely knew what I was doing, but thank God I had a few of my instincts left. I said I just wanted to be friends, he seemed fine with it, we talked for a while, he left. The next day I went into class and everyone was staring at me and nobody would talk to me. It took me two weeks to find out what was going on. I finally cornered this girl Sarah-Jane – we'd been pretty good friends, back in first year – and she said that they all knew what I'd done to him.'

She drew on her cigarette, hard and fast. She was looking at me, but not quite meeting my eyes; hers were too wide, dilated. I thought of Jessica Devlin's dazed, narcotised stare. 'The night I turned him down, he'd gone straight to these other girls' flat, girls from our class. He arrived in tears. He told them that he and I had been secretly going out for a while, that he'd decided it wasn't working out, and that I had said if he broke up with me I'd tell everyone he'd raped me. He said I'd threatened to go to the police, the papers, to ruin his life.' She looked for an ashtray, flicked ash, missed.

It didn't occur to me at the time to wonder why she was telling me this story, why now. This may seem strange, but everything did that month, strange and precarious. The moment when Cassie had said 'We'll have it' had set in motion some unstoppable tectonic shift; familiar things were cracking open and twisting inside out before my eyes, the world turning beautiful and dangerous as a bright spinning blade. Cassie opening the door to one of her secret rooms seemed like a natural, inevitable part of this massive sea-change. In a way, I suppose it was. It was only much later that I realised she had actually been telling me something very specific, if I had just been paying attention.

'My God,' I said, after a while. 'Just because you bruised his ego?'

'Not just that,' Cassie said. She was wearing a soft cherry-coloured jumper and I could see it vibrating, very fast, just above her breast, and I realised my heart was speeding too. 'Because he was bored. Because, by turning him down, I had made it clear that he'd got as much entertainment out of me as he was going to, so this was the only other use he had for me. Because, when you come right down to it, it was fun.'

'Did you tell this Sarah-Jane what had happened?'

'Oh, yeah,' Cassie said levelly. 'I told everyone who would still talk to me. Not one of them believed me. They all believed him – all our classmates, all our mutual acquaintances, which added up to just about everyone I knew. People who were supposed to be my friends.'

'Oh, Cassie,' I said. I was aching to go over to her, put my arms around her, hold her close until that terrible rigidity melted out of her body and she came back from whatever remote place she had gone to. But the immobility of her, her braced shoulders: I couldn't tell whether she would welcome it or whether it would be the worst thing I could do. Blame boarding-school; blame, if you prefer, some deep-seated character flaw. The fact is that I didn't know how. I doubt that, in the long run, it would have made any difference; but this only makes me wish even more intensely that, at least for that one moment, I had known what to do.

'I stuck it out for another couple of weeks,' Cassie said. She lit another cigarette off the end of the old one, something I had never seen her do before. 'He was always surrounded by this knot of people giving him protective pats and glaring at me. People were coming up to me to tell me that I was the reason why genuine rapists got away with it. One girl said I deserved to be raped so I'd realise what a horrible thing I'd done.'

She laughed, a small harsh sound. 'It's ironic, isn't it? A hundred psychology students, and not one of us recognised a classic psychopath. You know the strange thing? I wished I had done everything he claimed I had. If I had, then it would all have made sense: I would have been getting what I deserved. But I hadn't done any of it, and yet that made absolutely no difference to what happened. There was no such thing as cause and effect. I thought I was losing my mind.'

I leaned over – slowly, the way you would reach out towards a terrified animal – and took her hand; that much, at least, I managed to do. She gave a quick breath of a laugh, squeezed my fingers, then let them go. 'Anyway. Finally he came up to me one day, in the Buttery – all these girls were trying to stop him, but he sort of shook them off bravely and came over to me and said, loud, so they could hear him, "Please, stop ringing me in the middle of the night. What have I ever done to you?" I was completely stunned, I couldn't figure out what he was talking about. All I could think of to say was, "But I haven't rung you." He smiled and shook his head, like, *Yeah, right,* and then he leaned in and said – just quietly, in this chirpy businesslike voice – "If I ever did break into your flat and rape you, I don't think the charges would stick, do you?" Then he smiled again and went back to his mates.'

'Hon,' I said finally, carefully, 'maybe you should put in an alarm on this place. I don't want to scare you, but—'

Cassie shook her head. 'And what, never leave the flat again? I can't afford to start getting paranoid. I've got good locks, and I keep my gun beside my bed.' I had noticed that, of course, but there are plenty of detectives who don't feel right unless they have their guns within reach. 'Anyway, I'm pretty sure he'd never actually do it. I know the way he works – unfortunately. It's a lot more fun for him to think that I'm always wondering than to just do it and get it over with.'

She took a last pull on her cigarette, leaned forward to

stub it out. Her spine was so rigid that the movement looked painful. 'At the time, though, the whole thing freaked me out enough that I dropped out of college. I went over to France – I've got cousins in Lyon, I stayed with them for a year and worked as a waitress in this café. It was nice. That's where I got the Vespa. Then I came back and applied to Templemore.'

'Because of him?'

She shrugged. 'I guess. Probably. So maybe one good thing came out of it. Two: I've got good psychopath sensors now. It's like an allergy: you get exposed once, from then on you're super-sensitised.' She finished her drink in a long swallow. 'I ran into Sarah-Jane last year, in a pub in town. I said hi. She told me he was doing fine, "in spite of your best efforts", and then walked off.'

'Is that what your nightmares are about?' I said gently, after a moment. I had woken her from these dreams – flailing at me, gasping incomprehensible spates of words – twice before, when we had worked rape-murders, but she would never tell me the details.

'Yeah. I dream he's the guy we're after, but we can't prove it, and when he finds out I'm on the case, he . . . Well. He does his thing.'

I took it for granted, at the time, that she dreamed this guy followed through on his threat. Now I think I was wrong. I failed to understand the one crucial thing: where the real danger lay. And I think this may have been, in the face of stiff competition, my single biggest mistake of all.

'What was his name?' I asked. I was desperate to do something, fix this somehow, and running a background check on this guy, trying to find something to arrest him for, was the only thing I could think of to do. And I suppose a small part of me, whether through cruelty or detached curiosity or whatever, had noticed that Cassie refused to say it, and wanted to see what would happen if she did.

Cassie's eyes finally focused on mine, and I was shaken by the concentrated, diamond-hard hatred. 'Legion,' she said.

14

We pulled Jonathan in the next day. I rang him up and asked him, in my best professional voice, if he would mind coming in after work, just to help us out with a few things. Sam had Andrews in the main interview room, the big one with an observation chamber for line-ups ('Jesus, Mary and the Seven Dwarfs,' O'Kelly said, 'all of a sudden we've suspects coming out of the woodwork. I should've taken away your floaters sooner, got ye three off your lazy arses'), but this was fine with us: we wanted a small room, the smaller the better.

We decorated it as carefully as a stage set. Photos of Katy, alive and dead, spanning half a wall; Peter and Jamie and the scary trainers and the grazes on my knees across the other half (we had a shot of my broken fingernails, but it made me far more uncomfortable than it could possibly have made Jonathan – my thumbs have a very distinctive turn to them, and already at twelve my hands were almost man-sized – and Cassie said nothing when I slid it back into the file); maps and charts and every bit of esoteric-looking paperwork we could find, the blood work, timelines, files and cryptically labelled boxes stacked in corners.

'That ought to do it,' I said, surveying the final result. It was actually quite impressive, in a nightmarish way.

'Mm.' A corner of one of the post-mortem shots was peeling away from the wall, and Cassie absently pressed it back into place. Her hand lingered there for a second, fingertips lying lightly across Katy's bare grey arm. I knew what she was thinking – if Devlin was innocent, then this was wanton cruelty – but I had no room to worry about this. More often than we like to admit, cruelty comes with the job.

We had half an hour or so before Devlin got off work, and we were far too antsy to start on anything else. We left our interview room – which was beginning to freak me out a little, all those round watching eyes; I told myself this was a good sign – and went into the observation chamber to see how Sam was getting on.

He had been doing his research; Terence Andrews now had a nice big section of whiteboard all to himself. He had studied Commerce at UCD, and though he had graduated with only a 2:2 he had apparently gained a firm grasp of the essentials: at twenty-three he had married Dolores Lehane, a Dublin debutante, and her property-developer daddy had set him up in the business. Dolores had left him four years ago and was living in London. The marriage had been childless but hardly unproductive: Andrews had a bustling little empire, concentrated in the greater Dublin area but with outposts in Budapest and Prague, and rumour had it that Dolores's lawyers and the Revenue knew about less than half of it.

According to Sam, though, he had got a little over-enthusiastic. The flashy executive pad and the pimpmobile (customised silver Porsche, tinted windows, chrome, the whole enchilada) and the golf-club memberships were all bravado: Andrews had barely more actual cash than I did, his bank manager was starting to get restive, and over the past six months he had been selling off bits of his land, still undeveloped, to pay the mortgages on the rest. 'If that motorway doesn't go through Knocknaree, and fast,' Sam said succinctly, 'the boy's banjaxed.'

I had disliked Andrews well before I knew his name, and I saw nothing that changed my opinion. He was on the short side, balding badly, with beefy, florid features. He had a massive paunch and a cast in one eye, but where most men would have tried to conceal these infirmities he used them as blunt weapons: he wore the belly thrown out in front of him like a status symbol – *No cheap Guinness in here, sunshine, this was built by restaurants you couldn't afford in a million years* – and every time Sam got distracted and glanced over his shoulder to see what Andrews was looking at, Andrews's mouth twitched into a triumphant little smirk.

He had brought his lawyer with him, of course, and was answering about one question out of ten. Sam had managed, working his way doggedly through a dizzying pile of paperwork, to prove that Andrews owned large amounts of land in Knocknaree; upon which Andrews had quit denying that he'd ever heard of the place. He wouldn't touch questions about his financial situation, though – he clapped Sam on the shoulder and said genially, 'If I were on a cop's salary, Sam, boy, I'd be more worried about my own finances than anyone else's,' while the lawyer murmured colourlessly, in the background, 'My client cannot disclose any information on that subject' – and both of them were profoundly, smoothly shocked at the mention of the threatening phone calls. I fidgeted and checked my watch every thirty seconds; Cassie leaned against the glass, eating an apple and abstractedly offering me a bite now and then.

Andrews did, however, have an alibi for the night of Katy's death, and after a certain amount of aggrieved rhetoric he agreed to provide it. He had been at a poker night in Killiney with a few of 'the lads', and when the game wound up around midnight he had decided not to drive home – 'Cops aren't as understanding as they used to be,' he said, with a wink at Sam – and had stayed in the host's spare room. He gave the names and phone numbers of The Lads, so Sam could confirm this.

'That's grand, so,' Sam said at last. 'We'll just need to do a voice line-up, so we can eliminate you as the source of the phone calls.'

A wounded expression spread across Andrews's pudgy features. 'I'm sure you realise it's hard for me to go out of my way for you, Sam,' he said, 'after the way I've been treated.' Cassie started to giggle.

'I'm sorry you feel that way, Mr Andrews,' Sam said gravely. 'Could you tell me what aspects of your treatment have been the problem, exactly?'

'You've dragged me in here for most of a *business day*, Sam, and treated me like a *suspect*,' Andrews said, his voice swelling and quavering with the injustice of it all. I started to laugh as well. 'Now I know you're used to dealing with little knackers with nothing better to do, but you have to realise what this means to a man in my position. I'm missing out on some wonderful opportunities because I'm here helping you out, I may have lost thousands today already, and now you want me to hang around doing some voice what-d'you-call-it for a man I've never even *heard* of?' Sam had been right: he did have a squeaky little tenor voice on him.

'Sure, we can fix that,' Sam said. 'We don't need to do the voice line-up now. If it suits you better to come back and do it this evening or tomorrow morning, outside business hours, I'll set it up then. How's that?'

Andrews pouted. The lawyer – he was the naturally

peripheral type, I don't even remember what he looked like – raised a tentative finger and requested a moment to confer with his client. Sam turned off the camera and joined us in the observation room, loosening his tie.

'Hi,' he said. 'Exciting watching, yeah?'

'Riveting,' I said. 'It must be even more fun from inside.'

'I'm telling you. A laugh a minute, this boy. God, did you see that bloody eye? It took me ages to cop on, I thought at first he'd just no attention span—'

'Your suspect's more fun than our suspect,' Cassie said. 'Ours doesn't even have a twitch or anything.'

'Speaking of whom,' I said, 'don't schedule the line-up for tonight. Devlin's got a prior appointment, and afterwards, with any luck, he'll be in no mood for anything else.' If we were really lucky, I knew, the case – both cases – could be over that evening, with no need for Andrews to do anything at all, but I didn't mention this. Even the thought made my throat tighten irritatingly.

'God, that's right,' Sam said. 'I forgot. Sorry. We're getting somewhere, though, aren't we? Two good suspects in one day.'

'Damn, we're good,' Cassie said. 'Andrews high-five!' She crossed her eyes, swiped at Sam's hand and missed. We were all very keyed up.

'If someone hits you on the back of the head you'll be stuck that way,' Sam said. 'That's what happened to Andrews.'

'Hit him again and see if you can unstick him.'

'My God, you're politically incorrect,' I told her. 'I'm going to report you to the National Commission for Squinty Bastards' Rights.'

'He's giving me bugger-all,' Sam said. 'But that's grand; I didn't expect to get much out of him today. All I want is to rattle him a bit, and get him to agree to the voice line-up. Once we have an ID, I can put the pressure on.'

'Hang on. Is he *langered*?' Cassie asked. She leaned forward, breath misting the glass, to watch Andrews as he gestured and muttered furiously in his lawyer's ear.

Sam grinned. 'Well spotted. I don't think he's actually drunk – not drunk enough to get chatty, anyway, unfortunately – but there's a smell of booze off him, all right, when you get up close. If just the thought of coming in here got him shook enough that he needed a drink, he's got something to hide. Maybe it's just the phone calls, but . . .'

Andrews's lawyer stood up, rubbing his hands on the sides of his trousers, and waved nervously at the glass. 'Round two,' Sam said, trying to work his tie back into place. 'See ye later, lads. Good luck.'

Cassie aimed her apple core at the bin in the corner and missed. 'Andrews jump shot,' Sam said, and headed out, grinning.

We left him to it and went outside for a cigarette – it might be a while before we got another chance. There is a little overhead bridge crossing one of the pathways into the formal garden, and we sat there, our backs against the railings. The Castle grounds were golden and nostalgic in the slanting late-afternoon light. Tourists in shorts and backpacks wandered past, gawking up at the crenellations; one of them, for no reason that I could fathom, took a photo of us. A couple of little kids were whirling around the maze of brick trails in the garden, arms out superhero-style.

Cassie's mood had shifted abruptly; the burst of ebullience had dissipated and she was shut away in a private circle of thought, arms on her knees, wayward wisps of smoke trailing from the cigarette burning forgotten between her fingers. She has these moods occasionally, and I was glad of this one. I didn't want to talk. All I could think was that we were about to hit Jonathan Devlin hard, with everything we had, and if he was ever going to crack then it would be today; and I had absolutely no idea what I would do, what would happen, if he did.

Suddenly Cassie's head went up; her gaze moved past me, over my shoulder. 'Look,' she said.

I turned. Jonathan Devlin was coming across the courtyard, his shoulders set forward and his hands deep in the pockets of his big brown overcoat. The high, arrogant lines of the surrounding buildings should have dwarfed him, but instead they seemed to me to align themselves around him, swooping into strange geometries with him at their crux, imbuing him with some impenetrable significance. He hadn't seen us. His head was down and the sun, low over the gardens, was in his face; to him we would have been only hazy silhouettes, suspended in a bright nimbus like the carved saints and gargoyles. Behind him his shadow fluttered long and black across the cobblestones.

He passed directly beneath us, and we watched his back as he trudged towards the door. 'Well,' I said. I mashed out my cigarette. 'I think that's our cue.'

I got up and held out a hand to pull Cassie to her feet, but she didn't move. Her eyes on mine were suddenly sober, intent, questioning.

'What?' I said.

'You shouldn't be doing this interview.'

I didn't answer. I didn't move, just stood there on the bridge with my hand held out to her. After a moment she shook her head wryly and the expression that had startled me disappeared, and she caught my hand and let me pull her up.

We brought him into the interview room. When he saw the wall his eyes widened sharply, but he said nothing. 'Detectives Maddox and Ryan interviewing Jonathan Michael Devlin,' Cassie said, riffling through one of the boxes and coming up with an overstuffed file. 'You are not obliged to say anything unless you wish to do so, but anything you do say will be taken down in writing and may be used in evidence. OK?'

'Am I under arrest?' Jonathan demanded. He hadn't moved from the door. 'For what?'

'What?' I said, puzzled. 'Oh, the caution . . . God, no. That's routine. We just want to update you on the investigation's progress, and see if you can help us move things forward another step.'

'If you were under arrest,' Cassie said, dumping the file on the table, 'you'd know all about it. What did you think you might be under arrest for?'

Jonathan shrugged. She smiled at him and pulled out a chair, facing the scary wall. 'Have a seat.' After a moment, he slowly took off his coat and sat down.

I took him through the update. I was the one he had trusted with his story, and that trust was a small close-range weapon that I didn't intend to detonate until the right moment. For now, I was his ally. I was, to a large extent, honest with him. I told him about the leads we had followed up, the tests the lab had run. I listed for him, one by one, the suspects we had identified and eliminated: the locals who thought he was stopping progress, the paedophiles and confession junkies and Tracksuit Shadows, the guy who thought Katy's leotard was immodest; Sandra. I could feel the frail, mute army of photographs ranged behind me, waiting. Jonathan did well, he kept his eyes on mine almost all the time; but I could see the effort of will that went into it.

'So what you're telling me is that you're getting no-where,' he said eventually, heavily. He looked terribly tired.

'God, no,' Cassie said. She had been sitting at the corner of the table, chin propped on one palm, watching in silence. 'Not at all. What Detective Ryan is telling you is that we've come a long way, these last few weeks. We've done a lot of eliminating. And here's what we've got left.' She inclined her head towards the wall; he didn't take his eyes off her face. 'We've got evidence that your daughter's murderer is a local man with intimate knowledge of the Knocknaree area. We've got forensic evidence linking her death to the 1984 disappearances of Peter Savage and Germaine Rowan, which indicates that the murderer is probably aged at least thirty-five and has had strong ties to the area for over twenty years. And a lot of the men fitting that description have alibis, so that narrows it down even further.'

'We also have evidence,' I said, 'to suggest that this isn't some thrill killer. This man isn't killing at random. He's doing it because he feels he has no choice.'

'So you think he's insane,' Jonathan said. His mouth twisted. 'Some lunatic—'

'Not necessarily,' I said. 'I'm just saying that sometimes situations get out of hand. Sometimes they end in tragedies that nobody really wanted to happen.'

'So you see, Mr Devlin, that narrows it down again: we're looking for someone who knew all three children and had motive to want them dead,' Cassie said. She was tilting her chair back, hands behind her head, her eyes steady on his. 'We're going to get this guy. We're getting closer every day. So if there's anything you want to tell us – anything at all, about either case – this is the time to do it.'

Jonathan didn't answer immediately. The room was very quiet, only the soft drone of the fluorescent bars overhead and the slow, monotonous creak of Cassie rocking her chair on its back legs. Jonathan's eyes fell away from hers and moved past her, across the photographs: Katy suspended in that impossible arabesque, Katy laughing on a blurry green lawn with her hair blown sideways and a sandwich in her hands, Katy with one eye a slit open and blood crusted dark on her lip. The bare, simple pain on his face was almost indecent. I had to force myself not to look away.

The silence stretched tighter. Almost imperceptibly, something I recognised was happening to Jonathan. There's a specific crumbling in the mouth and spine, a sagging as though the underlying musculature is dissolving to water, that every detective knows: it belongs to the instant before a suspect confesses, as he finally and almost with relief lets his defences fall away. Cassie had stopped rocking her chair. My pulse was running high in my throat, and I felt the photographs behind me catch tiny swift breaths and hold them, poised to swoop off the paper and down the corridor and out into the dark evening, freed, if only he gave the word.

Jonathan wiped a hand hard across his mouth and folded his arms and looked back at Cassie. 'No,' he said. 'There's nothing.'

Cassie and I let out our breath in unison. I had known, really, that it was too much to hope for, so soon, and – after that first sinking second – I hardly cared; because now, at last, I was sure that Jonathan knew something. He had as good as told us so.

This actually came as something of a shock. The whole case had been so crowded with possibilities and hypotheticals ('OK. So say just for a second that Mark did do it, right, and the illness and the old case aren't related after all, and say Mel's telling the truth: who could he have got to dump the body?') that certainty had started to seem unimaginable, some remote childhood dream. I felt as if I had been moving among empty dresses hung in some dim attic and had suddenly bumped smack into a human body, warm and solid and alive.

Cassie eased the front legs of her chair to the floor. 'OK,' she said, 'OK. Let's go back to the beginning. The rape of Sandra Scully. When did that happen, exactly?'

Jonathan's head turned sharply towards me. 'You're all right,' I told him, in an undertone. 'Statute of limitations.' In fact, we still hadn't bothered to check this, but it was moot: there was no chance we would ever be able to charge him, anyway.

He gave me a long, wary look. 'Summer of eighty-four,' he said, finally. 'I wouldn't know the date.'

'We've got statements putting it in the first two weeks of August,' Cassie said, opening the file. 'Does that sound right to you?'

'Could well have been.'

'We also have statements saying that there were witnesses.'

He shrugged. 'I wouldn't know.'

'Actually, Jonathan,' Cassie said, 'we've been told that you chased them into the woods and came back saying, "Bloody kids." Sounds to me like you knew they were there.'

'Maybe I did. I don't remember.'

'How did you feel about the fact that there were kids out there who knew what you'd done?'

Another shrug. 'Like I said. I don't remember that.'

'Cathal says . . .' She flipped pages. 'Cathal Mills says you were terrified they'd go to the cops. He says you were, quote, so scared you were practically shitting your pants, unquote.'

No response. He settled deeper into the chair, arms folded, solid as a wall.

'What'd you do to stop them turning you in?'

'Nothing.'

Cassie laughed. 'Ah, come on, Jonathan. We know who those witnesses were.'

'You've one up on me, so.' His face was still braced into hard angles, giving away nothing, but a red flush was building across his cheeks: he was getting angry.

'And only a few days after the rape,' Cassie said, 'two of them disappeared.' She got up – unhurriedly, stretching – and crossed the room to the wall of photos.

'Peter Savage,' she said, laying a finger on his school picture. 'I'd like you to look at the photograph, please, Mr Devlin.' She waited until Jonathan's head came up and he stared, defiantly, at the picture. 'People say he was a born leader. He might have been heading up the Move the Motorway campaign with you, if he'd lived. His parents can't move house, do you know that? Joseph Savage got offered his dream job, a few years back, but it would've involved moving to Galway, and they couldn't bear the thought that Peter might come home some day and find them gone.'

Jonathan began to say something, but she didn't give him time. 'Germaine Rowan' – her hand moved to the next picture – 'a.k.a. Jamie. She wanted to be a vet when she grew up. Her mother hasn't moved a thing in her room. She dusts it every Saturday. When the phone numbers went to seven digits, back in the nineties – remember that? – Alicia Rowan went into Telecom Éireann's head office and begged them, in tears, to let her keep the old six-digit one, in case someday Jamie tried to ring home.'

'We had nothing—' Jonathan started, but she cut him off again, her voice rising, bearing down on his.

'And Adam Ryan.' The photo of my scraped knees. 'His parents moved away, because of the publicity and because they were afraid that whoever did this would come back for him. They've dropped off the radar. But wherever he is, he's been living with the fallout every day of his life. You love Knocknaree, right, Jonathan? You love being part of a community where you've lived since you were a tiny kid? Adam might have felt the same way, if he'd got the chance. But now he's out there somewhere, could be anywhere in the world, and he can't ever come home.'

The words tolled through me like the lost bells of some underwater city. She was good, Cassie: just for a split second, I was filled with such a wild and utter desolation that I could have thrown back my head and howled like a dog.

'Do you know how the Savages and Alicia Rowan feel about you, Jonathan?' Cassie demanded. 'They envy you. You had to bury your daughter, but the only thing worse than that is never having the chance to do it. Remember how you felt the day Katy was missing? They've felt that way for twenty years.'

'All these people deserve to know what happened, Mr Devlin,' I said quietly. 'And it's not just for their sakes, either. We've been working on the assumption that the two cases are connected. If we're wrong, then we need to know that, or Katy's killer could slip straight through our fingers.'

Something shot across Jonathan's eyes – something, I thought, like a strange, sick mixture of horror and hope, but it was gone too quickly for me to be sure.

'What happened that day?' Cassie asked. 'The four-teenth of August, 1984. The day Peter and Jamie van-ished.'

Jonathan settled deeper into the chair and shook his head. 'I've told you all I know.'

'Mr Devlin,' I said, leaning forward to him, 'it's easy to understand how this happened. You were utterly terrified about the whole thing with Sandra.'

'You knew she was no threat,' Cassie said. 'She was mad about Cathal, she wouldn't say anything to get him into trouble – and if she did, it would be her word against all of yours. Juries have a tendency to doubt rape victims, especially rape victims who've had consensual sex with two of their assailants. You could call her a slut and be home free. But those kids . . . one word from them could land you in gaol at any minute. You could never feel safe, as long as they were around.'

She left the wall, pulled a chair close beside him and sat down. 'You didn't go into Stillorgan at all that day,' she said softly, 'did you?'

Jonathan shifted, a tiny squaring of the shoulders. 'Yeah,' he said, heavily. 'I did. Myself and Cathal and Shane. To the pictures.'

'What'd you see?'

'Whatever I told the cops at the time. It's been twenty years.'

Cassie shook her head. 'No,' she said, a slight, cool syllable that dropped like a depth charge. 'Maybe one of you – I'd bet on Shane; he's the one I'd leave out, myself – went to the pictures, so he could tell the other two the plot of the film, in case anyone asked. Maybe, if you were smart, you all three went into the cinema and then slipped out the fire exit as soon as the lights went down, so you'd have an alibi. But before six o'clock, two of you, at least, were back in Knocknaree, in the wood.'

'*What*,' said Jonathan. His face was pulled into a disgusted grimace.

'The kids always went home for tea at half-six, and you knew it could take you a while to find them; the wood was pretty big, back then. But you found them, all right. They were playing, not hiding; probably they were making plenty of noise. You sneaked up on them, just like they'd snuck up on you, and you grabbed them.'

We had talked all this over beforehand, of course we had: gone through it again and again, found a theory that fit with everything we had, tested every detail. But some tiny slippery unease was stirring in me, twitching and elbowing – *Not like that, it wasn't like that* – and it was too late: there was no way left to stop.

'We never even went into the bloody wood that day. We—'

'You pulled the kids' shoes off, to make it harder for them to run away. Then you killed Jamie. We won't be sure how till we find the bodies, but I'm betting on a blade. You either stabbed her or cut her throat. Somehow or other, her blood went into Adam's shoes; maybe you deliberately used them to catch the blood, trying not to leave too much evidence. Maybe you were planning to throw the shoes into the river, along with the bodies. But then, Jonathan, while you were dealing with Peter, you took your eye off Adam. He grabbed his shoes and he ran like fuck. There were slash-marks in his T-shirt: I think one of you was stabbing at him as he ran, just missed him . . . But you lost him. He knew that wood even better than you did, and he hid till the searchers found him. How did that make you feel, Jonathan? Knowing that you'd done all that for nothing, and there was still a witness out there?'

Jonathan stared into space, his jaw set. My hands were shaking; I slid them under the edge of the table.

'See, Jonathan,' Cassie said, 'this is why I think there were only two of you there. Three big guys against three little kids, it would've been no contest: you wouldn't have needed to take their shoes off to stop them running, you could have just held down one kid each, and Adam would never have made it home. But if there were only two of you, trying to subdue the three of them . . .'

'Mr Devlin,' I said. My voice sounded strange, echoing. 'If you're the one who wasn't actually there – if you're the one who went to the cinema to provide an alibi – then you need to tell us. There's a big, big difference between being a murderer and being an accessory.'

Jonathan shot me a vicious *et-tu-Brute* look. 'You're out of your bloody minds,' he said. He was breathing hard through his nose. 'You – *fuck* this. We never touched those kids.'

'I know you weren't the ringleader, Mr Devlin,' I said. 'That was Cathal Mills. He's told us so. He said, and I quote, "Jonner would never in a million years have had the balls to think of it." If you were only an accessory, or only a witness, do yourself a favour and tell us now.'

'That's a load of shite. Cathal didn't confess to any murders, because we didn't *commit* any murders. I haven't a clue what happened to those kids and I don't give a damn. I've nothing to say about them. I just want to know who did this to Katy.'

'Katy,' Cassie said, her eyebrows lifting. 'OK, fair

enough: we'll come back to Peter and Jamie. Let's talk about Katy.' She shoved her chair back with a screech – Jonathan's shoulders leaped – and crossed, fast, to the wall. 'These are Katy's medical records. Four years of un-explained gastric illness, ending this spring when she told her ballet teacher it was going to stop and, hey presto, it stopped. Our medical examiner says there was no sign of anything wrong with her. Do you know what that says to us? It says someone was poisoning Katy. It's easily done: a little toilet bleach here, a dose of oven cleaner there, even salt water'll do it. It happens all the time.'

I was watching Jonathan. The angry flush had drained out of his cheeks; he was white, bone-white. That tiny convulsive unease inside me evaporated like mist and it hit me, all over again: he knew.

'And that wasn't some stranger, Jonathan, that wasn't someone with a stake in the motorway and a grudge against you. That was someone who had daily access to Katy, someone she trusted. But by this spring, when she got a second chance at ballet school, that trust was starting to wear a little thin. She refused to keep taking the stuff. Probably she threatened to tell. And just a few months later' – a sharp slap to one of the piteous post-mortem shots – 'Katy's dead.'

'Were you covering for your wife, Mr Devlin?' I asked gently. I could hardly breathe. 'When a child's poisoned, it's usually the mother. If you were just trying to keep your family together, we can help you with that. We can get Mrs Devlin the help she needs.'

'Margaret loves our girls,' Jonathan said. His voice was taut, over-tightened. 'She would *never*.'

'Never what?' enquired Cassie. 'She'd never make Katy sick, or she'd never kill her?'

'Never do *anything* to hurt her. Ever.'

'Then who does that leave?' Cassie asked. She was leaning against the wall, fingering the post-mortem photo and watching him, cool as a girl in a painting. 'Rosalind and Jessica both have a rock-solid alibi for the night Katy died. Who's left?'

'Don't you dare even suggest I hurt my daughter,' he said, a low, warning rumble. 'Don't you dare.'

'We've got three murdered children, Mr Devlin, all murdered in the same place, all very probably murdered to cover up other crimes. And we've got one guy smack bang in the middle of each case: you. If you've got a good explanation for that, we need to hear it now.'

'This is *unbefuckinglievable*,' Jonathan said. His voice was rising dangerously. 'Katy's – someone's after killing my daughter and you want me to give you an *explanation*? That's *your* bloody job. You're the ones should be giving *me* explanations, not accusing me of—'

I was on my feet almost before I knew it. I threw down my notebook with a flat smack and pitched myself forward on my hands, leaning across the table into his face. 'A local guy, Jonathan, thirty-five or over, been living in Knocknaree more than twenty years. A guy with no solid alibi. A guy who knew Peter and Jamie, had daily access to Katy, and had a strong motive to kill all of them. Who the fuck does that sound like to you? You name me one other man who fits that description, and I swear to God you can walk out that door and we'll never hassle you again. Come on, Jonathan. Name one. Just one.'

'Then arrest me!' he roared. He slammed out his fists at me, palms up, wrists pressed together. 'Come on, if you're so bloody sure, all your evidence— Arrest me! Come on!'

I cannot tell you, I wonder if you can imagine, how badly

I wanted to do it. My whole life was shooting through my mind as a drowning man's is said to – tear-sodden nights in a chilly dorm and bikes zigzagging look-Ma-no-hands, pocket-warm butter-and-sugar sandwiches, the detectives' voices yammering endlessly at my ears – and I knew we didn't have enough, it would never stick, in twelve hours he would walk out that door free as a bird and guilty as sin. I had never been so sure of anything in my life. 'Fuck this,' I said, shoving up my shirt cuffs. 'No, Devlin. No. You've been sitting here bullshitting us all evening, and I've had enough.'

'Arrest me or—'

I lunged at him. He leaped backwards, sending the chair clattering, finding a corner and throwing up his fists in the same reflexive movement. Cassie was on me already, grabbing my raised arm with both hands. 'Jesus, Ryan! Stop!'

We had done it so many times. It's our last resort, when we know a suspect is guilty but we need a confession and he won't talk. After the lunge and grab I slowly relax, shake off Cassie's loosening hands, still glaring at the suspect; finally roll my shoulders and stretch out my neck and sprawl in my chair, drumming my fingers restlessly, while she goes back to questioning him with a watchful eye on me for any sign of renewed ferocity. A few minutes later she starts, checks her mobile, says, 'Dammit, I have to take this. Ryan . . . just stay cool, OK? Remember what happened last time,' and leaves us alone together. It works; mostly I don't even have to stand up again. Ten times we'd done it, twelve? We had it as smoothly choreographed as any screen stunt.

But this wasn't the same, this was the real thing for which all the other times and all the other cases had been nothing but practice, and it infuriated me even more that Cassie didn't realise this. I tried to jerk my arm away; she was stronger than I expected, wrists like steel, and I heard a seam rip somewhere in my sleeve. We swayed in a thick, clumsy struggle. 'Get *off* me—'

'Rob, *no*—'

Her voice came to me thin and meaningless through the huge red roaring in my head. All I could see was Jonathan, brows down and chin braced like a boxer, cornered and waiting only a few feet away. I reefed my arm forward with all my strength and felt her stumble back as her grip slipped away, but the chair got under my feet and before I could kick it aside and reach him she had recovered, caught my other arm and twisted it up behind my back, one fast, clinical move. I gasped.

'Are you out of your fucking mind?' she said straight into my ear, low and furious. 'He *doesn't know anything.*'

The words hit me like a slap of cold water in the face. I knew that even if she was wrong there was nothing in the world I could do about it, and it left me breathless, helpless. I felt as if I had been filleted.

Cassie felt the fight drain out of me. She shoved me away and stepped back swiftly, her hands still tense and ready. We stared at each other across the room like enemies, both of us breathing hard.

There was something dark and spreading on her lower lip, and after a moment I realised it was blood. For a hideous, free-falling second I thought I had hit her. (Later I found out that I hadn't, in fact: when I pulled away, the recoil flung one of her wrists back to smack her in the mouth, cutting her lip on her front teeth; not that this makes much of a difference.) It brought me back to myself, a little. 'Cassie—' I said.

She ignored me. 'Mr Devlin,' she said coolly, as if nothing at all had happened; there was only the faintest hint of a tremor in her voice. Jonathan – I had forgotten he was there – moved slowly out of the corner, his eyes still on me. 'We'll be releasing you without charge for now. But I would strongly advise you to stay where we can find you and not to attempt to contact your rape victim in any way. Understood?'

'Yeah,' Devlin said, after a moment. 'Fine.' He yanked the chair upright, pulled his tangled coat off the back and threw it on in quick, angry jabs. At the door he turned and gave me a hard look, and I thought for a moment he was going to say something, but he changed his mind and left, shaking his head disgustedly. Cassie followed him out and whipped the door shut behind her; it was too heavy for a proper slam, it closed with an unsatisfying thump.

I sank into a chair and put my face in my hands. I had never done anything like this before, ever. I abhor physical violence, I always have; the very thought makes me flinch. Even when I was a prefect, with arguably more power and less accountability than any adult outside of small South American countries, I never once caned anyone. But a minute ago I had been tussling with Cassie like some drunk skanger in a bar brawl, ready to dogfight Jonathan Devlin on the interview-room floor, swept away by the over-whelming desire to knee him in the guts and beat his face to bloody pulp. And I had hurt Cassie. I wondered, with detached, lucid interest, whether I was losing my mind.

After a few minutes Cassie came back in, shut the door and leaned against it, hands shoved into her jeans pockets. Her lip had stopped bleeding.

'Cassie,' I said, rubbing my hands over my face. 'I'm really sorry. Are you OK?'

'What the hell was that?' She had a hot, bright spot of colour on each cheekbone.

'I thought he knew something. I was sure.' My hands were shaking so hard it looked phony, like an inept actor simulating shock. I clasped them together to stop it.

Eventually she said, very quietly, 'Rob, you can't keep this up.' I didn't answer. After a long time, I heard the door close behind her.

15

I got drunk that night, banjoed drunk, drunker than I'd been in about fifteen years. I spent half the night sitting on the bathroom floor, staring glassily at the toilet and wishing I could just throw up and get it over with. The edges of my vision pulsed sickeningly with every heartbeat, and the shadows in the corners flicked and throbbed and contorted themselves into spiky, nasty little crawling things that were gone in the next blink. Finally I realised that, while the nausea showed no signs of getting better, it probably wasn't going to get any worse. I staggered into my room and fell asleep on top of the covers without taking off my clothes.

My dreams were uneasy ones, with a clogged, tainted quality to them. Something thrashing and yowling in a burlap bag, laughter and a lighter moving closer. Shattered glass on the kitchen floor, and someone's mother was sobbing. I was a trainee again in some lonely border county, and Jonathan Devlin and Cathal Mills were hiding out in the hills with guns and a hunting dog, living wild and we had to catch them, me and two murder detectives tall and cold as waxworks, our boots mired deep in treacly mud. I half-woke fighting the bedclothes, sheets pulled away from the mattress into sweaty tangles, and was dragged down into sleep again even as I realised I had been dreaming.

But I woke up in the morning with one image brilliantly clear in my head, slapped across the front of my mind like a neon sign. Nothing to do with Peter or Jamie or Katy: Emmett, Tom Emmett, one of those two murder detectives who had paid a flying visit to Ballygobackwards when I was a trainee. Emmett was tall and very thin, with subtly wonderful clothes (now that I think of it, this is probably where I got my first immutable impression of how murder detectives are supposed to dress) and a face straight out of an old cowboy movie, scored and polished like ancient wood. He was still on the squad when I joined – he's retired now – and he seemed like a pretty nice guy, but I never managed to get past that first awe of him; whenever he talked to me I would instantly congeal into an inarticulate, schoolboyish mess.

I had been skulking in the Ballygobackwards car park one afternoon, smoking and trying not to be too obvious about eavesdropping on their conversation. The other detective had asked a question – what, I couldn't hear – and Emmett had shaken his head briefly. 'If he doesn't, then we've made a bollocks of the whole thing,' he'd said, taking a last crisp drag on his cigarette and extinguishing it under one elegant shoe. 'We'll have to go back. Right back to the beginning, and see where we went wrong.' Then they'd turned and gone into the station, side by side, shoulders hunched and secretive in their discreet dark jackets.

I had, I knew – there's nothing like booze for triggering abject self-reproach – made a complete bollocks of just about everything, in just about every possible way. But that barely mattered, because the solution was suddenly so clear. I felt as if everything that had happened throughout this case – the Kavanagh nightmare, the awful interview with Jonathan, all the sleepless nights and little treacheries of the mind – had been sent by the hand of some wise kind god to bring me to this moment. Here I had been avoiding Knocknaree wood like the plague, I think I would have interviewed everyone in the country and racked my brain till it exploded before it occurred to me to take a step back in there, if I hadn't been battered to the point where I had no defence left against the single blindingly obvious thing: I was the one person who beyond any doubt knew at least some of the answers, and if anything could give them back to me, it was (*right back to the beginning*) that wood.

It sounds facile, I'm sure. But I can't begin to describe to you what it meant to me, this thousand-watt bulb clicking on above my head, this beacon to tell me that I wasn't lost in a wilderness after all, that I knew exactly where to go. I almost burst out laughing, sitting there in bed with early-morning light streaming between the curtains. I should have had the mother of all hangovers, but I felt like I'd slept for a week; I was bubbling over with energy like a twenty-year-old. I showered and shaved and gave Heather such a cheerful 'Good morning' that she looked taken aback and slightly suspicious, and drove into town singing along to terrible chart music on the car radio.

I found a parking space on Stephen's Green – it felt like a good omen; they're unheard of at that hour of the morning – and did some quick shopping on my way to work. In a little bookshop off Grafton Street I found a beautiful old copy of *Wuthering Heights* – thick pages browning at the edges, rich red binding stamped in gold, 'For Sara, Christmas 1922' in faded ink on the title page. Then I went to Brown Thomas and bought a sleek, complicated little machine that made cappuccino; Cassie has a thing for coffee with froth on top, I had meant to get her this for

Christmas but had somehow never got around to it. I walked to work without bothering to move my car. It cost me a ridiculous amount of money in the meter, but it was the kind of sunny, buoyant day that encourages extravagance.

Cassie was already at her desk with a pile of paperwork. Sam and the floaters, luckily for me, were nowhere to be seen. 'Morning,' she said, giving me a cool warning look.

'Here,' I said, dumping the two bags in front of her.

'What's this?' she demanded, eyeing them suspiciously.

'That,' I said, pointing at the coffee gadget, 'is your belated Christmas present. And this one is an apology. I am so, so sorry, Cass – not just about yesterday, but about the way I've been all these last few weeks. I have been an utter pain in the arse and you have every right to be furious with me. But I absolutely promise that's over. From now on I will be a normal, sane, non-horrible human being.'

'That'd be a first,' Cassie said automatically, and my heart lifted. She opened the book – she loves Emily Brontë – and ran her fingers over the title page.

'Am I forgiven? I'll go down on my knees if you like. Seriously.'

'I would love to make you do it,' Cassie said, 'but somebody might see you, and the grapevine would blow a fuse on that one. Ryan, you little bastard. You ruined my perfectly good sulk.'

'You couldn't have kept it up anyway,' I said, enormously relieved. 'You would have cracked by lunchtime.'

'Don't push it. Come here, you.' She held out an arm, and I bent and gave her a quick hug. 'Thank you.'

'You're very welcome,' I said. 'And I really mean it: no more obnoxiousness.'

Cassie watched me as I took off my coat. 'Look,' she

said, 'it's not just that you've been a pain in the hole. I've been *worried* about you. If you don't want to deal with this any more – no, listen – then you could swap with Sam, go after Andrews and let him take the family. He's got far enough that any of us could take over; it's not like we're going to need help from his uncle or anything. Sam won't ask questions, you know what he's like. There's no reason for you to drive yourself nuts over this.'

'Cass, I'm genuinely, honest-to-God fine,' I said. 'Yesterday was a huge wake-up call. I swear on anything you can think of, I've worked out how to deal with this case.'

'Rob, remember how you said to kick you if you got too weird about this one? This is me kicking you. Metaphorically, for now.'

'Look, give me one more week. If by the end of next week you think I'm still not handling this, I'll swap with Sam. OK?'

'OK,' Cassie said finally, though she still looked unconvinced. I was in such a good mood that this unexpected protective streak, which normally would have given me the fidgets, seemed very touching; probably because I knew it was no longer necessary. I gave her shoulder a clumsy little squeeze on the way to my desk.

'Actually,' she said, as I sat down, 'this whole Sandra Scully thing has one major silver lining. You know how we've been wanting to get our hands on Rosalind and Jessica's medical records? Well, we've got Katy showing physical signs of abuse, Jessica showing psychological signs and now Jonathan admitting to rape. I think there's a good chance we've got enough circumstantial stuff to pull the records.'

'Maddox,' I said, 'you're a star.' This was the one thing that had been nagging at me, the fact that I had made a fool of myself by sending us off on a wild-goose chase. Apparently it hadn't been that pointless after all. 'But I thought you thought Devlin wasn't our guy.'

Cassie shrugged. 'Not exactly. He's hiding something, but it could be just abuse – well, not *just*, you know what I mean – or he could be covering for Margaret, or . . . I'm not as sure as you are that he's guilty, but I'd like to see what's in those records, that's all.'

'I'm not sure either.'

She raised an eyebrow. 'You seemed pretty sure yesterday.'

'Speaking of which,' I said, a little awkwardly, 'do you have any idea whether he's filed a complaint on me? I don't have the bollocks to check.'

'Because you apologised so nicely,' Cassie told me, 'I'm going to overlook that wonderful set-up line. He didn't say anything about it to me, and anyway you'd know if he had: you'd be able to hear O'Kelly all the way to Knocknaree. That's why I'm assuming Cathal Mills hasn't filed anything on me for saying he had a teeny weenie, either.'

'He won't. Can you seriously see him sitting down with some desk sergeant and explaining that you suggested he might have a limp mini-dick? Devlin's a different story, though. He's half off his trolley right now anyway—'

'Don't be bitching about Jonathan Devlin,' Sam said, bouncing into the incident room. He was flushed and overexcited, his collar twisted and a forelock of fair hair tumbling into his eyes. 'Devlin is The Man. Honestly, if I didn't think he might take me up wrong, I'd snog the face off him.'

'You'll make a lovely couple,' I said, putting down my pen. 'What's he done?' Cassie spun her chair around, a smile of anticipation starting on her face.

Sam pulled out his chair with a flourish, dropped into it and swung his feet up onto the table like a private eye in an old movie; if he had had a hat, he would have sent it spinning across the room. 'He's only after picking Andrews out of the voice line-up. Andrews and his lawyer nearly had a conniption about it, and Devlin wasn't best pleased to hear from me either – what the hell did ye say to him? – but they all did it in the end. I rang Devlin up – I figured that was the best way; you know how everyone always sounds different down the phone? – and I got Andrews and a bunch of the lads to say a few sentences from the phone calls: "Nice little girl you've got there," "You have no idea what you're messing with" . . .'

He shoved the lock of hair away with his wrist; his face, laughing and open, was triumphant as a little boy's. 'Andrews was mumbling and drawling and all sorts, trying to make his voice sound different, but my main man Jonathan picked him out in five seconds flat, not a bother on him. He was yelling at me down the phone, wanting to know who it was, and Andrews and his lawyer – I had your man Devlin on speaker-phone so they could hear it themselves, I didn't want any arguments later – they were sitting there with faces on them like a pair of slapped arses. It was brilliant.'

'Oh, well done, you,' Cassie said, leaning across the table to high-five him. Sam, grinning, held up his other palm to me.

'To be honest, I'm delighted with myself. It's nowhere near enough to charge him with the murder, but we can probably bring some kind of harassment charge – and it's definitely enough for us to hold him for questioning and see how far we get.'

'Have you kept him in?' I asked.

Sam shook his head. 'I didn't say a word to him after the line-up, just thanked him and said I'd be in touch. I want to let him worry about it for a while.'

'Oh, that's underhanded, O'Neill,' I said gravely. 'I wouldn't have thought it of you.' Sam was fun to tease. He didn't always fall for it, but when he did he got all earnest and stammery.

He gave me a withering look. 'And, as well, I want to see if there's any chance I can tap his phone for a few days. If he's our boy, I'd bet he didn't do it himself. His alibi checks out, and anyway he's not the type to mess up his fancy gear doing his own dirty work; he'd hire someone. The voice ID might get him panicky enough to ring his hit man, or at least say something stupid to someone.'

'Go through his old phone records again, too,' I reminded him. 'See who he was talking to last month.'

'O'Gorman's already on it,' Sam said smugly. 'I'll give Andrews a week or two, see if anything turns up, and then pull him in. And' – he looked suddenly bashful, caught between shame and mischief – 'you know how Devlin said Andrews sounded locked on the phone? And how we wondered if he was a little jarred yesterday? I think our boyo might have a bit of a drinking problem. I wonder what he'd be like if we went to see him at, say, eight or nine in the evening. He might be – you know . . . more likely to talk, less likely to call his lawyer. I know it's bad to take advantage of the man's failing, but . . .'

'Rob's right,' Cassie said, shaking her head. 'You've got a cruel streak.'

Sam's eyes rounded in dismay for an instant; then the penny dropped. 'Feck the pair of ye,' he said happily, and spun his chair round in a full circle, feet still in the air.

*   *   *

We were all giddy that night, giddy as children given an unexpected day off school. Sam, to our collective disbelief, had managed to coax O'Kelly into convincing a judge to give him an order to tap Andrews's phone for two weeks. Normally you can't get a tap unless there are large amounts of explosives involved, but Operation Vestal was still front-page news almost every other day – 'No New Leads in Katy's Murder (see p.5, "Is Your Child Safe?")' – and the high drama of it all gave us some extra leverage. Sam was jubilant: 'I know the little bastard's hiding something, lads, I'd put money on it. All it'll take is a few too many pints one of these nights, and bang! we'll have him.' He had brought a lovely buttery white wine to celebrate. I was light-headed with reprieve and hungrier than I'd been in weeks; I cooked a huge Spanish omelette, tried to flip it high like a pancake and nearly sent it into the sink. Cassie flew around the flat, barefoot below summery cropped jeans, slicing a baguette and turning Michelle Shocked up loud and slagging my hand-eye coordination – 'And someone actually gave this guy a personal firearm, it's only a matter of time before he starts showing it off to impress some girl and shoots himself in the leg . . .'

After dinner we played Cranium, a slapdash, improvised three-person version – I am at a loss for words to adequately describe Sam, after four glasses of wine, trying to mime 'carburettor'. ('C3PO? Milking a cow? . . . That little man out of Swiss clocks!') The long white curtains billowed and spun in the breeze through the open sash window and a sliver of moon hung in the dimming sky, and I couldn't remember the last time I had had an evening like this, a happy, silly evening with no tiny grey shades plucking at the edges of every conversation.

When Sam left, Cassie taught me how to swing-dance.

We had had inappropriate cappuccinos after dinner, to christen the new machine, and we were both hours away from being able to sleep, and scratchy old music was pouring out of the CD player; Cassie caught my hands and pulled me up from the sofa. 'How the hell do you know how to swing-dance?' I demanded.

'My aunt and uncle thought kids should have Lessons. Lots of them. I can do charcoal drawings and play piano, too.'

'All at once? I can play the triangle. And I have two left feet.'

'I don't care. I want to dance.'

The flat was too small. 'Come on,' Cassie said. 'Take your shoes off,' and she grabbed the remote control and turned the music up to eleven and climbed out the window, down the fire escape to the roof of the extension below.

I'm no dancer, but she taught me the basic moves again and again, her feet skipping nimbly away from my missteps, until suddenly they clicked into place and we were dancing, spinning and swaying to the sassy, expert syncopations, recklessly close to the edges of the flat roof. Cassie's hands in mine were gymnast-strong and flexible. 'You can too dance!' she called breathlessly, eyes shining, over the music.

'What?' I shouted, and tripped over my feet. Laughter, unrolling like streamers over the dark gardens below.

A window slammed up below us and a quavery Anglo-Irish voice screeched, 'If you don't turn that down at once I shall call the police!'

'We *are* the police!' Cassie yelled back. I clapped a hand over her mouth and we shook with explosive, suppressed laughter until, after a confused silence, the window banged shut. Cassie ran back up the fire escape and hung off it by one hand, still giggling, while she aimed the remote control through the window, changed the CD to Chopin's nocturnes, turned down the volume.

We lay side by side on the extension roof, hands behind our heads, elbows just touching. My head was still spinning a little, not unpleasantly, from the dancing and the wine. The breeze was warm across my face, and even through the city lights I could see constellations: the Plough, Orion's belt. The pine tree at the bottom of the garden rustled like the sea, ceaselessly. For a moment I felt as if the universe had turned upside down and we were falling softly into an enormous black bowl of stars and nocturne, and I knew, beyond any doubt, that everything was going to be all right.

16

I saved the wood for Saturday night, hugging the thought to myself like a child saving a huge Easter egg with some mysterious prize inside. Sam was down in Galway for the weekend, for a niece's christening – he had the kind of extended family that holds full-scale gatherings almost on a weekly basis, someone was always getting christened or married or buried – and Cassie was going out with some of her girl friends, and Heather was going speed-dating in some hotel somewhere. Nobody would even notice I had gone.

I got to Knocknaree around seven and parked in the lay-by. I had brought a sleeping-bag and a torch, a thermos of well-spiked coffee and a couple of sandwiches – packing them had made me feel faintly ridiculous, like one of those earnest hikers in technologically advanced fleeces, or a kid running away from home – but nothing to light a fire with: the people in the estate were still on edge and would have been on to the cops like a shot if they saw a mysterious light, which would have been embarrassing all round, and besides I am not the Boy Scout type; I would probably have burned down what was left of the wood.

It was a still, clear evening, long slants of light turning the stone of the tower rose-gold and giving even the trenches and heaps of earth a sad, ragged magic. There was a lamb bleating, far off in the fields, and the air smelled rich and tranquil: hay, cows, some heady flower I couldn't name. Sprays of birds were practising their V-shapes over the crest of the hill. Outside the cottage, the sheepdog sat up and huffed a warning half-bark, stared me out of it for a moment, then decided I was no threat and settled down again. I followed the archaeologists' bumpy trails, just wide enough for a wheelbarrow, across the site – I was wearing old trainers, this time, and ratty jeans and a thick jumper – to the wood.

If you, like me, are essentially a city person, then the chances are that when you imagine a wood you picture a simple thing: matching green trees in even rows, a soft carpet of dead leaves or pine needles, orderly as a child's drawing. Possibly those earnestly efficient man-made woods are in fact like that; I wouldn't know. Knocknaree wood was the real thing, and it was more intricate and more secretive than I had remembered. It had its own order, its own fierce battles and alliances. I was an intruder here, now, and I had a deep prickling sense that my presence had instantly been marked and that the wood was watching me, with an equivocal collective gaze, not yet accepting or rejecting; reserving judgement.

Mark's clearing had fresh ash in the fire-spot and a few new rollie butts scattered on the bare earth around it; he had been here again, since Katy died. I hoped devoutly that he wouldn't pick tonight to reconnect with his heritage. I took the sandwiches and the thermos and the torch out of my pockets, spread out my sleeping-bag on the compact patch of flattened grass where Mark had spread his. Then I walked through the wood, slowly, taking my time.

It was like stumbling into the wreck of some great ancient city. The trees swooped higher than cathedral pillars; they wrestled for space, propped up great fallen trunks, leaned with the slope of the hill: oak, beech, ash, others I couldn't name. Long spears of light filtered, dim and sacred, through the arches of green. Swathes of ivy blurred the massive trunks, trailed in waterfalls from the branches, turned stumps into standing stones. My steps were padded by deep, springy layers of fallen leaves; when I stopped and turned over a chunk with the toe of my shoe, I smelled rich rot and saw dark wet earth, acorn-caps, the pale frantic wriggle of a worm. Birds darted and called in the branches, and small warning scurries exploded as I passed.

Great drifts of undergrowth, and here and there a worn fragment of stone wall; muscular roots, green with moss and thicker than my arm. The low banks of the river, tangled with brambles (sliding down, on our hands and our backsides, *Ow! my leg!*) and overhung with elderberry clusters and willow. The river was like a sheet of old gold, creased and stippled with black. Slim yellow leaves floated on its surface, balancing as lightly as if it were a solid thing.

My mind sideslipped and spun. Every step set recognition thrumming in the air around me, like Morse code beating along a frequency just too high to catch. We had run here, scrambling sure-footed down the hillside along the web of faint trails; we had eaten streaky little crab apples from the twisted tree, and when I looked up into the whirl of leaves I almost expected to see us there, clinging to branches like young jungle cats and staring back. At the fringe of one of these tiny clearings (long grass, sun-dapples, clouds of ragwort and Queen Anne's lace) we had watched as Jonathan and his friends held Sandra down. Somewhere, maybe in the exact spot where I was standing, the wood had shivered and cracked open, and Peter and Jamie had slipped away.

I didn't exactly have a plan for that night, in the strictest sense of the word. Go to the wood, have a look around, spend the night there; hope something happened. Up until that moment, this lack of forethought hadn't seemed like an impediment. After all, every time I had tried to plan anything recently, it had gone spectacularly, galactically wrong; I clearly needed a change of tactics, and what could be more drastic than going into this with nothing and simply waiting to see what the wood gave me? And I suppose it appealed, too, to my sense of the picturesque. I suppose I've always had a yearning, in spite of the fact that I am temperamentally unsuited to the role in every possible way, to be a hero out of myth, golden and reckless, galloping bareback to meet my fate on a wild horse no other man could ride.

Now that I was actually there, though, this whole thing no longer seemed quite so much like a free-spirited leap of faith. It just felt vaguely hippie-ish – I had even considered getting stoned, in the hope that it would relax me enough to give my subconscious a sporting chance, but hash always makes me fall asleep – and more than vaguely dumb. I realised, suddenly, that the tree I was leaning against could be the very tree beside which I had been found, could still have pale scars where my fingernails had gouged into the trunk; realised, too, that it was beginning to get dark.

I almost left then. I actually went back to the clearing, shook the dead leaves off my sleeping-bag and started rolling it up. If I'm honest, the only thing that kept me there was the thought of Mark. He had spent the night here, not just once but regularly, and it didn't even seem to have occurred to him that this might be a frightening thing to do, and I couldn't stand the idea of letting him have one up on me, whether he knew about it or not. He might have had a fire, but I had a torch and a Smith & Wesson, although I felt slightly silly for even thinking of this. I was only a few hundred yards from civilisation, or at any rate the estate. I stood still for a moment, the sleeping-bag in my hands; then I unrolled it, wriggled into it up to my waist, and leaned back against a tree.

I poured myself a cup of whiskeyed coffee; the sharp, adult taste was oddly reassuring. The shards of sky dimmed overhead, from turquoise to glowing indigo; birds landed on branches and settled for the night, with brisk exclamations and bickerings. Bats shrilled across the dig, and among the bushes there was a quick pounce, a burst of scuffling, silence. Far away, on the estate, a child called something high and rhythmic: *Ally ally in free . . .*

It came to me gradually – without surprise, really, as if it were something I had known for a long time – that, if I managed to remember anything useful, I was going to take it to O'Kelly. Not right away, maybe not for a few weeks, I would need a little time to tie up loose ends and set my affairs in order, so to speak; because when I did it, it would be the end of my career.

Only that afternoon the thought would have been like a baseball bat to the stomach. But somehow that night it seemed almost seductive, it shimmered tantalisingly in the air before me, and I turned it over with a luxurious giddiness. Being a murder detective, the only thing on which I had ever set my heart, the thing around which I had built my wardrobe, my walk, my vocabulary, my life waking and sleeping: the thought of tossing it all away with one flick of the wrist and watching it soar into space like a bright balloon was intoxicating. I could set up as a private investigator, I thought, have a battered little office in some dingy Georgian building, my name in gold on a frosted-glass door, come to work when I chose and skate expertly around the edges of the law and harass an apoplectic O'Kelly for inside information. I wondered, dreamily, if Cassie might come with me. I could get a fedora and a trench coat and a wisecracking sense of humour; she could sit poised at hotel bars with a slinky red dress and a camera in her lipstick, to snare cheating businessmen . . . I almost laughed out loud.

I realised that I was falling asleep. This had not been part of my plan, such as it was, and I struggled to stay awake, but all those sleepless nights were hitting me at once, hard as a shot in the arm. I thought of the thermos of coffee, but it seemed like way too much work to reach out for it. The sleeping-bag had warmed against my body and I had adjusted myself around all the little lumps and crevices in the ground and the tree; I was deliciously, narcotically comfortable. I felt the thermos cup fall from my fingers, but I couldn't open my eyes.

I don't know how long I slept. I was sitting up and biting back a shout before I was even fully awake. Someone had said, clear and sharp and right next to my ear, 'What's that?'

I sat there for a long time, feeling slow waves of blood surging in my neck. The lights in the estate had gone out. The wood was silent, barely a whisper of wind through the branches overhead; somewhere a twig cracked.

Peter, whirling around on the castle wall and shooting out a hand to freeze me and Jamie on either side: 'What's that?'

We had been outside all day, since the dew was still drying off the grass. It was boiling; every breath was warm as bathwater and the sky was the colour of the inside of a candle flame. We had bottles of red lemonade in the grass under a tree, for when we got thirsty, but they had gone warm and flat and the ants had found them. Someone was mowing a lawn, down the street; someone else had a kitchen window open and the radio turned up loud and was singing along to 'Wake Me Up Before You Go-Go'. Two little girls were taking turns on a pink tricycle on the sidewalk, and Peter's prissy sister Tara was playing teachers in her friend Audrey's garden, the two of them yakking at a bunch of dolls lined up in rows. The Carmichaels had bought a sprinkler; we'd never seen one before and we eyed it every time they put it out, but Mrs Carmichael was a bitch, Peter said if you went in her garden she would smash your head in with a poker.

We had mostly been riding our bikes. Peter had got an Evel Knievel for his birthday – if you wound it up, you could make it jump piles of old *Warlord* annuals – and he was going to be a daredevil when he grew up, so we were practising. We built a ramp in the road, out of bricks and a piece of plywood that Peter's dad had in the garden shed – 'We'll keep making it higher,' Peter said, 'one brick more every day' – but it wobbled like crazy, and I could never keep myself from slamming on the brakes in the second before I took off.

Jamie tried the ramp a few times and then hung around at the edge of the street, scraping a sticker off her handlebar and kicking her pedal to make it spin. She had been late coming out that morning, and she'd been quiet all day. She always was, but this was different: her silence was like a thick private cloud all round her, and it was making me and Peter fidgety.

Peter flew off the ramp yelling and zigzagged wildly, just missing the two little girls on the tricycle. 'You big ding-dongs, you'll have us all killed,' Tara snapped over her dollies. She was wearing a long flowery skirt that puddled on the grass, and a weird big hat with a ribbon around it.

'You're not my boss,' Peter shouted back. He swerved onto Audrey's lawn and swooped past Tara, grabbing the hat off her head as he went. Tara and Audrey shrieked in practised unison.

'Adam! Catch!' I followed him into the garden – we would be in trouble if Audrey's mam came out – and managed to catch the hat without falling off my bike; I stuck it on my head and cycled no-hands around the dolly classroom. Audrey tried to knock me over, but I dodged. She was sort of pretty and she didn't look really mad, so I tried not to run over her dolls. Tara stuck her hands on her hips and started yelling at Peter. 'Jamie!' I shouted. 'Come on!'

Jamie had stayed in the road, bumping her front tyre rhythmically off the edge of the ramp. She dropped her bike, took a running jump at the estate wall and swung herself over.

Peter and I forgot about Tara ('You haven't a titter of sense, so you haven't, Peter Savage, just you wait till Mammy hears about your carry-on . . .'), braked and looked at each other. Audrey grabbed the hat off my head and ran, checking to see if I was chasing her. We left our bikes in the road and climbed the wall after Jamie.

She was in the tyre-swing, kicking herself off the wall every few swings. Her head was down and all I could see was the sheet of straight pale hair and the end of her nose. We sat on the wall and waited.

'My mam measured me this morning,' Jamie said in the end. She was picking at a scab on her knuckle.

I thought, puzzled, of the door-frame in our kitchen: glossy white wood, with pencil marks and dates to show me growing. 'So?' Peter said. 'Big swinging mickeys.'

'For *uniforms*!' Jamie yelled at him. '*Duh!*' She slid out of the tyre, landed hard and ran, into the wood.

'Sheesh,' Peter said. 'What's her problem?'

'Boarding-school,' I said. The words made my legs feel watery.

Peter gave me a disgusted, incredulous grimace. 'She's not going. Her mam said.'

'No she didn't. She said, "We'll see."'

'Yeah, and then she didn't say anything else about it ever since.'

'Yeah, well, now she has, hasn't she?'

Peter squinted into the sun. 'Come on,' he said, and jumped back down off the wall.

'Where are we going?'

He didn't answer. He picked up his bike and Jamie's and managed to wobble them both into his garden. I got mine and went after him.

Peter's mam was hanging out the washing, with a line of clothes-pegs clipped to the side of her apron. 'Don't be annoying Tara,' she said.

'We won't,' Peter said, dumping the bikes on the grass. 'Mam, we're going in the wood, OK?' The baby, Sean Paul, was lying on a blanket, wearing nothing but a nappy and trying to crawl. I poked him tentatively in the side with my toe; he rolled over, grabbed my trainer and grinned up at me. 'Good baby,' I told him. I didn't want to go find Jamie. I wondered if maybe I could stay there, mind Sean Paul for Mrs Savage and wait until Peter came back to tell me Jamie was going away.

'Tea at half-six,' Mrs Savage said, reaching out absently to smooth down Peter's hair as he passed. 'Have you your watch?'

'Yeah.' Peter waved his wrist at her. 'Come on, Adam, let's go.'

When something was wrong we mostly went to the same place: the top room of the castle. The staircase leading up to it had long since crumbled away, and from the ground you couldn't even really tell it was there; you had to climb the outer wall, all the way over the top, and then jump down onto the stone floor. Ivy trailing down the walls, branches tumbling overhead: it was like a bird's nest, swinging high up in the air.

Jamie was there, huddled up in a corner with one elbow crooked across her mouth. She was crying, hard and clumsily. Once, ages before, she had caught her foot in a rabbit hole when she was running, and broken her ankle; we had given her a fireman's lift all the way back home and she had never cried, not even when I tripped and jolted her leg, just yelled, '*Ow*, Adam, you thick!' and pinched my arm.

I climbed down into the room. 'Go away!' Jamie shouted at me, muffled by her arm and tears. Her face was red and her hair was tangled, clips hanging off sideways. 'Leave me alone.'

Peter was still on top of the wall. 'Are you going to boarding-school?' he demanded.

Jamie squeezed her eyes and mouth tight, but choked-up sobs broke through all the same. I could barely hear what she was saying. 'She never said, she acted like it was all OK, and all the time . . . she was just *lying*!'

It was the unfairness of it that knocked the breath out of me. *We'll see*, Jamie's mother had said, *don't worry about it*; and we had believed her and stopped worrying. No grown-up had ever betrayed us before, not about something that mattered like this, and I couldn't take it in. We had lived that whole summer trusting that we had forever.

Peter balanced anxiously along the wall and back again, stood on one foot. 'So we'll do the same thing again. We'll have a mutiny. We'll—'

'No!' Jamie cried. 'She's paid the fees and everything, it's too late – I'm going in two weeks! *Two weeks* . . .' Her hands balled into fists and she slammed them against the wall.

I couldn't stand it. I knelt down beside Jamie and put my arm around her shoulders; she shook it off, but when I put it back she left it there. 'Don't, Jamie,' I begged. 'Please don't cry.' The green and gold whirl of branches all around, Peter baffled and Jamie crying, the silky skin of her arm making my hand tingle; the whole world seemed to be rocking, the stone of the castle rolling beneath me like the decks of ships in films— 'You'll be back every weekend . . .'

'It won't be the *same*!' Jamie cried. Her head went back and she sobbed without even trying to hide it, frail brown throat turned up to the fragments of sky. The utter wretchedness in her voice cut straight through me and I knew she was right: it was never going to be the same, not ever again.

'No, Jamie, don't – stop . . .' I couldn't stay still. I knew it was stupid but for a moment I wanted to tell her I would go instead; I would take her place, she could stay here forever . . . Before I knew I was going to do it, I ducked my head and kissed her on the cheek. Her tears were wet on my mouth. She smelled like grass in the sun, hot and green, intoxicating.

She was so startled that she stopped crying. Her head whipped round and she stared at me, wide red-rimmed blue eyes, very close. I knew she was going to do something, punch me, kiss me back—

Peter leaped off the wall and dropped to his knees in front of us. He grabbed my wrist in one hand, hard, and Jamie's in the other. 'Listen,' he said. 'We'll run away.'

We stared at him.

'That's stupid,' I said at last. 'They'll catch us.'

'No, no they won't, not right away. We can hide here for a few weeks, no problem. It doesn't have to be forever or anything – just till it's safe. Once that school's started, we can go home; it'll be too late. And even if they send her anyway, so what? We'll run away again. We'll go up to Dublin and get Jamie out. Then they'll expel her and she'll *have* to come back home. See?'

His eyes were shining. The idea caught, flared, spun in the air between us.

'We could live here,' Jamie said. She caught her breath in a long, hiccupy shudder. 'In the castle, I mean.'

'We'll move every day. Here, the clearing, that big tree where the branches do that nest thing. We won't give them a chance to catch up with us. You really think anyone could find us in here? Come *on!*'

Nobody knew the wood like we did. Sliding through the undergrowth, light and silent as Indian braves; watching motionless from thickets and high branches as the searchers clumped past . . .

'We'll take turns sleeping.' Jamie was sitting up straighter. 'One of us can keep watch.'

'But our parents,' I said. I thought of my mother's warm hands and imagined her crying, distraught. 'They're going to be really worried. They'll think—'

Jamie's mouth set. 'Yeah, my mam won't. She doesn't want me around anyway.'

'My mam mostly only thinks about the little ones,' Peter said, 'and my dad definitely won't care.' Jamie and I glanced at each other. We never talked about it, but we both knew Peter's dad sometimes hit them when he got drunk. 'And anyway, who cares if your parents worry? They didn't tell you Jamie was going to boarding-school, did they? They just let you think everything was fine!'

He was right, I thought, light-headed. 'I guess I could leave them a note,' I said. 'Just so they know we're OK.'

Jamie started to say something, but Peter cut her off. 'Yeah, perfect! Leave them a note saying we've gone to Dublin, or Cork or somewhere. Then they'll be looking for us there, and we'll be right here all the time.'

He jumped up, pulling us with him. 'Are you in?'

'I'm not going to boarding-school,' Jamie said, wiping her face with the back of her arm. 'I'm not, Adam. I'm not. I'll do anything.'

'Adam?' Living wild, brown and barefoot among the trees. The castle wall felt cool and misty under my hand. 'Adam, what else are we supposed to do? Do you want to just let them send Jamie away? Don't you want to *do* something?'

He shook my wrist. His hand was hard, urgent; I could feel my pulse beating in its grasp. 'I'm in,' I said.

'Yes!' Peter yelled, punching the air. The shout echoed up into the trees, high and wild and triumphant.

'When?' Jamie demanded. Her eyes were bright with relief and her mouth was open in a smile; she was poised on her toes, ready to take off as soon as Peter gave the word. 'Now?'

'Relax on the jacks,' Peter told her, grinning. 'We have to get ready. We'll go home and get all our money. We need supplies, but we have to buy them a little every day, so nobody gets suspicious.'

'Sausages and potatoes,' I said. 'We can build a fire and get sticks—'

'No, no fire, they'd see it. Don't get anything that needs cooking. Get stuff in tins, spaghetti hoops and baked beans and stuff. Say it's for your mam.'

'Someone better bring a tin-opener—'

'Me; my mam has an extra one, she won't know.'

'Sleeping-bags, and our torches—'

'Duh, but that's not till the last minute, we don't want them noticing they're gone.'

'We can wash our clothes in the river—'

'– stick all our rubbish down a hollow tree so no one finds it—'

'How much money have you guys got?'

'My confirmation money's all in the post office, I can't get it.'

'So we'll get cheap stuff, milk and bread—'

'Ew, milk'll go off!'

'No it won't, we can keep it in the river in a plastic bag—'

'Jamie drinks chunky milk!' Peter yelled. He jumped at the wall and started scrambling up to the top.

Jamie leaped after him. 'I do not, *you* drink chunky milk, you—' She grabbed Peter's ankle and they tussled on top of the wall, giggling wildly. I caught up with them, and Peter shot out an arm and dragged me into the scuffle. We wrestled, yelping and breathless with laughter, balancing dangerously half over the edge. 'Adam eats *bugs*—' 'Screw you, that was when we were *little*—'

'Shut up!' Peter snapped suddenly. He shook us off and froze, crouched on the wall, hands out to silence us. 'What's that?'

Motionless and alert as startled hares, we listened. The wood was still, too still, waiting; the normal afternoon bustle of birds and insects and unseen little animals had been cut off as if by a conductor's baton. Only somewhere, up ahead of us—

'What the . . .' I whispered.

'Shh.' Music, or a voice; or just some trick of the river on stones, the breeze in the hollow oak? The wood had a million voices, changing with every season and every day; you could never know them all.

'Come on,' said Jamie, her eyes shining, 'come *on*,' and launched herself like a flying squirrel off the wall. She caught a branch, swung, dropped and rolled and ran; Peter was leaping after her before the branch stopped swaying, and I scrambled down the wall and chased behind them, 'Wait for me, wait—'

The wood had never been so lush or so feral. Leaves threw off dazzles of sunlight like Catherine wheels and the colours were so bright you could live on them, the smell of fertile earth amplified to something heady as church wine. We shot through humming clouds of midges and leaped ditches and rotten logs, branches swirled around us like water, swallows trapezed across our path and in the trees alongside I swear three deer kept pace with us. I felt light and lucky and wild, I had never run so fast or jumped so effortlessly high; one shove of my foot and I could have been airborne.

How long did we run? All the familiar loved landmarks must have shifted, turned out to wish us good speed, because we passed every one of them on our way; we jumped the stone table and soared through the clearing in one bound, between the whip of the blackberry bushes and the rabbits poking up their noses to see us go by, we left the tyre-swing swaying in our wake and swung one-handed round the hollow oak. And up ahead, so sweet and wild it hurt, drawing us on—

Gradually I became aware that under the sleeping-bag I was drenched in sweat; that my back, pressed against the tree trunk, was so rigid that I was shaking, my head nodding in stiff convulsive jerks like a toy's. The wood was black, blank, as if I had been blinded. Far off, there was a quick pittering sound like raindrops on leaves, tiny and spreading. I fought to ignore it, to keep following where that frail gold thread of memory led, not to drop it in this darkness or I would never find my way home.

Laughter streaming over Jamie's shoulder like bright soap-bubbles, bees whirling in a sunbeam and Peter's arms flying out as he leaped a fallen branch whooping. My shoelaces coming undone and alarm peals rising fiercely somewhere inside me as I felt the estate dissolving to mist behind us, are you sure, are you sure, *Peter, Jamie, wait, stop—*

The pittering sound was catching all through the wood, rising and falling, drawing closer on every side. It was in the branches high overhead, in the undergrowth behind me, small and swift and intent. The hairs rose on the back of my neck. *Rain*, I told myself with whatever was left of my mind, *just rain*, though I couldn't feel a drop. Off at the other side of the wood something screamed, a shrill witless sound.

Come on, Adam, hurry, hurry up—

The darkness in front of me was shifting, condensing. There was a sound like wind in the leaves, a great rushing wind coming down through the wood to clear a path. I thought of the torch, but my fingers were frozen around it. I felt that gold thread twist and tug. Somewhere across the clearing something breathed; something big.

Down by the river. Skidding to a stop; willow branches swaying and the water firing off splinters of light like a million tiny mirrors, blinding, dizzying. Eyes, golden and fringed like an owl's.

I ran. I scrabbled out of the clutching sleeping-bag and threw myself into the wood, away from the clearing. Brambles clawed at my legs and hair, wing-beats exploded in my ear; I shoulder-barged straight into a tree trunk, knocking myself breathless. Invisible dips and hollows flicked open under my feet and I couldn't run fast enough, legs crashing knee-deep through underbrush, it was like every childhood nightmare come true. Trailing ivy wrapped my face and I think I screamed. I knew beyond all doubt I would never get out of the wood, they would find my sleeping-bag – for an instant I saw, sharp as reality, Cassie in her red jumper, kneeling in the clearing among falling leaves and reaching out a gloved hand to touch the fabric – and nothing else, ever.

Then I saw a fingernail of new moon between racing clouds and knew I was out, on the dig. The ground was treacherous, it sideslipped and gave under my feet and I stumbled, flailing, barked my shin on a fragment of some old wall; saved my balance in the nick of time and kept running. There was a harsh gasping sound loud in my ears, but I couldn't tell whether it came from me. Like every detective, I had taken it for granted that I was the hunter. It had never once occurred to me that I might have been the hunted, all along.

The Land Rover loomed up radiantly white through the darkness like some sweet shining church offering sanctuary. It took me two or three tries to get the door open; once I dropped my keys and had to grope frantically in the leaves and dry grass, staring wildly over my shoulder and sure I would never find them, until I remembered I was still holding the torch. Finally I clambered in, banging my elbow off the steering-wheel, locked all the doors and sat there, gasping for breath and sweating all over. I was way too shaky to drive; I doubt I could even have pulled out without hitting something. I found my cigarettes, managed to light one. I wished, badly, that I had a stiff drink, or a large joint. There were huge smears of mud across the knees of my jeans, though I didn't remember falling.

When my hands were steady enough to push buttons, I phoned Cassie. It had to be well after midnight, maybe much later, but she answered on the second ring, sounding wide awake. 'Hi, you, what's up?'

For one hideous moment I thought my voice wasn't going to work. 'Where are you?'

'I just got home like twenty minutes ago. Emma and Susanna and I went to the cinema and then had dinner at the Trocadero and, God, they gave us the *loveliest* red wine *ever*. These three guys tried to chat us up, Emma said they were actors and she'd seen one of them on TV in that hospital thing—'

She was tipsy, but not actually drunk. 'Cassie,' I said. 'I'm in Knocknaree. At the dig.'

A tiny, fractional pause. Then she said calmly, in a different voice, 'Want me to pick you up?'

'Yeah. Please.' I hadn't realised, till she said it, that that was why I had rung her.

'OK. See you soon.' She hung up.

It took her forever to get there, long enough that I started imagining panicky nightmare scenarios: she had been splattered across the dual carriageway by a truck, got a flat tyre and been abducted from the roadside by human traffickers. I managed to pull out my gun and hold it in my lap – I had enough sense left not to cock it. I chain-smoked; the car filled up with a haze that made my eyes water.

Outside, things rustled and pounced in the undergrowth, twigs snapped; over and over I whipped round with my heart racing wildly and my hand tightening on the gun, sure I had seen a face at the window, feral and laughing, but there was never anything there. I tried switching on the roof-light, but it made me feel too conspicuous, like some primitive man with predators drawn by the firelight circling just beyond its glow, and I turned it off again almost at once.

At last I heard the Vespa buzzing, saw the beam of its headlamp coming over the hill. I got my gun back into its holster and opened the door; I didn't want Cassie to see me fumbling with it. After the darkness her lights were dazzling, surreal. She pulled up in the road, bracing the bike with her foot, and called, 'Hey.'

'Hi,' I said, stumbling out of the car; my legs were cramped and stiff, I must have been pressing both feet against the floorboards the whole time. 'Thanks.'

'No problem. I was awake anyway.' She was flushed and bright-eyed from the wind of driving, and when I got close enough I felt its cold aura striking off her. She swung her rucksack off her back and pulled out her spare helmet. 'Here.'

Inside the helmet I couldn't hear anything, only the bike's steady hum and the blood beating in my ears. The air flowed past me, dark and cool as water; cars' headlights and neon signs streamed by in bright lazy trails. Cassie's rib cage was slight and solid between my hands, shifting as she changed gears or leaned into a turn. I felt as if the bike was floating, high above the road, and I wished we were on one of those endless American freeways where you could drive on and on forever through the night.

★   ★   ★

She had been reading in bed when I rang. The futon was pulled out, made up with the patchwork duvet and white pillows; *Wuthering Heights* and her oversized T-shirt were tumbled at the foot. There were semi-organised heaps of work stuff – a photo of the ligature mark on Katy's neck leaped out at me, hung in the air like an after-image – scattered across the coffee table and the sofa, overlaid with Cassie's going-out clothes: slim dark jeans, a red silk handkerchief top embroidered in gold. The chubby little bedside lamp gave the room a cosy glow.

'When did you last eat?' Cassie asked.

I had forgotten about my sandwiches, presumably still somewhere in the clearing. My sleeping-bag and my thermos, too; I would have to get them in the morning, when I picked up my car. A fast finger ran down my neck at the thought of going back in there, even by daylight. 'I'm not sure,' I said.

Cassie rummaged in the wardrobe, passed me a bottle of brandy and a glass. 'Have a shot of that while I make food. Eggs on toast?'

Neither of us likes brandy – the bottle was unopened and dusty, probably a prize from the Christmas raffle or something – but a small objective part of my mind was pretty sure that she was right, I was in some kind of shock. 'Yeah, great,' I said. I sat down on the edge of the futon – the thought of clearing all that stuff off the sofa seemed almost unimaginably complicated – and stared at the bottle for a while until I realised I was supposed to open it.

I threw down way too much brandy, coughed (Cassie glanced over, said nothing) and felt it kick in, burning trails of warmth through my veins. My tongue throbbed; I had apparently bitten it, at some point or other. I poured myself another shot and sipped it more carefully. Cassie moved deftly around the kitchenette, pulling herbs out of a cupboard with one hand and eggs out of the fridge with the other and shoving a drawer shut with her hip. She had left music on – the Cowboy Junkies, turned down low, faint and slow and haunting; normally I like them, but tonight I kept hearing things hidden somewhere behind the bass line, quick whispers, calls, a throb of drumbeat that shouldn't have been there. 'Can we turn that off?' I said, when I couldn't stand it any longer. 'Please?'

She turned from the frying pan to look at me, a wooden spoon in her hand. 'Yeah, sure,' she said after a moment. She switched off the stereo, popped the toast and piled the eggs on top of it. 'Here.'

The smell made me realise how hungry I was. I shovelled the food down in huge mouthfuls, barely stopping to breathe; it was granary bread and the eggs were redolent with herbs and spices, and nothing had ever tasted so richly delicious. Cassie sat cross-legged at the top of the futon, watching me over a piece of toast. 'More?' she said, when I had finished.

'No,' I said. Too much too quickly: my stomach was cramping viciously. 'Thanks.'

'What happened?' she said quietly. 'Did you remember something?'

I started to cry. I cry so seldom – only once or twice since I was thirteen, I think, and both those times I was so drunk that it doesn't really count – that it took me a moment to understand what was happening. I rubbed a hand across my face and stared at my wet fingers. 'No,' I said. 'Nothing that does any good. I can remember all that afternoon, going into the wood and what we were talking about, and hearing something – I can't remember what – and going to find out what it was . . . And then I panicked. I fucking panicked.' My voice cracked.

'Hey,' Cassie said. She scooted across the futon and put a hand on my shoulder. 'That's a huge step, hon. Next time you'll remember the rest.'

'No,' I said. 'No, I won't.' I couldn't explain, I'm still not sure what made me so certain: this had been my ace in the hole, my one shot, and I had blown it. I put my face in my hands and sobbed like a child.

She didn't put her arms around me or try to comfort me, and I was grateful for this. She just sat there quietly, her thumb moving regularly on my shoulder, while I cried. Not for those three children, I can't claim that, but for the unbridgeable distance that lay between them and me: for the millions of miles, and the planets separating at dizzying speed. For how much we had had to lose. We had been so small, so recklessly sure that together we could defy all the dark and complicated threats of the adult world, run straight through them like a game of Red Rover, laughing and away.

'Sorry about that,' I said at last. I straightened up and wiped my face with the back of my wrist.

'For what?'

'Making an idiot of myself. I didn't intend to do that.'

Cassie shrugged. 'So we're even. Now you know how I feel when I have those dreams and you have to wake me up.'

'Yeah?' This had never occurred to me.

'Yeah.' She rolled over onto her stomach on the futon, reached for a packet of tissues in the bedside locker and passed them to me. 'Blow.'

I managed to work up a weak smile, and blew my nose. 'Thanks, Cass.'

'How're you doing?'

I caught a long shuddery breath and yawned, suddenly and irrepressibly. 'I'm all right.'

'You about ready to crash?'

The tension was slowly draining out of my shoulders and I was more exhausted than I'd ever been in my life, but there were still quick little shadows zipping past my eyelids, and every sigh and crack of the house settling made me jerk. I knew that if Cassie switched off the light and I was alone on the sofa the air would fill up with layers of nameless things, pressing and mouthing and twittering. 'I think so,' I said. 'Would it be OK if I slept here?'

'Sure. If you snore, though, you're back on the sofa.' She sat up, blinking, and started to take out her hair-clips.

'I won't,' I said. I leaned over and took off my shoes and socks, but both the etiquette and the physical act of undressing seemed way too difficult to negotiate. I climbed under the duvet with all my clothes on.

Cassie pulled off her jumper and slid in beside me, curls standing up in a riot of cowlicks. Without even thinking about it I put my arms around her, and she curled her back against me.

'Night, hon,' I said. 'Thanks again.'

She gave my arm a pat and stretched to switch off the bedside lamp. 'Night, silly. Sleep tight. Wake me up if you want to.'

Her hair against my face had a sweet green smell, like tea leaves. She settled her head on the pillow and sighed. She felt warm and compact, and I thought vaguely of polished ivory, glossy chestnuts: the pure, piercing satisfaction when something fits perfectly into your hand. I couldn't remember the last time I had held anyone like this.

'Are you awake?' I whispered, after a long time.

'Yeah,' Cassie said.

We lay very still. I could feel the air around us changing, blooming and shimmering like the air over a scorching road. My heart was speeding, or hers was banging against my chest, I'm not sure. I turned Cassie in my arms and kissed her, and after a moment she kissed me back.

I know I said that I always choose the anticlimactic over the irrevocable, and yes of course what I meant was that I have always been a coward, but I lied: not always, there was that night, there was that one time.

17

For once I woke first. It was very early, the roads still silent and the sky – Cassie, high above the rooftops with no one to look in her window, almost never closes the curtains – turquoise mottled with palest gold, perfect as a film still; I could only have been asleep an hour or two. Somewhere a cluster of seagulls burst into wild, keening cries.

In the thin sober light the flat looked abandoned and desolate: last night's plates and glasses scattered on the coffee table, a tiny ghostly draught lifting the pages of notes, my jumper hunched in a dark blot on the floor and long distorting shadows slanting everywhere. I felt a pang under my breastbone, so intense and physical that I thought it must be thirst. There was a glass of water on the bedside table and I reached over and drank it off, but the hollow ache didn't subside.

I had thought my movement might wake Cassie, but she didn't stir. She was deeply asleep in the crook of my arm, her lips slightly parted, one hand curled loosely on the pillow. I brushed the hair away from her forehead and woke her by kissing her.

We didn't get up till around three. The sky had turned grey and heavy, and a chill ran over me as I left the warmth of the duvet.

'I'm starving,' Cassie said, buttoning her jeans. She

looked very beautiful that day, tousled and full-lipped, her eyes still and mysterious as a daydreaming child's, and this new radiance – jarring against the grim afternoon – made me uneasy somehow. 'Fry-up?'

'No, thanks,' I said. This is our usual weekend routine when I stay over, a big Irish breakfast and a long walk on the beach, but I couldn't face either the excruciating thought of talking about anything that had happened the previous night or the heavy-handed complicity of avoiding it. The flat felt suddenly tiny and claustrophobic. I had bruises and scrapes in weird places: my stomach, my elbow, a nasty little gouge on one thigh. 'I should really go get my car.'

Cassie pulled a T-shirt over her head and said easily, through the material, 'You want a lift?' but I had seen the swift, startled flinch in her eyes.

'I think I'll take the bus, actually,' I said. I found my shoes under the sofa. 'I could do with a bit of a walk. I'll ring you later, OK?'

'Fair enough,' she said cheerfully, but I knew something had passed between us, something alien and slender and dangerous. We held onto each other for a moment, hard, at the door of her flat.

I made a sort of half-assed attempt at waiting for the bus, but after ten or fifteen minutes I told myself it was too much work – two different buses, Sunday schedules, this could take me all day. In truth, I had no desire to go anywhere near Knocknaree until I knew the site would be full of noisy energetic archaeologists; the thought of it today, deserted and silent under this low grey sky, made me feel slightly sick. I picked up a cup of dirty-tasting coffee at a petrol station and started to walk home. Monkstown is four or five miles from Sandymount, but

I was in no hurry: Heather would be home, with biohazardous-looking green stuff on her face and *Sex and the City* turned up loud, wanting to tell me about all her speed-dating conquests and demanding to know where I had been and how my jeans had got all muddy and what I had done with the car. I felt as if someone had been setting off a relentless series of depth charges inside my head.

I knew, you see, that I had just made at least one of the biggest mistakes of my life. I had slept with the wrong people before, but I had never done anything at quite this level of monumental stupidity. The standard response after something like this happens is either to begin an official 'relationship' or to cut off all communication – I had attempted both in the past, with varying degrees of success – but I could hardly stop speaking to my partner, and as for entering into a romantic relationship . . . Even if it hadn't been against regulations, I couldn't even manage to eat or sleep or buy toilet bleach, I was lunging at suspects and blanking on the stand and having to be rescued from archaeological sites in the middle of the night; the thought of trying to be someone's boyfriend, with all the attendant responsibilities and complications, made me want to curl up in a ball and whimper.

I was so tired that my feet, hitting the pavement, seemed to belong to someone else. The wind spat fine rain in my face and I thought, with a sick, growing sense of disaster, of all the things I couldn't do any more: stay up all night getting drunk with Cassie, tell her about girls I met, sleep on her sofa. There was no longer any way, ever again, to see her as Cassie-just-Cassie, one of the lads but a whole lot easier on the eye; not now that I had seen her the way I had. Every sunny familiar spot in our shared landscape had become a dark minefield, fraught with treacherous nuances and implications. I remembered her, only a few days before, reaching into my coat pocket for my lighter as we sat in the Castle gardens; she hadn't even broken off her sentence to do it and I had loved the gesture so much, loved the sure, unthinking ease of it, the taking for granted.

I know this will sound incredible, given that everyone from my parents down to a cretin like Quigley had expected it, but I had never once seen this coming. Christ but we were smug: supremely arrogant, secure in our certainty that we were exempt from the oldest rule known to man. I swear I lay down as innocent as a child. Cassie tilted her head to take out her hair-clips, made faces when they caught; I tucked my socks into my shoes, the way I always do, so she wouldn't fall over them in the morning. I know you'll say our naïveté was deliberate, but if you believe only one thing I tell you, make it this: neither of us knew.

When I reached Monkstown I still couldn't face going home. I walked on to Dun Laoghaire and sat on a wall at the end of the pier, watching tweedy couples on Sunday-afternoon constitutionals run into each other with simian hoots of delight, until it got dark and the wind started cutting through my coat and a uniform on patrol gave me a suspicious look. I thought about ringing Charlie, for some reason, but I didn't have his number in my mobile and anyway I wasn't sure what I wanted to say.

That night I slept as if I had been clubbed. When I got into work the next morning I was still dazed and bleary-eyed, and the incident room looked strange, different in sneaky little ways I couldn't pinpoint, as if I had slid through some crack into an alternate and hostile reality. Cassie had left the old case file spread out all over her corner of the table. I sat down and tried to work, but I couldn't focus; by the time I reached the end of each sentence I had forgotten the beginning and had to go back and start over.

Cassie came in bright-cheeked from the wind, curls chrysanthemum-wild under a little red tam-o'-shanter. 'Hi, you,' she said. 'How're you doing?'

She ruffled my hair as she passed behind me, and I couldn't help it: I flinched, and felt her hand freeze for an instant before she moved on.

'Fine,' I said.

She slung her satchel over the back of her chair. I could tell, out of the corner of my eye, that she was looking at me; I kept my head down. 'Rosalind and Jessica's medical records are coming in on Bernadette's fax. She says for us to come get them in a few minutes, and to give out the incident-room fax number next time. And it's your turn to cook dinner, but I only have chicken, so if you and Sam want anything else . . .'

Her voice sounded casual, but there was a faint, tentative question behind it. 'Actually,' I said, 'I can't make it to dinner tonight. I have to be somewhere.'

'Oh. OK.' Cassie pulled off her hat and ran her fingers through her hair. 'Pint, then, depending on when we finish?'

'I can't tonight,' I said. 'Sorry.'

'Rob,' she said, after a moment, but I didn't look up. For a second I thought she was going to go on anyway, but then the door opened and Sam bounced in, all fresh and buoyant after his wholesome rural weekend, with a couple of tapes in one hand and a sheaf of fax pages in the other. I had never been so glad to see him.

'Morning, lads. These are for you, with Bernadette's compliments. How was the weekend?'

'Fine,' we said, in unison, and Cassie turned away and started hanging up her jacket.

I took the pages from Sam and tried to skim through them. My concentration was shot to hell, the Devlins' doctor had handwriting so lousy that it had to be an affectation, and Cassie – the unaccustomed patience with which she waited for me to finish each page, the moment of enforced nearness as she leaned over to pick it up – set my teeth on edge. It took me a massive effort of will to disentangle even a few salient facts.

Apparently Margaret had been easily alarmed when Rosalind was a baby – there were multiple doctor visits for every cold and cough – but in fact Rosalind seemed to be the healthiest of the bunch: no major illnesses, no major injuries. Jessica had been in an incubator for three days when she and Katy were born, when she was seven she had broken her arm falling off a climbing frame at school, and she had been underweight since she was about nine. They had both had chicken pox. They had both had all their shots. Rosalind had had an ingrown toenail removed, the year before.

'There's nothing here that says either abuse or Munchausen's by proxy,' Cassie said at last. Sam had found the tape recorder; in the background, Andrews was giving a real estate agent a long, injured rant about something or other.

If he hadn't been there, I think I would have ignored her. 'And there's nothing that rules them out, either,' I said, hearing the edge in my voice.

'How would you rule abuse *out*, definitively? All we can do is say there's no evidence of it, which there isn't. And I think this does rule out Munchausen's. Like I said before, Margaret doesn't fit the profile anyway, and with this . . . The whole *point* of Munchausen's is that it leads to medical treatment. Nobody's been Munchausening these two.'

'So this was pointless,' I said. I shoved the records away, too hard; half the pages fluttered off the edge of the table, onto the floor. 'Surprise, surprise. This case is fucked. It's been fucked right from the start. We might as well throw it into the basement right now and move on to something that has a snowball's chance in hell, because this is a waste of everyone's time.'

Andrews's phone calls had come to an end and the tape recorder hissed, faintly but persistently, until Sam clicked it off. Cassie leaned over sideways and started collecting the spilled fax pages. Nobody said anything for a very long time.

I wonder what Sam thought. He never said a word, but he must have known something was wrong, he couldn't have missed it: all of a sudden the long happy studenty evenings *à trois* stopped, and the atmosphere in the incident room was like something out of Sartre. It's possible that Cassie told him the whole story at some point or other, cried on his shoulder, but I doubt it: she had too much pride, always. I think probably she kept inviting him round for dinner and ex-plained that I had trouble with child-murders – which was, after all, true – and wanted to spend my evenings unwinding; explained it so casually and convincingly that, even if Sam didn't believe her, he knew not to ask questions.

I imagine other people noticed, too. Detectives do tend to be fairly observant, and the fact that the Wonder Twins weren't speaking would have been headline news. It must have been all around the squad within twenty-four hours, accompanied by an array of lurid explanations – some-where among them, I'm sure, the truth.

Or maybe not. Through everything, this much of the old alliance remained: the shared, animal instinct to keep its dying private. In some ways this is the most heartbreaking thing of all: always, always, right up until the end, the old connection was there when it was needed. We could spend excruciating hours not saying a word to each other unless it was unavoidable, and then in toneless voices, with averted eyes; but the instant O'Kelly threatened to take Sweeney and O'Gorman away we snapped to life, me methodically going through a long list of reasons why we still needed floaters, while Cassie assured me that the Superintendent knew what he was doing and shrugged her shoulders and hoped the media wouldn't find out. It took all the energy I had. As the door closed and we were left alone again (or alone with Sam, who didn't count) the practised sparkle would evaporate and I would turn expressionlessly away from her white, uncomprehending face, giving her my shoulder with the priggish aloofness of an offended cat.

I genuinely felt, you see, although I'm unclear on the process by which my mind arrived at this conclusion, that I had been wronged in some subtle but unpardonable way. If she had hurt me, I could have forgiven her without even having to think about it; but I couldn't forgive her for being hurt.

The blood results from the stains on my shoes and the drop on the altar stone were due back any day. Through the submarine haze in which I was navigating, this was one of the few things that remained clear in my mind. Just about every other lead had crashed and burned; this was all I had left, and I held onto it with grim desperation. I was sure, with a certainty far beyond logic, that all we needed was a DNA match; that if we got it everything else would fall into place with the soft precision of snowflakes, the case – both cases – spreading out before me, perfect and dazzling.

I was aware, vaguely, that if this happened we would need Adam Ryan's DNA for comparison, and that Detective Rob would very probably vanish forever in a puff of scandal-flavoured smoke. At the time, though, this didn't always seem like such a bad idea. On the contrary: there were moments when I looked forward to it with a kind of dull relief. It seemed – since I knew I had neither the guts nor the energy to extricate myself from this hideous mess – my only, or at least my simplest, way out.

Sophie, who believes in multitasking, phoned me from her car. 'The DNA guys called,' she said. 'Bad news.'

'Hey,' I said, shooting upright and swivelling my chair around so that my back was to the others. 'What's up?' I tried to keep my voice casual, but O'Gorman stopped whistling and I heard the rustle of Cassie putting down a page.

'Those blood samples are useless – both of them, the shoes and the one Helen found.' She smacked her horn. 'Jesus Christ, idiot, pick a lane, any lane! . . . The lab tried everything, but they're way too degraded for DNA. Sorry about that, but I did warn you.'

'Yeah,' I said, after a moment. 'It's been that kind of case. Thanks, Sophie.'

I hung up and stared at the phone. Cassie, across the table, asked tentatively, 'What did she say?' but I didn't answer.

That evening, on my walk home from the DART, I rang Rosalind. It went against all my loudest instincts to do this to her – I had wanted, very badly, to leave her alone until she was ready to talk, let her choose her own time for this rather than forcing her back against the wall; but she was all I had left.

She came in on the Thursday morning, and I went down to meet her in Reception, just as I had that first time, all those weeks ago. A part of me had been afraid she would change her mind at the last minute and not show up, and my heart lifted when I saw her, sitting in a big chair with her cheek leaning pensively on her hand and a rose-coloured scarf trailing. It was good to see someone young and pretty; I hadn't realised, until that moment, how exhausted and grey and jaded we were all starting to look. That scarf seemed like the first note of colour I had seen in days.

'Rosalind,' I said, and saw her face light up.

'Detective Ryan!'

'It's just occurred to me,' I said. 'Shouldn't you be in school?'

She gave me a conspiratorial sideways look. 'My teacher likes me. I won't get in trouble.' I knew I ought to lecture her about the evils of truancy, or something, but I couldn't help it: I laughed.

The door opened and Cassie came in from outside, tucking her cigarettes into her jeans pocket. She met my eyes for a second, glanced at Rosalind; then she brushed past us, up the stairs.

Rosalind bit her lip and looked up at me, her face troubled. 'Your partner's annoyed that I'm here, isn't she?'

'Well, that's not really her problem,' I said. 'Sorry about that.'

'Oh, it's all right.' Rosalind managed a small smile. 'She's never liked me very much, has she?'

'Detective Maddox doesn't dislike you.'

'Don't worry about it, Detective Ryan, really. I'm used to it. A lot of girls don't like me. My mother says' – she ducked her head, embarrassed – 'my mother says it's because they're jealous, but I don't see how that could be true.'

'I do,' I said, smiling down at her. 'But I don't think that's the case with Detective Maddox. That had nothing to do with you. OK?'

'Did you have a fight?' she asked timidly, after a moment.

'Sort of,' I said. 'It's a long story.'

I held the door open for her, and we crossed the cobbles towards the gardens. Rosalind's brow was furrowed thoughtfully. 'I wish she didn't dislike me so much. I really admire her, you know. It can't be easy, being a woman detective.'

'It's not easy being a detective, full stop,' I said. I did not want to talk about Cassie. 'We manage.'

'Yes, but it's different for women,' she told me, a little reproachfully.

'How's that?' She was so young and earnest; I knew she would be offended if I laughed.

'Well, for example . . . Detective Maddox must be at least thirty, isn't she? She must want to get married soon, and have children, and things like that. Women can't afford to wait like men can, you know. And being a detective must make it hard to have a serious relationship, doesn't it? It must be a lot of pressure for her.'

A vicious twist of unease caught at my stomach. 'I don't think Detective Maddox is the broody type,' I said.

Rosalind looked troubled, little white teeth catching at her bottom lip. 'You're probably right,' she said carefully. 'But you know, Detective Ryan . . . sometimes, when you're close to someone, you miss things. Other people can see them, but you can't.'

That twist tightened. A part of me badly wanted to push

her, to find out what exactly it was that she had seen in Cassie and I had missed; but the past week had brought it home to me, with considerable force, that there are some things in this life we are better off not knowing. 'Detective Maddox's personal life isn't my problem,' I said. 'Rosalind . . .'

But she had darted off, down one of the carefully wild little pathways that ring the grass, calling back over her shoulder: 'Oh, Detective Ryan – look! Isn't it lovely?'

Her hair danced in the sun coming through the leaves, and in spite of everything I smiled. I followed her down the pathway – we were going to need privacy anyway, for this conversation – and caught up with her at a secluded little bench overhung by branches, birds twittering in the bushes all around. 'Yes,' I said, 'it's lovely. Would you like to talk here?'

She settled herself on the bench and gazed up at the trees with a happy little sigh. 'Our secret garden.'

It was idyllic, and I hated the thought of wrecking it. For a moment I let myself toy with the thought of ditching the whole purpose of this meeting, having a chat about how she was doing and what a beautiful day it was and then sending her home; of being, for a few minutes, just a guy sitting in the sunshine talking to a pretty girl.

'Rosalind,' I said, 'I need to ask you about something. This is going to be very difficult, and I wish I knew some way to make it easier on you, but I don't. I wouldn't be asking you if I had any other choice. I need you to help me. Will you try?'

Something crossed her face, a flash of some vivid emotion, but it was gone before I could pinpoint it. She clasped her hands around the rails of the bench on either side, bracing herself. 'I'll do my best.'

'Your father and mother,' I said, keeping my voice very gentle and even. 'Has either of them ever hurt you or your sisters?'

Rosalind gasped. Her hand flew to her mouth and she stared at me over it, eyes round and startled, until she realised what she had done, snatched her hand away and clasped it tightly around the rail again. 'No,' she said, in a strained, compressed little voice. 'Of course not.'

'I know you must be frightened. I can protect you. I promise.'

'No.' She shook her head, biting her lip, and I knew she was on the verge of tears. 'No.'

I leaned closer and put my hand over hers. She smelled of some flowery, musky scent decades too old for her. 'Rosalind, if something's wrong, we need to know. You're in danger.'

'I'll be all right.'

'Jessica's in danger, too. I know you take care of her, but you can't keep doing that on your own forever. Please, let me help you.'

'You don't understand,' she whispered. Her hand was trembling under mine. 'I can't, Detective Ryan. I just *can't*.'

She almost broke my heart. This fragile, indomitable slip of a girl: in a situation that would have crippled people twice her age, she was holding it together by the skin of her teeth, walking a slim tightrope twisted out of nothing but tenacity and pride and denial. That was all she had, and I, of all people, was trying to pull it out from under her.

'I'm sorry,' I said, suddenly horribly ashamed of myself. 'There may come a time when you're ready to talk about this, and when that happens, I'll be right here. But until then . . . I shouldn't have tried to push you. I'm sorry.'

'You're so kind to me,' she murmured. 'I can't believe you've been so kind.'

'I just wish I could help you,' I said. 'I wish I knew how.'

'I . . . I don't trust people easily, Detective Ryan. But if I trust anyone, it'll be you.'

We sat there in silence. Rosalind's hand was soft under mine, and she didn't move it away.

Then she turned her hand, slowly, and interlaced her fingers in mine. She was smiling at me, an intimate little smile with a dare lurking in the corners.

I caught my breath. It went through me like an electric current, how badly I wanted to lean forward and cup my hand around the back of her head and kiss her. Images tumbled in my mind – crisp hotel sheets and her curls falling free, buttons under my fingers, Cassie's drawn face – and I wanted this girl who was like no girl I had ever known, wanted her not in spite of her moods and her secret bruises and her sad attempts at artifice but because of them, because of them all. I could see myself reflected, tiny and dazzled and moving closer, in her eyes.

She was eighteen years old and she might still end up being my main witness; she was more vulnerable than she would ever be again in her life; and she idolised me. She did not need to find out the hard way that I had developed a tendency to wreck everything I touched. I bit down hard on the inside of my cheek and disengaged my hand from hers.

'Rosalind,' I said.

Her face had shuttered over. 'I should go,' she said coldly.

'I don't want to hurt you. That's the last thing you need.'

'Well, you have.' She slung her bag over her shoulder, not looking at me. Her mouth was set in a tight line.

'Rosalind, please, wait—' I reached out for her hand, but she whipped it away.

'I thought you *cared* about me. Obviously, I was wrong. You just let me think so because you wanted to see if I knew anything about *Katy*. You wanted what you could get from me, just like everyone else.'

'That's not true,' I began; but she was gone, clicking down the path with angry little steps, and I knew there was no point in going after her. The birds in the bushes scattered, with a harsh tattoo of wings, as she passed.

My head was spinning. I gave her a few minutes to calm down and then rang her mobile, but she didn't answer. I left a babbling, apologetic message on her voicemail; then I hung up and slumped back on the bench.

'*Shit*,' I said aloud, to the empty bushes.

I think it's important to reiterate that, no matter what I may have claimed at the time, for most of Operation Vestal I was not in anything resembling a normal frame of mind. This may not be an excuse, but it is a fact. When I went into that wood, for example, I went into it on very little sleep and even less food and a considerable amount of accumulated tension and vodka, and I feel I should point out that it's entirely possible that the subsequent events were either a dream or some kind of weird hallucination. I have no way of knowing, and I can't think of an answer, either way, that would be particularly comforting.

Since that night I had, at least, started sleeping again – sleeping, actually, with a level of dedication so intense it made me nervous. By the time I staggered in from work every evening I was practically sleepwalking. I would fall into bed as if drawn by a powerful magnet and find myself in the same position, still in my clothes, when the alarm clock dragged me awake twelve or thirteen hours later. Once I forgot to set my alarm and woke at two o'clock in the afternoon, to the seventh phone call from a very snotty Bernadette.

The memories and the more bizarre side effects had stopped, too; clicked off as sharply and as definitively as a light bulb burning out. You'd think this would be a relief, and at the time it was: as far as I was concerned, absolutely anything to do with Knocknaree was the worst possible kind of news, and I was a lot better off without it. I should have pretty much figured this out a while back, I felt, and I could not believe that I had been stupid enough to ignore everything I knew and prance gaily back into that wood. I had never been so angry with myself in my life. It was only much later, when the case was over and the dust had settled on the debris, when I prodded cautiously at the edges of my memory and came up empty; it was only then that I began to think this might be not a deliverance but a vast missed chance, an irrevocable and devastating loss.

18

Sam and I were the first ones in the incident room on Friday morning. I had taken to coming in as early as I could, going through the phone tips to see if I could find an excuse to spend the day elsewhere. It was raining hard; Cassie, somewhere, was presumably swearing and trying to kick-start the Vespa.

'Daily bulletin,' Sam said, waving a couple of tapes at me. 'He was feeling chatty last night, six calls, so please God . . .'

We had been tapping Andrews' phones for a week now, with results pathetic enough that O'Kelly was beginning to emit ominous, volcanic grumbling noises. During the day Andrews made large numbers of snappy, testosterone-flavoured calls on his mobile; in the evenings he ordered overpriced 'gourmet' food – 'takeaway with notions', Sam called it, disapprovingly. Once he rang one of those sex chat-lines you see advertised on late-night TV; he liked to be spanked, apparently, and 'Redden my arse, Celestine' had instantly become a squad catchphrase.

I took off my coat and sat down. 'Play it, Sam,' I said. My sense of humour, along with everything else, had deteriorated over the past weeks. Sam gave me a look and threw one of the tapes into our obsolete little tape recorder.

At 8.17 p.m., according to the computer printout, Andrews had ordered lasagna with smoked salmon, pesto and sun-dried tomato sauce. 'Jesus Christ,' I said, appalled.

Sam laughed. 'Nothing but the best for our boy.'

At 8.23 he had called his brother-in-law to arrange a round of golf for Sunday afternoon, with a few manly jokes thrown in. At 8.41 he had rung the restaurant again, to shout at the order-taker because his food hadn't arrived. He was starting to sound tipsy. There followed a period of silence; apparently the Lasagna From Hell had, eventually, made it to its destination.

At 12.08 a.m. he rang a London number: 'His ex-wife,' Sam said. He was at the maudlin stage and wanted to talk about what had gone wrong. 'The biggest mistake I ever made was letting you go, Dolores,' he told her, his voice thick with tears. 'But, sure, maybe I did the right thing. You're a fine woman, do you know that? You're too good for me. A hundred times too good. Maybe even a thousand. Amn't I right, Dolores? Don't you think I did the right thing?'

'I wouldn't know, Terry,' Dolores said wearily. 'You tell me.' She was doing something else at the same time, clearing plates or maybe emptying a dishwasher; I could hear the chink of china in the background. Finally, when Andrews started to cry in earnest, she hung up. Two minutes later he rang her back, snarled, 'You don't hang up on me, you bitch, do you hear me? *I* hang up on *you*,' and slammed down the phone.

'A real ladies' man,' I said.

'Bugger,' Sam said. He slumped in his chair, leaned his head back and put his hands over his face. 'Ah, bugger. I've only a week left on this. What the hell do I do if it's all sushi pizza and lonely hearts?'

The tape clicked again. 'Hello,' said a deep male voice, furred with sleep.

'Who's this?' I asked.

'Unregistered mobile,' Sam said, through his hands. 'Quarter to two.'

'You little fucking scut,' Andrews said, on the tape. He was very drunk. Sam sat up.

There was a brief pause. Then the deep voice said, 'Didn't I tell you not to ring me again?'

'Whoa,' I said.

Sam made a small inarticulate noise. His hand shot out as if to grab the tape recorder, but he caught himself and merely pulled it closer to us on the table. We bent our heads over it, listening. Sam was holding his breath.

'I don't give a tinker's damn what you told me.' Andrews's voice was rising. 'You've told me more than enough already. You told me it would all be back on track by now, do you remember that? Instead there's fucking . . . *injunctions* everywhere—'

'I told you to calm the hell down and let me sort it, and I'm telling you the same again. I've everything under control.'

'You do in your hole. Don't you dare talk to me like I'm your emp— your emp— your employee. You're *my* fucking employee. I paid *you*. Fucking . . . thousands and thousands and . . . "Oh, we'll need another five grand for this, Terry, a few grand for the new councillor, Terry . . ." I might as well have flushed it down the bog. If you were my employee you'd be *fired*. Out on your arse. Like *that*.'

'I got you everything you paid for. This is just a minor delay. It'll be sorted. Nothing's going to change. Do you understand what I'm saying?'

'Sorted, my *arse.* You double-dealing little cunt, you. You took my money and ran. Now I've nothing but a pile of worthless land and the police crawling all over me. How do they . . . how the fuck do they even know that's my land? I *trusted* you.'

There was a slight pause. Sam let his breath out in a small burst, held it again. Then the deep voice said sharply, 'What phone are you calling from?'

'That's none of your bloody business,' Andrews said sulkily.

'What were the police asking you about?'

'Some . . . just some kid.' Andrews stifled a belch. 'That kid who got killed out there. Her father's the fucker with the fucking injunction . . . the thick bastards think I had something to do with it.'

'Get off the phone,' the deep voice said coldly. 'Don't talk to the cops without your lawyer. Don't worry about the injunction. And don't ever fucking ring me again.' There was a click as he hung up.

'*Well,*' I said, after a moment. 'That certainly wasn't sushi pizza and lonely hearts. Congratulations.' It wouldn't be admissible in court, but it would be enough to put considerable pressure on Andrews. I was trying to be gracious, but a self-pitying part of me felt this was typical: while my investigation degenerated into an unparalleled collection of dead ends and disasters, Sam's skipped gaily onwards and upwards, success after tidy little success. If I had been the one chasing Andrews, he would probably have made it through the two weeks without calling anyone more sinister than his ageing mother. 'That should get O'Kelly off your back.'

Sam didn't answer. I turned to look at him. He was so white he was almost green.

'What?' I said, alarmed. 'Are you all right?'

'I'm grand,' he said. 'Yeah.' He leaned forward and switched off the tape recorder. His hand shook a little, and I saw a damp, unhealthy sheen on his face.

'Jesus,' I said. 'No you're not.' It struck me suddenly that the excitement of victory could have given him a heart attack or a stroke or something, he could have some weird undiagnosed weakness; there are stories like that in squad lore, detectives pursuing a suspect through epic obstacles only to drop dead as soon as the handcuffs click home. 'Do you need a doctor or something?'

'No,' he said sharply. 'No.'

'Then what the hell?'

Almost as I said it, the penny dropped. I'm amazed, actually, that I hadn't already caught on. The timbre of the voice, the accent, the little quirks of inflexion: I had heard them all before, every day, every evening; a little softened, lacking that abrasive edge, but the resemblance was there and unmistakable.

'Was that,' I said, 'was that by any chance your uncle?'

Sam's eyes snapped to me and then to the door, but there was no one there. 'Yeah,' he said, after a moment. 'It was.' His breathing was fast and shallow.

'Are you sure?'

'I know his voice. I'm sure.'

Regrettable though this may be, my main reaction was an intense desire to laugh. He had been so bloody earnest (*Straight as a die, lads*), so solemn, like a GI making a speech about the flag in some terrible American war movie. At the time I had found it endearing – that kind of absolute faith is one of those things that, like virginity, can only be lost once, and I had never met anyone who had retained it into his thirties before – but now it seemed to me that Sam had spent much of his life trundling happily along on sheer dumb luck, and I had a hard time working up much sympathy for the fact that he had finally stepped on a banana skin and gone flying.

'What are you going to do?' I asked.

His head moved blindly from side to side, under the fluorescent lights. He must have thought of it, surely: we were the only two there, one favour and one push of the Record button and the phone call could have been about that Sunday round of golf, anything.

'Can you give me the weekend?' he said. 'I'll take this to O'Kelly on Monday. I just . . . not right now. I can't think straight. I need the weekend.'

'Sure,' I said. 'Are you going to talk to your uncle?'

Sam glanced up at me. 'If I do, he'll start covering his tracks, won't he? Getting rid of the evidence before the investigation starts.'

'I assume he would, yes.'

'If I don't tell him – if he finds out that I could have given him the heads-up, and I didn't . . .'

'I'm sorry,' I said. I wondered, fleetingly, where the hell Cassie was.

'Do you know the mad thing?' Sam said, after a while. 'If you'd asked me this morning who I'd go to, if something like this happened and I didn't know what to do, I'd have said Red.'

I could think of nothing to say to this. I looked at his blunt, pleasant features and suddenly felt oddly disengaged from him, from the entire scene; it was a vertiginous sensation, as if I were watching these events unfold in a lighted box hundreds of feet below me. We sat there for a long time, until O'Gorman banged in and started shouting about something to do with rugby, and Sam quietly put the tape in his pocket and gathered up his things and left.

That afternoon, when I went for a smoke break, Cassie followed me outside.

'Have you got a light?' she asked.

She had lost weight, her cheekbones had sharpened, and I wondered whether this had happened unnoticed over the whole course of Operation Vestal or – the thought gave me a prickle of unease – just over the past few days. I fished out my lighter and handed it to her.

It was a cold, cloudy afternoon, dead leaves starting to build up against the walls; Cassie turned her back to the wind to light her cigarette. She was wearing make-up – mascara, a smudge of something pink on each cheek – but her face, bent over her cupped hand, still looked too pale, almost grey. 'What's going on, Rob?' she asked, as she straightened up.

My stomach plummeted. We've all had this excruciating conversation, but I don't know of a single man who thinks it serves any useful purpose, nor of a single occasion when it has had a positive result, and I had been hoping against hope that Cassie would turn out to be one of the rare women who can leave it alone. 'Nothing's going on,' I said.

'Why are you being weird at me?'

I shrugged. 'I'm wrecked; the case is a mess, these last few weeks have done my head in. It's not personal.'

'Come on, Rob. It is too. You've been acting like I have leprosy ever since . . .' I felt my whole body tighten. Cassie's voice trailed off.

'No, I haven't,' I said. 'I just need some space right now. OK?'

'I don't even know what that *means*. All I know is you're

freaking out on me, and I can't do anything about it when I don't understand why.'

Out of the corner of my eye I saw the determined set to her chin, and I knew I wasn't going to be able to dodge this one. 'I'm not freaking out,' I said, hideously uncomfortable. 'I just don't want to make things any more complicated than they already are. I am very definitely not capable of starting a relationship right now, and I don't want to give the impression—'

'*Relationship?*' Cassie's eyebrows shot up; she almost laughed. 'Jesus, is that what all this is about? No, Ryan, I don't expect you to marry me and have my little babies. What the hell made you think I wanted a *relationship*? I just want things to go back to normal, because this is ridiculous.'

I didn't believe her. It was a convincing performance – the quizzical look, the easy slouch of her shoulder against the wall; anyone else in the world would have been able to breathe a sigh of relief, give her an awkward hug and start back towards some variation of normal, arm-in-arm. But I knew Cassie's every tell and every quirk, as well as I knew my own hands. The quickening in her breath, that gymnast's brace of the shoulders, the infinitesimal tentative note in her voice: she was terrified, and this terrified me in turn.

'Yeah,' I said. 'Fair enough.'

'You know that. Right, Rob?' That tiny shake again.

'In this situation,' I said, 'I'm not sure going back to normal is a possibility. Saturday night was a big mistake, and I wish it had never happened, but it did. And we're stuck with it.'

Cassie flicked ash onto the cobbles, but I had seen the flash of hurt on her face, stark and shocked as if I had slapped her. After a moment she said, 'Well. I'm not sure it needs to be a mistake.'

'It shouldn't have happened,' I said. My back was pressed against the wall so hard that I could feel its protrusions digging into me, straight through my suit. 'It would never have happened if I hadn't been such a mess about other things. I'm sorry, but that's the reality of it.'

'OK,' she said, very carefully, 'OK. But it doesn't have to be a huge big deal. We're friends, we're close, that's why this happened, it should just bring us a little closer; end of story.'

What she said was eminently reasonable and sensible; I knew I was the one who sounded juvenile, melodramatic, and this just wound me even tighter. But her eyes: I had seen them look like that before, across a junkie's needle in a flat where no human being should live, and she had sounded very plausibly calm then, too. 'Yeah,' I said, looking away. 'Maybe. I just need some time to sort out my head. What with everything else that's been going on.'

Cassie spread her hands. 'Rob,' she said: this small clear puzzled voice, I'll never be able to forget it. 'Rob, it's just *me.*'

I couldn't hear her. I could barely see her; her face looked like a stranger's, unreadable and risky. I wanted to be almost anywhere else in the world. 'I should get back inside,' I said, throwing my cigarette away. 'Can I have my lighter?'

I can't explain why I gave so little consideration to the possibility that Cassie might have told the simple, exact truth about what she wanted from me. After all, I had never known her to lie, to me or to anyone else, and I'm not sure why I assumed with such certainty that she had suddenly started doing it now. It never once occurred to me that her wretchedness might actually be the result not of unrequited passion but of losing her closest friend – which I think I can, without deceiving myself, say that I was.

It sounds like arrogance, fancying myself some irresistible Casanova, but I truly don't think it was that simple. You have to remember that I'd never seen Cassie like this before. I'd never seen her cry, I could count on the fingers of one hand the times I'd seen her afraid; now her eyes were puffy and bruised-looking under the clumsy defiant make-up, and there was that flinch of fear and desperate appeal in them every time she looked at me. What was I supposed to think? Rosalind's words – *thirty, biological clock, can't afford to wait* – rubbed at me like a broken tooth, and everything I'd read on the subject (tattered magazines in waiting-rooms, Heather's *Cosmo* skimmed blearily over breakfast) backed them up: ten ways for 'thirty-something' women to make the most of their last chance, Awful Warnings on leaving childbearing too late, and, for good measure, the odd article on how you should never sleep with your friends because it inevitably led to 'feelings' on the woman's part, fear of commitment on the man's, tedious and unnecessary hassle all round.

I had always thought of Cassie as a million miles from these chick-lit clichés, but then (*sometimes, when you're close to someone, you miss things*), I had also thought we were the exception to every rule, and look how that had turned out. And I didn't intend to be a cliché myself; but remember that Cassie wasn't the only one whose life had gone haywire, I was lost and confused and shaken to the core, and I held onto the only guidelines I could find.

And then, too, I had learned early to assume something dark and lethal hidden at the heart of anything I loved.

When I couldn't find it, I responded, bewildered and wary, in the only way I knew how: by planting it there myself.

Now it seems obvious, of course, that even a strong person has weak spots and that I had hit Cassie's full-force, with all the precision of a jeweller fragmenting a stone along a flaw. She must have thought, sometimes, of her namesake, the votary branded with her god's most inventive and sadistic curse: to tell the truth, and never to be believed.

Sam showed up at my apartment on Monday evening, late, around ten. I had just got up and made myself toast for dinner and I was already half asleep again, and when the buzzer went I had an irrational, craven flash of fear that it might be Cassie, maybe a little drunk, demanding that we sort things out once and for all. I let Heather answer. When she banged irritably on my door and said, 'It's for you, some guy called Sam,' I was so relieved that it took a moment for the surprise to kick in. Sam had never been to my place before; I hadn't even realised he knew where it was.

I went to the door, tucking my shirt in, and listened to him clumping up the stairs. 'Hi,' I said, when he reached the landing.

'Hello,' he said. I hadn't seen him since Friday morning. He was wearing his big tweed overcoat; he needed a shave and his hair was dirty, falling in long dank streaks across his forehead.

I waited, but he didn't offer any explanation of his presence, so I brought him into the sitting-room. Heather followed us in and started talking – Hi I'm Heather, and it's lovely to meet you, and where has Rob been hiding you all this time, he never brings his friends home, isn't that very bold of him, and I was just watching *The Simple Life*, do you ever follow it, God it's mad this year, and on and on and on. Finally our monosyllabic replies got through to her: she said, in injured tones, '*Well*. I suppose you boys want some *privacy*,' and when neither of us denied it she flounced off, giving Sam a warm smile and me a slightly chillier one.

'Sorry for bursting in on you like this,' Sam said. He looked around the room (aggressive designer sofa cushions, shelves of long-lashed porcelain animals) as if it baffled him.

'That's all right,' I said. 'Would you like a drink?' I had no idea what he was doing there. I didn't even want to think about the intolerable possibility that it had something to do with Cassie: *She wouldn't have*, I thought, *surely to God she wouldn't have asked him to have a word with me?*

'Whiskey would be great.'

I found half a bottle of Jameson's in my kitchen cupboard. When I carried the glasses back into the sitting-room Sam was in an armchair, still wearing his coat, his head down and his elbows on his knees. Heather had left the TV on, with the volume off, and two identical women in orange make-up were arguing with silent hysteria about something or other; the light skittered wildly across his face, giving him a ghostly, damned look.

I switched off the TV and handed him a glass. He looked at it with something like surprise, then threw half of it back with one clumsy jerk of his wrist. It occurred to me that he might be a little drunk already. He wasn't unsteady or slurring or anything like that, but both his movements and his voice seemed different, rough-edged and heavy.

'So,' I said inanely, 'what's the story?'

Sam took another swallow of his drink. The pole lamp

beside him trapped him half in, half out of a pool of light. 'You know that thing on Friday?' he said. 'That tape?'

I relaxed a little. 'Yes?'

'I didn't talk to my uncle,' he said.

'No?'

'No. I thought about it all weekend. But I didn't ring him.' He cleared his throat. 'I went to O'Kelly,' he said, and cleared it again. 'This afternoon. With the tape. I played it for him, and then I told him it was my uncle on the other end.'

'Wow,' I said. To tell the truth, I don't think I had expected him to go through with it. I was, in spite of myself, impressed.

'No,' Sam said. He blinked at the glass in his hand, put it down on the coffee table. 'Do you know what he said to me?'

'What?'

'He asked was I off my fucking head.' He laughed, a little wildly. 'Christ, I think the man's got a point . . . He told me to erase the tape, call off the phone tap and leave Andrews the hell alone. "That's an order," that's what he said. He said I hadn't an iota of evidence that Andrews had anything to do with the murder, and if this went any further we would be back in uniform, him and me both – not right away, and not for any reason that had anything to do with this, but some day soon we'd wake up and find ourselves on patrol in the arse end of nowhere for the rest of our lives. He said, "This conversation never happened, because this tape never happened."'

His voice was rising. Heather's bedroom backs onto the sitting-room, and I was pretty sure she had one ear pressed against the wall. 'He wants you to cover it up?' I asked, keeping my voice down and hoping Sam would take the hint.

'I'd say that's what he was driving at, yeah,' he said, with heavy sarcasm. It didn't come naturally to him and rather than sounding tough and cynical it made him seem terribly young, like a miserable teenager. He slumped back in the armchair and raked his hair out of his face. 'I never expected that, you know? Of all the things I worried about . . . I never even thought of it.'

I suppose, if I'm honest, I had never been able to take Sam's whole line of investigation very seriously. International holding companies, rogue property developers and hush-hush land deals: it had always seemed impossibly remote and crude and almost laughable, some cheesy blockbuster starring Tom Cruise, not something that could ever affect anyone in any real way. The look on Sam's face caught me off guard. He hadn't been drinking, nothing like that; the double whammy – his uncle, O'Kelly – had hit him like a pair of buses. Being Sam, he had never even seen them coming. For a moment, in spite of everything, I wished I could find the right words to comfort him; to tell him that there comes a time when this happens to everyone and that he would survive it, as almost everyone does.

'What'll I do?' he asked.

'I have no idea,' I said, startled. Granted, Sam and I had been spending a lot of time together recently, but this hardly made us bosom buddies, and anyway I was in no position to give anyone sage advice. 'I don't mean to sound unfeeling, but why are you asking me?'

'Who else?' Sam said quietly. When he looked up at me I saw that his eyes were bloodshot. 'I can't go to any of my family with this, can I? It'd kill them. And my friends are great, but they're not cops, and this is police business. And Cassie . . . I'd rather not bring her into this. Sure, she's got enough on her plate already. She's looking awful stressed these days. You already knew about it, and I just needed to talk to someone, before I decide.'

I was fairly confident that I had been looking pretty stressed myself, these past few weeks, though I was pleased by the implication that I had been hiding it better than I thought. 'Decide?' I said. 'It doesn't really sound as if you have a lot of options here.'

'I've Michael Kiely,' Sam said. 'I could give him the tape.'

'Jesus. You'd lose your job before the article hit the presses. It might even be illegal, I'm not sure.'

'I know.' He pressed the heels of his hands into his eyes. 'Do you think that's what I should do?'

'I haven't the foggiest,' I said. The whiskey, on a near-empty stomach, was making me feel slightly ill. I had used ice cubes from the back of the freezer, the only ones left, and they tasted stale and tainted.

'What would happen if I did, do you know?'

'Well, you'd be fired. Maybe prosecuted.' He said nothing. 'They might have to have a tribunal, I suppose. If they decided your uncle had done something wrong, they'd tell him not to do it again, he'd be back-benched for a couple of years and then everything would go back to normal.'

'But the motorway.' Sam rubbed his hands over his face. 'I can't think straight . . . If I say nothing, that motorway'll go through, over all the archaeological stuff. For no good reason.'

'It'll do that anyway. If you go to the papers, the government will just say, "Oops, sorry about that, too late to move it," and go on their merry way.'

'You think so?'

'Well, yes,' I said. 'Frankly.'

'And Katy,' he said. 'That's what we're supposed to be *about*. What if Andrews hired someone to kill her? Do we just let him get away with it?'

'I don't know,' I said. I wondered how long he was planning to stay there.

We sat in silence for a while. The people in the next apartment were having a dinner party or something: I could hear a jumble of happy voices, Kylie on the stereo, a girl calling coquettishly, 'I *did* tell you, I so did!' Heather banged on the wall; there was a moment's silence, then an outburst of half-muffled laughter.

'Do you know what my first memory is?' Sam said. The lamplight shadowed his eyes and I couldn't tell what expression he wore. 'The day Red got into the Dáil, I was only a little lad, maybe three or four, but we all came up to Dublin to walk him in, the whole family. It was a gorgeous day, sunny. I had a new little suit on me. I wasn't sure what had happened exactly, but I knew it was important. Everyone looked so happy, and my dad . . . he was glowing, he was so proud. He put me up on his shoulders so I could see, and he shouted, "That's *your* uncle, son!" Red was up on the steps, waving and smiling, and I yelled, "That man's my uncle!" and everyone laughed, and he winked at me . . . We've still got the photo, on the sitting-room wall.'

There was another silence. It occurred to me that Sam's father might just possibly be less shocked by his brother's exploits than Sam expected, but I decided this would provide dubious comfort at best.

Sam pushed back his hair again. 'And there's my house,' he said. 'You know I own my house, right?'

I nodded. I had a feeling I knew where this was going.

'Yeah,' he said. 'It's a nice house – four bedrooms and all. I was only looking for an apartment, like. But Red said . . . you know, for when I've a family. I didn't think I could afford anything decent, but he . . . yeah.' He cleared his throat again, a sharp unsettling sound. 'He introduced me to the fella building the estate. He said they were old friends, the guy would give me a good deal.'

'Well,' I said, 'he did. There's not much you can do about it now.'

'I could sell the house, for the price I got it. To some young couple who'll never get a place any other way.'

'Why?' I said. This conversation was starting to frustrate me. He was like a big earnest bewildered St Bernard, gamely struggling to do his duty in the midst of a blizzard that made every laborious step completely useless. 'Self-immolation's a nice gesture, but it doesn't usually achieve very much.'

'Don't know the word,' Sam said wearily, reaching for his glass. 'But I get the idea. You're saying I should leave it.'

'I don't *know* what you should do,' I said. A wave of fatigue and nausea enveloped me. *God*, I thought, *what a week*. 'I'm probably the last person to ask. I just don't see the point of making a martyr of yourself and ditching your home and your career when it won't do anyone any good. You didn't do anything wrong. Right?'

Sam looked up at me. 'Right,' he said softly, bitterly. 'I did nothing wrong.'

Cassie wasn't the only one who was losing weight. It had been well over a week since I had eaten an actual meal, with food groups and everything, and I had been vaguely aware that when I was shaving I had to manoeuvre the razor into new little hollows around my jawline; but it wasn't until I was taking off my suit, that night, that I realised it was hanging off my hipbones and sagging away from my shoulders. Most detectives either lose or gain some weight during a big investigation – Sam and O'Gorman were both starting to look a little bulky around the middle, from too much snatched junk food – and I'm tall enough that this is seldom noticeable, but if this case went on for much longer, I was going to have to buy new suits or go around looking like Charlie Chaplin.

This is what not even Cassie knows: the year I was twelve, I was a big kid. Not one of those featureless spherical children you see waddling down the street on preachy news segments about the moral inferiority of modern youth; in photos I just look sturdy, a little chunky maybe, tall for my age and horribly uncomfortable, but I felt monstrous and lost: my own body had betrayed me. I had shot up and out until it was unrecognisable to me, some hideous practical joke I had to carry around every moment of every day. It didn't help that Peter and Jamie looked exactly like they always had: longer in the leg, all their baby teeth gone, but still slight and light and invincible as ever.

It didn't last long, my chunky stage: the food at boarding-school was, in keeping with literary tradition, so awful that even a kid who wasn't shaken and homesick and growing fast would have had a hard time eating enough of it to gain weight. And I hardly ate anything at all, that first year. At first the housemaster made me stay at the table on my own, for hours sometimes, until I forced down a few bites and his point, whatever it was, had been made; after a while I grew expert at slipping food into a plastic bag in my pocket, to be flushed away later. Fasting is, I think, a profoundly instinctive form of appeal. I'm sure I believed, in some inarticulate way, that if I ate little enough for long enough Peter and Jamie would be given back and everything would return to normal. By the beginning of my second year I was tall and thin with too many elbows, the way thirteen-year-olds are supposed to be.

I'm not sure why this, out of all the possibilities, should be my most closely guarded secret. I think the truth is this: I have always wondered whether this was the reason I was left behind, that day in the wood. Because I was fat; because I couldn't run fast enough; because, newly heavy and awkward, my balance shattered, I was afraid to jump off the castle wall. Sometimes I think about the sly, flickering line that separates being spared from being rejected. Sometimes I think of the ancient gods who demanded that their sacrifices be fearless and without blemish, and I wonder whether, whoever or whatever took Peter and Jamie away, it decided I wasn't good enough.

19

That Tuesday, first thing in the morning, I finally took the bus out to Knocknaree to pick up my car. Given the choice, I would have preferred never to think about Knocknaree again in my life, but I was sick of getting to and from work on jam-packed, sweat-smelling DARTs, and I needed to do a serious supermarket run soon, before Heather's head imploded.

My car was still in the lay-by, in pretty much the same condition as I'd left it, although all the rain had covered it with a layer of grime and someone had written ALSO AVAILABLE IN WHITE with a finger on the passenger door. I headed between the Portakabins (apparently deserted, except for Hunt in the office, blowing his nose loudly) onto the site, to retrieve my sleeping-bag and my thermos.

The mood of the dig had changed: this time there were no water-fights and no cheery shouting. The team was working in grim silence, hunched like a chain gang, keeping a hard, punishingly fast rhythm. I went through the dates in my mind: this was their last week, the motorway people were due to start work on Monday if the injunction was lifted. I saw Mel stop mattocking and straighten up, grimacing, one hand to her spine; she was panting, and her head fell back as if she didn't have the strength left to hold it up, but after a moment she rolled her shoulders, took a breath and heaved up her mattock again. The sky hung grey and heavy, uncomfortably close. Somewhere far away, on the estate, a car alarm's hysterical shrieking went ignored.

The wood was dark and sullen, giving away nothing. I looked at it and realised that I very badly did not want to go in there. My sleeping-bag would be sodden by now, and probably colonised by mould or ants or something, and I never used it anyway; it wasn't worth the immensity of that first step into the rich, mossy silence. Maybe one of the archaeologists or the local kids would find it and annex it, before it rotted away.

I was already late for work, but even the thought of going in made me tired, and a few more minutes wouldn't make much difference at this stage. I found a semi-comfortable position on a tumbledown wall, one foot up to brace myself, and lit a cigarette. A stocky guy with scrubby dark hair – George McSomething, I remembered him vaguely from the interviews – raised his head and saw me. Apparently this gave him an idea: he stuck his trowel into the ground, sat back on his haunches and pulled a flattened smoke packet out of his jeans.

Mark was kneeling on top of a thigh-high bank, scraping at a patch of earth with coiled, frantic energy, but almost before the dark guy fished out a cigarette he had clocked him and was leaping down off the bank, hair flying, and bounding over. 'Here, Macker! What the fuck do you think you're doing?'

Macker jumped up guiltily – 'Jesus!' – dropped the packet and fumbled for it in the dirt. 'I'm having a smoke. What's your problem?'

'You have it on your coffee break. Like I told you.'

'What's the big deal? I can smoke and trowel at the same time, it takes five seconds to light a fag—'

Mark lost it. 'We don't have five seconds to waste. We don't have *one* second. Do you think you're still in school, you fucking halfwit? Do you think this is all some kind of game, yeah?'

His fists were clenched and he was halfway to a street-fighter's crouch. The other archaeologists had stopped working and were watching, open-mouthed and unsure, tools suspended in mid-air. I wondered if it was going to turn into a brawl, but then Macker forced a laugh and stepped back, raising his hands mockingly. 'Relax, man,' he said. He held up the cigarette between thumb and finger and reinserted it into the packet with elaborate precision.

Mark kept staring until Macker, taking his time, had knelt down and picked up his trowel and started scraping again. Then he spun around and headed back towards the bank, his shoulders hunched and rigid. Macker scrambled stealthily to his feet and followed, mimicking Mark's springy lope, turning it into a chimpanzee's gallop. He got an edgy snicker from one or two of the others; pleased with himself, he held out his trowel in front of his crotch and thrust his pelvis at Mark's backside. His silhouette against the lowering sky was distorted, grotesque, a creature from some obscene and darkly symbolic Greek frieze. The air hummed with electricity like a pylon and his clowning set my teeth on edge. I realised I was digging my nails into the wall. I wanted to handcuff him, smack him in the mouth, anything to make him stop.

The other archaeologists got bored and stopped paying attention, and Macker gave Mark's back the finger and swaggered back to his patch as if all eyes were still on him. I was suddenly, fiercely glad that I would never in my life have to be a teenager again. I ground out my cigarette on a stone and was buttoning my coat and turning to go back to my car when the realisation slammed home in the pit of my stomach (sucker-punch, wicked drop through black ice): the trowel.

I stood very still for a long time. I could feel my heart-beat, quick and shallow, at the base of my throat. At last I finished buttoning my coat, found Sean among the huddled army jackets and picked my way across the dig towards him. I felt curiously light-headed, as if my feet were paddling effortlessly a foot or two above the ground. The archaeologists threw small swift glances at me as I passed: not inimical, exactly, but perfectly, studiedly blank.

Sean was trowelling earth away from a patch of stones. He had headphones on, under his black woolly hat, and he was bobbing his head gently in time to the tinny bam bam bam of heavy metal. 'Sean,' I said. My voice sounded like it was coming from somewhere behind my ears.

He didn't hear me, but when I took a step closer my shadow fell across him, faint in the grey light, and he looked up. He fumbled in his pocket, switched off the Walkman and pulled the headphones down.

'Sean,' I said, 'I need to talk to you.' Mark whipped round, stared, then shook his head furiously and attacked the bank again.

I brought Sean out to the lay-by. He hauled himself onto the bonnet of the Land Rover and pulled a greasy dough-nut wrapped in cling-film out of his jacket. 'What's the story?' he asked sociably.

'Do you remember, the day after Katharine Devlin's body was found, my partner and I brought Mark in for questioning?' I said. I was impressed with how calm my voice sounded, how easy and casual, as if this were only a small thing, after all. It becomes second nature, interrogation; it seeps into your blood until, no matter how stunned or exhausted or excited you are, this remains unchanged: the polite professional tone, the clean, relentless march as each answer unfolds into question after new question. 'Not long after we brought him back to the site, you were complaining that you couldn't find your trowel.'

'Yeah,' he said, through a huge mouthful. 'Hey, it's OK if I eat this, right? I'm starving, and Hitler will have a total cow if I eat during work.'

'That's fine,' I said. 'Did you ever find your trowel?'

Sean shook his head. 'I had to buy a new one. Bastards.'

'OK, think carefully,' I said. 'When was the last time you saw it?'

'Finds shed,' he said promptly. 'When I found that coin. Are you going to, like, arrest someone for stealing it?'

'Not exactly. What's this about a coin?'

'I found this coin,' he explained, helpfully. 'Everyone was all excited and stuff, because it looked old and we've only found like ten coins on the whole dig. I took it to the finds shed to show Dr Hunt – on my trowel, because if you touch old coins the oils in your hands could fuck them up or something – and *he* got all excited and started getting out all these books to try and ID it, and then it was half-five and we went home, and I forgot my trowel on the table in the finds shed. I went back to get it the next morning, but it wasn't there.'

'And that was the Thursday,' I said, my heart slowly sinking. 'The day we came to talk to Mark.' It had been a long shot, anyway, and I was surprised at how badly let down I was. I felt idiotic and very, very tired; I wanted to go home and go to sleep.

Sean shook his head and licked grains of sugar off his filthy fingers. 'Nah, before that,' he said, and I felt my heart rate start to pick up again. 'I sort of forgot about it for a while, because I didn't need it – we were mattocking back that fucking drainage ditch – and I figured someone had, like, picked it up for me and forgot to give it back. That day you guys came for Mark, that was the first time I needed it, but everyone was going, "No, I haven't seen it, uh-uh, wasn't me."'

'It's identifiable, then? Anyone who saw it would know it was yours?'

'Totally. It's got my initials on the handle.' He took another enormous bite of doughnut. 'I burned them on ages ago,' he said, in muffled tones, 'this one time when it was lashing rain and we had to stay inside for, like, hours. I have this Swiss Army knife, see, and I heated up the corkscrew with my lighter—'

'At the time you accused Macker of taking it. Why?'

He shrugged. 'I don't know, because he does dumb shit like that. Nobody was gonna *steal* it steal it, not with my initials on it, so I figured someone had just taken it to piss me off.'

'And do you still think it was him?'

'Nah. I only realised after, Dr Hunt locked the finds shed when we left, and Macker doesn't have a key—' Suddenly his eyes lit up. 'Hey, was it the *murder* weapon? Shit!'

'No,' I said. 'What day did you find the coin, can you remember?'

Sean looked disappointed, but he thought about it, staring into space and swinging his legs. 'The corpse showed up on a Wednesday, right?' he said eventually. He had finished his doughnut; he balled up the cling-film, tossed it in the air and swatted it into the undergrowth. 'OK, so it wasn't the day before that, because we were doing the fucking drainage ditch. The day before *that*. Monday.'

I still think about this conversation with Sean. There is something oddly comforting in the memory, even though it carries its own inexorable undercurrent of grief. I suppose that day was, though it still comes hard to acknowledge this, the pinnacle of my career. I am not proud of a lot of the decisions I made in the course of Operation Vestal; but that morning, at least, in spite of everything that had gone before and regardless of anything that came after, that morning I did everything right, as surely and easily as if I had never put a foot wrong in my life.

'Are you sure?' I asked.

'Yeah, I guess. Ask Dr Hunt; he logged it in the finds book. Am I, like, a witness? Am I gonna have to testify in court?'

'Quite possibly,' I said. Adrenalin had burned off the fatigue and my mind was speeding, throwing out permutations and possibilities like a kaleidoscope. 'I'll let you know.'

'All *right*,' Sean said happily. Apparently this made up for the murder-weapon disappointment. 'Do I get witness protection?'

'No,' I said, 'but I do need you to do something for me. I want you to go back to work and tell the others that we were talking about a stranger you saw hanging around a few days before the murder. I was asking you for a more detailed description. Can you pull that off?' No evidence and no back-up: I didn't want to spook anyone, not yet.

'Course,' Sean assured me, offended. 'Undercover work. Excellent.'

'Thanks,' I said. 'I'll get back to you later.' He slid down from the bonnet and bounced off towards the others, rubbing the back of his head through the woolly hat. He still had sugar around the corners of his mouth.

*   *   *

I checked with Hunt, who went through his logbook and confirmed what Sean had said: he had found the coin on the Monday, a few hours before Katy died. 'Wonderful find,' Hunt told me, 'wonderful. Took us quite a long time to . . . um . . . *identify* it, you know. No coin specialist on site; I'm medieval, myself.'

'Who has a key to the finds shed?' I asked.

'Edward VI base penny, early 1550s,' he said. 'Oh . . . the finds shed? But why?'

'Yes, the finds shed. I've been told it's locked at night. Is that correct?'

'Yes, yes, every night. Mostly pottery, of course, but you never know.'

'And who has a key?'

'Well, I do, of course,' he said, pulling off his glasses and blinking fuzzily at me as he wiped them on his jumper. 'And Mark and Damien – for the tours, you know. Just in case. People always like to see finds, don't they?'

'Yes,' I said, 'yes, I'm sure they do.'

I went back to the lay-by and phoned Sam. One of the trees was a chestnut, there were conkers littered around my car, and I peeled the prickly casing off one of them and tossed it into the air while I waited for him to pick up: casual phone call, maybe setting up a date for the evening, if anyone was watching and worried; nothing important.

'O'Neill,' Sam said.

'Sam, it's Rob,' I said, catching the conker overhand. 'I'm in Knocknaree, at the dig. I need you and Maddox and a few floaters down here as fast as you can, with a team from the Bureau – get Sophie Miller if you can. Make sure they bring a metal detector and someone who knows how to work it. I'll meet you at the entrance to the estate.'

'Got it,' Sam said, and hung up.

It would take him at least an hour to round everyone up and get out to Knocknaree. I moved my car up the hill, out of sight of the archaeologists, and sat on the bonnet to wait. The air smelled of dead grass and thunder. Knocknaree had closed in on itself, the far hills invisible under cloud, the wood a dark illusive smear down the hillside. Enough time had passed that children were being allowed outside to play again, I heard faint high shrieks of glee or terror or both coming from inside the estate; that car alarm was still going, and somewhere a dog was barking mindlessly, frenetically, on and on and on.

Every sound wound me a notch tighter; I could feel the blood trembling in every corner of my body. My mind was still going full tilt, whirring through correlations and shards of evidence, fitting together what I needed to say to the others when they arrived. And somewhere under the adrenalin was the inexorable realisation that, if I was right, then Katy Devlin's death almost certainly had nothing at all to do with what had happened to Peter and Jamie; not, at least, in any way you could enter into evidence.

I was concentrating so hard that I almost forgot what I was waiting for. When the others started arriving, I saw them with the heightened, shocked gaze of a stranger: discreet dark cars and white van pulling in with a near-silent rush, doors sliding smoothly open; the black-suited men and the faceless techs with their glittering array of tools, cool and ready as surgeons to peel back the skin of this place inch by inch and reveal the darker, seething archaeology underneath. The slamming of car doors sounded small and deadly precise, muffled by the heavy air.

'What's the story?' Sam said. He had brought Sweeney and O'Gorman and a red-haired guy whom I recognised, vaguely, from the blur of action in the incident room a few weeks earlier. I slid off the Land Rover and they moved into place around me, Sophie and her team pulling on their gloves, Cassie's thin still face over Sam's shoulder.

'The night Katy Devlin died,' I said, 'a trowel disappeared from the locked finds shed on the dig. The trowels they use consist of a leaf-shaped metal blade attached to a wooden handle five or six inches long, tapering inwards towards the blade, with a rounded end. This particular trowel, which is still missing, had "S.C." burned into the handle – the initials of the owner, Sean Callaghan, who claims he forgot it in the finds shed at five-thirty on Monday evening. It matches Cooper's description of the implement used to sexually assault Katy Devlin. Nobody knew it would be in the finds shed, which suggests that it was a weapon of opportunity and the shed may be our primary crime scene. Sophie, can you start there?'

'Luminol kit,' Sophie said to one of her mini-me's, and he broke away from the group and clicked open the back of the van.

'Three people had keys to the finds shed,' I said. 'Ian Hunt, Mark Hanly and Damien Donnelly. We can't rule out Sean Callaghan, either: he could have made up the whole story about leaving the trowel there. Hunt and Hanly have cars, which means if it's one of them he might have hidden or transported the body in the car boot. Callaghan and Donnelly don't, as far as I know, so either of them would have had to hide the body fairly nearby, probably on the site. We'll have to go over the whole place with a fine-tooth comb and pray there's some evidence left. We're looking for the trowel, for a bloodstained plastic bag and for our primary and secondary crime scenes.'

'Do they have keys to the other sheds, too?' Cassie asked.

'Find out,' I said.

The tech was back, with the luminol kit in one hand and a roll of brown paper in the other. We looked at one another and nodded and fell into step, a swift, primed phalanx moving down the hill towards the dig.

A case breaking is like a dam breaking. Everything around you gathers itself up and moves effortlessly, unstoppably into top gear; every drop of energy you've poured into the investigation comes back to you, unleashed and gaining momentum by the second, subsuming you in its building roar. I forgot that I had never liked O'Gorman, forgot that Knocknaree wrecked my head and that I had almost blown this whole case a dozen times, almost forgot everything that had happened between me and Cassie. This, I think, is one of the things I always craved from the job: the way that, at certain moments, you can surrender everything else, lose yourself in the driving techno pulse of it and become nothing but one part of a perfectly calibrated, vital machine.

We fanned out, just in case, as we crossed the site towards the archaeologists. They gave us quick, apprehensive glances, but nobody bolted; no one even stopped working.

'Mark,' I said. He was still kneeling on top of his bank; he leaped up in one fast, dangerous movement and stared at me. 'I'm going to have to ask you to bring all your team into the canteen.'

Mark exploded. 'Jesus *fuck*! Have you not done enough? What are you afraid of? Even if we find the fucking Holy Grail today, your lot will still level this place on Monday morning. Could you not leave us our last few days in peace?'

For a second I almost thought he was going to come at me, and I felt Sam and O'Gorman moving in at my shoulders. 'Settle down, boy,' O'Gorman said threateningly.

'Don't you "boy" me. We have till half-five on Friday and anything you want from us can wait till then, because we're going nowhere.'

'Mark,' Cassie said sharply, beside me. 'This has nothing to do with the motorway. Here's how we're going to work this: we need you and Damien Donnelly and Sean Callaghan to come with us right now. Non-negotiable. If you quit giving us hassle, the rest of your team can keep working, under Detective Johnston's supervision. Fair enough?'

Mark glared at her for another second, but then he spat into the dust and jerked his chin at Mel, who was already moving towards him. The rest of the archaeologists stared, wide-eyed and sweating. Mark snapped instructions at Mel in an undertone, stabbing a finger at various parts of the site; then he gave her shoulder a light, unexpected squeeze and strode off towards the Portakabins, fists shoved deep in his jacket pockets. O'Gorman went after him.

'Sean,' I called. 'Damien.' Sean bounded over eagerly and held up his hand for a high-five, gave me a knowing look when I ignored it. Damien came more slowly, hitching up his combats. He looked dazed almost to the point of concussion, but coming from him this didn't exactly set my alarm bells ringing.

'We need to talk to you,' I said. 'We'd like you to wait in the canteen for a while, until we're ready to take you back to headquarters.'

Both their mouths opened. I turned and left before they could ask.

We put them in the canteen, along with a flustered Dr Hunt – still clutching handfuls of paperwork – and left O'Gorman to keep an eye on them. Hunt gave us permission to search the site, with an alacrity that moved him further down the suspect list (Mark demanded to see our warrant, but backed off fast when I told him I'd be happy to get one if he didn't mind waiting around for a few hours), and Sophie and her team headed for the finds shed and started taping brown paper over the windows. Johnston, out on the dig, moved among the archaeologists with his notebook out, checking trowels and pulling people aside for brief tête-à-têtes.

'The same key fits all the Portakabins,' Cassie said, coming out of the canteen. 'Hunt, Mark and Damien have one each – not Sean. No spares. They all say they've never lost, lent or missed their keys.'

'So let's start with the sheds,' I said, 'and then we can work our way outwards if we need to. Sam, will you and Cassie take the tool shed? Sweeney and I will do the office.'

The office was tiny and crammed – shelves sagging with books and house plants, desk piled with papers and mugs and bits of pottery and an elephantine, obsolete computer. Sweeney and I worked fast and methodically, pulling out drawers, taking down books and checking behind them and stacking them back roughly in place. I didn't actually expect to find anything. There was nowhere here to stash a body, and I was fairly sure the trowel and the plastic bag had been either dumped in the river or buried somewhere on the dig, where we would need the metal detector and huge amounts of luck and time to find them. All my hopes were pinned on Sophie and her team and whatever arcane rites they were performing in the finds shed. My hands moved automatically along the shelves; I was listening, so hard it nearly paralysed me, for some sound from outside, footsteps, Sophie's voice calling. When Sweeney dropped a drawer and cursed softly, I almost screamed at him to shut up.

It was gradually dawning on me just how high I had staked on this. I could have simply rung Sophie and got her to come down and check out the finds shed, no need to mention it to anyone if it didn't pan out. Instead, I had taken over the entire site and pulled in just about every person who had anything to do with the investigation, and if this turned out to be a wild-goose chase I didn't even want to think about what O'Kelly would say.

After what felt like an hour I heard, outside, 'Rob!' I leaped up from the floor, scattering papers everywhere, but it was Cassie's voice: clear, boyish, excited. She bounded up the steps, caught the door handle and swung round it into the office. 'Rob, we've got it. The trowel. In the tool shed, under all these tarps—' She was flushed and breathless, and she had obviously completely forgotten that we were barely on speaking terms. I forgot it myself, for a moment; her voice sent the old, bright dart of warmth straight to my heart.

'Stay here,' I said to Sweeney, 'keep searching,' and followed her. She was already running back to the tool shed, feet flashing as she jumped the ruts and puddles.

The tool shed was a mess: wheelbarrows at various wild angles, picks and shovels and mattocks tangled against the walls, great teetering stacks of dented metal buckets and foam kneeling-mats and neon-yellow visibility vests (someone had written INSERT FOOT HERE, with an arrow pointing downwards, on the back of the top one), everything crusted in ragged layers of dried mud. A few people kept their bikes there. Cassie and Sam had been working from left to right; the left-hand side had that unmistakable post-search look, discreetly tidy and invaded.

Sam was kneeling at the back of the shed between a broken wheelbarrow and a heap of green tarpaulins, holding up the corner of the tarps with one gloved hand. We picked our way through the tools and squeezed in beside him.

The trowel had been jammed down behind the pile of tarps, between them and the wall; jammed hard enough that the point, when it caught halfway down, had gouged a rip into the tough material. There was no light bulb and the shed was dim even with the big doors open, but Sam shone his torch on the handle: SC, big uneven letters with Gothic serifs, charred deep into the varnished wood.

There was a long silence; only the dog and the car alarm, on and on in the distance, with identical mechanical determination.

'I'd say the tarps aren't used very often,' Sam said quietly. 'They were behind everything else, under broken tools and all. And didn't Cooper say she was probably wrapped in something, the day before she was found?'

I stood up and dusted bits of muck off my knees. 'Right here,' I said. 'Her family was going crazy looking for her, and she was right here all the time.' I had got up too fast, and for a moment the shed rocked around me and receded; there was a high white buzz in my ears.

'Who's got the camera?' Cassie said. 'We'll need to photograph this before we bag it.'

'Sophie's lot,' I said. 'We'll need them to go over this place, too.'

'And look,' Sam said. He shone the torch over at the right-hand side of the shed, picked out a big plastic bag half full of gloves, those green rubber gardening gloves with woven backs. 'If I needed gloves, I'd just take a pair out of there and throw them back in afterwards.'

'Detectives!' Sophie yelled, somewhere outside. Her voice sounded tinny, compressed by the lowering sky. I jumped.

Cassie started to spring up, glanced back at the trowel. 'Someone should probably—'

'I'll stay,' Sam said. 'You two go on ahead.'

Sophie was on the steps of the finds shed, a black-light in her hand. 'Yeah,' she said, 'definitely your crime scene. He tried to clean up, but . . . Come see.'

The two baby techs were crammed into a corner, the guy holding two big black spray-bottles, Helen with a video camera; her eyes were large and stunned over her mask. The finds shed was too small for five and the sinister, clinical incongruity the techs had brought with them turned it into some makeshift guerrilla torture chamber: paper covering the windows, bare light bulb swinging overhead, masked and gloved figures waiting for their moment to step forward. 'Stay back by the desk,' Sophie said, 'away from the shelves.' She slammed the door – everyone flinched – and pressed tape back into place over the cracks.

Luminol reacts with even the tiniest amount of blood, making it glow under ultraviolet light. You can paint over a splattered wall, scrub a carpet till it looks brand-new, keep yourself off the radar for years or decades; luminol will resurrect the crime in delicate, merciless detail. *If only*

Kiernan and McCabe had had luminol, I thought, *they could have commandeered a crop-spraying plane and misted the wood,* and fought down a hysterical desire to laugh. Cassie and I pressed back against the desk, inches apart. Sophie motioned to the boy tech for the spray, flicked on her black-light and switched off the overhead bulb. In the sudden darkness I could hear all of us breathing, five sets of lungs fighting for the dusty air.

Hiss of a spray-bottle, the video camera's tiny red eye moving in. Sophie squatted and held her black-light close to the floor, near the shelves. 'There,' she said.

I heard Cassie's small, sharp intake of breath. The floor blazed blue-white with frantic patterns like some grotesque abstract painting: spattered arcs where blood had burst outwards, blotchy circles where it had pooled and started to dry, great swipes and scrubmarks where someone panting and desperate had tried to clean it away. It glowed like something radioactive from cracks between the floor-boards, etched the rough grain of the wood in high relief. Sophie moved the black-light upwards and sprayed again: tiny droplets fanning across the bottom of the metal shelves, a smudge like a wild grabbing handprint. The darkness stripped away the finds shed, the messy papers and bags of broken pottery, and left us suspended in black space with the murder: luminescent, howling, replaying itself again and again before our eyes.

I said, 'Jesus Christ.' Katy Devlin had died on this floor. We had sat in this shed and interviewed the killer, smack bang on the scene of the crime.

'No chance that's bleach or something,' said Cassie. Luminol gives false positives for anything from household bleach through copper, but we both knew Sophie wouldn't have called us in here until she was sure.

'We've swabbed,' Sophie said briefly; I could hear the dirty look in her voice. 'Blood.'

Deep down, I think I had stopped believing in this moment. I had thought an awful lot about Kiernan, over the past few weeks: Kiernan, with his cosy seaside retirement and his haunted dreams. Only the luckiest of detectives makes it through a whole career without at least one of these cases, and some traitor part of me had insisted from the start that Operation Vestal – the last one in the world I would have chosen – was going to be mine. It took a strange, almost painful adjustment of focus to realise that our guy was no longer a faceless archetype, coalesced out of collective nightmare for one deed and then dissolved back into darkness; he was sitting in the canteen, just a few yards away, wearing muddy Docs and drinking tea under O'Gorman's fishy eye.

'There you go,' Sophie said. She straightened up and switched on the overhead light. I blinked at the bland, innocent floor.

'Look,' said Cassie. I followed the tilt of her chin: on one of the bottom shelves was a plastic bag stuffed with more plastic bags, the big, clear, heavy kind the archaeologists used for storing pottery. 'If the trowel was a weapon of opportunity . . .'

'Oh, for fuck's sake,' Sophie said. 'We're going to have to test every bag in this whole bloody place.'

The window-panes rattled and there was a sudden, wild thrumming on the roof of the shed: it had started to rain.

20

It rained hard all the rest of the day, the kind of thick, endless rain that can soak you to the skin as you run the few yards to your car. Every now and then lightning forked over the dark hills, and a distant rumble of thunder reached us. We left the Bureau gang to finish processing the scenes and took Hunt, Mark, Damien and, on the off-chance, a deeply aggrieved Sean ('I thought we were *partners* here!') back to work with us. We found them an interview room each and started rechecking their alibis.

Sean was easy to eliminate. He shared a flat in Rathmines with three other guys, all of whom remembered, to some extent, the night Katy had died: it had been one of the guys' birthday and they had had a party, at which Sean had DJ'd till four in the morning, then thrown up on someone's girlfriend's boots and passed out on the sofa. At least thirty witnesses could vouch for both his whereabouts and his tastes in music.

The other three were less straightforward. Hunt's alibi was his wife, Mark's was Mel; Damien lived in Rathfarnham with his widowed mother, who went to bed early but was positive he couldn't have left the house without waking her. These are the kind of alibis detectives hate, the thin, mulish kind that can wreck a case. I could tell you about a dozen cases where we know exactly whodunit, how and where and when, but there is absolutely nothing we can do about it because the guy's mammy swears he was tucked up on the sofa watching *The Late Late Show*.

'Right,' O'Kelly said, in the incident room, after we had taken Sean's statement and sent him home (he had forgiven me for my treachery and offered me a farewell high-five; he wanted to know if he could sell his story to the papers, but I told him if he did I would personally raid his flat for drugs every night until he was thirty). 'One down, two to go. Place your bets, lads: who do ye fancy?' He was in a much better mood with us, now that he knew we had a suspect in one of the interview rooms, even if we weren't sure which one.

'Damien,' Cassie said. 'He fits the MO, bang on.'

'Mark's admitted he was at the scene,' I said. 'And he's the only one with anything like a motive.'

'As far as we know.' I knew what she meant, or thought I did, but I wasn't going to bring up the hired-gun theory, not in front of either O'Kelly or Sam. 'And I can't see him doing it.'

'I'm aware of that. I can.'

Cassie rolled her eyes, which I actually found slightly comforting: a small savage part of me had expected her to flinch.

'O'Neill?' O'Kelly asked.

'Damien,' Sam said. 'I brought them all a cup of tea. He's the only one picked his up with his left hand.'

After a startled second, Cassie and I started to laugh. The joke was on us – I, at any rate, had forgotten all about the left-handed thing – but we were both wound tight and giddy, and we couldn't stop. Sam grinned and shrugged, pleased at the reaction. 'I don't know what ye two are laughing about,' O'Kelly said gruffly, but his mouth was twitching too. 'You should've spotted that yourselves. All this jibber-jabber about MOs . . .' I was laughing too hard, my face going red and my eyes watering. I bit down on my lip to stop myself.

'Oh, God,' said Cassie, taking a deep breath. 'Sam, what would we do without you?'

'That's enough fun and games,' O'Kelly said. 'You two take Damien Donnelly. O'Neill, get Sweeney and have another go at Hanly, and I'll find a few of the lads to talk to Hunt and the alibi witnesses. And, Ryan, Maddox, O'Neill – we need a confession. Don't fuck this up. *Andele.*' He scraped back his chair with an ear-splitting screech and left.

'*Andele*?' said Cassie. She looked perilously near to another bout of the giggles.

'Well done, lads,' Sam said. He held out a hand to each of us; his grip was strong and warm and solid. 'Good luck.'

'If Andrews hired one of them,' I said, when Sam had gone to find Sweeney, and Cassie and I were alone in the incident room, 'this is going to be the mess of the century.'

Cassie raised one eyebrow noncommittally. She finished her coffee – it was going to be a very long day, we had all been spiking ourselves up on caffeine.

'How do you want to do this?' I asked.

'You head it up. He thinks of women as the source of sympathy and approval; I'll pat him on the head now and then. He's intimidated by men, so go easy: if you push him too hard, he'll freeze up and want to leave. Just take your time, and guilt-trip him. I still think he was in two minds about the whole thing from the start, and I bet he feels terrible about it. If we play to his conscience, it's only a matter of time before he goes to pieces.'

'Let's do it,' I said, and we shook our clothes straight and smoothed down our hair and walked, shoulder to shoulder, down the corridor towards the interview room.

It was our last partnership. I wish I could show you how an interrogation can have its own beauty, shining and cruel as that of a bullfight; how in defiance of the crudest topic or the most moronic suspect it keeps inviolate its own taut, honed grace, its own irresistible and blood-stirring rhythms; how the great pairs of detectives know each other's every thought as surely as lifelong ballet partners in a pas de deux. I never knew and never will whether either Cassie or I was a great detective, though I suspect not, but I know this: we made a team worthy of bard-songs and history books. This was our last and greatest dance together, danced in a tiny interview room with darkness outside and rain falling soft and relentless on the roof, for no audience but the doomed and the dead.

Damien was huddled in his chair, shoulders rigid, his cup of tea steaming away ignored on the table. When I cautioned him, he stared at me as if I were speaking Urdu.

The month since Katy's death hadn't been kind to him. He was wearing khaki combats and a baggy grey jumper, but I could see that he had lost weight, and it made him seem gangly and somehow shorter than he actually was. The boy-band prettiness was looking a little ragged around the edges – purplish bags under his eyes, a vertical crease starting to form between his eyebrows; the youthful bloom that should have lasted him another few years was fading fast. The change was subtle enough that I hadn't noticed it back on the dig, but it gave me pause.

We started with easy questions, things he could answer with no need to worry. He was from Rathfarnham, right? Studying at Trinity? Just finished second year? How had the exams gone? Damien answered in monosyllables and twisted the hem of his jumper around his thumb, clearly dying to know why we were asking but afraid to find out. Cassie steered him onto archaeology and gradually he relaxed; he disentangled himself from the jumper and started drinking his tea and speaking in full sentences, and they had a long, happy conversation about the various finds that had turned up on the dig. I left them to it for at least twenty minutes before intervening (tolerant smile: 'Hate to say this, guys, but we should probably get back to business before we all three get in trouble').

'Ah, come on, Ryan, two seconds,' Cassie begged. 'I've never seen a ring-brooch. What does it look like?'

'They said it's probably going to be in the National Museum,' Damien told her, flushed with pride. 'It's kind of this big, and it's bronze, and it's got a pattern incised into it . . .' He made vague squiggly motions, presumably intended to indicate an incised pattern, with one finger.

'Draw it for me?' Cassie asked, pushing her notebook and pen across the table to him. Damien drew obediently, brow furrowed in concentration.

'Sort of like this,' he said, giving Cassie back the notebook. 'I can't draw.'

'Wow,' Cassie said reverently. 'And you *found* it? If I found something like that, I think I'd explode or have a heart attack or something.'

I looked over her shoulder: a broad circle with what appeared to be a pin across the back, decorated with fluid, balanced curves. 'Pretty,' I said. Damien was indeed left-handed. His hands still looked a size too big for his body, like a puppy's paws.

'Hunt's out,' O'Kelly said, in the corridor. 'Original statement says he was having his tea and watching telly with his wife all the Monday night, till he went to bed at eleven.

Bloody *documentaries*, they watched, some yoke about meerkats and one about Richard III – he told us every bloody detail, whether we wanted to know or not. The wife says the same, and the telly guide backs them up. And the neighbour has a dog, one of those little shites that barks all night; he says he heard Hunt shouting out the window at it, around one in the morning. Why he wouldn't tell the little fucker to shut up himself . . . He's sure of the date because it was the day they got the new decking in – says the workmen upset the dog. I'm sending Einstein home, before he has me driven mental. It's a two-horse race, lads.'

'How's Sam doing with Mark?' I asked.

'Getting nowhere. Hanly's narky as fuck and sticking to the shag-fest story; the girlfriend's backing him up. If they're lying, they're not going to crack any time soon. And he's right-handed, for sure. How about your boy?'

'Left,' Cassie said.

'There's our odds-on favourite, so. But that's not going to be enough. I talked to Cooper . . .' O'Kelly's face pulled into a disgusted grimace. 'Position of the victim, position of the assailant, balance of probabilities – more shite than a pigsty, but what it boils down to is he thinks our man's left-handed but he's not willing to say for definite. He's like a bloody politician. How's Donnelly doing?'

'Nervous,' I said.

O'Kelly slapped the door of the interview room. 'Good. Keep him that way.'

We went back in and set about making Damien nervous. 'OK, guys,' I said, pulling up my chair, 'time to get down to business. Let's talk about Katy Devlin.'

Damien nodded attentively, but I saw him brace himself. He took a sip of his tea, though it had to be cold by now.

'When did you first see her?'

'I guess when we were like three-quarters of the way up the hill? Higher up than the cottage, anyway, and the Portakabins. See, because of the way the hill slopes—'

'No,' Cassie said, 'not the day you found her body. Before that.'

'Before . . .?' Damien blinked at her, took another sip of tea. 'No – um, I didn't; I hadn't. Met her before that, that day.'

'You'd never even seen her before?' Cassie's tone hadn't changed, but I felt the sudden bird-dog stillness in her. 'Are you sure? Think hard, Damien.'

He shook his head vehemently. 'No. I swear. I'd never seen her in my entire life.'

There was a moment of silence. I gave Damien what I hoped was a look of mild interest, but my head was whirling.

I had cast my vote for Mark not out of sheer contrariness, as you might think, nor because something about him annoyed me in ways I didn't care to explore. I suppose when you come down to it, given the choices available, I simply wanted it to be him. I had never been able to take Damien seriously – not as a man, not as a witness and certainly not as a suspect. He was such an abject little wimp, nothing to him but curls and stammers and vulnerability, you could have blown him away like a dandelion clock; the thought that all this past month might have stemmed from someone like him was outrageous. Mark, whatever we might think of each other, made an opponent and a goal worth having.

But this: it was such a pointless lie. The Devlin girls had hung around the dig often enough, that summer, and they were hardly inconspicuous; all the other archaeologists had remembered them; Mel, who had stayed a safe distance from Katy's body, had known her straight away. And Damien had given tours of the site; he was more likely than any of them to have spoken to Katy, spent time with her. He had bent over her body, supposedly to see if she was breathing (and even that much courage, I realised, was out of character). He had no reason in the world to deny having seen her before, unless he was clumsily dodging a trap we had never set; unless the thought of being linked to her in any way scared him so badly that he couldn't think straight.

'OK,' Cassie said, 'what about her father – Jonathan Devlin? Are you a member of Move the Motorway?' and Damien took a big gulp of cold tea and started nodding again, and we skated deftly away from the subject before he had a chance to realise what he had said.

Around three o'clock, Cassie and Sam and I went out for takeaway pizza – Mark was starting to bitch about being hungry, and we wanted to keep him and Damien happy. Neither of them was under arrest; they could decide to walk out of the building at any moment, and there would be nothing we could do to stop them. We were trading, as we so often do, on the basic human desires to please authority and to be a good guy; and, while I was pretty sure these would keep Damien in the interview room indefinitely, I was far from convinced about Mark.

'How are you getting on with Donnelly?' Sam asked me, in the pizza place. Cassie was up at the counter, leaning over it and laughing with the guy who had taken our order.

I shrugged. 'Hard to tell. How's Mark?'

'Raging. He says he's spent half the year working his arse off for Move the Motorway, why would he risk scuppering the whole thing by killing the chairman's kid? He thinks this is all political . . .' Sam winced. 'About Donnelly,' he said, looking not at me but at Cassie's back. 'If he's our man. What would . . . does he have a motive?'

'Not that we've found so far,' I said. I did not want to get into this.

'If anything does come up . . .' Sam shoved his fists deeper into his trouser pockets. 'Anything you think I might want to know. Could you call me?'

'Yeah,' I said. I hadn't eaten all day, but food was the last thing on my mind; all I wanted was to get back to Damien, and the pizza seemed to be taking hours. 'Sure.'

Damien took a can of 7-Up, but he refused the pizza; he wasn't hungry, he said. 'Sure?' Cassie asked, trying to catch strings of cheese with her finger. 'God, when I was a student I'd never have turned down free pizza.'

'You never turn down food, full stop,' I told her. 'You're a human Hoover.' Cassie, unable to answer through a huge mouthful, nodded cheerfully and gave us the thumbs-up. 'Go on, Damien, have some. You should keep your strength up; we're going to be here for a while.'

His eyes widened. I waved a slice at him, but he shook his head, so I shrugged and kept it for myself. 'OK,' I said, 'let's talk about Mark Hanly. What's he like?'

Damien blinked. 'Mark? Um, he's OK. He's strict, I guess, but he sort of has to be. We don't have a lot of time.'

'Ever seen him get violent? Lose his temper?' I wiggled a hand at Cassie; she threw me a paper napkin.

'Yeah – no . . . I mean, yeah, he gets mad sometimes, if someone's messing, but I never saw him *hit* anyone, or anything like that.'

'Do you think he would, if he was angry enough?' I

wiped my hands and thumbed through my notebook, trying not to get grease on the pages. 'You're such a slob,' Cassie told me; I gave her the finger. Damien glanced between us, flustered and off balance.

'What?' he asked at last, uncertainly.

'Do you think Mark could get violent if he was provoked?'

'I guess maybe. I don't know.'

'What about you? Ever hit anyone?'

'What . . . no!'

'We should've got garlic bread,' Cassie said.

'I'm not sharing an interview room with two people and garlic. What do you think it would take to make you hit someone, Damien?'

His mouth opened.

'You don't seem like the violent type to me, but everyone's got a breaking point. Would you hit someone if he insulted your mother, for example?'

'I—'

'Or for money? Or in self-defence? What would it take?'

'I don't . . .' Damien blinked fast. 'I don't know. I mean, I've never – but I guess everyone's, like you said, everyone's got a breaking point, I don't know . . .'

I nodded and made a careful note of this. 'Would you rather a different kind?' Cassie asked, inspecting the pizza. 'I think ham-and-pineapple rules, personally, but they have some macho pepperoni-and-sausage thing next door.'

'What? Um – no, thanks. Who's . . .?' We waited, chewing. 'Who's next door? Am I, like, allowed to ask?'

'Sure,' I said. 'That's Mark. We sent Sean and Dr Hunt home, a while back, but we haven't been able to let Mark go yet.'

We watched Damien turn a shade paler as he processed this information and its implications. 'Why not?' he asked faintly.

'Can't go into that,' Cassie said, reaching for more pizza. 'Sorry.' Damien's eyes ricocheted, disorientated, from her hand to her face to mine.

'What I can tell you,' I said, pointing at him with a crust, 'is that we're taking this case very, very seriously. I've seen a lot of bad stuff in my career, Damien, but this . . . There's no crime in the world worse than murdering a child. Her whole life's gone, the entire community's terrified, her friends will never get over it, her family's devastated—'

'In bits,' Cassie said indistinctly, through a mouthful. Damien swallowed, looked down at his 7-Up as if he had forgotten it and started fumbling with the tab.

'Whoever did this . . .' I shook my head. 'I don't know how he can live with himself.'

'Tomato check,' Cassie told me, dabbing a finger at the corner of her mouth. 'Can't take you anywhere.'

We finished off most of the pizza. I didn't want it – even the smell, greasy and pervasive, was too much for me – but the whole thing was getting Damien more and more flustered. He accepted a slice, in the end, and sat wretchedly picking off the pineapple and nibbling on it, his head whipping from Cassie to me and back as if he were trying to follow a tennis match from too close by. I spared a thought for Sam: Mark was unlikely to be sent into a tailspin by pepperoni and extra cheese.

My mobile vibrated in my pocket. I checked the screen: Sophie. I took it out into the corridor; Cassie, behind me, said, 'Detective Ryan leaving the interview room.'

'Hi, Sophie,' I said.

'Hey. Here's the update: no signs that either lock was forced or picked. And the trowel's your rape weapon, all right. It looks like it's been washed, but we've got traces of blood in the cracks on the handle. We've also got a fair amount of blood on one of those tarps. We're still checking gloves and plastic bags – we'll still be checking gloves and plastic bags when we're *eighty*. We found a torch under the tarps, too. There are prints all over it, but they're all small and the torch has Hello Kitty on it, so I'm betting it's your victim's and so are the prints. How're you guys doing?'

'Still working on Hanly and Donnelly. Callaghan and Hunt are out.'

'Now you tell me? For Christ's sake, Rob. Thanks a bunch. We've gone over Hunt's fucking *car*. Nothing – well, obviously. No blood in Hanly's car, either. About a million hairs and fibres and blah blah blah; if he had her in there, he wasn't worried enough to clean up after himself, so we might get a match. Matter of fact, I doubt he's *ever* cleaned that thing. If he ever runs out of archaeological sites, he can start work under his front seat.'

I slammed the door behind me, told the camera, 'Detective Ryan entering the interview room,' and started clearing away the pizza things. 'That was the Technical Bureau,' I said, to Cassie. 'They've confirmed our evidence is exactly what we thought it was. Damien, are you finished with that?' I threw the pineapple-less slice of pizza back into the box before he could answer.

'That's what we like to hear,' Cassie said, grabbing a napkin and giving the table a quick wipe. 'Damien, do you need anything before we get to work?'

Damien stared, trying to catch up; shook his head.

'Great,' I said, shoving the pizza box into a corner and pulling up a chair. 'Then let's start by updating you on some of what we've found out today. Why do you think we brought the four of you in here?'

'About that girl,' he said, faintly. 'Katy Devlin.'

'Well, yeah, sure. But why do you think we only wanted the four of you? Why not the rest of the team?'

'You said . . .' Damien motioned to Cassie, with the 7-Up can; he was clutching it in both hands, as if afraid I might take that away too. 'You asked about the keys. Who had keys to the sheds.'

'Bingo,' Cassie said, nodding approvingly. 'Well spotted.'

'Did you, um . . .?' He swallowed. 'Did you, like, find something in one of the sheds?'

'Exactly,' I said. 'Actually, we found something in two of the sheds, but close enough. We can't go into details, obviously, but here's the gist of it: we've got evidence that Katy was killed in the finds shed on the Monday night and stashed in the tools shed through the Tuesday. There was no forced entry. What do you think that means?'

'I dunno,' Damien said, at last.

'It means we're looking for someone who had the key. That's Mark, Dr Hunt or you. And Hunt's got an alibi.'

Damien actually half raised his hand, as if he were in school. 'Um, me too. I mean, an alibi.'

He looked at us hopefully, but we were both shaking our heads. 'Sorry,' Cassie said. 'Your mother was asleep during the time we're looking at; she can't vouch for you. And anyway, mothers . . .' She shrugged, smiling. 'I mean, I'm sure your mammy's honest and everything, but as a rule, they'll say whatever it takes to keep their kids out of trouble. God love them for it, but it means we can't really take their word on something this important.'

'Mark's got the same kind of problem,' I said. 'Mel says she was with him, but she's his girlfriend, and they're not much more reliable than mothers. A little, but not much. So here we all are.'

'And if you've got anything to tell us, Damien,' Cassie said softly, 'now's the time.'

Silence. He took a sip of his 7-Up and then looked up at us, all transparent blue eyes and bewilderment, and shook his head.

'OK,' I said. 'Fair enough. There's something I want you to look at, Damien.' I went through the file, making kind of a big deal of it – Damien's eyes followed my hand, apprehensively – and finally pulled out a bunch of photos. I laid them out in front of him, one by one, taking a good look at each before I put it down; letting him wait.

'Katy and her sisters, last Christmas,' I said. Plastic tree, garish with red and green lights; Rosalind in the middle, wearing blue velvet and giving the camera an impish little smile, her arms around the twins; Katy straight-backed and laughing, wearing a white fake-sheepskin jacket, and Jessica smiling uncertainly down at a beige one, like a reflection in some uncanny mirror. Unconsciously, Damien smiled back.

'Katy at a family picnic, two months ago.' The snapshot with the green lawn and the sandwich.

'She looks happy, doesn't she?' Cassie said, aside to me. 'She was about to go off to ballet school, everything was just beginning . . . It's good to know she was happy, before . . .'

One of the crime-scene Polaroids: a full-length shot of her curled on the altar stone. 'Katy just after you found her.

Remember that?' Damien shifted in his chair, caught himself and sat still.

Another crime-scene shot, this one a close-up: dried blood on her nose and mouth, that one eye a slit open. 'Same again: Katy where her killer dumped her.'

One of the post-mortem shots. 'Katy the next day.' The breath went out of Damien. We had chosen the nastiest picture we had: her face folded down on itself to reveal the skull, a gloved hand holding up a steel ruler to the fracture above her ear, clotted hair and splinters of bone.

'Hard to look at, isn't it?' Cassie said, almost to herself. Her fingers hovered over the photos, moved to the crime-scene close-up, stroked the line of Katy's cheek. She glanced up, at Damien.

'Yeah,' he whispered.

'See, to me,' I said, leaning back in my chair and tapping the post-mortem shot, 'that looks like something that only a raving psycho would do to a little girl. Some animal with no conscience, who gets his kicks out of hurting the most vulnerable people he can find. But I'm just a detective. Now Detective Maddox here, she's studied psychology. Do you know what a profiler is, Damien?'

A tiny shake of the head. His eyes were still riveted to the photographs, but I didn't think he was seeing them.

'Someone who studies what kind of person commits what kind of crime, tells the police what type of guy to look for. Detective Maddox, she's our resident profiler, and she's got her own theory about the guy who did this.'

'Damien,' Cassie said, 'let me tell you something. I've said all along, right from day one, that this was done by someone who didn't want to do it. Someone who wasn't violent, wasn't a killer, didn't enjoy causing pain; someone who did this because he had to. He didn't have any choice. That's what I've been saying since the day we got this case.'

'It's true, she has,' I said. 'The rest of us said she was off her head, but she stuck to her guns: this wasn't a psycho, or a serial killer, or a child-rapist.' Damien flinched, a quick jerk of the chin. 'What do you think, Damien? Do you think it takes a sick bastard to do something like this, or do you think this could just happen to a normal guy who never wanted to hurt anyone?'

He tried to shrug, but his shoulders were too tense and it came out as a grotesque twitch. I got up and wandered around the table, taking my time, to lean against the wall behind him. 'Well, we'll never know for sure one way or the other, unless he tells us. But let's just say for a moment that Detective Maddox is right. I mean, she's the one with the psychology training; I'm willing to admit she could have a point. Let's say this guy isn't the violent type; he was never meant to be a murderer. It just happened.'

Damien had been holding his breath. He let it out, caught it again with a little gasp.

'I've seen guys like that before. Do you know what happens to them, afterwards? They go to fucking pieces, Damien. They can't live with themselves. We've seen it, over and over.'

'It's not pretty,' Cassie said softly. 'We know what happened, the guy knows we know, but he's scared to confess. He thinks going to gaol is the worst thing that could happen to him. God, is he ever wrong. Every day, for the rest of his life, he wakes up in the morning and it hits him all over again, like it was yesterday. Every night he's scared to go to sleep because of the nightmares. He keeps thinking it has to get better, but it never does.'

'And sooner or later,' I said, from the shadows behind

him, 'he has a nervous breakdown, and he ends up spending the next few years in a padded cell, wearing pyjamas and drugged up to the eyeballs. Or he ties a rope to the bannisters one evening and hangs himself. More often than you'd think, Damien, they just can't face another day.'

This was bullshit, by the way; of course it was. Of those dozen uncharged murderers I could name for you, only one killed himself, and he had a history of untreated mental problems to start with. The rest are living more or less exactly as they always did, holding down jobs and going to the pub and taking their kids to the zoo, and if they occasionally get the heebie-jeebies they keep it to themselves. Human beings, as I know better than most, can get used to anything. Over time, even the unthinkable gradually wears a little niche for itself in your mind and becomes just something that happened. But Katy had only been dead a month, and Damien hadn't had time to learn this. He was rigid in his chair, staring down at his 7-Up and breathing as if it hurt.

'You know which ones survive, Damien?' Cassie asked. She leaned across the table and laid her fingertips on his arm. 'The ones who confess. The ones who do their time. Seven years later, or whatever, it's over; they get out of gaol, and they can start again. They don't have to see their victims' faces every time they close their eyes. They don't have to spend every second of every day terrified that this is the day they're going to be caught. They don't have to jump a mile every time they see a cop or there's a knock at the door. Believe me: in the long run, those are the ones who get away.'

He was squeezing the can so hard that it buckled, with a sharp little crack. We all jumped.

'Damien,' I asked, very quietly, 'does any of this sound familiar?'

And, at long last, there it was: that tiny dissolution in the back of his neck, the sway of his head as his spine crumpled. Almost imperceptibly, after what seemed like an age, he nodded.

'Do you want to live like this for the rest of your life?'

His head moved, unevenly, from side to side.

Cassie gave his arm one last little pat and took her hand away: nothing that could look like coercion. 'You didn't want to kill Katy, did you?' she said; gently, so gently, her voice falling soft as snow over the room. 'It just happened.'

'Yeah.' He whispered it, barely a breath, but I heard. I was listening so hard I could almost hear his heart beating. 'It just happened.'

For a moment the room seemed to fold in on itself, as if some explosion too enormous to be heard had sucked all the air away. None of us could move. Damien's hands had gone limp around the can; it dropped to the table with a clunk, rocked crazily, came to a stop. The overhead light streaked his curls with hazy bronze. Then the room breathed in again, a slow, replete sigh.

'Damien James Donnelly,' I said. I didn't go back around the table to face him; I wasn't sure my legs would carry me. 'I arrest you on suspicion that, on or around the seventeenth of August of this year, at Knocknaree in County Dublin, you did murder Katharine Bridget Devlin, contrary to common law.'

21

Damien couldn't stop shaking. We took the photos away and brought him a fresh cup of tea, offered to find him an extra jumper or to heat up the leftover pizza for him, but he shook his head without looking at us. To me the whole scene felt wildly unreal. I couldn't take my eyes off Damien. I had razed half my mind in search of memories, I had gone into Knocknaree wood, I had risked my career and I was losing my partner; because of this boy.

Cassie went through the rights sheet with him – slowly and tenderly, as if he had been in a bad accident – and I held my breath in the background, but he didn't want a lawyer: 'What's the point? I did it, you guys knew anyway, everyone's gonna know, there's nothing a lawyer can . . . I'm going to gaol, right? Am I going to gaol?' His teeth were chattering; he needed something a lot stronger than tea.

'Don't worry about that right now, OK?' Cassie said soothingly. This sounded like a pretty ludicrous suggestion to me, in the circumstances, but it seemed to calm Damien down a little; he even nodded. 'Just keep helping us, and we'll do our best to help you.'

'I didn't – like you said, I never wanted to hurt anyone, I swear to God.' His eyes were locked on Cassie's as if his very life depended on her believing him. 'Can you tell them that, can you tell the judge? I'm not, I'm not some, like, psycho or serial killer or . . . I'm not *like* that. I didn't want to hurt her, I swear on, on, on . . .'

'Shh. I know.' She had her hand on his again, her thumb rubbing the back of his wrist in a soothing rhythm. 'Shh, Damien. It's going to be OK. The worst part's over. Now all you need to do is tell us what happened, in your own words. Can you do that for me?'

After a few deep breaths, he nodded, bravely. 'Well done,' said Cassie. She stopped short of patting him on the head and giving him a biscuit.

'We'll need the whole story, Damien,' I said, pulling my chair closer, 'step by step. Where did it start?'

'Huh?' he said, after a moment. He looked stunned. 'I . . . what?'

'You said you never wanted to hurt her. So how did this end up happening?'

'I don't . . . I mean, I'm not sure. I don't remember. Can't I just tell you about, like, that night?'

Cassie and I exchanged glances. 'OK,' I said. 'Sure. Start when you left work on the Monday evening. What did you do?' There was something there, obviously there was, his memory hadn't conveniently deserted him; but if we pushed him now, he might clam up altogether or change his mind about that lawyer.

'OK . . .' Damien took another deep breath and sat up straighter, hands clasped tightly between his knees, like a schoolboy at an oral exam. 'I took the bus home. I had dinner with my mother, and then we played Scrabble for a while; she likes Scrabble. My mother – she's sort of sick, she has this heart condition? – she went to bed at ten, she always does. I, um, I went to my room and I just hung out there till she was asleep – she snores, so I could . . . I tried to read and stuff, but I couldn't, I couldn't concentrate, I was so . . .' His teeth were chattering again.

'Shh,' Cassie said gently. 'It's over now. You're doing the right thing.'

He caught a jagged little breath, nodded. 'What time did you leave the house?' I asked.

'Um, eleven. I walked back to the dig – see, it's only really like a few miles from my house, it just takes ages on the bus 'cause you have to go all the way into town and then out again. I went round by the back lanes, so I wouldn't have to go past the estate. I had to go past the cottage instead, but the dog knows me, so when he got up I said, "Good dog, Laddie," and he shut up. It was dark, but I had a torch. I went in the tools shed and got a pair of, of gloves, and I put them on, and I picked up a . . .' He swallowed, hard. 'I picked up a big rock. From the ground, at the edge of the dig. Then I went into the finds shed.'

'What time was this?' I said.

'Like midnight.'

'And when did Katy get there?'

'It was supposed to be . . .' A blink, a duck of the head. 'It was supposed to be one o'clock, but she was early, maybe quarter to one? When she knocked on the door I almost had a heart attack.'

He had been frightened of her. I wanted to punch him. 'So you let her in.'

'Yeah. She had these chocolate biscuits in her hand, I guess she took them on her way out of the house; she gave me one but I couldn't – I mean, I couldn't *eat*. I just put it in my pocket. She ate hers and she told me about that ballet school and stuff for a couple of minutes. And then I said . . . I said, "Look on that shelf," and she turned round.

And I, um, I hit her. With the rock, on the back of her head. I hit her.'

There was a high note of pure disbelief in his voice. His pupils were dilated so widely that his eyes looked black.

'How many times?' I asked.

'I don't – I – God . . . Do I have to do this? I mean, I told you I did it, can't you just . . . just . . .' He was gripping the edge of the table, nails digging in.

'Damien,' Cassie said, softly but very firmly, 'we need to know the details.'

'OK. OK.' He rubbed a hand clumsily across his mouth. 'I hit her, just one time, but I guess I must've not done it hard enough, 'cause she sort of tripped forwards and fell down, but she was still like – she turned round and she opened her mouth like she was gonna scream, so I – I grabbed her. I mean, I was *scared*, I was really scared, if she screamed . . .' He was practically gibbering. 'I got my hand over her mouth and I tried to hit her again, but she got her hands in the way and she was scratching me and kicking and everything – we were on the floor, see, and I couldn't even see what was going on 'cause there was just my torch on the table, I hadn't turned on the light – I tried to hold her down but she was trying to get to the door, she kept twisting, and she was *strong* – I hadn't expected her to be strong, when she was . . .'

His voice trailed off and he stared down at the table. He was breathing through his nose, fast and shallow and hard.

'When she was so little,' I said, tonelessly.

Damien's mouth opened, but nothing came out. He had turned a nasty greenish-white, freckles standing out in high relief.

'We can take a break if you need one,' Cassie said. 'But sooner or later you're going to have to tell us the rest of the story.'

He shook his head violently. 'No. No break. I just want to . . . I'm OK.'

'Good,' I said. 'Then let's keep going. You had a hand over her mouth, and she was fighting.' Cassie moved, a tiny half-suppressed twitch.

'Yeah. OK.' Damien hugged himself, hands dug deep into the sleeves of his jumper. 'Then she twisted over onto her stomach and she was kind of crawling towards the door, and I – I hit her again. With the rock, on the side of her head. I guess I did it harder this time – adrenalin or something – 'cause she collapsed. She was unconscious. But she was still breathing, really loud, sort of moaning, so I knew I had to . . . I couldn't hit her again, I just couldn't. I didn't . . .' He was close to hyperventilating. 'I didn't . . . want to . . . hurt her . . .'

'So what did you do?'

'There's these, these plastic bags on the shelf. For finds. So I got one of them, and I . . . I put it over her head and kept it twisted till . . .'

'Till what?' I said.

'Till she stopped breathing,' Damien said at last, very softly.

There was a long silence, just the wind whistling eerily through the air vent and the sound of the rain.

'And then?'

'Then,' Damien's head wobbled a little; his eyes looked blind. 'I picked her up. I couldn't leave her in the finds shed or you guys would know, so I was going to take her out to the site. She was . . . there was blood all over the place, I guess from her head. I left the plastic bag on her so the blood wouldn't go everywhere. But when I got out to the site there was – in the woods, I saw this light, like a campfire or something. Somebody was there. I got scared, I was so scared I could hardly stand up, I thought I was going to drop her . . . I mean, what if they saw me?' His palms turned up to us in appeal; his voice cracked. 'I didn't know what to *do* with her.'

He had skipped the trowel. 'So what did you do?' I asked.

'I took her back to the sheds. In the tools shed, there's these tarps, we're supposed to use them to cover up delicate bits of the site when it rains? But we almost never need them. I wrapped her up in a tarp so that – I mean, I didn't want . . . you know, bugs . . .' He swallowed. 'And I put her under the rest of them. I guess I could've just left her in one of the fields, but that felt— There's foxes and – and rats and stuff, round there, and it might've been days before anyone found her, and I didn't want to, just to throw her *away* . . . I wasn't thinking straight. I thought maybe by tomorrow night I'd, I'd know what to do . . .'

'And then you went home?'

'No, I – first I cleaned up the finds shed. The blood. It was all on the floor, and on the steps, and it kept getting on my gloves and my feet and . . . I got a bucket of water from the hose and I tried to wash it off. It was – you could *smell* it . . . I kept having to stop 'cause I thought I was going to throw up.'

He looked, I swear, as if he expected sympathy. 'It must have been awful,' Cassie said, sympathetically.

'Yeah. God. It was.' Damien turned to her in gratitude. 'I felt like I'd been there forever, I kept thinking it was almost morning and the guys would be there any minute and I had to hurry, and then I thought this was a nightmare and I needed to wake up, and then I got dizzy . . . I couldn't even see what I was doing, I had the torch but half the time I was too scared to turn it on – I thought whoever was in the wood would see it and come look – so it was all dark, and *blood* everywhere, and every time there was a sound I thought I was gonna die, like actually die . . . There kept being these, these noises outside, like something was scratching at the walls of the shed. Once I thought I heard it, like, *sniffing* round the edge of the door – for a second I thought it could be Laddie, but he's chained up at night, and I almost – Jesus, it was . . .' He shook his head, dazed.

'But you got it cleaned up in the end,' I said.

'I guess, yeah. As much as I could. I just – I couldn't keep going any more, you know? I put the rock behind the tarps, and she had this little torch so I put it in there, too. For one second – see, when I lifted up the tarps the shadows did something weird and it looked like, like she was moving – God . . .'

He was starting to look green again. 'So you left the rock and her torch in the tools shed,' I said. He had skipped the trowel this time, too. This didn't bother me as much as you might think: at this stage, anything he shied away from became a weapon for us to use in our own time.

'Yeah. And I washed off the gloves and put them back in the bag. And then I locked up the sheds, and I just – I just walked home.'

Quietly and without restraint, as if it was something he had been waiting to do for a long time, Damien began to cry.

He cried for a long time and much too hard to answer questions. Cassie sat next to him, patting his arm and murmuring soothing things and passing him tissues. After a while of this I caught her eye, over the top of his head; she nodded. I left them to it and went to find O'Kelly.

'That little mammy's boy?' he said, eyebrows shooting up. 'Well, fuck me sideways. I didn't think he'd the bollocks for it. My money was on Hanly. He's after leaving, just now; told O'Neill to shove his questions up his hole and stormed out. Good thing Donnelly didn't do the same. I'll start on the file for the DPP.'

'We'll need his phone records and financials,' I said, 'and background interviews with the other archaeologists, college classmates, school friends, anyone close to him. He's being coy about the motive.'

'Who gives a fuck about the motive?' O'Kelly demanded, but the irritation didn't carry conviction: he was delighted. I knew I should be delighted myself, but somehow I wasn't. When I had dreamed of solving this case, my mental picture had never been anything like this. The scene in the interview room, which should have been the greatest triumph of my career, simply felt like too little too late.

'In this case,' I said, 'I do.' O'Kelly was right, technically – as long as you can prove that your boy committed the crime, you have absolutely no obligation to explain why – but juries, trained by TV, want a motive; and, this time, so did I. 'A brutal crime like this, from a sweet kid with absolutely no form; the defence is bound to try for mental illness. If we find a motive, then that's out.'

O'Kelly snorted. 'Fair enough. I'll put the lads onto the interviews. Get back in there and get me a cast-iron case. And, Ryan' – grudgingly, as I turned to leave – 'well done. The pair of ye.'

Cassie had got Damien calmed down; he was still a little shaky and he kept blowing his nose, but he was no longer sobbing. 'Are you all right to keep going?' she asked, squeezing his hand. 'We're nearly there, OK? You're doing great.' For a second, a pathetic shadow of a smile slipped across Damien's face.

'Yeah,' he said. 'Sorry about . . . sorry. I'm fine.'

'Fair play. You just let me know if you need another break.'

'OK,' I said, 'we'd got to the point where you went home. Let's talk about the next day.'

'Oh – yeah. The next day.' Damien caught a long, resigned, shuddering breath. 'The whole day was a total nightmare. I was so tired I couldn't even see, and every time anyone went into the tools shed I thought I was gonna faint or something – and having to act all normal, you know, laughing at people's jokes and acting like nothing had happened, and I kept thinking about – about her . . . And then I had to do the whole same thing that night, wait till my mother went to sleep and sneak out and walk back to the dig. If that light had been there in the wood again, I don't know *what* I'd've done. But it wasn't.'

'So you went back to the tools shed,' I said.

'Yeah. I put on gloves again and I got her – I got her out. She was . . . I thought she'd be stiff, I thought dead bodies were stiff, but she . . .' He bit down on his lip. 'She wasn't, not really. But she was *cold*. It was – I didn't want to touch her . . .' He shuddered.

'But you had to.'

Damien nodded and blew his nose again. 'I took her out to the site and I put her on the altar stone. Where she'd be, be safe, from rats and stuff. Where someone would find her before she . . . I tried to make her look like she was sleeping, or something. I don't know why. I threw the rock away, and I rinsed off the plastic bag and put it back where it was, but I couldn't find her torch, it was somewhere down behind the tarps, and I – I just wanted to go home . . .'

'Why didn't you bury her?' I asked. 'On the site, or in the wood?' It would have been the intelligent thing to do; not that this had anything to do with anything.

Damien looked at me, his mouth hanging a little open. 'I never thought of that,' he said. 'I just wanted to get out of there as fast as I could. And, anyway – I mean, just *bury* her? Like *rubbish*?'

And it had taken us a full month to catch up with this gem. 'The day after that,' I said, 'you made sure you were one of the people who discovered the body. Why?'

'Oh. Yeah. That.' He made a convulsive little movement, something like a shrug. 'I heard – see, I had the gloves on, so no fingerprints, but I heard somewhere that if I'd got one of my hairs on her, or fluff from my jumper or something, you guys could figure out it was from me. So I knew I had to find her – I didn't want to, Jesus, I didn't want to see her, but . . . All day I kept trying to figure out an excuse to go up there, but I was scared it would look suspicious. I was . . . I couldn't *think*. I just wanted it to be over. But then Mark told Mel to go work on the altar stone.'

He sighed, a tired little sound. 'And after that . . . it was actually *easier*, you know? At least I didn't have to pretend everything was fine.'

No wonder he had been spacy, during that first interview. Not spacy enough to ring our alarm bells, though. For a novice, he had done pretty well. 'And when we talked to you,' I said, and then I stopped.

Cassie and I didn't look at each other, didn't move a muscle, but the realisation shot between us like a jolt from an electric fence. One reason we had taken Jessica's Tracksuit Shadow story quite so seriously was that Damien had put the very same guy practically at the scene of the crime.

'When we talked to you,' I said, after only a fractional pause, 'you invented a big guy in a tracksuit, to throw us off.'

'Yeah.' Damien looked anxiously from one of us to the other. 'Sorry about that. I just thought . . .'

'Interview suspended,' Cassie said, and left. I followed her, with a sinking sensation in my stomach and Damien's faint apprehensive 'Wait – what . . .?' drifting after us.

By some shared instinct, we didn't stay in the corridor or go back to the incident room. We went next door, into the interview room where Sam had been questioning Mark. There was still debris strewn on the table: crumpled napkins, styrofoam cups, a splatter of dark liquid where someone had banged down a fist or shoved back a chair.

'All *right*!' Cassie said, on something between a gasp and a laugh. 'We *did* it, Rob!' She tossed her notebook onto the table and threw an arm around my shoulders. The gesture was quick and glad and unthinking, but it set my teeth on edge. We had been working together with all the old perfect understanding, slagging each other as if nothing had ever been wrong, but this had been purely for Damien's benefit and because the case demanded it; and I did not think I should be required to explain this to Cassie.

'Apparently, yeah,' I said.

'When he finally said it . . . God, I think my jaw practically hit the floor. Champagne tonight, whenever we're finished, and lots of it.' She let out a deep breath, leaned back against the table and ran her hands through her hair. 'You should probably go get Rosalind.'

I felt my shoulders tighten. 'Why?' I asked coolly.

'She doesn't like me.'

'Yes, I'm aware of that. Why should anyone go get her?'

Cassie stopped in mid-stretch and stared at me. 'Rob, she and Damien gave us the same exact fake lead. There has to be some connection there.'

'Actually,' I said, 'Jessica and Damien gave us the same fake lead.'

'You think Damien and *Jessica* are in on this together? Come *on*.'

'I don't think anyone's in on anything. What I do think is that Rosalind has been through just about enough for one lifetime, and that there's not a chance in hell that she was an accomplice to her sister's murder, so I don't see the point of dragging her in here and putting her through even more trauma.'

Cassie sat back on the table and looked at me. There was an expression in her eyes that I couldn't fathom. 'Do you think,' she enquired eventually, 'that that little sap came up with this all by himself?'

'I don't know and I don't care,' I said, hearing echoes of O'Kelly in my voice but unable to stop myself. 'Maybe Andrews or one of his buddies hired him. That would explain why he's dodging the whole motive thing: he's scared they'll go after him if he rats them out.'

'Yeah, except we don't have one single connection between him and Andrews—'

'Yet.'

'And we do have one between him and Rosalind.'

'Did you hear me? I said, *yet*. O'Kelly's on the financials and the phone records. When they come back, we'll see what we're dealing with and take it from there.'

'By the time the records come back, Damien'll have calmed down and got himself a lawyer, and Rosalind will have seen the arrest on the news and she'll be on her guard.

We pull her in right now and we play them off each other till we find out what's going on.'

I thought of Kiernan's voice, or McCabe's; of the vertiginous sensation as the ligaments of my mind gave way and I floated off into that soft, infinitely welcoming blue sky. 'No,' I said, 'we don't. That girl is *fragile*, Maddox. She is sensitive and she is highly strung and she just lost a sister and she has no idea why. And your answer is to *play her off* her sister's killer? Jesus, Cassie. We have a responsibility to look after that girl.'

'No we don't, Rob,' Cassie said sharply. 'No we don't. That's Victim Support's job. We have a responsibility to Katy, and a responsibility to try and find out the truth about what the hell happened here, and that's *it*. Anything else comes second.'

'And if Rosalind goes into a depression or has a nervous breakdown because we've been harassing her? Are you going to claim that's Victim Support's problem too? We could damage her for life here, do you understand that? Until we have something a whole lot better than a minor coincidence, we leave that girl the hell alone.'

'Minor *coincidence*?' Cassie shoved her hands into her pockets, hard. 'Rob. If this were anyone but Rosalind Devlin, what would you be doing right now?'

I felt a wave of anger rising inside me, sheer fury with a thick, tangled quality to it. 'No, Maddox. No. Don't even try to pull that. If anything, it's the other way around. You've never liked Rosalind, have you? You've been dying for a reason to go after her since day one, and now that Damien's given you this pathetic *shred* of an excuse, you're diving on it like a starving dog on a bone. My God, that poor girl told me a lot of women were jealous of her, but I have to say I gave you more credit than that. Apparently I was wrong.'

'Jealous of— Jesus *Christ*, Rob, you've got some nerve! I gave *you* more credit than to think you'd back off a fucking *suspect* just because you're sorry for her, and you fancy her, and you're pissed off with me for some bloody bizarre reason of your own—'

She was losing her temper fast, and I saw this with a hard pleasure. My anger is cold, controlled, articulate; it can smash a short-fuse explosion like Cassie's to pieces any day. 'I wish you'd keep your voice down,' I said. 'You're embarrassing yourself.'

'Oh, you think? You're an embarrassment to this entire fucking *squad*.' She jammed her notebook into her pocket, pages crumpling. 'I'm going to get Rosalind Devlin—'

'No you're not. For Christ's sake, act like a bloody detective, not like some hysterical teenager with a vendetta.'

'Yeah, I am, Rob. And you and Damien can do whatever you like, you can crawl up each other's arse and *die* for all I care—'

'Well,' I said, 'that certainly puts me in my place. Very professional.'

'What the fuck goes *on* in your *head*?' Cassie yelled. She kicked the door shut behind her with a bang, and I heard the echoes reverberate, deep and ominous, up and down the corridor.

I gave her plenty of time to leave. Then I went out for a cigarette – Damien could look after himself, like a big boy, for a few more minutes. It was starting to get dark and it was still raining, thick apocalyptic sheets. I turned up the collar of my jacket and squashed uncomfortably into the doorway. My hands were shaking. Cassie and I had had fights before, of course we had; partners argue as ferociously as lovers. Once I got her so furious that she slammed her hand down on her desk and her wrist swelled up, and we didn't speak for almost two days. But even that had been different; utterly different.

I threw away my soggy cigarette half-smoked and went back inside. Part of me wanted to send Damien off for processing and go home and let Cassie deal with that when she came back to find us gone, but I knew I didn't have that luxury: I needed to find out his motive, and I needed to do it in time to prevent Cassie from giving Rosalind the third degree.

Damien had started to catch up with events. He was almost frantic with anxiety, biting at his cuticles and jiggling his knees, and he couldn't stop asking me questions: What would happen next? He was going to gaol, right? For how long? His mother was going to have a heart attack, she had this heart condition . . . Was gaol really dangerous, was it like on TV? I hoped, for his sake, that he didn't watch *Oz*.

Whenever I came too close to the subject of motive, though, he shut down: curled in on himself like a hedgehog, stopped meeting my eyes and started claiming memory loss. The argument with Cassie seemed to have thrown me off my rhythm; everything felt terribly unbalanced and irritating, and try as I might I couldn't get Damien to do anything but stare at the table and shake his head miserably.

'All right,' I said at last. 'Let me get a little background straight. Your father died nine years ago, is that correct?'

'Yeah.' Damien glanced up tentatively. 'Almost ten; it's his tenth anniversary at the end of October. Can I . . . when we're finished here, can I, like, get bailed out?'

'Bail can only be decided by a judge. Does your mother work?'

'No. She's got this, I told you . . .' He gestured vaguely towards his chest. 'She gets disability. And my dad, he left us some . . . Oh God, my *mother*!' He shot upright. 'She's gonna be going crazy—What time is it?'

'Relax. We spoke to her earlier; she knows you're helping us with our enquiries. Even with the money your father left, it can't be easy to make ends meet.'

'What? . . . Um, we do OK.'

'All the same,' I said, 'if someone offered you a lot of money to do a job for him, you'd be tempted, wouldn't you?' Fuck Sam, and fuck O'Kelly: if Uncle Redmond had hired Damien, I needed to know now.

Damien's eyebrows drew together in what looked like genuine confusion. 'What?'

'I could name you a few people who had several million reasons to go after the Devlin family. The thing is, Damien, they aren't the kind to do their own dirty work. They're the type who use hired help.'

I paused, giving Damien a chance to say something. He merely looked dazed.

'If you're afraid of someone,' I told him, as gently as I could, 'we can protect you. And if someone hired you to do this, then you're not the real killer, are you? He is.'

'What – I didn't – *what*? You think someone *paid* me to, to . . . Jesus! No!'

His mouth was open in pure, shocked indignation. 'Well, if it wasn't for money,' I enquired, 'then why was it?'

'I told you, I don't *know*! I don't remember!'

For an extremely unpleasant instant, it occurred to me to wonder whether he might, in fact, have lost a segment of his memory; and, if so, why and where. I dismissed the thought. We hear this one all the time, and I had seen the look on his face when he skipped the trowel: that had been deliberate. 'You know, I'm doing my best to help you here,' I said, 'but there's no way for me to do that when you're not being honest with me.'

'I'm *being* honest! I don't feel good—'

'No, Damien, you're not,' I said. 'And here's how I know. Do you remember those photos I showed you? Remember the one of Katy with her face hanging off? That was taken at the post-mortem, Damien. And the post-mortem told us exactly what you did to that little girl.'

'I already told you—'

I leaned across the table, fast, into his face. 'And then, Damien, this morning, we found the trowel in the tools shed. How bloody stupid do you think we are? Here's the part you skipped: after you killed Katy, you undid her combats and you pulled down her underwear and you shoved the handle of that trowel inside her.'

Damien's hands went to the sides of his head. 'No – don't—'

'And you're trying to tell me that *just happened*? Raping a little kid with a trowel doesn't *just happen*, not without a damn good reason, and you need to stop fucking around and tell me what that reason was. Unless you're just one sick little pervert. Is that it, Damien? Are you?'

I had pushed him too hard. With dreary inevitability, Damien – who, after all, had had a long day – started to cry again.

We were there for a long time. Damien, his face in his hands, sobbed hoarsely and convulsively. I leaned against the wall, wondering what the hell to do with him and occasionally, when he stopped for breath, taking another desultory shot at the motive. He never answered; I'm not sure he heard me. The room was too hot and I could still smell the pizza, rich and nauseating. I couldn't focus. All I could think about was Cassie, Cassie and Rosalind: whether Rosalind had agreed to come in; whether she was holding up all right; whether Cassie was going to knock on the door, any moment, and want to put her face to face with Damien.

Finally I gave up. It was half past eight and this was pointless: Damien had had enough, the best detective in the world couldn't have got anything coherent out of him at this point, and I knew I should have spotted this long before. 'Come on,' I said to him. 'Get some dinner and some rest. We'll try this again tomorrow.'

He looked up at me. His nose was red and his eyes were swollen half-shut. 'I can go . . . go home?'

You've just been arrested for murder, genius, what do you think . . . I didn't have the energy for sarcasm. 'We'll be holding you overnight,' I said. 'I'll get someone to take you over.' When I brought out the handcuffs he stared at them as if they were some medieval implement of torture.

The door of the observation room was open, and as we passed I saw O'Kelly standing in front of the glass, hands in his pockets, rocking back and forth on his heels. My heart gave a great thump. Cassie had to be in the main interview room: Cassie and Rosalind. For a moment I thought of going in there, but I rejected that idea instantly: I did not want Rosalind to associate me in any way with this whole debacle. I handed Damien – still dazed and white-faced, catching his breath in long shudders like a child who's been crying too hard – over to the uniforms, and went home.

22

The land line rang at about a quarter to midnight. I dived for it; Heather has Rules about phone calls after her bedtime.

'Hello?'

'Sorry to ring so late, but I've been trying to reach you all evening,' Cassie said.

I had switched my mobile to silent, but I had seen the missed calls. 'I really can't talk now,' I said.

'Rob, for fuck's sake, this is *important*—'

'I'm sorry, I have to go,' I said. 'I'll be in work at some point tomorrow, or you can leave me a note.' I heard the quick, painful catch of breath, but I put the phone down anyway.

'Who was that?' demanded Heather, appearing in the door of her room wearing a nightie with a collar and looking sleepy and cross.

'For me,' I said.

'Cassie?'

I went into the kitchen, found an ice tray and started popping cubes into a glass. '*Ohhh,*' said Heather knowingly, behind me. 'You finally slept with her, didn't you?'

I threw the ice tray back into the freezer. Heather does leave me alone if I ask her to, but it's never worth it: the resultant sulks and flounces and lectures about her unique sensitivity last much longer than the original irritation would have.

'She doesn't deserve that,' she said. This startled me. Heather and Cassie dislike each other – once, very early on, I brought Cassie home for dinner, and Heather was borderline rude all evening and then spent hours after Cassie left plumping up sofa cushions and straightening rugs and sighing noisily, while Cassie never mentioned Heather again – and I wasn't sure where this sudden excess of sisterhood was coming from.

'Any more than I did,' she said, and went back into her bedroom and banged the door. I took my ice to my room and made myself a strong vodka and tonic.

Not unnaturally, I couldn't sleep. When light started to filter through the curtains, I gave up: I would go in to work early, I decided, see if I could find anything that would tell me what Cassie had said to Rosalind, start preparing the file on Damien to send to the DPP. But it was still raining hard, traffic was already bumper-to-bumper, and of course the Land Rover threw a flat tyre halfway down Merrion Road and I had to pull over and fumble about changing it, with rain pouring down my collar and all the drivers behind me leaning irately on their horns as if they would actually have been getting somewhere if it hadn't been for me. I finally slapped my flasher on the roof, which shut most of them up.

It was almost eight o'clock when I made it into work. The phone, inevitably, rang just as I took off my coat. 'Incident room, Ryan,' I said narkily. I was wet and cold and fed up and I wanted to go home and have a long bath and a hot whiskey; I did not want to deal with whoever this was.

'Get the fuck in here,' said O'Kelly. 'Now.' And he hung up.

My body understood first: I went cold all over, my breastbone tightened and it was hard to breathe. I don't know how I knew. It was obvious that I was in trouble: if O'Kelly just wants your basic chat, he sticks his head in the door, barks, 'Ryan, Maddox, my office,' and disappears again, to be in place behind his desk by the time you can follow. Phone summonses are reserved for when you are in for a bollocking. It could have been anything, of course – a great tip I had missed, Jonathan Devlin complaining about my bedside manner, Sam pissing off the wrong politician; but I knew it wasn't.

O'Kelly was standing up, his back to the window and his fists jammed into his pockets. 'Adam fucking Ryan,' he said. 'And it didn't occur to you that this was something I should know?'

I was engulfed by a wave of terrible, searing shame. My face burned. I hadn't felt it since school, this utter, crushing humiliation, the hollow clutch of your stomach when you know beyond any doubt you've been caught, snared, and there is absolutely nothing you can say to deny it or get out of it or make it any better. I stared at the side of O'Kelly's desk and tried to find pictures in the grain of the fake wood, like a doomed schoolboy waiting for the cane to come out. I had thought of my silence as some gesture of proud, lonely independence, something some weatherbeaten Clint Eastwood character would have done, and for the first time I saw it for what it essentially was: shortsighted and juvenile and traitorous and stupid, stupid, stupid.

'Do you have any idea of the extent to which you may have fucked up this investigation?' O'Kelly asked coldly. He always becomes more eloquent when he's angry, another reason I think he's brighter than he pretends to be. 'Have a quick think about what a good defence attorney could do with this, just on the off-chance that it ever gets as far as a courtroom. A lead detective who was the only eyewitness and the only surviving victim in an unsolved *related case* – Jesus Christ. While the rest of us dream about pussy, defence attorneys dream about detectives like you. They can accuse you of anything from being incapable of running an unbiased investigation through being a potential suspect in one or both cases yourself. The media and the conspiracy shower and the anti-Garda mob will go wild. Within a week, not one person in the country will remember who's supposed to be on trial here.'

I stared at him. The sucker-punch, coming out of nowhere while I was still reeling from being found out, left me stunned and speechless. This will seem incredible, but I swear it had never occurred to me, not once in twenty years, that I could be a suspect in Peter and Jamie's disappearance. There was nothing like that in the file, nothing. Ireland's 1984 belonged more to Rousseau than to Orwell; children were innocents, fresh from God's hand, it would have been an outrage against nature to suggest that they could be murderers as well. Nowadays, we all know there is no such thing as too young to kill. I was big for twelve, I had someone else's blood in my shoes, puberty is a strange slippery unbalanced time. Suddenly and clearly I saw Cassie's face, the day she came back from talking to Kiernan: that tiny twist to the corners of her mouth that said she was keeping something back. I needed to sit down.

'Every guy you've put away will demand a retrial on the basis that you have a record of withholding material evidence. Congratulations, Ryan: you just fucked up every case you've ever touched.'

'I'm off the case, then,' I said finally and stupidly. My lips felt numb. I had a sudden hallucinatory image of dozens of journalists yapping and screeching at the door of my apartment building, shoving microphones in my face and calling me Adam and demanding gory details. Heather would love it: enough melodrama and martyrdom to keep her going for months. Jesus.

'*No*, you're not off the fucking case,' O'Kelly snapped. 'You're not off the fucking case purely because I don't want any smart-arse reporter getting curious about why I gave you the boot. The word from now on is damage control. You don't interview a single witness, you don't touch a single piece of evidence, you sit at your desk and try not to make anything any worse than it already is. We do everything we can to stop this getting out. And the day Donnelly's trial is over, if there ever is a trial, you're suspended from the squad pending investigation.'

All I could think was that 'damage control' was two words. 'Sir, I'm so sorry,' I said, which seemed like a better thing to say. I had no idea what suspension involved. I had a fleeting image of some TV cop slapping his badge and his gun on his boss's desk, close-up fading to credits as his career went up in smoke.

'That and two quid will get you a cup of coffee,' O'Kelly said flatly. 'Sort the tips from the hotline and put them on file. Any of them mention the old case, you don't even finish reading them, you pass them straight to Maddox or O'Neill.' He sat down at his desk, picked up the phone and started dialling. I stood there staring at him for a few seconds before I realised I was supposed to leave.

I went slowly back to the incident room – I'm not sure why, I had no intention of doing anything with the hotline tips; I suppose I must have been on autopilot. Cassie was sitting in front of the VCR, her elbows on her knees, watching the tape of me interrogating Damien. There was an exhausted slump to her shoulders; the remote control dangled limply from one hand.

Something deep inside me gave a horrible, sick lurch. It hadn't even occurred to me, until that moment, to wonder how O'Kelly knew. It only hit me then, as I stood in the doorway of the incident room looking at her: there was only one way he could possibly have found out.

I was perfectly aware that I had been pretty shitty to Cassie lately – although I would argue that the situation was a complex one, and that I had my reasons. But nothing I had done to her, nothing I could do in the world, warranted this. I had never imagined this kind of betrayal. Hell hath no fury. I thought my legs were going to give way.

Maybe I made some involuntary sound or movement, I don't know, but Cassie turned sharply in her chair and stared at me. After a second she hit Stop and put down the remote. 'What did O'Kelly say?'

She knew; she already knew, and my final spark of doubt sank into something jagged and impossibly heavy dragging at my solar plexus. 'As soon as the case is over, I'm suspended,' I said flatly. My voice sounded like someone else's.

Cassie's eyes widened, horrified. 'Oh, shit,' she said. 'Oh, shit, Rob . . . But you're not out? He didn't – he didn't fire you or anything?'

'No, I'm not out,' I said. 'No thanks to you.' The first shock was starting to wear off, and a cold, vicious anger was surging through me like electricity. I felt my whole body trembling with it.

'That's not fair,' Cassie said, and I heard a tiny shake in her voice. 'I tried to warn you. I rang you last night, I don't know how many times—'

'It was a little late to be concerned about me by then, wasn't it? You should have thought of that before.'

Cassie was white to the lips, her eyes huge. I wanted to smash the stunned, uncomprehending look off her face. 'Before *what*?' she demanded.

'Before you poured out my private life to O'Kelly. Do you feel better now, Maddox? Has wrecking my career made up for the fact that I haven't treated you like a little princess this week? Or have you got something else up your sleeve?'

After a moment she said, very quietly, 'You think I told him?'

I almost laughed. 'Yes, actually, I do. There were only five people in the world who knew about this, and I somehow doubt that my parents or a friend from fifteen years ago picked this moment to ring my boss and say, "Oh, by the way, did you know that Ryan's name used to be Adam?" How stupid do you think I am? I *know* you told him, Cassie.'

She hadn't taken her eyes off mine, but something in them had changed, and I realised she was every bit as furious as I was. In one fast movement she grabbed a videotape from the table and threw it at me, a hard over-hand snap with her whole body behind it. I ducked reflexively; it crashed against the wall where my head had been, spun away and tumbled into a corner.

'Watch that tape,' Cassie said.

'I'm not interested.'

'Watch that tape right now or, I swear to God, by tomorrow morning I'll have your face plastered across every newspaper in the country.'

It wasn't the threat itself that got me; it was more the fact that she had made it, had played what had to be her trump card. It sparked something in me: a harsh curiosity, mixed – or perhaps this is only hindsight, I don't know – with some faint, dreadful premonition. I retrieved the tape from the corner, switched it into the VCR and hit Play. Cassie, her arms clasped tightly at her waist, watched me without moving. I swung a chair around and sat down in front of the screen, my back to her.

It was the fuzzy black-and-white tape of Cassie's session with Rosalind, the night before. The time-stamp showed 8.27; in the next room, I had been just about to give up on Damien. Rosalind was on her own in the main interview room, redoing her lipstick in a little compact mirror. There were sounds in the background, and it took me a moment to realise that they were familiar: hoarse, helpless sobs, and my own voice saying over them, without much hope, 'Damien, I need you to explain to me why you did this.' Cassie had switched on the intercom and set it to pick up my interview room. Rosalind's head went up; she stared at the one-way glass, her face utterly expressionless.

The door opened and Cassie came in, and Rosalind recapped her lipstick and tucked it into her purse. Damien was still sobbing. 'Shit,' Cassie said, glancing up at the intercom. 'Sorry about that.' She switched it off; Rosalind gave a tight, displeased little smile.

'Detective Maddox interviewing Rosalind Frances Devlin,' Cassie said, to the camera. 'Have a seat.'

Rosalind didn't move. 'I'm afraid I'd prefer not to talk to you,' she said, in an icy, dismissive voice I had never heard her use before. 'I'd like to speak with Detective Ryan.'

'Sorry, can't be done,' Cassie said cheerfully, pulling out a chair for herself. 'He's in an interview – as I'm sure you heard,' she added, with a rueful little grin.

'Then I'll come back when he's free.' Rosalind tucked her bag under her arm and headed for the door.

'Just a moment, Miss Devlin,' Cassie said, and there was a new, hard edge in her voice. Rosalind sighed and turned, eyebrows raised contemptuously. 'Is there any particular reason why you're suddenly so reluctant to answer questions about your sister's murder?'

I saw Rosalind's eyes flick up at the camera, just for a flash, but that tiny cold smile didn't change. 'I think you know, Detective, if you're honest with yourself,' she said, 'that I'm more than willing to help the investigation in any way I can. I simply don't want to talk to *you*, and I'm sure you know why.'

'Let's pretend I don't.'

'Oh, Detective, it's been obvious from the start that you don't care about my sister at all. You're only interested in flirting with Detective Ryan. Isn't it against the rules to sleep with your partner?'

A fresh spurt of fury shot through me, so violent it took my breath away. 'Jesus Christ! Is *that* what all this was about? Just because you thought I told her—' Rosalind had been shooting in the dark, I had never said a word about that to her or to anyone else; and for Cassie to think I would, to take this kind of revenge without even bothering to ask me—

'Shut up,' she said coldly, behind me. I clenched my hands together and stared at the TV. I was almost too angry to see.

On the screen, Cassie hadn't even flinched; she was tilting her chair back on two legs and shaking her head, amused. 'Sorry, Miss Devlin, but I don't get distracted that easily. Detective Ryan and I feel exactly the same way about your sister's death: we want to find her killer. So why is it, again, that you suddenly don't want to talk about it?'

Rosalind laughed. 'Exactly the same way? Oh, I don't think so, Detective. He has a very special connection to this case, doesn't he?'

Even in the blurry picture I could see Cassie's fast blink, and the savage flash of triumph on Rosalind's face as she realised she had got past her guard this time. 'Oh,' she said, sweetly. 'You mean you don't know?'

She only paused for a fraction of a second, just enough to heighten the effect, but to me it seemed to last forever; because I knew, with a hideous vortexing sense of inevitability, I knew what she was going to say. I suppose this must be what stuntmen feel when a fall goes horribly wrong, or jockeys coming off at full gallop: that oddly calm splinter of time, just before your body shatters against the ground, when your mind is wiped clean of everything except the one simple certainty: *This is it, then. Here it comes.*

'He's that boy whose friends disappeared in Knocknaree, ages ago,' Rosalind told Cassie. Her voice was high and musical and almost uninterested; except for a tiny, smug trace of pleasure, there was nothing in it, nothing at all. 'Adam Ryan. It looks like he doesn't tell you everything, after all, doesn't it?' I had thought, only a few minutes before, that there was no way I could feel any worse and still survive.

Cassie, on the screen, thumped the chair-legs down and rubbed at one ear. She was biting her lip to hold back a smile, but I had nothing left in me with which to wonder what she was doing. 'Did he tell you that?'

'Yes. We've got very close, really.'

'Did he also tell you he had a brother who died when he was sixteen? That he grew up in a children's home? That his father was an alcoholic?'

Rosalind stared. The smile was gone from her face and her eyes were narrow, electric. 'Why?' she asked.

'Just checking. Sometimes he does those too – it depends. Rosalind,' she said, somewhere between amused and embarrassed, 'I don't know how to tell you this, but sometimes, when detectives are trying to build up a relationship with a witness, they say things that aren't exactly true. Things that they think will help the witness feel comfortable enough to share information. Do you understand?'

Rosalind kept staring, unmoving.

'Listen,' Cassie said gently, 'I know for a fact that Detective Ryan has never had a brother, that his father is a very nice guy with no alcoholic tendencies, and that he grew up in Wiltshire – hence the accent – nowhere near Knocknaree. And not in a children's home, either. But, whatever he told you, I know he only wanted to make it easier for you to help us find Katy's killer. Don't hold it against him. OK?'

The door slammed open – Cassie jumped about a mile; Rosalind didn't move, didn't even take her eyes off Cassie's face – and O'Kelly, foreshortened to a blob by the camera angle but instantly recognisable by his spidery comb-over, leaned into the room. 'Maddox,' he said curtly. 'A word.'

O'Kelly, as I walked Damien out: in the observation room, rocking back and forth on his heels, staring impatiently through the glass. I couldn't watch any more. I fumbled with the remote, hit Stop and stared blindly at the vibrating blue square.

'Cassie,' I said, after a very long time.

'He asked me if it was true,' she said, as evenly as if she were reading out a report. 'I said that it wasn't, and that if it were you would hardly have told her.'

'I didn't,' I said. It seemed important that she should know this. 'I didn't. I told her that two of my friends disappeared when we were little – so she'd realise I understood what she was going through. I never thought she'd know about Peter and Jamie and put two and two together. It never occurred to me.'

Cassie waited for me to finish. 'He accused me of covering for you,' she said, when I stopped talking, 'and added that he should have split us up a long time ago. He said he was going to check your prints against the ones from the old case – even if he had to drag a print tech out of bed to do it, even if it took all night. If the prints matched, he said, we would both be lucky to keep our jobs. He told me to send Rosalind home. I handed her over to Sweeney and started ringing you.'

Somewhere at the back of my head I heard a click, tiny and irrevocable. Memory magnifies it to a wrenching, echoing crack, but the truth is that it was the very smallness that made it so terrible. We sat there like that, not speaking, for a long time. The wind whipped spatters of rain against the window. Once I heard Cassie take a deep breath, and I thought she might be crying, but when I looked up there were no tears on her face; it was pale and quiet and very, very sad.

23

We were still sitting there like that when Sam got in. 'What's the story?' he said, rubbing rain out of his hair and switching on the lights.

Cassie stirred, lifted her head. 'O'Kelly wants you and me to have another go at finding out Damien's motive. Uniforms are bringing him over.'

'Grand,' Sam said, 'see if a new face shakes him up a bit,' but he had taken us both in with one quick glance and I wondered how much he was guessing; wondered, for the first time, how much he had known all along and simply left alone.

He pulled over a chair and sat down next to Cassie, and they started discussing how to go at Damien. They had never interrogated anyone together before; their voices were tentative, earnest, deferring to each other and rising into open-ended little question-marks: Do you think we should . . .? What if we . . .? Cassie switched the tapes in the VCR again, played Sam bits of last night's interview. The fax machine made a series of demented, cartoonish noises and spat out Damien's mobile-phone records, and they bent over the pages with a highlighter pen, murmuring.

When they finally left – Sam nodding to me, briefly, over his shoulder – I waited in the empty incident room until I was sure they must have started the interrogation, and then

I went looking for them. They were in the main interview room. I ducked into the observation chamber furtively, ears burning, like someone diving into an adult bookshop. I knew this was going to be the very last thing in the world I wanted to see, but I didn't know how to stay away.

They had made the room as cosy as humanly possible: coats and bags and scarves thrown on chairs, the table strewn with coffee and sugar packets and mobile phones and a carafe of water and a plate of sticky Danishes from the café outside the Castle grounds. Damien, bedraggled in the same oversized jumper and combats – they looked like he'd slept in them – hugged himself and stared around, wide-eyed; after the alien chaos of a gaol cell, this must have seemed a bright haven to him, safe and warm and almost homey. At certain angles you could see a fuzz of fair, pathetic stubble on his chin. Cassie and Sam were chattering, perching on the table and bitching about the weather and offering Damien milk. I heard footsteps in the corridor and tensed – if it was O'Kelly he would kick me out, back to the phone tips, this no longer had anything to do with me – but they went past without breaking stride. I leaned my forehead against the one-way glass and closed my eyes.

They took him through safe little details first. Cassie's voice, Sam's, weaving together dexterously, soothing as lullabies: How did you get out of the house without waking up your mam? Yeah? I used to do that too, when I was a teenager . . . Had you done it before? God, this coffee's manky, do you want a Coke or something instead? They were good together, Cassie and Sam; they were good. Damien was relaxing. Once he even laughed, a pathetic little breath.

'You're a member of Move the Motorway, right?' Cassie

said eventually, just as easily as before; nobody but me would have recognised the tiny lift in her voice that meant she was getting down to business. I opened my eyes and straightened up. 'When did you get involved with them?'

'This spring,' Damien said readily, 'like March or something. There was a thing on the department noticeboard in college, about a protest. I knew I was going to be working at Knocknaree for the summer, so I felt sort of . . . I don't know, connected to it? So I went.'

'Would that be the protest on the twentieth of March?' Sam asked, flipping through papers and rubbing the back of his head. He was doing solid country cop, friendly and not too quick.

'Yeah, I think so. It was outside the Dáil, if that helps.' Damien seemed almost eerily at ease by this point, leaning forward across the table and playing with his coffee cup, chatty and eager as if this were a job interview. I'd seen this before, especially with first-time criminals: they're not used to thinking of us as the enemy, and once the shock of being caught has worn off they turn light-headed and helpful with the sheer relief of the long tension breaking.

'And that's when you joined the campaign?'

'Yeah. It's a really important site, Knocknaree, it's been inhabited ever since—'

'Mark told us,' Cassie said, grinning. 'As you can imagine. Was that when you met Rosalind Devlin, or did you know her before?'

A small, confused pause. 'What?' Damien said.

'She was on the sign-up table that day. Was that the first time you'd met her?'

Another pause. 'I don't know who you mean,' Damien said finally.

'Come on, Damien,' Cassie said, leaning forward to try

to catch his eye; he was staring into his coffee cup. 'You've been doing great all the way; don't flake out on me now, OK?'

'There are calls and texts to Rosalind all over your mobile-phone records,' Sam said, pulling out the sheaf of highlighted pages and putting them in front of Damien. He gazed at them blankly.

'Why wouldn't you want us knowing you guys were friends?' Cassie asked. 'There's no harm in that.'

'I don't want her dragged into this,' Damien said. His shoulders were starting to tense up.

'We're not trying to drag anyone into anything,' Cassie said gently. 'We just want to figure out what happened.'

'I already told you.'

'I know, I know. Bear with us, OK? We just have to clear up the details. Is that when you first met Rosalind, at that protest?'

Damien reached out and touched the mobile records with one finger. 'Yeah,' he said. 'When I signed up. We got talking.'

'You got on well, so you stayed in touch?'

'Yeah. I guess.'

They backed off then. When did you start work at Knocknaree? Why'd you pick that dig? Yeah, it sounded fascinating to me, too . . . Gradually Damien relaxed again. It was still raining, thick curtains of water sliding down the windows. Cassie went for more coffee, came back with a look of guilty mischief and a packet of custard creams swiped from the canteen. There was no hurry, now that Damien had confessed. The only thing he could do was demand a lawyer, and a lawyer would advise him to tell them exactly what they were trying to find out; an accomplice meant shared blame, confusion, all a defence attorney's favourite things. Cassie and Sam had all day, all week, as long as it took.

'How soon did you and Rosalind start going out?' Cassie asked, after a while.

Damien had been folding the corner of a phone-record page into little pleats, but at this he glanced up, startled and wary. 'What? . . . We didn't – um, we aren't. We're just friends.'

'Damien,' Sam said reproachfully, tapping the pages. 'Look at this. You're ringing her three, four times a day, texting her half a dozen times, talking for hours in the middle of the night—'

'God, I've done that,' Cassie said reminiscently. 'The amount of phone credit you go through when you're in love . . .'

'You don't ring any of your other *friends* a quarter as much. She's ninety-five per cent of your phone bill, man. And there's nothing wrong with that. She's a lovely girl, you're a nice young fella; why shouldn't you go out together?'

'Hang on,' Cassie said suddenly, sitting up. 'Was Rosalind *involved* in this? Is that why you don't want to talk about her?'

'No!' Damien almost shouted. 'Leave her alone!'

Cassie and Sam stared, eyebrows raised.

'Sorry,' he muttered after a moment, slumping in his chair. He was bright red. 'I just . . . I mean, she didn't have anything to *do* with it. Can't you leave her out of it?'

'Then why the big secret, Damien?' Sam asked. 'If she wasn't involved?'

He shrugged. 'Because. We didn't tell anyone we were going out.'

'Why not?'

'We just didn't. Rosalind's dad would've been mad.'

'He didn't like you?' Cassie asked, with just enough surprise to be flattering.

'No, it wasn't that. She's not allowed to have boy-friends.' Damien glanced nervously between them. 'Could you – you know . . . could you not tell him? Please?'

'How mad would he have been,' Cassie said softly, 'exactly?'

Damien picked pieces off his styrofoam cup. 'I just didn't want to get her into trouble.' But the flush hadn't died away and he was breathing fast; there was something there.

'We've a witness,' Sam said, 'who told us Jonathan Devlin may recently have hit Rosalind at least once. Do you know if that's true?'

A fast blink, a shrug. 'How would I know?'

Cassie shot Sam a quick look and backed off again. 'So how did you guys manage to meet up without her dad finding out?' she asked confidentially.

'At first we just met in town on weekends and went for coffee and stuff. Rosalind told them she was meeting her friend Karen, from school? So they were OK with that. Later, um . . . later we sometimes met at night. Out on the dig. I'd go out there and wait till her parents were asleep and she could sneak out of the house. We'd sit on the altar stone, or sometimes in the finds shed if it was raining, and just talk.'

It was easy to imagine, easy and seductively sweet: a blanket around their shoulders and a country sky packed with stars, and moonlight making the rough landscape of the dig into a delicate, haunted thing. No doubt the secrecy and the complications had only added to the romance of it all. It carried the primal, irresistible power of myth: the cruel father, the fair maiden imprisoned in her tower, hedged in by thorns and calling for rescue. They had made their own nocturnal, stolen world, and to Damien it must have been a very beautiful one.

'Or some days she'd come to the dig, maybe bring Jessica, and I'd give them the tour. We couldn't really talk much, in case someone saw, but – just to see each other . . . And this one time, back in May' – he smiled a little, down at his hands, a shy, private smile – 'see, I had a part-time job, making sandwiches in this deli? So I saved up enough that we could go away for a whole weekend. We took the train up to Donegal and stayed in this little B&B, we signed in like – like we were married. Rosalind told her parents she was spending the weekend with Karen, to study for her exams.'

'And then what went wrong?' Cassie asked, and I caught that tautening in her voice again. 'Did Katy find out about you two?'

Damien glanced up, startled. 'What? No. Jesus, no. We were really careful.'

'What, then? She was bothering Rosalind? Little sisters can be pretty annoying.'

'No—'

'Rosalind was jealous of all the attention Katy was getting? What?'

'No! Rosalind's not like that – she was happy for Katy! And I wouldn't *kill* someone just for . . . I'm not – I'm not *crazy*!'

'And you're not violent, either,' Sam said, slapping another heap of paper in front of Damien. 'These are interviews about you. Your teachers remember you staying far away from fights, not starting them. Would you say that's accurate?'

'I guess—'

'Did you just do it for the buzz, after all?' Cassie cut in. 'Did you want to see what it felt like to kill someone?'

'*No!* What are you—'

Sam moved round the table, surprisingly fast, and leaned in beside Damien. 'The lads from the dig say George McMahon gave you hassle, just like he did everyone else, but you're one of the few who never lost your temper with him. So what got you angry enough to kill a little girl who never did you any harm?'

Damien huddled wretchedly into his jumper, his chin tucked into his neck, and shook his head. They had closed in too soon, too hard; they were losing him.

'Hey. Look at me.' Sam snapped his fingers in Damien's face. 'Do I look anything like your mammy?'

'What? No—' But the unexpectedness of it had caught him; his eyes, wild and miserable, had flicked back up.

'Well spotted. That's because I'm not your mammy and this isn't some little thing you can get out of by sulking. This is as serious as it gets. You lured an innocent little girl out of her house in the middle of the night, you hit her on the head, you suffocated her and watched while she died, you shoved a trowel up inside her' – Damien flinched violently – 'and now you're telling us you did it for no reason at all. Is that what you're going to tell the judge? What kind of sentence do you think he's going to give you?'

'You don't *get* it!' Damien cried. His voice cracked like a thirteen-year-old's.

'I know, I know we don't, but I want to. Help me get it, Damien.' Cassie was leaning forward, holding both his hands in hers, forcing him to look at her.

'You don't understand! An innocent little girl? Everyone thinks she was, Katy was like some *saint*, they always thought she was so perfect – it wasn't *like* that! Just because she was a kid, that doesn't mean she was . . . You wouldn't believe me if I told you some of the stuff she did, you wouldn't even believe me.'

'I will,' Cassie said, low and urgent. 'Whatever you're going to tell me, Damien, I've seen worse on this job. I'll believe you. Try me.'

Damien's face was red, suffused, and his hands were shaking in Cassie's. 'She used to get her dad mad at Rosalind and Jessica. Like all the time, they were always scared. She just made stuff up and told him – like Rosalind had been mean to her or Jessica had touched her stuff or something – it wasn't even *true*, she just made it up, and he always just *believed* her. Rosalind tried to tell him this one time that it wasn't true, she was trying to protect Jessica, but he just, he just . . .'

'What did he do?'

'He hit them!' Damien howled. His head shot up and his eyes, red-rimmed and blazing, locked on to Cassie's. 'He beat them up! He broke Rosalind's skull with a *poker*, he threw Jessica into a wall and she broke her *arm*, he, Jesus, he *did* it to them, and Katy, she was watching and she *laughed*!' He ripped his hands out of Cassie's and swiped tears away furiously with the back of his wrist. He was gasping for breath.

'Do you mean Jonathan Devlin was having sexual intercourse with his daughters?' Cassie said calmly. Her eyes were huge.

'Yes. Yes. He did it to all of them. Katy . . .' Damien's face contorted. 'Katy *liked* it. How sick is that? How can anyone . . .? That was why she was his favourite. He hated Rosalind because she . . . didn't want to . . .' He bit the back of his hand and cried.

I realised I had been holding my breath for so long I was light-headed; realised, too, that there was a chance I might throw up. I leaned against the cool glass and concentrated on breathing slowly and evenly. Sam found a tissue and passed it to Damien.

Unless I was even stupider than I had already proven myself to be, Damien believed every word he was saying. Why not? We see worse in the papers every other week, raped toddlers, children starving in basements, babies' limbs ripped off. As their private mythology grew to fill more and more of his mind, why not the evil sister keeping Cinderella in the dust?

And, though this is by no means an easy thing to admit, I wanted to believe it too. For a moment I almost could. It made such perfect sense; it explained and excused so much, almost everything. But, unlike Damien, I had seen the medical records, the post-mortem report. Jessica had broken that arm falling off a climbing frame in full view of fifty witnesses, Rosalind had never had a fractured skull; Katy had died a virgin. Something like a cold sweat crawled across my shoulders, light and spreading.

Damien blew his nose. 'It can't have been easy for Rosalind to tell you this,' Cassie said gently. 'That was pretty brave of her. Had she tried to tell anyone else?'

He shook his head. 'He always said if she told he'd kill her. I was the first person she ever trusted enough to tell.' There was something like wonder in his voice, wonder and pride, and under the tears and snot and redness his face lit up with a faint, awed radiance. He looked, for a second, like some young knight setting off in search of the Holy Grail.

'And when did she tell you?' Sam asked.

'Sort of in pieces. Like you said, it was hard for her. She

didn't say anything till like May . . .' Damien flushed an even deeper red. 'When we stayed in that B&B. We were, um, we were kissing? And I tried to touch her . . . her chest. Rosalind got sort of mad and pushed me away and said she wasn't like that, and I was I guess kind of surprised – I hadn't expected it to be that big of a deal, you know? We'd been going out for like a month – I mean, I know that didn't give me any right to . . . but . . . Anyway I was just startled, but Rosalind got all worried that I was mad at her. So she . . . she told me what her dad had been doing to her. To explain why she'd got so freaked out.'

'And what did you say?' Cassie asked.

'I said she should move out! I wanted us to get a flat together, we could've got the money – I had this dig coming up and Rosalind could've got modelling jobs, this guy from a really big model agency had spotted her and he kept saying she could be a supermodel, only her father wouldn't let her . . . I didn't want her to ever go back to that house. But Rosalind wouldn't. She said she wouldn't leave Jessica. Can you imagine what kind of person it takes to do that? She went back to *that* just to protect her sister. I've never known anyone that brave.'

If he had been just a couple of years older, the story would have sent him lunging for the phone to ring the police, Childline, anyone. But he was only nineteen; adults were still bossy aliens who didn't understand, to be told nothing because they would charge in and ruin everything. It had probably never even occurred to him to ask for help.

'She even said . . .' Damien looked away. He was tearing up again. I thought, vindictively, that he was going to be in big trouble in gaol if he kept bawling at the drop of a hat. 'She told me she might never be able to, to make love with me. Because of the bad associations. She didn't know if she could ever trust anyone that much. So she said, if I wanted to break up with her and find a normal girlfriend – she actually said that, *normal* – then she'd understand. The only thing she asked for was, if I was going to go, I should go right away, before she started to care too much about me . . .'

'But you didn't want to do that,' Cassie said softly.

'Course not,' Damien said simply. 'I love her.' There was something in his face, some reckless and consuming purity that, believe it or not, I envied.

Sam gave him another tissue. 'There's only one thing I don't understand,' he said, an easy, soothing rumble. 'You wanted to protect Rosalind – that's fair enough, sure, any man would have felt the same. But why get rid of Katy? Why not Jonathan? I'd have been going after him, myself.'

'I said that too,' Damien said, and then stopped, his mouth open, as if he had said something incriminating. Cassie and Sam looked blandly back at him and waited.

'Um,' he said, after a moment. 'See, this one night Rosalind's stomach was hurting and finally I got it out of her – she didn't want to tell me, but he'd . . . he'd punched her in the stomach. Like four times. Just because Katy told him Rosalind wouldn't let her change the channel to watch some ballet thing on TV – and it wasn't even *true*, she would've changed it if Katy had asked . . . I just – I couldn't stand it any more. I was thinking about it every night, what she was going through, I couldn't sleep – I couldn't just let it keep *happening*!'

He took a breath, got his voice back under control. Cassie and Sam nodded understandingly.

'I said, um, I said, "I'm gonna kill him". Rosalind . . . she couldn't believe I would really do that for her. And yeah, I guess I was sort of – not joking, but like not totally serious about actually *doing* it. I'd never even thought about doing anything like that in my whole life. But when I saw how much it meant to her that I would even say it – nobody had ever tried to protect her before . . . She was almost crying, and she's not the kind of girl who cries, she's a really strong person.'

'I'm sure she is,' Cassie said. 'So why didn't you go after Jonathan Devlin, once you'd got your head round the idea?'

'See, if he died' – Damien leaned forward, hands gesturing anxiously – 'their mother wouldn't be able to look after them, because of money and because I think she's kind of spacy or something? They'd be sent to homes and they'd be split up, Rosalind wouldn't be there to take care of Jessica any more – and Jessica *needs* her, she's so messed up she can't do anything, Rosalind has to do her homework for her and stuff. And Katy – I mean, Katy would have gone and done the exact same thing to somebody else. If only Katy wasn't there, they'd all be *fine*! Their dad only, he only did stuff to them when Katy got him to. Rosalind said, and she felt so guilty about this – Jesus, *she* felt guilty! – sometimes she wished Katy had never been born . . .'

'And that gave you an idea,' Cassie said evenly. I could tell by the set of her mouth that she was so angry she could hardly speak. 'You suggested killing Katy instead.'

'It was my idea,' Damien said quickly. 'Rosalind had nothing to do with it. She didn't even . . . at first she said no. She didn't want me taking a risk like that for her. She'd survived it for years, she said, she could survive for six more, till Jessica was old enough to move out. But I couldn't let her just stay! That time he fractured her skull, she was in the hospital for two months. She could have *died*.'

Suddenly I was furious too, but not with Rosalind: with Damien, for being such a fucking cretin, such a perfect sucker, like some goofy cartoon character blundering obediently into the right place for the Acme anvil to drop on his head. I am of course fully aware of both the irony and the tedious psychological explanations of this reaction, but at the time all I could think of was slamming into the interview room and shoving Damien's face into the medical reports: *Do you see this, moron? Do you see a skull fracture anywhere here? Didn't it even occur to you to ask to see the scar before you slaughtered a child for it?*

'So you insisted,' Cassie said, 'and, in the end, Rosalind somehow came round.'

This time Damien caught the biting edge. 'That was because of Jessica! Rosalind didn't mind what happened to her, but Jessica – Rosalind was worried she was going to have a nervous breakdown or something. She didn't think Jessica could take six more years!'

'But Katy wouldn't have been there for most of that time anyway,' Sam said. 'She was about to go to ballet school, in London. By now she would have been gone. Didn't you know that?'

Damien almost howled, '*No!* I *said* that, I asked – you don't understand . . . She didn't care about being a dancer. She just liked everyone making a fuss of her. In that school, where she wouldn't have been anything special – she'd have dropped out by Christmas and come back *home*!'

Of all the things they had done to her, between them, this was the one that shocked me most profoundly. It was the diabolical expertise of it, the icy precision with which it targeted, annexed and defiled the one thing that had lain at Katy Devlin's heart. I thought of Simone's deep quiet voice in the echoing dance studio: *Sérieuse*. In all my career I had never felt the presence of evil as I felt it then: strong and rancid-sweet in the air, curling invisible tendrils up the table-legs, nosing with obscene delicacy at sleeves and throats. The hairs rose on the back of my neck.

'So it was self-defence,' Cassie said, after a silence in which Damien fidgeted anxiously and she and Sam didn't look at him.

Damien leaped on this. 'Yes. Exactly. I mean, we wouldn't even have thought of it if there'd have been any other way.'

'I understand. And you know, Damien, it's happened before: wives snapping and killing abusive husbands, stuff like that. Juries understand, too.'

'Yeah?' He looked up at her with huge, hopeful eyes.

'Course. Once they hear what Rosalind went through . . . I wouldn't worry too much about her. OK?'

'I just don't want her to get in any trouble.'

'Then you're doing the right thing by telling us all the details. OK?'

Damien sighed, a small, tired sigh with something like relief in it. 'OK.'

'Well done,' Cassie said. 'So let's keep going. When did you decide on this?'

'Like July. The middle of July.'

'And when did you set the date?'

'Only, like, a few days before it happened. I had said to Rosalind, she should make sure she had a, an alibi, you know? Because we knew you guys would look at the family, she had read somewhere that the family were always the main suspects. So this one night – I think it was Friday – we met up and she said to me, she'd arranged it so she and Jessica were sleeping over at their cousins' house the next

Monday and they'd be up till like two o'clock talking, so that would be the perfect night. All I had to do was make sure it was done before two o'clock; the, the police would be able to tell . . .'

His voice was shaking. 'And what did you say?' Cassie asked.

'I . . . I guess I sort of panicked. I mean, it hadn't seemed real up until then, you know? I guess I hadn't thought we were actually going to *do* it. It was just something we *talked* about. It was sort of like, you know Sean Callaghan, Sean from the dig? He used to be in this band only they broke up, and he's always talking about "Oh, when we get the band back together, when we make it big . . ." And, I mean, he knows they're never gonna *do* it, but talking about it makes him feel better.'

'We've all been in that band,' Cassie said, smiling.

Damien nodded. 'It was like that. But then Rosalind said, "Next Monday," and suddenly I felt like . . . it just seemed like a totally crazy thing to do, you know? I said to Rosalind, maybe we should go to the police or something, instead. But she freaked out. She kept saying, "I trusted you, I really trusted you . . ."'

'Trusted you,' Cassie said. 'But not enough to make love with you?'

'No,' Damien said softly, after a moment. 'No, see, she had. After we first decided, about Katy . . . it changed everything for Rosalind, knowing I'd do that for her. We . . . she'd given up hoping she'd ever be able to, but . . . she wanted to try. I was working on the dig by then, so I could afford a good hotel – she deserved something nice, you know? The first time, she . . . she couldn't. But we went back there the next week, and . . .' He bit his lips. He was trying not to cry, again.

'And after that,' Cassie said, 'you could hardly change your mind.'

'See, that was the thing. That night, when I said maybe we should go to the police, Rosalind – she thought I'd only ever said I'd do it so I could . . . could get her into bed. She's so fragile, she's been hurt so badly – I couldn't let her think I was just using her. Can you imagine what it would have *done* to her?'

Another silence. Damien wiped a hand hard across his eyes and got himself back under control.

'So you decided to go through with it,' Cassie said, evenly. He nodded, a painful, adolescent duck of the head. 'How did you get Katy to come to the site?'

'Rosalind told her she had this friend on the dig who'd found a, a thing . . .' He mimed vaguely. 'A locket. An old locket with a little painting of a dancer inside it. Rosalind told Katy it was really old and like magic or something, so she'd saved up all her money and bought it from the friend – me – as a present to bring Katy luck in ballet school. Only Katy would have to go get it herself, because this friend thought she was such a great dancer he wanted her autograph for when she was famous, and she'd have to go at night, because he wasn't allowed to sell finds, so it had to be a secret.'

I thought of Cassie, as a child, hovering at the door of a groundskeeper's shed: *Do you want marvels?* Children think differently, she had said. Katy had walked into danger the same way Cassie had: on the unmissable off-chance of magic.

'I mean, see what I mean?' Damien said, with a note of pleading in his voice. 'She totally believed that people were, like, queuing up for her autograph.'

'Actually,' Sam said, 'she'd every reason to believe that.

Plenty of people had asked for her autograph after the fundraiser.' Damien blinked at him.

'So what happened when she reached the finds shed?' Cassie asked.

He shrugged uncomfortably. 'Just what I already told you. I told her the locket was in this box on a shelf behind her, and when she turned around to get it, I . . . I just picked up the rock and . . . It was *self-defence*, like you said, or I mean defending Rosalind, I don't know what that's called—'

'What about the trowel?' Sam asked heavily. 'Was that self-defence too?'

He stared like a bunny in headlights. 'The . . . yeah. That. I mean, I couldn't . . . you know.' He swallowed hard. 'I couldn't *do* it to her. She was, she looked . . . I still dream about it. I couldn't do it. And then I saw the trowel on the desk, so I thought . . .'

'You were supposed to rape her? It's OK,' Cassie said gently, at the flash of queasy panic on Damien's face, 'we understand how this happened. You're not getting Rosalind into any trouble.'

Damien looked uncertain, but she held his eyes steadily. 'I guess,' he said, after a moment. He had turned that nasty greenish-white again. 'Rosalind said – she was just upset, but she said it wasn't fair that Katy would never know what Jessica had been through, so in the end I said I'd . . . Sorry, I think I'm gonna . . .' He made a sound between a cough and a gag.

'Breathe,' Cassie said. 'You're fine. You just need some water.' She took away the shredded cup, found him a new one and filled it; she squeezed his shoulder while he sipped it, holding it in both hands, and took deep breaths.

'There you go,' she said, when a little of the colour had

come back to his face. 'You're doing great. So you were supposed to rape Katy, but instead you just used the trowel after she was dead?'

'I chickened out,' Damien said into the water cup, low and savage. 'She'd done way worse stuff, but I chickened out.'

'Is that why' – Sam flicked the phone records with one finger – 'the calls between you and Rosalind dry up after Katy died? Two calls on the Tuesday, the day after the killing; one early Wednesday morning, one the next Tuesday, then nothing. Was Rosalind annoyed with you for letting her down?'

'I don't even know how she knew. I was scared to tell her. We'd said we wouldn't talk for a couple of weeks, so the police – you guys – wouldn't connect us up, but she texted me like a week later and said maybe we shouldn't get back in touch because obviously I didn't really care about her. I phoned her to find out what was wrong – and, yeah, of *course* she was mad!' He was babbling, his voice rising. 'I mean, we'll work it out – but, Jesus, she has every right to be mad at me. Katy wasn't even found till Wednesday 'cause I panicked, that could've totally ruined her alibi, and I hadn't . . . I hadn't . . . She trusted me so much, she didn't have anyone else, and I couldn't even do one thing right 'cause I'm a fucking wimp.'

Cassie didn't answer. Her back was to me; I saw the frail knobs of bone at the top of her spine and I felt grief like a solid weight dragging in my wrists and throat. I couldn't listen any more. That little gem about Katy dancing for attention had knocked all the anger out of me, knocked me hollow. All I wanted to do was sleep, drugged obliterated sleep, let someone wake me when this day was over and the steady rain had washed all this away.

'You know something?' Damien said softly, just before I left. 'We were going to get married. As soon as Jessica had, like, recovered enough that Rosalind could leave her there. I guess that's not going to happen now, right?'

They were with him all day. I knew what they were doing, more or less: they had the gist of the story, now they were going back over it, filling in times and dates and details, checking for any tiny gap or inconsistency. Getting a confession is only the beginning; after that you need to waterproof it, second-guess defence lawyers and juries, make sure you get everything in writing while your guy is feeling talkative and before he has a chance to come up with alternative explanations. Sam is the painstaking type; they would do a good job.

Sweeney and O'Gorman came in and out of the incident room: Rosalind's mobile records, more background interviews about her and about Damien. I sent them to the interview room. O'Kelly stuck his head in and scowled at me, and I pretended to be deep in phone tips. Halfway through the afternoon Quigley came in to share his thoughts on the case. Quite apart from the fact that I had no desire to talk to anyone, least of all him, this was a very bad sign: Quigley's one talent is an unerring nose for weakness, and, apart from the odd embarrassing attempt to ingratiate himself, he had generally left me and Cassie alone and stuck to battening on newbies and burnouts and those whose careers had taken sudden nosedives. He pulled his chair too close to mine and hinted darkly that we should have caught our man weeks earlier, intimated that he would explain how this could have been done if I asked with sufficient deference, sadly pointed out my unconscionable psychological error in allowing Sam to take my place in the interrogation, enquired about Damien's phone records and then cunningly suggested we should consider the possibility that the sister had been involved. I seemed to have forgotten how to get rid of him, and this increased my sense that his presence was not just annoying but horribly ominous. He was like a huge smug albatross waddling around my desk, squawking vacuously and crapping all over my paperwork.

Finally, like the bullies in school, he seemed to recognise that I was too wretched to provide value for money, so he bridled back to whatever he was supposed to be doing, an offended look spread over his large flat features. I gave up on any pretence of filing the phone tips and went to the window, where I spent the next few hours staring out at the rain and listening to the faint, familiar noises of the squad behind me: Bernadette laughing, phones ringing, the rise of arguing male voices suddenly muffled by a slamming door.

It was twenty past seven when I finally heard Cassie and Sam coming down the corridor. Their voices were too subdued and sporadic for me to make out any words, but I recognised the tones. It's funny, the things a change of perspective can make you notice; I hadn't realised how deep Sam's voice was, till I listened to him interviewing Damien.

'I want to go home,' Cassie said as they came into the incident room. She dropped into a chair and rested her forehead on the heels of her hands.

'Nearly over,' Sam said. It wasn't clear whether he meant the day or the investigation. He went around the table to his seat; on the way, to my utter surprise, he laid his hand briefly, lightly, on Cassie's head.

'How did it go?' I asked, hearing the stilted note in my voice.

Cassie didn't move. 'Grand,' Sam said. He rubbed his eyes, grimacing. 'I think we're sorted, as far as Donnelly goes, anyway.'

The phone rang. I picked it up: Bernadette, telling us all to stay in the incident room, O'Kelly wanted to see us. Sam nodded and sat down heavily, feet planted apart, like a farmer coming in from a hard day's work; Cassie lifted her head with an effort and fumbled in her back pocket for her rolled-up notebook.

Sort of characteristically, O'Kelly kept us waiting for a while. None of us spoke. Cassie doodled in her notebook, a spiky, vaguely sinister tree; Sam slumped at the table and gazed unseeingly at the crowded whiteboard; I leaned against the window frame looking out at the dark formal garden below, sudden little gusts of wind running through the bushes. Our positions around the room felt staged somehow, significant in some obscure but ominous way; the flicker and hum of the fluorescent lights had put me into an almost trancelike state and I was starting to feel as if we were in some existentialist play, where the ticking clock would stay at 7.38 forever and we would never be able to move from these predestined poses. When O'Kelly finally banged through the door, it came as something of a shock.

'First things first,' he said grimly, pulling up a chair and slapping a pile of paperwork on the table. 'O'Neill. Remind me: what are you going to do with this whole Andrews mess?'

'Drop it,' Sam said quietly. He looked very tired. It wasn't that he had bags under his eyes or anything like that, to anyone who didn't know him he would have seemed fine, but his healthy rural ruddiness was gone and he looked somehow terribly young and vulnerable.

'Very good. Maddox, I'm docking you five days' holiday.'

Cassie glanced up briefly. 'Yes, sir.' I checked, covertly, to see whether Sam looked startled or whether he already knew what this was all about, but his face gave away nothing.

'And Ryan, you're on desk duty until further notice. I don't know how the hell you three works of art managed to pick up Damien Donnelly, but you can thank your lucky stars that you did, or your careers would be in even worse shape than they are. Are we clear?'

None of us had the energy to answer. I detached myself from the window frame and took a seat, as far from everyone else as possible.

O'Kelly gave us a filthy look and decided to take our silence for acquiescence. 'Right. Where are we on Donnelly?'

'I'd say we're doing well,' Sam said, when it became clear that neither of us was going to say anything. 'Full confession, including details that weren't released, and a fair bit of forensic evidence. I'd say his only chance of getting off would be to plead insanity – and that's what he'll do, if he gets a good lawyer. Just now he's feeling so bad about it, he wants to plead guilty, but that'll wear off after a few days in gaol.'

'That insanity shite shouldn't be allowed,' O'Kelly said bitterly. 'Some eejit getting up on the stand and saying, "It's not his fault, Your Honour, his mammy toilet-trained him too early so he couldn't help killing that wee girl . . ." It's a load of my arse. He's no more insane than I am. Get one of ours to examine him and say so.' Sam nodded and made a note.

O'Kelly flipped through his papers and waved a report at us. 'Now. What's all this about the sister?'

The air in the room tightened. 'Rosalind Devlin,' Cassie said, raising her head. 'She and Damien were seeing each other. From what he says, the murder was her idea; she pressured him into it.'

'Yeah, right. Why?'

'According to Damien,' Cassie said evenly, 'Rosalind told him that Jonathan Devlin was sexually abusing all three of his daughters, and physically abusing Rosalind and Jessica. Katy, who was his favourite, encouraged and often incited the abuse against the other two. Rosalind said that, if Katy was eliminated, the abuse would stop.'

'Any evidence backing this up?'

'On the contrary. Damien says Rosalind told him Devlin had fractured her skull and broken Jessica's arm, but there's nothing like that on their medical records – nothing that indicates any kind of abuse, in fact. And Katy, after supposedly having regular sexual intercourse with her father for years, died *virgo intacta*.'

'So why are you wasting our time on this bullshit?' O'Kelly slapped the report. 'We've got our man, Maddox. Go home and let the lawyers sort out the rest.'

'Because it's Rosalind's bullshit, not Damien's,' Cassie said, and for the first time there was a faint spark in her voice. 'Someone made Katy sick for years; that wasn't Damien. The first time she was about to go off to ballet school, long before Damien knew she existed, someone made her so sick she had to turn down the place. Someone put it into Damien's head to kill a girl he'd barely seen – you said it yourself, sir, he's not insane: he didn't hear little voices telling him to do it. Rosalind's the only person who fits.'

'What's her motive?'

'She couldn't stand the fact that Katy was getting all the attention and admiration. Sir, I'd put a lot of money on this. I think that years ago, as soon as she realised Katy had a serious talent for ballet, Rosalind started poisoning her. It's horribly easy to do: bleach, emetics, plain table salt – your average household has several dozen things that can give a little girl some mysterious gastric disorder, if you can just convince her to take them. Maybe you tell her it's a secret medicine, it'll make her better; and if she's only eight or nine, and you're her big sister, she'll probably believe you . . . But when Katy got her second chance at ballet school, she stopped being convinced. She was twelve now, old enough to start questioning what she was told. She refused to take the stuff any more. That – topped off by the newspaper article and the fund-raiser and the fact that Katy was becoming Knocknaree's main celebrity – was the last straw: she had actually dared to defy Rosalind outright, and Rosalind wasn't going to allow that. When she met Damien, she saw her chance. The poor little bastard is a born patsy; he's not all that bright, and he'd do anything to make someone happy. She spent the next few months using sex, sob stories, flattery, guilt trips, everything at her disposal, to persuade him that he had to kill Katy. And finally, by last month, she had him so dazed and hyped up that he felt like he didn't have any other choice. Actually, he probably *was* a little insane by that time.'

'Don't be saying that outside this room,' O'Kelly said sharply and automatically. Cassie moved, something like a shrug, and went back to her drawing.

A silence fell over the room. The story was a hideous one in itself, ancient as Cain and Abel but with all its own brand-new jagged edges, and it is impossible for me to describe the mixture of emotions with which I had heard Cassie tell it. I had been looking not at her but at our frail silhouettes in the window, but there was no way to avoid listening. She has a very beautiful speaking voice, Cassie, low and flexible and woodwind; but the words she said seemed to crawl hissing up the walls, spin sticky dark trails of shadow across the lights, nest in tangled webs in the high corners.

'Got any evidence?' O'Kelly demanded, finally. 'Or are you just going on Donnelly's word?'

'No hard evidence, no,' Cassie said. 'We can prove the connection between Damien and Rosalind – we've got calls between their mobiles – and they both gave us the same fake lead about some non-existent guy in a tracksuit, which means she was an accessory after the fact, but there's no proof that she even knew about the murder beforehand.'

'Of course there isn't,' he said flatly. 'Why did I ask. Are you all three on board with this? Or is this just Maddox's personal little crusade?'

'I'm with Detective Maddox, sir,' Sam said firmly and promptly. 'I've been interrogating Donnelly all day, and I think he's telling the truth.'

O'Kelly sighed, exasperated, and jerked his chin at me. Obviously he felt Cassie and Sam were being gratuitously difficult, he just wanted to finish Damien's paperwork and declare this case closed; but in spite of his best efforts he is not a despot at heart, and he wouldn't override his team's unanimous opinion. I felt for him, really: I was presumably the last person he wanted to look to for support.

Finally – somehow I couldn't bear to say it out loud – I nodded. 'Brilliant,' O'Kelly said wearily. 'That's just brilliant. All right. Donnelly's story's barely enough for us to charge her, never mind convict her. We need to get a confession. What age is she?'

'Eighteen,' I said. I hadn't spoken in so long that my voice came out as a startled croak; I cleared my throat. 'Eighteen.'

'Thank Christ for small mercies. At least we don't have to have the parents there when we interrogate her. Right: O'Neill and Maddox, pull her in, go at her as hard as you can, scare the bejasus out of her till she cracks.'

'Won't work,' Cassie said, adding another branch to the tree. 'Psychopaths have very low anxiety levels. You'd have to stick a gun to her head to scare her that badly.'

'Psychopaths?' I said, after a startled instant.

'Jesus, Maddox,' O'Kelly said, annoyed. 'Less of the Hollywood. She didn't *eat* the sister.'

Cassie glanced up from her doodle, her eyebrows lifting into cool, delicate arcs. 'I wasn't talking about movie psychos. She fits the clinical definition. No conscience, no empathy, pathological liar, manipulative, charming, intuitive, attention-seeking, easily bored, narcissistic, turns very nasty when she's thwarted in any way . . . I'm sure I'm forgetting a few of the criteria, but does that sound about right?'

'That's enough to be going on with,' Sam said drily. 'Hang on; so even if we go to trial, she'll get off on insanity?' O'Kelly mumbled something disgusted, no doubt to do with psychology in general and Cassie in particular.

'She's perfectly sane,' Cassie said crisply. 'Any psychiatrist will say so. It's not a mental illness.'

'How long have you known this?' I asked.

Her eyes flicked to me. 'I started wondering the first time we met her. It didn't seem relevant to the case: the killer clearly wasn't a psychopath, and she had a perfect alibi. I considered telling you anyway, but do you really think you would have believed me?'

You should have trusted me, I almost said. I saw Sam look back and forth between us, perplexed and unsettled.

'Anyway,' Cassie said, going back to her sketching, 'there's no point in trying to scare a confession out of her. Psychopaths don't really do fear; mainly just aggression, boredom or pleasure.'

'OK,' Sam said. 'Fair enough. Then what about the other sister – Jessica, is it? Would she know anything?'

'Quite possibly,' I said. 'They're close.' One corner of Cassie's mouth went up wryly at the word I had chosen.

'Ah, Jesus,' O'Kelly said. 'She's twelve, am I right? That means the parents.'

'Actually,' Cassie said, not looking up, 'I doubt talking to Jessica would be any use either. She's completely under Rosalind's control. Whatever Rosalind's done to her, she's so punch-drunk that she can hardly think for herself. If we find a way to charge Rosalind, yeah, we might get something out of Jessica sooner or later; but as long as Rosalind's in that house, she'll be too terrified of saying something wrong to say anything at all.'

O'Kelly lost patience. He hates being baffled, and the charged, criss-crossing tensions in the room must have been setting his teeth on edge just as badly as the case itself. 'That's great, Maddox. Thanks for that. So what the hell do you suggest? Come on; let's hear you come up with something useful, instead of sitting there shooting down everyone else's ideas.'

Cassie stopped drawing and carefully balanced her pen across one finger. 'OK,' she said. 'Psychopaths get their kicks by having power over other people – manipulating them, inflicting pain. I think we should try playing to that. Give her all the power she can eat, and see if she gets carried away.'

'What are you talking about?'

'Last night,' Cassie said slowly, 'Rosalind accused me of sleeping with Detective Ryan.'

Sam's head turned sharply towards me. I kept my eyes on O'Kelly. 'Oh, I hadn't forgotten, believe me,' he said heavily. 'And it bloody well better not be true. You two are both in deep enough shite already.'

'No,' Cassie said, a trifle wearily, 'it's not true. She was just trying to distract me and hoping she would hit a nerve. She didn't, but she doesn't know that for sure; I could just have been covering very well.'

'So?' O'Kelly demanded.

'So,' Cassie said, 'I could go talk to her, admit that Detective Ryan and I have a long-standing affair, and beg her not to turn us in – maybe tell her we suspect she was involved in Katy's death and offer to tell her how much we know in exchange for her silence, something like that.'

O'Kelly snorted. 'And what, you think she'll just spill her guts?'

She shrugged. 'I don't see why not. Yeah, most people hate to admit they've done something terrible, even if they won't get in trouble for it; but that's because they feel bad about it, and because they don't want other people to think less of them. To this girl, other people aren't real, any more than characters in a video game, and right and wrong are just words. It's not like she feels any guilt or remorse or anything about having Damien kill Katy. In fact, I'm willing to bet she's over the moon with herself. This is her greatest achievement yet, and she hasn't been able to brag to anyone about it. If she's sure she has the upper hand, and she's sure I'm not wearing a wire – and would I wear a wire to admit to sleeping with my partner? – I think she'll jump at the chance. The thought of telling a detective exactly what she did, knowing there's not a thing I can do about it, knowing it must be killing me . . . It'll be one of the most delicious buzzes of her life. She won't be able to resist.'

'She can say whatever she bloody well likes,' O'Kelly said. 'Without a caution, none of it will be admissible.'

'So I'll caution her.'

'And you think she'll keep talking? I thought you said the girl's not crazy.'

'I don't *know*,' Cassie said. She sounded, just for a second, exhausted and openly pissed off, and it made her seem very young, like a teenager unable to conceal her frustration with the idiotic adult world. 'I just think it's our best shot. If we go for a formal interview, she'll be on her guard, she'll sit there and deny everything, and we'll have blown our shot: she'll go home knowing there's no way we can pin anything on her. This way, at least there's a chance she'll figure I can't prove anything and take the risk of talking.'

O'Kelly was grating a thumbnail, monotonously and infuriatingly, over the fake-wood grain of the table; he was obviously thinking about it. 'If we do it, you wear a wire. I'm not risking this on your word against hers.'

'I wouldn't have it any other way,' Cassie said coolly.

'Cassie,' Sam said very gently, leaning forward across the table, 'are you sure you're able for this?' I felt a sudden flare of anger, no less painful for being utterly unjustifiable: it should have been my place, not his, to ask the question.

'I'll be fine,' Cassie told him, with a little one-sided smile. 'Hey, I did undercover for months and never got spotted once. Oscar material, me.'

I didn't think this was what Sam had been asking. Just telling me about that guy in college had left her practically catatonic, and I could see that same distant, dilated look starting in her eyes again, hear the too-detached note in her voice. I thought of that first evening, across the stalled Vespa: how I had wanted to sweep her under my coat, protect her even from the rain.

'I could do it,' I said, too loudly. 'Rosalind likes me.'

'No,' O'Kelly snapped, 'you couldn't.'

Cassie rubbed her eyes with finger and thumb, pinched the bridge of her nose as if she had a headache starting. 'No offence,' she said flatly, 'but Rosalind Devlin doesn't like you any more than she likes me. She's not capable of that emotion. She finds you useful. She knows she has you wrapped around her little finger – or had you; whichever – and she's sure you're the one cop who, if it comes to it, will believe she's been wrongfully accused and fight her corner. Believe me, there's not a chance in hell she's going to throw that away by confessing to you. Me, I'm no use to her anyway; she has nothing to lose by talking to me. She knows I dislike her, but that just means she'll get an extra thrill out of having me at her mercy.'

'All right,' O'Kelly said, shoving his stuff into a pile and pushing back his chair. 'Let's do it. Maddox, I hope to God you know what you're talking about. First thing tomorrow morning, we'll get you wired up and you can go have a girly chat with Rosalind Devlin. I'll make sure they give you something voice-activated, so you can't forget to hit Record.'

'No,' Cassie said. 'No recorder. I want a transmitter, feeding to a back-up van less than two hundred yards away.'

'To interview an eighteen-year-old kid?' O'Kelly said contemptuously. 'Have some balls, Maddox. This isn't Al-Qaeda here.'

'To go one-on-one with a psychopath who just murdered her little sister.'

'She's got no history of violence herself,' I said. I didn't intend it to sound bitchy, but Cassie's eyes passed briefly over me, with no expression in them at all, as if I didn't exist.

'Transmitter and back-up,' she repeated.

I didn't go home that night until three in the morning, when I could be sure that Heather would be asleep. Instead I drove out to Bray, to the seafront, and sat there in the car. It had finally stopped raining and the night was dense with mist; the tide was in, I could hear the slap and rush of the water, but I caught only the odd glimpse of the waves between the swirls of erasing grey. The gay little pavilion drifted in and out of existence like something from Brigadoon. Somewhere a foghorn sounded one melancholy note over and over, and people walking home along the seafront materialised gradually out of nothingness, silhouettes floating in mid-air like dark messengers.

I thought about a lot of things, that night. I thought of Cassie in Lyon, just a girl in an apron, serving coffee at sunny outdoor tables and bantering in French with the customers. I thought of my parents getting ready to go out dancing: the careful lines my father's comb left in his Brylcreemed hair, the rousing scent of my mother's perfume and her flower-patterned dress whisking out the door. I thought of Jonathan and Cathal and Shane, long-limbed and rash and laughing fiercely over their lighter games; of Sam at a big wooden table amid seven noisy brothers and sisters, and of Damien in some hushed college library filling out an application for a job at Knocknaree. I thought of Mark's reckless eyes – *The only things I believe in are out on that there dig* – and then of revolutionaries waving ragged, gallant banners, of refugees swimming swift night-time currents; of all those who hold life so light, or the stakes so dear, that they can walk steady and open-eyed to meet the thing that will take or transform their lives and whose high cold criteria are far beyond our understanding. I tried, for a long time, to remember bringing my mother wild flowers.

24

O'Kelly has always been something of a mystery to me. He disliked Cassie, despised her theory and basically thought she was being an irredeemable pain in the arse; but The Squad has a deep, almost totemistic significance to him, and once he has resigned himself to backing one of its members he backs him, or even her, all the way. He gave Cassie her transmitter and her back-up van, even though he considered it a complete waste of time and resources. When I got in the next morning – very early; we wanted to catch Rosalind before she left for school – Cassie was in the incident room, being fitted with the wire.

'And take off the jumper, please,' the surveillance tech said quietly. He was small and blank-faced, with deft, professional hands. Cassie pulled her jumper over her head obediently, like a child at the doctor's office. Underneath she was wearing what looked like a boy's thermal vest. She had left off the defiant make-up she had been using for the past few days, and there were dark smudges under her eyes. I wondered whether she'd slept at all; I thought of her sitting on her windowsill with her T-shirt pulled around her knees, the tiny red glow of a cigarette blooming and fading as she drew on it, watching dawn lighten the gardens below. Sam was at the window, his back to us; O'Kelly was fussing with the whiteboard, erasing lines and redrawing them. 'And run the wire up under the T-shirt for me, please,' said the tech.

'You've phone tips waiting for you,' O'Kelly told me.

'I want to go with you,' I said. Sam's shoulders shifted; Cassie, head bent over the microphone, didn't look up.

'When hell freezes over and the camels come skating home,' O'Kelly said.

I was so tired that I was seeing everything through a fine, seething white mist. 'I want to go,' I repeated. This time everyone ignored me.

The tech clipped the battery pack to Cassie's jeans, made a tiny incision in the neck hem of her undershirt and slid the mike inside. He had her put her jumper back on – Sam and O'Kelly turned around – and then told her to talk. When she looked at him blankly, O'Kelly said impatiently, 'Just say whatever comes into your head, Maddox, tell us your plans for the weekend if you want,' but instead she recited a poem. It was an old-fashioned little poem, the kind of thing one might learn off by heart in school. Long afterwards, flicking through pages in a dusty bookshop, I came across these lines:

> About your easy heads my prayers
> I said with syllables of clay.
> What gift, I asked, shall I bring now
> Before I weep and walk away?
>
> Take, they replied, the oak and laurel.
> Take our fortune of tears and live
> Like a spendthrift lover. All we ask
> Is the one gift you cannot give.

Her voice was low and even, expressionless. The speakers hollowed it out, underlaid it with a whispery echo, and in the background there was a rushing sound like some far-away high wind. I thought of those ghost stories where the voices of the dead come to their loved ones from crackly radios or down telephone lines, borne on some lost wave-length across the laws of nature and the wild spaces of the universe. The tech fiddled delicately with mysterious little dials and sliders.

'Thank you for that, Maddox, that was very moving,' O'Kelly said, when the tech was satisfied. 'Right: here's the estate.' He slapped Sam's map with the back of his hand. 'We'll be in the van, parked in Knocknaree Crescent, first left inside the front entrance. Maddox, you'll go in on that motorbike yoke, park in front of the Devlins' and get the girl to come out for a walk. You'll go out the back gate of the estate and turn right, away from the dig, then right again along the side wall, to come out on the main road, and right again towards the front entrance. If you deviate from this route at any point, say so for the mike. Give your location as often as you can. When – Jesus, *if* – you've cautioned her and got enough for an arrest, arrest her. If you think she's sussed you or you're not going to get anywhere, wind it up and get out. If you need back-up at any point, say so and we'll come in. If she has a weapon, identify it for the mike – "Put the knife down," whatever. You don't have eyewitnesses, so don't pull your weapon unless you've no choice.'

'I'm not taking my gun,' Cassie said. She unbuckled her holster, handed it to Sam and held out her arms. 'Check me.'

'For what?' Sam said, puzzled, looking down at the gun in his hands.

'Weapons.' Her eyes slid away, unfocused, over his shoulder. 'If she says anything, she's going to claim I had her at gunpoint. Check my scooter, too, before I get on it.'

To this day I'm not sure how I managed to get myself into that van. Possibly it was because, even in disgrace, I was still Cassie's partner, a relationship for which almost every detective has a reflexive, deeply ingrained respect. Possibly it was because I bombarded O'Kelly with the first technique every toddler learns: if you ask someone often enough for long enough, when he is trying to do enough other things, sooner or later he will say yes just to shut you up. I was too desperate to care about the humiliation of this. Possibly he realised that, if he had refused, I would have taken the Land Rover and gone down there on my own.

The van was one of those blind, sinister-looking white things that regularly show up in police reports, with the name and logo of a fictitious tile company on the side. Inside it was even creepier: thick black cables coiling everywhere and the equipment blinking and hissing, ineffectual little overhead light, the soundproofing giving it the unsettling look of a padded cell. Sweeney drove; Sam, O'Kelly, the tech and I sat in the back compartment, swaying on uncomfortable low benches, not talking. O'Kelly had brought along a thermos of coffee and some kind of glutinous pastry, which he ate in huge methodical bites with no evidence of enjoyment. Sam scraped at an imaginary stain on the knee of his trousers. I cracked my knuckles, until I realised how irritating this was, and tried to ignore the intensity with which I wanted a cigarette. The tech did the *Irish Times* crossword.

We parked in Knocknaree Crescent and O'Kelly rang Cassie's mobile. She was within range of the equipment; her voice, over the speakers, was cool and steady. 'Maddox.'

'Where are you?' O'Kelly demanded.

'Just coming up to the estate. I didn't want to be hanging around.'

'We're in position. Go ahead.'

A tiny pause; then Cassie said, 'Yes, sir,' and hung up. I heard the buzz of the Vespa starting up again, then the weird stereo effect as, a minute later, it passed the end of the Crescent, only a few yards from us. The tech folded away his newspaper and made a minuscule adjustment to something; O'Kelly, across from me, pulled a plastic bag of pick-and-mix sweets out of his pocket and settled back on the bench.

Footsteps jolting the mike, the faint tasteful ding-dong of the doorbell. O'Kelly waved the bag of sweets at the rest of us; when there were no takers, he shrugged and fished out an iced caramel.

The click of the door opening. 'Detective Maddox,' Rosalind said, not sounding pleased. 'I'm afraid we're all very busy at the moment.'

'I know,' Cassie said. 'I'm really sorry to bother you. But could I . . . Is there any chance I could talk to you for a minute?'

'You had your chance to talk to me the other night. Instead, you insulted me and ruined my evening. I really don't feel like wasting any more of my time on you.'

'I'm sorry about that. I didn't – I shouldn't have done that. But this isn't about the case. I just . . . I need to ask you something.'

Silence, and I pictured Rosalind holding the door open and staring at her, gauging; Cassie's face upturned and tense, her hands deep in the pockets of her suede jacket. In the background someone – Margaret – called something. Rosalind snapped, 'It's for me, Mother,' and the door slammed shut.

'Well?' Rosalind enquired.

'Could we . . .' A rustle: Cassie shifting nervously. 'Could we maybe go for a walk or something? This is pretty private.'

That must have piqued Rosalind's interest, but her voice didn't change. 'I'm actually getting ready to go out.'

'Just five minutes. We can walk round the back of the estate, or something . . . Please, Miss Devlin. It's important.'

Finally she sighed. 'All right. I suppose I can give you a few minutes.'

'Thanks,' Cassie said, 'I really appreciate it,' and we heard them going down the pathway again, the swift decisive taps of Rosalind's heels.

It was a sweet morning, a soft morning; the sun was skimming off last night's mist, but there had still been wispy layers, over the grass and hazing the high cool sky, when we got into the van. The speakers magnified the twitter of blackbirds, the creak and clank of the estate's back gate, then Cassie's and Rosalind's feet swishing through the wet grass along the edge of the wood. I thought of how beautiful they would look, to some early watcher: Cassie windblown and easy, Rosalind fluttering white and slender as something from a poem; two girls in the September morning, glossy heads under the turning leaves and rabbits scampering away from their approach.

'Can I ask you something?' Cassie said.

'Well, I did think that was why we were *here*,' Rosalind said, with a delicate inflexion implying that Cassie was wasting her valuable time.

'Yeah. Sorry.' Cassie took a breath. 'OK. I was wondering: how did you know about . . .'

'Yes?' Rosalind prompted politely.

'About me and Detective Ryan.' Silence. 'That we were
. . . having an affair.'

'Oh, that!' Rosalind laughed: a tinkling little sound,
emotionless, barely even a speck of triumph. 'Oh, Detective Maddox. How do you think?'

'I thought probably you guessed. Or something. That
maybe we didn't hide it as well as we thought. But it just
seemed . . . I couldn't stop wondering.'

'Well, you *were* a little bit obvious, weren't you?' Mischievous, chiding. 'But no. Believe it or not, Detective
Maddox, I don't spend a lot of my time thinking about you
and your love life.'

Silence again. O'Kelly picked caramel out of his teeth.
'Then how?' Cassie said finally, with an awful note of
dread.

'Detective Ryan told me, of course,' Rosalind said
sweetly. I felt Sam's eyes and O'Kelly's flicking to me,
and bit the inside of my cheek to stop myself denying it.

This is not an easy thing to admit, but until that moment
I had held out some craven speck of hope that this had all
been a hideous misunderstanding. A boy who would say
anything he thought you wanted to hear, a girl made
vicious by trauma and grief and my rejection on top of
it all; we could have misinterpreted in any one of a hundred
ways. It was only in that moment, in the ease of that
gratuitous lie, that I understood that Rosalind – the Rosalind I had known, the bruised, captivating, unpredictable
girl with whom I had laughed in the Central and held hands
on a bench – had never existed. Everything she had ever
shown me had been constructed for effect, with the absorbed, calculating care that goes into an actor's costume.
Underneath the myriad shimmering veils, this was something as simple and deadly as razor wire.

'That's bollocks!' Cassie's voice cracked. 'He would *never* fucking tell—'

'Don't you dare swear at me,' Rosalind snapped.

'Sorry,' Cassie said, subdued, after a moment. 'I was just – I just didn't expect that. I never thought he would tell anyone. Ever.'

'Well, he did. You should be more careful about who you trust. Is that all you wanted to ask me?'

'No. I need to ask you a favour.' Movement: Cassie running a hand through her hair, or across her face. 'It's against the rules, to – to fraternise with your partner. If our boss finds out, we could both get fired, or reverted back to uniform. And this job . . . this job means a lot to us. To both of us. We worked like crazy to get onto this squad. It would break our hearts to be thrown off it.'

'You should have thought of that before, shouldn't you?'

'I know,' Cassie said, 'I know. But is there any chance you could – just not say anything about this? To anyone?'

'Cover up your little affair. Is that what you mean?'

'I . . . yeah. I suppose so.'

'I'm not sure why you feel I should do you any favours,' Rosalind said coolly. 'You've been horribly rude to me every time we've met – until now, when you want something from me. I don't like users.'

'I'm sorry if I was rude,' Cassie said. Her voice sounded strained, too high and too fast. 'I really am. I think I felt – I don't know, threatened by you . . . I shouldn't have taken it out on you. I apologise.'

'You did owe me an apology, actually, but that's beside the point. I don't mind the way you insulted *me*, but if you could treat me that way, I'm sure you do it to other people too, don't you? I don't know if I should protect someone who behaves so unprofessionally. I'll have to have a little think about whether it's my duty to tell your supervisors what you're really like.'

'The little bitch,' Sam said softly, not looking up.

'She wants a boot up the hole,' O'Kelly muttered. Despite himself, he was starting to look interested. 'If I'd ever given that kind of cheek to someone twice my age . . .'

'Look,' Cassie said desperately, 'it's not just about me. What about Detective Ryan? He's never been rude to you, has he? He's mad about you.'

Rosalind laughed, modestly. 'Is he really?'

'Yeah,' Cassie said. 'Yeah, he is.'

She pretended to think about it. 'Well . . . I suppose if you were the one chasing him, then the affair wasn't really his fault. It might not be fair to make him suffer for it.'

'I guess I was.' I could hear the humiliation, stark and uncamouflaged, in Cassie's voice. 'I was the . . . I was always the one who initiated everything.'

'And how long has this been going on?'

'Five years,' Cassie said, 'off and on.' Five years earlier Cassie and I had never met, hadn't even been posted in the same part of the country, and I realised suddenly that this was for O'Kelly's benefit, to prove herself a liar in case he had any lingering suspicions about us; realised, for the first time, quite what a fine and double-edged game she was playing.

'I would need to know it was over, of course,' Rosalind said, 'before I could think about covering up for you.'

'It's already over. I swear, it is. He . . . he ended it a couple of weeks ago. For good, this time.'

'Oh? Why?'

'I don't want to talk about it.'

'Well, that's not really your choice.'

Cassie took a breath. 'I don't know why,' she said. 'That's the honest-to-God truth. I've tried my best to ask him, but he just says it's complicated, he's mixed up, he's not able for a relationship right now – I don't know if there's someone else, or . . . We're not speaking to each other any more. He won't even look at me. I don't know what to do.' Her voice was trembling badly.

'Listen to that,' O'Kelly said, not quite admiringly. 'Maddox missed her calling. Should've gone on the stage.'

But she wasn't acting, and Rosalind smelled it. 'Well,' she said, and I heard the tiny smirk in her voice, 'I can't say I'm surprised. He certainly doesn't talk about you like a lover.'

'What's he say about me?' Cassie asked, helplessly, after a second. She was flashing her unarmoured spots to draw the blows; she was deliberately letting Rosalind hurt her, maul her, delicately peel back layers of pain to feed on them at her leisure. I felt sick to my stomach.

Rosalind held the pause, making her wait. 'He says you're terribly needy,' she said, at last. Her voice was high and sweet and clear, unchanging. ' "Desperate" was the word he used. That's why you were so obnoxious to me: because you were jealous of how much he cares about me. He did his best to be nice about it – I think he felt sorry for you – but he was getting very tired of putting up with your behaviour.'

'That's bollocks,' I hissed furiously, unable to stop myself. 'I *never*—'

'Shut up,' Sam said, at the same moment as O'Kelly snapped, 'Who gives a fuck?'

'Quiet, please,' said the tech politely.

'I did warn him about you,' Rosalind said, reflectively. 'So he finally took my advice?'

'Yeah,' Cassie said, very low and shaky. 'I guess he did.'

'Oh my God.' A tiny note of amusement. 'You're really in love with him, aren't you?'

Nothing.

'Aren't you?'

'I don't know.' Cassie's voice sounded thick and painful, but it wasn't until she blew her nose wetly that I understood that she was crying. I had never seen her cry. 'I never thought about it until – I just – I've never been that close to anyone. And now I can't even think straight, I can't . . .'

'Oh, Detective Maddox.' Rosalind sighed. 'If you can't be honest with me, at least be honest with yourself.'

'I can't *tell*.' Cassie was barely getting the words out. 'Maybe I . . .' Her throat closed up.

The van felt subterranean, nightmarish, walls tilting dizzily inwards. The disembodied quality of the voices lent them an added knife-edge of horror, as if we were eavesdropping on two lost ghosts locked in some eternal and unalterable battle of wills. The door handle was invisible in the shadows, and I caught O'Kelly's hard warning glance. 'You wanted to be here, Ryan,' he said.

I couldn't breathe. 'I should go in.'

'And do what? It's going according to plan, for whatever that's worth. Settle.'

A small, terrible catch of breath, on the speakers. 'No,' I said. 'Listen.'

'She's doing her job,' Sam said. His face was unreadable in the dirty yellow light. 'Sit down.'

The tech raised a finger. 'I wish you'd control yourself,' Rosalind said, with distaste. 'It's awfully hard to have a sensible conversation with someone who's hysterical.'

'Sorry.' Cassie blew her nose again, swallowed hard. 'Look – please. It's over, it wasn't Detective Ryan's fault, and he'd do anything for you. He trusted you enough to tell you. Couldn't you just – leave it? Not tell anyone? Please?'

'Well.' Rosalind considered this. 'Detective Ryan and I were very close, for a while. But the last time I saw him, he was awfully rude to me, too. And he lied to me about those two friends of his. I don't like liars. No, Detective Maddox. I'm afraid I really don't feel that I owe either of you any favours at all.'

'OK,' Cassie said, 'OK. OK. Then what if I could do something for you, in exchange?'

A little laugh. 'I can't think of anything I could possibly want from you.'

'No, there is. Just give me five more minutes, OK? We can cut down this side of the estate, down to the main road. There is something I can do for you. I swear.'

Rosalind sighed. 'You've got until we get back to my house. But you know, Detective Maddox, some of us do have morals. If I decide I have a responsibility to tell your superiors about this, you won't be able to bribe me into keeping quiet.'

'Not a bribe. Just – help.'

'From *you*?' That laugh again; the cool little trill I had found so enchanting. I realised I was digging my nails into my palms.

'Two days ago,' Cassie said, 'we arrested Damien Donnelly for Katy's murder.'

A fraction of a pause. Sam leaned forward, elbows on his knees. Then: 'Well. It's about time you took your mind off your love life and paid some attention to my sister's case. Who's Damien Donnelly?'

'He says he was your boyfriend, up until a few weeks ago.'

'Well, obviously, he wasn't. If he had been my boyfriend, I think I would have heard of him; don't you?'

'There are records,' Cassie said carefully, 'of a lot of phone calls between your mobiles.'

Rosalind's voice froze over. 'If you want a favour from me, Detective, then accusing me of being a liar isn't really the best way to go about it.'

'I'm not accusing you of anything,' Cassie said, and for a second I thought her voice would crack again. 'I'm just saying that I know this is your personal business, and you don't have any reason to trust me with it—'

'That's certainly true.'

'But I'm trying to explain how I can help you. See, Damien does trust me. He talked to me.'

After a moment, Rosalind sniffed. 'I wouldn't be too excited about that. Damien will talk to anyone who'll listen. It doesn't make you special.'

Sam nodded, one quick jerk: *Step one.*

'I know. I know. But the thing is, he told me why he did this. He says he did it for you. Because you asked him to.'

Nothing, for a long time.

'That's why I asked you to come in,' Cassie said, 'the other night. I was going to question you about it.'

'Oh, please, Detective Maddox.' Rosalind's voice had sharpened, just a touch, and I couldn't tell whether this was a good or a bad sign. 'Don't treat me as if I'm stupid. If you people had any evidence against me, I'd be under arrest, not standing here listening to you cry about Detective Ryan.'

'No,' Cassie said. 'That's the thing. The others don't know yet, about what Damien said. If they find out, then yeah, they'll arrest you.'

'Are you threatening me? Because that's a very bad idea.'

'*No.* I'm just trying to . . . OK. Here's the thing.' Cassie took a breath. 'We don't actually need a motive, to try someone for murder. He's confessed to doing it; we've got that part on the record, on video, and that's all we really need to put him in gaol. Nobody needs to know *why* he did it. And, like I said, he trusts me. If I tell him he should keep his motive to himself, he'll believe me. You know what he's like.'

'Much better than you do, actually. God. *Damien.*' Possibly this is a testament to my stupidity, but I still had the capacity to be taken aback by the note in Rosalind's voice, something far beyond contempt: rejection, utter and impersonal. 'I'm really not worried about him. He's a murderer, for heaven's sake. Do you think anyone will believe him? Over *me*?'

'I believed him,' said Cassie.

'Yes, well. That doesn't say much for your detective skills, does it? Damien's barely intelligent enough to tie his own shoelaces, but he came out with some story and you just took his word for it? Did you really believe that someone like him would be able to tell you how this actually happened, even if he wanted to? Damien can only handle *simple* things, Detective. This wasn't a *simple* story.'

'The basic facts check out,' Cassie said sharply. 'I don't want to hear the details. If I'm going to be keeping this to myself, then the less I know the better.'

A moment's silence, as Rosalind evaluated the possibilities of this; then the little laugh. 'Really? But you're supposed to be a detective, of some sort. Shouldn't you be interested in finding out what actually happened?'

'I know as much as I need to. Anything you tell me won't do me any good anyway.'

'Oh, I know that,' Rosalind said brightly. 'You won't be able to use it. But if hearing the truth puts you in an uncomfortable position, that's really your own fault, isn't it? You shouldn't have got yourself into this situation. I don't think I should be expected to make allowances for your dishonesty.'

'I'm – like you said, I'm a *detective*.' Cassie's voice was rising. 'I can't just listen to evidence about a crime and—'

Rosalind's tone didn't change. 'Well, you'll just have to, won't you? Katy used to be such a sweet little girl. But once her dancing started to get her all that attention, she got awfully above herself. That Simone woman was a terrible influence on her, really. It made me very sad. Someone had to put her in her place, didn't they? For her own good. So I—'

'If you keep talking,' Cassie snapped, too loudly, 'I'm going to caution you. Otherwise—'

'Don't you threaten me, Detective. I won't warn you again.'

A beat. Sam was staring into space, one knuckle caught between his front teeth.

'So,' Rosalind resumed, 'I decided the best thing would be to show Katy that she wasn't really anything that special. She certainly wasn't very intelligent. When I gave her something to—'

'You are not obliged to say anything unless you wish to do so,' Cassie broke in, her voice shaking wildly, 'but anything you do say will be taken down in writing and may be used in evidence.'

Rosalind thought about this for a long time. I could hear their feet crunching in fallen leaves, Cassie's jumper grating faintly against the mike at each step; somewhere a wood-dove cooed, cosy and contented. Sam's eyes were on me, and through the gloom of the van I thought I saw condemnation in them. I thought of his uncle and stared back.

'She's lost her,' said O'Kelly. He stretched, heavy shoulders rolling back, and cracked his neck. 'It's the bloody caution that does it. When I was coming up there was none of this shite: you gave them a few digs, they told you what you wanted to know, that was good enough for any judge. Well, sure, at least we can get back to work now.'

'Hang on,' Sam said. 'She'll get her back.'

'Listen,' Cassie said at last, on a long breath, 'about going to our boss—'

'Just a moment,' Rosalind said coldly. 'We're not finished.'

'Yes we are,' Cassie said, but her voice wavered treacherously. 'As far as Katy goes, we are. I am not going to just stand here and listen to—'

'I don't like people trying to bully me, Detective. I'll say whatever I like. You're going to listen. If you interrupt me again, this conversation is over. If you repeat it to anyone else, I'll make it clear to them exactly what kind of person you are, and Detective Ryan will confirm it. Nobody will believe a word you say, and you'll lose your precious job. Do you understand?'

Silence. My stomach was still heaving, slowly and horribly; I swallowed hard. 'The arrogance of her,' Sam said softly. 'The fucking arrogance.'

'Don't knock it,' O'Kelly said. 'It's Maddox's best shot.'

'Yes,' Cassie said, very low. 'I understand.'

'Good.' I heard the prim, satisfied little smile in Rosalind's voice. Her heels tapped on tarmac; they had turned onto the main road, heading down towards the entrance of the estate. 'So, as I was saying, I decided that someone needed to stop Katy from getting too full of herself. It really should have been my mother and father's job, obviously; if they had done it, I wouldn't have had to. But they couldn't be bothered. I think that's actually a form of child abuse, don't you – that kind of neglect?'

She waited until Cassie said tightly, 'I don't know.'

'Oh, it is. It made me very upset. So I told Katy that she should really stop doing ballet, since it was having such a bad effect on her, but she wouldn't listen. She needed to learn that she didn't have some kind of divine right to be the centre of attention. Not everything in this world was all about her. So I stopped her from dancing, now and then. Do you want to know how?'

Cassie was breathing fast. 'No. I don't.'

'I made her sick, Detective Maddox,' Rosalind said. 'God, you mean you hadn't even figured out that much?'

'We wondered. We thought maybe your mother had been doing something—'

'My *mother*?' That note again, that dismissal beyond contempt. 'Oh, please. My mother would have got herself caught within a *week*, even with you people in charge. I mixed juice with washing-up liquid, or cleaning things, or whatever I felt like that day, and I told Katy it was a secret recipe to improve her *dancing*. She was stupid enough to believe me. I was interested to see whether anyone would work it out, but nobody did. Can you imagine?'

'Jesus,' Cassie said, barely above a whisper.

'Go, Cassie,' Sam muttered. 'That's grievous bodily harm. *Go*.'

'She won't,' I said. My voice sounded strange, jerky. 'Not till she has her on murder.'

'Look,' Cassie said, and I heard her swallow. 'We're

about to go into the estate, and you said I only had till we got back to your house . . . I need to know what you're going to do about—'

'You'll know when I tell you. And we'll go in when I decide to go in. Actually, I think we might go back this way, so I can finish telling you my story.'

'All the way back around the estate?'

'You were the one who demanded to talk to me, Detective Maddox,' Rosalind said, reprovingly. 'You're going to have to learn to take the consequences of your own actions.'

'Shit,' Sam murmured. They were moving away from us.

'She's not going to need back-up, O'Neill,' O'Kelly said. 'The girl's a bitch, but it's not like she has an Uzi.'

'Anyway. Katy just wouldn't learn.' That sharp, dangerous note was seeping into Rosalind's voice again. 'She *finally* managed to work out why she was getting sick – God, it took her *years* – and she threw an absolute tantrum at me. She said she was never going to drink anything I gave her again, blah blah blah, she actually threatened to tell our parents – I mean, they would never have believed her, she always did get hysterical about nothing, but all the same . . . See what I mean about Katy? She was a spoilt little brat. She always, always had to have her own way. If she didn't get it, she ran to Mummy and Daddy to tell tales.'

'She just wanted to be a dancer,' Cassie said quietly.

'And I had told her that wasn't acceptable,' Rosalind snapped. 'If she had simply done as she was told, none of this would have happened. Instead, she tried to *threaten* me. That's exactly what I knew this ballet-school thing would do to her, all those articles and fundraisers, it was disgusting – she thought she could do whatever she liked. She said to me – this is exactly what she said, I'm not making this up – she stood there with her hands on her hips, *God* what a little prima donna, and she said, "You shouldn't have done that to me. Don't ever do it again." Who on *earth* did she think she was? She was completely out of control, the way she behaved to me was absolutely outrageous, and there was no *way* I was going to allow it.'

Sam's hands were clenched into fists and I wasn't breathing. I was covered in a sick, cold sweat. I could no longer picture Rosalind in my mind's eye; the tender vision of the girl in white had been blown to pieces as if by a nuclear bomb. This was something unimaginable, something hollow as the yellowed husks that insects leave behind in dry grass, blowing with cold alien winds and a fine corrosive dust that shredded everything it touched.

'I've run into people who tried to tell me what to do,' Cassie said. Her voice sounded tight, breathless. Even though she was the only one of us who had understood what to expect, this story had knocked the wind right out of her. 'I didn't get someone to kill them.'

'I think you'll find, actually, that I never told Damien to do anything to Katy.' I heard Rosalind's smirk. 'I can't help it if men always want to do things for me, can I? Ask him, if you want: he was the one who came up with every single idea. And, my God, it took him *forever*, it would have been quicker to train a monkey.' O'Kelly snorted. 'When the idea *finally* hit him, he looked like he had just discovered gravity, like he was some kind of *genius*. And then he kept having these doubts, it just went on and on – God, a few more weeks and I think I would have had to give up on him and start all over, before I lost my mind.'

'He did what you wanted in the end,' Cassie said. 'So

why did you break up with him? The poor guy's devastated.'

'The same reason Detective Ryan broke up with you. I
was so bored I wanted to scream. And no, actually, he
didn't do what I wanted. He made a complete mess of the
whole thing.' Rosalind's voice was rising, cold and furious.
'Panicking and hiding her body – he could have ruined
everything. He could have got me into serious trouble.
Honestly, he's just *unbelievable*. I even went to the bother of
coming up with a story for him to tell you, to put you off his
trail, but he couldn't even manage to get that right.'

'The guy in the tracksuit?' Cassie said, and I heard that
tautening at the edges of her voice: any minute now. 'No,
he told us that one. He just wasn't very convincing. We
thought he was making a big deal out of nothing.'

'You see what I mean? He was supposed to have sex with
her, hit her on the head with a rock and leave her body
somewhere on the dig or in the wood. *That* was what I
wanted. For God's sake, you'd think that would be simple
enough even for Damien, but no. He didn't get a *single one*
of those right. My God, he's lucky I just broke up with him.
After the mess he made of this, I should have put you
people onto him. He deserves whatever he gets.'

And there it was: all we needed. The breath went out of
me with a strange, painful little sound. Sam slumped back
against the side of the van and ran his hands through his
hair; O'Kelly gave a long, low whistle.

'Rosalind Frances Devlin,' Cassie said, 'I arrest you on
suspicion that, on or around the seventeenth of August of
this year, at Knocknaree in County Dublin, you did murder
Katharine Bridget Devlin, contrary to common law.'

'*Get your hands off me*,' Rosalind snapped. We heard
scuffling, the crunch of twigs snapping underfoot; then a

swift, vicious noise like the hiss of a cat, and something between a smack and a thump, and a sharp gasp from Cassie.

'What the fuck—' said O'Kelly.

'Go,' Sam said, 'go,' but I was already scrabbling for the door handle.

We ran, skidding around the corner, down the road towards the entrance of the estate. I have the longest legs and I outpaced Sam and O'Kelly easily. Everything seemed to be streaming past me in slow motion, swaying gates and bright-painted doors, a toddler on a tricycle gazing up open-mouthed and an old man in braces turning from his roses; the morning sunlight trickled down leisurely as honey, achingly bright after the dimness, and the boom of someone slamming the van door echoed on forever. Rosalind could have snatched up a sharp branch, a rock, a broken bottle; so many things can kill. I couldn't feel my feet hitting the pavement. I swung round the gatepost and threw myself up the main road, and leaves brushed my face as I turned onto the little path along the top wall, long wet grass, footprints in muddy patches. I felt as if I were dissolving, autumn breeze flowing cool and sweet between my ribs and into my veins, turning me from earth into air.

They were at the corner of the estate, where the fields met that last strip of wood, and my legs went watery with relief when I saw they were both on their feet. Cassie had Rosalind by the wrists – for an instant I remembered the strength of her hands, that day in the interview room – but Rosalind was fighting, intently and viciously, not to get away but to get at her. She was kicking at her shins and trying to claw her, and I saw her head jerk as she spat in Cassie's face. I shouted something, but I don't think either of them heard.

Footsteps thumped behind me and Sweeney streaked past, running like a rugby player and already pulling out his handcuffs. He grabbed Rosalind by the shoulder, spun her around and slammed her against the wall. Cassie had caught her barefaced and with her hair pulled back in a bun, and for the first time I saw in starkly allegorical relief how ugly she was, without the layered make-up and the artfully tumbling ringlets: pouched cheeks, thin avid mouth pursed into a hateful smirk, eyes as glassy and empty as a doll's. She was wearing her school uniform, shapeless navy-blue skirt and a navy-blue blazer with a crest on the front, and for some reason this disguise seemed to me the most horrible one of all.

Cassie stumbled backwards, caught herself against a tree trunk and regained her balance. When she turned towards me all I could see at first was her eyes, huge and black and blind. Then I saw the blood, a crazy web of it streaking one side of her face. She swayed a little, under the blurred shadows of the leaves, and a bright drop fell into the grass at her feet.

I was only a few yards from her, but something stopped me from moving closer. Dazed and unstrung, her face branded with those fierce markings, she looked like some pagan priestess emerging from a rite too bright and merciless to be imagined: still half somewhere and someone else, and not to be touched until she gave the sign. The nape of my neck prickled.

'Cassie,' I said, and held out my arms to her. My chest felt as if it was bursting open. 'Oh, Cassie.'

Her hands came up, reaching, and for an instant I swear her whole body moved towards me. Then she remembered. Her hands dropped and her head went back, her gaze skidding aimlessly across the wide blue sky.

Sam shoved me out of the way and pounded to a clumsy stop beside her. 'Ah, God, Cassie . . .' He was out of breath. 'What did she do to you? Come here.'

He pulled out his shirt-tail and blotted gently at her cheek, his other hand cupping the back of her head to steady her. 'Ow. Fuck,' Sweeney said, through gritted teeth, as Rosalind stamped on his foot.

'Scratched me,' Cassie said. Her voice was terrible, high and eerie. 'She *touched* me, Sam, that thing touched me, Jesus, she *spat*— Get it off me. Get it off.'

'Shh,' Sam said. 'Shh. It's over now. You did great. Shh.' He put his arms around her and pulled her close, and her head went down on his shoulder. For a second Sam's eyes met mine squarely; then he looked away, down at his hand stroking her tumbled curls.

'What the hell is going on?' demanded O'Kelly, behind me, in disgust.

Cassie's face, once it was cleaned up, was not as bad as it had initially looked. Rosalind's nails had left three wide dark lines scored across her cheekbone, but in spite of all the blood they weren't deep. The tech, who knew First Aid, said that there was no need for stitches and that it was lucky Rosalind had missed the eye. He offered to put plasters on the cuts, but Cassie said no, not until we got back to work and she had them disinfected. She was shuddering all over, off and on; the tech said she was probably in shock. O'Kelly, who still looked baffled and slightly exasperated by this whole day, offered her an iced caramel. 'Sugar,' he explained.

She was obviously in no state to drive, so she left her Vespa where it was parked and rode back to work in the front of the van. Sam drove. Rosalind went in the back, with the rest of us. She had settled down once Sweeney got the cuffs on her; she sat rigid and outraged, not saying a word. Every breath I took smelled of her cloying perfume and of something else, some overripe taint of rot, rich and polluting and possibly imaginary. I could tell from her eyes that her mind was working furiously, but there was no expression on her face; no fear or defiance or anger, nothing at all.

By the time we got back to work O'Kelly's mood had improved considerably, and when I followed him and Cassie into the observation room he didn't attempt to send me away. 'That girl reminds me of a young fella I knew in school,' he told us reflectively, as we waited for Sam to finish going through the rights sheet with Rosalind and bring her up to the interview room. 'Shaft you six ways till Sunday without blinking an eye, then turn around and have everyone convinced it was all your own fault. There's mad people in this parish.'

Cassie leaned back against the wall, spat on a blood-stained tissue and scrubbed again at her cheek. 'She's not mad,' she said. Her hands were still shaking.

'Figure of speech, Maddox,' O'Kelly said. 'You should go get the war wound seen to.'

'I'm fine.'

'Fair play to you, all the same. You were right about that one.' He clapped her awkwardly on the shoulder. 'All that about making the sister sick for her own good; would you say she actually believes that?'

'No,' Cassie said. She refolded the tissue to find a clean bit. ' "Believe" doesn't exist for her. Things aren't true or false; they either suit her or they don't. Nothing else means anything to her. You could give her a polygraph and she'd pass with flying colours.'

'She should've gone into politics. Hang on; here we go.' O'Kelly jerked his head at the glass: Sam was showing Rosalind into the interview room. 'Let's see her try to get out of this one. This should be good for a laugh.'

Rosalind glanced around the room and sighed. 'I'd like you to ring my parents now,' she told Sam. 'Tell them to get me a lawyer and then come down here.' She pulled a dainty little pen and diary out of her blazer pocket, wrote something on a page, then ripped it out and handed it to Sam, as if he were a concierge. 'That's their number. Thank you so much.'

'You can see your parents once we've finished talking,' Sam said. 'If you want a lawyer—'

'I think I'll see them sooner than that, actually.' Rosalind smoothed her skirt over her backside and sat down, with a little moue of distaste at the plastic chair. 'Don't minors have the right to have a parent or guardian present during an interview?'

There was a moment when everyone froze, except Rosalind, who crossed her knees demurely and smiled up at Sam, savouring the effect.

'Interview suspended,' Sam said curtly. He whipped the file off the table and headed for the door.

'Jesus Christ on a bike,' said O'Kelly. 'Ryan, are you telling me—'

'She could be lying,' Cassie said. She was staring intently through the glass; her hand had closed into a fist around the tissue.

My heart, which had stopped beating, resumed at double speed. 'Of course she is. Look at her, there's no way she's under—'

'Aye, right. Do you know how many men have landed in gaol for saying that?'

Sam banged the observation-room door open so hard it bounced off the wall. 'What age is that girl?' he demanded, of me.

'*Eighteen*,' I said. My head was spinning; I knew I was sure, but I couldn't remember how. 'She told me—'

'Sweet Jesus! And you took her word for it?' I had never seen Sam lose his temper before, and it was more impressive than I would have expected. 'If you asked that girl the time at half-two, she'd tell you it was three o'clock just to fuck with your head. You didn't even *check*?'

'Look who's talking,' O'Kelly snapped. 'Any one of ye could have checked, any time in the past God knows how long, but no—'

Sam didn't even hear him. His eyes were locked on mine, blazing. 'We took *your* word because you're supposed to be a bloody *detective*. You sent your own partner in there to get crucified, without even bothering—'

'I *did* check!' I shouted. 'I checked the file!' But even as the words left my mouth I knew, with a horrible sick thud. A sunny afternoon, a long time ago; I had been fumbling through the file, with the phone jammed between my jaw and my shoulder and O'Gorman yammering in my other ear, trying to talk to Rosalind and make sure she was an appropriate adult to supervise my conversation with Jessica, all at the same time (*And I must have known*, I thought, *I must have known even then that she couldn't be trusted, or why would I have bothered to check such a small thing?*). I had found the page of family stats and skimmed down to Rosalind's DOB, subtracted the years—

Sam had swung away from me and was rooting urgently through the file, and I saw the moment when his shoulders sagged. 'November,' he said, very quietly. 'Her birthday's the second of November. She'll be eighteen.'

'Congratulations,' O'Kelly said heavily, after a silence. 'The three of ye. Well done.'

Cassie let out her breath. 'Inadmissible,' she said. 'Every fucking word.' She slid down the wall to a sitting position, as if her knees had suddenly given way, and closed her eyes.

A faint, high, insistent sound came from the speakers. In the interview room, Rosalind had got bored and started humming.

25

That evening we started clearing out the incident room, Sam and Cassie and I. We worked methodically and in silence, taking down photographs, erasing the multicoloured tangle from the whiteboard, sorting files and reports and packing them away in blue-stamped cardboard boxes. Someone had set fire to a flat off Parnell Street the previous night, killing a Nigerian asylum-seeker and her six-month-old baby; Costello and his partner needed the room.

O'Kelly and Sweeney were interviewing Rosalind, down the hall, with Jonathan in the background to protect her. I think I had expected Jonathan to come in with all guns blazing and possibly try to hit someone, but as it transpired he hadn't been the problem. When O'Kelly told the Devlins, outside the interview room, what Rosalind had confessed to, Margaret whirled on him, mouth gaping open; then she drew in a huge gulp of breath and screamed, 'No!' hoarse and wild, her voice slamming off the walls of the corridor. 'No. No. No. She was with her *cousins*. How can you do this to her? How can you . . . how . . . Ah, God, she warned me – she warned me you would do this! You' – she stabbed a thick, trembling finger at me, and I flinched before I could stop myself – 'you, calling her a dozen times a day asking her out, and her only a child, you should be ashamed . . . And her' – Cassie – 'she hated Rosalind from the start, Rosalind always said she would try to blame her for . . . What are you trying to do to her? Are you trying to kill her? Then will you be happy? Oh God, my poor baby . . . why do people tell these lies about her? Why?' Her hands clawed at her hair and she broke down into ugly, wrenching sobs.

Jonathan had stood still at the top of the stairs, holding onto the railing, while O'Kelly tried to calm Margaret down and shot us filthy looks over her shoulder. He was dressed for work, in a suit and tie. For some reason I remember it very clearly, that suit. It was dark blue and spotlessly clean, with a slight sheen where it had been ironed too many times, and somehow I found it almost inexpressibly sad.

Rosalind was under arrest for murder and for assaulting an officer. She had opened her mouth only once since her parents arrived, to claim – lip trembling – that Cassie had punched her in the stomach and that she had only been defending herself. We would send a file to the DPP on both charges, but we all knew the evidence for murder was slim at best. We no longer had even the Tracksuit Shadow link to show that Rosalind had been an accessory: my session with Jessica had not in fact been supervised by an appropriate adult, and I had no way of proving that it had ever happened. We had Damien's word and a bunch of mobile-phone records, and that was all.

It was getting late, maybe eight o'clock, and the building was very quiet, just our movements and a soft fitful rain pattering at the windows of the incident room. I took down the post-mortem photos and the Devlins' family snap-shots, the scowling Tracksuit Shadow suspects and the grainy blow-ups of Peter and Jamie, picked the Blu-tac off the backs and filed them away. Cassie checked each box, fitted a lid onto it and labelled it in squeaky black marker.

Sam went around the room with a bin liner, collecting styrofoam cups and emptying wastepaper baskets, brushing crumbs off the tables. There were smears of dried blood down the front of his shirt.

His map of Knocknaree was starting to curl at the edges, and one corner ripped away as I took it down. Someone had got spatters of water on it and the ink had run in spots, making Cassie's property-developer caricature look unpleasantly as if he had had a stroke. 'Should we keep this on file,' I asked Sam, 'or . . .?'

I held it out to him and we looked at it: tiny gnarled tree trunks and smoke curling from the chimneys of the houses, fragile and wistful as a fairy tale. 'Probably better not,' Sam said, after a moment. He took the map from me, rolled it into a tube and manoeuvred it into the bin liner.

'I'm missing a lid,' Cassie said. Dark, shocking scabs had formed over the cuts on her cheek. 'Any more over there?'

'There was one under the table,' Sam said. 'Here—' He threw Cassie the last lid, and she fitted it into place and straightened up.

We stood under the fluorescent lights and looked at one another, across the bare tables and the litter of boxes. *My turn to make dinner . . .* For a moment I almost said it, and I felt the same thought cross both Sam's and Cassie's minds, stupid and impossible and no less piercing for any of that.

'Well,' Cassie said quietly, on a long breath. She glanced around the empty room, wiping her hands on the sides of her jeans. 'Well, I guess that's it, then.'

I am intensely aware, by the way, that this story does not show me in a particularly flattering light. I am aware that, within an impressively short time of meeting me, Rosalind had me coming to heel like a well-trained dog: running up and down stairs to bring her coffee, nodding along while she bitched about my partner, imagining like some star-struck teenager that she was a kindred soul. But before you decide to despise me too thoroughly, consider this: she fooled you too. You had as good a chance as I did. I told you everything I saw, as I saw it at the time. And if that was in itself deceptive, remember, I told you that too: I warned you, right from the beginning, that I lie.

It is difficult for me to describe the degree of horror and self-loathing inspired by the realisation that Rosalind had suckered me. I'm sure Cassie would have said that my gullibility was only natural, that all the other liars and criminals I'd encountered had been mere amateurs while Rosalind was the real, the natural-born thing, and that she herself had been immune purely because she had fallen for the same technique once before; but Cassie wasn't there. A few days after we closed the case, O'Kelly told me that until the verdicts came in I would be working out of the main detective unit, in Harcourt Street – 'away from anything you can fuck up', as he put it, and I found it difficult to counter this. I was still officially on the Murder squad, so nobody knew exactly what I was supposed to be doing in the general unit. They gave me a desk and occasionally O'Kelly sent over a pile of bureaucracy, but for the most part I was free to wander the corridors as I chose, eaves-dropping on fragments of conversation and evading curious stares, immaterial and unwanted as a ghost.

I spent sleepless nights conjuring up gory, detailed, improbable fates for Rosalind. I wanted her not just dead but obliterated from the face of the earth – crushed to unidentifiable pulp, pulverised in a shredder, burned to a handful of toxic ash. I had never suspected myself of this capacity for sadism and it horrified me further to realise that I would joyfully have carried out any of these sentences myself. Every conversation I had had with her spooled over and over through my head, and I saw with merciless clarity how skilfully she had played me: how unerringly she had put her finger on everything from my vanities through my griefs through my deepest hidden fears, and drawn them out of me to work her will.

This was, in the end, the most hideous realisation of all: Rosalind had not, after all, implanted a microchip behind my ear or drugged me into submission. I had broken every vow myself and steered every boat to shipwreck with my own hand. She had simply, like any good craftswoman, used what came her way. Almost with a glance she had assessed me and Cassie to the bone and discarded Cassie as unusable; but in me she had seen something, some subtle but fundamental quality, that made me worth keeping.

I didn't testify at Damien's trial. Too risky, the prosecutor said: there was too much of a chance that Rosalind had told Damien about my 'personal history', as he put it. He was a guy named Mathews who wears flashy ties and gets called 'dynamic' a lot, and he always makes me tired. Rosalind hadn't brought up the subject again – apparently Cassie had been convincing enough to make her drop it and move on to other, more promising weapons – and I doubted that she would have told Damien anything useful at all, but I didn't bother to argue.

I went to see Cassie testify, though. I sat at the back of the courtroom, which was, unusually, packed; the trial had been filling front pages and talk radio since before it even began. Cassie was wearing a neat little dove-grey suit and her curls were slicked down smoothly against her head. I hadn't seen her in a few months. She looked thinner, more subdued; the quicksilver mobility I associate with her was gone, and her new stillness brought her face home to me – the delicate, marked arches above her eyelids, the wide clean curves of her mouth – as if I had never seen it before. She was older, no longer the wicked limber girl with the stalled Vespa, but no less beautiful to me for that: whatever elliptical beauty Cassie possesses has always lain not in the vulnerable planes of colour and texture but deeper, in the polished contours of her bones. I watched her on the stand in that unfamiliar suit and thought of the soft hairs at the back of her neck, warm and smelling of sun, and it seemed an impossible thing to me, it seemed the vastest and saddest miracle of my life: I touched her hair, once.

She was good; Cassie has always been good in the courtroom. Juries trust her and she holds their attention, which is harder than it sounds, especially in a long trial. She answered Mathews's questions in a quiet, clear voice, her hands folded in her lap. On cross-examination she did what she could for Damien: yes, he had appeared agitated and confused; yes, he had seemed genuinely to believe that the murder had been necessary to protect Rosalind and Jessica Devlin; yes, in her opinion he had been under Rosalind's influence and had committed the crime at her urging. Damien huddled in his seat and stared at her like a little boy watching a horror movie, his eyes dazed and huge and uncomprehending. He had tried to commit suicide, using the time-honoured prison bed-sheet, when he heard that Rosalind was going to testify against him.

'When Damien confessed to this crime,' the defence barrister asked, 'did he tell you why he had committed it?'

Cassie shook her head. 'Not that day, no. My partner

and I asked him about his motive a number of times, but he either refused to answer or said that he wasn't sure.'

'Even though he had already confessed, and telling you his motive couldn't possibly have done him any harm. Why do you think that was?'

'Objection: calls for speculation . . .'

My partner. I knew from Cassie's blink on the word, from the tiny shift in the angle of her shoulders, that she had seen me tucked away there at the back; but she never looked my way, not even when the lawyers finally finished with her and she stepped down from the stand and walked out of the courtroom. I thought of Kiernan then; of what it must have been to him when, after thirty years of partnership, McCabe had that heart attack and died. More than I have ever envied anything in the world, I envied Kiernan that, that unique and unattainable grief.

Rosalind was the next witness. She tiptoed up to the stand, through the sudden flurry of whispers and journalistic scribbling, and gave Mathews a timid little rosebud smile from under her mascara. I left. I read it in the newspapers the next day: how she had sobbed when she talked about Katy, trembled as she recounted how Damien had threatened to kill her sisters if she broke up with him; how, when his barrister started digging, she had cried, 'How dare you! I *loved* my sister!' and then fainted, forcing the judge to adjourn the court for the afternoon.

She hadn't had a trial – her parents' decision, I'm sure, rather than hers; left to herself, I can't imagine she would have passed up that amount of attention. Mathews had plea-bargained her case. Conspiracy charges are notoriously difficult to prove; there was no hard evidence against Rosalind, her confession was inadmissible and she had of course recanted it anyway (Cassie, she explained, had terrified it out of her by making throat-slitting motions); and, besides, as a juvenile she wouldn't get much of a sentence even if by some chance she were found guilty. She was also claiming, off and on, that she and I had slept together, which left O'Kelly apoplectic and me even more so and brought the general confusion to a level nothing short of paralysing.

Mathews had played the odds and concentrated on Damien. In exchange for her testimony against him, he had offered Rosalind a three-year suspended sentence for reckless endangerment and resisting arrest. I'd heard, through the grapevine, that she'd already received half a dozen proposals of marriage, and that newspapers and publishers were having a bidding war over her story.

On my way out of the courthouse I saw Jonathan Devlin, leaning against the wall and smoking. He was holding the cigarette close against his chest, tilting his head back to watch the gulls wheeling over the river. I got my smokes out of my coat and joined him.

He glanced at me, then away again.

'How are you doing?' I asked.

He shrugged heavily. 'Much as you'd expect. Jessica tried to kill herself. Went to bed and cut her wrists with my razor.'

'I'm sorry to hear that,' I said. 'Is she all right?'

One corner of his mouth twitched in a humourless smile. 'Yeah. Luckily she made a balls of it: cut across instead of down, or some such.'

I lit my cigarette, cupping my hand around the flame – it was a windy day, purplish clouds starting to gather. 'Can I ask you a question?' I said. 'Strictly off the record?'

He looked at me: a dark, hopeless look tinged with something like contempt. 'Why not.'

'You knew, didn't you?' I said. 'You knew all along.'

He said nothing for a long time, so long that I wondered if he was going to ignore the question. Eventually he sighed and said, 'Not *knew*. She couldn't have done it herself, she was with her cousins, and I didn't know anything about this lad Damien. But I wondered. I've known Rosalind all her life. I wondered.'

'And you didn't do anything.' I had meant my voice to be expressionless, but a note of accusation must have slipped in. He could have told us on the first day what Rosalind was; he could have told someone years earlier, when Katy first started getting sick. Although I knew that quite possibly this would have made no difference to anything at all, in the long run, I couldn't help thinking of all the casualties that silence had left behind, all the wreckage in its wake.

Jonathan tossed away his cigarette butt and turned to face me, hands shoved into the pockets of his overcoat. 'What do you think I should have done?' he demanded, in a low, hard voice. 'She's my daughter too. I'd already lost one. Margaret won't hear a word against her; years ago I wanted to send Rosalind to a psychologist, about the amount of lies she told, and Margaret got hysterical and threatened to leave me, take the girls with her. And I didn't *know* anything. I would have had fuck-all to tell you. I kept an eye on her and prayed it was some property developer. What would *you* have done?'

'I don't know,' I said, truthfully. 'Quite possibly exactly what you did.' He kept staring at me, breathing fast, his nostrils flaring slightly. I turned away and drew on my cigarette; after a while I heard him take a deep breath and lean back against the wall again.

'Now I've something to ask you,' he said. 'Did Rosalind

have it right about you being that boy whose friends disappeared?'

The question didn't surprise me. He had the right to see or hear footage of all interviews with Rosalind, and at some level I think I had always expected him to ask, sooner or later. I knew I should deny it – the official story was that I had, legally if a little callously, made up the whole disappearance thing to gain Rosalind's trust – but I didn't have the energy, and I couldn't see the point. 'Yeah,' I said. 'Adam Ryan.'

Jonathan turned his head and looked at me for a long time, and I wondered what hazy memories he was trying to match to my face.

'We had nothing to do with that,' he said, and the undertone in his voice – gentle, almost pitying – startled me. 'I want you to know that. Nothing at all.'

'I know,' I said, eventually. 'I'm sorry I went for you.'

He nodded a few times, slowly. 'I'd probably have done the same thing, in your place. And it's not as if I was some holy innocent. You saw what we did to Sandra, didn't you? You were there.'

'Yeah,' I said. 'She's not going to press charges.'

He moved his head as if the thought disturbed him. The river was dark and thick-looking, with an oily, unhealthy sheen. There was something in the water, a dead fish maybe, or a rubbish spill; the seagulls were screaming over it in a whirling frenzy.

'What are you going to do now?' I asked, inanely.

Jonathan shook his head, staring up at the lowering sky. He looked exhausted – not the kind of exhaustion that can be healed by a good night's sleep or a holiday; something bone-deep and indelible, settled in puffy grooves around his eyes and mouth. 'Move house. We've had bricks through the windows, and someone spray-painted "PAE-DOPHILE" on the car – he couldn't spell, whoever he was, but the message came across clear enough. I can stick it out till the motorway thing is settled, one way or the other, but after that . . .'

Allegations of child abuse, no matter how baseless they may seem, have to be checked out. The investigation into Damien's accusations against Jonathan had found no evidence to substantiate them and a considerable amount to contradict them, and Sex Crime had been as discreet as was humanly possible; but the neighbours always know, by some mysterious system of jungle drums, and there are always plenty of people who believe there is no smoke without fire.

'I'm sending Rosalind to counselling, like the judge said. I've done some reading and all the books say it makes no difference to people like her, they're made that way and there's no cure, but I have to try. And I'll keep her at home as long as I can, where I can see what she's at and try to stop her pulling her tricks on anyone else. She's off to college in October, music at Trinity, but I've told her I won't pay her rent on a flat – she'll stay at home, if it's that or get a job. Margaret still believes she did nothing and you lot set her up, but she's glad enough to keep her at home a while longer. She says Rosalind's sensitive.' He cleared his throat with a harsh sound, as if the word tasted bad. 'I'm sending Jess to live with my sister in Athlone as soon as the scars on her wrists go down; get her out of harm's way.'

His mouth twisted in that bitter half-smile. 'Harm. Her own sister.' For an instant I thought of what that house must have been like for the past eighteen years, what it must be like now. It made a slow, sick horror heave in my stomach.

'Do you know something?' Jonathan said abruptly and painfully. 'Margaret and I were only going out a couple of months when she found out she was pregnant. We were both terrified. I managed to bring it up once, that maybe she should think about . . . taking the boat to England. But . . . sure, she's very religious. She felt bad enough about getting pregnant to start with, never mind . . . She's a good woman, I don't regret marrying her. But if I'd known what was – what it – what Rosalind was going to be, God forgive me, I'd have dragged her on that boat myself.'

I wish to God you had, I wanted to say, but it would have been cruelty. 'I'm sorry,' I said again, uselessly.

He glanced at me for a moment; then he took a breath and shrugged his coat closer around his shoulders. 'I'd better head in, see if Rosalind's finished up.'

'I think she'll be a while.'

'She probably will,' he said tonelessly, and plodded up the steps into the courthouse, his overcoat flapping behind him, hunching a little against the wind.

The jury found Damien guilty. Given the evidence presented, they could hardly have done otherwise. There had been various complicated, multilateral legal fights about admissibility; psychiatrists had had jargon-heavy debates about the workings of Damien's mind. (All this I heard third-hand, in passing snatches of conversation or in interminable phone calls from Quigley, who had apparently made it his mission in life to find out why I had been relegated to paperwork in Harcourt Street.) His barrister went for a double-barrelled defence – he was temporarily insane, and even if he wasn't, he believed he was protecting Rosalind from grievous bodily harm – which often generates enough confusion to be mistaken for reasonable doubt; but we had a full confession, and, perhaps more importantly, we had autopsy photos of a dead child. Damien was found guilty of murder and sentenced to life, which in practice usually works out at somewhere between ten and fifteen years.

I doubt that he appreciated the multiple ironies of this, but that trowel quite possibly saved his life, and certainly spared him various unsavoury prison experiences. Because of the sexual assault on Katy, he was considered a sex offender and sentenced to be held in the high-risk unit, with the paedophiles and rapists and other prisoners who would not fare well in general population. This was presumably something of a mixed blessing, but it did at least increase his chances of getting out of gaol alive and without any communicable diseases.

There was a minor lynch mob, maybe a few dozen people, waiting for him outside the courthouse after the sentencing. I watched the news in a dingy little pub near the quays, and a low, dangerous rumble of approval rose from the regulars as, on screen, impassive uniforms guided Damien stumbling through the crowd and the van pulled away under a hail of fists and hoarse shouts and the odd half-brick. 'Bring in the bloody death penalty,' someone muttered, in a corner. I was aware that I should feel sorry for Damien, that he had been fucked from the moment he walked over to that sign-up table and that I of all people ought to be able to muster up some compassion for this, but I couldn't; I couldn't.

I really don't have the heart to go into detail about what 'suspended pending investigation' turned out to mean: the tense, endless hearings, the various stern authorities in sharply pressed suits and uniforms, the clumsy humiliating explanations and self-justifications, the sick through-the-looking-glass sensation of being trapped on the wrong side of the interrogation process. To my surprise, O'Kelly turned out to be my most vehement defender, going into long impassioned speeches about my solve rate and my interview technique and all kinds of things he had never mentioned before. Although I knew this was probably due not to some unsuspected vein of affection but to self-protection – my misbehaviour reflected badly on him, he needed to justify the fact that he had harboured a renegade like me on his squad for so long – I was pathetically, almost tearfully grateful: he seemed my one remaining ally in the world. I even tried to thank him once, in the corridor after one of these sessions, but I only got out a few words before he gave me a look of such profound disgust that I started stammering and backed away.

Eventually the various authorities decided not to fire me, or even – which would have been far worse – to revert me back to uniform. Again, I don't put this down to any particular feeling on their part that I deserved a second chance; more likely it was simply because firing me could have caught the eye of some journalist and led to all kinds of inconvenient questions and consequences. They kicked me off the squad, of course. Even in my wildest moments of optimism, I had hardly dared to hope they wouldn't. They sent me back to the floater pool, with a hint (beautifully delivered, really, in delicate, steely subtext) that I shouldn't expect to get out of it again for a long time, if at all. Sometimes Quigley, with a more refined sense of cruelty than I gave him credit for, requests me for tip lines or door-to-door.

The whole process was, of course, nowhere near as simple as I'm making it out to be. It took months, months during which I sat around the apartment in a wretched nightmarish daze, with my savings draining away and my mother timidly bringing over macaroni and cheese to make sure I ate, and Heather buttonholing me to explain the underlying character flaw at the root of all my problems (apparently I needed to learn to be more considerate of other people's feelings, hers in particular) and give me her therapist's phone number.

By the time I got back to work, Cassie was gone. I heard, from various sources, that she had been offered a promotion to Detective Sergeant if she would stay; that, conversely, she had quit the force because she was about to be booted off the squad; that someone had seen her in a pub in town, holding hands with Sam; that she had gone back to college and was studying archaeology. The moral of most of the stories, by implication, was that women never really had belonged on the Murder squad.

Cassie had not, as it turned out, left the force at all. She had transferred to Domestic Violence and negotiated time out to finish her psychology degree – hence the college story, I suppose. No wonder there were rumours: Domestic Violence is possibly the single most excruciating job in the force, combining as it does all the worst elements of Murder and Sex Crime with none of the kudos, and the thought of leaving one of the élite squads for that was inconceivable to most people. Her nerve must have gone, the grapevine said.

Personally, I don't believe Cassie's transfer had anything to do with losing her nerve; and, though I'm sure this sounds facile and self-serving, I really doubt that it had anything to do with me, or at least not in the way you might think. If the only problem had been the fact that we couldn't bear to be in the same room, she would have found a new partner and dug in her heels, shown up for work a little thinner and more defiant every day, until we came up with a new way to be around each other or until I put in for a transfer. She was always the stubborn one, of us two. I think she transferred because she had lied to O'Kelly and she had lied to Rosalind Devlin, and both of them had believed her; and because, when she told me the truth, I had called her a liar.

In some ways, I was disappointed that the archaeology story had turned out to be untrue. It was an easy picture to imagine, and one I liked to think about: Cassie on some green hill, with a mattock and combats, her hair blown off her face, brown and muddy and laughing.

I kept a vague eye on the papers for a while, but no scandal concerning the Knocknaree motorway ever surfaced. Uncle Redmond's name showed up, well down the list, in some tabloid's chart of how much taxpayers were spending on various politicians' make-up, but that was all. The fact that Sam was still on the Murder squad tended to make me think that he had done as O'Kelly told him, in the end – although it's possible, of course, that he did in fact take his tape to Michael Kiely, and no newspaper would touch it. I don't know.

Sam didn't sell his house, either. Instead, I heard, he rented it out at a nominal rate to a young widow whose husband had died of a brain aneurysm, leaving her with a toddler, a difficult pregnancy and no life insurance. As she was a freelance cellist, she couldn't even draw the dole; she had fallen behind on her rent, her landlord had evicted her, and she and the children had been living in a B&B provided by a charity organisation. I have no idea how Sam found this woman – I'd have thought you would need to go to Victorian London for that level of picturesque, deserving pathos; he had presumably put in a character-istic amount of research. He had moved to a rental flat in Blanchardstown, I think, or some equivalent suburban hell. The main theories were that he was about to leave the force for the priesthood, and that he had a terminal disease.

Sophie and I went out once or twice – I did, after all, owe her dinner and cocktails several times over. I thought we had a good time, and she didn't ask any difficult questions, which I took as a good sign. After a few dates, though, and before the relationship had really progressed enough to merit the name, she dumped me. She informed me, matter-of-factly, that she was old enough to know the difference between intriguing and fucked up. 'You should go for younger women,' she advised me. 'They can't always tell.'

Inevitably, sometime during those interminable months in my apartment (hand after hand of late-night solitaire poker, near-lethal quantities of Radiohead and Leonard Cohen), my thoughts turned back to Knocknaree. I had, of course, sworn never to let the place cross my mind again; but human beings can't help being curious, I suppose, as long as the knowledge doesn't come at too high a price.

Imagine my surprise, then, when I realised that there was nothing there. Everything before my first day of boarding-school had apparently been excised from my mind, with surgical precision and this time for good. Peter, Jamie, the bikers and Sandra, the wood, every scrap of memory I had retrieved with such laborious care over the course of Operation Vestal: gone. I could remember what it had been like to remember these scenes, once upon a time, but now they had the remote, second-hand quality of old films I had watched or stories I had been told, I saw them as if from a vast distance – three brown-skinned kids in battered shorts, spitting on Willy Little's head from the branches and scrambling away, giggling – and I knew with cold certainty that over time even these deracinated images would shrivel up to nothing and blow away. They no longer seemed to belong to me, and I couldn't shake the dark, implacable sense that this was because I had forfeited my right to them, once and for all.

Only one image remained. A summer afternoon, Peter and me sprawled on the grass in his front garden. We had been trying, in a half-hearted kind of way, to make a periscope from instructions in an old annual, but we were supposed to have a cardboard tube out of a roll of kitchen towel, and we couldn't ask our mothers for one because we weren't talking to them. We had used rolled-up newspaper instead, but it kept buckling, so all we could see through the periscope was the sports page, backwards.

We were both in a really bad mood. It was the first week of the holidays and it was sunny, so it should have been a brilliant day, we should have been fixing the tree house or freezing our mickeys off swimming in the river or something; but on our way home from the last day of school on Friday, Jamie had said, to her shoes, 'Three months and I go to boarding-school.'

'Shut up,' Peter had said, shoving her, not hard. 'No you won't. She'll give in.' But it had taken all the shine off the holidays, like a huge black smoke-cloud hanging over everything in sight. We couldn't go inside because our parents were all mad at us for not talking, and we couldn't go into the wood or do anything good because everything we thought of felt stupid, and we couldn't even go find Jamie and get her to come out because she would just shake her head and say 'What's the point?' and make everything even worse. So we were lying in the garden, bored and itchy and annoyed with each other and with the periscope for not working and with the entire world for being a pain in the hole. Peter was pulling up blades of grass, biting the ends off and spitting them up into the air, in a restless automatic rhythm. I was lying on my stomach, one eye open to stare down at the ants bustling back and forth, and the sun was making my hair sweat. *This summer doesn't even count*, I thought. *This summer sucks.*

Jamie's door slammed open and she shot out like she had been fired from a cannon, her mother calling after her with a rueful smile in her voice and the door ricocheting shut with a bang and the Carmichaels' horrible Jack Russell exploding into high-pitched inbred hysteria. Peter and I sat up. Jamie skidded to a halt at her gate, head whipping round to look for us, and when we shouted to her she raced down the path, leaped over Peter's garden wall and tumbled flat on the grass with an arm hooked round each of our necks, bringing us down with her. We were all yelling at the same time and it took a few seconds before I figured out what Jamie was shouting: 'I'm staying! I'm staying! I don't have to go!'

The summer came to life. It burst from grey to fierce blue and gold in the blink of an eye; the air pealed with grasshoppers and lawnmowers, swirled with branches and bees and dandelion seeds, it was soft and sweet as whipped cream, and over the wall the wood was calling us in the loudest of silent voices, it was shaking out all its best treasures to welcome us home. Summer tossed out a fountain of ivy tendrils, caught us straight under the breastbones and tugged; summer, redeemed and unfurling in front of us, a million years long.

We disentangled ourselves and sat up panting, barely able to believe it.

'Seriously?' I said. 'For definite?'

'Yeah. She said, "We'll see, I'll have another think about it and we'll sort something out," but that always means it's OK but she just doesn't want to say so yet. I'm going *nowhere*!'

Jamie ran out of words, so she pushed me over. I grabbed her arm, got on top of her and gave her a Chinese burn. There was a huge grin straight across my face, and I was so happy that I thought it would never come off again.

Peter was on his feet. 'We have to celebrate. Picnic in the castle. Go home and get stuff and meet there.'

Rocketing through the house to the kitchen, my mother hoovering somewhere upstairs – 'Mam! Jamie's staying, can I take stuff for a picnic?' as I grabbed three packets of crisps and a half-package of custard creams and shoved them up my T-shirt – then out the door again, waving to my mother's startled face on the landing, and one-handed over the wall.

Coke cans fizzing and foaming over, and us on our feet on top of the castle wall to clank them together. 'We *won*!' Peter shouted up into the branches and the glittering bands of light, head thrown back and fist punching the air. 'We did it!'

Jamie screamed, 'I'm gonna stay here forever!' and danced on the wall like a thing made of air, 'forever and ever and ever!' And I just yelled, wild wordless whoops, and the wood caught our voices and tossed them outwards in great expanding ripples, wove them into the whirlpool of leaves and the jink and bubble of the river and the rustling calling web of rabbits and beetles and robins and all the other denizens of our domain, into one long high paean.

This memory, alone of all my hoard, did not dissolve into smoke and slide away through my fingers. It remained – still remains – sharp-edged and warm and mine, a single bright coin left in my hand. I suppose that, if the wood was going to leave me only one moment, that was a kind one to choose.

In one of those merciless little codicils that such cases sometimes have, Simone Cameron rang me not long after I got back to work. My mobile number was on the card I had given her, and she had no way of knowing that I was cross-checking joyriders' statements in Harcourt Street and no longer had anything to do with the Katy Devlin case. 'Detective Ryan,' she said, 'we've found something I think you must see.'

It was Katy's diary, the one Rosalind had told us she'd got bored with and thrown away. The Cameron Academy's cleaning lady, in an unaccustomed fit of thoroughness, had found it sellotaped to the back of a framed poster of Anna Pavlova that hung on the studio wall. She had rung Simone, agog with excitement, when she read the name on the cover. I should have given Simone Sam's number and hung up, but instead I left the joyriders' statements unchecked and drove down to Stillorgan.

It was eleven in the morning and Simone was the only person at the Academy. The studio was flooded with sunlight and the photos of Katy had been taken off the noticeboard, but one breath of that specific professional smell – resin, hard clean sweat, floor polish – brought it all back: skateboarders calling on the dark street below, rush of padded feet and chatter in the corridor, Cassie's voice beside me, the high singing urgency we had brought with us into the room.

The poster lay face down on the floor. Dusty sheets of paper had been taped to the back of the frame to form a makeshift pouch, and on top of them was the diary. It was just a copybook, the kind kids use in school, lined pages and the cover that grubby recycled orange. 'Paula, who found this, had to go on to her next job,' Simone said, 'but I have her phone number if you like.'

I picked it up. 'Have you read it?' I asked.

Simone nodded. 'Some. Enough.' She was wearing narrow black trousers and a soft black pullover and they somehow made her look more exotic, not less, than the full skirt and leotard had. Her extraordinary eyes had the same immobilised look they had held when we told her about Katy.

I sat down on one of the plastic chairs. 'Katy Devlin VERY PRIVATE KEEP OUT THIS MEANS YOU!!!' the cover said, but I opened it anyway. It was about three-quarters full. The handwriting was rounded and careful, just beginning to develop touches of individuality: strong flourishes on y's and g's, a tall curled capital S. Simone sat opposite me and watched, one hand laid over the other in her lap, while I read.

The diary covered almost eight months. The entries were regular at first, maybe half a page a day, but after a few months they became intermittent, two a week, one. Much of it was about ballet. 'Simone says my arabesque is better but I still have to think about it coming from the whole body not just the leg specially on the left the line has to go straigt through.' 'Were learning a new piece for the end of year show it has music from Giselle + I have fouettés. Simone says remember this is Giselles way to tell her boyfriend how he broke her heart + how much shell miss him this is her only chance so that has to be the reason for everything I do. Some of it goes like this' and then a few lines of laboured, mysterious notation, like some coded musical score. The day she got her acceptance from the Royal Ballet School was a wild, overexcited burst of capital letters and exclamation marks and stickers shaped like stars: 'IM GOING IM GOING IM REALLY REALLY GOING!!!!!!'

There were passages about things she did with her friends: 'We had a sleep over at Christinas house her mum gave us weird pizza with olives + we played truth or dare Beth fancies Matthew. I dont fancy anyone dancers mostly dont get married till after their career so maybe when Im thirty five or forty. We put on make up Marianne looked really pretty but Christina put too much eye shadow she looked like her mum!!' The first time she and her friends were allowed into town on their own: 'We took the bus + went shopping to Miss Selfrige Marianne + I got the same top but hers is pink with purple writing mine is light blue with red. Jess couldnt come so I got her a flower clip for in her hair. Then we went to Mac Donalds Christina stuck her finger in my barbcue sauce so I put some on her icecream we laughed so much the gaurd said hed put us out if we didn't stop. Beth asked him do you want some barbcue icecream?'

She tried on Louise's pointe shoes, hated cabbage and got kicked out of Irish class for texting Beth across the aisle. A happy child, you would say, giggly and determined and running too fast for punctuation; nothing special about her except dancing, and contented that way. But in between: terror rose off the pages like petrol fumes, acrid and dizzying. 'Jess is sad that Im going to ballet school she cried. Rosalind said if I go Jess will kill her self + it will be my fault I shouldnt be so selfish all the time. I dont know what to do if I ask Mum and Dad they might not let me go. I dont want Jess to die.'

'Simone said I cant get sick any more so tonight I said to Rosalind I dont want to drink it. Rosalind says I have to or I wont be good at dancing any more. I was really scared because she got so mad but I was mad too and I said no I dont beleive her I think it just makes me sick. She says Ill be sorry + Jess isnt allowed to talk to me.'

'Christina is mad at me on Tuesday she came over + Rosalind told her I said she wont be good enough for me once I go to ballet school + Christina wont beleive me I didnt. Now Christina and Beth wont talk to me Marianne still does though. I hate Rosalind I HATE HER I HATE HER.'

'Yesterday this diary was under my bed like always then I couldnt find it. I didnt say anything but then Mum took Rosalind + Jess to Auntie Veras I stayed home + looked all over in Rosalinds room it was inside her shoe box in her wardrobe. I was scared to take it because now shell know and shell be really mad but I dont care. Im going to keep it here at Simones I can write in it when I practise by myself.'

The last entry in the diary was dated three days before Katy died. 'Rosalind is sorry she was so horrible about me going away she was only worried about Jess + upset about me being so far away shell miss me too. To make up for it shes going to get me a lucky charm to bring me luck dancing.'

Her voice rang small and bright through the rounded Biro letters, swirled in the sunlight with the dust-motes. Katy, a year dead; bones in the grey geometric churchyard at Knocknaree. I had thought of her very little since the trial ended. Even during the investigation, to be frank, she had occupied a less prominent place in my mind than you might expect. The victim is the one person you never know; she had been only a cluster of translucent, conflicting images refracted through other people's words, crucial not in herself but for her death and the urgent firework trail of consequences it left behind. One moment on the Knocknaree dig had eclipsed everything else she had ever been. I thought of her lying on her stomach on this blond wooden floor, the frail wings of her shoulder-blades moving as she wrote, music spiralling around her.

'Would it have made some difference if we'd found this earlier?' Simone asked. Her voice made me start and set my heart pounding; I had almost forgotten she was there.

'Probably not,' I said. I had no idea whether this was true, but she needed to hear it. 'There's nothing here that ties Rosalind directly to any crime. There's the mention of her making Katy drink something, but she would have explained that away – claimed it was a vitamin drink, maybe; Lucozade. The same for the lucky charm: it doesn't prove anything.'

'But if we had found it before she died,' Simone said quietly, 'then,' and of course there was nothing I could say to that, nothing at all.

I put the diary and the little paper pouch into an evidence bag and sent them over to Sam, at Dublin Castle. They would go into a box in the basement, somewhere near my old clothes; the case was closed, there was nothing he could do with them unless, or until, Rosalind did the same thing to someone else. I would have liked to send the diary to Cassie, as some kind of wordless and useless apology, but it wasn't her case any more either, and anyway I could no longer be sure she would understand how I meant it.

A few weeks later I heard that Cassie and Sam were engaged; Bernadette sent round an e-mail, looking for contributions towards a present. That evening I told Heather someone's kid had scarlet fever, locked myself in my room and drank vodka, slowly but purposefully, until four in the morning. Then I rang Cassie's mobile.

On the third ring she said, blurrily, 'Maddox.'

'Cassie,' I said. 'Cassie, you're not actually going to marry that boring little bogger. Are you?'

I heard her catch her breath, ready to say something. After a while she let it out again.

'I'm sorry,' I said. 'For everything. I'm so, so sorry. I love you, Cass. Please.'

I waited again. After a long time I heard a clunk. Then Sam, somewhere in the background, said, 'Who was that?'

'Wrong number,' Cassie said, farther away now. 'Some drunk guy.'

'What were you on so long for, then?' There was a grin in his voice: teasing. A rustle of sheets.

'He told me he loved me, so I wanted to see who it was,' said Cassie. 'But he turned out to be looking for Britney.'

'Aren't we all,' said Sam; then, 'Ow!' and Cassie giggled. 'You bit my nose!'

'Serves you right,' said Cassie. More low laughter, a rustle, a kiss; a long contented sigh. Sam said, soft and happy, 'Baby.' Then nothing but their breathing, easing into tandem and slowing gradually back into sleep.

I sat there for a very long time, watching the sky lighten outside my window and realising that my name hadn't come up on Cassie's mobile. I could feel the vodka working its way out of my blood; the headache was starting to kick in. Sam snored, very gently. I never knew, not then, not now, whether Cassie thought she had hung up, or whether she wanted to hurt me, or whether she wanted to give me one last gift, one last night listening to her breathe.

The motorway went ahead on the route originally planned, of course. Move the Motorway stalled it for an impressive amount of time – injunctions, constitutional challenges, I think they might have taken it all the way to the European High Court – and a grungy bunch of unisex protesters calling themselves Knocknafree (including, I would be willing to bet, Mark) set up camp on the site to stop the bulldozers going through, which held things up for another few weeks while the government got a court order against them. They never had a hope in hell. I wish I could have asked Jonathan Devlin whether he actually believed, in the teeth of all the historical evidence, that this one time public opinion would make a difference, or whether he knew, all along, and needed to try anyway. I envied him, either way.

I went down there, the day I saw in the paper that construction had begun. I was supposed to be going door-to-door in Terenure, trying to find someone who'd seen a stolen car that had been used in a robbery, but nobody would miss me for an hour or so. I'm not sure why I went. It wasn't a dramatic final bid for closure or anything like that; I just had some belated impulse to see the place, one more time.

It was a mess. I had expected this, but I hadn't foreseen the scale of it. I could hear the mindless roar of machinery long before I reached the top of the hill. The whole site was unrecognisable, men in neon protective gear swarming like ants and shouting hoarse unintelligible commands over the noise, huge grimy bulldozers tossing aside great clumps of earth and nosing with slow, obscene delicacy at the excavated remnants of walls.

I parked at the side of the road and got out of the car. There was a disconsolate little huddle of protesters in the lay-by (it was still untouched, so far; the chestnut tree was dropping conkers again), waving hand-lettered signs – Save Our Heritage, History Is Not For Sale – in case the media showed up again. The raw, churning earth seemed to go on and on into the distance, it seemed huger than the dig had ever been, and it took me a few moments to realise why this was: that last strip of wood was almost gone. Pale, splintered trunks; roots exposed, thrusting crazily at the grey sky. Chainsaws were gibbering at the handful of trees that were left.

The memory smacked me in the solar plexus so hard it took my breath away: scrambling up the castle wall, crisp packets crackling in my T-shirt and the sound of the river chuckling somewhere far below; Peter's trainer searching for a foothold just above me, Jamie's blond flag flying high among the swaying leaves. My whole body remembered it, the familiar scrape of stone against my palm, the brace of my thigh muscle as I pushed myself upwards, into the whirl of green and exploding light. I had become so used to thinking of the wood as the invincible and stalking enemy, the shadow over every secret corner of my mind; I had completely forgotten that, for much of my life, it had been our easy playground and our best-loved refuge. It hadn't really occurred to me, until I saw them cutting it down, that it had been beautiful.

At the edge of the site, near the road, one of the workmen had pulled a squashed packet of cigarettes from under his orange vest and was methodically patting down his pockets for a lighter. I found mine and went over to him.

'Ta, son,' he said through the cigarette, cupping his hand around the flame. He was somewhere in his fifties, small and wiry, with a face like a terrier: friendly, non-committal, with bushy eyebrows and a thick handlebar moustache.

'How's it going?' I asked.

He shrugged, inhaled and handed the lighter back to me. 'Ah, sure. I've seen worse. Bleeding great rocks every-where, that's the only thing.'

'From the castle, maybe. This used to be an archae-ological site.'

'You're telling me,' he said, nodding towards the protesters.

I smiled. 'Found anything interesting?'

His eyes returned sharply to my face, and I could see him giving me a quick, concise appraisal: protester, ar-chaeologist, government spy? 'Like what?'

'I don't know; archaeological bits and pieces, maybe. Animal bones. Human bones.'

His eyebrows twitched together. 'You a cop?'

'No,' I said. The air smelled wet and heavy, rich with turned earth and latent rain. 'Two of my friends went missing here, back in the eighties.'

He nodded thoughtfully, unsurprised. 'I remember that, all right,' he said. 'Two young kids. Are you the little fella was with them?'

'Yeah,' I said. 'That's me.'

He took a deep, leisurely drag on his cigarette and squinted up at me with mild interest. 'Sorry for your trouble.'

'It's a long time ago,' I said.

He nodded. 'We've found no bones that I know of. Rabbits and foxes might've turned up, maybe; nothing bigger. We'd have called the cops if we had.'

'I know,' I said. 'I was just checking.'

He thought about this for a while, gazing back over the site. 'One of the lads found this, earlier,' he said. He went through his pockets, working from the bottom up, and pulled something out from under the vest. 'What d'you make of that, now?'

He dropped the thing into my palm. It was leaf-shaped, flat and narrow and about as long as my thumb, made of some smooth metal coated matt black with age. One end was jagged; it had snapped off something, a long time ago. He had tried to clean it up, but it was still patched with small, hard encrustations of earth. 'I don't know,' I said. 'An arrowhead, maybe, or part of a pendant.'

'Found it in the muck on his boot, at the tea break,' the man said. 'He gave it to me to bring home to my daughter's young fella; mad into the old archaeology, he is.'

The thing was cool in my palm, heavier than you would expect. Narrow grooves, half worn away, formed a pattern on one side. I tilted it to the light: a man, no more than a stick-figure, with the wide, pronged antlers of a stag.

'You can hang on to that if you like,' the man said. 'The young fella won't miss what he's never had.'

I closed my hand over the object. The edges bit into my palm; I could feel my pulse beating against it. It should probably have been in a museum. Mark would have gone nuts over it. 'No,' I said. 'Thank you. I think your grandson should have it.'

He shrugged, eyebrows jumping. I tipped the object into his hand. 'Thank you for showing it to me,' I said.

'No bother,' the man said, tucking it back into his pocket. 'Good luck.'

'You too,' I said. It was starting to rain, a fine, misty

drizzle. He threw his cigarette butt into a tyre-track and headed back to work, turning up his collar as he went.

I lit a cigarette of my own and watched them working. The metal object had left slender red marks across my palm. Two little kids, maybe eight or nine, were balancing on their stomachs across the estate wall; the workmen waved their arms and shouted over the roar of machinery till the kids disappeared, but a minute or two later they were back again. The protesters put up umbrellas and handed around sandwiches. I watched for a long time, until my mobile began vibrating insistently in my pocket and the rain started to come down more heavily, and then I put out my cigarette and buttoned my coat and headed back to the car.

AUTHOR'S NOTE

I've taken a number of liberties with the workings of the
Garda Síochána, the Irish police force. To pick the most
obvious example, there is no Murder squad in Ireland – in
1997 various units were amalgamated to form the National
Bureau of Criminal Investigation, which assists local officers in investigating serious crimes, including murder – but
the story seemed to require one. I owe David Walsh special
thanks for helping me with a wild variety of questions
about police procedure. All inaccuracies are mine and not
his.

ACKNOWLEDGEMENTS

I owe huge debts of thanks to a lot of people: Ciara Considine, my editor at Hodder Headline Ireland, whose unerring instincts, unfailing kindness and enthusiasm have helped this book forward, from start to finish, in too many ways to count; Darley Anderson, super-agent and dream-maker, who has left me speechless more times than anyone I know; his amazing team, especially Emma White, Lucie Whitehouse and Zoë King; Sue Fletcher of Hodder & Stoughton and Kendra Harpster of Viking, editors *extraordinaires*, for their breathtaking faith in this book and for knowing exactly how to make it better; Swati Gamble for her phenomenal patience; all at Hodder & Stoughton and Hodder Headline Ireland; Helena Burling, whose kindness gave me the haven in which to write this; Oonagh 'Bulrushes' Montague, Ann-Marie Hardiman, Mary Kelly and Fidelma Keogh, for holding my hand when I needed it most and keeping me more or less sane; my brother, Alex French, for fixing my computer on a regular basis; David Ryan, for waiving non-intellectual property rights; Alice Wood, for her eagle-eyed copy-editing; Dr Fearghas Ó Cochláin, for the medical bits; Ron and the Anonymous Angel, who by some grey magic always knew the precise moment; Cheryl Steckel, Steven Foster and Deirdre Nolan, for reading and encouraging; all of PurpleHeart

Theatre Company, for their ongoing support; and, last but so very far from least, Anthony Breatnach, whose patience, support, help and faith have been beyond words.